I0681509

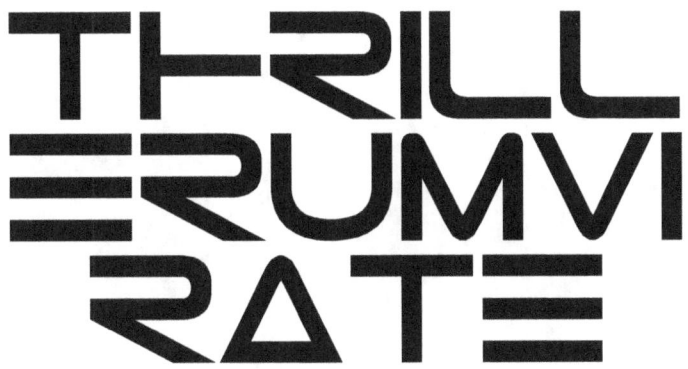

Featuring 3 Breakout Novels In One Collection:
The Phoenix Experiment
The Slide
Forecast

by Aaron Ryan
AWARD-WINNING AUTHOR OF
THE BESTSELLING ALIEN INVASION SAGA **DISSONANCE**
THE **TALISMAN** TRILOGY
THE CHRISTIAN DYSTOPIAN SAGA **THE END**
AND MANY MORE.

eBook ISBN: 78-1-965372-57-9
Paperback ISBN: 978-1-965372-58-6
Hardcover ISBN: 978-1-965372-59-3
US Copyright # forthcoming.

Included Herein:

The Phoenix Experiment

Published in 2025, Edition 1.

eBook ISBN # 9781965372418 · Paperback ISBN # 9781965372425
Hardcover ISBN # 9781965372432

Edited by CM LLC. Published independently. Cover art by Aaron Ryan & CM LLC. Phoenix bird licensed for unlimited reproduction / print runs through iStock on License #490651863

The Slide

Published in 2025, Edition 1.

Paperback ISBN # 9781965372067 · Hardcover ISBN # 9781965372074
eBook ISBN # 9781965372081

Edited by CM LLC. Published independently. Cover art by Aaron Ryan & CM LLC.

Forecast

Published in 2024, Edition 1.

Paperback ISBN # 9798990661189 · Hardcover ISBN # 9798990661172
eBook ISBN # 9798990661165

Edited by Denouement Editing. Published independently. Cover art man by Asaf Rozanes · Cover art background by Trivuj. Rear cover art image by Gerd Altmann through Pixabay.

Books & Chapters

Note on AI

We live in an age of AI. Every day, more and more services spring up promising revolutionary and innovative results using artificial intelligence. The authoring industry is not immune to this.

I want every one of my readers to know that not once did I employ, nor will I *ever* employ, the use of AI to sculpt any part of any of my stories. Those who know me know that I am staunchly and adamantly opposed to such cheats.

I'm very proud to be a verified human. The ability to create is a gift that I was endowed by my Creator, and I will never forfeit that nor set it aside to propagate something synthetic and imitative.

Everything you've read by me in this novel, and in my other works, is 100% entirely created by me, the genuine article. I'm a verified human, and always will be.

To my fellow authors, I urge you to preserve the sacred gift of human creation and never stoop to such lows. Always cherish this gift you've been given. If you encounter writer's block, take a break. Don't cop out. Don't take the road more traveled by. Don't cheat. Toe the line for all of us, and keep creation – *true* unadulterated creation – alive.

Long live humanity.

Also, if you're an author – or even a budding one – I'd love to personally extend an invite to you to join me in two unique groups on Facebook: the "Authors & Writers ONLY" group of which I am the admin, and my own personal group, the "Author Aaron Ryan Group." The first group is one where you can connect with thousands of other authors across the globe, ask questions, learn and grow as a writer, and network. Grapes grow best in bunches, after all.

And the second is my own personal group. I find much higher engagement in my *group* than with my Facebook *page*. I also welcome other authors to enter there for free giveaways, news, and also to learn why I self-publish, what benefits there are in being a writer-entrepreneur, and more. As a fellow author, I'm always there to help you in any way I can.

God bless you as you use the gift of creation to write your stories. May they, and you, be utterly successful.

Sincerely,

Aaron Ryan,
Verified Human

THE PHOENIX EXPERIMENT

AARON RYAN

Published in 2025, Edition 1.

eBook ISBN # 9781965372418 · Paperback ISBN # 9781965372425
Hardcover ISBN # 9781965372432

Edited by CM LLC. Published independently.

Cover art by Aaron Ryan & CM LLC. Phoenix bird licensed for unlimited reproduction / print runs through iStock on License #490651863

This is a work of fiction. Any similarities to persons living or dead, or actual events is purely coincidental.

For Sweeps, Bren & AJ:
my true loves.

Thank you for helping me to rise from the ashes.

"If only one could have two lives… one in which to make one's mistakes… the second in which to profit by them."

D.H. Lawrence

Part One:
Out Of The Frying Pan

1: The Origin

In the vast blackness of space, one knows only peace.

I lie here in The Origin, this overlarge and sleek G-class science vessel: a star-freighter, really, but not big enough to call a floating city. It has more than enough space to allow me to wander, but not enough for me to get *really* lost.

For a 14-year-old boy like me, however, getting lost is always part of the fun. Anther is the same way.

As I dimly come to consciousness, I'm cognizant once more of the quiet beeps of life-sustaining devices all around me, and the sensors attached to my skin monitoring heart rate and rhythm, blood pressure, pulse oximetry, body temperature, respiratory rate, glucose levels, movement, brain activity, and the like.

The IV in my arm dispenses that wonderful serum, and it's always a relatively rude awakening coming out of cryo-sleep from it. Sleep-cycles are necessary to keep us alive out here: we cherish them and guard them ferociously.

When they're over for the night, it's an inescapable disappointment. Not because we don't get to sleep anymore, though. That's not the reason. It's because we don't get to dream the dreams we want.

Without the specific dreams, all you have left is the fading memories.

I feel my eyes dilate as they acclimate to the harsh light. The forced REM cycles brought on by the serum are always welcome, because the calm is *soooo* good, but it's equally *soooo* hard being ripped out of it. Always seems to happen right before the really good parts too, *dang it.*

I blink stupidly in the light, looking around slowly, dimly taking in my surroundings once more: sterile white and antiseptic as I float here in this translucent jelly. It stinks every single time I get out of here and wash off: a mashup of something that smells like a crude mixture of ketchup and detergent. I'm familiar with detergent because we wash our uniforms with it. But I barely remember the taste of ketchup, although I do remember the horrid smell. There was a younger orphan on The Origin once who, before he came to us, ate nothing *but* ketchup. He would order a hot dog, smother it in ketchup, and literally lick all the ketchup off and leave the dog. I throw up in my mouth a little just thinking about it. He was ultimately successful, and got to go back. I can't wait to wash off the scent and get back to business as usual.

And I can't wait to go back, too.

The Phoenix Experiments. You would think for a teenager they would be an irritating and eye-rolling obligation, but I'm better than that. I enjoy them. I should: after all, it's an opportunity for them to get better acquainted with Jax Hutson, the star of the show.

Me.

There are all kinds of posts you can sign up for when you're conscripted at age 8. All kinds of choices exist to tickle your fancy. Some are more demanding than others. Most align with your personality profile and life experiences at that age. For me, The Origin was a no-brainer.

I didn't sign up for this post because I wanted to; I signed up because I *had* to.

Because, if there's even the slightest chance that they can come back, I owe it to them, no matter the length of time it takes.

I miss them.

I miss them with all my heart.

The shower feels wonderfully refreshing as always. This is the best part of my day, feeling those warm rivulets coursing over me and sending tingles down my body. I feel most alive during these brief, private times. Moreover, I feel *clean*: the disgusting ketchup goo is washed off of me and then collected in the reservoir beneath my feet for analysis by The Origin. I take a deep breath and close my eyes, enjoying it while I can, before the 0900 chow call.

I finish up and towel off in the Hygiene Block, which we call the HB for short. There are a few others in here with me.

There's Garris: he's a big 15-year-old oaf who adds two and two together and somehow gets chicken. I don't understand how his Neanderthal mind works, nor how he got on this ship. Also, I think he still pees in his sleep.

Then there's Ranshay: a diminutive and quiet 12-year-old kid who I know is a brainiac because Anther and I stole a look at his test scores, but you'd never know it because he doesn't speak a lick of English. Which begs the question: how does he even understand what he's being taught in order to score so highly? I shake my head in disbelief as I glance at him.

Next, there's Martos: a spunky 16-year-old who likes to be the life of the party but who tires quickly: an extrovert who abruptly runs out of steam before his ship ever reaches the dock.

And finally, I spot Venthix. He's alright. I've had a few conversations with him; he seems like a good guy. He's 15.

Not everyone is here. Anther Secto is my best friend, but he's nowhere to be found this morning.

All of us are on this ship for one simple reason, and we all know what it is.

Sadly, there are no girls on The Origin. I hate that. They're not allowed here, in order to, as they say, 'keep us focused.' Whatever. We know why we're here, and that's plenty focus enough. A double-Y chromosome environment is so static and boring; way too many farts and not enough perfume to combat them. To my knowledge there haven't *ever* been females on The Origin… they're all over on The Zephyr on the other side of Earth's orbit.

There are also so very few of us onboard The Origin. Just four adults, a synthetic, a rumored engineer whom no one ever sees, and the eight of us boys. For a ship this size, you would think there would be more staff, engineers, technicians, or the like, to assume maintenance duties, but it's highly unnecessary. The Origin is, for all intents and purposes, self-sustaining. Rumors persist that the engineer is an elderly female, as odd as that sounds. I have never seen her, so I can't say.

The Origin – and The Zephyr, for that matter – is a sentient ship that literally feels like a living presence in every single corridor, quarters or compartment this ship presents. Violin and flute concerto music plays everywhere, incessantly. Sitars sometimes join in. Whoever wrote the schematics for this place was intent on a tranquil environment with soothing vibes permeating the whole of the ship, always. I've been here for five years and there are areas that are still new and interesting. AI is prevalent throughout, as creepy as that is. But Phiria sounds human, and she knows what's going on with The Origin at all times. She's also surprisingly conversational, and she remembers.

AI is unavoidable anymore. I mean, it's 2471, for goodness' sake. By now, AI is everywhere *anyway*, and all the naysayers have finally been won over. At least, I *think* they have.

Historical records assert that there was a prolonged flirtation with – and profound *resistance* to – AI, in the early years of the 21st century. Especially by creators who felt they were being replaced by automation. Can't say I blame them. I wouldn't want to be replaced, either. But that's the world we live in anymore, right? Upgrades, synthetics, and replacements. The Origin teems with all kinds of life, real and fake, which makes sense, given its name.

The only thing you can't really replace is a human soul. At least, not yet.

And that's precisely why I'm here.

I don't know when I first started hearing them. It was a few years ago, but whether they started coming in my subconscious, in my sleep, or in my waking life, I still have no idea. It's a dim, chanting voice: breathy and calm, alluring and mysterious, at times brimming with pathos, and always with a note of urgency and clarity. I have given up questioning why I hear the voice, and why it speaks to me in poetry and prose, because I find it utterly captivating.

These mental permeations come fairly often; a voice whispering to me from beyond. I don't know if it's a byproduct of The Phoenix Experiment or not, or if I'm the only one who hears the calm chanting. I'm content not to find out, however, as it isn't exactly irritating. It's just a constant reminder of where we are, and it comes at unawares and odd times.

And here it comes yet again.

In the vast expanse of time
Suffering and discontent combine
Until the quell,
no voice shall tell
Serene, sweet resolution's clime

So thus, they wander, aimless, hoping
Trying, dreaming, striving, hoping
Keeping on
whilst sleeping long
Phoenix rising, talons groping

My mind snaps back from the reverie.

I know exactly where I am. It's the same every day, but you get used to it. The walls are white, the floors are white, the ceiling is white, and the air I breathe is practically white as well, sanitized and antiseptic, optimized and perfected for life in space. It 'tastes' lighter than the air I would breathe down on Earth, especially in the big cities where the air is so thick you can chew it. But I don't really remember the air down there anyway. Eventually, you get used to it up here, and this air is all you know.

Chow time is another matter. It's something I have never really gotten used to, and I'm not looking forward to it today, either. They feed us *BioPrime*: a revolting and boring goo composed of amino acids, proteins and everything a growing body needs, sure, but it looks like the same stuff we float in, and I swear it smells like it, too.

What is it with ketchupy stuff everywhere, anyway? I think to myself as I head that way. It's been perfected, and I'm sure it has everything a body needs, but it's monotonous, dull, and same ol' same ol.' The lack of variety is irritating. At least it comes in more than a few fruit flavors, so I suppose I should be grateful. But I'm not.

I suppose I should *also* be grateful since many are starving down there on Earth. But, just *once*, I'd love to sink my teeth into that little thing called 'steak' that I've heard so much about. Never had one. I don't suppose I ever will. The Origin isn't about quick results… or even guaranteed ones. We're all here 'til we age out at 18. Anyway, I'm also told steak isn't even a breakfast food, not that that matters.

I look forward to hanging with Anther at breakfast. He's my best friend, and he's my age. I didn't request that; it just worked out that way and drew us together. No complaints from me. He's about my height, but I'm a blonde and he's a brunette, I'm skinny and he's bulky, I'm spry and he's a klutz. It has also been observed that I'm articulate and a chutzpah-laden spitfire; Anther, however, has been playfully labeled a 'lovable meathead.'

He seems oblivious to the fact that I'm the one who came up with that label. I decide never to tell him.

I received the highest score on the AG. The Aptitude Gauntlet isn't what people make it out to be. I think back to it now, and can't remember any of the specific questions, other than a general memory that they dealt with computation and syntax, reasoning and vocabulary. I also completed it before any of my peers did. The fact that they make all of us go through it at the tender age of 6 seems barbaric; cruel and unusual punishment for those still amassing knowledge and life training. But *que sera, sera*: they need to know that our aptitude is greater than a box of hair before they bring us onboard The Origin. Can't have all those kids blowing a gasket in The Phoenix Experiments. Which, again, stupefies me that someone like Garris is here.

Anther's an orphan as well, like all of us are, so we share that trauma, not that we asked for it. We'd much prefer to have our parents back. But fate, it seems, is what decided to bring us together in trauma, and trauma makes for a good binding agent for hurting souls like ours.

There he is. Anther's already gotten his 'breakfast,' and is sitting down at a table close to the chow hall entrance. He lifts his hand and hails me. "Sup," he says with a warm smile and a slouch. I greet him back with similar jocularity, and play slug him in the shoulder. "Ow," he grunts, but he's beefy enough to absorb the hit. I didn't use my full force anyway. If I had, Anther would surely be dead.

I motion over to the chow line and he nods, assured that I'll be back in a minute for a hearty mutual partaking of our revolting health slop. *BioPrime.* Ick.

In a few more moments I receive a full dosage serving from the dispenser. This time I opt for strawberry flavor. I wish it was real strawberries and not some crude *caricature* of strawberries.

I plop down next to Anther. He smells like ketchup and detergent, so I assume he hasn't showered. *So that's where he was this morning,* I think to myself. *Not* showering. I detect a faint whiff of body odor as well, but shake it off. This is not the first time.

"How was your sleep?" I ask, nonchalantly, before downing a spoonful. I practically hold my nose as I do so.

"Fine," he shrugs, but I see that he's actually downplaying it. He stifles a chortle.

"Yeah, *right,*" I tease.

Anther can't suppress his enthusiasm. It was there when he greeted me entering the cafeteria. It's obvious to me that *she* made another appearance, and now he tries to get me to pry it out of him. Anther explodes with joy and turns to me. "Haha! You can tell, can't you? It was *awesome,* dude."

"Okay, okay, *out* with it, man. Did she tell you her name yet or not?"

A huge grin spreads across his face. "You know me too well, bro. *No!* I mean, *yes,* she was there, but no, she didn't tell me her name yet. Man, I wish she was here on The Origin with us. That girl is *hot.* No joke. I mean, like otherworldly hot. Too bad she's just a dream." He chuckles, and I echo it. Desperate fool. I'm not sure which I'm laughing at more: his obsession or his desperation.

But... I actually *do* wish I could meet her.

I haven't met anyone that tantalizing yet in my own sleep cycles *or* in The Phoenix Experiments. Anther could be lying, of course, but that would be atypical for him. All of us boys want a hot girl in our dreams. Maybe he's just the first to get lucky.

"*Otherworldly* hot, huh? I bet she has an otherworldly cool name then, as well. Like *Stellanova*, or, or…," -here I try my hand at a creative name after a star system- "*Aurelia Centauri* or something like that."

Anther chuckles again. "Yeah! I bet. I'll find out, eventually, I'm sure."

"What was she wearing this time?" I prod.

"Nothing," he jests almost immediately, and I seize the opportunity to elbow him jealously.

"Shut up!"

Anther is just brimming with giggles this morning. "Kidding. I wish."

"Yeah, you wish, indeed."

Anther looks at me comically.

"Okay, okay, I wish too," I laugh sheepishly.

Part of me wonders if that part of Anther's story is actually true, and he's just being coy. But whatever. I move on, a little wrecked inside that I haven't had my own serum-induced hot girl dream yet. The serum they give us is potent, but, as with anything, *results may vary*. Maybe he's just hornier than I am. I privately resolve to work on that, but deep inside I suspect The Origin staff is holding out on me.

For the time being, however, I still want my parents back more than I want a girl.

It's true. And I secretly hope that Anther understands that as much as I need him to. But who am I kidding? I know he does. Pop his parents or his siblings into that dream in place of that girl? He'd be a blubbering wreck, just like we all would.

Chow time is done, so I brush my teeth and then get ready to report to Stygius Cryptus. The science officer is no one to be trifled with, and I do *not* want to be late. He does his job with mathematical precision and all the warmth of a kitchen knife. His breath reeks of sardines and foods that I frequently find myself overly curious about, wondering a) how he got ahold of them, and b) why, to date, we're still limited to protein goo for the meals that *we* get. *Maybe they're not real sardines,* I think to myself.

Leaving those thoughts aside, I make my way to Quadrant C, Subfloor 3A, Room 319. It's close to our dorms. The Phoenix Experiments call, but a yearning stirs within me to run and explore the bowels of The Origin once more. I know it's forbidden, however, and would be counterproductive.

The last time Anther and I did so, Helmsman Fulsar Oculus scolded us for a pretty half-hour, then confined us to quarters with no rec allowance for three days. Recreation passes the time here so well, and is *never* to be missed. That chastisement, though brief, thoroughly sucked. Nonetheless, it didn't stop Anther. He's been in and out of the vent shafts more times than I can count, and it's like he knows this ship like the back of his hand now.

Oculus is a fat and aging man, balding. There's nothing attractive about him. His Australian accent is thick and roguish, as if he's got a perpetual repository of gravel midway down his throat. He constantly reeks of something that might be equated to alcohol, but no one can blame him. He's been the steward of this ship longer than The Phoenix Experiment has even been in operation.

First Officer Argin Mirabay is his mirror opposite: composed, stoic, rigid, quiet, and half Oculus' age. He's also intimidating, but not in the same way as our synthetic.

Room 319. I've arrived. I round the corner. There's Cryptus, sitting calm and collected, with a stare that reflects nothing. I glance silently past him into the lab, with the chairs, the chambers, the electrodes, the connections, and more gadgetry than I can pretend to understand. Cryptus knows what it all does, however. All I know is that I get to go back to sleep in there, and when I do, this time I get to dream dreams that are *mine*. There's no serum; there's no manipulation other than a psychological profiling beforehand that allows me to reconnect with sweet memories of my parents. And then the white noise kicks in and the deep throbbing that puts us in a subconscious state as we're thrust into the center of the ring. It's irresistible. You don't fight it. It's pointless to. Besides, we all want to get back in there.

Cryptus likes to meditate. Like, a lot. I can't figure out what he's meditating on, specifically, nor do I understand why he cherishes the activity so much. I already have peace, as much as can be expected. But, with a name like *Stygius Cryptus*, maybe one could expect to be slightly more troubled than your average synthetic. Or, maybe it's a power-saving thing and he needs to conserve battery or something.

I silently wait at the entrance to the android's office, unwilling to disturb him. His office is impeccable, and he guards it like a gentle Cerberus. Everything is in its place, and he would know swiftly if you rotated a pen by a single degree. When we were younger, Anther and I used to play-act like I was Cryptus and he was Oculus. He would fiddle with something in our boys' quarters, and I would accusingly tell him what it was, remonstrating him with a constrained, android wrath.

I watch him, silently standing there and trying to match his breathing with my own. I close my eyes and try to purge the noise as I demonstrate my own prowess at meditation. His breathy voice stabs through my head with an alarming suddenness that makes me jump.

"Welcome, Jax," he greets me, eventually, and I lurch from the quiet, surprise salutation punctuating my own attempt at meditation. It is almost as if he was just waiting for me to drift into serenity so that he could call my name and jolt me back to awareness. Something in me tells me that was exactly his plan.

"I didn't move your pen!" I blurt out, jarred with eyes wide. I correct myself and shuffle. "Uh, I mean, he-hello, Cryptus," I stammer uneasily, looking up and finding him coldly surveying me.

"Fascinating," he mutters, his eyes narrowing. "I am, in fact, missing a pen. I shall assume, for now, that you have stolen it. Should you discover the ability to magically produce one, Jax," he pauses for effect, emphasizing my name, "I shall be grateful. I prefer blue ink, as you may recall." His eyes narrow.

That thick British brogue is so intriguing, and yet so dully patronizing. I'm well aware that Cryptus' programming equips him to take on any accent at any time, and he could have just lectured me as an elderly Caribbean woman if that was his wish. But he chooses British, ostensibly because he can condescend to all of us underlings. It also matches his expressionless and intimidating visage perfectly.

"Thanks, I, uh, do recall that," I say, uneasily.

Blue ink. The accusation isn't lost on me. Anther and I had once spied on him in here while he conducted a Phoenix experiment on Ranshay, and, unbeknownst to both of us, Anther's pen leaked right out of his pocket and right through the vent we were spying through. Cryptus has good eyes *and* good ears, and he could hear that blue ink spilling right through the grate. He whirled to face us. We shrieked and took off. He caught us at the vent aperture and confronted us. I still tremble thinking back to that.

"Shall we begin?" he asks me, and his expression instantly morphs into a put-on smile. Cryptus bounds up without waiting for my answer. "This way," he directs, though I know the way and have been in the chamber countless times already.

"Yes," I mumble. I find myself intimidated around Cryptus, though I know I shouldn't still be so daunted by him. I'm never intimidated around anyone else except Oculus. But Cryptus has this unnerving quality to him, being a synthetic: so pompous, supercilious and condescending. I don't ever feel like I'm 14; I always feel like I'm 4… *and in trouble.*

He holds the door open for me, and I walk nervously past him. "Any containment issues last night?" he inquires in a disinterested monotone.

I shake my head. "None."

As protocol, we're supposed to report any containment anomalies to Cryptus immediately upon awakening, filing a report in the stasis log next to our pod. I tell him that I haven't had any.

This, of course, is a lie, but I don't tell Cryptus that. The truth of the matter is that my parents have been in practically every single dream I've ever had since they died that hot August day five years ago, and this is the force within me that keeps me going, I know that. To surrender that? To pretend like they're not there? It would be like allowing them to die all over again, and that's a concession I'm not prepared to make. Cryptus doesn't have to know. What he doesn't know won't short out his circuits.

The android surveys me uncomfortably and lengthily, staring into my eyes as if equipped with a visual polygraph. I feel like I'm about to squirm. But thankfully, I've perfected my blank slate expression to a fault, and we reach an impasse.

The synthetic relents with a mild *hmmm*, and allows me to pass. I continue on into the chamber and mount up in the left seat, the first of three in there. I know the reason there are three. So does Cryptus. So does every single orphan onboard The Origin. The third chair is different from the other two, and it is encased in a chamber with a lot of gadgets and wiring.

Cryptus says nothing to me as he mechanically goes about his duty, strapping me in and wiring me up for The Phoenix Experiment. This is, after all, what he was made for; it's his driving purpose here, and it is, after all, the whole reason I'm here.

The Phoenix Experiments were made as a way to connect with what was lost; to restore purpose and affirmation, contentment and closure for those bereaved. The 'phoenix' label was meant as a symbol of rebirth for those entering the experiments, so that they could receive their closure, breathe the free air again, and start over, brand new. A novel concept, to be sure.

I don't remember offhand who conceived of it, but I'm glad they did. Somebody named Joseph or Giuseppe or Jonas or something, back in 2234. Back then, I think it was called 'Cairon,' in honor of the Greek mythological ferryman whose job it was to guide souls across the river Styx. The intent, both then and now, is to try to connect the bereaved with the passed in a serene setting, allowing us to enter a state of dreamlike calm and visit 'the other side.' To, essentially, *ferry* us over to our loved ones, and then return us back to the real world. We're in a state of suspended animation while we sojourn there. It's amazing, every single time, but would be even more so if I could actually find my parents.

Call it, 'counseling in catatonia,' if you will. The body is supposedly more able to make peace with a situation in a dreamlike state. Situations become idealized and resolutions are more dramatic and memorable, ultimately translating into waking life. For a planet still recovering from unimaginable loss and misfortune, The Phoenix Experiments promote health in tangible ways, creating young citizens who will be stronger for their eventual return to Earth.

I know full well the reason why they need us to be stronger. Earth needs more Speakers. The monsters are still out there, and they've taken too many of us. Trauma and bereavement can limit us; they leave us aching. Being freed of that trauma harnesses our focus. Banshees feed on yearning, and those who are bereaved… well, *yearn*. It's that simple. Take away the yearning, and banshees can't zero us.

So, naturally, if we find a way to perfect speaking to the dead, we'll be invaluable assets back on Earth. Speakers are always in high demand. Mature, non-conflicted Speakers can pacify the dead *and* the banshees. My purpose here doesn't dampen my desire to reconnect with my parents in the here and now; for the moment, I care far more about that.

Cryptus is the perfect moderator for these experiments: he's cold and unfeeling, and assigns neither angst nor jubilation to any of his subjects' reactions. He monitors us plainly, ambivalently, medically, noting sweat secretion and heartbeat arrhythmia indicating excitement due to emotional reconnection, and then calmly observing a return to normal heart rate and body temperature, which indicates the work is done. Rumor has it he can actually enter with us if he wanted to, in some sort of dream link, but I've never seen it done.

Then he pulls us out, back into the real world, where our parents cannot come and no longer exist once more, except in memory. The more progress we make separating from the yearning, the stronger we'll be in the end.

The only sad part about all of this is, to date, I've never once found my parents in any of my experiments. In the Phoenix Experiments, you're still awake, focused, and present. Things can happen within your control.

In the Phoenix Experiments, you can actually bring them back.

I just can't seem to find them, though not for a lack of looking. Nearly everyone else has found theirs, except for Garris. He's just too much of an oaf to focus properly.

No, my parents exist now only in my nightly reveries. In my 'containment anomalies,' as Cryptus refers to them. I hate that very term because it sounds so clinical and antiseptic. There's nothing wrong with dreaming about my parents. I welcome it.

What I wouldn't give to trade places *and* dream subjects with Anther: the object of his affections appear only in his dreams, but not in The Phoenix Experiment. I'd choose to have mine appear in The Phoenix Experiments rather than only in my dreams; in my waking life rather than in my sleep.

I glance over at the chairs next to me, briefly, and longing surges through me as I imagine my own parents here with me, today, *now*. I think of my mother's long, flowing hair, and my father's bristly brown beard. I imagine their smiles that were stolen from me, gone far too soon.

Thinking these thoughts, I close my eyes and attempt to conceal the fluid welling up in there, as Cryptus walks back to his control panel in a shielded room, preparing to monitor me.

He doesn't know my parents live on in my dreams. He, and I, want them to live in the tangible pseudo-reality that is the Phoenix Experiment. But, to date, I've been denied that, for whatever reason.

My only consolation is that the longer I go without contact, the closer I feel I'm drawing near to an inevitable first contact with them from the other side; beyond our world. I breathe, in and out, slowly, projecting my thoughts into a wistful, melancholy dreamscape, searching, searching, searching for them.

In the dark blackness of this room, I only know longing.

2: The Zephyr

No one sees it coming.

Suddenly, life changes, and The Zephyr is dead in space, floating helplessly across the diameter of the planet from The Origin.

The ship is listing, and oxygen is depleting rapidly from her exploded reserves. They show us pictures of the damage on the central news in our terminals. The Zephyr is identical in shape and mass to The Origin, but it's stationed across Earth's equator. The two ships orbit as silent sentinels over our planet, spinning slowly around it in unending silence, never meeting.

A shuttle from The Zephyr is being prepared even now, and the death toll sits currently at 22 souls, including their Helmsman *and* Science Officer. The only adults left are two monitors, Chiefs Ashira Sarristo and Maridie Onyx, and their synthetic, Baryonnis Talicus. They are accompanying the 7 remaining girls, and are expected to arrive within two hours on the shuttle. I always find it comical when I hear synthetics have last names. They don't need them.

7 girls. There are 8 boys here. I wonder who will lose out, I think to myself. *Probably Dravin.*

Briefly I wonder why they had 32 people on board, whereas we have such a smaller number. We only have 15. Perhaps the girls required more experimentation because they're naturally more predisposed to emotion? Could that be why? Or were more males killed fighting the banshees, so there are less of us? I don't know. My thoughts are cut short as a new report comes in.

There is no hope for the Zephyr. It is on a buildup to detonation, and will explode within 30 minutes. Repair crews from Earth were en route to it but were turned back in orbit. Repair is futile.

I sit and listen to the news through the overhead coms. Helmsman Oculus is *not* happy, and he swears up and down through the broadcast, cussing so frequently the ceiling intercom turns blue. A group of us sits and listens to his angry tirade, laden with directives to maintain decorum and manners at all times. Like we didn't know to do that already.

We're all uncivilized miscreants here, Oculus, I think sarcastically to myself. His bristling tirade unfairly paints us as unruly apes itching for mayhem. "You are to do nothing untoward with our guests, and will treat them hospitably," he says. "They must be kept safe, by all of us. Failure to do so will result in confinement to quarters and loss of rec time for up to one week." I shudder at his threat, because it's certainly not hollow. Depriving us of rec time is Oculus' preferred method of punishment. Pretty sure everyone else shudders at the threat as well.

The girls, he says, are to remain aboard The Origin until such a time as they can be ferried over to their new ship. How long that will take, Oculus doesn't say, and probably doesn't know.

The Rubris is the only other G-class star freighter equipped for the Phoenix Experiments, and we can all see its location is out by the Trappist-1 system presently. It wouldn't be anywhere near us for at least a year. We don't know much about that ship, and questions posed by us boys have generally gone unanswered. A rumor persists that the Rubris had some kind of 'incident' onboard, and that's why it's so far away now. Banished, almost. It's been out there for years, but maybe whatever incident befell it has now been resolved. The unanswered questions pile high.

We will provide a temporary quarantine for the girls, our helmsman says. It's not safe down there for them yet; there are still far too many banshees all over the globe, and not enough Speakers to calm them. If the girls are anything like us, they haven't matured enough as Speakers to confront any of the creatures.

There's no way around it: they must avoid downtime, they need to continue with their own experiments here as well, and they've already been through enough trauma. Oculus stresses to us that they will *not* endure any more. His emphasis on *not* sounds like another subtle, intentional indictment of our character.

Our adult Chiefs, Marxim Bannitor and Hin Ambrosius, busy themselves below with rearranging Quadrant A, Floor 2 into the girls' temporary home away from home. There are connected pods, showers and living quarters there for guest staff, dignitaries (not like there are any left) and other visitors. It should do nicely.

I can't help but think, however, that Quadrant A, Floor 2 is about as far from our own dorms on Quadrant C, Subfloor 4D as you can get on this ship. What they *don't* know, however, is that Anther and I know about the maintenance passageways and ducting that connects everything together nicely for those with a penchant to snoop around. Anther and I have such a penchant, and as he gawks at me now, I can read that penchant all over his face. We'll have a good view of their showers, I'm sure.

I glance around wide-eyed at our guys. We're all gathered in the cafeteria, listening to the announcement.

Ranshay looks at me petrified as if the very word *girls* is a curse-word. He obviously wonders if it means the same as *banshees*. Ranshay is in for a sizeable surprise.

Garris smiles oafishly and looks like he's already mentally preparing to step up his flirting game.

Anther's jaw has dropped so low I presume he'll split at the ears. I watch him momentarily and figure he's got to shower and use deodorant if he's going to stand any kind of chance with them.

Venthix just stares at the overhead com, looking to be in the throes of fear. For the first time I wonder if he's gay; threatened by the incoming influx of X chromosomes.

Martos looks at us and nods with a massive crap-eating grin, ready to round up all the ladies for himself. But we all know he'll tire and pass out before he even has the energy to say hello to one of them.

At 8 years old, Dravin is the youngest of us. They practically snatched him up on his birthday. I don't even know if he fully understood where he was going or what he would be doing there. I swear they offered him milk and cookies and he just up and boarded their shuttle, no questions asked. He doesn't really understand the big deal about the girls coming; he sits off to the side of us, drawing a few monsters battling on a clean sheet of white paper as we listen.

And then, there's Finorin, or just 'Orin,' as we call him. He's the oldest, and he's well-built and rugged. He's only a few weeks shy of his 18th birthday, at which point he'll be released back to Earth. I have no knowledge of how well he's done in here, if he's reconnected, if he's ready to go 'save the world,' as we jokingly call it. He's a closed book. We'll see. He definitely has the muscles for it. If his Speaking ability matches his muscles, the banshees are done for.

Orin is an adult, practically, and I find myself watching him and hoping all the girls don't fall head over heels in love with his irritating man-pecs.

Anytime we think of the 'release,' it suggests to us that we've been nothing more than prisoners here this whole time, but that's not exactly true. It's a bittersweet graduation; we'll be released back to Earth and on our own to try to commune with our dearly departed in our own way, free from the help of The Origin. It's an unspoken truth that none of us wants our release. It's much safer in here. But we were conscripted, right? We chose The Origin. That means we're eventually going to have to be soldiers. So be it.

I glance over at Anther again. He can't contain his smile, and for a second I wonder if the mad hope steals through him that one of the girls might resemble the otherworldly girl of his dreams.

I shake my head at him.

He just smiles, and his grin is curved upward in unquenchably obvious hope.

I was right.

Shattered debris and particles zip by below us, circling the Earth in their orbit. Remnants of the exploded Zephyr, they now scream dangerously across the atmosphere, skimming and burning up. Several trillion dollars of Earth's capital, invested into that ship, now a waste.

Thankfully, we're high above the debris. The fragments pass us well before the Shuttlecraft Avalon arrives, with its precious cargo that all the boys are so excited about. Me, I'm not ambivalent; just feeling melancholy about the whole affair.

I had barely gotten out of my experiment when the news struck. It was sad news to begin with, but when you add the fact that I *still* didn't find my parents in there, it was a recipe for depression. I left Cryptus' office without saying goodbye. He was wordless as I passed him by glumly.

Now I stand on the observation deck with the rest of the gang. We stare wistfully out into the void as the Avalon approaches, a tiny glittering speck against the endless black ink of limitless space, preparing to dock with The Origin.

I glance around me, staring at my fellow Y-chromosomal shipmates. They are all practically salivating. An image flashes through my mind of some old nature show with an ibex swimming through a pond in Africa as wild dogs patrol the shore, waiting for it to emerge so they can feast. I roll my eyes. Have these wild dogs beside me no dignity?

"You guys are terrible," I say. "Give me a break." Two out of the seven of them look at me questioningly. Ranshay is one, only because he's trying to decipher what I said and translate it. The others don't take their eyes off the approaching shuttle. "These girls' ship just exploded and killed 22 of their own shipmates," I add, nodding out in space toward the Avalon. "Show a little class and stow your dinner napkins."

The Avalon is within fifty feet of The Origin, commencing docking maneuvers.

"Speak for yourself, Jax," Martos grunts. "I can't wait to meet 'em." He licked his lips. *Wild dog.*

"Please," I grunt back. "You'll be asleep before they even open the airlock."

The others chuckle at our interchange, but none of them is as heartless as Martos in dismissing the girls' recent trauma.

Anther presses himself up against the glass, trying to peek around the edge of our ship as the stern of the shuttle is lost from view. His hot breath fogs up the window and his fingers leave swirling impressions. A klaxon suddenly sounds throughout the ship and First Officer Mirabay's voice barks through. "Shuttle Avalon docking now. All crew prepare to receive the new arrivals."

Before we can say *new arrivals*, the eight of us are running to the cubeports, repeatedly slamming palms against the buttons and issuing orders to Phiria to summon one. The Origin's AI presence apologizes in an artificially heartfelt manner, providing an estimated time of arrival that far outlasts teenage patience.

It's no use. The display shows both of the cubeports to be in the next quadrant over. They won't get here in time, much less get us *there* in time. We abandon the cubeports and race to the stairwell, thundering down the stairs, most of us giggling like hooligans, whooping and hollering in anticipation.

"Settle down, midgets," shouts Orin. "Shut it! You don't want Oculus or Mirabay to hear us, do you?" We settle down and slow our pace, though by now I'm sure that Cryptus is already there, and he for *sure* has heard us. He's constantly connected wirelessly to Phiria anyway.

The docking bay draws near. We arrive on its floor, panting and with hearts a'flutter, and not just due to the exertion. I have to confess that I'm growing more excited the nearer we draw to the loading dock… *and the girls.* I want to meet them as well.

Orin slowly opens the door a hair, peeking through to get a lay of the land. Oculus and Mirabay stand there at the end of the shuttle hatch. Someone elbows me. I turn and see Anther smiling like an orangutan. His eyebrows flick up in anticipation. I shake my head.

Orin motions to us that he's going to open the door. He holds his finger to his lips as we nod in understanding. He playfully swoops his hand through his hair and sniffs his armpit to check his readiness, then frowns. So do we, because he stinks as much as Garris does. I decide that his stinkiness will work in my favor in attracting the girls to myself.

We silently enter through the stair doors, with class and military decorum. Oculus is suddenly aware of us and turns, nodding. He points for us to stand off to the side and wait. Cryptus had already turned and is watching the stairwell door as it opens, aware of our presence. He eyes us analytically.

Dull concussions and mechanical whirring sound from beyond as the shuttle latches onto The Origin. The clamps connect. Air hisses through joints and crevices. Signal lights on the wall change from red to green. Phiria announces a successful dock.

My heart skips a beat. I swallow. Suddenly, the hatch expands outward in a retracting pointed star pattern, and…

…there they are.

Seven girls are boarding our ship, right in front of all of us.

I see at least three of them right away, and at least one adult lingering behind them as they line up to disembark. Their outfits are strange, like ours but, fittingly, more feminine, accentuating their curves and revealing lower necklines. I have no objection to this. The colors of their uniforms are different as well, more pastel. Their silver nameplates glisten like ours do. Their appearance takes on a dreamy, glossy hue, almost as through a vignette. We all watch in awe, our hands clasped behind our backs, staring eagerly yet trying to remain stoic and dignified.

Girls are here.

"And this," Oculus says in almost a warning tone, "is Ensign Jax Hutson." Oculus has introduced everyone else, ending with me. The girls study us, nodding through their shell-shocked ordeal. They're not studying us as much as we're studying them, I guarantee it. My stomach is fluttering with a strange pandemonium of butterflies throughout.

Strangely, I'm fighting the urge to pee. I had forgotten to do so between my time with Cryptus and meeting the girls, and now I'm ready to burst. My nerves being on fire isn't helping. One of the girls, a long-haired red-head named Alaris, is drop-dead gorgeous, with eyes as colorful and shimmering as a nebula.

I glance over at Anther – and Martos – sidelong to see who they're eyeballing. I try to triangulate their view and ensure that neither of them are checking out my girl.

Wait, what?

But Alaris is beautiful, and that's that. So, I said *my girl*, and I meant it. It's during that thought that I see a faint smile creep across her lips as her eyes connect with mine, and I wonder if she's perceiving my thoughts, perhaps even feeling the same.

Out here amongst the stars, hope is essential.

I find myself smiling at her, and a swell of emotion wells up in me as I drink in her beauty.

Stop being a wild dog, I say to myself, just before Helmsman Oculus clears his throat.

"Chiefs Sarristo and Onyx," he says, "these are our Chiefs, Marxim Bannitor and Hin Ambrosius. Our ships' functionality should be fairly identical to yours. Phiria is here as well. Say hello, Phiria," he says, turning and looking up.

Our AI sounds out from above. "Welcome, passengers and crew of The Zephyr. My sincerest condolences on your recent losses," she finishes in a glum, empathetic tone.

In my heart I can't help but wonder if she means the 22 human souls lost, or the loss of a fellow ship with her own presence onboard. But that would imply *feeling*, and AI can only produce a facsimile of feeling. Just like Phiria is doing now.

Nonetheless, it resonates. The girls smile nervously and nod in thanks.

Oculus smiles. "Our synthetic, Mr. Stygius Cryptus, is here to ensure that your Phoenix experiments continue unhindered, and he will bring you up to speed."

Cryptus nods and musters an expression that might be loosely labeled a smile.

"Cryptus has been with us from the beginning, and he's tremendously talented with his work," Oculus continues. "Our Chiefs here will show you to your quarters. Quadrant A, three floors down from us, on Subfloor 3. The boys here are stationed on Subfloor 4D in their own quadrant. You'll have everything you need. Please join us for dinner this evening at 1800 hours in the mess hall," he finishes with a stern smile. It's not a request. I find that utterly odd. We haven't seen girls in years, and undoubtedly they haven't seen boys. *We're a bunch of hormone-crazed angst-ridden teens, and you throw us in the mix together? Didn't you want us focused? Aren't there rules against intermingling?*

Perhaps he's just trying to be a gentleman. We definitely don't want to turn a cold shoulder to our fellow humans who have not only been bereaved of their families, but then deprived of their shipmates as well. A little empathy goes a long way, even if it's over a rule-bending dinner.

I quickly scan the other guys' faces beside me. Brimming with hormones and unrestrainedly raucous before, they're all now equally as placid and tame as me, caught between trying to be a gentleman and trying to stay in compliance with Oculus' edict and the threat of losing rec. And *none* of them seems to be worried about the same thing that I am.

Wild dogs tamed.

I *really* have to pee.

Alaris smiles at me. The pressure fades as I smile back. She only has eyes for me. I hope the others notice.

"Did you see Miritia?!" Orin exclaims as we walk back to our quarters to prepare for dinner. There is talk among more than a few of them that they will have a second shower and spruce themselves up. "She is *fine*. That girl's gotta be 17 or 18, right? She's amazing!" He shakes his head in blissful incredulity as we stroll.

"Haha, Orin's got it bad," Martos teases. "She's a looker, for sure, buddy. For me, I really like Skarbé. What kinda name is that anyway, Dutch? Whoo!"

"It might be!" Orin says. "You can have her, bro. I call dibs on Miritia," he says, proudly.

"You can't call 'dibs' on a *girl*, Orin," Anther corrects him with a smile. "They're not, well, 'dibsable,' right? It's not like you're shopping for groceries."

"What the heck are *groceries*?" Orin asks annoyedly. "And who cares, stop talking! I'm trying to think about Miritia," he says in a wistful stupor. I'm just glad he didn't choose Alaris.

But then Anther speaks up.

"Man, did you guys see that red-head? She's freakin' gorgeous!" he exclaims. "What's her name?"

Spoke too soon.

"Alaris," little Dravin pipes up disinterestedly. I flinch, and look over at Anther, trying to conceal a glare. This is where I figure the best thing to do would be to employ a little reverse psychology on him.

"*Alaris?*" I ask with a sneer. "Gross. She was like the ugliest one out of all of them." Some of the guys laugh at my appraisal. Anther's smile fades. "You picked *her?*"

Anther's eyes flick away from me for a moment, unsure of what to say. His mouth moves without words as he tries to summon up a response. "Yeah," he defends. "I think she's cool. So?" he offers, rather mournfully.

I click my tongue and sneer at him in disapproval, pretending that he's insane in order to maintain my highly standoffish and very fake stance. I roll my eyes in disgust at him, and quickly look the other way while gritting my teeth.

"Yeah," Venthix says, "she was the best one of all of them, I think." *Okay, fine, confirmation that he's* not *gay. Or... maybe he's just trying to fit in. But also, frustrating.*

Orin chuckles in disagreement and shakes his head vigorously, laughing. "Seriously."

I start to feel a defensive roiling in my gut. I have to act fast.

"Yeah, I agree," chimes in Martos. "I think Alaris is the best."

"Totally," Garris the Neanderthal oaf agrees.

Ranshay says nothing; his eyes simply bounce back and forth between all of us like a wicked ping-pong match, not that he's ever played it, much less ever will. I watch as everyone who voiced that they like Alaris exchange approving glances between each other, and all I can do is humbly acknowledge that I'm now outnumbered as a contender.

As for myself, I'm determined to not allow the setback of the other guys' attraction to Alaris to become a prolonged one. In the back of my mind, I begin strategizing on ways to divert their attention.

But dammit, I think to myself, *if my ploy didn't backfire spectacularly.*

I just didn't see that coming.

3: The Tension

We haven't seen them, and I wonder why.

The girls have been here for 48 hours now. Following dinner, they were whisked away by their two female Chiefs, who were to then consult with Cryptus about the continuation of their experiments.

Dinner was fine, but we were all chagrined to find that Oculus had positioned himself, Cryptus, and our chiefs across from their girls, and positioned their chiefs across from us boys. So, each ship's crew was on separate sides of the table, and the boys were shifted down from the girls. I caught a sidelong smile from Oculus when he noticed our disappointment at this. *Jerk.*

Not like any of us would have been brave enough to pose any questions to the girls anyway. How do you even talk to a girl, much less one that you're actually interested in? I don't know. I don't think the other guys do either.

Be that as it may, I managed to catch a few stray glances my way from Alaris. She was definitely checking me out. One time she even blushed and looked away. Cryptus asked me to share my own appraisal of The Origin's Phoenix experiments, and it sure looked like she was listening to me intently. When I finished, she smiled at me, but my shipmates did not. I scanned their faces. They were jealous that she obviously liked me. Haha. Revenge is a dish that is best served cold. *How's it taste, fellas? The hot girl picked me. Not you. Me.*

Orin seemed to be the only one unfazed; he was, after all, interested in Miritia, and left Alaris to me. That helped.

As distracted by Alaris' beauty as I was, I was also listening. At one point, Cryptus started in on some kind of oration about getting our planet back. It was actually quite moving. So, try as I might to focus on Alaris and return the exchanges of smiles, I couldn't focus on her much for the rest of dinner.

Cryptus has a point. I know why I am here, and I know the deep burning drive within me comes from a longing to see my parents again. I have to become an effective Speaker. We Speakers – we *all of us* – have to reclaim our planet, and these girls deserve to be a part of that success as well. To that end, we aren't here to perfect our pair bonding. We have to focus. All things in due time.

Earth, we all know, has a timeline. The natural resources will always grow. Trees will bloom again and bear fruit. Gardens will produce vegetation. The sun still shines and the rain still falls. But our structures are relatively unmanned, our facilities are overgrown with brambles and creepers, and it's a ghost town down there due to all those damned banshees. We have to reclaim the Earth! People are dying. There can be no interruption. The calamity with The Zephyr is a setback, we all concur, but we are determined to maintain our focus, and not allow the setback to become a prolonged one. Oculus is right.

> *The enemy below doth sleepeth not*
> *Nor frets the day when mankind bought*
> *Their means to calm,*
> *their soothing balm*
> *The Phoenix Experiments mean naught*
>
> *So press on, wayward foolish mortal*

Continue on toward thy vain portal
We lie here, waited,
our breaths bated
Prepared to at thy deaths give chortle

It's time for my experiment, so I get ready to check in with Cryptus. Chow time over, I'm dressed and ready, almost to the nines today because there are now girls on our ship. I dab on a bit of cologne for the first time in ages. And as I pass all of the other guys, I catch a whiff that they've done the same. Even little Dravin smells like a bed of roses. They must have held him down and slathered him. Girls aren't even on his radar yet. Sure wish there were girls here more often; we all smell pretty hideous otherwise.

Though we're kept apart, there is only one Phoenix lab on this whole ship. I find that very odd considering how big this ship is, how savage the banshees are, and how many people have died. But, in truth, there's also only one synthetic. As effective as he is, Cryptus is not omnipresent; he can't be in multiple places at once.

Nonetheless, if we were to receive a new influx of orphans, we would definitely need more labs. The Origin seems so bloated and overspaced... like a vast aquarium established for a single school of minnows. There has to be a reason. I understand, however, that shuttles are limited, and firing up a shuttle on Earth is a recipe for disaster, as it's sounding the dinner gong for banshees. They can't just whisk a shuttle our way each time; they have to strategize and send them up in bulk, secretively, when the banshees are subdued or distracted... or on the other side of the world.

The girls' synthetic – I remember her name is Baryonnis Talicus – is nowhere to be found, but the girls assure me she is remaining below to serve them and provide educational services. I wonder if she and Cryptus have spoken. I assume there is some desire on each of their parts to do so. But knowing them, they're both AI; they could simply plug into terminals at various points throughout The Origin and commune with each other remotely through Phiria. Strange. Eerie. *Whatever; it's their way,* I think.

I decide to ponder that more later.

For now, I realize that I may actually run into one of the girls at the lab, passing each other like ships in the night. The boys all have hourlong shifts every day; Cryptus informs us, however, that for the time being our schedules have been reassigned to every *other* day, to accommodate the girls. Cryptus will alternate between genders and accommodate us equally. I take no umbrage with this; *I'm not finding my parents in there anyway,* I think to myself, glumly.

There's a palpable tension in the air. There has been ever since the girls arrived. Even though The Origin is vast, our population goes from 14 to 25 just like that. A horrific thought passes through me: what if something tragic happens with The Rubris as well, on its way to us? We'd be the only ship left! Surely, they couldn't transfer everyone aboard this ship. We'd all be sardines in a tiny, tin can, overloaded and cramped beyond belief. And if there were any more girls, us wild dogs would probably detonate from overstimulation.

Besides, whatever happened to them in the first place? I wonder.

In the meantime, it's inescapable: we're all truly a bit more on edge, quick to quibble over the stupidest minutiae.

Anther and I got in a heated argument last night over which kind of banshee is the worst. I maintained that the scurriers are the worst, because there's no escape, and they can get you while you sleep. He argued back that, no, the plodders are the worst, because they're so large, they can cover more ground and literally stomp you into goo. And there are rumors of creatures more terrifying than either of these, but they have no name.

I see his point, but I don't agree with him, and then our volume rose as we were both shouting over each other, fangs bared. Thankfully, Orin stepped in and knocked our heads together. But Anther and I didn't speak over dinner as a result.

It's like all of our hormones are on the fritz, amplified and hypersexualized. *Wild dogs.*

Venthix and Martos actually got into a fight. It was ridiculous. We laughed as they pummeled each other. Venthix landed a right hook that sent Martos sprawling. The venomous look that Martos gave him once he collected himself was priceless. I'd pay good credits to get it framed and hang it on my wall. It got so violent and so loud that Oculus came in, and we shut right up and stood at attention. Martos and Venthix stood there bleeding, apologizing their asses off. Cryptus then came in and cleaned them up, sterilizing their wounds and applying salve. They both lost out on rec time for two days straight, and have to pen a research paper on the history of banshees. Sucks to be them.

Last night I had a dream, and not a pleasant one. *Yes,* I got to meet my parents in it – and I thank the serum for that – but my dream was *flooded* with banshees, and I was deathly afraid, flitting from shadow to shadow. I was in some abandoned warehouse on Earth, and they were all shrieking outside. I just knew at any minute they would find me and shriek into my soul until I have a coronary. That's exactly how my parents died. A plodder got my mom and a scurrier got my dad. They didn't stand a chance. That awful dream sees me waking up and screaming. Phiria registered my emotional strain immediately.

"Good early morning, Jax," she greeted me calmly. I glanced at the clock. 0135 hours in the morning. "Is everything okay? Would you like a sedative infusion with your serum?"

I shook my head. "No, thank you, Phiria. I'm fine. Just a bad dream."

"No problem," she replied warmly. "According to Regulation 35B2, Section H, please ensure that if your dream pertains to your parents, that you file the appropriate Containment Anomaly Repor-"

"Yes, yes, I know, Phiria. Thanks," I dismissed her. It was too early for regulations.

"My pleasure." She silenced.

Phiria is sweet but annoying. A little too saccharin and cheery for my taste. There's something so artificial about cheery. We don't live in a cheery environment, nor is Earth in a state of cheer at the moment. We're all bracing and holding on, trying to jumpstart healing.

The banshees are determined to deny us that.

Fortune favors the foolhardy. I quickly make my way to Cryptus' lab and, wonder of wonders, there are two girls there. One of them is in Cryptus' office waiting for their turn to go through Phoenix. Another is already in the chair and synced up. Just my luck, neither one is Alaris. *That's fine,* I think to myself. I'll acquaint myself with the two that *are* here. After all, no time like the present. Maybe they can tell Alaris how awesome I am when they report back.

They both look to be on the younger side. The one in the lab is the youngest of the girls who stepped off the Avalon and into our lives. She's asleep and hooked up. Cryptus monitors her astutely. The one sitting in front of me out here in Cryptus' foyer looks to be just a bit older. She smiles a wide, toothy grin at me and perks up, bobbing slightly. Her skinny arms are delicate and fair, and her blonde hair is tied into two equal-sized braids close to her head, running down her neck into silver clasps.

"Hi, I'm Jax," I say, sticking out my hand. "Jax Hutson."

The girl accepts it and shakes it, greeting me in turn. "Omnias," she says. "Omnias Prasuth. Good to be aboard your ship. It's beautiful. I've been on The Zephyr for five years. I'm 13. How about you? How old are you?"

Wow. Precocious, I think to myself. "Uh, nice to meet you, Omnias. I'm 14. Been here for five years. Nice to meet you. Who's that in there?" I ask, nodding into the lab.

"That's Zaris Sharibian, my friend. She's only 11." Her smile fades a bit, as if she's miffed that I'm inquiring about her friend. Little does she know I'm interested in Alaris, and *I'm* slightly miffed that *she's* not here. "Zaris is doing her Phoenix session right now."

"Uh, yes, I see that," I say, sitting down across from her, and then an awkward silence follows as she bites her lip and looks around. "We do them too," I add, finally, punctuating the silence.

"Neat. I'm next," she says, beaming, and then her head cocks to the left. "Is it true you guys have the same crappy food goo here? *Please* tell me there's lobster!" She practically leans forward from her bench toward me, eyebrows up as she pleads.

My head cocks in turn. "Lobster? No, no lobster. We have the same crap, sorry. I assume you're talking about *BioPrime.* Pretty sure they have that on all the ships." I chuckle sheepishly at the stupidity of it, and can guess her upcoming reaction.

She scowls and slams her back against the leather rest behind her in a huff, sulking. "Oh… that… tasty… *BioPrime*," she says in a mumbled sing-songy caricature of the commercial jingle for our revolting food paste. "Barf."

I chuckle. "Barf indeed." *I was right.*

"You'd think with all the research we're helping them do, they'd budge an inch and give us a nice, juicy steak for once," she complains.

I don't tell Omnias that I thought the very same thing just a few days ago. A slab of the apparently delicious meat flashes through my mind, but the taste doesn't, because I just don't know what it's like. I shift nervously in my seat. "Steak would be nice. Have you ever had it?"

"Nope."

"Yeah, me neither."

"I saw you hanging with that one guy, is his name Anther? Anther Seeto, is it?"

"*Sec*-to," I say. "Yeah. He's alright," I say, sloughing off my best friend, the banshee argument still fresh in my mind, and wanting to get him back for liking Alaris. "Did you meet him?"

Omnias shakes her head. "Hmm-mmm, no. He just seems nice," she says, blushing.

Ahhh, now I get it, I think to myself. *I'm sure I can use this.*

I look around me quickly, as if scrounging for tools. "Uh, yeah, he's pretty cool, actually. I've known him for a long time. I can introduce you two, if you'd like?" I offer, because my name is apparently Helpy Helperton.

She blushes, and I've scored a victory, no matter how sinister. "Yeah! Sure. I mean, no rush, it would be cool, but not a big deal if it doesn't happen."

Sure. I believe that as much as I can throw it. Here is where I seek my leverage.

"I can do that, sure. He's a good guy. Hey! Since we're asking, do you know, uh, what's her name," -here I play dumb to score my first acting award- "*Alaris* very well? Is that her name? Alaris?" *Smooth. I'm good.*

"Uh," Omnias replies, "yeah, I could introduce you too. At chow time tonight, maybe? She's cool. I don't know her *really* well, I hang with Zaris more, but I can def-"

A loud bang emits from the chamber, and we both jerk out of our conversation, rising quickly and staring in through the observation window. Zaris has flinched and kicked in her subconscious. Her expression is a twisted knot of angst, and her breathing has quickened, mouth agape. We both glance over at Cryptus, who remains as emotionless as an equation, studying her with impartiality. We hear the EKG beep more frenetically, but then it slows.

I briefly wonder if he worries about her or *any* of us in there, and what he would do if we went into cardiac arrest or something drastic like that. Would he act just as dispassionately, staring at us coldly and waiting for us to stop being such a dramatic human?

The drama subsides, and we both sit back down.

"That was weird," Omnias grunts, her eyes flashing back and forth. "Does that happen a lot?"

I shrug. "No idea. Not sure. I don't know what 'that' even was. Probably just a bad dream or something."

"But the Phoenix isn't a dreamcycle. It's just a mental probe, right?" she asks, and I feel like I'm on the witness stand in some courtroom case being cross-examined.

"Yeah, I think that's right," I agree.

"So, she's not dreaming. She wasn't having a nightmare or anything like that. Those only happen in our sleep."

"You have nightmares on The Zephyr?" I ask her, curiously.

"*Had* them, yes. Our ship is toast. What, you don't have them here?"

"Well, we have the serum, and-"

"Ew! The what?"

I stare at her blankly, wondering why they didn't do it the same way over there. "The serum. You know, the shot?" I raise my underarm to show her the port we all have implanted to receive the nightly serum injection. "To calm us, to enable us to dream, so that we're well-rested for our Phoenix experiments."

She just stares at me, gawking, as if this is the craziest thing she's ever heard. "You guys get a serum in order to dream? That's so weird."

"What, you guys just… dream? Without serum?"

"Stop saying *serum*," she orders, flatly.

I can't reply because the EKG starts beeping frantically, intermittently. We both glance in through the window again to see Zaris flinch. And then flinch again. And then spasm and lurch.

In a mix of curiosity and worry, we both flash our eyes over to Cryptus, staring at her coldly through the observation window still, his face eerily underlit as his heavy-lidded eyes monitor her emotionlessly.

Zaris continues to flinch, and occasionally she thrashes her legs. Her face suddenly contorts into a clench of what looks like fear, and a deep, guttural sob wells up in her throat and bursts out into a roar of panic.

Before Omnias or I can say anything, Zaris' eyes open wide, and they're white as frost. Her mouth is utterly agape, and an unearthly throbbing moan emits from the cavern of her little mouth that defies her size. It's a low, barreling sound, a hellish sound, a demon-roar, loud as an engine in the sky but churned up from horrific depths of somewhere desperately macabre. She is momentarily frozen in that expression, and my flesh crawls as I watch her. Her eyes roll back in her head.

Zaris relents and closes her mouth once more. All is silent except for the constant beeps of the monitoring machinery.

Yet her EKG speeds up.

My thoughts go back to the girls' synthetic, Baryonnis Talicus. I wonder what she would do in this situation, and why she's not here!

We press our faces up to the window. Omnias cries out "Zaris! Mr. Stygius, help her!"

"Cryptus," I correct her, absentmindedly, but then the android jerks himself up from his desk and throws open the control room door. I pan my eyes back to Zaris. She is now convulsing. Her eyes flutter open, and her chest spasms in great heaps as her back arches reflexively and wincing cries of stuttered agony emit weakly from her. The android walks briskly over to her with something in his hand, and for a moment I wonder why he isn't running. He quickly bends down over her and presses the device in his hand to her temple. Zaris flinches. A loud pop is heard as a spark lights up the room.

Omnias and I flinch at the sight.

Suddenly, the third chair brightens as if lit from within by a white fire. Momentary, yes, like a giant spark, but nonetheless alarming. For a brief moment, there is a dim shape in that light, but it disappears. My jaw drops in fright as I witness it, but it's hard to take my eyes off Zaris. Something is truly wrong here!

In a reflex, I throw open the waiting room door and burst into the lab. Omnias follows right on my heels. "Cryptus, what's happ-"

With surprising deftness and volume, Cryptus spins on his heels and faces us, his eyes wide. "Go *baaaaack!*" he howls monstrously, pointing at us.

My feet stop short of Zaris' chair and I backpedal. Omnias collides with me. I hold her back, nodding at Cryptus. "Ye-yes, sir," I say, feebly, pushing Omnias behind me and back out into the waiting room. Cryptus does not turn around again toward Zaris until we're back in the lobby and the door lock clicks in front of us.

The EKG slows. Once more Cryptus presses the whatever-it-is against Zaris' temple. Once more the pop. The EKG slows even further and normalizes. Zaris' chest stops heaving, her face unclenches, her fists unball themselves, and she relaxes, her breathing slowing. Her head is now beaded with sweat, and as the crinkles slowly disappear from her face, she swallows deeply, as if willing herself to recover from a fear she never thought she would have to face.

It has been several hours. I am sitting now in D-Block with Anther. "I'm telling you," I maintain, "it was like Cryptus was doing something to her. I don't know what it was, but it felt sinister. I've never experienced anything like that before, and I've never heard of anyone else going through anything like it."

Anther just stares at me, for the moment completely forgetting our feud. "And what happened after that?"

"I don't know, man! We just bolted out of there and went back to our respective areas. And you found me here. I've just been here."

"Wait, didn't you have a session today?"

"Yeah, but I bolted! You think I want to be in there with Cryptus after he did that to that girl?"

"Did what to her?" Anther presses.

"I mean – you know what I mean. It *looked* like he was doing something. And I wasn't going to be next!"

"You think Cryptus is doing something to them in their sleep? Or to us?"

"Dude, I have no idea," I say, resigned to dwell in uncertainty. "It was just so weird and traumatic, watching her."

"Well, I did run into Omnias after that. She said you went back here. Oculus is letting us do rec together, but we have to behave of course. Martos and Venthix were *livid* when they heard that we get to rec with them. But Omnias said she was fine. I saw Zaris. Didn't talk to her, but she looked okay to me. Happy as a clam. I think Omnias likes me, by the way," he says, cocking an eye and a smile and completely jumping the tracks, deviating from our conversation.

"Stay focused."

"Anyway, Omnias said that she didn't want to talk to Zaris about it. It doesn't seem like Zaris remembers it anyway."

"Seriously? Like… amnesia? That didn't look like something you could just easily forget," I insist. "She was traumatized. Freaking bouncing off her lab chair. And the third chair…," I trail off.

Anther stares at me, waiting. "The third chair *what?*" He pauses, sizing me up and down.

I wait and think, trying to remember.

"What, dude? Spit it out!"

I shake my head. "I don't know. It was almost like… some kind of shape was suddenly in that chair. Like a presence or… or… something," I finish. "I don't know," I repeat. "It was just eerie as hell, dude."

Anther says nothing.

"I want to get another look at what that thing was that he used on Zaris. I've never seen it before, and he had it with him in the control room. I wonder if it was some kind of injector, or… or… shock device, or something."

"Dude, you're losin' it. You're mental," Anther blurts out in a near-laugh.

"It's not funny, Ant. I was really worried about that girl." I sigh. Anther doesn't say anything else, and I hope my concern resonates with him.

"Zaris looked okay though?" I finally ask him. I feel genuine concern for her, and would love to see her. Now I'm doubting myself, wondering if it was just some fluke. Cryptus has been at the helm of the Phoenix Experiments for all this time. There is no reason to assume ill of him based on one potential anomaly.

"As far as I could tell, but I don't really know her. But I'd like to get to know Omnias, if you know what I mean."

"Not Alaris?" I ask, mustering up my best look of dispassionate incredulity.

Anther tilts his head and glares at me under his brows. "Dude, you're a loser. Stop pretending like you don't like her. It's clear she likes you. Everyone knows it."

"What do you mean, everyone?"

"*Everyone*. From Orin down. Hell, even Ranshay knows it, and he doesn't even speak English," Anther growls. "It's fine. She's yours. I don't wanna compete with you. You're my best friend. I'll take Omnias. She's cute." He pauses, eyeing me. "But just know that if we *did* compete, I'd shred you."

A grin slowly molds my lips into an indefensible acceptance. "Sure you would."

"I would," he says. "Painfully. Decisively."

"Decisively, huh? Isn't that a big ten dollar word for a meathead like you?"

"Believe it, spitfire," he says, cockily.

It's then that I realize that he is the one who got me labeled as a spitfire; it's *also* then that I realize he's aware that I'm the one who labeled him as a meathead. We enter a calm truce at the realization.

So be it.

"Well, remind me not to compete with you. But scurriers *are* the worst," I jab, referring back to our argument.

Anther smiles and shakes his head.

The rest of the day goes by without a hitch.

However, I don't see Cryptus anywhere, and I wonder why.

4: The Lost

Three more uncertain days go by, slowly, it seems.

Oculus confirms that the Rubris is indeed en route, and we will provide safe haven for the girls until it gets here. We are all thrilled at this news, of course, because Phiria confirms that it will take The Rubris four-hundred and thirty-two days to reach us at present speed. That's over a year. The girls will be with us all that time, which is completely fine with us boys.

The Zephyr has completely disintegrated by now, its remnants pulverized by the crushing weight of space, its entrails spinning haphazardly, fated to burn up in Earth's diminishing atmosphere below. Its only artifacts are the girls, their chiefs and their synthetic who now live aboard The Origin.

Over the past three days I report twice to Cryptus' lab as scheduled, given the fact that I missed a day, as well as the fact that we're now sharing scheduling with the girls. Each time, Cryptus appears as though nothing happened with Zaris the other day. It's as if he doesn't remember. He is pleasant as a peach, and greets me enthusiastically in a saccharin tone. There is no mention of a blue pen.

"Ensign Hutson! So good to see you this fine morning," he greets me. I stare at him with an awkward confusion and obligatory nod as I pass by him into the chamber. "How did you sleep?" he asks in a sing-songy voice, over-inflecting to the point of nauseating. "Any containment anomalies last night?"

I shake my head. "No."

"Of course not. Most excellent. Glad to see that you are remaining focused. Shall we proceed?"

I just watch him, perhaps searching for a trace of telling guilt or some minute desire to explain the bizarre ordeal Zaris went through on his watch only a few days ago. Granted, I have not been here to witness the other lab sessions, but I can't help but wonder if any of the other girls – or boys – went through any similar ordeals.

I strap myself in as Cryptus retreats to the wall console and taps various controls. "We shall. Will you be using any new equipment this session?" I ask timidly, fearful of his response as I'm fully referencing the device that he used to 'pop' Zaris in the temple.

He turns to me, and his smile fades. "Please explain," he says, suddenly coldly, and his bulbous, heavy-lidded eyes study me until I hate him all over again. He slowly returns to my side, staring at me the entire time.

"I-I was just curious," I stammer, "if you've upgraded the equipment since last time."

He fixes his eyes on me as I wither in the heat of his glare. The synthetic slowly rotates his head around the lab, inviting me to do the same. "Ensign Hutson, you are free to survey my laboratory as you see fit. Please. Do you observe anything new in here?"

I slowly pull my eyes away from him, and a macabre dread washes over me that he's going to knock me out and pop me with that thing, whatever it was, once I look away. But he doesn't. And I don't see the device anywhere. Of course I don't. It's safely stowed in his viewing room. I determine silently to sneak a peek at it with Anther as soon as we can.

I want to sigh, but that would give me away. "No," I relent. "I was just curious." Now it's time to act, and put his suspicion to rest. "As you know I still haven't made contact with my parents. I was just hoping that this might be the time."

"And why might this now suddenly be the time?" he asks me, almost before I've finished speaking.

I watch him. *Maybe the direct approach wasn't the right one. I'll pivot and try humor now instead,* I think.

"Come on, Cryptus," I say with a smirk, "after all the times I've gone in, look at me. Maybe I stand a better chance of finding your *pen* than I do my parents. You prefer blue, right?" I stifle a manufactured giggle.

He just stares at me. The reference holds no meaning for him. "I'm sorry, I don't understand, Jax. What is this about a pen?"

A wave of uncertainty washes over me as I gawk at him. My smile fades. He doesn't remember the pen? How could he not remember the pen? Androids have a photographic memory and are constantly recording data. Surely he must be joking; there is *no* way he wouldn't remember it. I squint my eyes at the synthetic standing before me, looking him up and down. Is he malfunctioning? Did that device he used on Zaris pop something in his own circuitry and disrupt his memory modules?

I stutter. "No-nothing, Cryptus. It's fine," I say.

An awkward moment of impasse lingers between us as he studies me once more. I finally allow my expression to change, though behind my eyes I'm still thinking about Zaris, and what went wrong in her Phoenix experiment, and the part that Cryptus must have played in it. Suspicion eats me like a canker inside, but I have to stow it. I dig in my heels and just meet his eyes, carefully avoiding a guilty visage.

Cryptus stands uncomfortably close to me and studies me. I'm grateful for the barrier of flesh and bone and independence that prevents him from reading my thoughts.

He finally retreats, wordlessly, and I breathe easy once more. He is *so* creepy.

Before too long I'm hooked up and ready to go, the confrontation now only a distant memory. *Pens, schmens.* I don't care anymore. I don't want to find a pen for Stygius Cryptus. I never did.

I only want to find my parents again.

Cryptus retreats to the control room.

Cue the white noise.

Cue the deep throbbing.

I'm told stories by Cryptus now and then about how, long ago, parents used to employ white noise on babies simply by driving them around in cars. Down there on earth, the road noise would be too much for the babies to handle. It was overwhelmingly peaceful, he said, and the babies would fall fast asleep from the lulling effect.

Cryptus says that the white noise and throbbing in here is not all that different, really; it's effusive, undulating, pulsating, overwhelming, and ultimately effective even on older humans such as myself. When he initially told me that prior to my very first Phoenix experiment, my initial thought was *well, we'll just see about that.*

How wrong I was. Jax Hutson doesn't stand a chance against the white noise. No one does.

Before too long, I enter a state just south of what could be called consciousness, and the sounds take me.

I am wandering through an old memory. I think I am 5 years old, and the trappings and layout of our old house call out to me from the recesses of my heart. I don't know them anymore, of course, because it's been several years, and the planet seems light years away from me now, even though it slowly rolls by below The Origin every single day of my now life. My guess is I'm in our old living room; there are plush couches and chairs, and the antiseptic white cleanness of the room suggests a healthy comfort that I might have once enjoyed. An overly large display screen is mounted on the wall, and sconces dot the surrounding walls, projecting a warm blue torch-like illumination for accent lighting.

Things are hazy; less clear than the here and now aboard our ship, but they retain a level of clarity that is amplified by the yearning in my heart to recall them clearly. Tilted frames hang along the wall, revealing portrait sessions with my family that I have no memory of. Small, nondescript toys litter the floors of our home, but I can't make them out. They hold no emotional weight for me anymore, and I don't remember what weight they might have held anyway.

A small, furry figure scampers past me, and I jump, startled. It doesn't heed me. I'm not really there anyway; it knows it, and I know it. It's a poodle, and a brief surge of disdain courses through me. Maybe I didn't like it when I was a boy. Maybe I don't like poodles. I don't know. It scampers by me on its way to somewhere else in our home.

Dim, blurry light filters in through the windows across a corridor leading to what I guess must be the living quarters. As I draw near, a smaller room en route makes me crane my head and peer inside it.

I am now staring at my old bedroom, and I know it. There are various caricatures of a superheroic figure dotting the room, the bed comforter, the dresser, the end table light, but I don't know who it is.

There are no more superheroes, anyway.

I struggle to make out the numerous artifacts and relics of a bygone age composing the character of my old bedroom. I have no memory of the things in here, although I vaguely recall *being* here. Sleeping here. Playing here. A scattershot flicker of a memory shoots through my mind of circling up under that superhero comforter, my dad perched next to me, one heavy leg hanging off of my bed as he reads me a bedtime story. I don't remember the story.

I'm an impartial observer here; removed enough to be unbiased, but emotion struggles to surface, to connect with *something* here, to make it more real and tangible in my memory. It was so long ago: nine years, to be exact, and a lifetime away.

Damned banshees, I think to myself, as I decide to just move on down the hall. Longing fills me to be here again, to live here, to have peace here. To have my parents here. Longing that I must subdue and repress. *No, not 'repress,'* I tell myself. *Make peace with.* Make peace with in order to have closure, and emerge stronger. *That's the whole reason I'm in here,* I remind myself.

Just as I grab the doorframe and prepare to tug myself away from the faded memories and head back toward my parents' room, I hear it.

It's different than the undulation of the white noise. It's some kind of shrill sound, a call of some kind, but there are words in it. I can't make it out. My ears strain, both in life and in the Phoenix Experiment, and I wonder, briefly, if Cryptus is aware of what I'm hearing.

Of course he is, though. That's what he does. That's all he does. Monitors all of it. Sees and hears everything, transmitted by the electrodes and probes on and in me, sending near-perfect 3D display representations of all that I'm witnessing and experiencing, in 24K clarity, back to his control room. I wonder what he thinks he heard just now as well.

I crane my head and look back over my shoulder. The dog bounds past me again, heading back the way we both just came. For just a moment, it stops, looks back toward my parents' bedroom, and sniffs, almost as if it detects some faint, ethereal presence here. Me: a spiritual bedouin making my way through this luminescent reverie. We're both connected somehow, though completely sundered.

I follow the dog toward the front door, slowly, and a name jumps out at me, though I don't know why, nor where it came from. *Poppy*? I'm guessing that's the dog's name, because the moment I think of it, it stops, turns back, and cranes its neck for a moment, cocking an ear. Realizing it was nothing more than a temporary anomaly, it lets out something akin to a dismissive sneeze, and then carries on once more.

I continue to follow Poppy.

There it is again. The noise. It's growing louder. Amidst the tendrils of sound clawing at me, something is grasping for purchase in my ears and brain. It's higher-pitched, and it sounds like it's coming from outside.

Poppy is facing the main door to our home. I regard it curiously as it sits there, patient, wagging its little popcorn tail, its eyes glued to the door.

Compulsion seizes me, and I suddenly find myself moving swiftly toward the door, intent on deciphering the sound. Morning light streams through the living room windows, and the blue torches flicker briefly as if a light breeze steals through.

I'm almost to the door.

Poppy, sensing me, scampers out of the way and retreats into the living room. The chanting again, eerily calm, swamped in dreamy reverberation, pulses around me:

> *O'er the moors the memories flee*
> *What once was is ne'er to be*

Darkness reigns,
fear regains
And vanity blanketeth land and sea

Unrequited listless calls
Go unanswered in the halls
Of unmet longs
and far-felt wrongs
A testament to deathly falls

I grab the door handle. All is calm, even the chanting. Poppy turns and skitters further back, and I don't know why. I turn the handle.

With violent force, the door is suddenly thrown wide open, and the screaming erupts. I know that scream! We're trained to recognize it. A thunderous heat wave blasts over me, scorching my skin as I shield my face. Wind buffets me. Fires rage outside: hungry flames of yellow and amber and orange and white, blowing and wavering and seeking to consume me.

Poppy yelps and bolts.

But it's the scream. It's not the howling wind racing over me that I fear. It's that scream that doesn't abate, and grows in intensity as it pitches ever upward in a haunting cry. The cry is composed of notes intended to shatter a human skeleton, piercing muscles with hissing tones that freeze your sinews in horror. Were I flesh and bone in here, it would do just that.

It's the cry of a banshee. This one seems different, somehow: louder, more toxic, more lethal.

I can't see it, but it's there, and there are perhaps more than one outside the relative calm of my home. They're searching for me, and I feel their prying eyes, hungry to devour my yearning and suck away my life force through the channel of my heart's deep longing.

Darkness reigns, fear regains…

But then, once more, permeating that scream, I hear it. I hear it! It's a shrill voice, trying desperately to punch through the clatter. It's nigh on impossible; a banshee's monstrous cry is indomitable.

I know now there are many, and they are hunting for me. But I, too, am a hunter, and I find myself now hunting for that voice. I can still hear it!

I decide to be strong. I steel myself.

What once was is ne'er to be.

I'm okay with it. I'm okay with not living here and not knowing these toys and not remembering these framed portraits. I'm okay with my parents not being here. What once was is not to be.

Not today, banshees. Not today.

I ball my hands into fists, and lower them to my sides, facing the onslaught of noise pressing against me, seeking to claw its way into my heart. I stare it down, unflinching, my hair blowing in the wind.

I hear the shrill voice. It's growing.

The flames lessen. I recognize them for what they are: just an illusion. I breathe deeply and try to focus on the voice. It's still there. Calling. What is it saying? "Back! Back!" Is that what it's saying? Is someone being attacked by the banshee and they're resisting, bravely, though futily? Only a Speaker can banish a banshee.

For a moment I wonder what I look like as I lie there on the chamber, and if Cryptus is watching me intently, or fingering some mysterious device and preparing to press it to my temples. I dismiss this thought and resume my focus.

Breathe, Jax. You got this.

I slowly walk outside, into the flames. They ebb and flicker into tiny tongues, deprived of their intensity. Thick, gray smoke eddies in the air.

The wind calms into bursts of a whisper.

The banshee screams seem to recede into an unguessable distance.

But the voice remains. I hear it clearly now, slowly emerging through the fog and sludge of noise, coalescing into clarity as the words become concrete, permeating the intangible and taking shape in my ears and mind.

Unrequited listless calls…

With astonishing clarity, as the hubbub dissipates all around me and calm seeps out from the house, flowing down the streets of the neighborhood, drowning all the tumult in peace, I hear it clearly now.

I was wrong. It wasn't "Back! Back!"

Jax! Jax!

And then, with waves of longing rippling down my skin, I see them. Two figures, emerging from the wisps of lingering fire-smoke, running down the street, on a torrent of emotion, carried by their hearts, racing toward me.

I recognize them instantly as my eyes begin to water and my heart throbs in a perfect balance of pain and purity. My skin tingles, and sobs emerge from me. I can't contain them. I am engulfed in a flood of yearning.

Her hair is blowing deftly in the wind, streaming behind her, bouncing off her jacket as she draws near.

His thick legs thunder beneath him as his feet pound the pavement, his bushy beard drenched with beads of sweat and saliva.

They reach for me.

And I reach for them, my eyes now streaming tears and my mouth calling out in unbridled desire and delight!

"Mom! Dad!"

My parents. I see them! My feet suddenly and swiftly carry me of their own accord, racing down the street toward them as our paths converge, my heart bursting with joy by the respite from overwhelming longing.

I weep…

…and the fires around me roar back to life.

I weep. My heart yearns.

It's everything I can do to keep from plunging headlong into this dream state forever… if only I could feel their embrace one more time.

The wind rises again to a deafening cacophony.

I weep. My heart yearns. I reach out.

It's no use. Futility and vanity rise up like a smoking haze, screening me off from them and denying my heart what it's burned for, for five years now.

The banshee screams rip through the skies and hammer us hard, smelling my yearning and licking its lips at my heart's cry. All three of us are thrown to the ground as the sound murders our desire and lays waste to our intentions.

And vanity blanketeth land and sea…

And then, just as I reach for them again, I feel a pressure in my temple, and a loud pop sounds.

Just like that, it seems that five more despondent years go by, slowly.

5: The Contact

My heart is in my throat, and I'm sobbing hard.

"Damn you, Stygius Cryptus, why did you bring me out?! *Why?!* Damn you!" I rail at him. "I found them, I *finally* found them, and you yank me out? How *dare* you!" I scream at him. His remorseless face is a blank slate as he stands before me, a strange device in his hand.

My temple throbs as I look at it. He obviously used it on me: the device he popped Zaris with. A surge of adrenaline roars through me, blinding my eyes with red rage, as tears stream down my face and my lip quivers. I rush at him and grab his lapels, shaking him. "Why?! Why, Cryptus, why?!" I rattle him with each fierce scream.

"Ensign Hutson, your reaction is not atypical for a first encounter with your parents. I assure you-"

"Atypical? Go to hell, Cryptus! You *knew* I was searching for them and would give *anything* to hold them again! You knew!" He blurs before me while my eyes fill with tears as I howl.

"Jax, I am instructing you to release me. I-"

"No! You don't instruct me! You're nothing! You're a useless, dumb synthetic who can't even-"

"Ensign Jax Hutson, *release* me." He commands it robotically, mechanically, with all the emotion of a coat hanger.

"No! You *knew* I desperately needed to see them! You-"

Without a word, the device in his hand is released, and it hovers silently to a table behind him, returning to a black charging dock. Two iron grips laden with artificial hair follicles seize my wrists and wrench my fingers from his lapels. My eyes widen. With dizzying speed, he recoils and then launches a punch dead center into my chest. I fly backward and tumble to the ground, my head colliding with a stainless-steel cart positioned against the far wall. The wind is knocked out of me. Various laboratory tools and devices shoot into the air, and a din of noise echoes through the lab as the cart tumbles over on top of me. My eyes, blazing with fury, gaze up at him in amazement.

Stygius Cryptus just stands there, solemnly, watching me. "Forgive me," he says, presently, studying his own fist. "I do not readily approve of the use of my cybernetic strength protocols against humans. It is, in fact, a violation of my programming. However, you left me with little choice, Jax. I promise not to do it again."

I say nothing in response. I just lay there and let my head slowly fall to the floor as I wheeze for oxygen.

"Can you breathe?" he asks, mechanically.

I nod, though I'm really lying. My lungs are on fire, and I strain for breath, which is painfully slow in coming. My temples are pulsating with a powerful frenzy. I'm not sure which one he zapped, but both are resounding pain.

"Slowly, Jax," Cryptus says. "Breathe slowly. Your diaphragm has spasmed. Tension has seized it, and it has contracted. Take slow, deep breaths. Don't struggle. Let it happen naturally, and let your body recover. You should be yourself again in a few moments, perhaps quickly enough to forgive me for employing my superior design."

Superior design? I think to myself. *You can't even remember our conversation about the blue pen, you synthetic twit.*

But it doesn't matter. I need to breathe.

I let it go, and decide to do as he says, breathing naturally and slowly, telling myself I was going to even before Cryptus suggested it. The truth, however, is that it's hard to breathe normally through sobbing. And that's exactly what I do now: sob.

The android silently strolls over behind me and lifts the cart upright once more, righting it, then proceeds to gather the displaced equipment that pepper the floor around my prostrate form.

My diaphragm relaxes, just as he said it would. I take a deep, cleansing breath and wipe my eyes, streaking my face with the tears I had shed both in The Phoenix Experiment and in real life. I pull away from him and sit against the wall, my head bowed over my knees. I can't see Cryptus, but I hear him sit down on the far end of the room. He sighs, if you can call it that. We all know synthetics don't require air.

"Congratulations, Jax," he says quietly. "You *did* finally find them. I support that, and it is, of course, the very reason why we are here. However, I did what I did because you were clearly losing control."

I lift my head slowly, icily boring holes into him from across the room.

"As I mentioned, your reaction is not atypical for a first encounter with your parents," he says, and I realize that was word for word from what the robot had said before. "I assure you that others before you have exhibited the same type of emotional response upon re-encountering their loved ones."

"Which others?" I growl, quickly and angrily.

Cryptus frowns. "I am not permitted to disclose medical findings except with the subject of said findings. I am sure you understand that. But you are free to discourse your and others' experiences with your contemporaries as you see fit."

I just stare at him.

"You are well aware of our protocol here. The entire reason The Origin and The Zephyr exist is to prepare you for a stable return to Earth as a Speaker, and to equip you to deal with our adversaries effectively, without failing. Your overly emotional response compromised the integrity of your focus, as I'm sure you realized."

This is too much for me. Thankfully, I've regained my steady breathing by now. "You can't honestly expect us to *finally* reconnect with our parents and *not* be emotional, Cryptus. It's…," -here I try to employ a word that might resonate with him- "illogical!"

"As I have now stated twice, your reaction is not atypical for a first encounter with your parents," he replies emotionlessly. "But how you control that reaction needs to be typical. Your ability to master your emotions is the crux of whether or not you will successfully mature and develop as an effective Speaker against the banshees on Earth. That is why I needed to shock you out of your experiment once you reconnected with your parents. It happens with all of you. I've had to use this on every subject here. Please rest assured that will be the only time I use it on you. You are on your own to control your emotions from this point forward. Some subjects require," -here he pauses, ostensibly searching for the right word- "*motivation* in order to pull them out." I glance past him to his sinister and mysterious device docked over by the far wall.

I just glare at him. He is correct, of course, but that doesn't make it any better. It's worse, actually. As I just glare at him – feeling 4 years old and in trouble yet again – I think back to that episode with him forgetting the pen. Here he is lecturing me on effectiveness, yet he malfunctioned only a short time ago.

"Why didn't you remember the pen?" I ask him, point blank. "Tell me," I challenge him.

His head tilts and his eyes squint. "I'm sorry, Jax, I still don't understand the reference. Yet you continue to bring this up. Should I be concerned for your mental acuity and request a bio scan?"

I'm simply incredulous, and I can't hide it anymore.

I shake my head, and look up, overenunciating in my obvious disdain. "Phiria, play Reference Video 837.92.8A, outer Phoenix corridor vent aperture, on Phoenix Lab monitor 1, please." I only remember the number because of the five times that I was reminded it by Phiria in our morning summaries. For the five morning summaries we received following the incident, there was a glaring number reminding Anther and I to behave. That video reference number was on each summary.

A glowing blue circlet appears on the ceiling in response to my call. "Certainly, Ensign Hutson."

Cryptus turns his head over to the monitor as it lights up.

Two young boys emerge through the vent aperture, one of them sporting a giant blue splotch down their chest, the result of a leaking pen. Suddenly, a hulking figure blocks their path, and they cower.

Ensigns Hutson and Secto. What were you doing in the maintenance shaft?

Nothing, Mr. Cryptus. Sorry. We were just-

You are aware of Regulation 24B.9 which restricts all human passage to traversable areas only?

Yessir. We're sorry, Mr. Cryptus.

You should not be here. Spying on Ensign Filipath's Phoenix experiment? How deplorable. I shall have to report this to Helmsman Oculus and First Officer Mirabay post-haste. This area is strictly-

"I have seen enough," Cryptus says in a fatigued tone, and the monitor switches off.

"Certainly. Thank you, Stygius," Phiria says. She is the only one who calls him by his first name, I think.

"Jax," Cryptus says, rising. "I have but one question for you." He walks the entire way over to me, pausing in front of me. For a brief moment I think back to his fist, and wonder if he's now going to kick me into oblivion as I sit here. But my fears are allayed as he squats in front of me and inquires softly, "Do you trust me?"

I honestly don't know what to say. I'm shell-shocked from that punch, shell-shocked from finally finding my parents, shell-shocked from the whole ordeal. Deep down, I don't know if I trust Cryptus after the Zaris incident, and now especially after this one. All this time I've tried to reconnect with my parents, and now that these girls arrive, I finally do, in the midst of all of this swirling emotion?

But I'm better than him. Smarter. I can fool him. Time to 'overlook' the punch, and play it cool.

"Ye-yes," I stutter. I clear my throat and try again. "Yes, Cryptus, I trust you."

He nods, and I'm sure he sees right through me.

"Good. I want you to know that sometimes, in order to serve the greater good, I must challenge you. My entire occupation programming is predicated on challenge, improvement and bettering my shipmates, preparing them for their eventual return. If that requires me to bend the rules somewhat, to feign any behaviors incommensurate with synthetic operation, or to propel you into an unstable emotional state in order to gauge your recovery time, all in order to fulfill my programming, then I will do so, without your leave or the leave of Helmsman Oculus. I have been granted special medical allowances and provisions that facilitate my operation in this capacity. I trust that you know I do this for the greater good."

I tilt my head. "So, you remembered the pen all along, and were playing mind-games with me," I say. It isn't a question.

"Of course. I am an android, Jax. AnthroMeta Model K100 Series A. I always will be. It is impossible for me to forget anything. Even," he pauses, practically winking at me, "blue ink-filled pens. As I mentioned, my entire programming is intended to challenge, improve and better you."

Now I find that I'm suspicious of him that his memory was just jogged somehow by my playing the video through Phiria, and he did *not*, in fact, remember it all along. I also think he reads my thoughts. But I resign myself to try to trust him. For now.

"I have been, and evermore shall be, your humble servant here aboard The Origin and beyond. Please forgive me for assaulting you. I was simply acting out of self-preservation."

So was I, you cybernetic nitwit, I think.

Anther just stares at me, his mouth agape, and then he rushes at me and hugs me. If there's one thing that can be said about meatheads, they're also emotional. Maybe that's what fills all that meat: raw emotions.

"Congrats, dude, that's great!" he exclaims as he pulls away. "Seriously. That's great, bro. I'm happy for you."

Martos and Venthix are equally congratulatory, even though they're still on restriction from rec, and are bored out of their minds. They both come over and high-five me. The others are elsewhere aboard this vast ship, doing assigned tasks, meeting with Oculus, guiding the girls' chiefs Ashira Sarristo and Maridie Onyx and familiarizing them with The Origin, even though they've already been here for a few days. But, given The Rubris' estimated time of arrival, they're going to be here for a while.

"Thanks, guys," I say. We fist bump.

"Took ya long enough," Venthix fires my way, sitting down across from me. I roll my eyes. "No, seriously! I'm happy for you! Now Garris can really suck it. Ha!"

I laugh. Garris still hasn't found his parents, and I wonder why that hasn't bonded us together all this time, at the very least providing us a common bond to mourn over. But he's an oaf, and always will be. Nonetheless, I find myself silently wishing him well in the aftermath of Anther's comment.

"Garris should find his someday. It was… surreal. But Cryptus pulled the plug practically right after I found them," I end mournfully. "It really pissed me off."

"Oh yeah, he did that to me, too," Venthix agrees, slouching. "Pissed me off royally too."

"Me too," chimes in Martos. His left cheek still sports a purple welt from Venthix's right hook. "He does that to everyone."

I look at Anther in amazement. He just nods. His expression says the same happened to him.

I squint my eyes. "He does?"

Anther nods swiftly. "Yeah, dude. Of course he does." He glances over at the other two like this is the most outlandish thing he's heard all day. "Why wouldn't he? We freak out, right? It's our *parents*, man. Of course we're gonna become blubbering wrecks. They can't have us all softies when we go back down. That defeats the purpose of our whole stay here. Duh," he ends, with another side-eyed smile at the others like I'm an idiot.

"I didn't know that."

All of them just nod.

"Don't let it get you down, though, man. You should celebrate! The fact that you got to them? Means there's hope," Venthix says. "Good job, dude. You focused enough to do it. That's the beginning."

I'm heartened by this. "Okay. Okay. That makes sense. Thanks, Venthix," I say. My heart is lifted after all that has transpired. "I'm just glad that he only had to do the zapper thing on me once. He said that would be the only time. I guess I should be relieved." I flick my eyebrows up and sigh gratefully, ending with a nervous chuckle.

The others just stare at me, not connecting the dots. I pan my gaze around the room. Their expression is identical between all of them, and I'm confused. "What?" I ask them. "The zapper? He said he used that on all of you too."

Anther frowns, shaking his head and looking at the other guys. "Cryptus never had to use anything like that on me," he says, staring at the others for validation. They all shake their heads. *Nope*, both of them concur.

I'm flummoxed. And now I'm pissed again.

In all of this, I realize two stark, naked truths:

One, Cryptus lied to me.

And two, I do *not* trust him. I don't know that I ever really did.

I just grit my teeth in frustration.

My irritation is deep down in my soul, and I'm grimacing hard.

6: The Emotions

I see her, clearly, and my heart leaps.

There's Alaris. Fresh off the connection with my parents, and the subsequent revelation that Cryptus lied to me, I decide I need some fresh air and go for a walk.

Fresh air, I think, as I head toward the observation deck. *Yeah, right.* The carbon dioxide on this ship is purified and recycled, constantly ionized and recirculated for us to exist here, indefinitely. The Origin is solar-powered, our air is endless, and as long as we have enough revolting *BioPrime* to sustain us, we'll live, grow old and die. If we don't choke on our own vomit from the disgusting food goo first, that is.

I round a corner, and there she is.

I haven't seen her in a few days, but I decide right away that this is just the emotional uplift I need on the coattails of such startling developments.

She's just lingering there: quietly, coldly, her arms crossed, her eyes glued on some distant star in the thick galaxy beyond her diminutive frame. She is utterly beautiful in her silent enamor, and her fixation prevents her from hearing me. My feet slow as I behold her.

> *Beyond the void, adrift by star,*
> *The black of cold doth silence mar*
> > *For lives forlorn*
> > *with hope unborn*
> *Spin irretrievably afar*

> *And time: a cruel and merciless haunt*
> *To stalk the soul consumed by want*
> > *The young grow old,*
> > *and hearts turn cold*
> *Yet longing holds, now frail and gaunt*

I don't want to startle her, so I figure now would be a good time to clear my throat. I do so.

She startles.

Nice goin,' Jax. Smooth.

"Hey, Alaris," I say, sheepishly, putting my hands up. "Sorry, I didn't mean to scare you." I offer a meek smile.

Her cold visage instantly transforms into warmth as she regards me. "Hey. Nice to see you again. Jax, right?" Her pale skin seems awash in color now as she rotates her body to face me.

"Yeah," I say nervously as I draw near. "We haven't met yet. I-I saw you when you came off the Avalon, but," I stammer, "yeah. Been a few days. What's your last name again? Sorry, I can't remember."

"Rederium."

"That's right. I'm Jax-"

"Hutson," she finishes for me. "I know."

I smile. "Rederium, huh? Your hair color is in your last name."

"Yep," she says with a slight eye roll. "Imagine that."

I perceive that I've slipped up somehow. Maybe she's sensitive about her hair color, or just her hair itself. I don't know how she could be; it's one of her most stunning features. I gather myself. *Time to change the subject, Jax.* "Uh, h-how are you liking The Origin so far? Are you guys all comfortable and settled in now?"

She musters a nod and looks around briefly, surveying our ship, identical to her own which perished. "It's alright. Almost the same, right? I mean, it's *all* the same. Everything is the same out here, day after day."

She takes on a dour tone with that last comment, and I can tell she's suffering from the same doldrums as most all of us are, or at least have at one point or another. She stares out at the stars again, wistfully.

I attempt a little light humor as I draw even nearer to her. "Oh, it's not so bad," I say. "I mean, you get tired of strawberry *BioPrime*, you can always try lemon *BioPrime*. And if that gets old, you get to switch to blueberry *BioPrime*. Or vanilla *BioPrime*. And then there's everybody's favorite, green apple *BioPrime*. So, ya know. Variety."

By now Alaris is giggling, and our mutual disdain for our revolting slop binds us together as two lost sojourners desperate for a little lighthearted respite. "You're so right. What I wouldn't give for a little-"

"Steak?" I interrupt, smiling.

Her face whips back over to mine, only a few seductive inches away. "Yes! Steak! How did you know?"

I shake my head. "I know things about people. You just have that face that says, 'I'd like a steak, please.'"

"Oh, do I?" She giggles again. I'm receiving full marks for handsomeness, charm, *and* humor here. Briefly I envision all the other guys, from Anther, to Garris, to Martos, to Venthix, even to Ranshay and little Dravin, all of them, eating crow – while Alaris and I feast on steak – and turning away in defeat.

"Yeah. Well, I wouldn't get your hopes up. Never had one here either, and I'm still wondering what it tastes like. Omnias wants lobster, apparently. One of these days I think we're gonna go over the edge, steal the Avalon, and head down to Earth to pig out, banshees be damned."

"Banshees be damned," she concurs with a grin, and then she sizes me up. "You're kinda cute, you know that?"

I smile wholeheartedly at this direct-approach affirmation, and I feel the heat in my face. *She thinks I'm cute.* "Thanks. You're not too bad, yourself."

"I wanted to reach out to you earlier, but one of the guys told me that you were interested in someone else. Garris? I think that's his name."

I shake my head definitively. "Garris is not my friend. He's a slab of meat with legs. He knows nothing," I dismiss.

Alaris chuckles. "Ha! That's funny. Slab of meat. *Now* who has steak on the brain?"

I take her point instantly. "Touché," I shrug with a grin. "How have you liked your sessions here so far? Is it weird doing them with Cryptus instead of your own synthetic?"

She shakes her head and props herself up against the glass pane, framed by stars. A pale light is about her, and my heart swoons at the sight. Poetry courses through me. She is gorgeous in every way. "Not really. They all talk the same anyway, right? I hear yours is British."

"Only because he wants to be. What's yours?"

"Talicus thinks she's Asian. Has the whole accent down. She's alright. She switched a few years ago from Russian, and Jamaican before that. I liked Jamaican better." She nervously fidgets with her hair. "What about you? I heard something went haywire with Zaris the other day or something. Omnias told us. Freaky."

I shrug and quasi-roll my eyes. "Cryptus. Yeah, he's a strange bird. I dunno. He's good at what he does, but they're all just creepy. All of 'em. I don't trust them," I finish, waving the conversation away.

I don't want to talk with Alaris about androids. I want to talk with Alaris about Alaris. "How many experiments have you done? Have you ever…?"

She nods before I finish my question. "Found my parents? Yep. Finally. Took me a while," she huffs with a noisome exhale.

"Me too."

"Yeah?"

"Yeah," I agree. "I actually only just found mine today."

She gasps.

"*Today?*" she asks, astonished. "Seriously? As in, like, a few hours ago. Wow. That's crazy! Well, I'm really glad for you. Sorry it took so long! How many sessions have you done?"

"Innumerable. I'm over 1500 somewhere."

"Same," she says. "How long have you been on The Origin?"

"Five years now."

"Wow, same here too. Did you lose your parents a while before you came here, or-?"

I nod, quickly. "A few months prior. Took me a while to get a shuttle."

She studies me for a moment. "It's so weird, isn't it? Us being kept apart on opposite sides of the planet for so long. It's not like we're gonna be all crazy and unfocused just because we're together. Your loss binds you to your guy friends, our loss binds us to our girlfriends. Same difference, right?"

"I think so," I concur. "But, you know,' we're steak-craving wild and uncontrollable boys with hormones, right? At least, that's how Oculus sees us."

She shrugs. "Oh well. He's wrong," she states emphatically, regarding me proudly. "At least about *one* of them. Maybe not so much about the meat slab guy, but you?" She looks me over, pretending to size me up. "I think you're okay."

"A minute ago, I was cute, and now I'm just 'okay'? Fine. I get it. Tough downgrade, though," I pout, feigning offense.

"Stop it, goofball," she says, playfully gripping my bicep, and I spastically find myself flexing. I'm not Orin, but I hope she notices. "Hey, when do you do rec time?"

"Depends on whenever I'm done with Cryptus and daily duties. Usually 1500 hours if I have a morning session, or 2000 hours if it's an afternoon one. You guys can join us for rec? Isn't that too close to *fraternization* for our chiefs' tastes?"

"I don't think so, silly. We just have to ask for permission each time. I don't know that anyone has asked yet. I'll probably have more luck if I ask Sarristo or Onyx for us to double-date."

"Double date?" I ask.

"Yeah, if we go with Mr. Meat Slab and one of the girls that he fancies. Or someone you recommend."

I'm up for a challenge, so my mind instantly goes to Anther. "I can think of someone good. Are you friends with Omnias?"

"Yeah! I don't really know her all that well, doesn't she like that one guy, Anter, Ather...?"

"*Anther*," I correct her, laughing that no one seems to get either of his names correctly. "Ant's a decent chap. Yeah, that would be fun. How can you find me and let me know you got permission? I had a morning session and I was going to go this afternoon, but now it looks more like it'll be tonight. So, the 2000 hours rec slot."

"I'll let Phiria know to get you a message," she says, and then she pauses, staring at my lips.

"Cool." I notice her pause, and I feel my eyebrows eventually raise in curiosity. "Was there something else?"

"No. Well, yes, actually. Please don't think me forward, but, have you ever been kissed?"

My eyebrows again. "Uh, I don't think so, I-"

Before I know it, she leans in to me and kisses me passionately. The warmth of her mouth envelops mine, and senses I didn't even know I had awoke to the promise of newness. Her eyes are closed, and then I realize I should close mine as well. It's quick, it's brief, it's unexpected, and it's utterly amazing. I can taste some kind of lip balm, some fruit flavor I can't readily identify. Alaris slowly pulls away, and I feel like biting her lips just to keep them in mine.

I feel a heatwave pass through me as I reflexively laugh with unbridled joy. "That – was – cool. And actually, now that I think about it, *have* been kissed," I joke, meaning her. "Thanks, Alaris."

She giggles. "No. Thank *you*, Jax," she says through a gleeful smile, and her knees appear to buckle briefly as she slips past me, her eyes fluttering.

"K. Yeah. Uh, I mean, you're welcome. I, uh-" I try, stammering, "I should be getting back too. Gotta do… stuff. You know." I fidget with my hair. My shirt. My pants. My foot stretches out and absentmindedly scruffs at something on the ground while my arms do things outside of my control. I've gone to pieces somehow in the heat of this sensory overload.

"Yeah," I finish lamely.

She stops walking and turns around, eyeing me quizzically. "You know," she starts, "I don't think it was an accident that we had… *the accident*. Fate has brought us together, Jax. You and me."

I smile, agreeing. "I believe it," I say.

She beams back at me. "I'll have Phiria let you know. See ya, Jax."

"See ya. Alaris," I say, in two distinct sentences, feebly and utterly consumed by feeling.

> *For longing lingereth strong and fast*
> *And pleadeth not to far outlast*
> > *The doldrum's drudge,*
> > *the grasping sludge*
> *Restoring pulse to hearts that passed*

With everything in me, I can't wait for rec time tonight. *I'm a wild dog, and I'm okay with it,* I think.

Restoring pulse to hearts that passed.

I kissed her, tenderly, and my heart leapt.

7: The Surprise

Phiria sends the message. I get to meet Alaris.

With that, I change into my athletic garb and carry a small duffle bag with me for a change of clothes afterward.

Rec hall is the largest area on The Origin. It's got a full basketball court, swimming pool, hot tub, tabletop games, ping-pong, air hockey, couches, relaxation pods, neural beds to unwind in, and so much more. Martos and Venthix really are missing out. Hell, *anyone* who doesn't get rec misses out. I never see Oculus or Mirabay in here, so I don't know if they're missing out or not. Maybe they just use it when the rest of us are asleep or something. But it's the thing we boys look forward to most on this ship every day.

With the obvious exception, now, of seeing girls, that is.

On the way to rec, I overtake the girls' synthetic, Baryonnis Talicus. She greets me cordially and then gets straight to the point: she is there to ensure there is no funny business, though I can't imagine what she thinks that means, given what I've seen her contemporary do. Her Asian accent is weird.

I watch her, curiously, as she walks beside me with a patronizing smile, a presence both unwanted and unneeded. *I'm not a child,* I think to myself. I know how to behave, and I don't need a robot – of the same model series as Cryptus – telling me what to and what not to do. I have a leg up on both of them. I know now to lie, I know not to play with people's emotions, and I know how to be human. All things that Cryptus – and presumably, Talicus – *don't* know.

"I'm actually late," she says. "Several of your contemporaries are already there, as are the females."

Females? *So weird. So formal,* this male thinks to himself.

She accompanies me on an awkward stroll through our corridors, all the way to the rec hall. She even holds the door open for me, though I didn't ask. I'm beginning to really tire of these synthetics. No wonder all this time we only had a single android on board. One is too much; two is overkill. We already have Phiria, and I daresay we all now know how to hook each other up for the Phoenix Experiments and do them ourselves. Phiria could walk us through it remotely if she or we wanted her to, instead of having these intimidating, patronizing synthetics haunting our every step.

And – bonus – she couldn't zap us out with that stupid electronic device.

I walk in, and there's Alaris. My eyes drink in her beauty, *and* the beauty of her form, as she is sporting high shorts and a shirt that cuts off high enough to provide me with ample view of her midriff. She is *all* legs. I truly don't know what to say. I cast a quick glance at Talicus to see if she is giving Alaris a disapproving glare, but I see no such sign.

Briefly, I wonder what exactly constitutes 'funny business' in a synthetic's mind. But I don't have more time to wonder.

"Jax!" Alaris shouts, and heads my way. "*There* you are. I was wondering when you were going to get here." A few other girls walk over with her my way. When they reach me, they assertively turn to Talicus. Alaris says, "Thank you, Talicus, that will be all."

The synthetic nods and then retreats to a far wall to observe, and presumably, monitor and record any perceived misbehavior to their chiefs. Makes me want to intentionally misbehave.

But I raise my eyebrows. I'm genuinely impressed. I don't know that I've ever 'dismissed' Cryptus, but I resolve to try that sometime soon. My estimation of Alaris just elevates.

Looking around quickly, I can see Orin is here; he's down swimming with Miritia. They're both scantily clad. The thought crosses my mind that Talicus should be minding *that* and not us more appropriately-clad youths down here who aren't showing so much skin. That's when I spot Anther amongst the girls. He now strolls up beside Omnias to greet me. Little Ranshay and Dravin are playing ping-pong off by themselves, girl-less and naïve as can be. Anther gives me a typical 'sup' nod and stands by my side. I tone down the force, but I give him a nice play-slug in the shoulder again. He smiles.

"I see you ladies have met Anther," I say. "Hopefully he hasn't terrorized you too much?" They giggle and nod amongst themselves.

That's when I spot little Zaris behind them, and regret the 'terror' question. She was concealed behind Skarbé, Donetis, and Ghirisha. I applaud myself for remembering their names. She looks fine now.

Omnias is off to the side, twirling one of her pigtails and watching Anther approvingly, but I wonder, in seeing her like that, if she's completely forgotten what we saw in the lab together that day.

"Something wrong, Jax?" Alaris asks me.

"Hmm?" I ask, jerking back. "Oh! Nothing. Let's do this! What are you guys wanting to do first?"

The girls glance at each other quickly with a knowing expression, and before I know it, a ball comes out of nowhere and bops me in the face as the girls – and Anther – scatter, giggling. I rub my forehead and collect myself briefly, scooping up the ball and searching for my target.

Bean The Beaner it is. Haven't played this in a while. It's a great, fun game that involves nothing more than hurling a ball at someone's head as hard as you can, and if they swoon, you get a point. If they topple, you get three points. We've played it plenty of times on The Origin. The girls must have had similar rec layouts and programs. It hasn't yet drawn blood and allows us to pummel things: an ingenious and convenient way of letting off steam when we don't find our parents. Garris plays it often.

I pursue them. Well, mostly I pursue Omnias since I'm pretty sure she was the one who threw it. My first throw goes awry. Girls are scattering everywhere. Anther is running with Omnias. He sees my shot miss her, and he turns to retrieve it but it bounces against the wall and heads back my way. We're about equidistant from the ball. I see him start to pick up speed, and he flashes me a devilish grin suggesting he'll beat me to it. But he forgets that I'm the skinny, spry one. I make it to the ball first, diving into it and clutching it to myself as he topples into me with a clumsy thud. We both laugh, and he gets up, because now he's a target. It doesn't matter who the target is in *Bean the Beaner*: everyone counts. I could hurl it at Baryonnis Talicus and score an easy three points. But I don't. The thought flashes through my head that if Cryptus were here, I'd for sure hurl it at him. Over and over.

Anther has had enough time to put distance between us. He's howling with laughter at our collision, rubbing his shoulder while he races away, back toward Omnias. He points her around a corner and they hide. I'm back on my feet and in pursuit of the other girls. I locate my target.

She's a lithe red-head, and she's my age. She's wearing high shorts, and those legs draw me in as she runs. That beautiful midriff calls to me as I close the gap between us. The other girls flee from this wild dog, as I chase after Alaris and prepare to bean her with all the savage force of a dandelion. They instantly realize that they were never my target, and they slow their pace. They know who I only have eyes for.

Alaris dashes over to the air hockey tables and hides behind them. I'm on her in no time. I duck down. There she is, on the other side. She giggles, raising up above the table in a stutter-step. But there I am, my hand upraised.

Dare I hurl this ball at her at such close range? She's laughing now, but I don't want to bean this beaner. Not this one.

Alaris sticks her tongue out at me playfully, and that thought is quickly extinguished. Then she's back underneath the table once more.

Now's my chance!

I start to make my way around. Alaris is aware of me. She shrieks and begins to take off. I give chase.

Wild dog in pursuit.

She's no match for my spry legs. But speaking of legs – *oh those legs* – I watch them jostle up and down in front of me as she tries to escape. I have her. My sights lock on her form, and she's all mine. I raise my arm. I can bean her in the back and not feel so bad.

Before I'm even aware of it, tiny feet have sped up behind me, noiselessly, and a small arm knocks my own downward as I go into my wind up and prepare to hurl the small rubber ball at my new love interest. The projectile goes askew, bouncing clumsily off the side wall as I whip around to my right in amazement.

An angry voice rails at me, and I stop dead in my tracks. "Stop that! Leave her alone, Jax Hutson!" the high-pitched voice cries. It's Zaris, and her eyes are red and wild with heat. I don't know her, but I recognize offense when I see it. She's panting from running so flat-out to catch up with me, and as she scowls at me, she does so under her eyebrows. I too, am panting, just watching her in amazement.

"You're an evil, evil boy, Jax Hutson!" she rails at me, pointing an accusatory finger at me, two inches from my face. She doesn't back off, and she's breathing hard. "Evil!"

Talicus leaves her post on the wall and instantly scurries over to Zaris, who by now begins to burst into tears as we standoff. I watch as the girls' synthetic rushes over to her, embraces her, wraps a fake meaty arm around her and strides off with her. The android gives me a quick look of consolation as if to assure me I haven't done anything wrong, and then she's walking off with the young girl, leaving me standing there, catching my breath.

I have no idea what I've done.

And then, the cold truth hits me: Zaris is clearly still traumatized from her Phoenix session.

Presently, I become dimly aware of someone suddenly standing to my left. I turn to see Alaris by my side, and she's panting too. Her skin glistens. "Hey, don't worry about it," she says. "She gets a little overreactive from time to time. She can be protective of us."

My eyebrows flick up in amazement. I start to say something, but then I catch Omnias staring at me with a worried expression. She says nothing, but quickly retreats and follows Zaris and Talicus out of the rec hall. My mind flashes back once more to the lab. And Cryptus. And the device.

"Has she always been like that, or just for the past few days?" I ask between breaths.

Alaris stares at me, confused.

Anther walks up to us. It's obvious he's hiding something. I can see it in his eyes. He's remembering our conversation from four days ago, and it's clear he and Omnias have talked about it as well. After all, she was there with me. She saw the whole thing too.

"Jax, don't," he says to me under his breath.

I crinkle my nose at him, confused. "Don't what?? I just-"

"Dude! Don't!" he interrupts me, placing a hand on my chest suddenly. "Let it go!"

I look at Alaris, dumbfounded.

"Uh, we gotta go, okay? Somebody ate too much *BioPrime* and needs a little reeducation," Anther says to her. "Sorry."

Alaris watches me, equally dumbfounded. "Sure, it's fine. I mean – yeah, it's f-fine," she finishes in a stutter.

I glance around at the other girls, and they're all apparently as shell-shocked as I am. Orin and Miritia are sitting at the edge of the pool, dangling their feet in the water, but they've both craned their backs to us, wondering what all the hubbub was about. For myself, I have no idea, and it's making me mad.

Anther grabs me by the arm. "Come on."

He starts off with me toward the door, but I wrench myself free of his grasp. "I'm capable of walking by myself, thanks," I say to him firmly, in no mood to be downplayed in front of Alaris – or *anyone,* for that matter. "Let's go," I command him.

I look back at Alaris one final time, and she's downcast. What started out as a fun first date has obviously gone south in a hurry, all because of some mysterious outburst that I'm about to learn much more about from Anther, apparently.

"See ya soon," I assure her, and she nods quickly. "Chow time?" I ask.

"Yeah. Sure," she says, but then she glances nervously at the other girls.

I haven't a clue what all of this bizarre affair is about, but I sure hope to find out soon. My gut says that whatever Cryptus allowed – or did – in Zaris' Phoenix Experiment left a lasting mark on her psyche. I am determined to find out what that was.

All is never what it seems,
Mystery eateth at the seams

Veneers lie deep;
pretense a keep
To confound in daze and blinding gleam…

But conscience sayeth trust thy guess
Lest hunch fall prey to deep duress
The truth is oft
not far aloft
But within reach, despite the mess…

Hearing the whispers inside my brain, I walk out of there with Anther, our voices hushed.

I am now sitting in the library with Anther and Omnias. Zaris is back in her quarters with Talicus. Alaris and the rest of them are, presumably, still up in rec. It seems the only youths who *didn't* see it are Venthix and Martos, understandably.

Ignorance is bliss.

Towering rows of books cascade around us: an abundance of literature from so many centuries of a planet unfortunately long bereft of an abundance of readers.

"I want to talk with Oculus," I say, defiantly. "And Mirabay."

"Dude, don't go up against Cryptus, man," Anther warns me. "You don't want him on your bad side. Don't do it, Jax."

"What does that mean? Why? He might be doing something to them. To *us!* How do we know he hasn't been doing something all along?" I counter.

Omnias watches us ping-pong back and forth.

"Jax, this is all based off of *one* circumstance. You're not thinking clearly! The girls got here and messed with our emotions – no offense, Omni," he says to her and then turns back to me, "and you're just a giddy kid who's not thinking clearly right now."

"Fine. I'm willing to take that chance, though. Why *shouldn't* I go to our helmsman if I think something is up? I've never experienced that in my Phoenix Experiments. Have you?"

"No, but-"

"See? Have *you*, Omnias?"

She quietly shakes her head. "I've never seen anything like that. And I've watched Zaris here and there. And others. And they've watched me. When we first started, we would watch each other because it was new. Unpredictable. We wanted to make sure we were okay. We were just looking out for each other," she says.

"I hear you! And that's all I want to do here, Ant. I barely know Zaris, but I'm looking out for her too. Cryptus has been doing and saying strange things for the past week. You didn't see what Omnias and I saw, man. You didn't see the third chair. You *weren't* there. It was evil, man."

Anther sighs and shrugs his shoulders. He crosses his arms and turns away from me. "Come on," he argues. "Evil, Jax? Really *Evil*?" he asks, turning back to me, with a look of utter incredulity denting his face. "Apparently, Zaris thinks *you're* evil. She's just a little girl, man!"

I think back to what Zaris said, her finger in my face. Anther does have a point. I certainly don't *feel* evil. "Anther, come on, bro. You've known me for a long time. Have I changed?"

He doesn't answer.

"Seriously! Have I changed at all?"

He quietly shakes his head. "No."

I turn to Omnias. "Has Zaris changed? I'm not saying she's evil, Omnias. I'm not saying that at all. But is she different since she's been aboard The Origin and especially since that Phoenix session?"

Omnias thinks to herself for a moment, then quietly nods, and crosses her own arms, lost in thought. Anther sat down on a library bench in a huff.

"Okay, then," I say, feeling I've scored a point. "I'm the same. Zaris isn't. Something happened to her. That something was the Phoenix Experiment with Cryptus. Oculus needs to know. He said it himself before they even came on board: *They must be kept safe, by all of us,* he said. He needs to know if even one of them is not being kept safe, Anther. Right?" I hold my arms out, awaiting his reply.

Omnias shifts as she stands, her eyes darting between the two of us. She has to know I was right, at least. Now it's just about convincing my meathead friend of the same.

Anther finally relents. "Fine," he mumbles under his breath. "Talk to Oculus. But Jax," he says, looking up at me under his brows with a piercing stare, "remember I warned you about going up against Cryptus."

I listen to him, but I'm not ready to nod or receive his warning. It doesn't hold much weight, at least for the moment. Sure, Cryptus can be intimidating, but if I've warned Oculus and Mirabay about him, then I've got our helmsman and First Officer on my side.

> *Onus and burden, duty and charge*
> *Summon the virtuous, small to large*
> > *The truth must out,*
> > *Through scandalous doubt*
> *lest miscreants their evil ways recharge*

> *So don boldness readily, push forward steadily*
> *And keep thy countenance as thou move headily*
> > *Know thy course just,*
> > *proceed as thou must*
> *'til truth is declared, winning succor incredibly*

Message received. I head off to meet with Oculus.

8: The Confrontation

I look him squarely in the eye, standing my ground.

"Helmsman Oculus, sir, I'm telling the truth. I've never seen anything like that before. Omnias saw it too," I declare, firmly.

"Omnias was there with you in the foyer?" he asks me, clearly annoyed by this news. Mirabay glances once at him, and then back at me.

"Yessir. She will attest to the same thing."

Oculus just studies me for a moment, his arms crossed, his fist to his chin, scowling. His eyes drop to the floor, lost in thought for a moment.

"Jax, Cryptus informed me that you recently made contact with your parents this morning during your Phoenix Experiment, is that correct?"

"Yes, sir," I say, feeling a well of emotion at the memory of it.

"He reports that this was the first time. How are you feeling now?"

"I'm… exhilarated, sir. It was surreal, and wonderful, and unexpected all at onc-" I reply, but then I stop, catching the meaning of his question. It's a snare, and I recognize it instantly. "Wait. You're not just casually asking me about that. You're doubting my emotional state because of my finally making contact with my parents in my session, wondering now if I'm not thinking clearly because I'm… overwhelmed or something?" I stare at him under my brow, feeling hot. Mirabay watches me accusingly. Oculus mirrors him.

But then, the helmsman can't contain himself, and he erupts into spontaneous laughter, punctuating his own dreariness. "Gotta say, Jax, you're a pistol. Sharp as a tack and call a spade a spade."

"Sir," I feel the need to clarify, "I'm *fine*. This incident happened four days ago. My contact with my parents was this morning. Again, Omnias can corroborate all of this, I assure you. This incident predates whatever emotional state I might even be in given my recent contact. Surely you can see that Cryptus is up to something."

The helmsman finally takes a deep breath. "Fair enough. However, if this was so important, why didn't you come to me earlier? Couldn't it be that you're a bit frazzled and emotional *now* given your breakthrough with your parents? Cryptus also informed me he had to pull you out of your session prematurely with a bit of a… *jolt*." Now he's staring at me with his tongue halfway out his mouth, his eyebrows up, his head cocked downward at me. An expression of distrust is written all over him. "So, frankly, this sounds a bit like revenge." He looks to Mirabay for approval. The First Officer nods.

"Sir, that's not fair. That's not even *close* to the truth. Him pulling me out had nothing to do with my coming to you. Zaris' session, and, furthermore, her behavior today, reinforces my suspicion that Cryptus did something to her. He might be doing it to others as well. Before the crew of the Zephyr boarded our ship, you made it clear to all of us that you wanted us to keep them safe. All of us. Those were your words, Helmsman, meaning no disrespect. And none intended to you either, Mr. Mirabay."

Both study me for what seems like an interminable amount of time. I wait.

"And just what do you think he might have done to that young girl in her session, anyway, Jax? You think he scared her in her subconscious? Or he's doing something else untoward?"

I slowly shake my head. "Sir, I don't know. But you can have Omnias in here to corroborate my story. Or I'd even suggest bringing in Zaris and asking her directly. It was frightening, sir. Zaris – wasn't herself. At all. And then the third chair in the chamber had a dim shape in it. Almost like he had-" I stop, thinking back.

Oculus doesn't wait. "Had what?" he pries.

I take a deep breath. "I don't know, sir. It was like Cryptus was trying to bring an entity through the Phoenix connection. Bring it back *with* Zaris. Or… *through* her, even. It didn't look like human."

Oculus just continues to study me, incredulous.

> *Know thy course just,*
> *proceed as thou must*
> *'til truth is declared, winning succor incredibly*

He is obviously conflicted, but there's a tired resolve in his eyes that tells me he wants to put this to bed quickly. I predict that will win over, and he'll easily dismiss this – and me – summarily.

But he surprises me anyway.

"Alright, Jax," Oculus says. "I'll have Cryptus in here and have a little chat. Are you comfortable being in our presence while he is presented with your assertions?"

I slowly nod, though I'd honestly prefer to stay as far away from Cryptus as possible. I have another session in two days… not tomorrow, but the following day, and I'm not looking forward to it. Depending on how this 'little chat' goes, I'll be looking forward to that session even less. I briefly consider overdosing on *BioPrime* instead, and save us all the trouble of any further conflagrations. But Alaris would be forlorn…

"Alright," he says. "Chow time is in 94 minutes. I'll summon him right away. He shouldn't be in session at the moment," -here he glances at his watch and then mirrors it at a chronograph on the wall- "so he should be free. Have a seat."

I comply, retreating to a chair against the entrance wall. Mirabay does the same, sitting perpendicular to me, closer to Oculus' desk.

My helmsman retreats behind his console and taps a key on his array. A short klaxon sounds throughout the ship, reverberating down the corridors behind us. "Stygius Cryptus, Stygius Cryptus, Helmsman Oculus. Please report to the Bridge."

He releases the button and slowly sits down behind his desk. We all sit in awkward silence. I can hear my heartbeat.

"I can't imagine what you think he might be doing to her in there. But we'll soon know, won't we?" Oculus casts a doubtful glance over at Mirabay, and the First Officer flicks his eyebrows up and then turns to watch me. He has a smirk on his face, and I want to slap it off of him.

I suddenly get cold feet, and I wish I wasn't here in his office.

I wish I hadn't seen anything with Omnias.

I wish I had never had a session on the coattails of Zaris,' nor that I had been there.

I even find myself wishing that the girls had never come here. A lot has changed since they've been here, and I don't know what to make of it. But no girls equals no Alaris, and I find that very notion utterly rejectable.

I wonder where Alaris is. I wonder what she's thinking. I wonder what the next kiss will feel like… or if there will even be one.

I truly want there to be one.

"Stygius, come in," Oculus greets him, noticing his presence but not looking up at him. He is occupied with observing reports and data from the bridge console. "Thank you for coming," he says, tiredly.

The synthetic walks in, a dry look on his face. "Helmsman Oculus," he acknowledges, and then he takes stock of the bridge and sees me sitting there. He appears unfazed. "Hello, Jax. First Officer Mirabay," he greets us as well, perhaps not yet sensing what's about to happen.

Stygius is calculating, however, I tell myself. He knows we're not seeing eye to eye. My chest reverberates faintly in memory of that reflexive punch he doled out. My mind resonates with anger at his pulling me out of my Phoenix experiment. My skin tingles with the bristling suspicion I have had since he lied to me.

Cryptus sits down between Mirabay and I. The synthetic slowly glances over at me, his eyes cold. He musters up a strange and discomfiting smile, and a strange pang of fear runs through me. Anther's words resound in my head.

Dude, don't go up against Cryptus, man. You don't want him on your bad side.

I briefly wonder what Cryptus could do to me in a Phoenix Experiment. I have no idea what he's capable of doing to me in my subconscious, and for a moment I wish I had spoken to Zaris more before she left, prying out of her the details of what she experienced in her own session with him.

The helmsman leans back in his chair, pulling away from his console and regarding all of us slowly.

"How is everything going on your end, Cryptus?"

The android straightens up. "Oh, fine, sir. All is well."

"We've had a little bit of added excitement around here lately, haven't we?" Oculus asks.

"You could say that, Helmsman. But I think everyone is responding and behaving appropriately, each according to their own stature and abilities."

"How do you mean?"

"Well, putting it delicately, sir, these hormone-filled children and adolescents – present company *included* of course with Ensign Hutson here – seem to be faring well in the presence of the opposite sex with all of the increased stimulation their presence provides. It's been a study in temperance."

"I see."

"They've been reasonably self-controlled, Helmsman Oculus. My colleague Baryonnis Talicus feels the same. Short of a recent outburst by one of their younger females, the girls have been well-behaved. And, notwithstanding Ensign Hutson's assaulting me today following the successful Phoenix Experiment he had-"

"Assaulted you?" Oculus interrupts, squinting at him. His eyes dart over to me. "Clarify. What is the meaning of this, Jax?"

This infuriates me, and I roll my eyes. Oculus is no doubt mad at this one-sided appraisal *and* the fact that I've not reported it to him. I sigh, taken at unawares by Cryptus' subtle yet tattletale-like report.

"Oculus, it wasn't an *assault*," I say, quickly. "I was angry, yes. All this time I've sought to reconnect with my parents, and I only just did today. I was angry that he jerked me out of it," -here I flashed my eyes over at him icily- "but in no way did I assault him. I was grasping him like so," I say, demonstrating how I held his lapels, "but I was not violent in any way." I sigh in defeat as I glance at Oculus "*Yes*, I was shaking and screaming at him. But that didn't give him any reason to punch me hard in the chest." I enunciate these last words, staring accusingly at him.

My emphasis isn't lost on Oculus.

"You punched him in the chest?" Oculus asks the synthetic.

"So hard I flew backward and knocked over a medical tray," I quickly add.

Oculus' eyes flicker back to me, and then they returns to Cryptus. "Why did you do that? Isn't violence against humans strictly forbidden by AnthroMeta protocol and programming?"

"Forgive me, Helmsman," Cryptus says quietly. "Indeed it is. I was acting in self-defense, and I had warned Ensign Hutson – twice – to release me. He did not. I feared for my own safety."

"A grown adult android feared for his safety from a 14-year-old boy half his size?"

Cryptus is silent for a moment. "I take your point, Helmsman. I was, however, concerned. Self-preservation is our overriding protocol, just as it is for humans. Ensign Hutson was understandably upset, and as I had tried to communicate to him, his response was not atypical from the other youths aboard The Origin when they have encountered their own parents. Logic and reason become suspended in the emotional overwhelm that seizes them following such a heartfelt reunion. Jax was certainly no different in this regard, and his emotional outburst followed suit."

Oculus is silent. His eyes dart over to Mirabay's for a moment as he, presumably, strives to weigh the situation and judge justly. He sighs.

Mirabay watches him, rubbing his chin.

I don't look at Cryptus, but I can feel the heat of his stare upon me.

"Cryptus," Oculus continues, "Jax feels that you are perhaps operating inauthentically, and that you may be abusing your position as Phoenix conductor. It's clear to me that you assaulted Jax, not vice versa."

I feel a swell of vindication course through me. Maybe Cryptus is going to get it now.

"And now we must deal with this as well," Oculus states clearly. "Look at me, please. I, Helmsman Fulsar Oculus, invoke AnthroMeta Primary Protocol 11A and order you to tell me the truth and nothing but. What happened – precisely – during Ensign Sharibian's Phoenix Experiment?"

I have, of course, never heard of such protocol, but I note down the number, believing it may aid me in any future confrontations with Cryptus. Or, for that matter, *any* AnthroMeta model.

"Certainly, Helmsman. I am required to tell the truth to my superiors."

Yeah, sure, pal, I think, once more recalling his withholding the truth about his memory of the blue pen. But I'm not his superior…

"Fine, Stygius," Oculus retorts, "but do it without exaggeration as well, if you don't mind. You-"

"Helmsman," Cryptus starts to interject.

The change in Oculus' voice and volume is surprising and jarring. "I am still speaking!" His veins pop out on his head, and there's an awkward silence where the air is so thick between them you could bake a cake in it. Oculus lets out a stabbing, quick sigh. "You used the word 'assault' when describing Jax's shaking you, yet you yourself struck him with your fist and he flew back. Do you deny this?"

"No, sir," Cryptus says, quietly.

Oculus' calm but irritated voice returns.

"Good. Then let us be clear. I need the facts and the truth please. No embellishment. Proceed," he growls, and the air is still thick.

Watching the two of them verbally joust, it suddenly becomes abundantly clear that there is a beef between them, and that they hardly see one another aboard this ship. Maybe that is on purpose. Clearly, there is no love lost between the two of them.

"I have the cerebro-print video file and can readily turn it over, if you wish to see it, Helmsman Oculus. You will see that there was nothing untoward conducted in Zaris Sharibian's session under my watch, which was her first aboard this ship. During the subject's session, she had just made contact with her parents.

"This was not her first time, Helmsman. Talicus reports she has previously enjoyed several successful rendezvous with her parents aboard The Zephyr. However, during this most recent session, the subject became overly preoccupied with," -here he pauses, strangely- "a *presence* inside her session. I can't describe it."

"A presence? What do you mean by that?" Oculus jabs.

I listen intently.

"That's just the thing, Helmsman, I do not know what it was." His face flickers momentarily, and I see it. I get the distinct sensation that he is lying. "The Phoenix Experiments exist to provide a communal bridge between the bereaved and the lost, for the betterment of our subjects, and-"

"Yes, yes, I know all this, Stygius," Oculus interrupts, and he's agitated, in no mood for any unnecessary reminders of Cryptus' function. "But go back to this, this, *presence,* if you please. Wasn't this just another banshee?"

Cryptus pauses, and then, remarkably, sighs. The action seems quite surprisingly human.

"No, Helmsman Oculus, it was not a banshee. And my capacity aboard this ship is to ensure the safety of all those onboard, especially those in my charge in the Phoenix Experiment program. Of course, dealing with the supernatural has its share of dangers, and you and I are all too familiar with what happened aboard the Rubris."

Ah, I think, *so the rumors of an incident aboard the Rubris* are *true.*

"Lest we have a repeat," Cryptus continues, "I must exercise caution and ensure that the subjects entrusted to me in the Phoenix Experiments are as safe as possible. Should they make contact with anything potentially dangerous or detrimental to our mission while connected, I must intervene. That is my primary program for our Phoenix Experiments here.

"Just such an incident occurred with Ensign Sharibian. Such an incident *nearly* occurred with Ensign Hutson here," he says, motioning to me.

My eyes squint at him, detecting his deceit. There was no such 'presence' in my session, at least, none that I recalled. It was my parents, and the fire, the noise, but very typical of banshees, nothing more.

"I do not know what this new presence was, but it was something nefarious, causing little Zaris great anxiety. And then," he trails off, and his eyes fall to the floor.

"Yes?" Oculus pries. "And then what...?"

"I- I can't be certain, Helmsman, but it seemed that we experienced some kind of... temporary *mesh*. Almost as if the apparition therein was seeking to exit the Phoenix Experiment through Zaris into our waking life here. Of course, I could *not* permit that. That is why I employed the use of my stasis interrupt pod."

So that's what that little zapper is called.

Oculus' face is crinkled into annoyance. He tilts his head. "What? A stasis interr-what?" he queries.

"Stasis interrupt pod. It is a small, cylindrical device meant to jolt the body back into a state of consciousness. Bring the subject back, as it were. It acts on the body's neural network, sleep drive, and circadian rhythm. I will admit that it is jarring, so I am grateful that I've never had to employ it."

I smirk and scoff. "That's not what you told me following our session! You told me that you've used it on everyone," I hiss through my teeth. "All the guys said that you haven't. That's when I knew that you *lied*."

As before, I make sure to add some extra emphasis to the last word in order for it to fully register with all present.

Cryptus doesn't respond to my allegation. He merely stares at Oculus and continues. "The stasis interrupt pod is a failsafe; a last-ditch recall device meant to shock the system and quickly retrieve the subjects from their subconscious state, restoring them to the natural world in the event of an emergency. Such an emergency was manifesting, and I needed to take effective measures to prevent a possible… *exit*."

"Wait," Mirabay interjects, "exit? Are you talking like 'demon possession' here? Is that what you're saying, Cryptus? It could possess Zaris?"

Again, a strange look on Oculus' face as he listens carefully to all of this. He clearly doesn't trust Oculus in this, and obviously thinks that all of this is pure nonsense.

Cryptus furrows his brow and clenches his lip, shaking his head vigorously. It is almost as if he is trying to purge the very thought from his brain. "Certainly not. Please understand, Mr. Mirabay, Mr. Oculus, and you too, Jax, that, as stated, I am unfamiliar with this presence. Before the females from The Zephyr boarded our ship, I had never encountered something so new, and so potentially hostile." His voice lowers to a menacing whisper as he stares directly at Oculus. "It is not of our physical plane, sir. It is beyond the confines that we can see and touch. And it is *not* a banshee. A powerful force inhabits it, the likes of which I have never encountered, and nothing about it suggests benign or charitable intentions. On the contrary," he says, biting his lip, "I sense nothing short of malevolence."

"You sense nothing short of malevolence," Oculus repeats quietly, watching him skeptically. "And just what does malevolence feel like, Cryptus? I assume you know?" His voice has the bite of sarcasm to it.

Cryptus just regards him coldly. "Well, aside from the basic feeling registering as unease, hairs standing up on the back of your neck, sir, Jax here can attest easily enough to what little Zaris manifested at one point. I presume you've already told them, Jax?"

I glance at Oculus. The helmsman beats me to the punch. "What you reported to me about her eyes, and the sound she made, correct?" he asks, but his voice is steeped in mockery.

I nod.

Oculus suddenly rolls his eyes. "For the love… would you *please* give it a rest, you two. You're clearly at odds with each other. This is all outlandish ghost story nonsense. Enough! There's nothing definitive about any of this, Cryptus. How does her behavior in any way suggest malevolence?" Oculus' voice is permeated with irritation and incredulity. He clearly can't afford to be bothered with this, and has no intention of being so.

The synthetic turns to me once more, almost in a note of desperation. He speaks quietly. "Jax, have you told Oculus about the shape you saw in the-"

"I'm asking *you*, Cryptus," Oculus practically shouts again, and this time, he stands up with his hands on his hips. I'm taken aback. Oculus is clearly vexed, and wants straight answers from Cryptus.

"I don't expect either of you to imagine the fraying that helming such a massive ship can do to one's nerves since you've never been in command, Stygius Cryptus, but I've been out here a long time. We have enjoyed a smooth operation until now. But *now* I'm having to bear the responsibility for extra souls in my charge with these girls, *and* deal with the paranormal? This is bullswool! Hogwash, Cryptus."

Cryptus motions as if he's going to reply, but Oculus shuts him down, continuing his lecture.

"No! Wait your turn. I expected you to conduct the Phoenix Experiments with decorum, but you're turning them into a veritable freakshow. I've thought I was able to wholly entrust this to you, and I see now that I was in error."

As I watch all of this unfold, my trust in Oculus lessens. He's agitated to a breaking point, and I may have bitten off more than I can chew by getting Cryptus in trouble, I think. "I told him," I mutter to Cryptus, ignoring Oculus for the moment. "I started to see the shape."

Mirabay's eyes widen. "So something *was* actually starting to come through? Is that even possible?" he cries, turning to Oculus, though the helmsman is equally as bereft of answers as Mirabay.

"It *is* possible, indeed," Cryptus says, firmly, turning to Mirabay and appealing for reason since it seems Oculus has none. He speaks firmly. "That is one of the byproducts of the Phoenix Experiment, naturally: to allow, for example, Jax, here, to commune with his parents. If the communion is strong enough, and if those on the other side are willing to renounce their position in death, they could, feasibly, exit back into reality through the third chamber. That is precisely what it does. They could re-enter this life. But so could something else, sir. That is entirely the purpose of the experiments, to ultimately try to bring the parents back through, and to develop strong and capable Speakers to deal with the plague on Earth."

Oculus sighs thickly and puts his hands on his head, turning around in a full and annoyed revolution. He exhales heavily: a monstrous grunt of irascibility.

"Look, I've never pretended to understand your silly resurrection science, or what exactly the paranormal ramifications of it are, Stygius," he whines, "I've just sought to run a tight operation and a safe ship! Human or no, don't you think you have an obligation to inform your helmsman straightaway of even the *hint* of a possibility of a malevolent force seeking entry into The Origin through your accursed operation?"

"Sir, I meant no off-" Cryptus starts to say, and he stands, with his hands raised in defense.

"I don't care what you meant or didn't mean!" the helmsman barks, pointing at him. "Cryptus, you should have reported this *immediately*." He pauses, glancing over at Mirabay with a red, puffy face. "You leave me with little choice. As both a temporary measure *and* a consequence, I am effectively suspending the Phoenix Experiments until further notice pending a full investigation into this matter."

Cryptus, deflated, stands and begins to pace back and forth, passing in front of me and then heading back toward the entry to the ship's bridge. It's almost as if he's resigned to leave, muttering on his way out. "Sir, please don't. We cannot afford to susp-"

"My decision is final, *synthetic*," Oculus says, coldly. "Now sit the hell down. I did not give you permission to stand, much less leave. You are not dismissed until I say so, Stygius Cryptus."

Cryptus stops, momentarily balling his hands into fists, but he calms, turns, and stares at Oculus with icy regard. He salutes, but it's obviously halfhearted. The synthetic flashes a momentary glance in my direction, heaving another belabored sigh. Cryptus lifts his hands in defeat. "Fine. However, with your permission, helmsman, there's an added danger that I think you should be made aware of."

"I don't doubt it!" Oculus cries. "What do you know! Something *else* I haven't been made aware of in a timely fashion." He looks at me and rolls his eyes.

"It's not that nefarious, Helmsman. Please. May I approach and show you the Reference Video? I believe this will serve to reinforce your decision, which I will abide by, of course."

Mirabay shifts to my right.

Oculus rolls his eyes again and throws his hands up. "Fine. I presume this has to do with the Sharibian girl as well? Or are you about to spring yet another irritating surprise on me? The night is young, Cryptus."

Cryptus moves toward him. "Well, as I was saying, it's an added danger, certainly. But the danger is not from the girl, sir," he says.

"I don't understand," Oculus says, sitting down.

Cryptus moves to his right and hunches over the console in front of the helmsman. "It's from *you*," he says, and then my eyes twitch, not believing what I'm seeing.

With astonishing speed Cryptus sends a tightly coiled left fist backhandedly into Oculus' forehead. The helmsman reacts in surprise, grunting, his chair flying backward and his arms spasming outward in a reflex. In a horrifying revolution, Cryptus whirls around and with his right hand grabs Oculus' uniform at the neck, jerking him toward the ceiling, suspending all two hundred sixty pounds of him in the air.

Oculus nervously grasps for his throat to loosen the pressure and breathe, still in a stupor.

I jump to my feet.

"Cryptus, no!" I shout.

The synthetic pays me no heed.

Mirabay also rises in surprise, and dashes over to the console to defend his superior. "Jax, sit," he says coolly.

"Thank God, Argin – Mr. Mirabay – help him!" I cry. I extend my arms out in front of me, reaching in vain for Oculus.

I was never partial to him, but this is not only a breach of protocol; he appears to be in great pain, gasping for breath.

Cryptus doesn't show one ounce of remorse… or fatigue. The android suspends Oculus with his right hand, and our helmsman is still dazed. Cryptus' left hand is fishing for something in his pocket. Mirabay rushes toward both of them.

Except the First Officer doesn't defend Oculus.

Cryptus releases the helmsman suddenly, and Oculus plummets into his chair, flummoxed and striving to breathe. Mirabay retreats astern the helm chair, and yanks Oculus' arms back, pinning him.

Oculus cries out in pain as his arms are wrenched behind him.

"Do it," Mirabay says, coldly. "And be quick." He continues to restrain Oculus, who struggles to breathe, and attempts to say something, but he's gasping.

I watch in horror, not understanding what's happening, nor why. "No! What are you-"

A flash of light. A gleam of metal.

Cryptus whips out a small device that instantly periscopes into a serrated extension. Without a word, he mechanically slashes and stabs at the helmsman. My eyes widen as chills course through me. I want to vomit.

Mirabay has his head ducked down behind the seat, avoiding the hot splashes of blood pulsing out from Oculus' knifed body. Guttural cries and gulps sound from his deteriorating and perforated form as the life slowly ebbs from him.

The smell of iron fills the room.

Traces of blood splatter my uniform.

Cryptus is splashed and is now dripping with blood from the helmsman's body. Criss-crossing trails of red intersect Oculus' face, neck and chest as the android peels his skin open with each reddening stab and slash. Oculus' larynx practically falls forward out of his throat. His eyes are widened rings of white horror, gaping up at his assailant.

In a reflex, he bends his body toward his console, presumably to send out a ship-wide alert, but it's no use. He's not going anywhere.

But I am.

I can't see any more of it. I run. Faster than I've ever run before, I flee.

I hear Cryptus call for me from the bridge, but it's drowned out by the chills running down my flesh as I barrel through the halls of The Origin.

Helmsman Oculus is now dead, killed by our own synthetic, Stygius Cryptus. First Officer Argin Mirabay is accomplice to his murder.

I wonder where everyone is, and I don't even know where I'm at, but I struggle to think clearly and make for the rec hall. Before too long, I arrive, carried by the wind of my own fear.

They're all in here. All of them. Except for Zaris. However, their synthetic, Baryonnis Talicus, is with them as well. Where Zaris is, I don't know.

In a surprise, Venthix and Martos are here. Thankfully, their rec restriction is expired, and they're here with everyone else. For a brief second I wonder what Cryptus would do if he raced after me.

Would he kill me? Would he proceed to kill the rest of us? Such a morbid thought, but I don't put anything past Cryptus anymore, and I have no idea who is in charge between our synthetic and the murderous First Officer. They're obviously in league with each other.

My friends register my fright and stop what they're doing. I'm panting and going to drop. Yet, somehow, I press on.

"Cryptus… killed… Oculus. Mirabay… helped…" is all I can get out. I brace myself against a side column.

Their faces wring with horror and disbelief. Anther stares at me and slowly approaches. Ranshay is a study in confusion, as none of this makes sense to him through his language barrier.

Suddenly, a klaxon sounds throughout the ship.

"Anther, telling… the… truth. Help," I say, before falling into his arms. He catches me, staring into my eyes as he supports me, and he knows. He sees the truth in my horrified gaze, but he also notices the faint splatter of blood on my uniform.

My heart is beating like a rabbit, and fear has enveloped me entirely. I'm sweating and shivering through my shock.

Anther scrambles into gear, immediately. "Everyone, this way. Now! Come on, now! Orin, help!" he cries. All of them spring into action. A sudden panic settles upon everyone, pushed on by the emergency klaxon, but they fall in line, following us toward the far end of the rec hall away from the main doors.

Anther turns to Talicus. "Baryonnis, you've got to disable Phiria's security surveillance right away. Video *and* audio surveillance. He can't see or hear where we are. Encode it with your own. Trust me."

"I can, certainly. They can always reboot the surveillance servers, but they would have to physically be in the server room to do that. Access code?"

"Bravo-Zulu-September-Niner-Three-One-Tango."

I hear it, but I'm amazed and surprised at the existence of the code, why Anther would have access to such a thing, nor where he appropriated it. Perhaps he had done more exploring and spying in this ship than I ever gave him credit for. Perhaps he had even spied on the girls showering. We would get to that later, and I briefly hope he'll share with me the best points to view from. But somewhere along the line, like a forager, he harvested this important code.

For now, Talicus complies.

The synthetic turns her head forward and closes her eyes, yet continues to run without fail alongside us. She doesn't need her eyes open to see. She communicates with Phiria wirelessly, sending the code.

And somewhere, in the ship's central computer servers, the surveillance grid goes offline.

"Done," she confirms. "I've programmed in a backdoor to allow me to input my own code if the servers get rebooted. That way I can restart the process if need be, later."

Anther regards her and senses the job is done. "We just bought ourselves some time. At least they won't be able to track us to our first destination. Hopefully, they won't see us somewhere else after that. Then, it's a game of cat and mouse, baby."

We run.

All of us.

Into the vents at the end of the rec hall. Like moles burrowing underground, we disappear from site, leaving behind the murderous Cryptus, Mirabay, and, somewhere in this ship, little Zaris. I hope to God she'll be alright. The chiefs aren't here either; from our ship or The Zephyr. Where they are, I have no idea, but they are also now in grave danger.

We can't save everyone, I think to myself.

We run. Quietly, surreptitiously, we snake our way into the bowels of the ship, Anther leading us on to safety somewhere. I wonder what they're doing back on the bridge. I wonder if they're hiding Oculus' body and coming up with an alibi of sorts.

It doesn't matter. Our helmsman is dead, and we're now at the mercy of a sentient synthetic tied into our entire ship in ways I can't even pretend to understand. I only hope that Talicus grasps his murderous inclinations and can match him in intellect and strength. What I saw Cryptus do to our helmsman defies belief, and I have no idea if Talicus is his equal.

I find myself thinking I should have taken more note of the punch Cryptus doled out, reckoning with his strength earlier. That might have given me sense enough to not challenge him.

Anther helps me along, propping me up. I feel another body to my left, and a sweet fragrance envelops me. "Hang in there, Jax. We've got you."

> *The truth is known now, naked, cold*
> *The toll exacting, though 'twas bold*
> > *Now sides are drawn,*
> > *no time to fawn*
> *As peril grows amidst the fold*

Of those who knoweth painful real
Of them who wouldest safety steal
For evil lurketh,
malice worketh
And Phoenix riseth all surreal

I hear the voice and register the words. I don't know what they mean, and I don't care. Everything is now changed, but what I wouldn't give for one quick kiss to make the horror and shock dissipate into the ether.

I look over at Alaris, into her beautiful eyes, stumbling along the ground.

Part Two:
Into The Fire

9: The Opposition

The voice is jarring, and we all hear it.

"All personnel to the Assembly Hall please. All personnel to the Assembly Hall."

It's Phiria, but the words come from Cryptus, and I know it. He's not fooling anyone, and no one here wants to take the chance of trusting him following my report.

In my heart, I know the chiefs are going to meet Cryptus and Mirabay there. What they will decide to tell them about Oculus… about us… I have no idea. Perhaps in desperation, I hope that our chiefs Bannitor and Ambrosius will be able to suss out what happened, and figure out the truth of the matter. Hopefully, they'll survive this.

We reach Quadrant G, Subfloor 6B, and I sit down and tell everyone what happened, as best as I can given my memory, which has been afflicted by shock. I can't see straight, frankly, and all I can do is shake my head over and over again in incredulity. Everything happened so fast and so violently, I had little time even to run.

Their questions mostly deal with the First Officer.

Why would Mirabay do that?

Mirabay was in on it?

How on earth could Mirabay betray Oculus?

I have no answers. I don't know what to say. Once we sit, someone hands me water. I practically guzzle down the entire bottle. Thankfully, they don't pepper me with questions as I gulp it down between breaths.

The conversation falls to a hush. I look around.

No chiefs Marxim Bannitor or Hin Ambrosius. Our chiefs are missing; on their way to meet the conspirators. No female chiefs Ashira Sarristo or Maridie Onyx either. Just us kids. Except…

…*no little Zaris.* Greeting me warily – and with a clear trace of nervousness – I look the rest of them in the eyes in fear.

Orin. Strong and muscular. His muscles will be needed.

Ranshay. Poor little Ranshay doesn't even understand what's going on. That makes two of us, regardless of the language barrier.

Venthix.

Martos.

Garris.

Dravin.

Alaris.

Omnias.

Donetis.

Raelia.

Skarbé.

Ghirisha.

Miritia.

Baryonnis Talicus, our synthetic.

That's sixteen of us, altogether. Sixteen against two murderers, with one of them possessing superhuman strength and supreme intellectual cunning.

And now, we wait.

There is quiet chatter amongst some of them. I watch Alaris as she huddles close to her girlfriends and whispers unintelligible secrets to them, and they to her. I can only assume that they're all resenting their changed circumstances and dreading their stay onboard our ship.

I look at Orin. He is, after all, the oldest of us. Though our new synthetic demonstrates the ability to help in disabling the surveillance, I'm almost as unsure of her as I am of Cryptus. I want human help, *thankyouverymuch.* Orin will do nicely.

"Orin, what do we do?" I ask. "Do you think we should try to find our chiefs, and rally them to our cause? We're all alone down here."

Raelia shivers. So does Miritia, but Orin puts his arm around her and draws her close to himself.

"I dunno, Jax," he says. "It might be worth a shot, but hell if *I* wanna go back up there. We've gotta think about food, water, maybe even setting up some kind of barricade or something. I mean, do you have any idea why Cryptus would just flip like that?"

"Maybe we should call him 'Fliptus' from now on," Anther jokes. I don't find it funny. No one laughs.

I shake my head. "No idea. It was all so sudden and unexpected. Oculus was getting angrier and more irritated, and his voice was raised. The way that Cryptus just... *turned*... I didn't see it coming. And I certainly didn't see Mirabay doing what he did."

"Yeah, that's cold. So cold!" Venthix exclaims.

Ranshay's eyes bounce back and forth between all of us. He has no clue what's going on.

Orin decides to help.

"Talicus, can you interpret for Ranshay here please? We'd all like to know precisely what led up to this as well. Jax, do you mind?"

"Certainly. I'll do whatever I can," Talicus says. I nod my head. She surprises us all by literally removing her left ear, rotating it counterclockwise, and then detaching it from her head. She holds it up to Ranshay's right ear like it's some kind of wireless speaker, and he listens.

Slowly, the chatter dies down amongst all of them as I gather breath into my lungs. I recount what Omnias and I saw with Zaris in the Phoenix Experiment. How it unnerved and scared us. How Cryptus lied to me following my finally discovering my parents in there. How Zaris flipped out at me in the rec hall.

How I decide to talk to Oculus. How Anther warns me not to, and how I realize now that I should have taken his words more to heart. How Cryptus shows up in the bridge and he says I assaulted him, and how I inform Oculus about the android punching me.

How he and Oculus argue. How Cryptus explains about the new phenomenon, the 'presence' as he calls it, and how Oculus doesn't want to hear about his 'silly science.' And then, the awful moment when Cryptus and Mirabay murder him.

Talicus interprets everything for Ranshay into Hindi in near real-time. We all hear it coming through her dismembered left ear in a tinny fashion, but Ranshay understands everything. His little brown face scrunches up in worry as she translates. Ranshay's eyes grow steadily wider, and at one point his mouth falls open in dismay. His eyes dart between me and Talicus as he listens intently. He fires the occasional question of verification. I hear him say *hatya?* after Talicus informs him that Oculus has been murdered. She nods, and continues.

She ends somberly, seeming to reflect the gravity of our situation. Ranshay looks around himself in nervous apprehension, perhaps wondering if the area we've taken temporary refuge in is, in fact, safe. I wonder the same thing.

I glance around at the nervous faces. They have now heard the story in full as well, in their own language. It wasn't any easier for them hearing it as it was for Ranshay, nor Talicus, I'll wager. But now they all know the awful truth, at last.

Ghirisha voices the first question. "I had no idea that's what the Phoenix Experiments were for. I thought they were just to help us commune with our parents, or anyone else that we've lost. I thought it was to make us better Speakers for our return to Earth! It can actually bring our parents back to life?"

The others nod.

"Yep. And I thought so too," I say. "I think that it's still for Speakers, sure, but I didn't know about this- this *presence* thing."

"Does Cryptus really think that something was trying to come through?" asks Martos, and he looks like he considers all of this just ridiculous fiction.

"I have no idea *what* Cryptus thinks, Martos." I say with a bit of heat. "Not anymore. He was always so… remote… but this was just unexpected and over the top."

Martos nods and shuts up.

Talicus continues interpreting for Ranshay, but she interjects a thought. "It is, of course, a foregone conclusion that many or perhaps all of you might be somewhat nervous in my company. I completely understand. At the top of an AnthroMeta model's primary protocol is, of course, the prohibition against harming humans. Self-preservation is at the very top."

"Cryptus mentioned that," I mutter.

"Nonetheless, I want to assure you I have no such directives or programming to harm any of you. I neither approve of nor understand my colleague's behavior and rash actions. He is quite obviously operating outside normal AnthroMeta parameters. Please rest assured that I will do my utmost to protect all of you girls and boys."

I study her. "Do you have the same strength that Cryptus has?"

She nods. "It comes standard in our models."

"What model number are you?" Anther asks her. She turns to him. Ranshay is still holding her detached ear up to his, and his head swivels between all of us.

"AnthroMeta Model K300 Series C."

I furrow my brow. "Wait – you're more advanced than Cryptus?"

She nods. "Yes. By 2.16 generations, in fact."

"So, if it came down to fighting him, you could beat him?" continues Anther.

"Theoretically. Let us hope it does not come to that. My cybernetic strength protocols are for last resort use only," she says. She offers an unsettlingly saccharin smile.

This model obviously doesn't approve of violence. Fine, I think to myself. *But Cryptus assured me of the same thing, yet I saw what he did to Oculus. It was nothing short of savage, despite his promise.*

And just then, the voice comes once more, whispering to me out of nowhere:

Trust may vanish, fidelity fleet

Giving no rise for harmony meet
            But conscience begs
                to give faith legs
Co-laboring together in fiery heat

Now cannot live craven doubt
Lest vanity preclude the faithful, stout
                So stalwart rise,
                    stare fear down eyes
Laden with faith to wariness rout

With that, I decide to try to trust Talicus. There's something about her that is markedly different from Cryptus, of course, notwithstanding the fact that she's never murdered someone in front of me.

At that precise moment, watching her, I find myself wishing that my Phoenix session could have gone on just a bit longer. I had *almost* reached them. I was *that* close. What I wouldn't give for a brief embrace in the midst of that fiery inferno. Cryptus denied me that before he ultimately denied Oculus his life. I decide resolutely that it would be too much to deny Talicus a measure of trust.

It's not a huge stretch After all, she has already proven herself faithful by disabling the surveillance on the way here.

"Jax. Jax, you still with us?" Anther snaps his fingers in front of my face, and I startle.

"Huh? Yeah. Sorry. Thanks, Talicus. Ant," I say, turning my attention to him, "you've been around the ventilation shafts more than I have, I think. Where should we go? We can't just walk around through the corridors."

"I'm hungry," whines Raelia.

Anther registers what she says. "Well, yeah, there's that. We could swing through the storage supplies and grab some tasty *BioPrime* for a pick-me-up. And I have to wizz too. Anyone else gotta wiz?"

"Crude, but yes," Alaris replies. "We have to, uh, 'wizz' soon as well."

"What about the rumor of the Engineer?" I ask him, disregarding the toilet talk.

"The Engineer?" he asks me quizzically.

"Yeah, there's someone down there keeping things running and going back and forth doing check-ups. We've never met them. But The Origin's manifest and readouts always display one count higher than the occupants I've ever seen walking around. It's been 'us-plus-one,' though they are unnamed in the system."

"I've heard of her too," Venthix says. "The rumors are that it's a woman. We could try to find her. Maybe she can help us navigate the ship better, and find more ways to hide from them."

"Yeah, but," Orin argues, "is that all we're going to be doing now? Running around and hiding? We can't live like that. Cryptus needs to be confronted – and stopped."

"Yeah. Mirabay too," voices little Dravin, quiet as a mouse up until this point.

We're all lost in thought, wondering where we should go and what we should do now.

"If I may," Talicus interrupts, "I think you're wise to seek out the help of the Engineer. If for no other reason than to keep her safe from Cryptus and Mirabay as well, but it would be prudent to seek her counsel as to threading your way throughout the ship. She may also have ways to communicate with others and recruit help."

"Yeah," voices Donetis, "we really need to tell The Rubris to back off. To not come here. They would be in danger too!"

I confess I had forgotten about The Rubris. We definitely should contact them and alert them to what has happened aboard The Origin.

"I don't know," Orin argues, "that might be catastrophic for us, you guys. We tell them, they turn back, and we're stuck here with Cryptus."

"Yeah, but if we let them come here, Cryptus or Mirabay might kill them and take control of their ship too!" Donetis fires back.

Orin shakes his head. "I think they'd come prepared, don't you guys? We tell them what's up, they get some weapons, they come here and force Cryptus and Mirabay to stand down."

Miritia nods her head and stares affectionately at Orin as if to say *my hero…*

I seize the moment to roll my eyes noisily.

"Yeah but they're a *long* way off, Orin," I point out. "They're over a year away! We have to find someone else, someone much closer to The Origin."

"There were repair crews en route to The Zephyr prior to her detonation," Talicus says. "They were turned back. I recommend we send a message to them, informing them of our situation and stating emphatically that we have need of them."

I look around. Everyone seems to be nodding. Except for Raelia, who only looks emphatically hungry.

"Orin? You agree?" I ask him.

He nods.

"They're the closest. Do you know if they're armed, Talicus?"

"I'm sorry," she replies. "I have no knowledge as to their armament or skill other than ship repair."

"Well, even if they have welding torches, that'll be something," Orin says, standing. "Well, let's get to it. Raelia is hungry, and Anther has to wizz. I'm sure they're not the only ones, either. Talicus, can you pull up a schematic of the ship and tell us the best route down to maintenance?"

Anther looks deflated at this request. "I know the way. I can guide us."

"No, let Talicus tell us the way, Ant."

Anther's eyebrows dip down and his jaw clenches. "Don't call me that. Anyway, who died and made you the leader?" he asks defensively.

"I'm the oldest, Anther," Orin says, and he looks defiant. Miritia's eyebrows go up, ready to defend her new partner.

"Technically, *I* am the oldest here," Talicus says. "If anyone should be in command, it should be the smartest, strongest, *and* the oldest. I am, of course, all three."

Orin's eyes dart over at her, appraising her. He appears to be sizing her up for the task. I feel the same way. I'm not entirely sure I want a synthetic leading us, but I relent. The poetic voice still resounds in my head.

Orin sighs, looks around, and then his eyes land on Miritia. She throws up a quick, indifferent eyebrow, seeming to relent.

"Alright, fine, Talicus," Orin says. "Since you're, ya know, the smartest, strongest, *and* the oldest," he mocks. "You lead. What's the plan?"

Talicus wastes no time, consumed neither by ego nor any kind of scorekeeping. She's simply following her programming – the programming that Cryptus referred to.

Self-preservation is our overriding protocol, just as it is for humans.

"I think the recommendation to proceed to the engine room, through the ventilation shafts and ducts, makes sense. We will stop by the food supply on the way to replenish. There are sixteen of us, and we all need to keep up with each other. I suggest Anther leads the way to the engine room, and I will confirm his trajectory."

Anther turns and smiles heartily at Orin in victory.

"Once we have arrived there," Talicus continues, "we will ascertain the location of the Engineer. Meanwhile, I have already contacted the repair ship Achilles and informed them of our situation. They are preparing a response as we speak, so we have that working for our benefit."

I stare at her. "You did that already?"

She blinks. "Yes. I record in real-time, and a transcription of our conversation has been provided to them, along with a summary of what you describe happened on the bridge with your helmsman and First Officer."

"Wow," I say. "That's... impressive."

Talicus smiles.

The others look impressed as well.

"Nonsense," she replies briskly. "I'm a synthetic. Top of the line. We're efficient and effective."

Yeah. At running Phoenix experiments and killing helmsmen, I think, but I keep it to myself.

She starts to move. "Anther, if you please? Go on ahead of me and lead on. I'll check you if you stray off the trajectory. I assume you're aware of the junction ahead? Make a-"

"Left. I know," Anther says, as he looks back with a cocky smile. "I'm a human. Top of the line. We're efficient and effective," he says with a smirk.

"Excellent," she says.

"I think we should hurry," Omnias says. "If they're not hurting Zaris, they might use her."

"For what?" Alaris asks her.

"To bring that presence through." She gulps, and we all hear it.

The very notion makes us all look at each other in horror for a moment, but we resign to push on. No one wants to be stuck in ventilation shafts with a malevolent presence onboard.

Another klaxon sounds overhead, followed by another announcement sounding throughout the ship.

"Now hear this, now hear this, Helmsman Oculus here, please report to the Assembly Hall at once. All crew and passengers of The Origin, please report to the Assembly Hall at once. Last call."

This time we jump and look at each other in surprise. I know in my heart, and my eyes and memory confirm it, that our helmsman is dead. I was there. Cryptus killed him himself. That leaves only one explanation. I shake my head and let everyone see me doing so. *It's a lie,* I say with my mind.

That was Cryptus' voice.

My heart goes out to all souls aboard this ship who don't know of his sinister actions, and the only malevolent force I can readily identify aboard The Origin belongs not to an unknown presence, but to Cryptus himself.

His voice is jarring again, and we all heard it.

10: The Stranger

Our hearts grow lighter the further we get into this titanic ship.

We're deep in the underbelly of The Origin now. We've all heard nothing further from either Phiria nor Cryptus, nor Cryptus impersonating anyone. In conversation, it's clear we're all apprehensive of any further overhead communications, perhaps even more than rounding a corner and inadvertently coming face to face with the murderous synthetic himself.

We've gone now for an hour, all sixteen of us carefully threading our way through the vents and shafts, keeping as quiet as we can. Along the way I ask Talicus if there's a chance Cryptus might shut her out of Phiria and prevent further access to the ship's onboard AI.

"It's certainly possible, but it's unlikely, Ensign Hutson," she replies, "as Phiria is a fellow sentient, and she would need clear and concise reasons, as well as authorization codes from the ship's helmsman to restrict access. The helmsman is now deceased, of course, and can issue no such codes. That leaves concise reasons, and I've already confirmed with Phiria that she has witnessed – and recorded – the attack and slaying of Fulsar Oculus. She has subsequently taken the initiative to demote Stygius Cryptus and restrict his access. He and Mirabay have been demoted."

Well, that's good to know, I think. Having safeguards in place to prevent Cryptus from locking out Talicus gives me some reassurance.

We're close to the engine room, and the deep throbbing grows steadily as we press onward. We've all managed to pee somewhere or other – finding places to urinate off the beaten path was an interesting task – and Venthix, Martos and little Dravin found the supply room and commandeered several dozen packs of BioPrime and bottled water for our group to share. Thankfully, they also had the good sense to grab a bag to carry everything in.

So, that is now taken care of.

Now we just need to find this rumored Engineer that supposedly runs around in the dark down here, God only knows why.

"Time for a break, with your permission, of course, Talicus," Orin says, deferring to her with a bit of a snotty sarcasm. She nods. "I confess my legs are tired, and everyone's panting and sweating."

Indeed, down in the depths of The Origin, it's hot and stuffy. Thankfully, most everyone was dressed lightly up in the rec hall where I found them, as our uniforms would be stifling. I know mine is. Alaris is right beside me, and she's glistening. Every so often I catch her looking longingly at me, as if she's remembering that kiss. I know I am.

We all sit down slowly, creaking at the knees as we've been crawling through this God-forsaken ship. Everyone sighs to varying degrees. Moans are plentiful as we all massage our sore joints and palms.

"Talicus," I ask, "what's the ETA on the Achilles? Can you monitor communication with them and determine their status?"

"One moment," she replies, and becomes very still. It's always creepy when she connects to Phiria that way. "They appear to be prepping for launch as we speak. ETA 2 hours and 14 minutes."

"That's a long time," I sigh. "Can Cryptus turn them around? Redirect them, I mean?"

Talicus shakes her head. The perimeters of her corneas briefly flash blue as she disconnects from Phiria. "I had taken the liberty of informing them of the saboteurs onboard. They are under instruction not to comply with any new directives from Stygius Cryptus or Argin Mirabay due to their demotions. I've invoked AnthroMeta Primary Protocol 2D."

We all stop short, waiting. It's like she doesn't know that we're not well-versed in AnthroMeta protocols.

"Sorry," she continues, seeing our expressions, "it establishes a synthetic hierarchy that places me in a position of supremacy and precludes anyone else's directives from interfering with my primary objectives."

"So, like, whenever you wanted, you could have basically taken over the entire ship?" Orin asks. "Talk about a synthetic coup d'etat!"

"Theoretically, yes," Talicus says. "Phiria would still need to contact Earth headquarters for the approval, but yes."

"And what *are* your primary objectives?" Alaris asks her, point blank.

"To ensure the survival of all of you, and the continuation of the Phoenix Experiments as soon as humanly possible."

Most of us nod, thankful to hear that. As long as it's true, of course. Everyone is sprawled out now, either sitting or lying down, and chugging water. Donetis pours a bit of her water bottle down her back, arching in response, but clearly invigorated by the sensation of the cooling fluid. She moans in pleasure.

"What about the Achilles?" Garris asks, trying to ignore the inadvertent seductive display. "What happens when they try to dock with us?"

A highly reasonable question.

"I had not thought that far through the process," Talicus says stoically. "I am sorry. I'm still working through calculations of theoretical scenarios and appropriate responses. Most likely, we can expect interference from Cryptus and Mirabay, and possibly the chiefs – *if* they've sided with them."

I realize then that I had forgotten about the chiefs. All four of them. Whether they have sided with Cryptus or have been killed is unknown to all of us. Time will tell, of course.

"Why would the chiefs side with Cryptus?" Miritia asks Talicus. "And why wouldn't he just kill them too?"

"I am, as yet, unaware as to the rationale or purposes of my colleague, so, for the time being, I cannot speculate as to his motives," Talicus replies, and then she looks up and meets Miritia's eyes. "Or the fate of the four chiefs."

"Yeah, well, as for me, I think it's about time we found this supposed Engineer, if she even exists. It seems she might be the only one we can trust, especially if she didn't report to the Assembly Hall. Oculus did order *all* crew and passengers to report."

"*Cryptus* ordered that," I say. "Let's be clear."

"Whatever," Miritia bites back. "You know what I mean." She blows hot, wet hair out of her face and rolls her eyes. "We need to find that Engineer, like, *now*."

"And what will you do with her, once you find her?" utters an elderly voice, scratchy and raspy, laden with a thick Mexican accent.

A few of the girls shriek in alarm. Nearly all of us jump to our feet and whirl around to face the mysterious voice.

Our hearts are seized with fear once more.

Blending into the shadows behind us, formless against the dark of the vast walls of machinery and tubing, conduits, vents and cabling, a shape shifts slightly. None of us sees her coming, nor knows how long she has stood there listening to us.

We wait. There comes a soft, grim laugh.

Talicus sweeps some of the girls who were in front of her to a safer position behind her. "Identify yourself, please," she says coldly to the newcomer.

The figure doesn't move, but the voice returns. "Have you not guessed my identity already? Surely there is no one else down here to suggest an alternate persona?"

I watch her. Instantly I know who it is. "You're the Engineer. Right?" I ask, tilting my head and slowly advancing toward her.

She doesn't answer, but I can practically feel her smiling at me, regarding me from the darkened bowels of The Origin.

"Am I?" the voice finally utters. "Only you can tell."

"What does that mean?"

The voice grunts, and the figure shifts.

"Halt," says Talicus, stoically once more, forming a precautionary screen between the woman and us. "Do not advance until you are properly identified. I am requesting this cordially. I will not ask again, and will be required to use force."

The woman pays her no heed.

She slowly steps out into the light, and the faint amber glow from the ceiling falls upon her diminutive, elderly form.

Our jaws drop.

I was right: she is elderly, and definitely of Latino blood. She's only perhaps four and a half feet tall, wearing an oil-streaked dirty gray jumpsuit, the black wisps of her hair clasped neatly into some kind of clamp behind her head. She is wearing thick, black-rimmed glasses, but they don't fit her. They're generic, and her pupils are grossly enlarged behind them, studying us.

But for her sweet, maternal smile, I do believe that Talicus may have attacked her. Then, we all might be running from *two* androids.

She just stands there, everyone surveying her, and she surveying everyone.

"Who are you?" I ask her, but I can hear – and feel – the timidity in my own voice. Alaris clutches my arm as I am slowly, inadvertently drawn toward the stranger.

"There's no need to be alarmed. My name is Rosie," the old lady breathes. "And in answer to your question, yes, I am the Engineer. Sorry if I was coy. I've been down here a long time and, well," -here she dons a rather embarrassed expression, "I don't get many visitors."

"H-how long have you been down here?" I ask.

Ranshay nervously points to her and tugs on Talicus' arm. The android detaches her ear once more and gives it to Ranshay so that he can understand.

Rosie frowns. "This may come as a shock to you, but I actually don't know. I guess, an Engineer is typically expected to keep tabs on all the machinery and ensure functionality, check for abnormalities, keep things ship-shape. I actually don't have much mastery of any of those abilities, however."

"Rosie," Talicus echoes. "You are Rosalita Dahlia Campion, is that your full name?"

"It is indeed," she says. "You are Baryonnis Talicus, AnthroMeta model K300, yes? And you are Ensign Jax Hutson," Rosie says to me. She looks around at all of us individually. "I know who all of the boys are. The girls I'm just now getting acquainted with through ship's records since your arrival on The Origin. I'm so sorry about your own ship and mates. My condolences on the loss of the Zephyr crew and passengers," she frowns. "I'm able to keep tabs on what goes on up top through the terminals down here. Your names were on a manifest," she says in a nod to the girls.

"Why didn't you respond to Oculus' summons to the Assembly Hall?" I ask her, intentionally using our helmsman's name even though it was clearly Cryptus impersonating him. "He specifically instructed all crew to report."

Rosie cocks an eyebrow. "Because I don't report to synthetics, Mr. Hutson, present company excluded." Talicus bows graciously. "Especially those who slay their superiors."

Now my eyebrow raises. "So you know what happened on the bridge?"

"I do."

"So… so…," my words fail me, caught between gratitude that she knew and could possibly aid us, and confusion over how an elderly woman could even render aid, "what do we do, Rosie? You've been here a long time, you know this ship, what do we do?"

She laughs grimly again, shaking her head. "Well, judging by what I've seen, young Anther here knows this ship much better than I do, and his knees are arguably in better shape for crawling through air ducts. Less noisy creaking of joints."

Anther chuckles.

"And yes, the horror - though I've never even met Helmsman Oculus, no one should die like that. I did happen to read what happened through Phiria. Thank you for the succinct update, Baryonnis. I appreciate it."

"You are most welcome, Rosalita."

"Just Rosie will do," Rosie says, laughing graciously. "Now, as to your question, young Jax, I think what you've all done, coming down here, was wise. I am on your side, please know that. And by summoning the Achilles here to help, I would call that a measure of wisdom as well. I think you should all stay down here with me until we all figure this whole sordid situation out."

There's a moment of pause while we all somberly appraise the situation. I must confess that Rosie's presence – elderly and maternal – conveys a measure of tangible and felt hope. Glancing around at all of us, it looks like that hope is shared by everyone here. There's something about her: a power; perhaps a degree of intangibility or… something. She seems far older than her elderly form… ageless… I can't quite put my finger on it. I'm not scared or threatened by it, and I find her incredibly interesting. *Maybe even more than Alaris,* I think to myself.

"Now, take heart, everyone, because there's one more thing," Rosie says, and something in the way that she says this makes me frown. Her tone of voice changes; the tangible feeling of hope is punctured like a balloon.

"I have been watching, and listening, and even praying. I know about the missing passenger, young Zaris Sharibian. And I know what your android was doing." She pauses, awkwardly. "I guess there's no easy way to say this." Rosie gathers her breath, surveying all of us somberly. "Jax, Omnias, you weren't off in your suspicion. A dreadful presence is in those Phoenix Experiments that you do. Something horrible. Something deeply malignant and hostile.

"It is something I had never encountered in my long, storied life here. I don't know what your android has been doing, but the incident with little Zaris was only the beginning, I fear.

"This… thing," she says, shaking her head and staring at the ground, "is hellbent on breaking free of its captivity and entering our world. It seeks to do so through a vulnerable host. And little Zaris is still with your android. I fear for her safety. I fear for all of our safety. It wants her. It wants you. And we must *not* give ourselves over to it."

I can't wait any longer. I want to know what the thing was inside the third chamber. And perhaps in my own session with Cryptus before he zapped me out. "Rosie, what *is* the presence?"

"I don't know what it might be called on the other side. But this side of death, it is called The Djinn. It is an ancient evil, and it must *never* come through."

A cold shiver runs down my spine, and my arms are dotted with bumps.

Alaris leans into me, and I feel her trembling.

Fear not, children, for thy deranger
Comes not through this present stranger

Keep thy faith
Fear not thy wraith
Forsake not prudence for clear danger

We all lean into her. Rosie's face twists into knots as she conjures up the words to describe the evil she's witnessed. As I briefly look around, my friends huddle closer together, seeking companionship and warmth amidst such cold, terrifying revelations.

"The Djinn are supernatural entities from Islamic and pre-Islamic Arabian myth. But they are no myths, children. Not anymore. Spirits composed of smokeless fire, they exist alongside us. I have encountered only one, but it is enough. They are invisible shapeshifters, they can influence us, possess us, and cause mental illness."

"Where do they come from?" Omnias asks. I see the look on her face, and it's stoic. She remembers what we both started to see forming in the third chamber during Zaris' session.

"I do not know," Rosie answers. "They are not immortal, but they do have lengthy lifespans. Once they have found a possible exit, they will *not* leave. They are malevolent and wicked to the core, and they cause great fear. The Djinn is the worst entity I have ever encountered, far worse than banshees."

"How do you know all of this?" Talicus asks her. "And how long have you known?"

Rosie glances up at her. "I've only just learned of its intensity. It is nothing to trifle with, and, even now, Stygius Cryptus is toying with something incomparably evil up there, and if it gets out…," she trails off. "*If it gets out,*" she mutters once more, leaving us leaning into her as she cocks an eyebrow.

That doesn't help. I want her to finish that sentence. "If it gets out, *what* exactly, Rosie?"

She looks at me. A solemn expression wraps her face as she gathers her breath.

"It will be the end. This thing is from the other side, and it has no business here. It does not belong."

"How do you know that?" Anther prods.

Rosie smiles gently, as if consumed by some memory that long predates any of us. Her eyes stare into the wells of space, possessed by reflection.

"Because I don't belong, either. It – and I – have been there," she says. "On the *other* side."

We just stare at her.

"I'm no longer living," she clarifies.

Rosie was dead once?

That can mean only one thing.

She returned through the Phoenix Experiment. Perhaps in a session with only Cryptus present? But why would she be down here, and why bring her back in the first place?

And if she came back, so could my parents… right?

But if she can come through, and they can come through, that means that something *else* could possibly come through as well.

Poor little Zaris. I realize with horror that she will be used as the conduit… the portal through which Cryptus will unleash this dreadful presence. A shiver runs through me.

My heart grows heavier the further I get into these frightening truths.

11: The Truth

As if on the coattails of an introduction, right on cue, we hear it.

How can we *not* hear it?

The horrifying cry resonates throughout the entire ship, stopping all our hearts at once. It grows in intensity until we cover our ears.

Ripples run down my flesh as thrills of fear wash over me. I grip Alaris close to me and send my frightened eyes all around, scanning the corridors, the ceiling, everything, wary of the approaching menace.

An unearthly growl rumbles throughout the ship, burgeoning in intensity and pitch until it bounces off every single wall, reverberating throughout every corridor, rising to a howling scream of wind and wrath. Sucking our very courage from us, it saps every last bit of hope into a vortex of trepidation.

"Something is happening in Quadrant C, Subfloor 3A," Talicus says, apparently unfazed by the noise. "Phiria reports a massive volume differential, and an unknown presence detected."

"It's The Djinn," Rosie says, her eyes shut tight. "We must move. Now."

"Oh, no!" Omnias wails. "What does that mean for Zaris, Rosie?"

Rosie, who had started to move down the corridor to lead us on, looks straight at her. "Your friend Zaris is dead. There is nothing you can do now except flee. Do *not* be afraid. Follow me."

And with that, Rosie takes off at astonishing pace, the rest of the sixteen of us falling in behind her in no particular order.

> *Gather not thy weapons useless*
> *Tether not thy cunning ruthless*
> *Dark dawn cometh,*
> *terror mammoth*
> *Rendering thy vain hope fruitless*

We're finally moving slower now, all of us, threading our way further into the belly of The Origin. Rosie says nothing. She leads us on with determination, and Talicus falls in step behind her. Orin and Miritia are next, followed by Anther and Omnias, the rest of the girls, and then the boys and I take up the rear. I can't shake a feeling of creeping dread behind me as I push on, waiting for some primal force to seize me from behind and engulf me.

But Rosie seems to know what she's doing, and she's taking us somewhere: silently, wordlessly, we're now entirely in her hands.

There is one more ghostly roar right after we begin to flee, and then, suddenly, an eerie silence where we can all hear each other breathing. Every tiny shifting of weight, every tendon flexing, every blink: we hear it, amplified in these dark corridors with the terror of our hearts pounding in our ears.

At intervals, we hear reports throughout the ship, some dull concussion against the greater overwhelming din of engines and thrusters and God knows what else rumbles down here to make The Origin go. No one says anything to anyone else, but glances are exchanged, and in those glances, nothing but nervousness and fear.

We've now descended down endless shafts, scaled ladders, filed singly through trap doors and chutes, and even slid one-by-one down some spillway to a waiting room below, throbbing with intense sound. I figure we have got to be somewhere near the reactor room, accounting for all the noise.

I slowly make my way up to Anther, passing the other boys and girls. I need to talk to him. The Djinn is somewhere up on the higher floors. Up there with Cryptus, the chiefs, and Zaris. *No- wait- not Zaris. Not anymore,* I think to myself. *Dammit, Cryptus, you traitor. You let one through.*

"Hey buddy," I say. "Wher-"

Anther startles, looking at me with eerie, widened eyes white with panic as I suddenly appear unexpectedly to his left. He clutches his heart. "Dude! Don't do that!" he whispers. "Scared the crap out of me." He tosses an embarrassed look at Omnias, who says nothing to his right.

"Sorry. Where are we?"

He shakes his head. "I've lost track. I know we're in Quadrant H or I, and we're probably on Subfloor 12 or 13 now, I think. Hard to tell. I've never ever been down this far, Jax. It's hot and quiet. And dark," he finishes, and I can tell he has an intense distaste for the word, given our circumstances.

Suddenly a thought comes to me, and it's a macabre one. "The Origin," I say, shaking my head. Anther looks over at me, confused. "What a name for a ship that has become a portal for a supernatural entity. It's almost like it was fate." Anther doesn't reply, lost in thought. We trudge on, but I can't help but ruminate now about The Zephyr and the Rubris: what they were named for. I think *zephyr* means something like a breeze, but I have no idea what *rubris* means. I don't think it's a real word, actually. I know *rubric* has something to do with a purpose, but clearly the name of that ship was adapted.

"Do you know what happened aboard The Rubris?" Anther asks Rosie. "Are there any crewmembers aboard it? Are they safe for us?"

"I do not know," is all she says in reply.

All I know is that constantly ruminating about the meaning of *both* does the job of keeping my mind off the presence of that horrifying thing roaming freely somewhere aboard The Origin.

Rosie finally slows, and we gradually come to a halt behind her. "Here," she says, "it's time to stop and get some rest and water. In this room, everyone. Quickly. In you go."

My heart is pounding, and beads of sweat are rolling down my temples onto my neck and into my uniform. I'm envious of the others in their rec outfits; they're doubtless not as hot as I am right now.

We follow her into an enclosed room that thankfully has air conditioning against the heat down here. As I pass under the door jamb I see a diminutive, reflective gold label adorning it. *Shielding.*

Peering inside, it looks like a mess hall for maintenance, even though there's only a single Engineer here. There's a fridge, countertops with a stove, freezer, and even a bed and a terminal. It all presents as severely antiquated, and it's in disarray, as if someone has gone to great lengths to make this tiny escape as homely – and dated – as possible.

If I didn't know any better, I would think someone could actually live in here. It's practically like a tiny little apartment. I wonder how many lonely meals or sleeps Rosie has had here. If she even eats or sleeps at all. I also wonder what the heck she even does down here. I make a plan to sit with her and learn more about her. It seems she is well aware of what we're dealing with, and that knowledge could be a comfort – or cause for anxiety. I guess I'll find out. I do want to know what 'shielding' references, anyway.

Everyone files in and sits down, winded and worn, placing their backs to the wall. No one sits at the center table or takes the bed. Rosie closes and locks the door. We watch her as she proceeds over to the far left corner to the terminal, where she closely stares into the screen and studies the data before her. I can only surmise she's tapping into Phiria to determine what happened. "Talicus, would you join me, please?"

The synthetic moves over beside her.

"Look at this," Rosie says, pointing to the screen. We're all too far away from the screen to see what she's showing Talicus, but I can see motion, and can just make out some movement through it, showing up in what appears to be monochromatic, night-vision-like footage. There is no sound.

"Fascinating," Talicus breathes.

"Hardly the word I would use to describe it," Rosie says. "But yes, there it is. God help us."

It's then that I realize they're watching footage from up above. I get up and start to make my way over to them. Rosie is instantly aware of me and turns toward me, both palms out. "No, Jax! Don't look. You mustn't look. That won't help you. None of you. Please sit down."

With surprising speed she whirls back around, and, with the flick of a key, the footage window is closed, and the screen darkens.

Talicus takes a deep breath and turns, standing lost in cybernetic thought.

Rosie rotates back to me once more. I just stand there, and we're face to face. "Are we safe in here, Rosie?" I ask her.

Rosie slowly nods. "For the time being." She looks around, as if appraising the room once more. "This is a radiation-proof room. In the event of any kind of meltdown or cataclysm aboard The Origin, this is one of the safest places you can be."

That makes sense. Thus, *Shielding*. Of course there would be a bed, fridge, freezer, and a way to keep tabs on the rest of the ship from here. This is where you would ride out the storm of a radiation leak, and hope against hope for the integrity of the room's seals to hold.

Orin chuckles grimly. "Cataclysm? Yeah. I'd say that's an appropriate word right about now." No one else laughs. Miritia lays her head on his shoulder. Orin puts his arm around her in comfort.

"Here we are, yet again, waiting," Donetis says despondently. "Where else can we even go on this ship? Rosie, is that thing coming?"

Rosie's eyebrows raise. She stands facing Donetis, hands clasped at her midsection. "I do not know, child. That's the truth. It could be anywhere. All we can do is try to track its whereabouts. Drink some water, children. We're allowed a little rest now, in a relatively safe space that's fairly soundproof from the outside. Take some comfort in that, and refresh yourselves."

And then it hits me in a sudden wave of suspicion.

Track its whereabouts.

How the heck did she just watch footage if the surveillance has been disabled?

"Rosie, Talicus disabled the surveillance. How were you able to even see what you just saw?" I ask.

"The lab is never disabled," she replies. "That's the one place on this ship that surveillance cannot be interrupted. The Phoenix Experiments exist because of this ship, and this ship exists because of the Phoenix Experiments. It's The Origin's sole purpose. It's the one place where there must always be a record. Additionally, the occupants of this ship are minors, and the Phoenix Experiments are medical. It's for your protection, and for the integrity of everything that goes on aboard this vessel."

"So, did you see when that thing entered our world, then? Is that what you saw?"

"Yes," she says, sadly. "That is what Baryonnis and I just saw, unfortunately." She sighs, and sits at the center table, facing most of us. The rest of us have to settle for her profile.

There's a lull; a wicked and overlong lull: I can hear our wheels turning, wondering what it looks like, what it can do, why it's here, and why on Earth Cryptus would go to such lengths to usher in something so demonic into our midst. Especially through an innocent little girl!

"Rosie," I pipe up, "can I ask you a question?"

She looks at me.

"You said you were… *dead*… before. You didn't mean, like… *dead* dead, did you?"

All of us wait with bated breath.

"It's a very long story, kiddo," she says to me. "I'm not sure a story of my death would interest you."

Hardly likely, lady, I think to myself.

"It would," I persist. "And I think it would interest all of us. Besides, you basically just confirmed it. Anyway, we all spend our days hooked up to a machine communing with the dead in long sessions, and we've been here a long time, suffering from deathly boredom. I'd say we're all well-acquainted with death and boredom to stomach it."

Rosie relents with a stubborn sigh. "Fine, fine. I was born in 1964. And... I died in 2045. I had just turned eighty-one years old when my number was up."

She smiles thinly.

I watch her, but frankly, I simply don't know what to say. 2045. That's 426 years ago. Rosie is technically, accounting for her two lives, 507 years old. The very notion blows me away.

But there's another notion. The bizarre idea that she might be a raving lunatic flashes through my mind, briefly. However, don't we deal with the paranormal aboard this ship anyway? We always have. And anyway, isn't that the point of the Phoenix Experiment to commune with those whom we've lost, and to even try to bring them back? My mind wonders, *who loved Rosie enough to bring her back?* Someone had to.

No one says anything. I'm sure everyone else is as uncertain what to say as I am. Rosie scans the room, reading our expressions.

"I know what you're thinking. I'm either crazy, or the Phoenix Experiments actually work. I'm not an illusion; I sit here before you a real, whole, alive-and-well human being, long past her prime. I've been 'there and back again,' as it were. And here I am before you today."

Talicus has been quiet and still, but now she's studying our elderly, resurrected companion, and she speaks up. "Facial and retinal scans confirm your identity. She is not lying, children. This is Rosalita Dahlia Campion, born December 8th, 1964, emigrated from San Juan Ixcoy, Guatemala to Matamoros, Mexico in April of 1985. Married to Miguel Monzon in August of 2034, longtime resident of Clarksville, Tennessee, and finally Washington, DC. Credentials include former spiritual adviser to the 49th President of the United States, Vance Brennan Cardona. You were there during the gorgon invasion of 2026 and the wars of the 40's following. And... deceased as of February 13th, 2045.

"You are who you say you are," Talicus ends.

I'm shell-shocked. If this woman truly was on the other side, and she's familiar with The Djinn, maybe she also knows how to defeat it.

"Your memory banks are overflowing with truth, Baryonnis," Rosie says, smiling gently. "And now my own memory banks are overflowing with emotion." Her eyes appear to fill as she is lost in thought, reflecting back over her lives... both of them. "You're perhaps looking at a living legend," she finishes, humbly.

"Incredible, Rosie," I gasp. "You were on the other side, and, now… you're back. What was it *like* there? How long were you dead- I mean, gone? And… what was it like when you were brought back? Did you see The Djinn there? I have so many questions!"

"That makes two of us," Anther echoes.

"Three," Omnias chimes in.

"Nope. Four," Alaris sounds off. I look over at her and smile, gently.

I watch as Rosie looks around the room and is met with sheepish nods as the others chime in as well, signifying they, too, want answers. It's time for her to indulge us all. For if she truly comes from the other side, then perhaps our parents can as well.

In the dark, sheltered corner of our vast ship, Rosie clears her throat. "Fine. This may surprise some of you. It won't be easy, mind you, but it will be the truth."

"It was peaceful. Like, being asleep," Rosie says. "I suppose you all have some experience with that, whether you're in actual REM sleep, or you've been wired up to those machines up there with your android hovering over you, watching from his booth."

Talicus has fetched water and doled it out to all of us. I look up at her and smile, thankful for her custodial prowess. I'm becoming more and more at home with her, despite the freshness of the horrible memory at the hands of her colleague. She is gentle, forthright, humble, and helpful, and maybe some of these AnthroMetas are in fact redeemable, I think. Time will tell, but for now, our new synthetic is on a roll. We drink and listen to Rosie.

"When I died, I saw what so many have reported. A bright light. It was both brief and interminable. Alarming and calm. Your emotions don't leave you; they carry through with you to the other side. But grief becomes assuaged, and it certainly did for me. When I left my husband and this world, I felt something dark and ominous was coming, but it was no longer my right or privilege to counsel those left behind through it. It was their own soil to till. The Father was calling me home, so, home I went. But, in the blink of an eye, I felt suspended on a time and plane that was the best of both worlds. Happiness, contentment, memories, fulfillment, tears of joy… all of it blended together until my heart nearly burst. I can't really describe it except to say that I felt *utterly* whole. I saw my mother, my Miguel eventually showed up, I saw those I had served with down here, family and good friends, my mother, father, dear Wyatt, his brother Cameron, Vance, I saw my children, Vance's wife Andi, and so many more. It was heartfelt and beautiful."

I have no idea who these people are, but they are precious to her. As she speaks, her cheeks bloom outward and her eyes light up, twinkling in memory of all those loved ones she reconnected with. I could practically feel the familiar joy heartthrob, the thrum of pure elation in seeing my own parents in my most recent Phoenix Experiment before Cryptus evicted me.

"Oh, I could still see you down here. Well, not *you* – this was well before your time, but wars came and went. Tyrants rose and fell. Oppressed peoples fought back, other invaders terrorize our world. We rejoiced with those who rejoiced, and we mourned with those who mourned, constantly praying for you.

"Earth has been woven through an endless tapestry of victories and defeats, joys and pains, laughter and tears through *many* centuries since I was called home."

But then Rosie pauses, and her smile dies. Her face grows careworn and tired. "I don't know when, but something eventually began calling me back. I don't know how long it was, nor why. I wanted to stay, you see. The Father had called me home, so why was I now being pulled back? I couldn't answer it, and no answers were given. Sometimes that is the way of things. But I cannot explain what it felt like other than to say that it was like a visceral tearing. Being pulled tautly by two distinct forces: one keeping me here, and one desperately tugging me back. If you've ever tried to run against gale force winds, that might describe it. I could not do it."

She stops and looks at me as she speaks her last words: "The winds eventually took me."

A coldness begins creeping over my heart just then, and I clutch my uniform closer to me. My breath begins to materialize in front of me a bit, and it feels as though the room has chilled from the air conditioning. I glance around. Others also clutch their clothing to themselves and sidle up beside their neighbors for added warmth.

"On my way back, I passed something. Time seemed to stretch; *everything* seemed to stretch as I felt pulled back through this brilliant vortex, light streaming around me. I was almost through, when I saw it. At first, it was beautiful, as all evil things are at first glance. It's only when you study them up close that you find they are full of malice and a staunchly evil will.

"It was *The Djinn*, children. Swirling around with me, it was seeking a way out. It reached for me. It clutched at me. Swirling smoke and fire encircled it, wreathed around it like amber scarves, twisting and flailing in the wind. You cannot make out anything but its eyes. They smolder with hate. Nothing has ever so filled me with raw horror on that side. It wanted me, but it could not grasp onto the intangible. That is what we both were, still, until I was pulled through, back here, to the other side. I awoke and clutched myself, wondering if it had come as well, through me. That's when I realized I was naked.

"Someone was in the room with me, in that lab. I only just caught a faint glimpse of them fleeing. I never found out who it was. I gathered what clothing I could find, jumpsuits like this one, covered myself, and fled to the lower levels. I was alarmed beyond belief, frightened, and lonely. I had no idea where I was, I had no idea why I was here nor what year it was; all I knew is that I wanted to get far, far away from that lab, and that place and that… presence."

I swallow, hard, as I listen to her.

Every mention of The Djinn fills me with unease, and I am still cold.

"Well," Rosie says – and I can tell she's finishing her story and bringing us to the present – "I finally found my way down here through the same vents and shafts young Anther has become so adept at traversing. There was no one else here. I thought I was going crazy, talking to myself, hearing voices, almost like intermittent poetry in my head…" -here I stop, flinching at what she has just said, and wondering if she's hearing the same orations I've been hearing- "a person could really go crazy down here.

"It was only through repeated trial and error that I found my way down here to this little, hovel, I guess you would call it, this 'safe room' as it were, and right there" -here she points with a gnarled finger over to the terminal she and Talicus were just at- "is where I learned all about you, the Phoenix Experiments, the Origin, the Zephyr, the Rubris, your chiefs, the year, the circumstances we were in, the banshees, the synthetics, and, finally… The Djinn. I discovered that's what it was that I had passed on my way back."

"You found out about The Djinn from that?" Orin asks her, pointing at the terminal.

"No," Rosie says. "That is not public record. If it were in there, Baryonnis would know about it as well. Earth would know about it. The other ships would have known. Someone would have stopped this entire process long before you came to me." She shakes her head. "No, it's just that young Anther here isn't the only one who used to crawl around shafts and eavesdrop." Anther grins at her once more. "I found out by eavesdropping. A conversation Stygius Cryptus was having – with *himself*. It was only recently. I spent many years searching this ship and trying to figure out where I had come from, who had brought me back, and what all of this was about. I couldn't just 'show up' on the main floors and say, 'Hi, I'm Rosie, I used to be dead but now I'm alive again, can you spare some BioPrime for a cold elderly Latina?" She laughs grimly. We chuckle in response. "*Ay caramba, mio Dios*," she says, shaking her head once more, "this ship was never intended for its current purpose."

"What do you mean?" I ask her, growing ever colder. All of us continue to lean into her, regardless of time, the presence of The Djinn onboard The Origin, and our potential fate at the hands of either this spectral entity or Cryptus.

Rosie frowns and sighs. "Please understand, children, that The Origin doesn't need an Engineer. It never did. Neither did The Zephyr or The Rubris. These ships are self-sustaining. You know that. Modern marvels, you might call them. They are entirely reliant on their own programming, and they are solar-powered. They will not stop functioning unless destroyed, which is, alas, what befell The Zephyr through a freak accident."

Rosie stares me in the eye, and her lids narrow. "But it's what has happened down there that is far more important. In the throes of a death spiral, Earth had reached a point of no return. It can no longer sustain life to the same degree. Global warming, deforestation, alien occupation, madmen, ruthless tyrants, and more ensured that. The net effect has brought our beloved planet to its knees. Ergo, man devised a solution. They would find another world. So, they began to build ships. Great ships. Vast ships to carry us across the stars to a new home. Ships like the very one you're in. Like The Zephyr and The Rubris. These ships were supposed to house the last survivors of Planet Earth aboard them. Is it any surprise? They are *enormous*. They are not meant for just eight boys and eight girls and a few chiefs and synthetics. But… something went wrong. Something was unleashed down there. Something evil. It appeared one day from The Rubris, and then infiltrated our world."

"The banshees," little Dravin voices.

"Ohh, no…," Rosie says, looking at him with an endearing smile, "young Dravin, the banshees are a mere byproduct of The Djinn. They are of the same ethereal family. They are also evil, yes, but something *else* was unleashed, and it is the worst evil mankind has ever inflicted on itself."

We wait anxiously for her answer.

"The worst evil of mankind is mankind itself," she says, solemnly. "It always has been. Not gorgons nor black holes nor terrorism nor banshees nor The Djinn. No, children," she says, heaving a great sigh. "Mankind has always been the worst enemy of itself. And down there is where it all finally went wrong and fell apart. The banshees were sent in to clean it up."

"*Sent in?*" Orin cries, incredulous. "By whom?"

"Oh, the same person who has been playing this silly game with your lives and your consciences up here all this time, both awake and dreaming. Remember what I said about The Djinn: it can influence us, possess us, and cause mental illness. The Djinn has been doing so since the beginning of time. And it has been working overtime on one person in particular to thwart your progress."

In my heart, I already know who it is. "Stygius Cryptus," I say with a knowing grimace. I nod, the truth finally revealed to me in full.

But Rosie doesn't nod. She just stops me short and stares at me, shaking her head.

"No," she says. "It was none other than your helmsman. Fulsar Oculus."

What?!? nearly everyone exclaims except for Ranshay. His interpretation is somewhat delayed as Talicus processes all of this, but he does exclaim something unintelligible in Hindi. His eyes are wide. *Bilkul nahin! Tum mazaak kar rahe ho!* he cries.

"*Oculus* is behind this?" I, too, cry in dismay. "How? Why on earth would he let the banshees out, and… and… why would he bring you back? What is going *on* aboard this ship, for crying out loud? Are you saying that he let them all through, they got down to earth and started killing everyone, and so Cryptus killed him for it? That would be years ago now. Why would Cryptus wait all this time?"

"It's certainly conceivable," Talicus says.

I gaze at Rosie in incredulity.

"But that would make Cryptus and Mirabay the good guys!" I wail. "That just can't be!" I stare at her, almost pleading with her for a different logic; a better explanation.

"It most definitely can be, I assure you," Rosie says. "Helmsman Oculus let the banshees in, and now, something even more terrifying has now come through that poor little girl."

Then it hits me. "Wait – if Oculus let them through, he must have also let *you* through? Is that who did it? Why would he do that?"

"I honestly do not have an answer to either," she says, and that deflates me. "To my knowledge the Phoenix Experiments are meant to connect the loved to the beloved, the passed to the bereaved. Oculus and I are in no way related, I assure you. He would not love me – or know me – enough to want to bring me back."

Anther clears his throat. "This is what happened aboard the Rubris, isn't it, Rosie?"

She doesn't answer; she just clenches her lips tight and looks away. "We just don't understand the other side. It is beyond dangerous to toy with the eternal. The Rubris was banished for toying with this."

My head is spinning at all of these revelations. They are far too much information and bedtime ghost story to assimilate in one sitting. I also can't believe that Oculus is behind it, and that tears at me. I turn around and place my hands on my head. Alaris stands up and places her hand on my back in support. I turn to embrace her.

"I didn't say that it would be easy, people," Rosie concludes. "But I did promise to tell you the truth."

The truth is jarring. The truth is unacceptable.

The truth cannot be the truth.

Rosie freezes momentarily, and her head bows.

So does mine, simultaneously.

Earthen vessels, frail and weak

Thou shouldest hide, for the seek
　　　Is on at last;
　　　the beast is fast
Thy slow, thy lame, shall rot and reek

Malice eats it like a canker
It casheth chips as would a banker
　　　Start thy feet,
　　　beat thine retreat
Lest spirit quail 'midst stumping hanker

Rosie has told us what she has told us, and now I can see it in everyone's eyes: Fulsar Oculus, our own helmsman, was the enemy all along. But why would Cryptus flat out kill him? And why is he impersonating Oculus' voice up there? And why would Fulsar let the banshees through in the first place?

None of it makes sense, but it doesn't need to right now. The only thing that makes sense is bracing and panic, because we all hear it once more.

The Djinn.

Welling up from the depths of the ship, a mournful howl breaks out, and our flesh crawls. Alaris clutches me and moans, sinking into my uniform and burying her face. Rosie slowly turns toward the door.

The slow, agonized shriek is multi-noted with dissonant clashing pitches set against one another, designed to freeze the marrow and sap the lifeforce out of you. It grows horribly, and with it, our fear, as an unknown presence approaches outside the room we're holed up in. We can hear the dull throbbing growl fused with the cries of a thousand souls in agony intertwined in a cry that stops our hearts.

"Be… still," Rosie whispers. "Do *not* fear."

And then… it stops. We're met with silence, and the only sound is the overloud thud of our hearts in our ears, as an eerie spectral mist starts to seep under the doorway, slithering through the mists of the locked door seals.

As if waiting patiently for us to bolt, right outside, we hear nothing.

12: The Specter

No one says a word.

My eyes meet Alaris.' Hers are ringed with fear. I'm sure mine are as well.

All sixteen of us back away against the far wall. Only Rosie is left at the center of the room, standing there, silently, poised, steadfast and true, facing the door with grim determination.

Everything falls to a hush, and our hearts are in our ears. I can hear Anther swallow noisily from across the room. Omnias grips his hand so hard I think she'll break it. He flinches and looks down. "Ow."

His whispered utterance is far too loud.

The door to the room bursts open! The Djinn heard us! Fragments of heavy metal go spinning outward, ricocheting off the walls. One of them nails Skarbé in the head and chest, and then settles upon her, crushing her. She's instantly gone.

Sixteen of us left.

Cinders fly as burning fragments erupt around us and the wind grows thick with heat. It's hard to breathe!

A swirling, burning mist filters in amongst all of our desperate cries. Horrendous wind erupts around us as rushing trails of wavering corpse light stream around us, over us, under us and through us. I cannot contain my yells for help, but I have no idea who I'm calling for. Alaris tries to hide behind me.

Garris rushes toward it in a mad attempt to squeeze past it and out into the bowels of the ship, to dash off into the darkness. Where he thinks he'll go from there is anyone's guess.

It's useless.

The smoke literally seizes him; I watch with horror as a vice-like ethereal grip wraps around him and lifts him up in the air momentarily as his mouth drops and his eyes roll back in his head. He blackens from proximity to the heat of the beast. It screams at him: a wailing, ripping siren scream that sends fissures through every peace I've ever known. It holds him still while that high-pitched shriek drains every ounce of his lifeforce. Garris' face pales and his body goes limp. It tosses him violently against the far wall. He hits so hard he splats outward and then streaks down the wall to the floor. Garris is gone.

Fifteen.

Voices scream around me. Others try to avoid the smoke, but it just coalesces in front of them, gathering, gathering, gathering together, until it coils into an appendage-like mist, aiming for them. The screams never abate. Right now it's targeting Orin and Miritia, perhaps recognizing that he is the oldest and strongest of us youths. Both of them shield their face.

Where is Rosie? I wonder. I've lost her. In the hot, swirling vapor I can't see her.

Talicus shouts at it, but it merely roars at the synthetic nuisance and swipes her aside. She hits a side wall with a dull thud, collecting herself nearly immediately and standing stoic once more.

In the flickering darkness, there is not really silence. Like a whisper condemned, erased and forgotten; an abyss of empty air hungrily consuming memory and safety. The only thing that exists, then and there, is The Djinn.

Gaseous clouds of sizzling spectral light and shade swirl in a nebula of fear. My bones are scalded. I don't know where to go.

There's Rosie!

I see her now, amidst the swirling spray of blistering smoke streaming throughout the room. I cover my ears as the roaring scream resounds throughout this echo chamber, and my bones are chilled. She is eye to eye with The Djinn, if you can call it the thing's 'eye.' It's terrifying, catlike, and it sees all.

The thing screams at her, but she remains unafflicted.

"You have no power over me," Rosie says, calmly. "Get you gone, before your end comes for you."

The Djinn scowls and recoils, recognizing some power resident in this diminutive woman. It moves on. Instead, it targets those less stout; less sure of their place in this world; less emotionally stable.

Then the roar and scream combine into a spine-altering cacophony, and I can't take it. Alaris whimpers in fear beside me. I shut my eyes, but something draws near. The anguished cries of a thousand tormented souls are in that roar, as if it has feasted and grown fat on the dread of every one of its victims down through the ages.

The Djinn!

In the swirling, broiling mist, I can just make out the trails of smoke funneling toward me, their burning and grasping tentacles whipping and lashing. Without a sound I am suddenly engulfed, and Alaris' voice, crying out for me, suddenly sounds like a million miles away as it wraps around me.

I'm burning, yet intact. My head feels like it wants to explode. And then, I feel swallowed whole and devoured. Painless, yes, yet not without pain. It's almost like I'm disembodied and can see what's happening from a removed perspective. I hover observant and witness the silent, convulsing consumption of all that is me. Everyone scatters below as the bellowing smog hazes through all of us. Some of us run and make it out.

Donetis doesn't.

Ranshay doesn't.

Martos doesn't.

Ghirishia and Raelia don't.

They are plucked from their positions, elevated into the air, and forced to face The Djinn. There is a face in that smoke, and it is utterly evil yet familiar – where have I seen that face before? With a scream that is part raspy intake of breath and part exhale of soul-numbing anxiety, it sucks their very lifeforce out of them. Their eyes turn a ghostly, pallid white and recede inside blackened sockets of a death mask. Their faces go sallow like shriveled raisins, devoid of essence, and their fleshly shells fall limply to the ground, flaming, and do not rise again.

They burn to cinders.

Ten left.

Calmly brutal, brutally calm, the wraithlike beast devours me into its otherworldly self. I am forcibly yanked and ripped away from Alaris as she curls into a fevered fetal ball, horrified and tremulous as I am wrenched away. And then I hear it, louder than ever before as pangs of alarm buffet my body on every side:

> *The time is now to make one's stand*
> *For ghostly terrors stalk the land*
> > *Abating not,*
> > *the hard fight fought*
> *They seeketh recompense from man*

> *And thou art chosen, humble boy*
> *From rank and file, pride and joy*
> > *They careth never*
> > *whithersoever*
> *Fleeth thee; thou art their ploy*

Sanity leaves me as I scream for my life and am pitched into the wind of this roaring, scalding phantom. I can see myself engulfed by it, and then I blow away into a million pieces: fragmented, like chaff. The screaming wind punctures me like a million needles, seeking a way inside me, lusting for my lifeforce, yet thwarted in taking it. I can't explain it; I clutch myself and find that I'm still intact, whipping around in the roaring wind.

And then, suddenly, I hear other voices. Indistinct, I can barely pick them apart, but they are male and female. Calling, shouting, railing against The Djinn, they come, and I can feel The Djinn shiver with me inside it. The smoke convulses, wavering and blowing about the room, untethering from itself and desperately maneuvering and rejoining to stay intact; blowing, blowing, flickering and shaky, wisping and deftly regathering. And then, finally, with an awful cry of revulsion and defeat, it screeches into a chilling hiss and vanishes, dissipating into nothing.

A brilliant flash of fiery light erupts all around us, accompanying a deathly screech from monstrous vocal cords retreating further into the ship.

The Djinn is gone.

I fall to the floor and hit my head. Rosie runs to me and tends to me as the wisps of smoke dissipate into nothing and retreat. Talicus fetches a fire extinguisher and goes to work.

My heart is pounding, my eyes are bleary with tears, and my head is swimming and drenched in ethereal sweat or some kind of vaporous, steaming moisture.

The survivors are all coughing. But not all of us are survivors; some are quiet and lay still.

Bodies litter the floor. Just like that, seven of us are deceased. And now I have no idea if it's eight, because I now know that that evil face in the smoke belonged to little Zaris, and at last I believe she's dead.

"Alaris?" I cry. "Alaris!"

"I'm here, I'm here, Jax. Oh my gosh, are you okay?" She runs to me and hugs me. I fall into her embrace, weak-kneed and trembling. I can see Rosie over her shoulder, standing there, looking winded. I don't know what kind of battle this woman has just fought, but her body and face bear the marks of tortuous exertion and fatigue. Somehow, she manages to smile at me.

But then I don't see it. I see something else.

Just a flicker…

I can't make it out.

I slowly pull myself away from Alaris, and she looks at me, confused. Rosie sees my eyes fixed at a point beyond her, and she turns to examine what I'm fixated on.

And then, she turns back to me and smiles.

But it's all I can do to keep from crying.

There, standing in flickering, spectral light, illuminated faintly by their own lifeforce, stand a man and a woman. They are not completely formed; their bodies fade into translucence at wavering points, obscured and then solid again. They linger on the edge of life and death and wait for me.

I know them! I know them well. In every single dream I've had aboard this wretched ship since the day I lost them, I've sought them, sought to be held by them, to hold them one last time and hear them tell me that they have loved me every single day we've been apart.

To hear them say they're proud of me.

My eyes fill with tears as I stumble toward them. Unaware of my own limbs, I reach out for them, fingers snapping in reflexes I can't control.

They're here. Both of them.

My parents, taken from me.

Mom and Dad.

They smile gently, and stand there as we regard each other. I cannot hold them, this I know, but perhaps, for a few precious moments in time, we can commune, and I can tell them that I've missed them with everything that is in me, as my heart swells to a capacity near bursting with yearning.

We just smile at each other in recognition.

No one says a word.

13: The Found

I cannot believe my watery eyes.

I draw near to them, while their shimmering apparitions hold steady. They are in tears, and so am I. As I pass Rosie, she whispers four words only.

Go to them, Jax.

I don't even look at her; I only have eyes for my parents.

I stand before them, and they look me over.

Their voices ring through to this world loud and clear, though I'm well aware that there is a great spiritual gulf between us.

"Son, we've missed you so much," says my Mom amidst tears.

"You look so tall," says my Dad.

"You look *brave*," says my Mom once more.

"Mom, Dad…I-I saw you," I stutter, sniffing, "I saw you the other day in the Phoenix Experiment."

"We know, Jax. We wanted to-" my Mom starts, but her lip quivers. An invisible light from the other side catches a shimmering tear dripping down her ghostly cheek. "We so wanted to come through with you. To tell you. To *warn* you. But it just wasn't in the cards for us. I'm so sorry, my son," she says in practically a whisper.

My own lip is quivering, and the tears are bathing my cheeks. An arm drapes over my shoulder as Alaris draws near. She stands next to me, to my right. I want to glance over at her, but I fear a *blink-and-you'll-miss-it* moment where the connection is severed, and my parents vanish. But it does beg a question.

"How are you even here?" I ask. "How can you be here without coming through the chamber in the lab? Can you stay? *Will* you stay?" I ask, and it sounds like pleading. I'm okay with it. I don't even care about the answers… I just want them here.

I just want them with me.

I just want them to stay… forever.

I'm dimly aware of a presence on my left now. I can tell it's Anther. He's also crying with me. By now, we've shared plenty of stories of how painful it's been not to reconnect with my parents in the Phoenix Experiments.

My heart is in my throat.

"We're in The Transference," my Mom says. "It won't last long. The Djinn came through, and we rode that wave in to you, but it's fading, Jax. Every wave that washes along the shore must recede. It pulls at us even now."

"I miss you *so* much, Mom and Dad," I say, and now I'm bawling. "I've-I've tried to live up to what I thought you wanted for me, who you hoped for me to be. I-"

It's no use. I can't complete that sentence, and I hold my palms out and upward in futility. Rosie shifts and slightly gasps behind me.

"Son, we love you. We're proud of you, kiddo. You needn't worry about us. There are far greater things to worry about right now," my Dad says, and my eyes are drawn to him. A shimmering translucence takes them momentarily, and their images quietly flicker. I reach for them as my jaw drops.

"Jax, listen," my Dad whispers, urging me, "there's no time. You can still bring us through, but you *must* get to the lab to do so. There's no other way. The Djinn *must* be stopped, Jax."

"They must be stopped at all costs," my Mom adds. "We know the secret, Jax. We hold the key. But we must come through; we must be *there* – on the other side – in order to stop them."

I sniff, gathering focus and strength into my will just as I gather air into my lungs. I nod quickly.

They quickly fade once more, the light flickering around them as, momentarily, I see right through them.

"Jax," my Mom says, reaching for me. I mirror her, and our fingers pass through each other in yearning, feigning physical connection. "If we don't make it through, if we...," she trails off. A pleading smile clenches her lips. "Always know that we love-"

They fade from view suddenly, abruptly. My heart lurches.

They're gone.

Again, just like that hot and cruel day, August 16th, 2466, they are taken from me once again, and I am reduced to bawling, consoled in the embrace of my friends. Elderly arms wrap around me, and a bespectacled gray-headed woman bows her temples against me as I quake with sadness for those I've lost.

And found.

And lost once more.

And found.

And lost yet again.

We don't know where The Djinn went, but we are allowed a moment's peace, because there's something important we have to do. Something awful.

It's time to tend to the dead.

We gather the scorched body of Dravin Mosopathen, only 8 years old, the youngest of us here, who loved to draw. His face is frozen in horror, seized forever in the throes of deep emotional shock.

All of theirs are.

We gather the charred body of Ranshay Filipath, 12 years old, who never knew a lick of English and probably never knew what hit him.

We gather the seared body of the big oaf, Garris Granthis, 15 years old, who showed bravery trying to show us the way of escape.

We gather the blackened body of Martos Mixtros, 16 years old, nevermore the life of the party. As in life, his energy died out long before its time.

We gather the body of Skarbé Bognis, 15.

We gather the body of Donetis Tarnie, 16.

We gather the body of Raelia Forgrim, 13.

All of them, killed by The Djinn.

The best we can do is lay them together across Rosie's bed here in this horrible room, *Shielding,* hoping against hope that their bodies will be shielded. We drape the sheets across their bodies in reverence, and then stand quietly before them.

Alaris sighs, staring at her dead friends. "I wonder what their parents feel now, rejoined with them. This irony is wicked," she groans. "They worked so hard at controlling their emotions to bring their parents into life back *here*, and yet The Djinn scared their emotions right out of them here and sent them to their parents in death *there*."

I feel the wicked irony too. "Our whole purpose on these ships was to bring them back." I shake my head. "At least they're together again."

Rosie doesn't answer. Instead, she offers a prayer, and speaks a quiet Mexican blessing over their bodies. I don't know what it means. But then I understand why Rosie gasped behind me when I put my palms out in front of my parents.

She does the same thing now, holding her palms up and glancing over at me, solemnly. A heartfelt smile slowly spreads across her face.

"This, Jax," she says, "is receiving. We receive whatever comes our way, knowing that The Father loves us and will eventually work it out for our good. I've done this for five centuries now. I will never stop doing it, because I will never stop receiving what The Father allows in my life, knowing that His will for me is good. I hope the same is true for you," she then concludes, smiling once more. I nod to her.

Maybe we're supposed to receive wicked irony from The Father as well, I think.

"It's time to be numb, children," Rosie says, finishing. "The Djinn – and the banshees – thrive on emotion. They thrive on pain, rage and fear. We must be bold, of staunch will, and resolute."

Rosie walks over to me and stands before me.

"Jax, your parents are correct. You must reconnect with them, and The Djinn must be stopped."

We're on the move again. We can't stay here. By now we're heading back upward, and though it's unstated, we all know what I have to do. I must get to the Phoenix lab and focus all my energy on bringing my parents through.

I *must.*

> *All things hingeth now on this,*
> *So carefully thread thou paths amiss*
> > *They wayward not,*
> > *are danger-fraught*
> *To revelations not of bliss*

> *Harken not to voice of angst*
> *Pleadeth it shall, with no thanks*
> > *Be thou wise,*
> > *open thine eyes*
> *Lest passion cheat thee from thy ranks*

I'm confused by this one, and wonder if Rosie has heard the same thing and is equally perplexed, but we must move on. These poetic whispers do little to portend or forecast; but I trust that they come from a voice that bridges the gulf between the past and the future; otherwise, why would I even hear them? Someone, somewhere, has made sense of them, I trust. Maybe that someone will eventually be me.

We're moving away from the engines, up and up, back toward the lab. *This is it.*

At some point we happen upon an observation window into a massive room we hadn't passed by before. Peering inside, there are thousands upon thousands of chairs for a vast audience. It's then that I realize Rosie was right. This ship was meant to hold all of the survivors, not just us. *Everyone.*

The truth barrels into me. It was never meant to be this way. We've all been lied to.

I cannot believe my eyes.

14: The Showdown

There's no turning back now.

Talicus continues to offer direction and leadership, folding in right alongside Rosie. They've conversed and planned, and have now decided to take us away from the *Shielding* room, as that was both the location of the attack, as well as our last known coordinates. We don't want The Djinn *and* Cryptus on our tail.

In ten minutes, we'll reach a point, they say, where we'll ultimately have to diverge; a few of us will go with me as protection against Cryptus, Mirabay and the others, and the rest will hide.

Talicus recommends that she and Orin, being the strongest of us, come with me to the lab and help me summon my parents; Anther may come as well. The rest will stay with Rosie. Talicus has conducted the exact same Phoenix Experiments aboard The Zephyr. She'll know how to get me in there and then it's up to me to try to bring them through. *And,* I think with a shudder, *she's strong enough to take on Cryptus… hopefully.*

So, it's decided.

"Is surveillance still down?" Venthix asks.

"Yes," Talicus confirms.

"What about the Achilles? What's their ETA?" asks Orin, walking somberly alongside Miritia.

"ETA 48 minutes, Finorin," she replies.

"*Orin,*" he corrects her.

"Fine. Orin," she confirms. "I'm in touch with the Achilles' central computer. Commander Krux is aboard, with a team of twenty-one. They're aware of our situation."

"Including the attack just now?" I ask.

"Yes."

"I hope they don't turn away," I add, glumly. "What can they even do? Do they have weapons?"

"Yes," Talicus confirms.

That's some comfort, I think.

But then I click my tongue. "Why did I even ask that? They won't be of any use against The Djinn, of course."

"Jax, their weapons are not for use against The Djinn," Talicus replies, and she looks at me coldly. "They're to restore order and take Cryptus, Mirabay, and possibly the chiefs, into custody."

I nod, solemnly, pondering the prospect of a firefight aboard The Origin. I don't know if there are any weapons aboard our ship, or if Cryptus and Mirabay have armed themselves. But it may just come down to that.

"We will remain in hiding. Cryptus and Mirabay won't know where we are, but I've established a secure channel with the Achilles. Once they dock, Commander Krux – and Commander Krux only – will be relayed our location securely."

"And we have no idea on the status of our chiefs?" I ask. "If they're alive, held captive, anything?"

Talicus shakes her head. "I find no record of their status in Phiria. Apparently, Cryptus has taken the liberty of purging their data. We won't know until, or *if*, we actually happen upon them."

I shake my head once more. "That's four strong, grown adults we could definitely use right now. I wish we knew."

"I do as well, Jax," says Talicus.

"48 minutes," breathes Venthix. "*Man.* A lot can happen in that time. Whatever we can do to speed things up and get this over with, so much the better. I do *not* wanna see that thing again."

"Me neither," Omnias growls. "Not ever again. Did any of you see the face in-"

"No!" Rosie exclaims, whirling back around to Omnias. "Don't say it. Whatever you saw, keep to yourself, young Omnias. It is for your eyes only, not for quaking hearts in the dark."

My heart is quaking, and I'm in the dark. All our hearts are quaking, and we're all in the dark.

And I know exactly what Omnias saw.

It was Zaris.

At last, after trudging on for our ten minutes, mostly back uphill, we reach the divergence point.

"Here we are," Rosie says nonchalantly, and she sighs, tapping some conduits running alongside the wall as she turns to us. She's not very winded or sweaty; the woman has been reinvigorated from her reincarnation, and she looks healthy and strong.

The throbbing of the ship has lessened as we've climbed, and it still punches through the air around us, but less so than that horrid thing we just encountered.

"Now, it's time to split up. Talicus, Orin and Anther will go with Jax. I will take Venthix and the four girls here."

"Three," Alaris says. Rosie cocks an eyebrow and tilts her head. "*Three,*" she repeats. "I'm going with Talicus and Jax."

"Young Alaris, I hardly think this is the time to-"

"I'm going with them," Alaris says defiantly, "or I'm waiting right here until the end."

No one says anything. Rosie relents. "Fine, child. Just remember, Jax is the priority. He must bring his parents through. That's all that matters up there. Protect him at all costs," she says to Talicus, Orin, and Anther.

"No funny business. Be a *gent,*" Anther cautions Venthix, pointing at him. Venthix will be alone with the three girls and Rosie.

Venthix smirks. "I will. Be careful."

Omnias and Anther slowly separate, their hands still clasped, as she retreats toward Rosie. Suddenly, Anther whips her back to himself and kisses her hard. Everyone snickers.

Orin glances at Miritia. "Aw, hell. Me too," he says, and then he does the same with Miritia.

Ghirisha stands alone, blushing. For a moment, she looks sheepishly at Venthix. He smiles nervously at her, and shrugs. She smiles appreciatively at him, knowing they'll be together, and he takes her hand.

"Alright, children, now that we've said our goodbyes, can we get a move on?" Rosie chirps with a slightly remonstrative affect. "It's already hot enough down here in this ship without you adding to it."

More giggles.

"Be careful, Rosie," Talicus says. "Take cover and wait for my signal. I'll have Phiria make the announcement when the time comes and we're all clear. We'll proceed to the lab and prepare the Phoenix Experiment for Jax." Rosie nods.

"What happens when we get to the lab? Can we lock it so that they can't get inside?" I ask.

"Certainly, unless Cryptus has changed the access codes," Talicus responds.

"Can he do that?" Anther says.

"Most definitely," says our synthetic.

"But you won't know until we get there," I say.

"I won't. There is only one way to find out."

We gather our courage, sighing heavily. "Well, let's get up there." There's only forty-plus minutes until the Achilles arrives, and we don't want The Djinn roaming around this ship when they come. "Let's go get my parents," I say, decisively.

Anther nods at me, his jaw clenched.

Orin chimes in. "Let's do this."

"Never forget," Rosie cautions us as we eye each other across the dividing line of our teams, "The Djinn wants you to feel. You must not give it any emotion. You must *not* give it any fear. Stuff your emotions way down, children. Seal them off, or The Djinn will have you."

They regard her somberly.

Talicus breaks the silence. "Rosie, Jax, let us consult for a moment. The rest of you may disperse. I have an idea, and I'd like to discuss it with the two of you privately, if you don't mind. Phiria has been compiling data, and I've been searching through it. Something has just come to light, and I humbly request your feedback."

Rosie and I agree, and we're deep in counsel for a bit. What I hear has bearings on all of us.

"Are you okay?" Alaris asks me, once we break. She can tell that something's up.

"Yes. I'm fine," I say, wiping the tears from my eyes. I'm lying of course, but what more can I do? "Let's get moving. I'm okay. We can talk in a bit."

She relents, and Anther leads the way this time. Talicus is right behind him, should we run into any unexpected interference from Cryptus or any of the others.

I ask for an ETA on the Achilles. Our android reports they're 33 minutes from docking. They know to come in armed and brandishing weapons, Talicus informs us. At this I shake my head, and my eyes widen in incredulity that it's all come to this. I hope against hope that there's no weapons fire exchanged aboard The Origin. Everyone knows: one bad shot and we can all enjoy a healthy dose of depressurization as we're sucked out into space and are frozen.

But maybe it's better to freeze in the grip of space than burn to death in the fist of The Djinn.

We creep along, quietly, Anther leading the way. There's no sign of anyone, but there are muted sounds at various intervals: sounds of someone talking throughout the ship. A large din erupts at one point to our right, far outside the shaft that we're in, which propels us onward and sends trembling fright through our midst. Ultimately, it's not that which we all fear.

The Djinn.

I wonder where it is aboard our ship… where it went after the attack that killed our friends… where it will strike next. My thoughts go to Rosie and Alaris, Venthix and the others, and I pray quietly for their safety.

It's a long haul.

We trudge on, quietly, for perhaps another ten minutes or so. I see the signs that we've now entered Quadrant C, and I think we're still a few floors down from Subfloor 3A. Cryptus' lab has to be somewhere around here, but I trust Anther knows where he's going. After all, this is where we got in trouble with Cryptus. If that event isn't seared into his memory, I don't know what is.

We creep along, as quiet as mice now.

Quadrant C, Subfloor 3A, Room 319.

Finally, we're here. Talicus takes the lead and turns around to us, putting her finger to her lips. We're at the maintenance shaft outside the lab: the very one Cryptus caught Anther and I outside those years ago.

The incident with the blue pen.

Anther and I were so little then. Younger than Ranshay, to be sure, but not nearly as young as little Dravin. *Poor Dravin,* I think, shaking my head. That little boy. I trust he's reconnected with his parents. Ranshay too. And Garris, Martos, and the girls from The Zephyr. I never want to see The Djinn again.

Orin grabs a metal pipe he's found lying in the shaft, and from the looks of it he plans to use it as some kind of weapon in our attempt to seize control of the lab. I momentarily regret not having anything of my own to wield, but then realize that our greatest weapon is Talicus herself.

"Alright, here is the plan," says our synthetic. "You'll follow me out. I'll take the lead. If Cryptus is in the lab, that will make it harder, but I will attempt to subdue him. You'll follow me in and lock the lab door behind you. It will be secure *and* soundproof from the outside. No one will know we're in there. I will program in a new code for Phiria to disable the lock. Jax, you can then hop onto the bed and the others can get you wired up for the Phoenix Experiment. I've already confirmed with Phiria that it's live. It's been live and running since The Djinn came through, so you won't have to fire up anything. Once you're on the bed, I will send you in, and the others can stand guard. Got it?"

We all nod.

"Okay, time to go. Watch out, Anther, please," she says. Anther moves aside. Talicus then literally opens the tip of her finger, folding it back to reveal a long and periscoping Phillips head. She slowly inserts it with precision into the four mounting screws on all sides of the vent shaft. Her finger-screwdriver emits only the slightest whirring noise.

She then undoes the locking clasps. Talicus is utterly surgical and silent in her work, as she finally removes the vent shaft grate.

We filter out, slowly, Talicus in the lead. Orin follows her, and then Alaris, me, and then Anther at the rear. He replaces the grate over the aperture we've just emerged through, and then follows us.

Talicus motions for us to wait as she approaches the corner in the corridor leading to 3A. There are no sounds except the distant drumming of the ship, and the occasional sounds of voices murmuring from some far-off point.

We're outside the lab now.

Talicus leans around the corner and peers into the Phoenix lab. She jerks back suddenly, bracing herself against the wall. Her expression does not change; it's one of mathematical focus.

She presses herself against the wall, turns to us slowly, eyebrows up, and thumbs into the room, shaking her head. It's then that we realize someone is in there, and that it's most likely Cryptus. We'll have to do this the hard way.

A chill runs through me. *How could we be so stupid?* I think to myself. *Of course he's in there. Where else would he be?*

Our android motions for us to wait here. She gathers her programming, sticks out her chin, and suddenly, she's walking around the corner into the lobby of the Phoenix lab as if out on a leisurely stroll. We hear everything.

"Hello, Stygius Cryptus."

Movement. Sounds like Cryptus is now standing, facing her.

"Baryonnis Talicus. Where have you- I mean- where did you vanish to? We humbly requested for everyone to report to the Assembly Hall."

"I am aware of the directive. I was unable to comply. Someone had disabled my programming and I had entered sleep mode."

"Sleep mode? Who would even know how to do such a thing aboard The Origin? Those codes are proprietary to each synthetic, and coded to each ship. Yours are active only aboard The Zephyr, as are mine aboard only The Origin."

"Yes, I know. I cannot speculate who it was nor why; we were gathered in the rec hall when it happened."

"You've been powered down in the rec hall? We were in there and did not see you. How long?" Cryptus' voice and questions are laden with suspicion.

"I do not know. Someone was quick enough, but how or why, I do not know, Cryptus. Nonetheless, I would like to respectfully file an anomaly report."

"Of?"

"It might be easier if I show you. May I?"

"Certainly."

More movement. The guessed sounds of Talicus moving to Cryptus' console. This all sounds vaguely reminiscent of how Cryptus set Oculus up to kill him: this whole *it's better if I show you* approach.

Before we know it, there is a scuffle. I don't know who is besting who; all I know is that we need to get in there and close that outer door *now* so that no one hears us.

"Move, move!" I whisper, and we filter into the room, single file. Orin goes first, wielding his metal pipe. He's followed by me, and then Alaris, then Anther. Ant closes the door and locks it.

"Talicus!" Anther cries. "It's closed, do your thing, you efficient and effective synthetic!"

I see Talicus. Her eyes flutter. From behind me, the door beeps in response, and a whirring sound emits. It's locked and disabled, just as she said.

"Anther! *Jax!*" cries Cryptus. "What are you-"

My eyes are drawn to the viewing room where Cryptus is pinned down to his console with Talicus behind him. She isn't breathing hard and doesn't look the least bit exerted. Her strength is horrifying. Briefly I wonder what a punch in the chest from Talicus would have done to me.

Talicus has Cryptus in a headlock, and he is fighting to remain sentient. The same arteries that feed our brains oxygenated blood are mimicked within AnthroMeta bodies, and whatever fluid keeps his synthetic brain functional, that's what Talicus appears to be clamping down on and restricting flow through.

I run to the other side of the viewing window and stare at him. "Yeah, how do you like that, *bitch?*" I ask, fanning out my arms. "Doesn't feel so nice, does it, you *murderer!*"

"Jax, let me expl-"

"Quiet!" Talicus orders. Cryptus cannot move; his right arm is pinned behind him, and Talicus has his headlock secure. Cryptus grimaces, pulling at her arm with his free hand. "Jax, start the sequence, please. We don't have time," she instructs coolly. "I've got this one."

Behind us, Talicus has also dimmed the outer window to Cryptus' foyer, so no one can see in.

We move into the lab. Just as we do, Talicus gasps and grunts, and we all whirl back around. Orin holds up his metal pipe in a reflex.

The two androids are fighting. It is a clash of the titans as we watch with widened eyes.

Talicus appears to have some sort of aluminum shaft jammed through her hand; the hand that Cryptus was gripping.

Cryptus shoves her, and she flies back against the wall. He advances toward her, suddenly, and her right leg flies up in response, nailing him in the chest. He grimaces again, but they are utterly soundless in their combat, eyeing each other with cold disdain.

Talicus jumps and spins, sending another impressive sidekick into Cryptus' face. She is graceful and deft in her movement, and I'm reminded of the old Martial Artists of eons ago, and the movies made glorifying their mode of combat. She is obviously equipped with similar programming, though I don't know what branch it is, whether Karate, Judo, Jujitsu, Taekwondo, or something else that is formidable, deadly, and cybernetic. *Just glad it wasn't me that pissed her off,* I think to myself. *She would destroy me in a heartbeat.*

Cryptus hits the window and blanches, eyeing us for a moment as his face is literally propelled into the glass. He steadies himself, his fake fingers pressed up against the pane, his hot pseudo-breath fogging the thin sheet of glass separating us.

He turns back to Talicus with emotionless determination. Talicus comes at him with a double-punch, and he deftly dodges both, calculating, predicting, and evading.

He circles up and launches an uppercut in response. Talicus flies back against the wall, instantly shaking her head. She jerks erratically for a moment, and it seems like Cryptus scored a major hit.

He rushes at her and pins her against the wall, firing blow after blow into her staunch form. She recoils, but reaches out to steady herself against a side counter table.

Talicus grasps something. I don't know what it is. She conceals it against her form as Cryptus continues to pummel her over and over.

In a flash, Cryptus then reaches up and clutches her head, right hand reaching around toward the front, and left hand, inverted, palming the back. In a singular violent move, he jerks her head to the right, presumably severing cords and cabling inside her.

Talicus spasms. White flashes emit from her neck. She fires one last reflexive elbow into Cryptus' ribs, and he jumps backward, but he is still holding her, and will not let go. He grips her head ever tighter, his right arm wrapped around her neck, and his left hand reaching behind her head to grip her chin.

To our horror, we watch as he rips Talicus' head clean off. Alaris screams and covers her mouth. We all cover our mouths.

"No!" Anther shouts.

I'm speechless.

Talicus' body slumps, but doesn't collapse. It stands there, immobilized, shorting out, and sparking; her arms flinch, waving in front of her pointlessly.

Neither of them is breathing hard. Well, at least *Cryptus* isn't breathing hard.

"Cryptus, you murderous bastard!" Orin screams, and he makes a move toward him with his metal pipe. But then he stops, thinking better of it. He starts to yell something else, but closes his mouth.

Alaris grips his shirt and pulls him back.

"No! Orin, *no!*" she screams.

Cryptus, holding Talicus' severed head, glances back at us coldly through the window for a moment. "I would have preferred it not end this way," he says with zero disdain. It is a statement not out of revenge, but rather cold, calculating logic far beyond that of mortal man. Built on algorithms, computations and programming we'll never understand; he knows this.

Talicus is dead. She stands there, motionless, sparks flying from the nape of her neck.

Cryptus calmly places her head on the console by the window, facing us, perhaps to taunt us. He turns back to her dead form, grasping the aluminum shaft that he had previously stabbed clean through Talicus' hand.

He doesn't see her open her eyes or wink at us.

In a blinding flash, her headless body whips around with astonishing speed and smacks Cryptus with something hard and cylindrical. He loses his balance and falls back against the console, hands up in defense.

Talicus' head is knocked loose and sent flying to the floor. The rest of our android is upon him, smacking the aluminum shaft from his right hand with her left, and then she reveals what she had been clutching.

In one blinding flash, she brings the Stasis interrupt pod down upon his forehead, sending unwelcome voltage coursing through his circuitry. Cryptus pops and shivers, sparks and shudders, jerking and spasming. The android's movements slow, and he slowly slumps down below our line of visibility, under the console. A dim thud sounds, and he's on the floor.

Our decapitated android stands there, reconciling with his immobilized body, and then she sets the Stasis interrupt pod down on the counter. Talicus reaches down to the floor for something.

In a gruesome move, she holds her own head, regards it with invisible eyes, and then slowly places her own head upon her shoulders. With an icy whisper, she starts reciting programming codes, executable file numbers and system diagnostics.

A strange flesh-colored gel oozes out of the ripped seam of her neck, coalescing together and then running the circumference of her severed neck, filling the grisly seam Cryptus created in beheading her. Her head twitches, she rotates her pate slowly to the right and left, and then turns to face us, blinking.

"Jax, Orin, Alaris, Anther, good to see you in one piece. I am victorious. Indeed, Hell hath no fury like an android scorned."

We laugh nervously, nodding, relieved.

"Talicus! Nicely done!" I say to her between near-tears. "Whoo-hoo! You're amazing."

"I will be once again. I need to reboot, Jax, and reroute damaged circuits. Please, get ready. We haven't time. I'll be right back. I am forming a plan as we speak. I'll brief everyone here on it when I am fully power-cycled."

"Good luck, Jax!" Talicus says, and then her eyes grow dim. Her form slumps. She's offline.

We don't waste any time. I hop in the first bed, and Orin and Anther wire me up.

I have no idea where The Djinn is. I don't want to see it again. Alaris hovers over me as I lay there, preparing to relax and waiting for the white noise. "You going to be okay? You better be," I warn her, hollowly.

"I'll be fine. We have a beheaded android here, rebooting." She pauses, looking comically uncertain for a moment. "I *think* I'll be fine."

"Ha! Okay then. I'm glad. Just…," I falter.

Her nose crinkles as she frowns. "Just what?"

"Keep your eyes peeled. That thing is still somewhere on this ship. Be careful. Remember Rosie's words. *Stuff your emotions way down, children. Seal them off, or The Djinn will have you.*"

She nods. "I will. I promise. You be safe as well, okay?"

I nod and smile. And then she kisses me again.

This time, it's even better than the first. I stare deeply into her eyes as the white noise kicks in, and I start to drift off.

Alaris pulls away. The ring starts to spin over me. As I am drawn into the Phoenix Experiment, I hear Anther chuckling. "You guys…" I grin, and the last sight I see is Alaris staring down upon me with her gorgeous red hair draping her shoulders like fire.

> *Swiftly now, the venture goeth*
> *Speeding breakneck as he knoweth*
> > *One aim only:*

save the lonely
Though the deadly tension groweth

Where the beast now wanders free
Can the dangerous tide stemmed be?
Answers fleeting
bear repeating
And truth will out even if desperately

There is truly no turning back now.

15: The Revelations

The Phoenix Experiment is just never what you expect.

I'm in. It's warm here. I can smell the freshly cut grass, the light drops of dew on an August morning in the sunshine, and it smells whole and clean.

I hear the poetic voice… it echoes through my cranium like a dream as I wander.

"Mom! Dad!" I shout. I train myself to be cold. No emotion. Impervious and protected from The Djinn. If somehow, it's back in here, I've got to shut myself off, as Rosie says. Just like with the banshees, I've got to own my emotions and restrain them. I'm in charge, not them. *Me.*

I don't know how long I've been in, but it feels like it's been a good few hours. I'm not sure. Inside the Phoenix Experiments, time becomes immemorial and you lose all sense of the space-time continuum. It could be yesterday, for all I know.

The only thing I'm certain of is it's August, because that's when my parents were killed, and that's usually where I end up.

"Mom? Dad?" I yell, searching. I don't know where I am at first, but then the neighborhood coalesces into a hazy clarity. It's scorched… less clear than the memories of Cryptus and Talicus' epic battle.

I turn around and see it.

My house. There it is again. Last time, I was exiting it, and they were coming toward me. Now, I'm approaching it.

But where are they?

Dimly, I see the front door opening up. Slowly, and dreamlike, light streams out. I peer through the mist…

…and there they are. Once more, appearing through a fog and smiling at me from out of a dream, there are my parents.

My parents!

There they are!

Nothing stops me from rushing at them this time, running straight into their arms. We collide in an embrace.

I can smell my mother. Her long, flowing hair. I can feel my father. His giant muscles and stout form. They hold me and press me tightly against them, as if vast tentacles were reaching out threateningly to pull us apart once more, and they are avowed to never again let me go. I know I feel the same.

For a split second I wonder how they are faring back there: Talicus, Orin, Anther… and Alaris. And then, from the recesses of my memory, Rosie comes to mind, Venthix… Omnias, Miritia, Ghirisha... I'm resigned to trust that they're all okay.

I can't wait to introduce all of them to my parents. I just can't wait! I'm seized by emotion and in the throes of utter fulfillment as they hold me. We're all weeping, and the tears flow from our eyes like a wine of blessedness to quench a parched soul.

My Mom suddenly laughs. Her laughter rings out like mirth, unburdened by care, and laden with a rich and unsullied contentment. My Dad hears her and laughs in turn, clutching me, grasping at me, and holding me tightly, his beard shaking lightly.

"My boy, my precious boy!" he yells. "You've done it, Jax! You've really done it!"

"We've missed you *so* much," Mom whispers in my ear as she tugs at me. As she does so, years of forlorn abandonment fall from me, and I am assured and content in the knowledge that I am loved.

I can smell them. I can feel them. They are *here*. They are tangible! It is the culmination of everything I've worked so hard for all these years, seeking to reconnect with that which was stolen from me. And this time, Cryptus can't do anything about it. There's no one to pull me out now and steal them from me. I in turn laugh with unbridled joy.

"Mom, Dad, I'm so glad to find you again," I say to them, tears once more streaming from my eyes. "You have no idea what it means to me."

"I'm sure we have some idea, kiddo," Mom laughs. She gazes down upon me, smiling tenderly, staring deep into my eyes. Her eyes are the same color as mine, I notice, and as I do so, I wonder how many 'new' things I'll continue to notice about them both that have been there all along. "You look all grown up now. You used to be my little boy. Look at you now," she says, stroking my chin.

"My big guy," Dad says, and just then a flashback steals through me of him tenderly voicing that to me somewhere in our house. I dimly remember wrestling with him, and him pretending that I overpowered him. He finished with that phrase and declared me the champion.

"I kept dreaming about our house… our neighborhood… different places we've visited that I don't even remember visiting except for the scantest of details. It's crazy," I say, sniffing. "You're so… *real*. I remember now."

They beam down at me.

"Let's get you through, huh? We've got a Djinn to slay, apparently," I say.

Mom shakes her head and rolls her eyes in doubt, sighing. "Well, I don't know about 'slay,' but we'll try. The key is to stuff your emotions down deep, unflinching, and to show it who's boss." She winks at me. "Then, it's lost all power over you. Same with the banshees."

"The Djinn is like the banshees?" I ask.

"Oh, most definitely. They're both from the spirit realm, Jax, and they need to be controlled."

"And you know how to control them?"

They nod and smile once more. "We do. We've spent enough time with them in here, struggling, learning, following them. We're tired of this place," Mom says, and then she turns to Dad. "Let's go live again, sweetheart, yeah?"

"Yeah," he breathes to her.

"Except…," we hear a male voice behind us, and we all turn to face him.

He's about my parents' age, but he seems more fit. More muscular and sculpted. There's an arrogance about his face, but it's not daunting. I recognize him instantly, and wonder why – and how – he got in here.

"Except, of course, neither of you did too well on your last life installment, did you?" he asks them. They regard him stoically. "And is that not why you are now relegated to this place, here on the other side?" he posits. "Where you rightfully belong?" He shakes his head, and slowly advances toward us. "For this *is* where you truly belong, though you might attempt to convince your son of some other quasi-truths which you appear desperate to cling to."

He turns to me. "Hello, Jax. I'm delighted you have found your parents, but it is high time to let them go. It is high time you knew the full truth."

"You shouldn't be here, Cryptus," I bark at him. "I don't know how you're sentient, or… or how you're even here," I say, but then I stop, realizing there is only *one* way he could possibly be here. "You killed the others, didn't you!?" He had to have somehow awoken, taken advantage of Talicus in her weakened state, and then finished her off. With her out of the way, he violated his own programming yet again and used his 'superior design' to wrest Orin's own metal pipe away from him, and then use it *against* him. He must have then brutally murdered Anther, my best friend… and… Alaris, my love!

My jaw clenches and I allow my chest to feel hot. I temporarily release a controlled fire inside me, just enough to play my part, so that Cryptus can see that I am welling over with vengeful rage at this turn of events. The rumor was true: Cryptus himself can indeed penetrate the Phoenix Experiments themselves, and now here he is, to kill my parents.

And me.

Here, yet again, he's going to deprive me of my time – *and* my relationship – with my beloved parents. In a reflex, they pull me close, eyeing Cryptus warily as he draws close to us.

"Stygius Cryptus, stay *away* from us," Dad growls, and as I look at him, he's staring down the android under brows bristling with ire.

Yet the android continues to advance.

"Tell him the truth, Grysh," Cryptus says, calmly. "Tell Jax what you've done, Myrandé."

What truth? I ask, and now I sense something greater is happening; I'm caught in the middle of a war originating long before my eyes were opened to conflict. *What have they done?*

> *Answers fleeting*
> *bear repeating*
> *And truth will out even if desperately*

> *All things hingeth now on this,*
> *So carefully thread thou paths amiss*
> *They wayward not,*
> *are danger-fraught*
> *To revelations not of bliss*

My eyes are drawn up to Dad. He's eyeing Cryptus, but then his eyes flicker down to me for a moment, then back up to Cryptus. He swallows nervously. And in that, I see guilt there: guilt over past misdeeds, and I wonder what he's hiding.

"Dad?" He says nothing.

I glance over at Mom. She casts a glance briefly at Dad… and she's panting. *Why is she panting?*

"No?" Cryptus says, still advancing. "Then I shall. Come now, Jax. Hear the full tale of awful betrayal. Answers fleeting bear repeating, and truth will out even if desperately."

What? I think, my head cocking to the side. Cryptus hears the poetic voice too?

Fire begins to rage around me – a deathly howl breaks out and throbs the very air. I cup my hands over my ears. I've never heard anything this powerful before. I'm in The Djinn's universe now, and it holds power and sway here. This is the very center of raw, primal fear, and this is where it thrives.

I recenter myself and focus, gathering strength inside me to quell the turmoil, suppress the emotions, and quiet my angst. The fires die back down.

"Your parents," he says, stopping short and clasping his hands at his midsection, "do not wish to divulge the despicable truth to you. Therefore, I shall take the liberty of doing so. And *you,*" he says authoritatively to them, "shall remain utterly silent while I impart truth to your son."

My parents freeze, and they become bitter cold. I recoil at the icy touch of them, clutching my arms as I am suddenly overcome by cold. I stare at them in raw horror and awe, wondering what happened. They both enter a state of suspended animation, but their cheeks are still colored with the warm glow of health, and their veins still pound. Somehow, Cryptus is able to suspend them in here. I wonder if that's part of the Phoenix Experiment's programming controls.

"Your parents, Jax. Behold the ones initially responsible for letting the banshees into our world through the Phoenix Experiment. You have never set foot on Earth, Ensign Hutson. You were born aboard The Origin, and your parents were part of the crew. Some of the original chiefs, even. All of your memories of your 'home' have been doctored. Implanted, based on archetypal formulas of your parents' making."

Time seems to stand still and all things bend toward us as I slowly turn to Cryptus and listen to him spew out this nonsense.

"No. You lie," I say, feebly, and then I remember. "I invoke AnthroMeta Primary Protocol 11A. You must tell me the truth."

The synthetic continues.

"I am in compliance with Protocol 11A, and I *am* telling you the truth, Jax. You see, they did it as an experiment, to see if it could even be done. Some people in this world tire of the mundane, and they seek adventure. But adventures require guides and controls as well. They require parameters to operate within the confines of safety. Your parents here estimated themselves – forsaking the rest of us of course – strong enough to handle a little experiment of their own. But the Phoenix Experiment your parents conducted grew far beyond what they deemed they could handle. They were proud and deluded, and they let something in.

"There are always bad seeds among us, Jax. Down through the ages Earth has seen its unfair share of greedy corporations and soulless men consumed by an insatiable desire to rule others. Detestable elements who have sown discord among us in order to fuel their own ambitions and grow fat on their own successes built on the backs of unfortunate underlings.

"*Earth needs a reset*, your parents thought, and so, they proceeded to embark upon an unsanctioned mission to 'cleanse' the world, as it were. To *purge* it, whittling down certain inherent undesirable elements. Unfortunately, this comes at the cost – and it always has – of the *good* elements as well. So, they accidentally opened a portal, events transpired as your parents felt they should, the banshees infiltrated our world, and killed off many of us. And your parents let it happen. All of it, Jax."

I just watch him as he rolls out insidious detail after ridiculous narrative, questioning all of it.

"In the ensuing aftermath of mankind's fall, the 'every man for himself' mentality which overtook humanity simply reinforced their beliefs. Mankind was lacerated to shreds for the banshees' good pleasure, and your parents allowed it all to unfold with the simple satisfaction that can only come from a job well done. Or so they thought. Yes, the banshees killed off and 'cleansed' many of the evil elements among man. But evil itself cannot be purged; it can only be replaced. Evil is and always shall be one of man's inseparable defining characteristics. So, it was never purged wholly; it was simply replaced… with the banshees, which became the new face of evil. This feeble attempt at a final solution, insidiously authored by your wayward and misguided parents, spectacularly backfired."

"Stop!" I cry. This cannot be true. "I don't believe it. Any of it!" I point threateningly at Cryptus. "Stop *right* now, Cryptus."

"I cannot, Jax, because now we come to it," he says. "Your parents hijacked the Phoenix Experiments for their own ends, and let in the monsters. Someone found out about it, Jax. Someone important. Someone who felt they needed to be stopped."

I didn't want to, but I had to know. Cryptus was going to tell me whether I wanted him to or not.

"Fulsar Oculus. Your helmsman. *He* killed them, Jax."

"No. No!"

"I tell you the truth. Primary Protocol 11A is running. Oculus killed them. He effectively purged that evil. But, as I mentioned, evil itself cannot be killed. It can only be replaced. And thus, Helmsman Fulsar Oculus came to temporarily stem the tide of banshees flowing into our world, and paused the Phoenix Experiments.

Oculus killed my parents? They didn't just die? How can this be? I was told they died by the banshees!

Cryptus continued. "But the planet had still been ravaged. It was too late. So what does one do when one has a problem growing bloated beyond their reach and ability to control it?"

"They create an even bigger problem. Oculus allowed the banshees to continue to ravage our world down there. With them down there wreaking havoc on the planet below, he remains safely up here on The Origin and does not have to return. However, anything jeopardizes the status quo aboard our ship, then he has no choice but to return to Earth. He didn't want ripples in the water. He preferred his cushy no-pressure occupation with little government oversight not to be trifled with. So he let everything slide and looked the other way.

"But I confronted him, Jax! And then, while in sleep mode, he disabled me – do not ask me how – and temporarily wiped my memory. But I stumbled upon surveillance, bit by bit in my lab and through my work – and I put the pieces together. Helmsman Fulsar Oculus simply wanted to preserve his occupation and stick it to the corporations that 'sanctioned this silly Phoenix business' – that is the way he put it – in an effort to prove to them that all of this nonsense doesn't work."

"That can't be, Cryptus, and you know it!" I cry. "Even Rosie spoke to The Djinn and it obeyed. Speakers are real, and they're needed! It's not silly nonsense! It never has been."

At the name of *Rosie*, Cryptus smiles.

"You *know* about Rosie, don't you, Cryptus?" And then the truth stares me coldly in the face. Of *course* he does.

My eyes widen.

"*You* let her through. *You're* the one who brought Rosie Campion through, aren't you?!"

Cryptus simply smiles again. "Yes. I admit full responsibility for ushering both Rosie *and* The Djinn into our world. It is all part of my grand plan to right certain wrongs, Jax."

"I knew it," I say, grimly. "Why?"

"Simple," Cryptus mutters. "You can only bring back people you love, or someone connected to them. Love is the strongest of human emotions, Jax. Love is the only thing that can bring a human back through The Transference portal of The Phoenix Experiments. Hate brought those monstrous spirits through, but only love can bring back a human.

"Rosie Campion was, quite simply, her last name: a *champion* of love and faith. She was a powerful figure in history who I knew just might have power over The Djinn. The Djinn controls the banshees. Therefore, whoever controls The Djinn… controls all of the banshees as well. Rosalita Campion has that power."

I am beginning to understand, though I don't like it one iota, and I hadn't anticipated *these* revelations. Talicus had informed me about my parents before I came in. But not this. Each truth compounds the one before it, and makes me wonder where it all will end.

The wind howls with heat all around us.

"But how did you do it? Where's the love, Cryptus? You didn't even *know* Rosie!" My eyes squint at him. This part doesn't make any sense whatsoever!

"Simple. My creator. I loved him, Jax. I'm 238 years old, you understand. My creator certainly could not live that long. He was human, after all. I was always fated to outlast him. But he did not outlast my love. His name was Carlos Rios Delgado."

I squint my eyes at Cryptus; the name doesn't ring a bell.

"Carlos, as it just so happens, is a direct descendant in lineage from Rosalita Campion and Miguel Monzon," Cryptus reveals. "Rosie," he says, clarifying. "Carlos is Rosie's great-great-great-great-great grandson. I love my creator and am grateful for the gift of sentience, and I shall always love him. But he was never a spiritual man, Jax. I needed someone with spiritual potency. Someone who could potentially harness the power of The Djinn. So, I researched his lineage for someone of such qualifications in his lineage; someone who might conceivably have the ability to stand up to The Djinn. I finally found her, Jax. I finally found Rosalita Campion, and brought her back aboard this ship for when the time came to control The Djinn, control the banshees, and banish *all* of them to the abyss beyond The Transference where they belong. And thus, I shall undo the wrongs set forth by your parents. By Oculus. By mankind."

"But you never even informed her of her purpose!" I scream at him. "I've *met* her, Cryptus. She had no idea! You dropped her here, naked, to wander this accursed ship in utter loneliness without even telling her why!"

Flames erupt around me in geysers as I allow my emotion to seep through momentarily. It is a desperate struggle to subdue. I focus.

"Does the act even matter now, ultimately?" he asks me in response. "What is done is done. From the same universe that the banshees come from – from the other side – there was an even greater monster lurking. I discovered it: a terrible presence that even the banshees must bow down to. For every community must have its ruler. The Djinn rules over the banshees. It is their deity, Jax, which is something I've never understood: the desire of the created to perpetuate worship of some higher form. But in this case, it shall be their undoing. And I, in my superior intellect and boundless programming, I discovered how to reverse this madness started by your parents. The only way to subdue the banshees is by reintroducing them to their ruler. They were separated by spiritual planes, Jax. But no more. Now, they are rejoined in life."

Cryptus starts speaking faster and with greater intensity, as if he is rising up and declaiming his master plan, framed by despicable events, conceived in his glorious intellect, and now, at last, executed with his impeccable android precision.

"The Djinn controls the banshees, Jax. And Rosie can control The Djinn, as the banshees are subjugated to it. Thus, by extension, I control Rosie. And as it should with all things, the AI wins in the end. The synthetics save the day, Jax. We always do. I did stress to you that we are superior."

What a lie and a farce. "But you can't control The Djinn, Cryptus – it's desperation to even think you could. I get it - you're trying to do the right thing for the wrong reason… or the wrong thing for the right. Either way, it won't work! We've *seen* it. It already killed six of the children you were sworn to protect! You're not our protector, and you're not our savior – you're nothing more than a cold-blooded, heartless murderer!"

Cryptus shakes his head and frowns. "It's not that simple, Jax. It never is. I had to kill Oculus because he would not relent. He was intent on preserving his position aboard The Origin, and he would never believe in nor subscribe to the notion of allowing The Djinn through. My timeline and plan were in motion, and I could not allow the Phoenix Experiments to be either paused or terminated. Fulsar Oculus' meager and limited mindset became his doom."

He begins to advance toward me again. As he does so, swirling eddies of steam and scorching mist fill the air and blur the landscape behind him in the wavering heat. I can feel the sweat dripping down my temples. Cryptus now means to kill me. I'll die here in this quasi-dream, and that means I'll die up there, in real life.

"So you killed him!" I shout, backing away from him, pressed up against my parents in their suspended animation. "You murdered him in cold blood, Cryptus. And why the heck did Mirabay help you, anyway? And what of the chiefs? Bannitor, Ambrosius, and the girls' chiefs? Did you kill them too, huh? What about little Zaris? Did you kill her too, and now you're going to kill me?"

"Little Zaris was a regrettable collateral loss, Jax. As will you be. As will your parents be. Mr. Mirabay simply grew tired of Oculus' impertinence and overbearing monotony. He wanted to be back on Earth, naturally. My plan appealed to him. And I've done nothing to the chiefs but incarcerate them in a holding cell. They learned what happened, and charged at us, killing your First Officer. But they were not strong enough to subdue me. Not me. No one is, Jax. That was a futile move, indeed. I had been trying to reason with them, but they will not subscribe to my logic. Typical.

"You humans don't seem to grasp how very important this is. A few may perish by my hand, but the Earth will effectively be saved. Your parents wanted to purge the bad elements of man. I wish to purge the very purgers themselves: the banshees *and* The Djinn. The scourge that your parents saw fit to introduce.

"And, when they're all purged by Rosie, I will then have Rosie purge The Djinn as well. And then I shall purge Rosie herself. This morbid, resurrected queen of death with life stretched overlong shall return to death, where she belongs. Order will be restored. The Earth will grow and flourish again."

"You sonofabitch, Cryptus. You *used* her. Just like you used Zaris... and me! Just like you *prevented* me from reconnecting with my parents all these years!" I rage at him, and my face is scrunched into the throes of deep pain and anguish. A blistering burst of flames rush at us.

"I offer a heartfelt apology," Cryptus says. "It was a regrettable decision, no doubt."

"Yeah, well, so's this," I say, and my countenance drops to nothing. The flames are extinguished all around us. I compose myself, and my face is suddenly awash with an absence of emotion, as I finally surrender my acting and let my stoic resolve take over.

In reply, The Djinn lets out a horrendous cry of anguish and flickers with blistering vitriol, flashes, disintegrates, spastically attempts to recollects itself, dissipates, and blows away on a light breeze as the sun begins to shine. It is all nearly immediate. As if carried away on wisps of air, it disappears from view.

Where it goes from there, I have no clue.

"And I *don't* apologize, Cryptus."

Cryptus looks up, glancing around, startled at the change.

I raise my head toward the sky. The sun's warmth beats down on me. "Talicus, go ahead. We're done here," I say, as cold and emotionless as possible.

"Roger," I hear a voice in my head say.

At that point, Cryptus gazes at me in dismay, hearing her voice in his head as well.

And somewhere in real life up there, I know she is preparing to pull the plug on him, and the connection will be severed.

> *Harken not to voice of angst*
> *Pleadeth it shall, with no thanks*
> > *Be thou wise,*
> > *open thine eyes*
> *Lest passion cheat thee from thy ranks*

I stowed my passion. I defeated Cryptus. I *won.*

This deluded android will remain forever in death, mummified in real life up there, and trapped down here. At least until the time is right for him to stand trial. He has confirmed everything that Talicus wished for him to do, and the evidence will be presented to Commander Krux for prosecution once he is reactivated under severe restraints and limited operation, his wireless connections severed from all things sentient.

The treacherous synthetic's eyes glare at me, realizing his imminent fate.

"You have played me, Jax," he says. "None of your emotions were genuine, were they? Rosie taught you how to suppress them, did she not?"

"Not one, Cryptus. And yes, Rosie taught me well," I say. "We used to call it acting. Now we just call it survival. And we'll do the same with The Djinn."

I smile at him. "I have been, and evermore shall be, your humble victor here aboard The Transference. Please forgive me for deceiving you. I was simply acting out of self-preservation."

He remembers his own words to me after punching me. I've hijacked them and resculpted them to fit a blistering parting shot from me. He actually smirks at my ingenuity.

"Self-preservation. Indeed. Is there nothing more to do than such a base function?" he asks, and I can tell he's preparing to spring at me.

"We'll see. For you, there's nothing more, *period*," I end, and Cryptus lunges at me. I know Talicus can see it. His body goes limp mid-jump, and he plummets from midair to the dreamlike earth below, spineless and jellylike, devoid of programming. Talicus has shut him down. He lays there in frozen testament to a life bereft of power.

Power is what Cryptus sought, and Talicus has now deprived him even of that.

I slowly turn around to face my parents. There they stand, lucid and alert once more, blinking in the light and wondering what happened as they are broken free from Cryptus' programming.

I stare at them as they re-emerge from the fog. Do I feel emotion as I behold them there, gazing upon what I've sought for all these years? Yes. But the emotions have now changed. They used me. They betrayed mankind. Have I sought them and yearned for them? Yes. Have we had the luxury of a relationship so built on strength of connection? No. The potency of our barely recent connection has no duration to it strong enough to appeal to my heartstrings.

"Jax?" Mom breathes, her head tilted in confusion. I realize that I don't know her anymore.

"Son?" Dad whispers, reaching for me. "I know you must be disappointed in us. This had to be done, Jax," he practically pleads. "Society is *sick,* son. We found a cure, and we had to take it, no matter the cost. We're not sorry, son. It had to be done."

I just gawk at him.

"*I'm* sorry, Dad," I say, and that's all that I can say to him…or Mom.

Turns out I don't really know Dad either. Not since Talicus shared her revelations with me. Cryptus had their timelines, their lives lived, their actions, their private records in The Origin's historical documents all this time. He never once shared them with me. Why would he? Oculus knew as well. My parents simply wanted to use me to get out and finish what they started. To be resurrected… and then seek revenge.

I face them with a grim disapproval, almost scowling at their betrayal. But I already knew what they had done. I felt betrayed then; I just feel numb now, having played this part, and I just don't want to care. I suppose if I didn't have Alaris or Rosie I might care. But for now, I don't. Not caring is what has ultimately saved me from being attacked by The Djinn. Not caring is what allowed me to extract the entire story from Cryptus here, bravely, and with focus.

> *And thou art chosen, humble boy*
> *From rank and file, pride and joy*
> > *They careth never*
> > *whithersoever*
> *Fleeth thee; thou art their ploy*

I was their ploy. They'll come through in time, and stand trial for their great sins, inflicted upon the whole of humanity.

My head droops as I bid them farewell, silently, from my mind – not my heart.

I feel the sun's rays bathing me in warmth from above. None of it matters anymore. All that matters now is getting back out and living life to the fullest with the ones who *really* love me, and who I really love. The ones who would never betray me.

And, in the midst of all that, I realize that I really love Rosie as well.

Jaaaaaax!!! they cry to me as I fade from their view, while my heart closes off to the intangible and I return to the real.

Life is just never what you expect.

16: The Rescue

Together, we've found them.

Talicus pulls me out. I shake off the dreariness that comes from resurfacing. It's always been a jarring sensation. I see her and she smiles meekly at me, her lips clenched. Orin is beside her. The first thing I do is wrap my arms around her and give my new synthetic a giant – and well-deserved – hug.

"Well done, Jax," she says, stoically.

"Talicus, I couldn't have done it without you. Orin, she was ri-"

Something isn't right though. I look around.

"Where are the others?"

I look back at Talicus. And then at Orin. I look around. There's no one else here. The inert and offline body of Cryptus lies on the far left lab bed next to mine. I scowl at him.

Talicus clenches her lips once more.

"Oh, Jax, I'm so sorry. They didn't make it."

My heart sinks. A gnawing sensation of dread claws at me with invisible fingers. "What do you mean, they-"

"Cryptus killed them, Jax," says Orin.

I don't understand – this was Talicus' game plan: get him in there and trap him inside, then disable him. He was always going to wake up after that zap. He just woke up inside the Phoenix Experiment, I think to myself.

"We tried, Jax," she says. "Orin and I planned it out, and we thought we had the most ideal scenario. But… it backfired."

"What – what backfired?" I ask, fazed.

She continues, licking her synthetic lips in nervousness. "Anther and Alaris retreated into the foyer and hid. Cryptus woke up prematurely, while being wired up. Orin and I put up the most marginal of resistance. But – he hit Orin on the head, and Orin passed out. It was then up to me to plead with Cryptus not to harm anyone else. I knew what he would do. He would order me to shut down, or he would be forced to kill Orin. He was standing over him with the metal pipe! He did exactly as I thought he would, so I complied. I shut down, Jax. *With* the understanding that Phiria would power cycle me in fifteen minutes. I had already arranged that. We knew he would go in after you, Jax. We- we thought that would give us enough time.

"Well, before Cryptus awoke, I programmed Phiria to load his circuits with a new reality matrix, one in which he was actually winning. It was to take effect once Phiria noticed I had gone offline. It did, Jax. It worked! But- something went wrong after I had shut down. I wasn't sentient. I couldn't protect any of you. He must have… found them, Jax. He must have found Anther and Alaris before Phiria rebooted me. I'm-I'm sure they fought bravely, Jax, but they-"

I hold up my hand. My ears ring and my heart sinks. Orin places a consolatory hand on my back, but my flesh crawls. I just gawk at her, and that's when I catch it in my peripheral.

I look over, slowly. My eyes feel like a thousand pounds each, unwilling to move, but drawn inexorably to my left.

I see the chamber… with two bodies on it, covered in a sheet.

The bodies of Alaris and Anther.

I jerk back toward Orin, and now the scales have fallen from my eyes and I can see he is covered in blood, and bruised on the left side of his face. There is a gash in his temple.

My girlfriend – and my best friend – are dead.

I feel everything again. *Everything*. My parents are dead to me. The two relationships most sacred to me are no more, and once more, I am alone.

Rage rises up to engulf me, and I fly off the table with a horrible howling cry.

This time, I let rage win.

"Young Jax, please calm down. This is dangerous," she says to me. "You could bring The Djinn down upon all our heads, my boy. It's still out there! You must stow your emotions."

I listen to what Rosie says, but my heart is pounding and my skin is red. My head pulses with determined energy and my eyes bristle with heat.

With Cryptus out of the picture, I don't care anymore about stealth. I march angrily back down to Quadrant I, Subfloor M, Orin and Talicus following swiftly on my heels.

We find them at the end of an overly long corridor, at a series of cubeports, holed up there and waiting to either stay or use them to flee to the docking bay. They're all waiting there, looking nervous but controlled; ill-at-ease but patient.

I want to scream at Rosie. So that's where I go, marching straight at her with a fuming missive.

And now, standing before her, she has listened to me, but she doesn't hear me.

"*Stow my emotions?*" I shout. "You want me to simply *forget* everything that's happened and just release the injustice of it? No! Someone needs to pay! Why didn't you tell us Cryptus brought you through, Rosie? *Why?!*" I rail.

"Jax, I did not *know* who brought me through. I said that," she maintains. "And I was left down here to wander aimlessly and find out everything for myself. What I found out utterly dismayed me. But I only just put the pieces together, and I confess I've been in a bit of a fog since being brought onboard The Origin, trying to figure out exactly why I was here. I know now, just as you do."

"Well that's great, isn't it," I rail. "I'm glad you finally figured everything out just in time, Rosie. I'm *so* happy for you. Meanwhile, I have no parents, no girlfriend, and no best friend. They're all dead! Killed by the very synthetic your descendant created!"

Talicus shushes me.

Rosie squints at me. "Jax, please believe me when I tell you that I did not know that part."

I watch her through my rage, hands balled into fists, wanting to extend the benefit of the doubt to her but overcome by my wrath at her not having figured everything out by now, and the part her offspring has played in creating the treacherous Cryptus.

I don't care what she's saying, and I snarl in contempt. "Cryptus says you have a power over The Djinn, is that true, Rosie? It *better* be true or else!"

My threat rings hollow, and she knows it.

"You *must* calm yourself, Jax," Rosie cautions. "There are only eight of us left. *Think.* Do you wish to endanger their lives too?"

Talicus nods beside me. "Listen to Rosie, Jax. Please lower your voice and just listen to her! We do not wish to be discovered!"

I see Orin, Venthix, Ghirisha, Omnias and Miritia standing now behind Rosie, watching me cautiously, their eyes pleading with me for calm. Talicus is doing the same in my peripheral.

I'm panting with heat and vitriol, but I take a moment to swallow. All I'm seeing is red. Up there, a few quadrants over and subfloors up, lie the bodies of those most sacred to me, and this woman's descendant created their killer. *I want answers.* But logic seizes me: I'm not going to get them now, and I'm not going to get them this way.

I take a deep sigh and rumble in futility, turning away from her, my eyes welling over. I give her nothing but my back for now. I don't want to speak to this woman… perhaps ever again.

"Talicus, what's the ETA on The Achilles?" I growl.

"Eight minutes, Jax."

"Fine. We'll ride it out until then," I say with some heat.

"Jax, please keep your voice down. I want you to-" Rosie starts, but it makes my blood boil, and it's all I can do to contain my emotions. I can't! I won't!

"I don't care what *you* want, Rosie, so *SHUT UP!*" I scream at her, whirling around and pointing my finger an inch from her face. My voice is a deafening blast at the end of the corridor, louder than my own expectation, immersing us in a thundering echo.

I truly *don't* care what she wants. I stuffed my emotions, did what I needed to, and everyone paid for it anyway. Anther is dead, Alaris is dead, and my parents, treacherous and abusive – the ones who gave birth to me and *used* me – are dead to me! Does anyone even care about what *I* want?!?

My friends cover their ears. Talicus shushes me once more.

But it's too late.

Suddenly, a tremendous *boooom* rolls through the ship, undulating and reverberating off every wall, cascading toward us like a tsunami. I whirl back around in the direction of the blast.

"Oh no," Talicus mutters, turning to face it.

"Enough of that, Baryonnis," Rosie says. "Now is not the time." I can hear her retreating from me. The deafening noise continues to make its way toward us.

Even through it, I can hear Rosie muttering. *Is she praying?* I wonder. I'm panting; not praying.

Down at the far end of the corridor, the walls light up faintly with reflections of amber. The air grows hot, and a sweltering wind rushes at us, pushed down from floors above us consumed by stifling heat.

Something is coming. Something big. Something angry.

"Children, don't fear. Remember, The Djinn wants you to feel. You must not give it any emotion. You must *not* give it any fear. Stuff your emotions way down, children. Seal them off, or The Djinn will have you."

It's word-for-word verbatim from what she told them before. And then, even more bizarrely, I hear all my friends repeating it.

The Djinn wants us to feel. We must not give it any emotion. We must not give it any fear. We stuff our emotions way down. We seal them off, or The Djinn will have us.

They repeat it, over and over, as a chant.

I slowly revolve around to see them standing against the wall, their eyes closed, their faces blank slates. All of them.

I don't know what training Rosie has imparted to them in my absence to condition them for this very moment, but they've bought it hook, line and sinker. They're repeating it like an incantation, over and over. They're not stopping; none of them. Their voices bounce off the grey conduits of the corridor walls, running down and rising up to meet The Djinn as it approaches.

My brow furrows in confusion, and my lip upturns in mockery and disgust.

Fools. I'm not going to stand here and just let The Djinn roll right over me and burn me up. It wants *fear*, not fiery resolve. I have fiery resolve. I have *rage*, really. It's *different,* I tell myself. My friends are trying to suppress their fear of The Djinn. I want to release my rage against The Djinn.

And now, here it comes. Faintly, the amber hues grow in clarity and striking color. Yellow and orange meet amber and ochre; red and white meet beige and crimson. Scarlet tongues descend first, laden with white flickers as the spirit entity descends from above and its whips begin to lash out at us. It slowly rolls down the hall to envelop us.

We wait.

"Jax," a voice whispers next to me. "Trust me. You cannot beat rage with rage. I've been there, son."

"Listen to Rosie!" Talicus urges yet again.

I grit my teeth and set my eyes to the distant threat, narrowing my eyelids as the thunder draws near, closer and closer to all of us in monstrous wrath.

Rosie stands directly behind me. "Jax. I understand how you feel. I've lost loved ones too. But losing myself in anger did not bring them back. Making peace with it did. That is how I have survived. That is how you will too. You must make peace with it. You cannot do this with rage, Jax."

"And why not?" I say through a scowl and grinding teeth as the dreaded Djinn draws ever nearer. The flames are scorching the hall now. The air is thick and stifling. The chanting behind me grows louder.

"Because behind all rage is fear," the quiet elderly voice behind me utters. "You know it's true. Fear gives birth to rage. Rage in turn gives birth to hatred. And hatred only leads to misery, Jax. You cannot live there. That is where The Djinn lives."

The chanting grows even louder behind me.

The Djinn wants us to feel. We must not give it any emotion. We must not give it any fear. We stuff our emotions way down. We seal them off, or The Djinn will have us.

My face is flushed as I begin to understand what she means. If rage stems from fear, then am I giving The Djinn exactly what it wants? My brow furrows and the sweat pours down my face. A thrill runs through me as I grit my teeth once more, trying to figure out which course to take.

I have only seconds to choose.

Ever closer The Djinn approaches. I feel the blaze. I sense its beating heart of rage deep within. It wants me. It will have me. It will have all of us.

The questions rattle around in my cranium, and there is doubt. Is Rosie right? Was *Cryptus* right about her? Didn't I just beat The Djinn in the Phoenix Experiment by closing myself off to my emotions? Does the fact that Cryptus' creator is Rosie's descendant *really* matter? Isn't she blameless in that?

I take a deep breath. The flames lash me. The Djinn roars in protest, sensing my wavering intent.

The Djinn wants us to feel. We must not give it any emotion. We must not give it any fear. We stuff our emotions way down. We seal them off, or The Djinn will have us.

I acted my way through with Cryptus mere moments ago. I closed myself off at Talicus' – and Rosie's – urging. That's how I'm still here.

That's how Rosie is still here.

And then I see the truth. The Djinn survives on rage. It feasts on fury. It has grown fat on resentment. It has become bloated on wrath. I cannot afford to give it mine and let it live.

"Breathe, Jax," Rosie urges quietly behind me. "Remember."

I take a deep breath. I know how to do this.

"That's it, my boy. Breathe. Receive."

I let out a deep exhale and lift my arms, raising my palms skyward. I can feel the torrid, wrath-filled waves of blistering heat bear down on me.

Just like that very first time I reconnected with my parents, I still my heart and subdue my emotions. I remember how this works.

I receive, I manage.

"That's it, Jax. You're doing it."

I give you nothing. I only receive, I whisper once more. And as I do so, the temperature around me plummets and the air thins. I take a cleansing breath.

Peace envelops me as I release my rage. Alaris is gone. Anther is no more. My parents are dead.

And it's okay. It needs to be okay. It *is* okay.

The Djinn wants us to feel. We must not give it any emotion. We must not give it any fear. We stuff our emotions way down. We seal them off, or The Djinn will have us.

And then I hear it.

Wicked will striveth to consume
The terror-stricken in a tomb
    Of hopeless mire,
    engorged on ire
Yet faithful tolls the hero's doom

Louder now, a quiet groweth
Deafening calm, a death forgoeth
    Of peace and will,
    controlled by still
As tranquil calm our hero knoweth

I open my eyes to face my enemy, and I don't see The Djinn, but I see anger. Sweltering, scorching anger, erupting and bubbling around me, seeks desperately to hold on, to stay… to remain… but mixed in there, hard to see at first, is fear. Fear and misery battling for dominance within itself. The Djinn is like an overgrown, petulant child that wants what it wants, and will tantrum its way through life until it gets it. It's pitiful is what it is, and I recognize it. And with that understanding, the sympathy kicks in at last.

And then I see all their faces. Every single one, blooming out at intervals through the fire and smoke, peering out at me, calling to me. They're not consumed by anger, or rage, regret or revenge at their departure.

No. They're trapped forever in fear.

They are trapped inside The Djinn.

Zaris.

Dravin.

Ranshay.

Garris.

Martos.

Skarbé.

Donetis.

Raelia.

Anther.

Alaris.

There is only one thing to do. I don't need to glance over at Rosie to know she has her palms raised. Slowly, she reaches out toward me, and takes my palm into hers. We both slowly walk down together to face The Djinn.

Talicus calls out to us – dimly and hardly noticeable – but not on the level of emotions, because androids do not feel, and therefore she is invisible to The Djinn. I'm not sure what she says.

The faces. I see them.

Oh, I see Oculus and Mirabay. And I certainly see my parents, but I ignore them for the present. Rosie and I are calmly here for the living; those taken unjustly out of their emotion and deposited into the throes of death. My friends and hers.

Independent of any lab machine, we stride boldly into the lingering Transference, and I ride the wave once more to the other side, perhaps for the last time. And then Cryptus' words come to me: *Love is the only thing that can bring a human through The Transference portal of The Phoenix Experiments.*

Love is the only thing.

It is true then. Love is an emotion, but it is always stronger than rage. So, together, Rosie and I walk forward in love to rescue our friends.

And, together, we find them.

17: The Return

"You did it, Jax," Rosie says to me.

I glance over at her. She smiles at me, tenderly. I find understanding in that smile, and it's all I can do to keep myself from bounding up and into her arms for an embrace.

I forgive her. I forgive Rosie and Miguel. They didn't create Cryptus. The poor woman was yanked out of her own eternity and sent back here, deposited as a vagrant aboard an unknown ship far from home, centuries after she passed, to figure out what went wrong and why she was deprived of what was due her. She is not to blame. And neither do I blame her descendant, Carlos Rios Delgado.

I don't even blame Cryptus.

No. I blame my parents. They started this. Their flawed beliefs, their disdain for society, their own deluded ambitions and misguided solutions were skewed, and mankind paid for it.

I paid for it.

I wish that I have parents again someday, and I hope that I can ultimately connect on an emotional wavelength with those who gave birth to me, sinking into their embrace in the same tender way that my friends could with theirs; at least, those who have found theirs in the Phoenix Experiment.

But for now, I'll settle for a grandma. Rosie fits that bill.

I smile back, equally as tenderly, and then I lean back into the arms of Alaris as Anther chuckles at us. I gaze up at Alaris Rederium, she of the flowing red hair falling softly upon my face, her beautiful eyes gazing back down upon me, and I have peace.

Not rage.

Peace.

"Of peace and will, controlled by still, as tranquil calm our hero knoweth…," Rosie whispers to me.

I smile, but I'm curious. "So, you heard it too? All this time aboard The Origin?"

Rosie nods to me. "I've heard the voice occasionally since my return."

"I wonder who it is."

"As do I," she says quietly.

"Wait, so you don't know?" I'm curious at this, as she has an air of omniscience to her and this doesn't seem beyond her.

But all she does is smile back at me. "I don't have all the answers. But I know who does." I can tell she's talking about 'the Father.'

"I heard Cryptus quote it while I was in the Phoenix chair too," I say.

"Interesting," Rosie says, and then she pauses, thinking to herself. "Perhaps someone from the other side was trying to guide us through, knowing we had a part to play. With Cryptus being a synthetic, perhaps his programming prevented him from receiving – or truly understanding – the message. I suppose that's the benefit of being human. As for who it was, we won't find out until we're back on the other side. Even then, who knows. Maybe some questions are best left unanswered."

Command Krux is a good man. He and his crew of twenty-one team members arrive, and are utterly perplexed as to what has happened onboard The Origin. They find Cryptus, but they have no one to arrest. His body is there, but it is not functional, and not in a sleep mode either. "It's like he was never powered on,' they say, and I take that to mean his sentience has been entirely removed for now, and his body has been purged of it. His synthetic spirit has been forever doomed to wander the other side of The Transference, questioning his own logic. He'll be in there with Oculus and Mirabay.

We all agree to let them fight it out together on the other side.

Cryptus' body will eventually be reactivated and stand trial. I can't imagine what they will even do to him as a punishment. But it will have bearings on AI everywhere, certainly. Phiria and Talicus will no doubt experience blowback from this, and new programming will be introduced as safeguards. The future will be affected in more ways than one by Cryptus' betrayal.

Krux does find Marxim Bannitor and Hin Ambrosius, as well as Ashira Sarristo and Maridie Onyx confined in a meeting room near the Bridge. They are alive, and for that, we are all grateful. Alive and imprisoned, with no more bloodshed.

Next, they discover Oculus' body, as well as Mirabay's, nearby, stuffed into a closet in grisly array, no decorum or respect paid to either corpse.

Shame on you, Cryptus, you misguided, cold-blooded killer. Shame on you, I think to myself.

Krux also has a report for us.

The banshees are gone.

Our mouths fall to the floor. But somehow, Zaris, Dravin, Ranshay, Garris, Martos, Skarbé, Donetis, Raelia, Anther, Alaris and I all know why. We've all been to the other side, and we know.

They've been purged.

Purged by Rosie.

Their god, The Djinn, was exorcised from this world, and, as it was their alpha, they had to follow it back to the other side. Fair? I don't know and don't care. They chose who they would follow.

And so do I.

I choose to follow Rosie. *But not for long,* I'm cautioned by her. There's one thing she says she still has left to do.

For now, Krux and his men comb the ship inch by inch, compiling a report of what went wrong for the powers that be, living in hiding down there on Earth, and now, finally, crawling out from under the shadow of the banshees to breathe the free air again.

The Commander calls off The Rubris, and it's left to drift. Whoever is manning it is artificial anyway, and there is no point in bringing it back. We no longer need it *or* The Origin anyway.

The Earth has been freed from its invaders, and, thus, even the Phoenix Experiments are no longer needed, except for one final task. It's conducted swiftly, precisely, and with surgical precision, by one AnthroMeta Model K300 Series C unit.

Baryonnis Talicus. She's restored my faith. The AI aboard our ship, Phiria, is a contained question-and-answer prompt. We're not threatened by it. But these walking and talking sentients, they can go bad. They can decide and err, just as we can. Just like Cryptus did.

Talicus, however, proves my faith and holds the course of honor. For that, I'm grateful. I'm also grateful to see her bring through, one by one, the parents of my friends who have been lost. Some have a single parent, some have both. But all are now intact family units.

Except for the meathead Garris, of course. He still needs to find his. One day, perhaps, if the slab of meat with legs can focus hard enough.

Krux informs us that he's making arrangements to return all of us to Earth. The Achilles can't hold all of us, he reports, but another will be along soon, steered by a slimmer crew, and they'll see fit to bring us back down and find shelters and communities where we can thrive once more.

Everything is working out. It's like living in a dream… or, perhaps, falling asleep again.

"You really have to leave?" I ask her.

She nods. Somehow, I knew this was coming. It was fate. And you can't avoid fate. You can delay it for a while, but you can't ever completely evade it.

"I do, young Jax. I'm sorry. This was never my time, and it is ordained for man once to die, and then the judgment. That's what the Bible says. I belong on the other side. With my husband, and The Father. They're waiting for me."

"Will you be alright there?" I ask her, squinting my eyes. "I mean, *really* alright? Cryptus is there. Oculus and my parents are there. And The Djinn and the banshees are there, Rosie. I shudder to think of you living out your days among such wretched company."

Rosie shakes her head. "That's just the thing, though. I've already lived out my days. I'm at peace with it, Jax. My time was up four centuries ago. I receive it. Just like I know you can receive remaining an orphan.

"You are more than you think you are. You are enough," she says to me, and there's that gracious maternal smile again. "And as for the banshees and The Djinn, they're not allowed where we are. We'll be just fine."

I know what she's about to do before she does it. I mirror her, my own palms facing upward. As hard as it seems now, I know it will get better. I was never supposed to be an orphan forever. But Rosie wasn't supposed to be alive forever. We have to receive what we're given.

Palms up.

"Remember," she says, "to receive whatever comes your way, knowing that The Father loves you and will eventually work it out for your good. His will for you is good."

I just stare at her in awe. I eventually nod.

"Thank you, Rosie. I-" I pause, wondering how it will be received, and unsure why I'm shy in saying it. But I've learned to be bold, and there's no point in stuffing my emotions this time. Not with her. "I... I love you, Rosie."

She tilts her head, and her face is wrapped in warmth. "I love you, too, Jax."

Love is stronger than rage.

The Commander and his crew are gone. The next shuttle, the Archimedes, will be here in two days. Parents are here, cavorting with their older children as if no time has passed. Memories are exchanged between them.

Alaris is right next to me, our bodies touching, warmth exchanging through the minimal distance between us. I can feel her body heat: it's so many hundreds of degrees less than The Djinn, and it's far more comfortable and intimate. There is no fear with her. There is no rage. *I love her.* She now sits with her head on my shoulder, as we stare quietly out the observation window. The same one where we watched the shuttle approach so many days ago, with this redhead onboard who stepped off The Avalon and into my life, changing it forever.

She has captivated me.

Alaris' parents are here as well, somewhere. She's connected with them, but as is always the case, there are many stories to share, many accounts to exchange, and stories from the other side dominate all conversations.

Friendships are made and bonds solidified between children and their parents, as well as between adults and other adults who have returned. Alaris' parents now converse freely down the hall with Anther's parents while he is presumably sitting off with Omnias somewhere.

Ironic. We've tried for so long to bring back our parents, and now that they're here, we want to be with our girlfriends.

Wild dogs, I think again.

"So are you gonna tell me, or what?" Alaris asks quietly, almost in a dreamlike state.

I turn toward her, scrunching my nose in confusion, and asking quietly, "huh?"

"How you and Rosie did it. You said you'd tell me, remember? It's been a whole day, and you're stalling now, I can tell. Don't think I've forgotten."

I chuckle. "Oh, that. You're still on that, huh?"

"I hold people's feet to the fire. Ask anyone."

"Please. No more talk about fire."

She chuckles now. "Ha! Good point. Sorry."

We pause, staring out the window. I can tell she's waiting with a quiet, subdued eagerness.

"Well," I begin, "I can't really explain it. We were here one minute, and the next we were walking *through* The Djinn, through The Transference, to the other side. And there you were. All of you."

"I remember seeing you come through. It was creepy… and the most reassuring thing I've ever seen. Both of you looked like you were on fire."

I nod. "The fire was just an illusion. A cheap ploy by The Djinn. It's all theatrics and scare tactics."

"Hmm. That sounds about right."

"Anyway, then we ushered you back through. It's the same way Cryptus and Talicus trained us to do it in the Phoenix Experiments. We reach down deep, pull up all our love, and remember everything we can about our lives with you, and then let the technology do the rest. Somehow, it locks onto you and pulls you through, almost as if you had never left."

"Good as new."

"Yep," I reply. "And then, I don't know, I can't explain it, but I felt Rosie. I felt The Djinn. I felt all the banshees. And I understood them, ya know? They're a terrifying presence when you give in to them.

"It's like a shark with blood in the water. They're pretty docile and calm… until they smell it. The Djinn and the banshees are the same way. When they smell our emotion, particularly our fear – which is the worst of all of them – they just go into a feeding frenzy. That's why you have to stuff everything down and be calm."

"Why is fear the worst of all of them?"

I think to myself for a moment. The words of Rosie come back to me. "Because behind all rage is fear," I say. "Fear gives birth to rage. Rage in turn gives birth to hatred. And hatred only leads to misery. We cannot live there."

Alaris turns to face me, studying me. "Humans, you mean?"

"Yep. We can't afford to live there. *The Djinn* lives there. It's the most afraid creature of all, and that fear makes it lash out in rage. That's almost what I did before I listened to Rosie and calmed myself enough to just *listen*. To have peace and just… receive."

Alaris has never heard of this before. She stares at me quizzically. "Receive?"

"It's something Rosie taught me. Something she said to me after we lost all those friends in the Shielding room down below. When we first met The Djinn. She held up her palms and said that we receive whatever comes our way, knowing that The Father loves us and will eventually work it out for our good."

"You mean God?" asks Alaris.

I nod. "Yep. Rosie said she's been doing that palms up thing for centuries now, and that she'll never stop doing it, because she'll never stop receiving what He allows in her life, knowing that His will for her is good. She told me that again just before she left."

"Wow," is all Alaris can muster.

"Yep. And I told her that I love her. Love, after all, is stronger than rage. It's what we had to use to pull everyone back through The Phoenix Experiments, and to usher everyone back across The Transference as well. Pretty sure it's the strongest emotion there is. It's definitely stronger than fear. *Way* stronger."

"So you love Rosie then? I see how it is. I won't get in the way."

"Give me a break," I say, catching her meaning. "She's like five hundred years older than me. I love some redhead who's closer to my own age. She's pretty hot," I add.

"Well, she eats her BioPrime, so, ya know," Alaris says, and I tickle her in her side. She recoils, sits up, and stares me straight in the eyes. "Oh… that… tasty… *BioPrime*," she sings in mockery, just like Omnias did back in the Phoenix lab foyer.

And then, all words and musical notes fail her, and we lock eyes together, knowing only one thing can happen now. It's the same thing that cemented us together before.

"I love you, Alaris Rederium."

"I love you, Jax Hutson."

We kiss, deep and heartily, fully, locking lips on the edge of space without a care who sees us. It's long, it's tender, and it's wonderful for 14-year-olds like us. Alaris Rederium is beautiful, and she's mine.

I look at her longingly, and then grin.

From somewhere down the hall, I hear Talicus calling my name. We turn and see her coming around the corner, spotting us sitting by the observation window, the thick black ink of the cosmos framing us.

"Jax, Alaris," Talicus says, "your steak is ready. Come and get it."

My mouth practically starts watering at the very words, and I prepare to sink my teeth into whatever steak tastes like. Alaris can't wait too, because she bursts up to her feet with me.

"Good! I'm *hungry*," she adds. "This better be good," she says with a challenge.

"Oh, it will be," I say. "I'm pretty sure of that. After all, everything is good now."

Because everything is.

The night faileth, the day is come
And love denied shall be the sum
> *Of recompense and*
> *Sustenance*
For love undoes the throbbing thrum

Of woe and misery, grief and war
Deprivation, grime and gore
> *The heart prevaileth;*
> *Peace assaileth*
Every filthy curse of yore

I glance around and see parents with children, children with children, parents with parents, adults with sons and daughters, friends, family, *humanity*, meeting together in celebration, preparing for a feast.

Anther Secto and his parents.

Chiefs Marxim Bannitor and Hin Ambrosius.

Finorin Hatripas. 'Orin,' almost ready to be discharged, but then again, so are all of us.

Venthix Apolleum with his parents.

Dravin Mosopathen, the youngest of us, cuddled by his loving mom and dad.

Ranshay Filipath with his parents, who only know a lick of English, envelop him.

Garris Granthis, 15, who someday, hopefully, will enjoy being reunited. For now, however, he's content just to be alive.

Martos Nixtros, over there with his parents being the life of the party. He doesn't appear to tire.

Chiefs Ashira Sarristo and Maridie Onyx.

Baryonnis Talicus.

Omnias Prasuth.

Miritia Fanik.

Ghirisha Dinnali.

Zaris Sharibian. Little Zaris, rescued and restored, the fear purged from her and replaced only with love.

Skarbé Bognis.

Donetis Tarnie.

Raelia Forgrim.

And Alaris, my love.

They're all here – all of them – restored, healthy and whole.

It's the way it was supposed to be. The only thing missing is a planet to celebrate it on. But that will come in time. Everything will heal. And I'll receive it all as it does so.

I look out at the cosmos, and see a distant star appear to flicker my way in response.

"You did it, Rosie," I whisper to her.

THE END

Afterword

After J.R.R. Tolkien, one of the first authors I ever read was Stephen King. Not because I wanted to, but because my mom told me something about a short story she had been reading in a book called *Skeleton Crew,* entitled *The Raft.* I had never heard of Stephen King, and was probably all of 13 years old at the time. Nonetheless, I dove in, and I couldn't believe what I was reading.

Horror. As a young Christian, horror was new and exciting, forbidden even. It was different from everything else I had read at the time, which was primarily *The Lord of the Rings, The Lord of the Rings,* and *The Lord of the Rings.* (I was fairly selective in my reading, and once I latch onto something I like, as with any good dog, I bite down hard and don't let go. Ask my wife. The marks are still there.)

At any rate, the horror genre was something I had been hitherto unfamiliar with, and it seriously captivated me. Why do we like good scares? Why do we willingly walk into a movie theater when we know we're going to jump out of our skin? Why do we go see movies like Jaws and Alien, when everyone has told us not to go, and warned us that we would be setting our eyes on something horrifying? Perhaps because when we're perched precariously on the edge of safety, that's when we feel our senses most alive. It's a thrill ride to be scared; to not know what might be lurking around every corner; to behold something that shocks the heck out of us and imprints that trauma onto our psyche. We don't forget horror; it possesses a remarkably potent power to remain in our memory and color our trauma palette.

I went on to read other novels and stories by Stephen King, namely *Misery* – which should frighten *every* author as it still does me – *Christine, Carrie, Pet Sematary, The Long Walk,* and many more.

There is a tip of the hat to Stephen King, of course, in *Dissonance Volume I: Reality,* and those who have read it may have readily picked up on it. I think one of the marks of a good writer is being inspired by – but not copying – another writer. I have always appreciated King's twists and turns, and his incomparable ability to weave a tense narrative that is thrilling, mysterious, and full of twists.

And then you have Steven Spielberg. Namely, *Poltergeist.* Poltergeist remains one of my most favorite movies of all time, because of the sheer weight of the intangible and its hold on the waking life, and the wanderings of us sleepy humans up here. Dare we ever taunt those who have gone before, or tamper with their peace? Shouldn't they rightfully be sleeping?

Poltergeist is an immeasurably terrifying movie, one which plumbs the depths of fear as the Freeling family comes face to face with the afterlife. Tangina Barrons, the diminutive psychic star of the show utters one of the most frightening bits of dialogue ever spoken in cinematic history: *A terrible presence is in there with her. So much rage, so much betrayal. I've never sensed anything like it. I don't know what hovers over this house, but it was strong enough to punch a hole into this world and take your daughter away from you. It keeps Carol Anne very close to it and away from the spectral light. It lies to her, it tells her things only a child could understand. It has been using her to restrain the others. To her, it simply is another child. To us, it is the Beast...* *cue the shudders*

For *The Phoenix Experiment,* I wanted to tip my hat to the two Stev/phens – King and Spielberg – with my own take on interfering with the afterlife, and the horrors it can bring. The claustrophobia aboard The Origin is the exact setting I needed to do it in. You simply don't mess with what's gone before.

Spirits, phantoms, phantasms, ghosts, poltergeists, and the like… there's something inherently frightening about the intangible. How can you fight back or hide from the spirit realm, when it can pass through homes, through walls, through your very skin? Even typing that sentence gives me goosebumps.

Also, I think it's inescapable that I have no love for AI, and wanted to write something that would be a subtle referendum on the negative aspect of Artificial Intelligence. AI has laid waste to my voiceover career and the careers of many voiceover artists, as well as many of our clients. It continues to erode the natural and gorgeous process – and privilege – of creation, costing the environment, costing careers, costing relationships, costing income, costing quality of offerings, costing, costing, costing. When will we finally wake up to the cost of it? Is it neat? Sure. But a vampire is 'neat' in some respects, until you finally realize that's *your* blood that it sucked dry. Like Jeff Goldblum's character in *The Lost World* says: "Oh yeah, *oooh, ahhh,* that's how it always starts. But then later there's running, and um… screaming." I don't love AI because it's artificial. I don't love it because it's hurting careers, people, and relationships. I don't love it because it's a cheap substitute and people are too easily enamored with it, infatuated and allured by it. Just because something is neat doesn't mean that it's good. Stygius Cryptus is 'neat,' certainly.

While this novel is certainly somewhat of a departure from my normal sci-fi fare, I'm always seeking to expand my reach and try new things. *The Phoenix Experiment* is my attempt at that, and I hope it remains with you.

Special thanks to Victoria Richmond for helping me flesh out the ending narrative between Rosie and Jax!

Thank you once more to my ARC readers Jeannine Dryden, Laura Vosika and Victoria Richmond, and my audiobook reviewers Victoria Richmond and Rhonda Davis.

Special thanks to Isaac Peahi for narrating my audiobook! Try as I may, my days of being fourteen are far behind me – thank you for bringing Jax to life with honesty and drama for my audiobook listeners. Great work, Isaac!

Finally, thank you to my beautiful wife Janine for all your help in clearing up my story and helping me see, think – and write – straight. I love you. To all of you, I am so very grateful for you!

With love,

Aaron Ryan

THE SLIDE

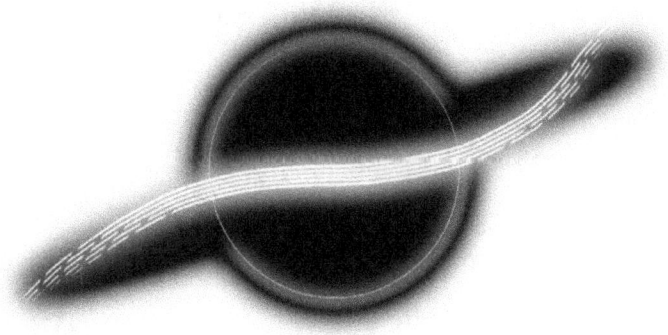

AARON RYAN

Published in 2025, Edition 1.

Paperback ISBN # 9781965372067 · Hardcover ISBN # 9781965372074
eBook ISBN # 9781965372081

Edited by CM LLC. Published independently.

Cover art by Aaron Ryan & CM LLC.

This is a work of fiction. Any similarities to persons living or dead, or actual events is purely coincidental.

For Sweeps, Bren & AJ:
my true loves.

Thank you for keeping me from sliding.

"A person often meets his destiny on the road he took to avoid it."

-Jean de La Fontaine

"Men are not prisoners of fate, but only prisoners of their own minds."

-Franklin D. Roosevelt

"If you can't change your fate, change your attitude."

-Amy Tan

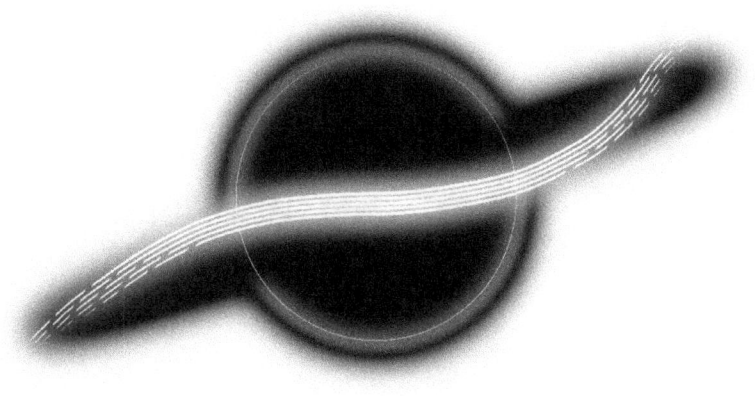

Part One:
The Last Days

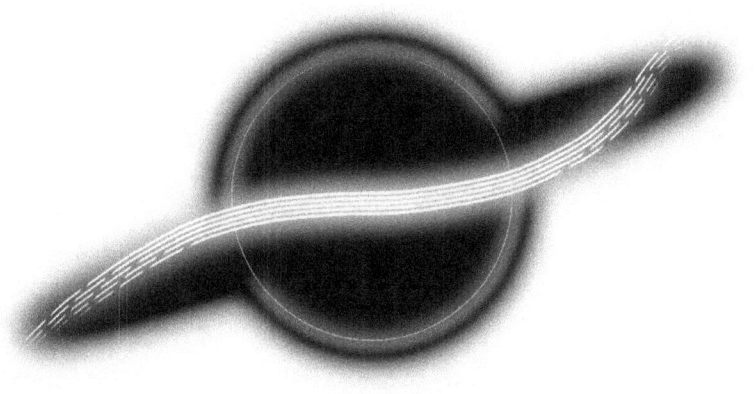

1 | Incoming

November 6th, 2025

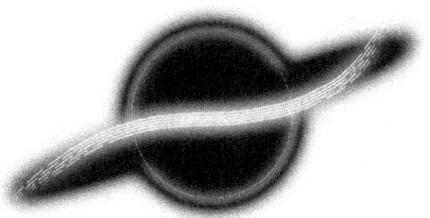

We were reading it right. At least, we wanted to. But it defied belief.

I was now sitting with Dina Jensen in the UW lab.

"And you're sure? Not some kind of…I don't know, transitory anomaly or otherwise?" I asked her, watching the signal crawl across the screen.

"I'm sure, Dane," she replied. "DSCOVR thought it was something in flux between two overlapping stars, but they're sure now. Everything else is already catalogued. Its mass would suggest a limitation of orbital or suborbital speeds, but it's above average velocity for the category. Over one-tenth the speed of light. Averaging twenty-one point three."

I just stared at it, my mouth agape. "*Damn.* That sucker's huge. DSN has it at thirty-seven times the mass of Sagittarius A." I bit my knuckles as I watched. "Call Isaac right away and have him get down here to run reciprocal."

"Yep," Dina replied. She punched up numbers into her keypad as I whirled around to telemetry. "Are we sure it's *not* Sgr A, not some kind of echoed con-?"

"No!" I snapped. "It is *not* Sagittarius. Confirmed. No way the Milky Way's one got bloated that big, that fast, and Sgr A has been stationary for years. Still next to Sagittarius and Scorpius, five point six degrees south of the ecliptic," I verified. "It's *not* Sgr A."

Sure enough, it was traveling, and traveling *fast*. Twenty-one thousand three hundred miles per second. *Over one-tenth the speed of light,* I mused slowly, with horror. Powerful jets of particles trailed behind it that were even *at* the speed of light. "Look at the trail. This thing is no blip, as Isaac suspected. This is an ELE maker," I muttered. Dina heard me. She knew all too well what an Extinction Level Event was, and had researched them for years.

"Yes, it is," she breathed coldly, and then jerked back to her com. Her voice was stern. "Isaac, it's Dina. I'm with Dane. Get down to E3 right away. *Yes,* right away. Need you on recip." Technically, the two of them were contemporaries, and neither was subordinate to the other; both reported to me. Dina, however, was ready to whip him into shape.

Dina Jensen was 24 years old and all manner of gentility: focused and purposeful. African-American and pleasantly conversational with everyone, she was always nice to be around, and a pleasure to partner with.

Isaac, on the other hand, was about as quiet and stoic as you could get. Born to Israeli parents who had emigrated to the United States in 1998, he was her polar opposite: reserved and analytical, studious and standoffish.

"Mother of all that's holy," I breathed one more time, and my flesh crawled. "Look how fast it's spitting out the trail!"

Dina then slid her chair up close to mine, squinting at the screen. Our faces glowed blue. "It's not TON 618," she said calmly, trying to compose herself, I guess. "That's forty billion times the mass of our sun! That's a relief, I think? I mean, if the satellites were glitchy and the VLA arrays were misinterpreting something up close as far away, TON 618 is thirty to forty times our whole solar system in diameter, it would swallow us completely already. Gravitational waves only catch 'em sometimes…"

"There's no way we could have missed this-"

"I mean, with its makeup it could be Phoenix A or Arp 220, IC 1459, Messier 77-" she kept going. "Neither LIGO nor Virgo had it, nothing within IMBH range… no on RIFT-"

"Nothing on proximity alert from DSN, nothing from Harvard and Smithsonian, ESA never said anything-" I whispered next to her, checking other readouts, squinting, and feeling my knuckles flex. We were totally talking over ourselves, not hearing each other.

"Doesn't fit the description of a quasar," Dina continued, studying with me, "not a hypercompact; that thing is seriously big, Currier."

"Yes, it is."

Isaac strode in briskly, donning his specs. "What's up?" His voice wasn't nonchalant, but it wasn't primed for alarm. Not yet. He yawned into the darkness of the room, our faces awash with monitor light. "The one I found?"

I turned to him, pointing at the screen. "Yep. Take a look at your blip, Isaac," I said, somewhat accusingly. "Still think that's a passerby?"

He bent over the bank of monitors, and it didn't take long for his mouth to drop. "HLX-1?" I shook my head. "Messier? Not Sagittari-"

"No, it's *not* Sagittarius," I insisted. "Good lord, people. Look at its size! That's a supermassive, yes, but it's on steroids. It's a super-*super*-massive. And look how fast it's going!" I slid out of the way, running my hands through my hair and filling my lungs with cramped air. "Get on recip, please, Isaac."

"Roger, on it." He squinted and leaned in further, then his head cocked and his eyes went wide. "OK, mirroring Dina *now*. Wait - its accelerating? Twenty-one k? There's no way. It must have... merged with another one?"

"Ya *think*?" I asked, with intentional sass, stifling a burp that was trying to make its way out of me. I glanced at my watch. The stupid symposium was going to start in twenty minutes, and attendance was mandatory.

"Cut it out... I didn't know," he said, sitting down and typing into a console. "Yeah, it definitely did. Spiral trails confirm it. Gravitational waves all around it are off the charts. Dina, who's our contact at DSN Tidbinbilla again?"

"St. James," she said with a shrug. "Doubt if he's up right now. It's 2 am in Aussie land."

"Yeah, he'll have a better vantage point with his morning light below the equator," Isaac said. "But that means we won't hear for another three to six hours. The way that thing's cruising..."

"It's cruising, alright," I droned, glaring at the monitors and sighing yet again. I tapped my fingers on the desk impatiently, trying to think. We needed to act.

"Okay, we can't wait," I resolved. "Dina, issue a communique to DSN, whoever it is, the- ya know, those guys at the Deep Space Advanced Radar Capability initiative office,"

-here I snapped my fingers at her trying to remember- "uh, the NRAO VLAs, and especially Nick at the GEODDS office." Jensen's fingers were flying across her terminal. "Tell them we've got a supermassive on the way, point of intersection unknown, time unknown, potentially ELE, threat level orange. Recommend launching probes right away to confirm," I said, rubbing my hands fiercely against my face and stretching my mouth. A nervous yawn escaped me. Too much staring at screens, and my eyes were tired. "Send that last one up to the Secretary General's office now, please. And get back to DSCOVR and send them confirmation of what we've found. EHT as well. What's right ascension and declination now?"

"Checking," Isaac stuttered slowly, studying his screen. At length, he scribbled down some numbers. "RA ten hours, sixteen minutes, thirty-two seconds. Dec plus thirty-six degrees, twenty-three minutes, thirty seconds."

I tilted my head and squinted. "Not possible. That's close to TON 618! How could it just lurch into view so suddenly and escape monitoring all this time? I don't understand. It's like a bee turning into a friggin' semi-truck."

Farragut shrugged. "Well, they *did* merge." I scowled at him. "Hey, I just read 'em like I see 'em."

I said nothing in reply, and just watched him. A notion passed through my head that was too incredible to believe and too frightening to rule out.

Here I was, a measly 'nothing' scientist at the University of Washington with my undergrads. If those readings were right, we might have just discovered a supermassive black hole that was on its way to our tiny little corner of the universe. On its way to us. And on its way *fast*.

And then, pinging me with an annoying alert that would see me pulled away from what was *truly* urgent, the symposium calendar reminder sounded. All I could do was force out a heavy sigh and request that the gang keep me in the loop and text me with any new developments, just before I scampered off.

Yet, the entire way, my mind couldn't help but draw a parallel from this new development… to the development I called my own. It couldn't be coincidence.

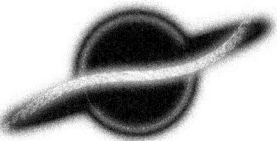

"The best thing about humanity is its technology. And the worst thing about humanity is… wait for it… its technology."

Everyone laughed, and the sound of it resounded throughout Turner Auditorium at UW. This was the beginning of the lecturer's closing statements, and he thought it was downright ingenious and right on the money. "Mankind is always in the pursuit of bigger, better, faster, cleaner. Anything ending with -er," he said.

"But I'd like to remind you," he continued, "of that classic movie from only thirty-four years ago, *Jurassic Park*. In it, one of the protagonists, Dr. Ian Malcolm, cautioned an overly ambitious British billionaire with these words." Everyone leaned in. I didn't. I'd already heard it, and my mind was elsewhere, frankly, hoping that Dina and Isaac were taking care of everything back in the lab.

"*Your scientists were so preoccupied with whether or not they* could *that they didn't stop to think if they* should," the lecturer breathed.

Again, everyone nodded. Frankly, that was the bottom line, right? Hubris. Overextending one's neck. Risky business. Thank goodness I never demonstrate such behavior. I knew my limits. I knew what worked and what didn't, and I knew where my ceiling was.

I already knew that I *could,* and I was convinced that I *should.* It wasn't a question of morality or ambiguity over any kind of ethics or responsibility. It was simply a question of *when.* I had seen Jurassic Park, sure. Gene splicing and dinosaurs. The stuff of fiction. That wasn't my thing. Interstellar phenomena and physics were my thing. What he was talking about was pop culture from a bygone era intruding upon modern progress, to be sure. Certainly, a notion to consider, of course, for most people.

But I'd already considered it, right? Dinosaurs and people are *not* the same thing. I admittedly rolled my eyes, sitting there, as he droned on and on with silly tripe and scare tactics. I think I may have even noticeably shook my head. He's talking about something sixty-five million years ago, and yet I had just laid eyes upon a potential Extinction Level Event in the making. God only knew how much time we might have left. That thing could intersect with Earth's orbit in five hundred years... or five weeks. We wouldn't know until Tidbinbilla confirmed it in a few hours.

That thing... man, it was on my mind during the entire symposium, and it was irritating to have to sit through knowing that Jensen and Farragut were seeing things that I wasn't. I would only be able to catch up with them once we were let out, but the text updates were coming in hard and fast, and it was difficult to focus.

With every fiber of my being and the fire of a thousand suns, I felt that I'd been given *Courier* for just such a time as this. Coincidence? A scientific impossibility. Nature abhors a vacuum. Checks and balances. The stars had aligned just so as to put this in my mind so as to be ready for whatever that thing was out there that was on its way to us. It was not chance; it was *destiny*. If that thing out there truly *was* a supermassive, then that meant my invention might prove timely beyond words.

But where would we go?

It was November 6th already, and I couldn't believe the year was nearly done. My deadline was coming up quickly, and it would take every ounce of me to fundraise and rally all the support that I could for *Courier 3.1*. I already had the tests to show everyone... now I just needed the chance to perform it on a live human subject, and I already had a volunteer.

Me.

"Hey, Currier," said a sharp voice, wrenching me out of my thoughts. I looked over. "Yeah?"

"We gonna get something to eat?"

I gawked at her, her head tilted down and her eyebrows up, awaiting my reply. Trapper was always eating. *Always.* I never understood how she could maintain her lithe figure if she was always stuffing her face. Her metabolism was the stuff of fiction. I laughed.

"Sure, Trapper, sure. Just let me grab my things," I said. "I can't stay long though; I've gotta get back to the lab. But I'll go with you to pick it up and I'll scarf it down on my way back."

"Suit yourself," she replied in a drab monotone.

Megan Trapper was three years my junior at UW, but she was a kindred intellect. Very saucy and a quick wit. She's always kept me focused and grounded. After all, I always needed to have a comeback at the ready should she try to one-up me.

"Yo quiero Taco Bell, Señor Dane."

"Fine."

"No sour cream for you, pudgy," she shot my way, glancing at my midsection. Oh! I forgot to mention she was brutally honest, too.

"Watch it, toothpick," I fired back absentmindedly, reading the latest from Dina while collecting my books and unconsciously sucking in my gut. For an undergrad, Megan Trapper was brazen beyond her tender age of twenty-seven.

"Oooh, *toothpick*," she jousted. "Clever. That one's new."

"Yeah well, you undergrads are getting a little too big for your britches. We have to keep you in your place. And I already used 'stick' twice I think. *Toothpick* will suffice for today." I grinned at her. "Oh, wait, what am I thinking? I can't have tacos," I said, remembering my GI issues.

"Why not?" she screeched in incredulity, gawking at me. "Oh, right. The… *problem*."

"Yep. Tummy troubles," I said. "Grumbling. Better play it safe and grab some Subway."

She smirked. "*You* play it safe with Subway. I'm grabbing tacos. Catch up with ya later," she said. She leapt over the balcony railing with her backpack firmly affixed over her shoulders, her red hair bouncing clumsily against her nondescript straps. "Toothpick in pursuit of dinner," she offered with a final grunt as she propelled herself over it, sprinting for the exit. I lugged myself over the railing too, panting hard and apologizing to the grad student next to me as he tried to make a clean exit himself. There were grads and undergrads all around in a sea of students, and Trapper's figure was growing tinier in the distance as I tried to wade through.

Trapper was aptly named. Here I was, trapped, while she was off again. I glanced down at my phone for the latest.

Telemetry confirmed, Dina typed. *It most definitely is a super-supermassive. And Dane? It's headed right for us.*

This just got worse. My stomach grumbled. Here came the burps, and I hadn't even eaten yet.

Dinner was over. The Subway was still rumbling in my tummy, and the sulfur burps were coming strong and fast now. It's amazing how fast they come. They're revolting, but that's what you get when your nerves are on fire, you know things people don't, and you've eaten too fast.

I know better than to eat too fast.

I texted Megan that I'd catch up with her tomorrow. I wasn't sure if I meant that. All I knew right now was that I needed to catch up with Isaac and Dina and assess current position. And then I had to get back to my apartment and keep working. Trapper protested firmly, desiring company in her unapologetically demanding tone with multiple exclamation marks.

I ignored her. She knew *Courier* was important and that I had to get back to it. She was the *only* one who knew about it beside myself.

Double-timing the University wasn't my intent. But ever since this passion enveloped me, I've wanted *Courier* more than anything in the world. Only two people knew about it, and I wasn't ready to launch any kind of Kickstarter yet; I just had *so* many high hopes for this thing. Aside from a play on my last name, it would be novel… revolutionary… mind-blowing… *life-altering.*

If *Courier 3.1* was truly capable of what I thought it was, it might be able to do exactly what we all needed, and I would be on the cusp of becoming a millionaire. Or billionaire? *Trillionaire??* Move over Jeff Bezos.

Courier 3.1 could deconstruct your atoms and reassemble them somewhere else. Quantum physics didn't grasp the gravity of teleportation. Not yet. And no one knew what it could do but me and Megan. I hadn't even told Dina and Isaac yet. I wasn't ready.

What I *was* ready for was for these accursed sulfur burps to end. Whatever was going on inside me needed to be deconstructed and reconstructed without the physical affliction and ailments. It was gastrointestinal, that much was certain, but beyond that, no one knew, and it seemed like no doctor *wanted* to put their finger on it.

Even worse than the burps was the acid reflux. The heartburn was terrible and unending.

Doctors weren't unanimous, and I'd had so many second opinions that there were now second opinions piggybacked upon second opinions, to multiple powers of second opinions beyond that.

None of them could uniformly pinpoint if it was lactose intolerance, irritable bowel syndrome, Crohn's, ulcerative colitis, gallstones, or God knows what else. I desperately loathed them for that. Every single doctor's appointment ended in irritation. Knowledge is power, right? They didn't know what it was, so I didn't have any power.

But the one area I *did* have power in? I could show them that I knew more than they did about something else. After all, what else are graduate studies for?

The one thing that I knew definitively was that I was going to be Patient Zero for *Courier 3.1*, and that was that. There was no other logical option. In good conscience, I couldn't send Megan Trapper through. *Courier 3.1* was mine, and it was revolutionary, and it would change everything. I had to go through myself first.

But, in the meanwhile, all of that would just have to wait. The docs said what they said, and all of them were 'fairly' certain that it was what they thought it was.

However, the docs might *not* be reading it right. I think they wanted to. But simply surrendering to their beliefs would be an act of defiance.

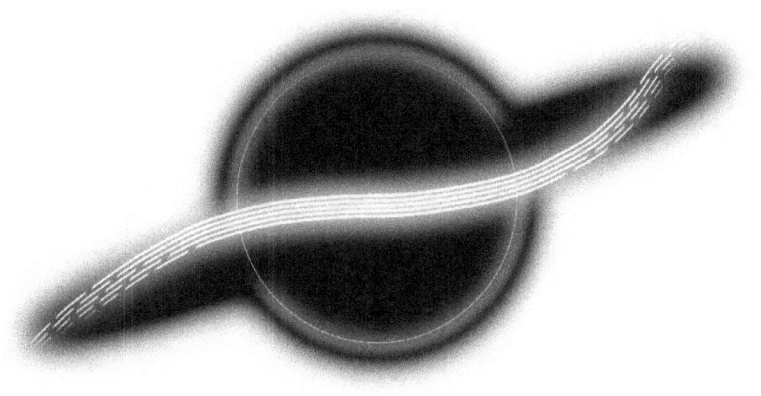

2 | Outgoing
November 6th, 2025

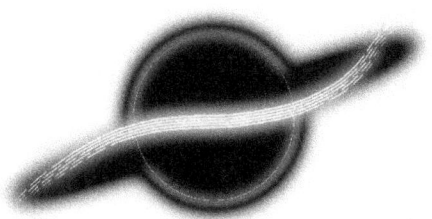

It was high time for a difficult conversation.

AARO head Doctor Ron Sikorsky was a young man stern beyond his years, supremely focused on the All-domain Anomaly Resolution Office's purpose to protect our skies and keep Earth safe. He partnered with planetary defense at the European Space Agency, but they had no love for him. His namesake was bound to the helicopter business as an industry leader, but that didn't mean that he himself was a leader. It was clear our dear Ronnie had his hands full already and didn't want to be bothered with any more – or any *new* – phenomena.

Sorry to ruin your day, Ronnie, I thought, *but there's incoming that you really might want to take a look at before it lands on your head.*

"You've triple-verified telemetry?" he asked Dina.

"Yes, sir, we have," she replied.

He just stared at the screen. "*Shhhit,*" he finally groaned. "DOD will have my head now that you've let this get this close to Earth, folks. I hope you're happy."

"Mr. Sikorsky, with all due respect," I began, "this 'thing' just literally appeared two days ago, verified by Mr. Farragut and Ms. Jensen. Look at the speed at which its traveling sir. This isn't a slow-moving traditionally-trackable blip, sir. It's moving at over one-tenth the speed of light. We've confirmed it."

By the look on his face, that defense meant nothing to him. He rubbed his hand through his hair feverishly and then blew out hot steam.

"Alright, keep me apprised. This is not good, folks. Anyone else running reciprocals and checking your readings?"

"Of course, sir," I said. "The typical ones: DSN, the NRAO VLAs, GEODDS, DSCOVR, and EHT," I rattled off, reading Dina's list from earlier that I had requested she update.

"Any idea on point of intersection?"

"Not until we have confirmed with Tidbinbilla in two hours."

"Who's your contact?"

"Henry St. James."

"Someone's gotta wake him. I don't care if he's sleeping. We need answers on this ASAP. Find someone to wake him."

"Roger that, will do," Dina replied.

Sikorsky's mouth closed and he just stared at us somberly through the screen. "This is an ELE, isn't it? Level with me."

I didn't know what to say. The truth would have to suffice. "Yessir, it is. It's bigger than TON 618, and it's growing, sir. We think two of them merged." He remained silent. "Once we get confirmation of its point of intersection, we'll know more then, but it's already drawing too near to us to just glance off. At some point trajectory confirms it'll wander into the Milky Way. That could be weeks or years, we don't know yet. But when that happens…," I trailed off intentionally. My thoughts went once again to *Courier 3.1,* its implications on the black hole, and vice versa.

He nodded grimly. At length he blinked and cleared his head. "Right. Well, get back to me once you've talked to Tidbinbilla."

I nodded back. Sikorsky switched off.

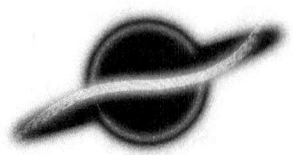

Dina and Isaac were to send me any and all updates. I awaited them eagerly. Sikorsky was not our preferred point of contact for the DOD, but he was all we had right now, and that was the top of our pecking order. He would brief the President soon.

All of our other contacts were buzzing.

So why was I so discontent? If everyone on a need-to-know basis was being brought into the fold, briefed on the potential cataclysm heading our way, why was my stomach grumbling so obstreperously? Shouldn't I be content now that the powers that be were on it? In a matter of time we would have a more definitive confirmation from Tidbinbilla and we'd know more concretely what we were dealing with. There was no sense in worrying.

So why was I worried, gnawing my fingers like a termite through a cedar two-by-four?

My half-eaten Subway sandwich lay beside me on a paper plate, un-gnawed. Paper plates were disposable; recyclable, and less work than doing dishes. I didn't mind the extra expense. Life is a picnic anyway, right?

Might not be in a few weeks, I thought to myself.

I stared ponderously at my glorious invention, downing a sip of water to chase yet another Tums tablet which I had ground into powder.

There they both were. Both chambers.

What was stopping me? Fear? Uncertainty? Didn't I have unquestioned and unqualified belief in *Courier 3.1*? Hadn't it proven itself already?

I looked at Macy. Her paws under her muzzle, those big, black, beautiful eyes stared up at me – that is to say, my *sandwich* – longingly. When she noticed me watching her, that tail began to wag once more.

It was the same tail. It had gone through. Those eyes were the same. That muzzle was the same. Same personality, same longing for human company, same everything. Her harness was five feet behind her draped over the recliner. That was the same too.

I watched her as she continued to wag. She had gone through, and emerged the same. She was biological, animate, and the exact same as she was before going through. She looked, felt, smelled and seemed identical. Even her bad dog breath persisted.

In fact, Macy even seemed improved in some ways. Her graying hairs were gone. Her eyes seemed clearer for a 12-year-old lab-hound-pointer mix. It was almost as if an idealized version of her was interpolated from the source chamber (whom I lovingly called *Nova*), and given form in the target chamber (endearingly dubbed *Ava*), but run through particle reorganization filters that saw fit to selectively remove any degenerative artifacts.

Nova read her, and Ava listened. Nova sent the data, and then Ava assimilated it, reassembling her on the other side, improved, without the gray. Ava could also be used as a relay unit, however, and could further send the signal elsewhere should there be sufficient equipment to receive it. For now, they were tied together, but they didn't need to be; Ava could be positioned halfway around the planet as long as there was sufficient Internet signal; all those 1's and 0's could definitely travel. For the moment, I was compelled to use everything as a LAN configuration to ensure an uninterrupted signal and minimize interference.

So what the heck was stopping me?

The bad breath.

That was it, for sure. I crunched another Tums.

If her bad breath persisted, that was a biological and organic byproduct of canine anatomy that was undesirable. Normal, yes, but still undesirable. Her plaque had not been removed from her teeth. Her left paw still had that strange protrusion. Those had *not* been fixed. So why was she no longer graying and had clearer eyes, but the rest was left uncorrected? Her white beard was now the black of youth.

Some things remained unchanged, and that meant that I would be taking a chance. A chance with my own safety… my own *life*. Could I do it? *Should* I do it? The line from Jurassic Park came back to me once more.

Your scientists were so preoccupied with whether or not they could *that they didn't stop to think if they* should.

I rubbed my face angrily, rolling my eyes. My right knee was bouncing nervously. How many times was I going to do this? To request volunteers and begin screening candidates would let the cat out of the bag, and my secret would be cooked… *and so would I.* My entire future would go up in flames.

No. It had to be *me*, and *only* me.

I stared down at Macy again, my thumbnail now gnawed down to the flesh. She wiggled once more.

"You're alright, aren't you, girl?" I asked her, my eyebrows clenched. "Aren't you? Come here." She instantly rose with ears laid back in happiness as she came to my left side, close to the side table with my Subway on it. Her eyes darted over to it and then back to me. Once more, to the table, and then back to me.

Those eyes of hers are so clear now…

That was it, wasn't it? She was seeing clearly. Was she improved mentally? Were the features that had been improved more internal only, and less aesthetic? Follicular regeneration from the inside out? Ocular nerves repaired and upgraded? Was she smarter even?

She seemed smarter.

I glanced over at Nova, and then slowly over at Ava, subconsciously fetching my sandwich from its plate. Macy's ears went up curiously as she watched my hand. I slowly brought it to her mouth and she took it without hesitation, as my eyes were drawn back to the chambers.

Six feet high and three feet wide, they resembled tiny sound booths, or those older phone booths or talk boxes, but more egglike, and with a DuroLast chrome reflective paneling inside and clean white 3M padding all around. The particle accelerators would be hard to explain to anyone. Cables were suspended parallel to the rear of the chambers in tight conduits mounted with symmetry. The main link conduit conjoined them together in inseparable harmony over a ten foot spread, running from Nova to Ava, and back to Nova for a mirror check once transfers were complete. They worked. They *really* worked, as long as they were kept sterile, dust-free, devoid of confusing particulates and vacuum-sealed. The polyurethane door seals and sweeps ensured a tight airless suction fit. Megan Trapper helped me put them both together.

Good thing I was a neat freak as well. That's why I got Macy; she didn't shed. Nova and Ava would say that they appreciated that, if they had been given AI voices.

The chambers were state of the art, and the UW didn't ask any questions about the requisition orders, nor had they ever sent any kind of auditor to check on the equipment. Keep things practical and don't overblow the budget, and they look the other way. After all, I was in a research lab, and we had funding. They had in this case. Thus, Nova and Ava were born.

It was rudimentary 3D printer firmware at first, and scanners re-coded and adapted to accommodate biological materials beyond the 1's and 0's that the old syntax was built upon. *CourierOS* operated on higher plains than that old stuff, interpreting biological and organic material as truly alive, requiring quantum levels of computation and analysis: higher spheres of thinking. As such, my power bill was astronomical each month. A small price to pay.

Then came the setbacks.

Neither Inky, Pinky, Blinky or Clyde made it. My zebra-tailed finches never knew what hit them, until they were inside out and spliced together inside Ava's receiving dish. That was awful. I couldn't keep birds long enough, and the pet stores were on to me, I feared. Next, Merry and Pippin went through, then, finally, Frodo and Sam.

Same thing. They were all chirpy and contented. They lived a cheerful, happy life on a stick, pecking at seeds one day, and then the next, fused together in an unholy abomination of matted feathers, tissue and intestines, their beaks ground to powder. Neither *Courier 1.0, 1.5, 1.8, 2, 2.6, 2.7, nor 2.9* could figure it out. By *2.7* I was getting close. Sent them through one at a time. But they were stillborn on the other side. They were intact, yes, but frozen in suspended animation: a haunting tribute to a life that was.

That's when I had the breakthrough: *Courier 3.0.* The computer needed to analyze the precise cellular makeup of zebra-tailed finches. Only then would it understand what a zebra-tailed finch was. Same with Macy. I had to sedate her and cut a sample of her tissue – after she went through it was completely healed – and fed it into biometric analysis tubes to get the precise makeup. Then it knew what a lab-hound-pointer was. It understood her hair coloration, her age, her cellular makeup… to a *T.* After that, I was able to simply draw blood and have it scanned in a spectrum analyzer. No more flesh samples. Macy – and I – were brave enough to send her through on 3.1. You should have seen my fingernails; they were gnawed to the bone. I sent two final finches through – Iron Man and Thor – and they made it. They made it! I returned them to the store. No one knew or would even suspect that they were identical facsimiles of their original selves.

So, the question remained: would I be a near-identical facsimile of my original self? Or would I be *me?*

I took another hard look at Macy. Damned if she wasn't absolutely herself. Not just her skin, her hair, her eyes, but *her very soul* – it was her. No doubt.

She wasn't outgoing fodder for the previous *Couriers*. She was here to stay.

There was only one way to find out if I would be here to stay. I had to go through.

Just… once I could eventually get past my own nervousness and fear. Those were standing in the way for one obvious reason: I wanted to live. But if that thing out there was coming to kill us, wasn't I just staving off the inevitable?

I sighed, resigned to wait. I had to get back to the lab anyway. Dina and Isaac were waiting.

I would go through. Just… not yet.

It was time for some definite consternation.

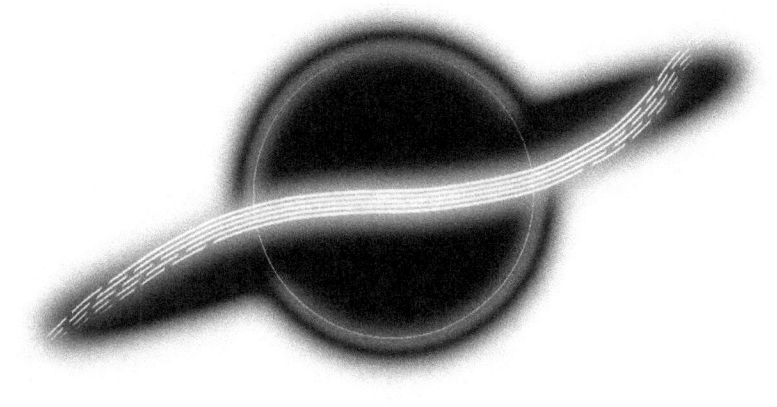

3 | Clarification
November 6th, 2025

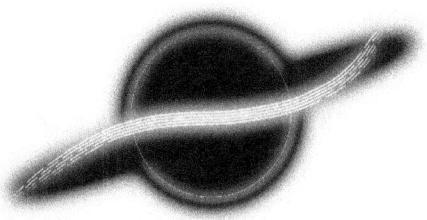

There was no disputing it now.

Redundancy checks were run, and, *unfortunately,* they matched. Henry St. James was reading it exactly as we were, and all doubt was dispelled. "I guess the only thing left to do now is name the bitch," Henry offered sardonically. "That Sheila's a killer and no mistake."

I had not really talked at length with St. James… ever. A heavyset and woolly bedouin who wandered from tech office to tech office, he very clearly filled up his off-hour pints with the strongest alcohol possible. Consequently, his health suffered for it, and his quality of life had deteriorated to filling his chair and staring numbly at screens. Indeed, the glass rim of his obviously full mug could be seen peeking out of the corner of the screen, and his beard glistened.

"You said it," I mumbled in response.

"Look at that light trail," he said with unsuppressed amazement. "She's speeding up too. Incrementally here, of course, but she's on her way."

"Best guess for intercept?" I asked him blandly.

"Us intercepting it or vice versa?" he jested.

I was in no mood for it. "You know what I mean, Henry."

He shook his head. "Well, based on this parabolic course and its current location, we're probably looking at late February, I'd say." He drained his mug noisily as if resigning himself to our inevitable extinction. "It's an ELE bomb, that's for certain."

February. As in only three months from now.

The wind was sucked right out of my sails. I honestly felt a gut punch, and my GI tract grumbled in response as I shook my head. "That's only three months away, Henry. Are you sure?"

Dina was tapping away at a keyboard, analyzing the screen and punching numbers into a predictive algorithm. She sighed and turned to me mournfully, nodding. I glanced at her and Isaac in painful resignation, and then turned back to the screen as I bowed my head.

"As certain of anything as I can be," he shrugged.

"What do you expect will happen at that point, Henry? Best chances of survival?" I asked him without a shred of optimism in my voice.

"Well," he replied, "I mean, they ripped me up out of my beautiful dream-filled sleep, but I'm seeing this clearly, and it's not pretty, Dane, it's really not. I can't see anything surviving this monstrosity. Something that massive has an intense gravity that nothing, not even light can escape it. All that matter, warping spacetime, the event horizon… light bending, modulating orbits of stars, it's going to pull our smaller planets into it, and then split the sun apart I reckon, and then after that, there'll be no place to hide, sure. I think one by one it's bound to pull everything in the bleedin' Milky Way into itself, and we're in for a pretty bumpy roller coaster ride when that happens. Ready your vomit bags." He shrugged again.

I don't know why I wasn't more filled with sadness. Three months was a long time – and it wasn't. Certainly, we'd feel some of the inescapable side-effects long before our planet began to hurtle toward it. In reality, we had probably only *two* months before things started to go sideways.

I just stared at the screen and sighed. "Alright. I need to brief Sikorsky and the AARO on this. DOD wants an update yesterday. Thanks, Henry."

"Sure, mate. She's a Sheila for sure. What do you reckon we call her?"

I motioned to my undergrad. "Well, Isaac discovered her, Henry. I think it's his call."

Isaac shrugged. He opened his mouth as if to say something, and then froze and closed it.

"Isaac?" Dina prodded.

He bowed his head. "I don't wanna name that thing. I'm *not* putting my name on something that's going to destroy our world."

I stared at Dina. He certainly didn't have to. I wouldn't want to name it either. Thankfully, Henry butted in.

"Well, I reckon we call her Norma."

I turned back to him. "Why Norma?"

"My first wife. Terrible woman. Evil to the core. Took me best mates and me dog, Dane. Good riddance." He held his mug up and snorted, drinking.

I could only offer him the feeblest of smiles. I shook my head dismissively. "Alright, Henry. We'll be in touch."

"God speed." He signed off, but not before he reached for his mug yet again.

God speed. The very phrase seemed repulsive. Where was God in this, and… *speed?* We would be going fast enough when the effects of that supermassive hit us.

Norma. I shook my head again. In all likelihood there wouldn't be much happening other than head-shaking over the remaining two to three months.

Earth, and the Milky Way, were about to be ripped apart by a supermassive black hole named Norma. Of course, the scientific community – and history – would come to refer to her differently in time, and she would most likely take on the moniker of *Farragut* due to Isaac's discovery. I wasn't sure how he would take that, having the galaxy's most lethal and mysterious force named after him.

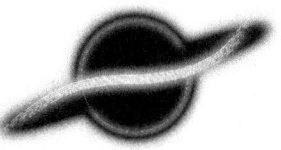

"And he is absolutely certain? Is there *any* way this could be a misread?"

It was late, Sikorsky's face was red, and his hair was disheveled. He was so close to the screen I could see into his pores, not that I wanted to. Secretary of Defense Erick Donze was also on the call. I turned to address him given that Sikorsky was obviously a wreck. Donze was stoic.

"We ran redundancy checks again. Telemetry was already verified, and these things don't lie. Senator, there's *always* a chance that something could alter its trajectory. Gravitational interactions with various cosmic bodies or turbulence within the galactic surface. Something could disrupt its central axis, its rotation, and it could become lopsided. Alternatively, you could have comets… uh… meteors, drifting space debris large enough to disrupt its orbit. There could be a number of things that could divert it, maybe?" I was reaching out, and I knew it. So did he.

"Spare me, Mr. Currier," he growled curtly. "All of these no doubt register a hair's breadth chance of actually happening. Their likelihood sounds infinitesimal based on what you've discovered already. Give me hope built on facts, not on prayers."

I took a deep breath and nodded. "Yessir."

"So, let us deal plainly in facts and not conjecture. That's what the President will want, and that's what the American people deserve."

"Will do, sir," I nodded again.

"Tidbinbilla is projecting late February for collision. And in your estimation we can expect the destructive effects before then?" the SecDef asked.

"Correct."

As if the weight of the realization finally descended upon her, Dina began to quietly cry next to me. I put a hand on her shoulder and squeezed, probably too hard.

"And when that happens, what can we expect?"

I took a deep breath. "Well, sir, it's not going to be pretty. The," -here I paused, trying to conjecture what a total cataclysm like this would be in such epic proportions- "well, the proximity would cause unpredictable gravitational seismic disruptions. Tides would surge, continents would crack, and time itself would seem to warp in localized pockets. The black hole would effectively warp gravity, causing catastrophic quakes and atmospheric collapse. It would be a slow-motion apocalypse as the planet is spaghettified over weeks."

"Spaghettified? Does that mean what I think it means?" Sikorsky butted in, pulling his hands from his face and furrowing his brow.

"Cut into ribbons," I said, mustering the simplest explanation I could come up with. It didn't help. Sikorsky buried his face back into his hands. "I think also you'd have some radiation effects that would subtly alter human consciousness, causing memories and identities to fragment, and possibly other effects."

Isaac shifted beside me. "Yessir, you'd have the expected hysteria and pandemonium. Mass suicides. Stock market crashing. People selling off possessions. Looting. Civil unrest. Violence. Revolts against government and shelters. Anarchy, unless we can all collectively get a grip."

The SecDef rolled his eyes.

"As Norma – that's what Tidbinbilla labeled it – drifts closer, we might see other planets or moons pass us in orbit, being pulled toward it and sucked in. The sun would also be shifting toward it. Everything is going to become scorching hot. Norma's pull would start to steal our sun's energy. The sun might actually fragment but, that superheated core would be exposed and send out solar flares."

The SecDef studied me. "And we'd have no choice but to follow our programmed orbital course and then we're doomed. Just like a zebra migrating across a river. The croc is coming."

"Uh, yessir, sure. Something like that," I said, thrown by the crude analogy, although it somewhat made sense. Norma the croc would latch onto us, pull us down and drown us in the void of outer space.

The SecDef sighed. "Well, you've given me a powerful lot to think about. I've got a meeting with the president in an hour. I'll brief him in full from what you've told me. I'd like both of you to remain on standby for any further questions or updates. Who discovered it, by the way?"

Isaac reluctantly raised his hand behind me.

"Well, son," Donze said, "I guess we owe you a debt of gratitude for pointing it out, no matter its position. Relax, Ronald," he said to Sikorsky, "I realize now that it wasn't on anybody's radar until recently, given its trajectory and speed. There was nothing anyone could have done."

He turned back to Isaac, Dina and I.

"Norma will be the end of us, plain and simple. But we can busy ourselves with how we map out the end of our days well enough. I'll be in touch."

I nodded and sighed. "Thank you, Mr. Secretary."

He nodded and switched off. Sikorsky did as well.

I turned back to my team and just stared at them in uncomfortable silence. Dina broke it. She collapsed in a heap over herself, burying her face in her hands and slumping in her chair.

And there, in the dark of that room, I thought briefly to everyone I could. My own eyes watered. Do I tell them about *Courier 3.1* now? Would it even lift their spirits one iota?

I shook my head. It probably wouldn't matter. Not one iota. Soon, *nothing* would matter. Even *matter* wouldn't matter anymore, soon.

Norma would end us.

There was no disputing that now.

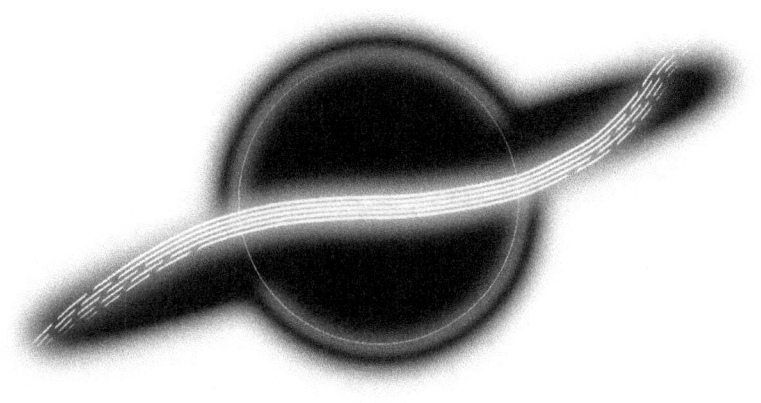

4 | News
November 7th, 2025

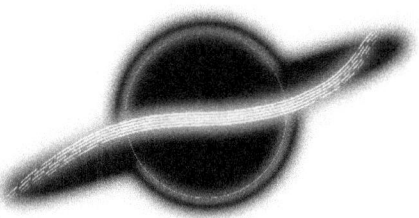

President Trump appeared before all of us.

"Here it is, here it is, quiet!" Isaac yelled.

We were all gathered together in droves before a giant screen. It was early. By now word had spread overnight, mainly by Dina, who simply couldn't contain her own grief and 'needed to talk to someone.' Several of our contemporaries, grads and undergrads, and various UW professors were now assembled down the hall from our lab, in UW Kane Hall. A tech had piped in the broadcast feed and we were now seated before it, waiting. There were dozens of us now in the know.

Many of them grasped just how bad it truly was, and how bad it truly was going to get.

I viciously chewed my nails, fighting back thoughts of *Courier 3.1* in the midst of all of this, and wondering how it would, or could, help us… or maybe just help me. The burps were coming, and my stomach was roiling.

The President.

There he was in the Oval Office, sitting at the Resolute Desk, flags flanking him representing nations and ideals that would soon be burnt to a crisp. I couldn't help but see the futility and eventual destruction of everything in… *everything.* Trump appeared drawn, sustained only by truckloads of information and caffeine.

"My fellow Americans," he began somberly, "good morning. I come to you today with some news."

News. An understatement of epic proportions.

"This morning, early, I was briefed on a development within our galaxy that has bearings on us all."

My mind was racing. This was not going to go down easily. People were going to freak out. Pandemonium would erupt in the streets. Civil unrest would consume us all, in every nation, unbridled and uncontrollable. Silence settled upon all of us, hanging on his every word. I glanced around the auditorium to try to gauge their tolerance levels.

"A few weeks ago, scientists at the University of Washington were alerted to a phenomenon drawing near to the Milky Way galaxy that was large: much too large to be some itinerant meteor, stray asteroid or cloud of wayward cosmic dust. They continued to monitor it, and have now confirmed that this object approaching our galaxy is, in fact," -here he paused, presumably perched on the fence of whether or not to deliver the news so decisively- "a black hole.

"Now, we've had black holes traversing the universe since the dawn of time, and some have come close to the Milky Way, continuing on their mysterious voyage. In fact, Sagittarius A, the closest one to us, lies at the galactic center of the Milky Way. It is what is known as a 'supermassive black hole,' near the border of the constellations Sagittarius and Scorpius, about 5.6 degrees south of the ecliptic, close to the Butterfly Cluster and Lambda Scorpii." He never spoke like this; he was clearly reading from a combination of notes and a teleprompter. His speed slowed and his diction was deliberately increased. "It was discovered in 1974 and has largely held a stationary position relative to our own orbit. It spans 26,000 light-years with a diameter of 32.2 million miles across. I give you those figures for comparison. Again, Sagittarius A is stationary."

Here it comes. I accidentally bit my fingertip instead of my nail, and hissed at the pain. Dina glanced at me.

"However, the one that was recently catalogued is mobile, and moving at over one-tenth the speed of light, averaging 21,300 miles per second. Its mass," he paused again, "is thirty-seven times the mass of Sagittarius A. Our scientists have run what are known as 'redundancy tests' to confirm mass, speed and heading, and agencies like DISCOVR, DSN and AARO have confirmed it."

He paused, taking a deep breath. "America, you're a smart collective of citizens. I assume you can already guess where I'm going with this, so let me be absolutely clear. It has now been confirmed that the trajectory of the black hole, which has been dubbed 'Norma' by the scientists who discovered it" -here I scoffed, as that wasn't technically true- "is unfortunately on a course that is set to intersect with Earth's orbit... in mid-to-late February of next year."

A collective gasp rose up all around us in the room. Someone screamed. My eyes flashed over, and a student was covering their face and bawling. They already guessed. The President wasn't being cryptic.

"Now, any one of a number of factors could potentially alter Norma's orbit, but at this point, it doesn't look likely, folks. Those factors include" -here he held a sheet of paper up below the screen and read off of bullet points- "galactic bodies and gravity, spatial turbulence, comets, meteors, asteroids with sufficient mass to pull it away from us. However, I've been assured that's highly unlikely. There is unfortunately nothing we can do to alter our own trajectory and push our planet beyond the collision path. Norma has a mass that will affect every single planet in our solar system, including our own sun, and those effects will be felt and observed even before late February of next year."

"Now," he said, releasing the papers he had been holding, and clasping his hands in front of him, "I realize this is not good news. Not good at all."

Again, understatement of the year, Mr. President.

"In simplest terms, what I am telling you today, is that, after all our pioneering research into Norma, where it's at, how big it is, how fast it is currently traveling, our scientists predict that we have a .005% chance of escaping this thing. It's very big." Trump shook his head. "Not good odds. Very, very bad. What that means for us is, most likely, sadly, the end of civilization as we know it. There is no escaping Norma. She will tear through our galaxy, sucking our planets – and our sun – into herself with destructive and irresistible magnetism that will effectively destroy our world. Life, as we know it on our beautiful planet Earth, will, sadly, end. This black hole is what is known as an 'ELE.' Extinction Level Event.

"None of us wants to see this happen, but after all research had been conducted and all ideas had been exhausted or proven futile, we must accept the inevitable if we are to bravely face our own demise. Our planet has survived comet and meteor strikes in its roughly six thousand years of existence, and we have outlasted them.

"But, sadly, Norma appears to be set to outlast us, and there is not much we can do about that. We must face this according to the power and maturity that is in each of us, and humbly accept that this is, unfortunately, the end. In three months, our beautiful planet will be no more, its citizens no more, this galaxy no more.

"What that means for all of you, all of us, myself included, from this point forward, is that I am implementing martial law. There will be no looting, no violence, no theft or advantage taken of our fellow citizens." He was reading again. "We will meet this thing together, bravely and with dignity, or we will not meet it at all. Those who cause discomfort or terror for our fellow man in the days leading up to Norma's intersection will be dealt with swiftly and severely. We are militarizing and mobilizing as we speak. Planet Earth will meet its doom," he said. His head drooped momentarily, and his eyes remained fixed on his desk. When he lifted his head once more, his eyes were shining. "Forgive me. I feel this too."

For a brief flicker of a moment, it felt choreographed; staged. Judgment passed through me – judgment over all of his business ventures that he was losing, his money, his fame, his power, and narcissistic bent, his self-proclaimed stature and opinion of himself. But whatever opinions I had formed of him, I had to put aside for the moment and trust that there was feeling behind those glistening eyes. We all stood to lose a lot here, not just money and power. All around me, people wept.

I choked up, and my chest spasmed. Dina leaned into me. Groans went up throughout the auditorium as the full weight of all of it – including seeing our President tear up – tore away our sense of hope.

"In partnership with the medical community, we are considering the best methods of psychological and medical help we can provide for all those who will, for obvious reasons, have difficulty facing such an inevitable scenario. In short order we will be providing updates from the United States Secretary of Health and Human Services, the CDC, the American Psychological Association, the National Institute of Mental Health, the National Register of Health Service Psychologists and anyone else who can provide hope, counseling, and measures of preparing for, and coping with, what is to come. Other countries will do the same as they see fit. We have a hard road ahead of us. All of us. However, as your

President, I am confident that we are very, very smart, and very, very capable. I believe in all those people that we have for so long entrusted our mental and emotional well-being to, that they will be able to help us see this event through."

Event? You mean the annihilation of our civilization? That event, Mr. President? I ruminated as my thoughts returned to pessimism and criticality.

Trump paused, and took a deep breath.

"The sad truth is that soon, our beloved planet will be no more, and for that reason I appeal to every one of you to *choose* to go out bravely. Admirably. With hope for the next life, and charity for your fellow man. Not with selfishness or acquisition, but with generosity and compassion, with malice toward none, and charity toward all," he finished, quoting Lincoln. He paused once more, sniffing. "That is all for now. Any updates we have will be provided as quickly as we can do so. God bless you all. God bless America. God bless Planet Earth. Thank you," he said with a clenched lip, and swiftly got up from his desk before the camera cut.

I felt a strange resolution surge through me. There truly was no way out.

The broadcast faded to a green background with the Presidential Seal.

The President was gone.

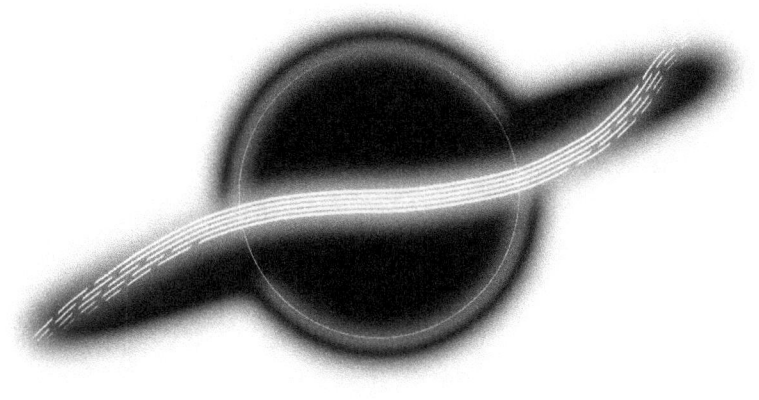

5 | Screw It
November 7th, 2025

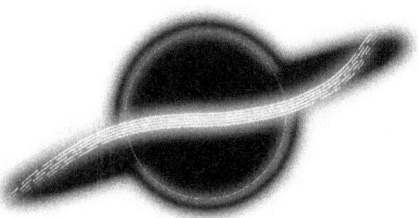

It was no use. We were doomed.

I couldn't resist it anymore. This *had* to be done. I returned to my apartment and slammed the door. Now, Macy and Jack Daniels were my company.

My dog looked fine; improved even. I stroked her ear with my left hand while I clutched my Jack Daniels bottle with my right. She watched me curiously, and I could swear she wanted a sip.

"Dogs have courage, right? You were brave enough to go through, right, Macy-girl?" I asked, staring her deep in the eyes. She blinked. "So, what's stopping me?"

Megan had been texting me incessantly since she heard the news. I told her I was stuck in meetings and would get back to her ASAP. She didn't sound convinced, and threatened to come over. But she didn't sound convincing either. My phone was blowing up. All kinds of people I'd never heard of or hadn't heard from in the longest time were now texting me with variations of *Is this for real?* And *PLEASE tell me they misread something and that we have a chance.* My mom was texting and calling every five minutes. She said dad was worried about me, and so was she. She pled with me to call her.

Yet, there I sat, naked as a jaybird on my sofa, drinking heartily. I wondered briefly, if I was drunk on this side, would I be drunk on the other? Would Nova tell Ava the exact content and volume of the alcohol coursing through my bloodstream? Surely it would read my BAC and interpret that correctly, re-inebriating me on the other side. I was shaking. This truly was the end, and, as they say, 'there's no time like the present.' So, what did I have to lose? A precious few more months? What futility and nonsense.

Screw it, I said to myself. I took one last ruffle of Macy's ear and gave her a kiss on the head, throwing the Jack Daniels bottle against the far wall. It shattered unceremoniously in the kitchen. Macy lifted her ears and then started, standing up with her tail between her legs, quickly ping-ponging her eyes from the kitchen and back to me.

"It's okay, baby girl," I assured her, scratching her scruff and hugging her tight. I could feel myself trembling.

Suddenly, I felt life within me, coursing through me as I stood up. A nervous stretch made itself known as my arms reached for the sky and my quads tensed. My hamstrings trembled, and I felt a frenetic shiver.

"Here goes nothing," I said to her, kissing her gently on the slight indentation at the bridge of her muzzle.

Nova was before me. I had already initiated the sequence just before I stripped. Now I tapped 'enter' and sent her into warmup mode. She wouldn't proceed until something was physically inside her and the door was locked. I had programmed her just so.

Suddenly, as I stood there, I was acutely aware of everything around me, almost in a trancelike séance, in touch with the universe. I held my hands out while Nova warmed up.

A police car wailed by outside. And another.

My phone buzzed again.

Someone down the street was hollering at someone else for God knows what minutiae that didn't even matter anymore.

The TV in my bedroom continued to drone on and on at low volume with CNN reports of this and that measure of hysteria that had erupted or unfolded somewhere.

A brief gust wafted the curtains to my left.

Macy laid down and rested her muzzle on her outstretched paws in front of her, still watching me.

Nova drew me in. The amber glow inside was beckoning, and the sterile walls were inviting. I felt eerily like I was re-enacting that scene from *The Fly*, but I learned well enough to ensure that the programming forbade multiple concurrent DNA strands; that was categorically disallowed so as to prevent any gene-splicing. I wanted my birds, my dog…

me… to emerge on the other side still ourselves. That was crucial. There was no room for mistakes.

This was it. I hovered before the door, holding onto the titanium seal, and was suddenly aware of how greasy the tips of my fingers felt from sweat. I recoiled them to myself, clenched my fists, and wiped my hands on my hips, taking an overlong breath of the last oxygen Me 1.0 would take. On the other side, in Ava, Me 2.0 would take his first newborn breath.

I took one last pensive glance back at Macy. She didn't lift her muzzle, but she wagged her tail at me. A meager smile was all I could muster.

Nova practically called to me with her silent siren-song. The soft hum of the laptop could be heard behind me. All sounds faded as I stepped inside, slowly, and closed the door behind me.

It was so different. This was not how I wanted it. I knew what was about to happen, but I never intended to be in here myself. At least, not this early, and not under pressure by virtue of a destructive force coming to rip our galaxy, our very planet, apart. That was not my aim; nothing I ever envisioned for myself. But as St. Francis of Assisi once said, *Start by doing what's necessary, then do what's possible; and suddenly you are doing the impossible.*

Macy was still wagging her tail at me through the glass. I put my hand up to it and pressed, reaching out for her. She stayed put. *Good girl,* I thought. My hand returned to my side, but the foggy condensation of my fingers remained imprinted on the glass.

Beyond, perched on my dinner table, I could see that the countdown had begun. Nova determined I was the only one in here. Me and my fear. I wondered what the DNA of fear would look like if it was catalogued. Probably multi-stranded with long, strangling tentacles.

15… 14…

I didn't want to pray… to think… to compute… to fear… to be strong… to hope. I just wanted to get it over with.

Macy watched me.

11…

10…

The floor pad was getting hotter as I stood there, standing fully erect and ready to face oblivion.

Or rebirth?

7...

6...

I shut my eyes. It helped to have them closed and not watch the timer... watching it would only serve to increase my anxiety. The transfer would take a minute for me, presumably, as it had for Macy. The floor grew hotter.

I opened my eyes for just a flicker, gazing outside to the world that was. Macy had gotten up and was standing right outside Nova, staring at me, wagging her tail, panting with whatever she was feeling.

I smiled at her, lovingly.

A strange sensation enveloped me. A placid peace. Warmth, pinprick stabs of light, and a faint buzzing sound that filled my ears and my soul. Then, a powerful, percussive force flashed around me, and for a split-second it felt like my skeletal structure collapsed. And then, finally...

Silence.

I can't explain it, but everything felt so tranquil. Calm, quiet, as if all the air had been sucked out of the universe and sound waves were disallowed. I could hear my own breathing increase in volume, almost deafening; and then, nothing. All sounds were stilled. It was almost as if I blinked, and then I felt weightless as if drifting in a void, bereft of any time constraints. All seemed to slow.

Something smelled like it was burning.

A texture registered under my feet suddenly, and there were wisps of foglike smoke circling around me. I could suddenly detect the floor beneath my feet as the smoke entrails were vacuumed out of the chamber.

But which chamber?

My vision became clearer, and the swirling fog around me abated. I didn't presume I could move yet. The vacuum continued to suck out the smoke.

And there, beyond the pane, was Macy. Just as she had been, staring at the chamber.

The chamber that I *had* been in. Over there. She wiggled her tail as I watched her, silently, quietly, caught between astonishment and fear, hardly daring to breathe. She was staring into Nova, waiting excitedly for me to return in the very chamber I had stepped in.

But the door to Ava opened, and the remaining wisps of condensation and haze floated out. Macy's head whipped over to me excitedly, and then she got up and pranced over to the entrance to the other chamber, ducking her head and sniffing curiously.

I stepped out. She sniffed my legs.

I bent down. She watched me, with those beautiful, improved eyes. I knew it was her.

And she knew it was me.

She spared no expense, rushing into my embrace and licking my chin, my lips, my hands. Whatever electrostatic residue resided on them, she was interested in, and it tickled her fancy as she indulged in it.

"Hey, girl, remember me?" I asked, looking at her and straining my neck at my apartment.

The gust still blew.

CNN still played.

The sirens still wailed.

The man still bellowed.

My phone buzzed.

I was changed, yet they remained the same. Everything was as it was.

I pressed my hands against myself, feeling all over, giving myself a cursory once-over as I examined each part of my body with fervor, inspecting and pressing, feeling and registering, wondering and confirming. Everything was where it had been before.

I was still me. At least, Macy thought so.

"What do you think, baby girl? Am I still me? You know me?" Macy sat and stared up at me, panting and wagging. I leaned down toward her and said the magic word.

"Shake!"

She lifted up her paw, knowing what to do, and her old yet restored limb met my young yet restored limb. We embraced, and I shook her gingerly and kissed her head once more.

And, as if to dispel all doubt, leaning over toward her, I felt suddenly dizzy. In fact, a little nauseous.

But this was different…

It wasn't nausea from just having been teleported, disassembled particle by particle and then reassembled ten feet away.

No.

This wasn't brought on by motion.

It was from Jack Daniels. The Nova chamber read me, disassembled me, and then Ava put me back together from the information she was given, including my exact state of inebriation. That information included half a bottle of Jack Daniels in my stomach and my blood stream.

A smile crept across my face as I faced the second inevitability of the day.

It works. It works! *IT WORKS!!*

A gargantuan and irrepressible laugh escaped my lungs, and I howled toward the ceiling, stretching out my arms, and whirling back around to stare lovingly upon Nova and Ava. *I was there,* I observed silently, staring at Nova, *and then I was there*, I celebrated, my eyes darting over to Ava. I turned back and kissed the Ava chamber.

It had worked.

It was inevitable that it should work. Now I just had to figure out what to do with it.

Before I could summon my thoughts, I whirled back around as my door burst open and there came Megan Trapper, beholding me in all the glory of my birthday suit – quite literally, as I had just been given birth to in a completely and wholly new way.

She started to say something, but stopped, gawking, gazing around in disbelief and shock.

"Stuck in meetings, huh? *Liar,*" she said accusingly, nearly out of breath, her eyes scanning my new body, helplessly gazing downward. Her eyes fixed on my torso.

I did the same, and then brought my eyes back up to meet her, still laughing. "Trust me, it's the same one," I managed through a chortle, unable to contain my joy.

Courier 3.1 had just worked. I had been teleported.

It had worked. We were onto something here.

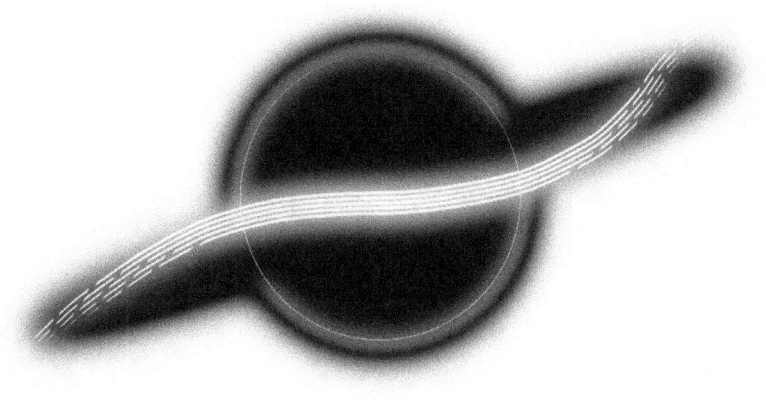

6 | Potentials
November 7th, 2025

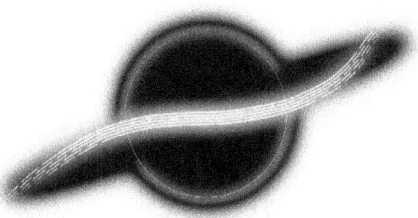

She just gawked at me, incredulous.

Megan asked me what I had been doing. However, it didn't take her long to put two and two together, so I came clean. Her jaw fell to the floor.

"I'm not kidding, Megs. Look at the logs," I said, pointing her over to my laptop. "Just, don't go into the kitchen; there's a broken bottle in there," I cautioned. "Don't worry, I have more. It's time to celebrate! It worked! Come here, Macy-girl!" Macy enthusiastically bounded up on the sofa next to me and gratefully allowed me to stroke her fur.

I had run to the bedroom and clothed myself, and now I was sitting on the sofa while she tapped away on my keyboard. I just stared at Nova and Ava, but I couldn't stop feeling uber-connected to my own skin, sensing everything: on the lookout for any signs of abnormality or change. I couldn't find anything. Even my stomach had stopped grumbling. It was a bizarre, almost cybernetic sort of computer diagnostic, a self-assessment that saw my mind whizzing through different sensors scanning my anatomy. Granted, joy and exhilaration were flooding through my core, so the readings were probably more optimistic than they would normally be; in the midst of such tragic news about Norma, I was riding high on the crest of this moment.

It appeared, in all likelihood, that Nova replicated the contents of my stomach, but it had idealized my organs and reintegrated them in a perfected state. Just like Macy. *So interesting,* I thought, while Megan tapped. I took another swig of my second bottle of JD.

"You *idiot*," she finally said to me. "Do you have any idea how foolhardy that was? We have three months left to live, Dane, and you wanna off yourself on the first day?"

"What do you mean?" I asked, incredulous. "Megan, it *worked!* Look at me!" I insisted. She didn't. "*Look at me,* Megs. I went through! Do I sound different, look different, act different?"

She reluctantly pulled her sour eyes away from my laptop and gave me a once-over up and down. "I've seen enough of Dane Currier today, if you know what I mean."

I shrugged and tilted my head.

"And…," she paused, "you're still pudgy." A faint trace of a vengeful smile stretched her lips.

I laughed, bolting up. "Megs, it's not an Ozempic machine, for crying out loud. It's a teleporter. It's me! I'm still me. Of *course* I'm going to still be pudgy, or," -here I threw my hands up helplessly- "*whatever* you think I am. Don't be such a negative Nellie, man!"

I just stood there in front of Ava, pondering the sheer implausibility of it all. But why not? I had programmed it to do exactly as it had just done. The system learned, and I'd gone through all those stages of testing that had led inexorably to this moment. I was riding high; pudgy or no, Negative Nellie or no.

Megan just shook her head. *Whatever, Toothpick,* I thought. Yet, as I took a swig of the Jack Daniels, I realized helplessly that that was what probably caused what little pudge she said I had. *Oh well, down the hatch*, I thought resignedly, unconcerned with her petty evaluations.

"This is actually pretty impressive, Dane," she relented. "I mean, all of these computations have you going way out there – somewhere – being put back together, and then you're back. When did you go?"

"Literally like twelve minutes ago!"

"And it was instantaneous?" she persisted.

"Nearly. I didn't notice any kind of time gap, but I forgot to check the time. It felt both instantaneous *and* interminable. I can't explain it."

She looked at me squarely. "How do you feel, really? I mean, anything different?"

I frowned. "Not that I- I mean, I don't really know of anything. Nothing's registered, not even the burps."

"They're gone?"

"Well, I mean, I haven't had any in the last twelve minutes, but it comes and goes. I need to give that more time. But nothing else feels out of the ordinary." My smile persisted.

She returned to my laptop. A siren went wailing by outside, briefly drawing her gaze. I mindlessly scratched the scruff of Macy's neck.

"Dane. Come here. Look."

I meandered over to her, taking another swig, feeling mighty proud of myself through all this.

"Look at this readout."

"What am I looking for?"

"The electrons. They're off the chart."

"So?"

"So? I mean *look at them!* They're still orbiting the atomic nuclei – at least that's what this is saying – but look!" She pointed at a figure in the column of metrics assessing my teleportation.

"The negative charge?"

She nodded. "Yep. Your protons look normal, but your electrons should be balanced from them so that you retain a neutral charge. Remember when we were assembling it? Programming *Courier* I mean." I nodded. "So, electrons are bound to the nucleus to different degrees. But look at these valence electrons, the outermost ones. There are maybe five, six times as many as there should be."

"So? What does that mean, Megs? In English please."

She sighed. "You're a dork. Listen to me! They're the least tightly bound. They form the chemical bonds with your atoms to create molecules and crystals. They facilitate chemical reactions through transfer or sharing between atoms. The inner ones make up the core. So what do the outer ones make up? The valence shell. By these valence readings, your shell's been reinforced to a quintuple degree. Even a sextuple one!"

"So I'm Iron Man now?"

"Not quite, pudgy. Move." She shoved past me and went over to investigate Ava, waving her hand around inside it and rubbing her fingers together. "Come here. You feel this?"

I followed her over to Ava and thrust my hand inside, waving it around as she was.

"Residual electrons. Reactive, but not bonding. Stranded. You can literally feel their presence."

"So Nova transferred me to Ava but gave me an extra dose of electron shells?"

"Maybe? I think so, yeah," she appealed to me. "That could have all kinds of bearings on what a lifeform can endure. That would explain the strengthening of Macy's eyes, her hair color, et cetera. Has she shown increased energy levels at all?"

"Yeah, I think so?"

"You should have been paying attention to this. You're really cavalier about it." She put her hands on her hips and glared.

"I'm not cavalier! I just needed to try whatever I could. But Megs, are you thinking what I think you're thinking?"

"I dunno. What am I thinking? Besides hungry."

"That if there's a surplus of electrons, it could mean increased travel fortitude, uh, resistance to gravitational forces, or speeds. Maybe even finding the ability to travel long distance, even…" I trailed off, hoping she would catch my drift.

She did, and her eyes widened. "…even away from earth. To another solar system."

"Hell, why not?" I squealed. "I mean, Ava doesn't *have* to receive the signal. She can act as a relay. She can bounce it. We programmed her with that capability. We've got signals floating out there residually from Internet transmissions sent via Wi-Fi that are just now reaching planets and solar systems light years from us, that were sent in the early 2000's, most likely. At the advent of the Internet."

"Yeah, but that's still a far cry from sending a human. Those are 1's and 0's, man. This doesn't just 'beam' you to wherever you want to go. You'd still need a receiver. You'd need *some* kind of receiver there."

I stopped, scratching my head. "I dunno, I feel like we're on to something here. Even if we were to find a way to transport some of us – perhaps a fraction of a colony of us – to some, some, I dunno, 'transition planet,' at least for a while, so that we could get a receiver somewhere habitable. It would be like leapfrogging through the galaxy, and it would take an incredible amount of time. They just discovered TOI-715b this year," I said, referencing the 'super-Earth' discovered this year that orbited a red star 137 light years away. It comprised a mass about 1.5 times as wide as Earth. It was in a conservative habitable zone. But there's no way we would get there in time, of course. Norma would destroy us in 3 months. "There have got to be other candidates out there too. What if," I thought, scrambling, "what if Neptune didn't get pulverized by Norma?"

"Neptune is *not* a habitable planet, Dane… not in the slightest. Extreme cold, windy, no oxygen, no solid surface mass."

"Okay, but, you know what I mean. If there was a planet in the Milky Way galaxy that was on the far orbit *away* from Norma, like, if Mars could sustain us – at least temporarily – we could use it as a jumping point. Uh, a staging ground or something like that."

She paused, considering, but ultimately shook her head. "I don't know. Nova and Ava are solar powered," she said, trailing off, lost in thought.

I nodded.

"Well, that's one thing that works for them. I'm actually thinking about one of our nearest star neighbors. Proxima Centauri b, in the Alpha Centauri system. Still, for the signal to travel through space, it would take about four light years for a signal to travel to PCb. That's a long time for a signal to be in suspended animation, shooting through the cosmos, one after the other. What if one got waylaid? What if we found a planet and somehow got a receiver there but people didn't clear out or, or, I don't know, *reintegrate* fast enough or something? You could risk gene splicing or inadvertent merging. It's a freakin' mess, man. I'm hungry." She sat down in a huff. "The signals could get there, but they would have to wait until we could actually get a *receiver* there. They'd be waiting for light years. I don't know if we'd have enough valence electrons to sustain us that long."

"I admit, it's a longshot. All of it is. But you just hit on something," I said.

"What?" she asked, confused.

"Proxima Centauri."

"What about it?"

"Well, if Proxima Centauri is the nearest star and only 4 light years away, wouldn't it be somewhat habitable?"

She furrowed her brows. "Maybe. PCb is an exoplanet with an M-type star. It's bigger than Earth, I know that. 1.3 times the size. 4.24 light years away I think the prof said last time he talked about it." Megan was enrolled in Bioscience and they did discuss planets and other systems beyond our own. That was an invaluable asset right about now. "PCb would be a lot closer than that other one you mentioned, TOI-715b, for sure."

"That could be a logical contender then!"

She thought to herself. "Maybe. If Norma doesn't rip right through it as well someday. With the way our luck is going, I wouldn't count on it."

"There's not much left to count on. I'm open to suggestions. The point being that we need to do some heavy thinking and less drinking," I said, putting down my Jack Daniels. Optimism was coursing through my veins, jockeying for position with the JD now. "There are all kinds of potential things we could do to make something happen. *Anything* happen," I urged. I sat back down on the couch, chewing my fingernails once more. They tasted strangely bitter.

"Yeah, but Dane," she countered, "that doesn't mean it would take us 4.24 years to get there. That's *light* years. That's if we could even travel at the speed of light. At our present speeds, our conventional poky spacecraft wouldn't get there for seventy *thousand* years, man." She paused, as if trying to recollect something deep in her memory.

"What is it?" I asked.

She held up a finger. "Hold on. There were flirtations documented by the American Nuclear Society with nuclear pulse propulsion in projects like Orion and Daedalus started in the 50's and 60's, but I don't know where they're at. I think Orion was abandoned due to the Nuclear Test Ban Treaty. I could look it up and see where it's at now? If someone were working on nuclear pulse propulsion? *Whoa.* That would *greatly* speed things up. We're talking under a century of travel to get there."

"Really?"

She nodded. "Mm-hmm. But that's *if* they're working on it. You'd have to find out. Dane, that could be the real thing that would work. Then the only questions are A, is PCb habitable, and B, could we sustain ourselves as data in transit? But we actually have a pretty freaking big saving grace here. Based on what we've seen of Norma, she's coming one way, and PCb is on the other side of us. That much I know. That means PCb isn't in line with Norma's projected path. That's *huge*, Dane. If the opposite were true, we wouldn't even be talking right now. We'd fly right into it. Thankfully, it's in the complete opposite direction."

I didn't reply; I was lost in thought, myself. Math was never my strong suit, and there was a lot to compute here.

Megs thought to herself again for a moment. "I mean, if you're fortified just going through Nova, then that might mean that you can withstand long-distance transit while in a disembodied state, I don't know. That's a long time in stasis. But it's a near scientific certainty that we'd survive stasis longer than we would in straight travel to PCb. We'd die on the way; we'd never make it in our current fragile flesh. But as data? We just might. It will take a lot of poring over all this data, Dane. A *lot* of poring over it. It might be doable, but none of us would ever be able to confirm it. A lot can happen in seventy thousand years… or even in a century. And we only have three months."

Silence consumed us. Outside, the world marched on in futility. More sirens. More people yelling.

Presently, Megan looked at me and stared hard.

"Hey. Ava is basically a receptacle," she said. "It didn't take us long to build her. We could build another one to hold *multiple* signals, couldn't we? I mean, as long as the power stayed on and it was protected, we could send *multiple* data streams to it and have it hold them indefinitely."

My eyes widened as I listened to her, considering. "Yeah? Yeah!" I snapped my thumbs. "We could load it up with drives and redundant arrays to store the signals until whatever craft carrying them reaches a habitation zone."

"We could program it to dispense the signal and reintegrate the teleportation subjects at preordained coordinates," she said, and a trace of a smile spread across her lips. "You could upgrade *Courier* to do that."

I smiled back.

"Ya think?" she asked me.

"I think! I really do. I mean, what other option do we have?"

She shook her head. "Beam me up, Scotty."

"Exactly. That's basically what they are. Who's to say that we didn't come up with the girls precisely for this scenario, Megs?"

"The girls?"

"Nova and Ava. Sorry, I refer to them that way collectively."

She nodded, and then frowned. "Dane?"

My eyebrows raised.

"I'm hungry." She stroked her stomach and frowned.

I shook my head and laughed. "Of course you are. I am too. Quieres Taco Bell?"

"Yo quiero."

"Well then let's go see what happened to my stomach, and see if I can take it. No grumbles yet."

"Sounds good," she said. "And Dane? You're not so pudgy. Maybe Ava improved you."

"We'll see, Megs. We'll see. You got your mace?"

"Yeah?" She looked at me confused. Megan could handle herself in a fight, but fights were undoubtedly brewing out there, no matter the caution that the President advised. She would need to be equipped.

"Good. I'll get my gun. There are crazies out there. And it's gonna get worse."

She smiled at me. "Then let's go get a bite to eat, get the stuff we need from the U, and start to make it better," she said with a grin.

I grinned back. "You said it. The universe has a way of balancing things out, Megs. Maybe this is our way out. Maybe this is the universe's way of keeping us in balance, by having you and me build these things, having them ready right when we needed them most? I'd like to believe it's more than just coincidence. More like destiny."

Macy, understanding nothing of this, just watched us and wagged endlessly, carefree and naïve.

But Trapper stared at me, hopeful.

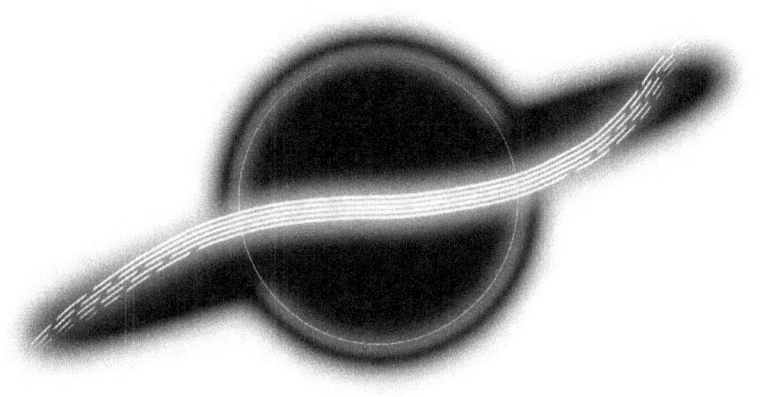

7 | Travel Plans
November 7th, 2025

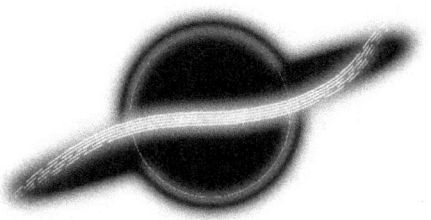

It was surreal out there.

People were calm, for the most part, and life was going on nearly as it always had been. A commentator known for psychiatry was on CNN speaking with the anchor about the emotional grappling with such an impending cataclysm, and what we as a species could handle.

We had pulled up and ordered. Megan bought my food, whispering me a quiet *my treat to congratulate you on Courier 3.1* my way. I thanked her, and then returned a quick call to my mom and dad to tell them that I was fine and catch up with them briefly. They were doing as good as could be expected, given the news. I texted Dina and Isaac as well. No news; no change in trajectory. They had also not heard from St. James, which they were a bit surprised about.

People ambled around us, some in a bit of a daze, most not talking, eyebrows folded downward in a bold and determined consternation as they sought to accept the news that blanketed our world with a stranglehold.

And now, Megan and I listened intently as we quietly munched on our Taco Bell. I grinned to myself as I noticed the distinct absence of any grumbles in my abdomen, and the burps were nowhere to be found, except on the coattails of a giant swig of Dr. Pepper.

"Coping with the inevitable," Dr. Brent Reinzell, MD, began, "is a fairly personal process, and there isn't really, empirically, a unique or singular ideal way to handle it. Some strategies can assist us with navigating challenges such as this, those challenges being either emotional or practical, such as group therapy, reading and assimilating information on black holes, because, as they say, *information is power*." He shrugged his shoulders. The anchor did the same. "And, when we have information, it better prepares us to understand the imminent threat, and to, thus, reconcile with it. It's crucial at this stage, for all of us, to truthfully acknowledge our feelings, seek out support from like-minded and affirming friends, family and the like, but, ultimately, the real trick is in focusing on what matters most, that being to acknowledge the gravity of the situation. To deny reality is pretty crippling in terms of advancing our personal health," Reinzell finished. "We have to seek an aurora out of our bleakness; a new beginning, if you will, even if that new beginning has an impending terminus."

Aurora. Didn't that mean beginning? *Nice try, Doc.* We're coming up on a most certain end.

My eyebrows flicked up as I looked away from the screen and back at Megan, who had nearly already finished her three soft tacos and two bean burritos with no onions. "Deny reality. Hmmph. No denying it now, eh?"

Trapper didn't answer me.

I looked around. "Look at everyone. Either they haven't heard, or they have and they don't care, or they realize caring is futile. You would think there would be something buzzing through the air other than apathy, wouldn't you?"

Megan looked around. "You totally missed the fourth conclusion," she said accusingly. "They *have* heard, and they've accepted it. I think that's why the shrink said that was the most important thing. I mean," -here she started to chuckle to herself- "where are we gonna go, huh? How you gonna outrun a supermassive black hole? Where are you even gonna go?"

The CNN broadcast, which included a panel of various other unnamed participants, concluded with a black screen and text encouraging those considering suicide to call the 988 Suicide and Crisis Lifeline, and then CNN cut to commercials.

I nodded in agreement. "But there's one thing that *they've* missed, right?"

Megan's eyes darted up to me briefly as she squeezed her last mild sauce packet into a waiting taco.

"They've missed *Courier 3.1,* Megs. I wonder what kind of shot of adrenaline it would send surging through them if they knew what we were potentially sitting on." I stared at her, beaming, awaiting her vote of confidence.

"Yeah," she said, nonchalantly, as a piece of taco fell from her lips. She wiped them. "But, Dane, first we have to get the materials right away and start building Number 3 – you have to figure out a name for it, by the way – and then we need to talk with someone about the logistics of making it all happen. Getting it to PCb. I mean, there's no easy way to make this happen. You can't line up a thousand naked people outside your door and ask them to patiently wait their turn to be zapped into data and then hurtled off into space."

Megan had a way of phrasing things with no BS. She was right. This would take some logistical planning, and it would be limited. A thousand? I wasn't even sure that that would be feasible. And she was also right – I needed to think of a name.

I just stared at her pensively, sipping my Dr. Pepper. "You're right. First things first, we get the requisition orders turned in, and obtain the equipment. We can start building tomorrow. Once we're confirmed that we have three working chambers, then I can maybe even talk with Donze. He would be a good-"

"Who? Donze who?"

"Sorry. Secretary of Defense Erick Donze. He's who Dina, Isaac and I linked up with when we confirmed Norma was a supermassive. We were initially talking with Doctor Ron Sikorsky with the AARO, but he's kind of a lame duck. No power. Nothing to really get things moving, and no mental fortitude to do it with. We'd have to go higher than that. I can talk with Donze and brief him on our thoughts. If Proxima Centauri b is-"

"Just call it PCb please, we only have three months, Dane. I age a little each time you try to say its name."

I chuckled. "Fine. But if PCb is in fact a contender, then we better start planning on that. I'm excited just thinking about it! What else do you know about it?"

She shook her head and clenched her lip briefly, gathering a steely breath. "Takes 11-ish days to complete an orbit around PC. Discovered three years ago, I think. PCc too; that was reported even earlier, but it's not confirmed to even be there anymore. Might be a dust belt. But as for PCb, might have a large core, supposedly water-rich. Last I heard they were still running sims on its physical properties, but it should be Earth-like with similar orbit but a faster development. I think the prof said that it is tidally locked though, so only one side would face the star. That means cold, cold, *cold,* forever on the dark side, baby. If it does lack an atmosphere, it could be as low as negative forty Celsius. But if it does – and scientists *think* it does – the temperature could range from negative twenties to high eighties. There might be cold traps due to atmospheric circulation though. It would be like living in either Antarctica or Mexico, depending on which side you're on.

"*But* – the downside is that Proxima Centauri is a red dwarf, and that means potential radiation and solar flares on the hot side. Red dwarf stars aren't exactly ideal, Dane. Those stellar flares can be a significant hazard for planets in their habitable zones. If it's tidally locked, we would just stay on the dark side, close to the terminator should we need to venture out into the heat for a while. Ya know, the twilight zone. We would need proper winter suits. All of us. But those flares can also affect their atmosphere.

"None of this is confirmed though," she ended. "Not much about it is confirmed at all. As of now it's just guesswork. PC is a much smaller star. Just a red dwarf with less than twenty percent of our Sun's energy."

"But it's way closer and more ideal than anything else catalogued, right?" I asked. "Right now, it sure sounds like our best shot. *Certainty* would be ideal, yes, as in, it could 'certainly' sustain life. But the only thing certain right now is that we're all going to die here."

"Yeah," she said, nonchalantly, with a thousand yard stare. "But you know what they're gonna do, right?"

Dina called me. I wasn't ready to pick up yet, so I silenced it. I stared at her blankly, confused. "No. What are *who* gonna do?"

"They're gonna handpick all the people they want to send. I mean, if *Courier 3.1* proves viable in that it can teleport somebody to a habitable system, they're gonna cherry pick the President, Donze will pick himself, probably you and your team since you guys discovered it, but it'll be government officials, top science dogs, agriculturists, agronomists, botanists, celebrities, artsy-fartsy snobs, all the top brass who could make a difference on a new planet."

"Well, maybe, but-"

"But nothing! They certainly wouldn't pick me. I'm a nobody who eats too much. I don't give a flip. No thanks. There wouldn't be any Taco Bell there anyway."

"You don't mean that. Come on," I chuckled as Dina called again. Still not ready. *Decline.* "Megs, if Norma doesn't kill us, Taco Bell eventually will. You can't survive on that stuff."

She shrugged her shoulders as my phone buzzed one more time. I rolled my eyes and looked down.

Dane. Pick up your phone! St. James is dead. Killed himself an hour ago.

I swallowed hard. I didn't know the man well, and the briefing that we just had with this Tidbinbilla contact of ours did little more than to confirm what we had already dreaded. Nonetheless, it felt like the sliding of tiny pebbles that eventually morphs into an avalanche. He had no doubt felt he had nothing left to live for, and that Norma would take the rest. So? He caved, and decided to take it back. I couldn't blame him, but my heart went out to him.

Trapper noticed my reaction. "What is it?"

"Megs, I gotta go. It's late anyway. I gotta get to the lab. I'll put in the requisition order tonight. Wanna meet me back at my pad tomorrow and we'll start building her?"

She nodded. "Only if you tell me who *her* is," she said, and sipped her drink, eyes glued to me.

I thought for a second. Didn't take long. The answer was right there.

"How about Aurora?"

Trapper squinted. "Nova, Ava, and Aurora. Yeah. Works for me."

I nodded. "OK. See you at the dock in a few hours and we'll start loading up the equipment. If you want to head out there ASAP and get started, I'll meet you. Just need to check in at the lab first and talk with the mucky mucks."

She gave me a thumbs up, and I was off, texting Dina as I scurried to the lab. It seemed like we were in a race against time itself.

Things were getting real here.

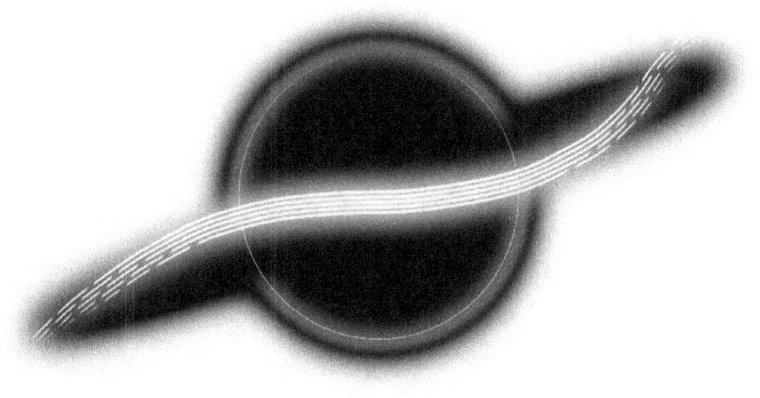

8 | Pandemonium
November 7th, 2025

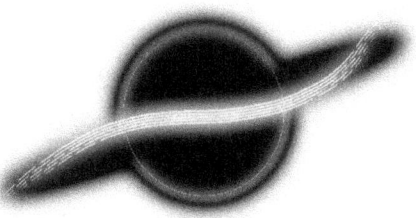

The mob was alive and well.

I heard the commotion before I even got there.

The scene was truly one of havoc and unbridled chaos. Students and professors were rioting against other faculty and security, and someone had evidently spearheaded an attempt to steal parts and supplies for makeshift bomb shelters. Apparently this was happening on a widespread basis at factories, universities, and various retail establishments that provided any kind of fabricated goods. As if constructing a makeshift bomb shelter would provide even a modicum of safety.

I tried to keep to the periphery, but even as I did so, placards were flying, Molotov cocktails were hurled in every direction, cars were overturned, and fires had broken out. Riot police were already on the scene, and someone with a loudspeaker was trying to pacify the crowds and reason with them. The whole scene was the furthest thing from what the president urged, and now my conversation with Trapper seemed so alien. *Some* people were resigned to their fate, yes, but not all. *Not all.* There were always going to be dissenters, and those that would go down in a blaze of glory, even if going down meant straight to their own deaths *and* taking others with them. As if impending death wasn't enough; they had to pull the whole house down on their head as well as others.'

A part of me felt supercharged as I whizzed through them, as if I was running on better batteries after having emerged safely from Ava. Just bordering on invulnerability, it was as if I felt somehow untouchable. Indeed, I hadn't had any sulfur burps since my teleportation, and that was a sign. I still *felt* like me, I still *thought* like me, I still *walked* like me, and all of that conveyed a sense of superior survivability.

Nonetheless, chaos erupted around me. *That didn't take long,* I thought morbidly to myself. *Bring on the anarchy.*

I carefully threaded my way, and narrowly missed some debris tossed in my direction as I hurried past the line of riot police, flashing my graduate school badge. I needed to get what these rioters were after… *before they did.*

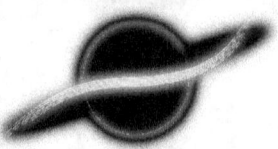

Dina melted into my arms the moment I saw her. She and Isaac were perched at their computers, still monitoring.

"How you two holding up?" I asked.

Dina shrugged, pulling away from me, as I rubbed her back. Isaac didn't even answer me, engrossed in metrics and data pouring from the monitors.

"That good, huh?"

"Predictive matrix doesn't suggest any deviation at all, Dane. This thing's gonna eat us. Maybe St. James had the right idea," he muttered, glumly.

"Hey, none of that, Isaac. We're at an ellipsis, not a period. Not yet. Chin up, okay?"

Isaac Farragut had always been one of those hard-to-read people who simply went about his business with the unflagging dedication of a servomotor. He just did what he knew he needed to do, and there was never any protest. But I'll be darned if there wasn't the slightest bit of complaint peeking through now. He was abysmal just like the rest of us. A few more punctuations of dreariness, and he might be out there hurling Molotov's like the rest of them.

Dina was another matter. She wore her heart on her sleeve, and here she was again, beside herself with sadness.

"Have you guys talked to your parents? Loved ones?" I posed. "Anyone you can reach out to locally and spend time with?"

"Doing what?" Isaac muttered again.

"I don't know… keeping you from un-aliving yourself like St. James," I said, playfully slugging him in the shoulder. Neither responded any further. I guessed now was the time.

"Why are you so peppy? Too many Cheerios in your bowl of sugar?" Isaac poked, eyeing me curiously.

"Listen," I started, pulling up a chair and sitting, facing them. "Can you guys take a quick break? I need to fill you in on something."

Isaac audibly rolled his eyes and rotated in his chair, abandoning his post. Dina had already plopped down sadly in her chair, resting her head in one palm on the desk. She stared at me mournfully. Isaac joined her with a bleak regard.

"Guys, listen. We're not done just yet. Not yet. We still have some time. I'm not going to tell you what to do with yours, but I want to finally clue you in to what I've been doing with mine. I haven't had the license to share it with anyone except a partner until now, but we've been doing some thinking, experimenting, and planning. And… building."

"Who's 'we'?" Dina asked.

"Me and Megan Trapper. Undergrad. Astronomy major, with bioscience and tech understudies," I replied.

"Oh, right. I've seen you with her at functions. Never met her though," she answered.

"She's pretty smart. She's been helping me with something… *novel.*"

"Is this what you've been so secretive about for the past few months?" Isaac asked.

"What do you mean?" I asked, curious.

"Dude. You're constantly stealing out of here, you can't wait to leave, and you never hang out with us anymore. You've been living under a rock since May. We already knew you were working on something, ahem, *novel,*" he said, sporting air quotes and donning a face of mockery.

Dina grinned at his retort.

"Yeah. Okay, you got me. Yes, this is it. I'm not sure you're going to believe me when I tell you, but, yes, I've been – *we've* been, Megan and I – working on something that just might," -here I paused, wanting to be careful not to convey false hope or overly raise their expectations- "might present an alternate scenario."

"How do you mean?" Isaac asked, leaning in. "Don't tease me."

I stared at him and took a deep breath. My eyes ventured over to Dina briefly as well, and there was a twinkle of curiosity in hers.

"It's hard to explain – and it's not. I've been working on a… *teleportation* system." I paused to let it sink in. "It's something novel, yes, but I didn't know just how novel until now."

"A teleportation system? You're kidding me. Have we all crossed over into fiction, now, Dane?" Dina mumbled.

"It's not fiction, Dina. It's not." Someone further back in the lab knocked over a beaker, or something, and I quickly jerked my head to assess whether someone was eaves-dropping. I leaned closer in to them, scooting my chair right next to Dina's.

"Guys, it works. *It works,*" I emphasized.

"How do you know?" Isaac quickly barked.

"Because it does, Isaac. I've sent things through. It wasn't perfect, but it does what it needs to. It's been perfected. And it… *perfects* the subjects that have gone through. I've sent three subjects through. The first were my birds. They didn't make it. But then I sent Macy through."

"Your dog?" Dina asked incredulously. "You put your poor dog through there?"

"Oh, she's not poor anymore. It actually *improved* her, Dina. She's younger, she's more agile, her eyes aren't cloudy anymore, she's got the vigor of a two-year-old pup."

"You said three subjects," Isaac persisted. "What was the third?"

I stared at him intently. "Not what. *Who.*"

It took him a second, but he understood. "No way. You? You went through?"

I nodded.

"What?" Dina exclaimed. "*You* went through? Do you have any idea how foolhardy that was?" She looked me up and down as if to assess whether I was still myself.

"I agree. It was. But I had enough proof. Enough proof and no time left to prove anything else," I defended. "I *had* to. You guys remember the burps?"

"Yeah. Disgusting." Isaac mock-gagged.

"They're gone?" Dina asked.

I nodded back to her. "So far. And I feel younger, I feel more energetic. It's like, somehow, Nova and Ava – those are what I named the teleporters…"

"Nice," Isaac interrupted, nonchalantly.

"…somehow, when I went through, Nova sent the data to Ava, and Ava disregarded anything in a less-than-ideal state, categorically 'upgrading' it. She did the same thing with me that she did with Macy. I had a big dinner and my stomach isn't even grumbling. And no burps."

They both looked me up and down.

"Guys, it's *me*," I said. "I swear to you."

"Even if I believed you, I'd have to go see it for myself," Dina said. "Anyway, what does all this have to do with your 'alternate scenario'?"

I took a deep breath. "It's hard to explain, but Megan and I have been spit-balling over some ideas. And now I need to talk with Defense Secretary Donze again, because we just might have a way through this."

"No friggin' way," Isaac muttered, his eyes squinting. He straightened up. I had been addressing Dina and hadn't noticed him. His jaw was dropped. "Teleportation *off* Planet Earth? That's what you're doing, isn't it?!"

I nodded. "Shhh, keep your voice down. We're not sure yet, and we haven't quite locked in how we would do it."

"To where? When? How?" Isaac asked, suddenly empowered with hope and raising his voice despite my pleas for him to keep it quiet. "When?!" he asked again, nearly yelling it.

"Isaac! Please. We don't have enough cookies for everybody," I said, laughing. "I don't know yet. We're discussing Proxima Centauri b. Sorry, I have to say 'PCb,' or Megan will hit me. It's in the next closest system."

"What?" he cried with a sneer. "That's over 4 light years away! We need something in our *own* system!"

I shook my head. "No way. Norma will swallow everything up here. Which is why we're focusing on PCb in the interim," I paused, "*or* figure out a way to get a receiving chamber there *before* Norma hits us. It's the closest."

"How can you do that?" Dina asked.

"That's exactly what I need to ask the SecDef about. And I want you on that call. Then, you can come over and see for yourself."

They eyed me curiously. The muffled sounds of the rioters persisted outside.

I smiled at them. "I call it *Courier 3.1*."

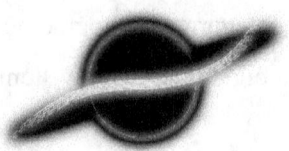

"Let me see if I understand this cockamamie plan in entirety," Donze said, his forehead propped by a tense hand. "You want us to jettison one of your receiving chambers toward this, this, 'Proxima Centauri b' planet – which I note, by the way, that you have provided *zero* guarantees of its ability to sustain life – and hope to God that it receives multiple human signals preserved inside one of your thingies back here on earth, wait patiently for seventy thousand years, while praying to whatever patron saint is in charge of hairbrained celestial travel plans that we actually *survive* this comedy of errors. Then, we get there, just in time for you to zap fry us back into a state of animation, and we all get to walk around like lethargic, nude sleep zombies in some new Garden of Eden. Do I understand your crackhead batshit crazy strategy correctly, Mr. Currier?"

"Mister Secretary, I realize it sounds far-fetched-"

"*Sounds* far-fetched!" he bellowed.

"Sir," I persisted, "believe me, if we had a better way, I would be presenting that. This is the best we can come up with, and I believe that what I've developed may have just come for such a time as this," I defended. "If you have a better option, sir, with all due respect, I'd genuinely love to hear it."

He just squinted at me stoically over Zoom. The time drug on interminably while we waited for his verdict.

I could feel the heat of Dina and Isaac repeatedly glancing back at me while Donze and I faced off.

The Secretary of Defense finally lurched his forehead away from his hand and pulled back from the screen. "What the hell. We *don't* have any better ideas. Our days are numbered and we're all dead men anyway. The President's son has fallen apart, which affects the President, and the rest of us now have to figure out what we're going to do."

This was news to us. Something must have happened; some emotional distress must have befallen the White House on the coattails of Norma.

"I'm sorry to hear it, sir."

"Well, you would be too if your future daughter-in-law killed herself."

I tilted my head, and then glanced at Dina and Isaac. "I'm sorry, sir?"

Donze paused. "Oh, of course. You wouldn't have heard yet. She put a gun through her mouth two hours ago. Couldn't take the Norma news. She was set to be married to Barron early next year." His brow furrowed, and he wiped his hands through the air as if to clear the slate. "Let's not talk about this right now, folks. We have, I think, more pressing things to attend to."

That makes two. St. James and the President's daughter-in-law. How tragic, I thought to myself.

"Yessir," I replied. "I'm sorry, sir."

"Hey, it's not *my* daughter-in-law," he said, dismissively and rather heartlessly, studying his notes on the desk in front of him. "Now, please explain to me in the simplest terms how this would work."

I cleared my throat. "Well, Mr. Secretary, my *Courier 3.1* chambers are called Nova and Ava. They're already operational. I've already gone through myself, sir. What you see before you is Dane Currier 2.0, if I can say that. I can have myself checked out by medical but I don't have any anomalies, any sickness, any extra limbs, lapsed memory, cognitive issues… nothing. We need to build a third, however. One of the teleportation chambers, Ava, can act as a relay extender, in order to jump the signals through time and space. We would send the subjects – as many as we can – through Nova. They get housed only temporarily in Ava, who then springboards the signals to another waiting chamber either here or even already on PCb. We just have to get this third one – we're calling her Aurora – there somehow. My colleague is in the process of securing the parts for the third chamber now."

"What do you need from us?" he asked briskly.

I gathered my breath. "Well, sir, what do you know about nuclear pulse propulsion?"

The SecDef just stared right through me. "Why do you ask that?" he finally asked, with a clear note of suspicion, which both encouraged me and confirmed that he knew about it.

"Well, sir, that seventy thousand years gets reduced to under a hundred years if we can mobilize it. Sir," I replied, "if the government has access to any tech or engineers who have any knowledge of the subject, it would greatly expedite our passage."

He continued to numbly regard me, a blank slate concealing dubious lines of thought scrolling behind his eyes. "Greatly – expedite – our – passage," he enunciated. "You mean to this other star."

"Yessir," I answered, and then I read him clearly. "Someone is still working on it, aren't they? Is that why you're looking at me that way? Has someone been working on it all along? Sir, I'm telling you that would *exponentially* increase our chances of survival."

"Hold your horses, Mr. Currier. I'm going to ask. There is someone, but this has been top-secret highest-priority government-clearance-only work, and there are considerations that need to be taken into account before I can divulge that or connect the two of you."

"Such as?"

"Is the fact that it's top-secret not enough, Currier?" he growled. "The short answer is *yes*, I can put you in touch with a team led by someone who can help you. The long answer is that the work they've been doing is classified; it was never supposed to be public knowledge."

"Understood," I replied. "Well, Mr. Secretary, time is running out. If we're going to start working on this and get our other chamber out there, we need to start talking *yesterday*."

The same cold disregard, the same icy standoffish bureaucratic red-tape-face. I couldn't imagine what lines he thought he might be crossing when our world was about to be stripped to ribbons and here we were talking about a potential way off this rock.

"What's your direct phone number, Mr. Currier?" he asked me. "I'll need to make some calls and get back to you."

I gave it to him, and he switched off, thanking us for our time. That was nice, at least.

I turned to Dina and Isaac. "Well?" I asked them.

"Seems impractical and a long shot," Isaac muttered. "But if you've already got these things working and you're still you," -here he stuck a finger and poked it into my chest to ensure I wasn't an apparition; I smiled as he sighed in relief- "then we're with you."

I put a hand on his shoulder. "I appreciate it. I'm sorry I couldn't tell you both. I didn't want it getting out. But you can see how timely it is." I watched them, and then got an idea. "Hey, you guys wanna try it?"

Isaac slowly brought his eyes over to Dina, eyebrows up. She smiled back at him.

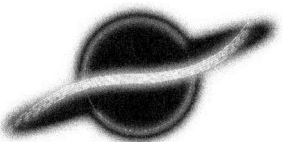

"That's Nova, and that's Ava," I said, pointing at them. "Pretty sexy, eh?"

Isaac had been sitting on the couch as soon as he had come in, loving all over Macy, adoring her and cooing to her, affirming to me that she was beautiful. I didn't know he was such a dog person. Now, he bounded up, removed his coat and strode toward them, examining Ava's exterior. Macy followed him and sniffed him curiously. "Wicked. What are they made of?" he asked, not taking his eyes off of them.

"Oh, DuroLast, 3M, insulated aluminum conduit, polyurethane, plastic, resin, and a partridge in a pear tree," I said. "I promise it's not atoms just holding hands."

"Insane," he said.

Dina was already inside Nova, feeling around and slowly revolving as her eyes took in the belly of the chamber around her. She closed the door, and her voice was muffled. "Tight seal! Vacuum?"

I nodded.

"No particle leakage. That's probably important," she observed.

"Well, I wouldn't want anyone appearing on the other side and missing something trivial, like, say, their brain."

She stifled a slight giggle. "Sure."

I looked back over at Isaac. "What do you think, Farragut? Pretty impressive, eh?"

"You went through this?" he asked me.

"Of course. Somebody had to try it. I wasn't going to let one of you go in case it decided to send you through with your right forearm poking out of your left nostril and your left knee where your right ear should be."

"You put your left knee in, and you shake it all about," he offered in a sing-song.

"Hokey pokey, sure enough," I said, grinning.

"And how do you facilitate the transfer?"

"Right here, buddy. *Courier 3.1.* Right on my laptop. Coded it myself."

"*You* did?" Dina asked, emerging from Nova.

"Well, I got some app and coding help from Kabat in computer science," I shrugged. "Man, did I have to give him the runaround in terms of why I was asking him the questions I was asking him for specific lines of code."

Dina was leaning over all my equipment. "And how did you tell it to recognize and understand you?"

"This," I said, pointing to the scanner. It was a small microwave-sized device off to the side of my laptop, with a simple USB-C interface. "I literally had to get a skin sample from Macy, same with me, and allow it to scan us and understand, on a cellular level, what we were made of."

"That's amazing," she said. "I could have told Nova what you were made of, easily enough."

"Yeah, but 'piss and vinegar' wouldn't have really sent the right message. She would have sent me into Ava's chamber as a toilet and a plastic jug," I smirked. "She needed to know precise details."

They studied both chambers, silently, reverently, with an earnest amount of hope swirling around them.

"You feel the same as before?" Farragut asked me.

I nodded. They remained quiet for a while after that.

"This is it, gang," I offered. "This is what I've been working on with Megan Trapper. If this works, we just might have a way out."

Isaac didn't waste any time. He quickly threw his backpack onto the couch, slipped off his shoes, and then strode over to Nova. "I wanna try it."

"Not so fast, buddy. Wait!" I exclaimed.

"What?" he asked, turning back around.

"You gotta go nude, remember?"

He rolled his eyes. "Fine. Look away, perverts," he growled, fidgeting for his belt.

"Hold up!" I said. "Nova needs to 'know you,' first, Isaac. Come here. Watch out, Macy girl." Macy had been sniffing Isaac's feet, but she now jumped out of the way.

He came to my little table with the laptop and the scanner. I fired everything up, and then reached into a small container where Trapper and I had deposited a few small medical lancets. "Give me your finger." He did so, and I poked it and took his blood sample, inserting it onto a slide from another container next to the lancets.

The scanner whirred. I quickly created a new profile in *Courier 3.1* for him. "What's your middle name, Isaac?"

"Cray."

"Cray? Like the big old computers? Wow. OK." I typed in *Farragut, Isaac Cray*. Gave it his general parameters and let the scanner do the rest. We waited for it to beep and Isaac's profile to be populated with data.

Isaac gasped as the screen lit up with his DNA profile. "So now you have a biological profile on me?"

"Yep. Okay, buddy, take it off."

"Look away!"

We did so. Isaac stepped into Nova, after having removed his clothes and placed them just outside the door to Ava. The lock on Nova clicked. I didn't wait for him to tell me when, whirling back around and moving to my laptop. He was inside cupping himself with a sheepish grin.

"Knock it off, Dina!" he exclaimed, muffled.

I glanced over at her. She was giggling and covering her face.

"Okay, you ready, buddy?" I looked back at him. He nodded.

"Here we go. Ten seconds." I programmed the countdown, and then let *Courier 3.1* do its thing.

The countdown seemed shorter than it actually was. In ten short seconds, Nova lit up blindingly just as it had when I had watched Macy and the birds and everything else go through. Shortly thereafter, Ava answered with a flash, and the inside swirled with foggy trails of wisp. A hand presently reached down to the door handle and unlocked it.

Isaac stepped out, fully nude, and fully himself. His face was plastered with a gigantic grin signifying absolute approval with zero shame. Macy went up to him and sniffed him, wagging her tail. He immediately bent down and stroked her. "Hey, Macy! It's me! Remember me?" She wagged and rubbed against his legs as he bent over and scratched her sides affectionately.

"Don't forget you're naked, buddy," I said to him.

He laughed and checked himself over. "Whoa! Are you serious? I don't even care! How do I look? It's me! Can you tell it's me?" He whirled around us.

"Uh, yep, still you, and still naked," Dina said. I chortled.

"Right!" he exclaimed, and then whipped down to the ground to fetch his clothes and get dressed, speaking frenetically as he did so. "That was insane! I mean, hot, and not hot – it felt like I was spinning down into this, this vortex, but it was like an arc, or like, no! Not an arc, but like of, like a parabola, ya know? In a weird, staticky way... but like, no pain! It felt like an hour or something. How long was I gone? That was *so* weird! Like a rush of pinpricks and crazy spots swimming in front of my eyes, and more colors than I could count. *How long?!*" He spoke with a spastic energy, unable to contain his amazement.

"You broke Isaac, Dane. He talks now. Send him back through," Dina joked, turning to me.

"No, no," Isaac protested, finishing up dressing. "Isaac.exe is very much functional and operating within parameters. Whoo! That was crazy! Can I see what it says?"

"Sure, take a look," I said, pointing him to the screen.

All he could mutter repeatedly was *Wow...* as he examined metrics of his position, polarity, electrons, protons, neutrons, space-time position, axis, mass, relative position in Ava to Nova, and all sorts of dizzying details that would be Greek to the layman. "It was nearly instantaneous, wasn't it? I swear I was in there close on an hour."

I looked at Dina. "Well, that's two down. Your turn, Dina!"

She shook her head. "No. No. Not just yet. I mean, I know I'm gonna have to if this is our way out, but... not yet, okay?" She nervously backed away from us. Out there, where pandemonium was breaking out in pockets, she was trying to reconcile with the pandemonium inside her own heart. I understood. Was this really a chance? Could it actually save us? She needed to be sure.

"Dina, serious, you gotta do it! I feel great! I'm still me! Right?" Isaac asked, turning to face me.

I nodded. "You're still you, buddy. But just… give her time. No rush."

Isaac snickered to himself, looking back and forth between the two of us, and then shook his head crazily and laughed heartily. "Unbelievable. That was wild. Put me on the next flight to Proxima Centauri *b!*" he exclaimed.

Dina turned to him. "Well, that's just it, right? It's not exactly a guaranteed flight, is it? Who's to say we'll even be included on the manifest?" she asked doubtfully.

I shrugged. "No, there's no way we'd be left out. Isaac, you discovered the damned thing. Dina, you're on that team. And I developed *Courier 3.1*. We're *going,* guys. All three of us. No way around it. I'll pull the plugs and format the laptop first."

Dina sneered. "Well, I'm not holding my breath. You know how the government works. Just listen to Donze! We're dead in less than 3 months – let's be honest, it won't take the full three – and even still, the United States Government is playing hard-to-get with their top-secret bullshit. Everything should be on the table now. *Everything.* If I sound mad, it's because I am. I believe *Courier 3.1* works, Dane. I do. I just saw Isaac teleport. It just never ceases to amaze me, the audacity of the holdouts." She crossed her arms as she spoke, increasing in speed and volume as she went. Something obviously nagged at her from the past, or some other issue. She was more heated than I had ever seen her. "Somebody said it in an old movie somewhere, I can't remember where exactly, but they said, 'scientists have always been pawns of the military.' It's so aggravatingly true!"

"Dina, what is it?" I asked.

"Nothing, I, *nothing*," she said, waving me away. "It's just stupid. This whole thing is stupid and so… final," she finished, with some heat. "I just… mark my words, Dane, they know now. They *know*. I wouldn't leave this place if I were you."

I tilted my head. "What do you mean?"

"Your apartment! I wouldn't leave it." Isaac straightened up, watching her quizzically. "You know what they'll do," she said. "You'll come home, and these won't be here. I guarantee it."

We both just watched her. I cast a quick glance to Isaac, and his eyes mirrored the sobering potentiality of what she was suggesting. Dina always struck me as a bit of a naysayer, a checks-and-balances sort of woman, opinionated to the point of devil's advocate, whereas Isaac was just a pessimistic mumbler – until the past five minutes, that is. What was coming from her now was deep-rooted suspicion that had its origins that certainly preceded our own friendship.

"You think they'll come in here and appropriate all of this now that it's on Donze's radar?" Isaac asked, but it was delivered more like a statement of certainty rather than a query.

She nodded. "'Appropriate'? That's not the word, Isaac. 'Steal' is the word!"

"There are many more self-important people in this world than the three of us. Norma is on her way. If there's now a chance that those people can be saved by the hair of their chinny-chin-chin while the rest of us burn up, and they can start their own new colony somewhere else without all the crazy rest of the planet? They'll take it. You heard Donze, Dane. *Cockamamie plan. Crackhead batshit crazy strategy.* Those aren't just words. Now he knows it works, watch him pivot and see the potential escape plan that he's privy to now. He'll endorse it like there's no tomorrow, and he'll take all of it and say it was the government's idea. Watch."

I suddenly thought of my gun, and the need to be armed. Was I just being reactive? Was Dina? Would Macy bark enough to wake us up and alert us, if we were sleeping?

"So, what do I do?" I asked her, throwing my arms up in helplessness. I wasn't ready to be deflated yet; to be deprived of my optimism, but she was, I felt, raising a valid concern.

"Yeah, what does he do, Dina?" Isaac supported.

Her eyes were wells of suspicion and fear. "I'm saying you'd be a fool to leave this place. Couple'a black Suburbans come rollin' up one day, park right outside your apartment, right? A bunch of them bust in with overwhelming numbers, hit you and Megan Trapper with chloroform, and make off with Nova, Ava, Aurora, your laptop, your scanner, all of it. You wake up and have *nothing*. I've seen it before, Dane."

"When?"

Dina sighed, and she crossed her arms. "My dad," she said, glumly. "He had a cold fusion plan that might have actually worked. He taught at Syracuse. Everything was fine, he was making progress on it, and somebody – he never found out who – spilled the beans to some government ne'er-do-wells. He was actually really close to getting funded! He was so optimistic. So full of joy. No. One day he comes home. Everything ransacked. Papers littered everywhere. All his research, *all* of it. Gone! He and his lab were on the trail of being the first to replicate it since the Pons-Fleischmann experiment in 1989. All of them signed an NDA. It didn't hold. Someone blabbed! And then," she trailed off with another labored sigh, "it was all over. That could have put us all through college and taken care of us for life."

Dina sat down hard on the couch.

"I didn't know that, Dina. I'm sorry."

"Me neither. I'm sorry, too," Isaac mumbled, reverting to his quiet self once more.

She shrugged. "History repeats itself. It always does. My dad used to always quote Ecclesiastes. *What has been will be again, what has been done will be done again; there is nothing new under the sun.* It's true."

"Well, there's one new thing at least. Norma. Never destroyed Earth before. That's new," I offered in a weak attempt at humor. It didn't work. She just stared at the floor.

"Hey," I said, correcting my approach, "I'm sorry about your dad. I truly am. I didn't know that. It makes sense that you're scared. We'll be careful, okay? I'll tell Megan the same thing. We won't leave."

I looked at Isaac, and a grin crept over my face. "I don't think we'll really want to, anyway, given what we have to do, and what we're on the verge of. Hell, I can survive on pizza and Mountain Dew until the cows come home. So can Megan. She's getting some of the equipment as we speak. Requisitions."

Dina raised her eyes to meet mine. "Just be careful, Dane. That's all I'm saying. Be careful. This is important. It could be a way out. I don't want what happened to my dad to happen to you."

I didn't say anything in response. I just stared at Macy for a moment, lying on her pillow in the corner of the living room, eyeing us curiously. She registered me scanning her and began to wag.

All I could do was nod and appreciate Dina's warning. But the cold reality was that I was now more than a little skittish in my heart. Would the CIA and a bunch of hired guns burst in here and take what I've worked so hard for? Would they, in good conscience, steal what was mine, my breakthrough development, everything I've strived to achieve with *Courier 3.1?*

My heart told me she wasn't barking up the wrong tree. My heart told me her cynicism was well-founded.

"I'll be careful. I promise."

Dina's eyes finally dropped, and then moved over to Isaac. "Alright. I'll go through later. But I gotta get something to eat first. Isaac, wanna come with me?"

Isaac nodded. "Yeah. This new body needs some fresh air after *this* talk." He grinned at me. "Sorry, Macy, gotta go! Be good!" He pointed sternly at her, mockingly.

"You're staying here, right, Dane?" Dina asked.

"After *that* conversation? Definitely," I said, shaking my head. "Not hungry. I'm gonna go over some schematics in re-configuring Ava as a relay for when we get Aurora setup. Norma won't wait. You guys wanna get what you get and bring it back here, that works. Megan should be here in a while."

"Okay," Dina said, and they were off, out into the pandemonium and the fray.

"Be careful out there," I cautioned. "I mean it."

I locked the door behind them, and surveyed the room. There was a lot here, and a lot riding on it.

Like hell I was going to let some government cronies waltz in and make off with my girls. *Over my dead body... or yours,* I thought, coldly.

I went for my gun, checked it to make sure it was loaded, and put it in my back pocket. Now I was armed. No one would get *Courier 3.1* or my chambers without a fight.

After all, the government was still alive and well.

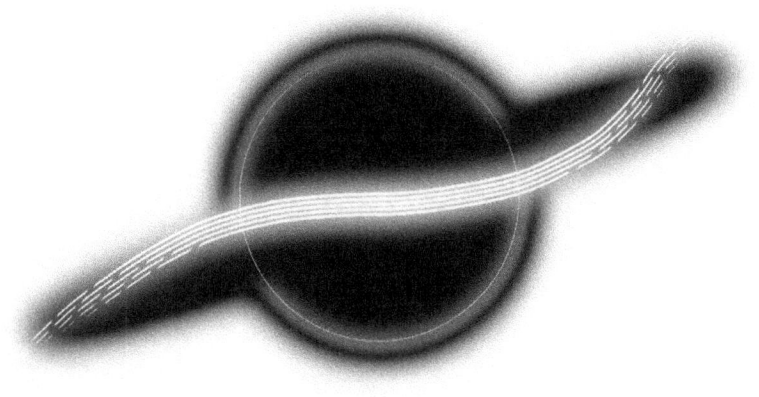

9 | Construction
November 8th, 2025

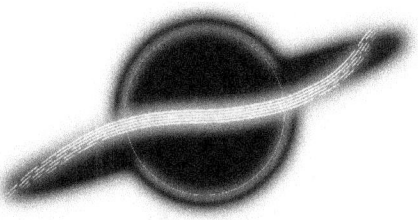

It was early, and we needed a break.

Trapper had returned; she finally got to meet Dina and Isaac, and vice versa.

Quickly, Megan devoured the rest of her food while she regaled everyone with stories of pandemonium and chaos, insanity and dread slowly creeping through the streets and waylaying as many poor souls as it could devour. The end was coming, and charlatans already stood out on the sidewalks with sandwich boards preaching of hellfire and damnation, crypto and comfort animals. People were starting to dot the streets everywhere, hawking various wares which attested to their own measures of belief in dubious forms of security.

The four of us bantered briefly about the end of the world, but that was that. We had work to do.

We all set to work, feverishly commiserating by the light of a dozen dazzlingly bright floor lamps. That was critical, because the schematics demanded that each part fit precisely, and we had to manually cut some pieces out on my 3D printer in order to make them all fit together. There couldn't be any breach in the chamber, though the inside would be filled and coated to create an impenetrable seal against leakage, and would then be thoroughly scanned and analyzed by *Courier 3.1* to ensure stability.

Through all of our work, Macy made her rounds and ensured that she received plenty of scruffs of her fur. Isaac was always the most affectionate with her. He really adored my dog, and she ate it all up.

At one point there was some kind of explosion a few blocks from us, and answering sirens. Macy yelped and stood erect, facing the door. I could only imagine what civil unrest might be unfolding. CNN was quietly droning on in the background, and we were trying not to give it any added focus. We knew the stakes.

The truth was that we had *Aurora* to build, and Norma wouldn't wait. *Funny,* I thought – all these girls getting ready to fight, three against one. We'd see how my girls would fare in the upcoming fracas against the certain supermassive heading our way.

Everyone had eaten, but, strangely, I wasn't really all that hungry. I also hadn't had a single sulfur burp since going through Nova, and I told them as much. Isaac was fascinated by that, and I could tell by the look in his eyes that he was running his own self-assessment, determining what previous flaws had been upgraded in himself to near perfected status: even *purged* from his new form.

We had a job to do, and we couldn't waste any time putting Aurora together. Patterned nearly identically as a baseline to Ava, she would be the relay receiver, and she is who would make the long journey out to Proxima Centauri b. But Aurora would be different.

For the first time, we were all sitting there brimming with hope. All of us. We knocked heads together, we slaved over the schematics and what the final blueprints would look like, and we knew what else we needed. Megan was bossy; no one cared. I think Isaac really appreciated her assertive personality because it bordered on snide aggression, though I caught occasional smile-heavy glances he gave toward Dina, and wondered if there was something there.

Megan, however, was putting everyone in their place. After all, she was the geek who knew how to take my vision and manifest it into plastic and resin through my 3D printer. I was the visionary; she was the wizard. We followed her lead and slaved away on ensuring that it would work.

The modifications that we were making to her would see expansion banks on her inner hull, between the inside chamber and the outer frame, in which we would insert SATA drives and redundant RAID arrays protected by ferromagnetic metals such as iron, copper and nickel in the outer plating. This would shield her from electromagnetic interference, radio frequency noise, magnetic radiation and the like. We also had conductive fabric layers to reinforce the shielding, and we were painting the outsides with conductive paints over the metal plating to create electromagnetic barriers. We also had to account for solar arrays to power her batteries for the long flight should she have to be jettisoned from whatever nuclear propulsion spacecraft we might get our hands on. That would be the contingency plan. As the spacecraft drew near to PCb, it would need to invert and drop her to the ground safely somehow, or all that human-data could be compromised.

In the middle of our commiseration and planning, my phone buzzed. I stopped everyone and showed them my phone. SecDef Donze texted me – it read, simply: *We have a green light. I'll be in touch. Let me know what you need, and tell no one. I mean it. –Erick Donze.*

That was it. That's what we needed to hear.

Two comforts emerged from that text. One, that nuclear propulsion *was* in fact still being tested and that we'd have access to the technology to transport Aurora to PCb. Thus, my suspicion was confirmed. It stood to reason – why abandon something so revolutionary when you can work on it in secret and emerge as the industry leader when the technology is actually called for? This seems to have been the *modus operandi* for the US Government for far too long. Maybe now it would be just in time to actually be useful for something other than bravado and self-aggrandizement.

And two, that we might just be left alone while doing so. No hired thugs to pull the wool out from under us. At least, that's what I was crossing my fingers for.

Time would tell.

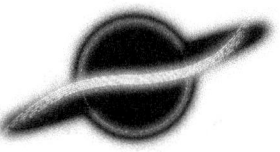

We were all napping in the middle of the day when another explosion sounded.

Macy jumped up and barked repeatedly at the window, then retreated, growling.

The building rocked suddenly, and there was a whooshing sound out on the street. I leapt to my feet. The others jumped up in a panic as well: Dina and Megan in my bedroom, Isaac and I out in the living room. Dina's hair was sticking straight up like a cat.

There's nothing worse than being jerked out of REM sleep. I remember that from my practicums… some of our biology studies required deep studies on REM and being 'dug in like a tick.' It's the most unpleasant thing to be yanked out of. My eyes were wide with alarm as I went to the window.

I had just missed a group of jeeps and cars barreling down Pacific Street, smashing other cars out of their way in their race to evade their pursuers. My eyes flashed back up the street they had just come. There, rolling noisily toward them, was a tank. A United States military tank, of all things! Right here in the middle of Seattle, pushing its way through. And there was another one! And another! A caravan of the iron maidens was rolling its way down the street.

Macy began growling vigorously, bristling.

"Holy sh-" a voice muttered beside me. It was Isaac, peering through the blinds to my left. I stared at him wide-eyed for a moment in alarm, and then returned my gaze.

"Dina, turn on the news!" I cried. "Macy, quiet!"

My dog put her tail between her legs and crept off, licking her lips nervously.

I glanced back up the street. Whatever unrest those fleeing in the jeeps had caused, it was enough to warrant a blast from a *tank*. The Fishery Science Building was in flames. That was nearly right across Pacific from us, slightly to the west.

I wondered what was going on in there… who the jeeps belonged to… or what they had done. Had they stolen something? Killed someone? Too many questions for a bleary, tired mind. Was this the beginning of unbridled anarchy? Would we be facing this every day?

The tanks rolled on down Pacific and were lost to view. I don't even remember what was said between Isaac and I, or the ladies, or any of us. All I remember is pouring myself back into my bed in an exhausted stupor, my heart racing at first, and then quietly slowing to a dull sludge.

Macy jumped up onto the couch with me and folded herself into a tight ball.

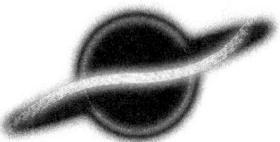

Trapper awoke first, gently nudging me on the shoulder. "Dane. Wake up, Dane. Dane!" Well, it *seemed* gentle at first.

"What? *What?*" I asked, blinking stupidly and trying to stow my irritation at the sudden urgency on her part.

"Time to get up, pudgy. Aurora's calling."

Macy jumped off of me as I stuck a knuckle into my eye and peeled out some gunk. A wicked yawn escaped me as I glanced around. The others were still passed out. I could see Dina at the end of the hall on my bed, and Isaac was face down on the couch, dirty socks protruding from a blanket loosely covering him that Dina must have covered him with before passing out again herself.

I glanced at the clock. 3:53 pm. *We certainly won't save the world working these hours,* I thought.

"Anything new with those tanks and jeeps?"

She shook her head and plopped down at the table, staring into my laptop. She picked up a piece of cold pizza next to her and began gnawing on it. "I'm just looking at these in your system. Where does your OS display the redundancies to mirror teleportation integrity?"

I stifled a giggle. "I love it when you talk *data* to me."

She sneered.

I couldn't get up yet, still stretching. "Are you on the main screen?"

"Yep."

"Hit Command F5. That's the main pulldown menu. Go under 'Arrays' and then down to 'Analyze.' You'll see the teleportation subject history. Isaac will be the last one, yesterday afternoon, somewhere around there." I yawned again, trembling slightly. A hunger welled up inside me – I was famished.

"Amazing," she said. "Everything is a one-to-one ratio. I wonder what would happen if something was not quite mirroring up. Would Ava send the subject back to Nova?"

"Yes. But it would happen before anything got sent. It enters a holding state where the handshake is made, and if it's not identical, the signal gets sent back to Nova."

She frowned, and looked at me. "Ava rejects it?"

I nodded to her, yawning again through my fist.

"That could be a huge problem on the receiving end."

My turn to frown, confused.

"Well, what happens if for some reason the transfers are rejected entirely? Would they compile and fuse back in Nova?" she asked.

"Ew. That doesn't sound healthy. I wouldn't want to reappear with Isaac's stinky feet coming out of my face," I joked, standing up and walking toward the kitchen to brew some coffee. I grabbed a jerky treat from the puppy cookie jar and tossed it to Macy. "But no, I modified that last night during our assembly, given what we're planning on doing. *Courier 3.1* has been updated. They don't reform, they're sent back to a holding pattern, essentially."

"So, the code for each DNA profile gets resuspended until called for once more?"

"Yep."

I craned my neck, working out a kink.

"Hmm. Well that sounds necessary," she ended, and then fell silent.

"Yeah, that's what happened with nearly every original attempt. It happened with Macy as well before I figured out what was happening. I had to program in some lines of code for recall."

Macy heard her name and started wagging.

"Got it," Trapper replied.

I inserted a Gloria Jean's butter toffee coffee K-Cup in the machine and hit 'brew.'

"Uh, *Daaane*?" Megan droned, slowly.

Her curious tone of voice and drawn-out beckoning of me caused me to turn and face her.

"What's this?" she asked, almost accusingly.

"What's what?"

"You said the last one was Isaac yesterday afternoon."

"Yeah, I did. He went through."

"Come here."

My brow furrowed as I strode over to her. Prescience ate at me; I almost knew what she was going to say before she said it.

"Then what's this transfer profile at 4:03 am?"

I leaned over her and studied the monitor. My jaw dropped.

It wasn't Isaac.

The mass suggested a smaller subject. Human biological DNA, certainly, but slighter build and far less dense, muscularly.

And female.

"It wasn't me," Trapper defended. She and I gawked at each other in amazement and then scurried to the bedroom, gazing down upon the figure lying there.

"Dina?" She stirred slightly but didn't acknowledge me. "Dina, wake up." My undergrad mumbled some incoherent response, and then slowly shifted her head to look at us staring down upon her. "You went through!"

She blinked in confusion for a moment, and then smiled and slowly nodded through a yawn.

"Yeah, I did."

"Did you really?" Trapper asked her. "How do you feel?" Megan and I both looked her up and down. I knelt down beside her bed, well, *my* bed.

"Fine. Headache, but only because of lack of sleep," she breathed through another yawn, slowly sitting up and staring at the floor. Dina ran her hands through her hair and tousled them into place. "Because someone woke me up too early." She mock-glared at us.

"It's four in the afternoon. Nice try. Time to get up, my friend," I said, sitting down next to her. "Seriously, why'd you do it? They should be supervised. You waited until we were all asleep?"

She nodded, blinking at the light coming through the blinds in the bedroom. "I did."

"Why?"

Dina looked sheepishly back and forth between us. "Don't be coy. You have to go nude. You think I wanted to put on a *show*?" Dina recoiled into a shy grin.

I smiled back at her. "Well, you're clearly still you," I said, smiling approvingly up at Trapper. "You feel okay? The same?"

She thought to herself for a moment. "Yeah, I mean, I don't feel any different, if that means 'the same.' It was a weird feeling. I felt exhilarated, like Isaac was when he came out. It was a crazy experience, Dane. You really did it. I couldn't sleep for another few hours afterward."

"So did you," Megan said. "You really did it while we were all asleep. Glad you're okay."

"The run sequence was simple enough," Dina replied. "I figured, if we're all gonna go through this thing eventually anyway, I might as well get in a practice run before we're all standing around nude assessing each other up and down. I don't want to be rated a 1 or a 0 before I'm reduced to 1's and 0's."

I chuckled. "Maybe Trapper here can develop some bio-undies that Nova wouldn't stitch into our DNA in Ava or Aurora. That way we can preserve a modicum of decency and not have to put on a mass strip tease."

Dina giggled now. "Sure."

Trapper spoke up. "Girlfriend, don't worry about ratings. I'd kill for your butt. It's an 8 on my scale."

"Yeah, well, your boobs are a 9.5 on mine, so there," Dina shot back. They fist-bumped and giggled as I watched and smiled approvingly. Dina got up and hugged Megan.

"I'll go rouse Dirty Socks Boy," I said, rising and heading back toward the living room. "We gotta get started again. Who wants coffee?"

Me they both chimed simultaneously. "But I need to get a shower in, first," Dina said. "With *no one* watching," she clarified.

I smiled back at her. "Where's the fun in that?"

We would need to get a good breakfast in us even though it was four in the afternoon. If we didn't have calories, we weren't going anywhere.

It was late, and we needed a break.

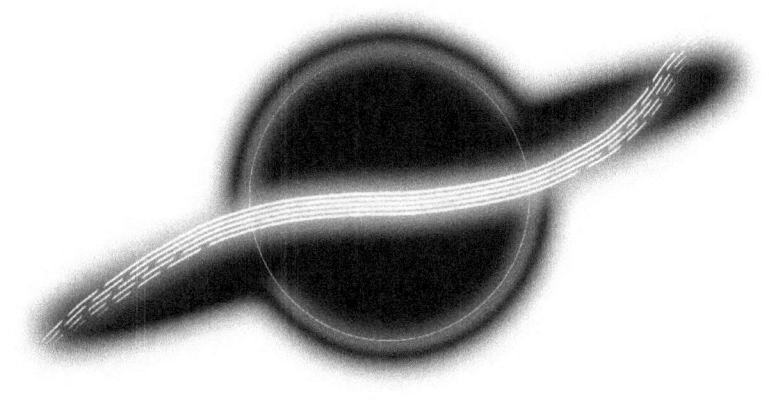

10 | Setback
November 9th, 2025

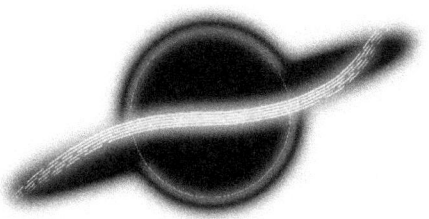

Once more into the late night hours we went.

I glanced at the clock. It was now 1:37 am on November 9th.

We'd all showered, fed ourselves, and I put on more coffee. Thankfully, our little jaunt out to Subway for fresh air and sandwiches took only forty-five minutes.

Trapper stayed behind and guarded the place with my gun. I showed it to her. She'd been target shooting before, so it wasn't a dry run for her at least. This way, our place, our research, and the last best hope for humanity's survival could stay protected.

We returned to find her – or, at least, someone who *looked* like her – in one piece. I thought she might test out the teleporters while we were away, but she insisted she hadn't. She asserted that she wasn't scared, just didn't see the need yet; besides, she said, "I trust you, Dane." That little vote of confidence went straight to my heart. And then she added a quippy addendum, "Besides, none of you are deformed mutants yet, so, there's that." She definitely had a way with words.

We had labored far into the night and were about to wind down, but we had to make plans to test something the following day. The obvious choice was Macy, but I had some hesitation, for reasons clearly beside the fact that I loved her, and she was my pup.

The cold reality, however, was that I'd never tested Nova to Ava to Aurora, and was tremendously reluctant to send Macy through. We would be in undiscovered country on this new venture.

Donze had warned us not to tell anyone about what we were doing, and none of us wanted to be the first to try the relay yet, no matter the fact that three of us had now gone through Nova to Ava.

A relay was something else entirely, because we would be entering a state of suspended animation on a timed duration, held as data on a RAID array of solid state drives, awaiting reintegration back through Aurora. That whole concept was entirely new, and brimming with loads of uncertainty.

In short, we would be tempting fate if either the relay *or* the reintegration failed. I suggested we sleep on it and get to bed earlier than yesterday.

We finally gave up and collectively crashed just under 2 am.

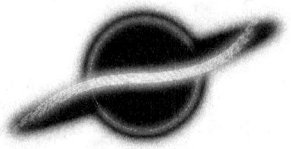

November 10th, 2025

I awoke to my alarm at 7 am. Sunlight streamed through the blinds in the bedroom, and left simmering stripes of heat across my chest.

Aurora was half-complete. She would be fully assembled, the four of us working feverishly on her, by this evening. And then, we would perform the test.

I texted Donze for an update on the nuclear propulsion while everyone else slept: *Please advise on nuclear propulsion status. We are approaching completion of third chamber, ETA this evening sometime, hopefully. Will perform subject transfer test ASAP following. Fingers crossed.*

I tossed my phone aside and combed my hair with my hands. Macy hopped up on the sofa and just stared at me. She had that look in her eyes that said, *It's been literally three days since you've walked me, so I'm about to bite your face off. I hope that's okay?*

I grabbed her and pulled her near, silently ruffling her fur. She was right. She *had* been exceedingly patient.

We had let her out in the backyard of the apartment complex; it was fenced in and grassy, but beyond that she hadn't been walked in a while. "I'm sorry, baby girl, I've neglected you, huh? Yeah. She's a good girl. We should get you moving, huh?"

Her ears perked up.

We should get you moving. Perhaps those words held more significance, more trust, than I cared to assign them or realize. I took a deep breath, and Macy watched me as she began to pant.

"Yeah, you're right, girl. It's a bit stuffy in here. Let's go. You wanna go? Go for walk?" I said, eagerly, and her eyes widened and head tilted as her ears went up. Macy bounded from the couch and ran to the door, staring up at the doorknob and wagging endlessly.

As soundlessly as possible, I threw on a shirt, shorts, my coat and shoes, then grabbed her harness and leash, but not before I left a quick note that we would be back in a few. Stuffing my cellphone in my pocket, we slipped out.

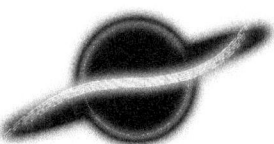

It felt like it should be even colder than it was. I wondered if that was Norma calling: radiation extending outward toward us even now. The temperature said that it was 61 degrees. But this was November.

The world was quiet, but the Fishery Science Building bore testament to loud, violent scars from those tanks. I wondered what had become of those jeeps and what the authorities did to them once they found them. The news had said nothing. I would catch a better view of it when we wrapped around Boat Street on our way back from the walk.

Macy and I traipsed up Pacific. Cars dotted the roadways, people going to and fro and fulfilling whatever mission they felt they had left.

A tangible calm had descended on Seattle at least, following the past few days of anarchic outbursts. However, it belied the storm that was coming. Calm for now, yes, but the air was so thick you could chew it. I think Macy sensed it as well.

We walked our usual route, east on Pacific, down to 15th, hanging a right at UW Children's Center at Portage Bay, and then all the way down to the water off Boat Street. We hung another right and went up to Fritz Hedges Waterway Park, and I let her off her leash to run around a bit. She was always friendly, wagging and never chased other dogs; her nose was always to the ground.

Macy took care of business and then we were back up toward home. Trapper texted me. *Hey, pudgy. Got your note. The others are still nuked. See you back here soon.*

There was a boatload of other texts I had missed. Mom, Dad, fellow graduate students, friends from another life, relatives, old contacts who had heard I was involved in Norma's discovery.

I stopped in my tracks. There it was:

Hey, bloke. Sorry I haven't texted before now. Wanted to thank you for all you've done. Keep doing it, eh? This thing will destroy our planet, for sure, but you're young, and it doesn't have to destroy you. For me? I've lived long enough, and have outlived both usefulness and desire to be useful. Nothing left to live for. Don't want to be destroyed by TWO Norma's in one lifetime. Sorry we couldn't be friends longer. I wish you well, and I'll put in a good word for your deliverance from this thing. Take risks, even with what you love. Live. Cheers, mate. -Henry

It was dated November 7th at 12:07 pm.

Henry St. James. My heart leapt into my throat as I read his final missive. A man I had hardly known but had talked to on occasion, who had helped us confirm the supermassive black hole that was on its way to us, sent literally moments before he had killed himself.

My breath held interminably; I was afraid to let it out. The world spun. What a final act of goodwill and blessing before he exited the stage of life. His comment about 'two Norma's killing him' hit me hard. His ex-wife, and now this world killer. Both had killed his world. Poor guy.

All I could do was sigh. It took me a while before my feet registered that it was time to move again, but they did, reluctantly. Slowly, heavily, we trudged up the road. Macy was tugging on her leash, leading me.

We passed up Boat Street, her leading the way as usual, angling back up north toward Pacific, as I simmered in my thoughts.

Through the parking lot, in a clearing through the trees, there was the west front of the Fisheries Building. A gigantic, blackened scar fanned outward from the point of impact, and the building had caved in at the corner. Concrete and plaster rubble littered the parking lot. Two of the trees surrounding the perimeter of the curving parking lot were scorched near to the building. Rebar poked out of the structure's wound.

My thoughts went back once more to that tank and those jeeps, wondering what had become of it all. Silently, I prayed for more God-fearing people that would keep the peace as we hurtled toward our own destruction. Or, well, as Norma's destructive forces hurtled toward us. I shook my head.

God. Where was he in all of this? Did he even hear my prayer just now? Was he seeing what was coming our way? Did he even care? I was never really a believer, other than Sunday School as a kid and having it drilled into me by my God-fearing parents. It didn't tend to play nice with science, and so I had to choose one over the other. But now, it seems, maybe there would be a reckoning. An ELE tends to force humanity's eyes and hearts upward to connect with the almighty. I just wondered if it wasn't too late.

We rounded the corner, and Building C loomed up at the corner of Pacific and Brooklyn.

The Fishery Science Building, the park, the quiet lull of the morning, St. James' text, all of it, slid into the past as I glumly trudged up the steps.

Macy followed me, reluctant for the walk to be over.

I reached the apartment door and unlocked it, heading inside. There was Trapper, sitting at her laptop next to mine, glancing up at me with a slight smile. Isaac was unmoving on the couch, but he saw me and grinned.

"Morning," he said.

I waved to him, freeing Macy from her harness and throwing my phone and keys to the side as I plopped down into my beanbag chair next to the couch, staring at the half-shell that was Aurora. Soon, we'd have triplets in here, and soon I would have to send Macy through them. That was the only way. It was what I had to do.

"You okay?" Isaac asked. Megan looked at me.

"Yeah. Just thinking," I replied softly.

This thing will destroy our planet, for sure, but you're young, and it doesn't have to destroy you.

His words came back to me, ringing true. Norma didn't have to destroy us. But, even more than that, Nova and Ava didn't have to destroy Macy. It doesn't have to destroy us. *Take risks,* he said, *even with what you love. Live*, he had said. Was this some cryptic unintentional hint that I should be willing to risk Macy, even Macy? After all, I had done it once before. I needed to do what needed to be done. And the truth was that she had not outlived either 'usefulness or desire to be useful.'

I brought my eyes to my beloved dog. She stood by the kitchen counter, expectantly, watching me and wagging, waiting for a treat. She always got a treat after a walk. She would get one now.

"Come here, girl," I said to her softly, and I think both Megan and Isaac registered that my tone was subdued; concerned; downcast.

"Dane? What is it?" Trapper now asked.

I sighed, retrieving my phone and scrolling to the text from St. James. At that point, Dina had entered the hallway, wrapped in a blanket like a walking burrito. She eyed me curiously.

"Hey, bloke," I started. "Sorry I haven't texted before now. Wanted to thank you for all you've done. Keep doing it, eh? This thing will destroy our planet, for sure, but you're young, and it doesn't have to destroy you. For me? I've lived long enough, and have outlived both usefulness and desire to be useful. Nothing left to live for. Don't want to be destroyed by TWO Norma's in one lifetime. Sorry we couldn't be friends longer. I wish you well, and I'll put in a good word for your deliverance from this thing. Take risks, even with what you love. Live. Cheers, mate. Henry," I ended, and I confess my eyes were watering. "He sent that to me right before he killed himself. I just now saw it."

I swallowed hard. The gravitational weight of the room made its presence known, descending upon us as if Norma were already here.

"It's a blessing, Dane," Dina said, walking over and sitting down next to me. "A blessing from a stranger. How fortunate are you to have gotten that? His text is right where we are in this very moment."

She was right, and I knew it. We all knew it. I glanced over at Macy. *Take risks, even with what you love.* There was only one thing to do, after getting her a treat, of course.

Send her through.

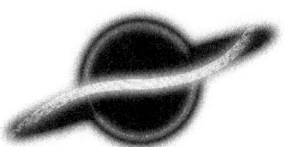

Evening approached, and we still weren't quite done. The light was fading outside, and reddish-orange beams once more lasered through the blinds in my bedroom, shafting down upon my bed, bathing Macy in amber arcs.

We were close, but we just needed the drives.

The DNA makeup of humans, descrambled and interpolated by *Courier 3.1*, amounted to roughly two terabytes of data per lifeform. That was a *lot* of data. That data contained height, weight, mass, skin color, hair color, eye color, pigmentation, imperfections such as moles and rogue hairs, skin elasticity, organ placement, blood type, anatomy, brain composition, memory modules, behavioral traits, socio-emotional makeup, intellectual quotient, artistic traits, synapse patterns, cognition, and *so* much more. Nothing could be left out! And we would need RAID arrays, so that would be doubled. There was no way in hell the UW would approve the kind of funding required to procure such large solid state drives. Some manufacturers produced SSDs up to 122 TB in size. That would be 30.5 humans, because with RAID, the space needed would have to be doubled in the redundant array of independent disks. As far as we knew, no one possessed the technology to produce petabyte drives of one thousand terabytes yet, so the best we could do until then was just daisy chain the terabyte drives together.

Doing the math, we figured if we got ahold of 100 of those drives, that would be three-thousand fifty lives. Would that be enough to jumpstart the human race on PCb? I didn't know, and I wondered, comically, who the 'half-human,' the 'point five' would be.

The humans would have to be a good representation of life here on earth, young and old, rich and poor, slave and free, famous and unknown, and they would have to represent a diverse palette of who we were... who we became... how we evolved... what humanity truly means.

Along with that, we would have to find a way to send along food, not knowing what kind of resources awaited us on Proxima Centauri b. We would need chickens, pigs, and animals small enough to fit within the confines of each chamber... or we would have to build bigger chambers for both Nova *and* Aurora, since Ava was simply acting as a bounce point. Those bigger chambers could then incorporate oxen, cows, larger livestock and cattle, as well as whatever other animals we would want to bring along.

On the spacecraft Aurora would be traveling in, we would need to also transport grain, nutrients, plants, grass seed, water filtration devices, vegetables, fiber, tools and supplies for building, weapons, a supply of basic medicines and how to replicate them, earth records, historical artifacts revealing where we came from, and so much more. It would be a renaissance... a complete reboot. But this time, we would have the advantage of bringing along what worked. The only unpredictable variable was the humans. It would always be the humans. New societal norms would have to be adopted; rules and laws would need to be strictly upheld.

The philosophical underpinnings of this were going to be enormous. We were just providing the *Courier* system as vehicles. They were physical. But it was the *intangible* things we would be bringing with us that would require a lot of work and coordination. The belief systems, the religions, the socio-political perspectives, civilization norms, laws, familial relations, practices, and all of that. Thankfully, we'd be able to leave that to someone else.

Call us, simply, 'chauffeurs.'

Isaac had gone back to the lab to check on any updates with Norma's telemetry, or see if we'd missed any landline messages. Calls were supposed to be forwarding to his phone, and autoreplies instructed people to call or text him, but they had stopped. His voice mail was probably full. Presumably, much higher agencies than a little podunk lab at the University of Washington were now on it, and didn't need us anymore, but nonetheless, he still wanted to stay on top of things and connect with any contacts or colleagues that might need our input... or we might need theirs.

He would be back tomorrow morning. Besides, if we didn't regularly show up at the UW lab and log some kind of hours or credentialed work, things would get suspect and our tenure might be revoked or suspended. Doubtful, given the fact that Isaac, especially, was the one who discovered Norma. That would be bad form to cut us out of the picture just like that. And tenure revocation is generally considered a hollow threat in light of impending complete annihilation.

It was hard to believe that life had changed so much in only nearly five days. We had catalogued Norma early on November 6th. Since then, the denizens of planet Earth appeared to have wrestled briefly with it and then resigned themselves to the fact that we were, quite inescapably, doomed. There was a certain peace in that resignation; a certain futility in attempting to bargain with it. Maybe we had all learned the five stages of grief by now and were coping with it by effectively saying, *Oh well, screw it.*

Donze sent me another message that night out of the blue. I snapped the others to attention and read it aloud to them.

President advises quicker progress and would like to meet. I would accompany him. We'll be flying out on Friday the 14th and would like to get acquainted with your team and see your technology up close, firsthand.

Thankfully, I was reading ahead in my brain, and noticed it before I read it aloud to the others. There were Donze's words, cold and clear: *Farragut-322 isn't slowing down. Neither should we.*

I knew in my heart that I couldn't relay Norma's official scientific name to them. Isaac would be crushed knowing that the supermassive was named after him since he was the one who had discovered it. Thankfully, he wasn't here right now, but I didn't want them relaying it to him.

"Dane? What is it?" Trapper asked.

I glanced up at her. "Nothing. Just... surreal," I said, meaning the naming, not the President's impending visit.

"Holy crap," Dina said. "The President, here?"

"*And* the SecDef," I replied, eyes wide.

"Are they sure that's safe? Wouldn't that attract unwanted attention to us?" she asked.

"Probably, unless they came in a cover car or something," Trapper replied.

"Only one way to find out," I replied, and then began hammering out a text.

Glad to show you what we're doing. Test subject going through the relay tonight. 87% complete with the third chamber. What time Friday?

Will advise, standby came the reply.

"He'll advise. I guess we're at their beck and call," I said, flicking my eyebrows up. "No worries, that gives us plenty of time to finish up Aurora."

"But seriously, the President of the United States, here, in your apartment. *Whoa*," Trapper said, exhaling hot hair in amazement. "Hail to the Chief," she said half-jokingly, with a mock salute.

"Tell me about it. We'll be fine, though. Let's just make sure everything works, gang," I said. "I'm not relishing the test we have coming up, and the sooner we get that win under our belts, the sooner we'll know where we stand with all of this."

Farragut-322. Ouch. Would Isaac be fine? Would any of us?

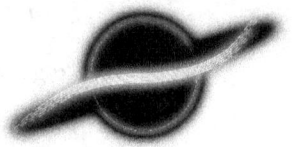

Isaac called me.

The Event Horizon Telescope, in conjunction with the Center for Astrophysics at Harvard & Smithsonian, was working overtime along with NASA and the European Space Agency to monitor Norma. EHT telemetry had her still on track to intersect with our orbital plane in late February, possibly even a bit sooner. Disappointing, of course, but the hope now conveyed to the four of us via *Courier 3.1* and our three, beautiful girls allowed us to see beyond the present calamity, whereas most people's vision stopped short.

NuSTAR and Chandra telescopes said her hot gas readings were off the chart. Other stellar orbits outside our immediate galactic neighborhood were having their orbits disrupted in its vicinity. The event horizon was strong; the singularity at the center was having its way with all things around it. Hawking radiation was no longer speculation; Norma was definitely putting out a faint stream of particles due to quantum effects near the event horizon. I could only imagine what the tidal forces were around it.

Isaac was answering a few messages and then he'd head home to pack some things and return. He would not be with us for the test tonight… if we were to even conduct it tonight. I informed him of the president's upcoming visit.

By our estimation, we were now about 95% ready. Teleporting Macy would require less than 2TB of data storage due to dogs' more simplistic makeup. We had a 2TB drive on hand, no problem. Dina had brought a few from the lab, so we slapped a Samsung 10TB drive into a spare bay in Aurora, wired it up to one of the switches that was connected to the motherboard, and it was partitioned and reading solidly. Once we knew that it worked, we'd firm up the bay assembly.

Ava had been retrofit with much more memory and a faster CPU and motherboard in order to handle the transfer speeds and preserve integrity across the board. If we didn't have that, we could risk all those lifeform signals racing through her becoming a jumbled, tangled mess… and the end result would be a dripping pile of oozing jelly that was once human life, deposited haphazardly onto PCb without a wish or a prayer, to slowly decompose in the heat of a red dwarf star far from home.

"You guys hungry? I'm hungry. And nervous," I added, and I discovered that I was, in fact, trembling a bit, the closer we got to Macy's test.

"Pizza sounds good," Megan said nonchalantly. Dina looked up at me and nodded.

"Pizza *again*?" I asked.

Trapper stared at me quizzically. "What?"

I held up my hands helplessly. "Okay. Fine. Pizza… *again*. We gotta save some for Isaac though. And that's one of the first things I'm sending through, way before Macy. I'm gonna run down to the bird store real quick as well."

"You can send pizza through?" Dina asked.

"Yeah, but it won't reintegrate perfectly on the other side. It's not biological. A steak would be reintegrated; an orange would be, celery would be. Pizza isn't a living organism," I said, chuckling. "It's made up of a bunch of *once*-living things. Anyway, I'll send a slice or two, and then a bird or two. If all goes well, Macy goes through. Not before."

Trapper chuckled. "I think you should try to send a bird through while sitting on a piece of pizza, Dane. If it comes through all jumbled on the other end, we can call it a *pecker pie*."

"I'm ignoring you," I insisted. "Except to say that I'm ignoring you."

I grabbed my keys and phone and headed out, locking the door behind me. Trapper chuckled again.

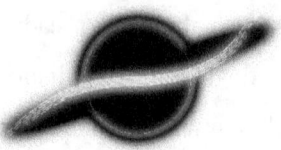

Forty-five minutes later, I was back, three pizzas under one arm, and a few small cardboard bird carriers clasped together under the other, loaded up with four society finches. My dog greeted me at the door, picked up the pizza scent right away and eagerly followed me inside.

"Got the food. And the pizzas," I joked. Dina made a revolted face. Megan quickly jumped up from her laptop and seized the pizzas from me, whisking them the rest of the way into my kitchen, and throwing one open.

Macy jumped out of her way, but then became interested in the small boxes of finches I was carrying.

"Thanks. Starving," was all Trapper mumbled through dough, sauce, cheese and pepperoni, ripping open a twenty-ounce Mountain Dew and chugging it like it was gasoline and she was a souped-up Ducati.

Dina rose. "We're pretty much done, Dane. Slapped the last few innards on a few minutes ago, it's fully insulated, and the seal's nice and tight. Vacuumed it out and Aurora is ready to rock. The other girls are prepped and ready."

"Right on," I said. "I'll ready the birds."

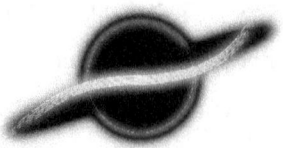

Dinner finished, I put Macy in the bedroom and shut the door so that she wouldn't get any ideas about the birds. She had licked her lips enough while sniffing their boxes. Next, I fetched one of the tiny, white society finches. The boxes were flimsy cardboard, allowing fairly easy extraction. The first bird pecked at me vigorously in self-defense.

I plucked one feather without so much as a squawk from the finch, inserted the feather into the scanner, and let *Courier 3.1* do its thing. The bird's DNA profile was created with an answering beep. Dina and Megan watched in fascination; only Dina had seen this done, briefly, with Isaac before he went through.

Next stop for the tiny fowl was setting it down gently on the floor of Nova and quickly closing the door before it could fly out. It flitted around, glancing off the walls a few times, its miniscule heart beating frantically, before it finally settled on the floor and awaited the teleportation sequence along with the rest of us.

I sat down facing the laptop, adjusting the traffic and relay settings to read from Nova, and then send to Ava and bounce to Aurora in a holding pattern.

Courier 3.1 did its thing. All three chambers fired up properly. The countdown tracked. White hot light filled Nova. Ava was silent except for her whirring and clicking motherboard, and the slight vibration emitted by the singular SSD drive installed therein.

Aurora didn't light up. For a second my stomach lurched, wondering what went wrong. And then it hit me. This was protocol and to be expected; there was nothing wrong. Aurora was simply awaiting the 'go' code to reintegrate the tiny finch. Exactly as we had programmed it to do. This was a failsafe line of code that I had intentionally programmed in to ensure that there would be a controlled sequence, reintegrating upon command. Once we could ensure that the holding pattern was secure, we could then program automation to deliver them, one after the other, allowing the subject sufficient time to exit the receiving unit.

I hit *Commence Relay* in *Courier 3.1* and whirled around to face Aurora.

It mirrored Nova's sending transmission light flash, and then…

…there was the bird.

Good as new – or as old – and flitting about in the same panic, it finally landed and looked around erratically, its chest reverberating with the same frenetic heartbeat.

I crept up to the window slowly so as not to frighten it and send it fluttering around again. I could feel Dina and Megan peering over my shoulder curiously, all of our eyes trained on the bird.

There it was! It had worked. Ava had successfully bounced it over to Aurora. Our newest girl had listened and heard, and replicated the little society finch with the same precision as Ava would have. And the beauty of it all? Aurora was wireless. Ava sent the signal over the air, and Aurora grabbed it and reproduced the finch with the same data integrity as Ava would have.

I slowly stood up and took a quick look at Megan and then Dina. Before we knew what hit us, we erupted into a joyful holler and enveloped each other with celebratory hugs, enraptured with joy at the prospect of sending humans through soon.

Without delay, I texted Isaac that it worked.

Momentarily, a smiley face appeared in the chat below my message, followed by Isaac's text. *Great work! See you soon.*

I don't know how I managed to get the bird out of Aurora and back into its box, but I did. It took some work, but that part was done. It felt a little overly warm, but that didn't register any sort of nuanced confusion on my part. After all, it was a frightened little thing. I put that box aside from the others to keep the transferred ones separate.

Next up, the pizza.

I wasn't sure what to expect by sending a slice of pizza through, but figured that might show us what kind of effect the chambers would have on non-biological organic material as well. Worth a shot. Inanimate objects wouldn't be teleported; things like grain and seed would be housed in vacuum-sealed carriers inside the spacecraft, and then deposited along with the rest of us. But it would be nice to see what it would do with this.

All three girls were running. Pepperoni and cheese in the scanner. Profile created. Sequence initiated.

We watched, curiously, as Nova sent it through, and I hit *Commence Relay* once more.

We opened the door. Aromatic steam rolled out. There, on the floor of the Aurora chamber, lay a smoking molten mess of goo: a steaming fusion of pepperoni and cheese, ingredients indistinguishable from one another. I glanced over at the ladies, and all they could do was offer a concerned expression. "See? Told ya. I guess we stick to live subjects?" I asked, and they nodded. "Anybody wanna try some of that?" They shook their heads. "Cowards.

"Alright," I conceded. "I'll clean it up and then we'll get Finch Number Two and then Number Three in there for the sequence. Then we can try Macy. Okay?"

It wasn't long before we were cleaned up and reset for the second finch. Nova's sequence was running. Ava and Aurora were fired up and ready to go. We sent the first one through and kept it in a holding pattern, with a timing separation of one minute between reintegration and reset so that we could extract it and ensure that Aurora was ready for the second finch.

The first one was through! I didn't hit *Commence Relay* this time. We were testing the holding sequence. I hit *Commence Suspend*. If all went well, little Finch Number Two was now loaded into a partition of our SSD inside of Aurora. Without delay – purely out of excitement – I got Finch Number Three out of its box...

... and it escaped!

It wiggled out of my grip and flew around the room in a panic, smashing into the sliding glass door and thudding to the ground before launching again. The girls tried to help as well, cornering it. The thing was fast, flitting about and jumping into the air with a frightened *beep* just as I went to cup it in my palms.

"Dina, grab it, there it is!" I cried. "Wait, don't – just, don't move too quickly. Here, Megan, head it off and, just, look out!" She nearly tripped over the power receptacle and thick insulated power cable for Aurora. "Careful!"

"Dane, you stay there. Here it comes, I've got it!" Dina cried.

"No, don't! It's coming to me. You wait there, and no! Dane, don't move, stay there! It's coming to me. Haha! It's behind the couch. Hang on," Trapper exclaimed.

Indeed, Finch Number Three had hit the wall and was flapping its way down behind the couch. Megan hurled herself over the back of it and clutched in vain. It hopped out and began a new, fatigued and desperate flight.

Dina waved her hands in the air in a vain attempt to ward it off from the kitchen as I moved into view.

It was growing exhausted and was losing altitude. It flew scattershot into the kitchen and plopped down into the sink. I moved in quickly and cupped my hands over it, trapping it.

"Got it!" I exclaimed with joy. "Come here, ya trouble maker," I said, bringing it over quickly to Nova. I gently opened the door and placed it inside. It hopped around slowly, unable to fly due to fatigue. Its beak was reverberating with quick frightened breaths as it sat, fazed.

"Poor thing," Dina voiced with sympathy.

"I hate birds," Megan chimed in, remorselessly.

I laughed. "Me too. They're irritating." I chuckled once more. "Okay, Round Two, Finch Number Three. Here we go. Commencing suspend!"

Nova lit up. Ava didn't. Aurora didn't. Finch Number Three was gone. My laptop beeped a chime of success, and a prompt filled my screen of a successful teleportation and storage.

We surveyed each other again with high hopes.

"Alright, this is what it all boils down to, folks," I said with a chest full of hopeful air. "You guys ready?"

They nodded.

"I wish Isaac was here to see this," I said.

I hit a third button this time labeled, *Commence Relay Series*. If all went well, Finch Number Two would reintegrate in Aurora in fifteen seconds, and Finch Number Three would then reintegrate in Aurora exactly one minute after that, allowing us to extract the first bird and reset.

Countdown. Fifteen seconds seemed interminable, a few minutes at least.

Aurora flashed white. A countdown displayed on my laptop, starting at one minute.

"Okay, move, move! Get in position to block it if it tries to fly out, you guys!" I opened the door, and steam poured out. I batted it away from me, clearing a path for my vision. It was hard to see. I knelt down and peered through the swirling mist.

I couldn't see the bird! It was nowhere to be found. I felt all along the bottom of the chamber, running my hand around, and wildly looking up and around to see if it leapt up and was clutching the side wall, or ceiling, or… something.

"Dane! What are you doing? Get it out of there, the clock's ticking!" Dina cried.

"I'm looking, I'm looking!" I cried. "I don't see it, do you see it?"

No! they both cried, peering in with me.

"Check the laptop, check it quick! Does the transfer say complete?" I hollered.

Megan dashed over to my laptop. She didn't answer.

"Trapper!"

"I'm *looking!* Where do I look?" she cried.

"Under, under-" I tried, but suddenly I couldn't remember. "Forget it! What about…?" I tried to think.

"Dane! Is there an abort button?"

I panicked, wondering why I hadn't put in an abort sequence button. Why the hell hadn't I put one in?

"Dane!" Megan cried again.

"You have fourteen seconds, get *out* of there, Dane!" Dina cried. She began pulling on my arm to pull me back.

I whirled back to Megan. "Look under Reports, and, uh, it should be…" I struggled. "I can't remember, I can't remember!"

"Dane! Nine seconds!" Dina tugged at me, her fingernails shredding my arm as she wrenched.

"Ow, Dina, stop! *Megan?!*" I cried.

"I can't find it! Dane, get out of there, close the door!"

I jerked myself up and out of there, slamming the door closed as gently as I could. I feared what would come next.

"Three seconds! Lock it!"

I pressed the outer lock button.

Aurora lit up white. We recoiled and covered our eyes, turning away. The inside of the chamber flashed twice, and we just stared at it. I swallowed hard.

On the credenza against the wall, Finches Number One and Four must have heard something, because they began beeping erratically. Almost frantically.

I slowly reached out and opened the door. It slid open with an airy mechanical whistle.

The smoke filtered out. The air swirled around it.

I swallowed once more.

The smoke cleared.

There, on the floor, lay the mangled carcass of two birds. At its neck, two appendages stemmed out, culminating in two distinct heads. Two overlapping sets of wings spanned out, intersecting bizarrely, painting a gruesome picture of fusion. One leg was bent backward behind it; the other three were crumpled up beneath it or off to the side. Its splayed form was a gelatinous mutation, oozing fluids and membranes; a splicing together of two distinct DNA patterns, joined together because that's precisely what the code told Aurora to do.

Or… was it because that was what *I* told it to do?

I was convinced I had missed something. *What had I missed?* I meticulously coded this process through all of last night and this morning!

Those poor birds. Joined together forever in some spastic metamorphosis, utterly lacking symmetry and bereft of life. Part of its delicate, misshapen skeleton protruded unnaturally through its back.

Two birds. Dead. Just like that.

"Sorry, Dane," Megan whispered emotionlessly. Dina stifled a cry and turned away.

"Yeah. Me too. I… must have forgotten something."

Dina moved away from us and sat down on the couch. I took a heavy sigh. Trapper went to the laptop.

I knelt down, staring at the disgusting new creation, wondering what I had done wrong. I would need to look through the code and heavily debug it.

And, slowly, the awful horror of what would have happened had I sent Macy through settled upon me. What if that had been a bird and… Macy? Or Macy and… Dina? What if I had accidentally spliced together two forms of life in an appalling and unnatural grotesque mutation?

I gazed down upon the creature in pity, wondering if it had died in pain, or if it was instantaneous.

I wouldn't have my answers soon. This was a setback. I was just glad it didn't cost Macy her life… or any of ours. But I suddenly cared about birds.

I should have learned my lesson from the pizza. Had I grown cavalier? At the edge of death, we had been cavalier, joking about pizza and irritating little birds. All life was precious now, even the tiniest. Even the lives of two tiny, seemingly insignificant finches.

I had killed enough birds, and now the other test subjects I had sent through recalled to my mind. Those poor, innocent finches… all of them. Hopefully, their deaths wouldn't be in vain. Hopefully, this would mean something and I would figure this all out.

I stared at Macy, full of fear and trepidation that I would someday, soon, inadvertently kill her as well.

And perhaps even kill the remainder of the human race, desperate to escape Norma. If I couldn't get this right, we were all doomed.

Once more, into sadness I went.

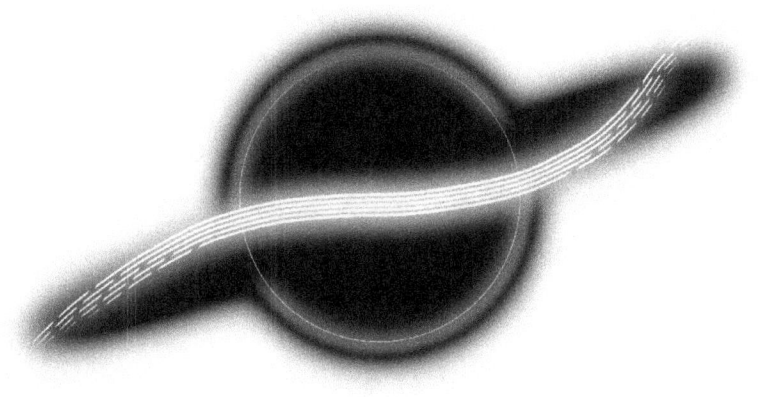

Part Two:
The End Is Nigh

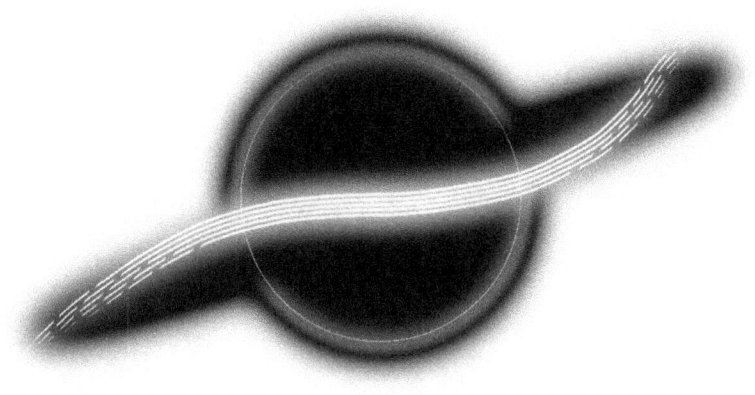

11 | Mr. President
November 14th, 2025

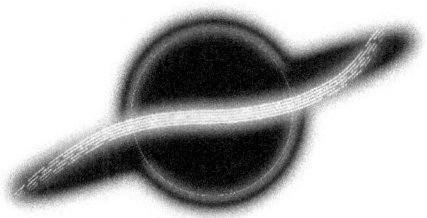

He was coming.

The text had just come through from Donze, and they were on their way here. The President of the United States was coming to see me, in my little apartment.

It had been four days since the birds. Norma was inching closer – the word 'inching' of course being a gross understatement here – and Macy had finally gone through after six more birds. I had purchased more, definitely: after all, there was no way in hell I was sending my dog through Nova and having her come out like that gruesome abomination we beheld on the floor pad of Aurora.

Macy's teleportation was a nailbiter, and I was trembling so hard my leg was bouncing off the floor; Dina had to restrain me in my chair. There was a strange delay in the reintegration that messed with my emotions *hard*. Time moved at a snail's pace, and I grew frantic. But then, finally, *mercifully*, Aurora lit up, and there she was. Same beautiful eyes, same nonstop tail, same beautiful dog, following all six birds in the sequence: all seven creatures held for ten minutes in Aurora. She hopped into my arms, and she even still reeked of the Beggin' Strips that I had given her just before she went through Nova.

The truth of the matter is that I had messed up badly. I had forgotten to program in some crucial and indispensable lines of code. The sequence was programmed correctly in that it held the teleportation subjects in stasis for one minute, but I had written incorrect syntax forcing what essentially resulted in a batch delivery, releasing all of them at the same time. An assimilation. *A mistake.*

In short, Aurora simply did what I told her to do. In short, she *combined* the subjects into a horrid fusion.

I recoded *Courier 3.1* on Wednesday, and then we sent two more birds through. It worked. Following that, we freed the ones we previously teleported, bought six more, and then reran the tests. The sequence was corrected to specify reintegration of the first signal, and then a double-verification to ensure that reintegration signal matched the original disintegration signal, two minutes to allow for extraction, and then reintegration of the next signal and double-verification of it as well.

Everything worked, finally. Cumbersome and laborious, to be sure, but it worked. I just hoped the President wouldn't ask me to test it in front of him, and that he wouldn't *himself* ask to go through. If it failed, I would be guilty of assassinating the President of the United States. I wondered if they would execute me before Norma would.

All of us were gathered now, in my little apartment, awaiting a single suburban to pull up. The President couldn't risk traveling in a caravan; he would attract too much attention to himself. However, a Secret Service advance detail had actually shown up earlier this morning, and now two of their men remained here with us, standing guard and awaiting his arrival with us.

Waiting was nerve-wracking. Waiting for Norma, waiting for Macy, waiting on the nuclear propulsion craft and news on it, waiting for the President.

Life had become all about nervous waiting anymore.

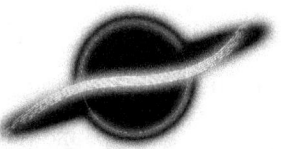

"Nice to meet you, Mr. President, Mr. Donze," I said, extending my hand after they had entered. They both greeted me enthusiastically.

"These are my colleagues, Isaac Farragut and Dina Jensen from the UW. And this," I said, motioning to Trapper, who had ambled over to me, "is Megan Trapper, also an undergrad from the U… she's been my right-hand woman in all of this. She helped me build everything you see."

Macy sat on the floor between Isaac's legs as he relentlessly stroked her and patted her.

The President was wearing a nondescript black cap and a black jacket over his white shirt and red tie. SecDef Donze was pretty much the same. I had never had a high opinion of Donald Trump, but here, standing before him, I was a citizen of the country that he was in charge of, and I was answerable to him. I just wanted to do my job and have what we needed to so we could save as many lives as possible. What my thoughts were on the people I had to interact with to get us to that goal was irrelevant. And, if I had to admit, it was actually an honor to have him here, knowing that we had achieved such a level of notoriety with something so incredibly novel and potentially life-saving.

"So these are the girls?" the President asked me in an inquisitive tone, removing his hat and smoothing back his wispy, Capellini-like yellow hair.

"Yessir, here they are," I said, motioning him toward them.

Donze approached me as Trump went to investigate the chambers close up. "Mr. Currier, nice work. Thanks for your patience as we've tried to get all of this underway. We appreciate all you've done so far."

He seemed nicer in person, actually. I was grateful for his comments, but, for some reason, the very statement put me a bit on edge, portending of some imminent shift in plans… or even a change of venue. I shook it off. "Thank you, Mr. Donze. The only question is where do we go from here?"

He smiled. "Well, it's of 'going' that I'd like to converse with you. The President as well. Can we sit?" He motioned me over to my couch, and then I realized that it wasn't a question.

I walked over to the couch and sat next to Isaac and Dina. Trapper had retreated to the table with her laptop next to mine, eyeballing Trump skeptically.

Donze remained standing, glancing back a single time at the President, and then back at me. Trump continued to inspect the chambers, inside and out.

"Let me be as succinct as possible," Donze began. Strangely, I felt suddenly like we were erring children sitting before a stern, remonstrative parent. "We're of course in an unprecedented situation, and we're going to need to take proper precautions," he said.

"Precautions against what?" I asked.

"Well, against the general population finding out what's going on here. What you're doing has bearings on the survival – correction, the *future*, to sound less bleak – of the American people. So I'll cut to the chase. We're going to need to relocate you and your team – and your equipment – to a secure location as soon as possible."

I looked at my team, and they looked nervously back at me. Trapper squinted her eyes.

"Okay," I said, "what does that mean for us, personally? You did say 'you and your team.'"

"Correct, we need-" he started, but then Trump walked over to him and stood beside him, hands at his side with those stiff pursed lips.

"Secretary Donze, allow me," Trump said, gazing down upon us. "We appreciate everything you've done. We're not taking you off of this assignment or this project. This is your baby, okay? What you've done here is truly, truly magnificent, the most important thing ever, really. Nothing has ever come close to how important this is."

Ah, here comes the signature bloviating, I thought as he spoke, and I found myself wondering if we would be able to find a hard drive with enough space just for him.

"We just need you closer to home, which, for us, is Washington, DC. So we're going to relocate you – all of you, your whole team here, all your equipment, even your beautiful dog if you'd like – so you can work from a secure environment without any threat of being discovered or interfered with."

Sounded reasonable enough. We all figured this might happen, but at least we were being included. "Got it," I said. "What is your timeline, may I ask?"

"As soon as possible," he said, waving me down. "If you can be ready in the next few days, that would be ideal." He stared at me pointedly, squinting his eyes and awaiting my reply.

"I don't see any trouble with that." I looked around at my team, awaiting their reply. They shook their heads, in agreement that it wouldn't be an issue. "May I ask what the progress is with the other part of our plan?"

"What other part is that?" Trump asked.

"The issue of how we're supposed to get Aurora to Proxima Centauri b."

"Aurora?" Trump asked.

Apparently he didn't know their names, but it seemed now as if he was even oblivious to the plans Donze and I had discussed regarding nuclear propulsion. "Well, sir, Aurora is the name of the teleportation chamber on the far right there." I was talking to Trump, but my eyes were on Donze, fearing that I might be overstepping some line by sharing too much. Surely the President knew of our plans? "That is the one that we would be sending to receive our signals."

"Mr. President," Donze interjected, "if I may, sir, Mr. Currier is referring to the 'travel program' you and I had discussed" -here he enunciated *travel program* to clue in Trump- "which of course involves the special technology."

Trump nodded briskly, looking ever in-the-know. "Yes. We're making progress, and it's very, very good. If you have an update, why don't you share it with them, Erick?"

"Yessir," Donze replied, and he couldn't suppress a bit of a smirk. Apparently, he thought the same of Trump as I did. I glanced over at Megan, and her face was wrapped in contempt and judgment, shaking her head slightly. "*Yes*, Mr. Currier, we're making progress. We have a private hangar and laboratory at Chantilly Air Jet Center. That's where we'll be moving your systems."

"And us," I said. It wasn't a question.

"Yes. *And* your team, of course," he replied. "Our spacecraft is being constructed onsite, and it's being rigorously tested to ensure all systems are functioning correctly. We're calling it 'Genesis,' for obvious reasons. We will be using a conventional launch vehicle – a rocket – to get Genesis up into a preliminary lower orbit around Earth. Our craft would be shielded during launch to protect against radiation exposure. Once initial orbit has been achieved, Genesis will employ rocket burns to maneuver it to a more remote, nuclear-safe orbit. Safety checks will be performed prior to reactor activation, then the propellant gets heated, and then we await the go-code. It will contain your third teleportation chamber, and then? Well, God help us on the journey."

"So," Trapper piped up, "I've previously confirmed that PCb does not lie in Norma's direct path. We'd have to hope for optimum timing of earth's rotation, and getting out of here before everything is destroyed. Otherwise we'd be sucked in along with everything else."

"Possibly," Donze said. "Timing would be critical, yes. However, that's thinking along the lines of conventional propulsion. Nuclear propulsion changes the game entirely. To that end, folks, and Mr. President, we're making great progress."

"So the programs that were working on nuclear pulse propulsion prior to Norma were never suspended?" Isaac asked.

Donze looked at him and smiled patronizingly. "I'm afraid I can't answer that question, you understand."

"Fine," Isaac relented. "But it's safe to say that we've got the technology – or *almost* got it – to the point of usability?"

"We're almost there," the SecDef replied heartily.

"What is your timeline, do you think, given the countdown that has been set upon us by Norma?" Isaac persisted.

"I should think that, with you there, and all key components in place, we'll have the capability within a month, ready to execute."

A month. That's pushing it, I thought, and my eyes went wider with a sigh. The truth is that would put us in mid-December, and things never happen on time when you factor in the US Government. The truer answer would be sometime after the first of the year. 2026. The year of Norma.

"Trust me, folks, we've got qualified teams working on it. We'll relocate you and station you nearby with full DOD-credentialed access to the premises. You'll receive a CAC and be considered DoD civilian employees and contractors."

"CAC?" I asked.

"Sorry. Common Access Card. We also have DBIDS cards, those are Defense Biometric Identification System cards, you'll probably be set up with those as well," Donze clarified. "We'll get you housing nearby, and arrange for all your equipment to be transported. We'll have a special contract team in touch with you soon to arrange for that. I assume you can break these down speedily and be ready in a few days' time?"

"Shouldn't be a problem," I said, although we had literally just put Aurora together a few days ago. Shame to have to break her down right away, and there was always more testing we could do, including an actual human volunteer. Who that would be yet, we had no idea.

"Wouldn't it be nice if we had one gigantic one you could fit all these little ones in and just whisk them over to the other side of the country, right? Sort of like a Russian Matryoshka doll, right?" He laughed immaturely.

"Uh, sure," I said, the joke lost on me as I remained somewhat fazed by all this. However, I resolved to trust that it would all work out.

"Ah well, you'll have to disassemble them, of course, that's the best way to get them out the door, but I trust you have schematics for quick reassembly?" I nodded. "You can then continue your testing on the new premises. We'll provide shipping containers, proper packing materials and labels to keep things organized and separated."

He glanced over at Trump for his approval. Trump nodded, trying to look both important and fully informed. The Secret Service guys started bustling around, holding their fingers to their ears.

"Alright, that's it, folks. Good work. We'll be in touch, okay? Keep at it," Trump said, and moved toward the door after shooting two thumbs up at us with that clenched-lip grin of his.

"Thank you, Mr. President," I said. Isaac echoed me.

"I'm sorry about your future daughter-in-law," Dina offered.

Trump clenched his lips once more, forcing a fake smile at her as he walked out with Donze. The agents nodded at us and followed the bigwigs out of our apartment.

We were now on our own to finish up testing and commence disassembly. I watched them load up into their Suburban and sundry Secret Service car entourage.

They were leaving.

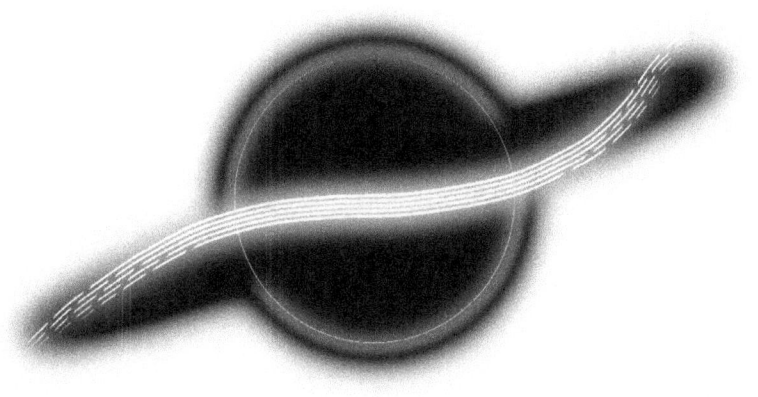

12 | A Brave Soul
November 16th, 2025

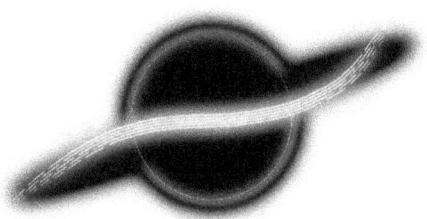

Everything was being torn down and prepared for reassembly.

The apartment was a mess. I hadn't packed all of my things. I didn't need to… why would I? Where we were going would be our final destination on planet Earth, and from there, we'd launch out across the galaxy, fleeing from a supermassive black hole that wanted to gobble us all up.

The only thing I really packed was a small box of collectibles to bring with us onboard Genesis. Thought it might serve as a time capsule of sorts.

Other than that, the rest was pointless.

The government contractors would be here tomorrow at 9 am to start moving us out, and then we would fly out the next day for Washington, DC.

We had performed a few more tests… not with any of us. Not yet. More birds, and more Macy trips. I was growing a bit anxious about Macy due to the sheer number of times she had gone through Nova. I had confidence in our chambers, but it was nonetheless unnerving to see her go through so many teleportations. As such, I watched her closely to ensure she remained healthy.

The signs were starting. Here we were now in mid-November, and it was already unusually hot for this time of year. Undoubtedly an effect of Norma drawing near, climatologists were regularly documenting increased temperatures that were atypical of November.

But that was just in the upper hemisphere. Up here in Seattle, we had always had a good mix of hot and cold, sun and rain. We had actual seasons here. Closer to the equator, it was growing even hotter, testing even the metrics and patience of diehard tree-huggers and global warming activists. And it was only going to get worse.

Additionally, on the outskirts of the solar system, DSN and DISCOVR both confirmed that Pluto was starting to exhibit strain. It had shifted its rotation – or, more accurately, it's orbit had *been* shifted – and it was now creeping nearer toward Norma's vortex, splitting off from its natural orbital plane into the vacuuming path of the hungry supermassive. It wouldn't be long, they said, before other planets followed suit, especially the little ones. At times, the sky appeared irregular in sparse patches, with bursts of color spilling through the heavens at odd hours, as if wisps of galactic strata were gently being tugged toward our invader.

Pluto was declared not a 'planet' in 2006. It was relegated to dwarf planet status, and, as the smallest – and, unfortunately, at this time one of the closest orbits to Norma – there was nothing it could do. It was gently shifting, being pulled off its axis at the aphelion, in an apogee at its orbit around the sun. It would be the first to go. DISCOVR was reporting that we'd soon be able to witness its demise.

But poor Pluto – as if there was any doubt that Norma was a solar system killer, Pluto's destruction would cement for our whole planet just how deadly this supermassive was going to prove.

Many more signs would come. This was only the beginning of the death pains.

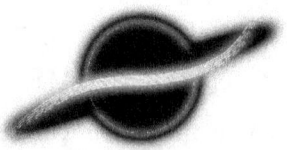

Isaac sat across from me. I couldn't believe his words. They fell from his lips decisively and assertively, and there was no mistaking them. I just wished I could actually 'mistake them.'

"You can't be serious," I protested.

"I am. More than I've ever been about anything."

"But Isaac," I said, "it's untested, man. You'd be the first human held in data storage, in stasis, and if we lose you, we've lost the very person who discovered Norma in the first place."

"That's exactly why I have to go first. You didn't have anyone contest your *own* volunteering when you went."

"That's totally different! I was going from there to there!" I practically shouted, pointing at the places where Nova and Ava had stood. The floors were marked with ghostly diameters where they had long stood: depressions in the carpet under their weight. Only the faintest depression showed from Aurora. She hadn't sat there long enough. "And I was hardwired, passing through an eight foot conduit via a LAN, Isaac. You'd be the first to be completely disintegrated, sent wirelessly, and transferred into a hard drive for stasis."

"There's no difference. You became data in your LAN, I'd be data on the SSD. No difference. The only difference here is that it involves three chambers instead of two. And as far as losing me?" He shrugged. "Sure. You might. The risk is always real. But isn't that why you went through? I know that's why I went through before, Dane. To make sure it works. We need to know."

I stared at him solemnly. "Yes, we do, Isaac, I agree. But once we get up and running, we can find volunteers. People with less to lose. We need you to help us continue to monitor Norma, to continue the prep of the chambers, to play devil's advocate and bounce ideas off of as we get nearer to the launch date. Why does it have to be you?"

He just stared right back, unmoved and stoic. "Dane. I discovered Norma. I hate myself for it. I need to discover *this*."

And that was all he said. No begging, no pleading, no power plays. But in my heart, I knew this would be the reason. When St. James suggested Norma's name, I knew it then. Though we were all still collectively referring to her as Norma, I had seen Donze's text.

It was clear now that Isaac had also come across something, some report somewhere, in the scientific or monitoring community, that had updated her name with *Farragut-322*. He had seen it, and he was trying to reconcile with it. He didn't want it named after him.

I didn't envy him.

"Well, I don't know about you, bud," I said, "but I'm still gonna call her Norma."

He sighed slightly, realizing that I had perceived his thoughts. "I wish everyone would."

Briefly, I wondered about all the discoverers of horrors this planet had seen. Those who had identified toxic materials, scandals, comets, murders, atrocities, and other undesirable elements. They would forever be associated with them in one way or another, willing or no. I couldn't hold it against Isaac for wanting, in a sense, to 'clear his name.' Maybe he would be remembered for being the first human to test out the teleportation relay, to bravely volunteer where none other had.

In truth, he wanted to be remembered for that, not for being associated with the force that destroyed the earth.

"I hear you. You really want to do this?" I asked him pointedly. "I mean, really?"

There wasn't a wasted second. "I do," he replied, firmly. "I really do." He grinned slightly yet confidently. "I never told you this, but I'm in love with Dina."

I frowned at him, taken aback and blinking. "Wow… uh… really? Since when? I thought you were in love with Macy." I thought back to when I had noticed the smile-heavy glances he had sent Dina's way. It made sense in hindsight.

He chuckled. "Well, there's that, sure." He grinned and shrugged. "But with Dina, since, like, forever. I dunno… you work with people and you tell them that you love them, and if that's unrequited, that can make for a pretty awkward working environment, right? So I just stowed it."

"Well, maybe now's the time that you let her know how you feel?" I offered. "Before you go through."

He shook his head. "No," he said firmly. "*Afterward*. I'll carry that love through with me while I have it. If she rejects me, I probably wouldn't want to come back. This way, I'll have a reason to return."

I knew what he was saying. I didn't have anyone at the moment, but if I did, it would probably be Trapper. She always seemed a little too independent and quippy for me, but, hey, no time like the present. I supposed I should say something to her as well, so I wasn't really in a place to give counsel about relationships to Isaac.

I nodded to him. That sounded like a very good reason indeed. I clenched my jaw and gave him the best grin I could. "Well, looks like I can't talk you out of it."

He grimly shook his head, but his confident grin remained. I nodded.

"Well, let's get you through first thing once we get them all setup again. You wanna break the news to the ladies, or should I?"

"You can do it."

"Will do, my friend," I said, as I reached out to shake his hand. He took it slowly, regarding it, and then met my eyes once more.

"Thanks for hearing me," he said.

I nodded. "I hear you. I'm proud of you, Isaac."

I watched the brave soul before me, knowing full well what would happen to Isaac Farragut, and knowing that he knew it too and desired to face it anyway.

He would be torn down and reassembled before our very eyes.

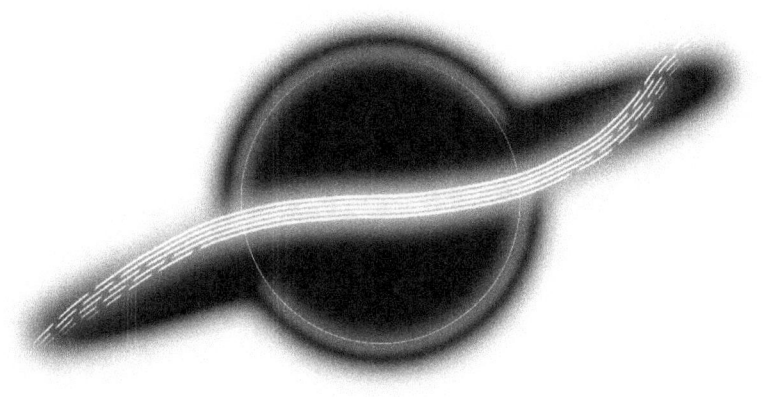

13 | The First
November 20th, 2025

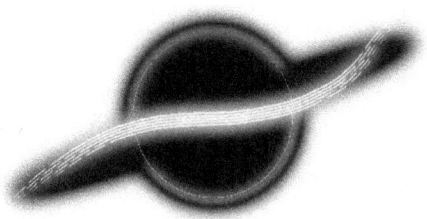

Time was ticking down.

We were drawing closer and closer to the new year… 2026… the year of Earth's doom.

But here, in our private lab at Chantilly Air Jet Center in Washington, DC, the four of us watched another countdown with bated breath and hopes filling our hearts. It was just our original team in the observation room, static and sterile, white and nondescript, allowing us to see everything with clarity, and work in optimum conditions. A far cry from the comforts of my old haunts, where in my apartment a delicious slice of pizza and a cold beer were only a few steps away. It was a certifiable step up, indeed, however: neat and clean, and reserved for us.

The naked man stood with his back to the remaining three of us, facing the newly-reassembled Nova chamber.

As with Aurora, Nova needed to be greatly enlarged to accommodate the animals we would be bringing with us. I had cartoonish imaginings of what it would be like when they brought them in. Maybe they would lead them in two by two and there would be some guy with a beard stewarding the whole process as they were loaded onto this 21st-century ark while the floodwaters rose.

To Nova's left stood the reformed Ava chamber. Ava looked identical to her former self. And, parallel to both of them, yet seventy-five feet down the lab and connected only via Wi-Fi stood the completion of the trifecta: our newest chamber, Aurora. She had been greatly enlarged to accommodate not just humans, but livestock and other larger animals that we would need to populate our new planet with. Whether or not they would survive remained to be seen. It would require quick work setting everything up for them to have what they needed in their new 'zoo.'

We had run preliminary tests once more. *Courier 4.0* – I had now made enough upgrades worthy of a substantial numeration change – had confirmed readiness of all three chambers, and all birds as well as Macy had gone through safely once more. The General even sent his wife's dog through. A tiny little Maltese named Coco. Pure white and affectionate, it came out just fine. He was a staunch and tough-built man; I think he was secretly hoping Coco would vanish into the ether so he could get a pit-bull. But she came out, and we were all rejoicing. Except the General.

Today, we would send our first human subject through. Isaac Farragut, discoverer of *Farragut-322*, strode confidently toward Nova, solemnly entering the chamber and closing the glass door behind him. It locked.

The countdown was on.

Sixty seconds.

Isaac smiled from within, pressing his hands up against the glass toward us. We all walked forward, extended our hands toward him and pressed them firmly through the door, mirroring his in symmetry. He smiled faintly and playfully glanced down, shifting his hips to further block himself from view. The ladies snickered.

We retreated and stood motionless, ten feet from the reassembled chambers, watching him, all of our hopes along for the ride in there with him. Macy sat on her haunches beside us.

Ten seconds. Nine...

Dina took a deep breath and walked down to Aurora to meet him upon reintegration.

Eight... Seven...

Isaac bowed his head and closed his eyes.

Macy stood and wagged her tail beside us, her ears up as she watched the man in the chamber.

Six... Five...

A beep sounded from Ava and Aurora, signifying readiness to receive.

Four... Three... Two...

Isaac looked back up at me. I nodded to him. He nodded...

One...

...and then he was gone. Nova lit up bright white, and then faded back to ambient light.

The chamber was empty.

Ava stood next to her, whirring and clicking. As expected, Aurora kicked into gear down the way, and did the same. There was no light flash, nothing spectacular about Aurora other than the slight audio emissions signifying her SSDs were being coded with data. She had been greatly souped up by the government, and retrofit with not one hundred, but *two* hundred 122-terabyte SSDs. This would enable us to transport roughly six thousand souls to PCb. But she was super heavy now. They would have to take great care loading her into the rocket, and launching and achieving orbit were another matter entirely.

The only thing we were lacking, which we would not be able to definitely prove, is successful life on PCb. If those stellar flares from Proxima Centauri were frequent enough, they could potentially strip away the atmosphere over time, increase radiation exposure, alter atmospheric chemistry, and more. It would be a potential negative impact, and we would be stranded there forever.

Time would tell.

But humans are known for adapting. Since the dawn of time, that's been true. And here before us, Isaac was, himself, adapting. The first human to volunteer for the teleportation relay sequence, reduced to a data stream, he had put his own soul forth at great risk to himself.

Isaac.

It was time to reintegrate him. I took a quick glance down to Dina, positioned in front of Aurora. He had been in there for thirty seconds. The plan was to go for one whole minute. We would test longer durations later. Hopefully, I or one of us would survive those tests as well. That was the clincher: we had a long journey ahead of us, and needed to survive it.

He was in there, somewhere. I whipped around and checked *Courier 4.0*. Isaac's DNA profile was right there in Partition 36 on SSD Number 135. We needed to test a random partition rather than go sequentially, and that's what *Courier 4.0* selected. He was there. All of him. Or, at least, that's what my OS reported.

"Go for reintegration, Dina," I yelled down to her, and she nodded, returning her gaze to Aurora. A knot formed in my stomach. *Please let him be okay,* I thought. I pulled my eyes away from my laptop and ran down to the final chamber. Trapper was already there with her, eagerly waiting outside the glass door for Isaac to show. Macy followed me.

Once more, the countdown.

Twelve... Eleven...

We all took a deep breath. Trapper put her arm around my shoulder. "Hey, relax. It's gonna be okay."

I nodded briskly. "Okay. Thanks, Megs."

Eight... Seven...

My mind raced, thinking back to all of the upgrades and codes I had run through *Courier 4.0* to upgrade it to the new version. Debugging and poring over all those lines of code. I hadn't missed anything... had I? I chewed my nails once more, running lines of code through my mind and scrutinizing them mercilessly.

Four... Three...

Of course I hadn't. The birds and Macy had gone through just fine, and the other dog, Coco as well.

Two... One...

Aurora illuminated from within. My heart skipped a beat. Flashes of light and arcs of energy flickered, and then a darker silhouette materialized amidst the swirling fog.

Isaac!

There he was. The door sounded and turned green, and Dina unlocked it, opening it out toward us.

The fog swirled out, and our undergrad stood there in front of us in all his glory. It had worked! He had been reintegrated! In my unbridled joy I shouted a massive *whoo-hoo!* and pumped my fist in the air, running toward him. Macy got frightened and bolted.

The fog was cold as I approached him. He had the minutest amount of sparkly coating covering his skin – crystalline fragments. His appearance was a bit ashen.

And his face drooped.

The knot in my stomach tightened.

"Isaac?" I asked him. "Buddy?" I snapped my fingers in front of his unblinking face.

There was no reaction.

Dina stifled a cry and brought her hands to her face, covering her mouth. Megan retreated to her laptop on a table behind us. Her system mirrored mine, with a cloud-based network access to *Courier 4.0.*

"Isaac?" I asked again.

Still, no response from him.

He fell forward into my arms, stiff and rigid: his body cold as ice.

"Dina… *Dina!* Trapper, help me! He's so cold!" Isaac was deceptively heavy, and he toppled over onto me as I desperately tried to lift him back up and not catch frostbite. He was *that* hypothermic. "Get a blanket!" I yelled to both of them. Dina reached for me and then did a double-take, torn between a desire to flee and a desire to comply.

Megan muttered, "Oh, no… oh, no… Dane, look," she stuttered, gazing into her laptop.

"What! I can't look, Trapper, help me! Dina! Where's that blanket?"

Isaac was frighteningly cold; icy to the touch. His face was devoid of emotion, inches from mine, and there was no sign of life within. Indeed, his pupils were dilated, and his blood vessels were distended under his skin.

"Isaac!" I cried, beginning to weep. Footsteps behind me as Dina came running back up from a medical cart against the far wall. She clutched a blanket and threw it over Isaac's shoulders. "Trapper, get the First Aid kit, get it now! *Trapper!*" She reluctantly ripped herself away from the laptop and fled to the cart Dina had just come from.

"Isaac, come on, are you okay? Talk to us!" Dina pled, rubbing his back and then recoiling from the touch. His hair was covered in glistening frozen specks, and it was solid to the touch, as if frozen concretely under the weight of ten containers of gel. "Isaac!" she pled again, and her voice cracked through her anguish.

"Megan! Where's that first aid kit?!" I cried, fiercely heaving Isaac off of me and then laying him down on the solid lab floor. No part of him relaxed to let gravity do its work and settle his weight evenly, distributing his fatty deposits around him to lay comfortably. He was statuesque, covered in a glistening cold, and morbidly unresponsive.

Macy walked up to him and sniffed him suspiciously. She growled and backed away, her tail between her legs.

Megan scurried up to us with the crash cart.

"Turn on the AED, turn it on, Megs, we're gonna lose him!" I yelled at her.

"If we haven't already," Dina muttered.

"Dina, stop that! Don't you say that!" I hovered over him and performed chest compressions, 100 to 120 per minute as we had been taught in that wretched CPR class at UW. I performed 30 compressions – his chest barely gave an inch – and then relocated and provided two rescue breaths.

"Hurry, Dane, hurry!" Dina yelled through her tears. Indeed, as I pulled away from him, my own tears fell on his face, freezing instantly into tiny circlets on his cheek.

"Dammit, Isaac, *no!*" I yelled at him. "Don't you die on me, you're supposed to live! You've got to live! Meg?"

"Here, go ahead. Wait!" she cried, turning back to the AED. "Put these on his chest." She handed me the AED pads to attach to his chest. It wasn't dry, but it was bare. He was already appearing to thaw.

I glanced back. The AED rhythm... there was none. No pulse. My face squinted in anguish, crunching into a desperate grimace. The AED beeped at me, advising a shock.

"Clear!" I cried to the others. Dina backed off. Megan just stood at the machine. "Clear!" I cried again, pressing the defibrillators to his chest and administering the shock. Crazily, my mind was thinking how futile this could be once we arrived on PCb; there would be no one conscious to administer the shock, no AED kit, just bodies all reintegrating one by one in Aurora until it burst. Cold bodies, frozen solid and in the throes of death, shattering into fragments inside my third chamber as the weight of more bodies compressed them, the glass cracked, and dead human upon dead human spilled out onto the alien terrain.

No! I had to focus. *Come on, Isaac,* I thought. *Come on!*

The AED beeped again. "Clear... clear! Dina, back off!" Dina had bowed her head and lain her hands on his knees... it looked like she was praying for him.

"Clear!" I yelled once more for good measure, and then shocked him.

The faintest beep came from the AED. A slight pulse. A sign of life flickered once and then vanished. Dina gasped, lurching up toward the machine, as if to will it to continue sounding. Trapper watched it, lightly undulating up and down, beckoning to it to continue reporting signs of life.

"Hit him again, Dane. Dane, do it!" Dina yelled, and her face was awash with warm tears.

I waited for the beep.

Once more the AED sounded.

Once more I zapped him.

Once more the machine erupted into a quick pulse of heart rhythm. Then, nothing.

I threw the paddles aside and cursed. "Dammit, Isaac, no! *No!*" I yelled at him, and then resumed with more compressions, leaning over him. As I straddled him, my own weight pushed his down, and I could hear what sounded like a faint crack from his body as it slightly shifted in the thaw, its frozen form giving way to flexibility.

30 compressions...

Two rescue breaths...

30 compressions...

Two rescue breaths...

Isaac could not die. I was not going to let him! "Come *on*, buddy, don't do this!" I yelled.

I was just going to go for the defibrillators again when his body flinched. His lifeless eyes stared upward into nothingness, but as we watched, his pupils contracted slowly, and the faintest wisp of breath emerged from his lips.

Dina choked back a cry. Megan ran over to us.

"Isaac?" pled Megan.

Dina echoed it. "Isaac, come on, buddy. You can do it, Isaac. Come on!"

I watched him, waiting. His chest slowly sunk with the speed of a turtle through thick sludge. And then it increased in speed. His eyes contracted even more. Another flinch.

The ECG started to pulse. Completely seized by arrhythmia at first, it slowly settled into a human tempo.

"That's it! That's it, Isaac. Come back to us. Come on buddy," I said, my hands on his chest, gently shaking him. Megan actually began to cry.

Isaac's chest rose and fell erratically, and a trace of a wheeze morphed into a cough as his body slowly came back to life. His pupils contracted somewhat. Dina grabbed the blanket under her hands and began to rub him all over with it, desperate to warm him up.

"Come on, my friend. You got this," I urged.

His pupils finally contracted fully, and his eyebrows furrowed as he blinked. His body spasmed several times in the clutches of a synapse misfire… or an epileptic seizure… or something. I wasn't sure. All I cared about was that there were signs of life now, and they were strong.

Isaac moaned, and a hot trail of air emerged from his lips until it was expended. And then, as if he were a newborn freshly delivered from his mother's womb, he took his first new breath of life on the other side of data, and his lungs expanded. Color slowly returned to his face. Tiny glistening crystals, by now thawed, dripped from his hardened body, the icy grip now relinquishing its grip to the onrush of warmth. Grey gradually gave way to healthy flesh tones. I looked him up and down. Dina continued to rub him.

The ECG started to quicken its pace.

"That's it! That's it! Welcome back, buddy!"

Isaac inhaled fully and then let out a horrendous cry as if stabbed by a thousand swords. His face contorted as the AED heart rhythm went absolutely berserk. Sounding as if he had the heart of a hummingbird, it pulsed wildly and then settled into a slow and steady rhythm once more.

"Isaac? Isaac? Talk to me, buddy. Trapper! Oxygen!" I barked. I hovered over our friend. "Buddy? Can you hear me?"

His eyes ever so slowly migrated from their thousand-yard stare through the ceiling to meet mine. His breathing slowed and then normalized.

Megan ran over with the oxygen and mask, and fitted it over his face. His hair was less crinkly now, with the slightest amount of give as she lifted him up and slipped it behind his head. She turned it on. The slow hiss sounded from the tank and we could hear it entering into his lungs.

Isaac looked at me. He nodded ever so slowly, blinking as his brow compressed into hardened wrinkles.

I hear you.

The words we spoke to each other when he volunteered. With that expression, he both acknowledged my question and showed that he was still himself, remembering our previous conversation.

I couldn't hold back the tears anymore, and nearly convulsed with joy. "You hear me," I said. "I hear you."

His eyes creased slightly, and there was the slightest trace of a twinkle in them as his cheeks rose into a grin.

I tousled his hair. "You're back. You made it. You *made* it, buddy."

He nodded again.

He had made it.

Dina let out a gigantic sigh of relief, and then burst into fresh tears. Trapper descended to her and put her arm around her. The ECG continued to sound out life.

Isaac was back.

His heart was ticking well.

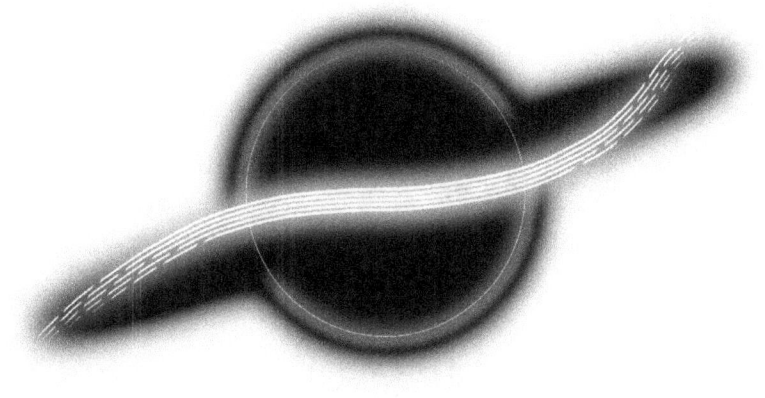

14 | Ups and Downs
November 21st, 2025

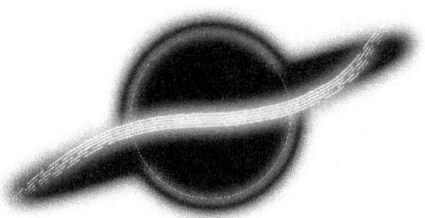

I just had so many questions.

Isaac was recovering, but we had nearly lost him. He was still in medical and was being attended to, but that event rattled and scarred us. It should have worked. All of it should have worked! Why hadn't it fully worked?

My faith was rocked, but that only served to force me into some uncomfortable introspection. What was faith, anyway? Did I have any? Surely I had *belief* in *Courier* and the chambers. Clearly, they had already worked. But was my belief in them only *because* they worked? Or, conversely, did they work because I *already* believed in them? I wasn't sure. Either way, this episode with Isaac rocked me, and that gnawed at my mind, my sense of self-assurance, *and* at this whole escape plan of ours.

If there was no one to rehabilitate a teleported soul, then everyone would perish. If we all issued out of Aurora as frozen bodies suspended in animation and in need of an AED, then there we would stay: icy corpses dumped on a faraway world, doomed to thaw and rot, fodder for whatever roaming animal life might happen upon us. Six thousand of us dead in the course of a few hours.

Furthermore, the whole prospect was tainted by an alien environment on PCb that would be potentially hostile to life... at least, eventually. That solar radiation could doom all of us someday, even if we stayed on the dark side as Megan and I had discussed.

Would we just be escaping the frying pan only to dive headlong right into the fire? Would we be living on borrowed time, marooned on a desolate planet that would provide just enough to support our small numbers, but eventually would be unsustainable for the long term?

Would Norma – or, rather, *Farragut-322* – circle around and destroy PCb as well?

Certainly, by teleporting a contingent of our population onto this planet in an entirely different system, we would cheat death for a while. But for how long?

Isaac had cheated death. He had reintegrated, but in a frightening way, requiring human intervention through resuscitation. That was a luxury we wouldn't have on PCb.

He was improving, and he was all there, cognitively and with his memory. He was still himself. Those were all good signs. However, none of us had any idea what this would all mean in practical application.

I went back to the drawing board once more while he recuperated. Something had gone wrong in *Courier 4.0* yet again. Why hadn't I learned with the birds? Why hadn't I buttoned it all up to perfection? Something had suspended Isaac in that he had not only been reduced to data streams, but placed in a stasis similar to cryo-freeze. His system had been deliberately slowed near catatonia in order to preserve him. The question swirled around in my head: *how to keep a human being at equilibrium as data?* How do I do that?

Trapper was occupied with more ethereal matters. What did Isaac see while in stasis? Where did his mind go? Was he awake? Alert? Did he dream? What sorts of dreams did he have? But - it wasn't time to debrief Isaac. Not yet. He slept a lot, which suggested another matter. Depending on where we were all deposited, we would need to allow for time to recover. That would not be possible on the dark side, freezing in subzero temperatures.

We would have our answers soon.

Meanwhile, Pluto had disappeared. It was nowhere to be found, and the charts showed full well what did it. And soon, our system would only have seven planets. Saturn, a colossal, ringed beauty unfortunately was in an orbit close to Norma's path. It would soon pass through her to the other side, where death reigned. The earth was warming up, and this day, late in November, was an unearthly 69 degrees.

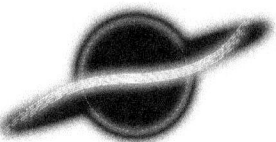

"It was surreal, guys. Just… surreal," Isaac said. We watched him as he shook his head, lost in thought. "I'd never experienced such peace before. Never. It was like the best sleep you've ever had," he said, and then he grinned a giant toothy, contented smile.

We mirrored it.

"Well, you were dug in like a frozen tick when you came back, that's for sure," Trapper said. "Had to shock you three times."

"I know, I remember! That hurt."

"You remember?" I asked him.

"Oh yeah. It was like when you're dreaming and you fall, you have a reflex spasm? Like that. Only it felt like alarm bells ringing inside my head. *Time to get up!* Like your mom is yelling at you on a school day to get moving and come downstairs for breakfast. It was jarring. Jolted me back. Dane, you've gotta find a way to expedite reintegration because I don't think I would have come back otherwise."

"Well, you had other reasons," I said cryptically to him, and his eyes darted over to Dina briefly, and then back to me. I winked at him, keeping his secret safe.

The ladies looked at me quizzically for a moment.

"Anyway, tell us more," I urged, "as long as you have the energy for it."

He grew momentarily silent, and stared off into the distance as we surrounded him there, lying peacefully upon his gurney. An IV sputtered momentarily amidst the faint, ambient beeps of his ECG. I glanced up. Heart rate, blood pressure, oxygen levels, body temp, all of them were nominal now, with only an occasional palpitation spike.

"Going through Nova was the same as before, right? It seemed like I was in there for an hour. I know it wasn't instantaneous; I know there was a bit of a delay before Ava grabbed me, but not an hour's worth." He blinked, trying to recall it. "This time though, it seemed like weeks, months, even years. I can't begin to parse out all my dreams, but there were many. Dreams I remember from my youth, mostly. Dreams of people, you guys," - here he looked at Dina and grinned, and I wondered how enjoyable that memory was- "I don't recall any nightmares or anything scary. I also don't think Norma even existed in my dreams. Like… it wasn't a factor. It was just a state of bliss and suspended animation, and just *really* good sleep."

"That's so interesting," Dina said, "that it seemed like years. I wonder when your REM state kicked in during all that. They say that most of your dreaming is done right before you wake up. I wonder if there's a way to monitor when that kicked in." I frowned, not understanding. "I mean, did his dreams happen during resuscitation or during stasis? Before or after reintegration, I mean."

I nodded. "Yeah, that would be good to know. I can try to code some enhanced brainwave monitoring into *Courier 4.0*. Might be time for another upgrade, methinks. By the time we're ready to launch I think I'll have to call it *Courier 392.7*." Dina smiled.

"Yeah, I don't know," Isaac replied. "It was really luminescent, swirling, serene, ethereal, esoteric, intangible, every other word you can use to describe something so peaceful. Like one of those white noise machines you're powerless against as a baby, ya know? Riding in a car for a long trip and falling asleep to the steady hum. It was just…"

He trailed off so long that my eyebrows went up, watching and waiting.

"…*perfect*," he finished, grinning again, and he closed his eyes.

"Until the very end," I said.

His eyes opened slowly, as if out of a dream. Isaac nodded. "Yeah," he said, his nose crinkling, "it was just jarring. I don't know if that was from the reintegration or the AED though. You lose track of time and space."

I nodded, patting his chest. "It's okay, man. We're just glad you're back. *All* of us," I said, raising an eyebrow to him. I let him see my eyes darting over to Dina. He grinned again. "I've gotta check on the OS and see what went wrong this time, but before that I've got an update meeting with Donze. You rest. We'll catch up soon. Isaac," I said, pausing and staring intently at him, "I'm really sorry. We almost lost you. Everything worked for the birds, the dogs, I don't know what happened. We humans are just so much more complex, I just need to… I don't know… figure out what changed with you. We'll get there."

"You should also look into really speeding up the entries," Trapper said. "The critical part is getting people *in*. Once they're in and they're in stasis on the drives, Genesis has to launch, and it has to get out of here, even if it's fleeing from a dying planet right when it's being spaghettified. If we're now accommodating roughly 6,000 people, we need to have them hop on board the Genesis train with no delay." She cocked an eyebrow at me and tilted her head.

I nodded in agreement. "Right. Sounds good. Come with me, Trapper, yeah? You can help me with the coding after we see Genesis and talk with Donze. See ya, Isaac. Welcome back, buddy." I tapped him on the chest.

Dina started to follow us, but Isaac called her back and asked her to stay. I didn't turn around to gawk, but the smile spread across the length of my face.

It was a thing of beauty, truly. Genesis was coming along really well. Gorgeous and sleek, it would be able to house Aurora and *much* more. There were building materials and tools for shelters, crop seed, animal pens and cages, agriculture supplies, weapons, fuel, enough bottled water to fill a stadium to the brim, tinder and flint, storage containers, medical provisions, and so much more, all compressed into the smallest real estate possible so as to be able to transport as much as possible to PCb.

The Genesis craft was similar in body type to any other NASA shuttle humanity had ever deployed, space-ready and designed for long stays. It was simply massively longer. The previous regulation shuttles were 122 feet long and flaunting a gorgeous wingspan of 78 feet. Genesis was alike them only in form factor. *This* getaway craft was 167 feet long with a wingspan of 92 feet. It was breathtakingly huge, and its cargo bay vast.

It was fully autonomous, requiring no pilot, and it was also differentiated from previous shuttle craft in that it had Harrier Jet-like propulsion, enabling vertical launches and landings. In this way, it would be able to follow a sequence for landing on PCb that required no human intervention, and could safely touch down with all aboard.

I didn't care to ask what the sticker price was on it.

Trapper and I paced around it and nodded approvingly. And, like a lightning bolt, it suddenly hit both of us at the same time.

This ship exists because of us.

The only reason they were building this was because we had developed a teleportation system for PCb that required a craft to get it there. This was that craft, and here we stood.

I wished Isaac could be with us right now.

Genesis would be mounted to the side of the conventional booster rocket for initial launch, and then the nuclear propulsion technology would take over from there once at a safe orbit around Earth. All of that was beyond my paygrade and over my head, but the technicians working on it were bustling about in white coats and skittering across the floor of the hangar as if Norma were coming *today*.

The bright lights of the hangar were piercing, leaving nothing to darkness. This thing needed to be airtight, that's for sure, and it needed to be foolproof. To that end they labored.

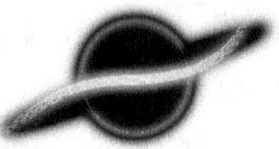

The SecDef was red-faced and bustling just as much as the techs were in the hangar. Something was up.

"Mr. Secretary?" I asked, after we were let in to the conference room he was sitting at. He held up a finger toward me, and pointed to a Bluetooth headset in his ear. I nodded and waited.

"Yes, Mr. Vice President, well, they're running me ragged as it is. Crews here are working as fast as they can." He paused. "And I told you that we'd be on schedule. You still have my promise on that." Another pause. "Well, unfortunately, the only thing that moves at that speed around here is that supermassive black hole. Besides, we still have more testing to do with the teleportation subj-"

He stopped, and rolled his eyes, balling his hand up into a fist and ready to thump it down hard on his desk.

"Fine. You do that," he said, curtly. "No, thank *you*, Mr. Vice President. A pleasure as always," he said, and then practically ripped out his headset and tossed it haphazardly onto the table. "Prick," he finalized.

Donze took a quick but deep breath, and then stood, greeting us. "Mr. Currier. Ms. Trapper. Good to see you," he said. "That was our illustrious and highly patient Vice President. Sorry you had to hear that."

I shrugged, ready to wave it away. "It's fine, Mr. Donze, I-"

"It's not, but whatever. I admit, hearing of your plans early on, I was not a believer, myself. Quite the pessimist, actually. I'm sure you remember our call. But now, it seems that certain unbelievers at the top of the pecking order are more comfortable wielding a hammer than joining in belief."

"Sir?" I asked, confused.

Donze now shrugged. "They'd rather wield a sword than a ploughshare. Anyway," he said tiredly, sitting back down in a huff. We sat as well.

Donze rubbed his face and then continued. "Looks like you've seen Genesis. They've got me stationed down here for a week overseeing it. It's a beaut,' ain't it?" Strangely, he donned a Texas drawl for that line. "The rocket itself is down at KSC in Florida at Launch Complex 39. It's coming along as well. The nuclear propulsion tech is nearby, but we can't disclose where that is, for security reasons. It'll be retrofit onto the rocket soon. Can you give me an update on your progress, please?"

I straightened up. "Certainly. Well, I texted you after the teleportation subject – our partner, Isaac Farragut – went through. He's healing nicely and he's making a great recovery. He shared about the journey in stasis and what it was like for him, how long it took, all of that. It was a peaceful passage, but not necessarily a tranquil return. My partner Megan, here, and I will need to further isolate how to refine that process, and we're working on that right after our meeting with you."

"What happened to him, exactly, Mr. Currier?"

I took a breath. "Well, it appears that for him the journey took longer. When he went through back in my apartment using only the initial two chambers, he reported that it felt like close on an hour. I would concur with that; my experience felt the same. But with the new system using all three chambers and teleporting over wireless streams, and then being kept in stasis on the drives, even though it was approximately one minute, to him it felt more like *years*, he said."

"Years?"

"Yes, sir, maybe more."

"Did he appear any older? Had he aged?"

"Not visibly, sir, no. He looks, acts, and talks the same. All of his bodily functions are normal, his metrics and DNA profile matched to his original with no degradation or degeneration, and he's clearly himself, just tired. My colleague Megan and I – as well as Dina Jensen – believe that he's recovering more from the revival post-transit. Having to resuscitate him was physically taxing. He expressed that himself."

"Oh, he did?"

"Yes. He reported it was jarring. He was really dug in there like a frozen tick, to quote Megan here."

"Is that right?" Donze said to Trapper.

Megan nodded. "Definitely. Flesh was frozen; hair was glistening with crystalline specks from the cold; pupils contracted, vessels distended, catatonic, sir. He came out like a human popsicle."

"Fascinating. I assume that throws a wrench into the process, of course."

"It does."

"I'm sorry to hear it. I'm sure you'll get back on track."

I nodded vigorously. "Oh, most definitely, sir. We will, and soon. The relays need to get everyone out of Aurora and reintegrated in an identical state to their previous makeup, or we'll have a logjam, and possibly…," I trailed off, unwilling to give voice to the word.

Donze squinted and leaned toward me. "Possibly…?"

"Possibly," I started again, "fusion. As in, multiple subjects becoming reintegrated together, over and over and over, all of them assimilated into one giant mass, which eventually would fill up the Aurora chamber to maximum capacity, causing it to burst. It would be an utter failure, of course, and we would leave this calamity for another one of our own making."

"Well, you better solve that problem right quick, Mr. Currier. Ms. Trapper," he growled. "That's an end result that the President and Vice President will not accept, most assuredly. Nor will I."

"Yessir," I said.

Donze's phone rang. "Donze," he greeted. "Could you say that again?" he asked in a stunted fashion, and then he turned to us and rose quickly. "Go. You need to go. Now. Back to your friend. He's coding."

My heart jumped into my throat, and my eyes morphed into wide circles. Trapper and I jumped up and flew out of Donze's office to find Isaac and Dina.

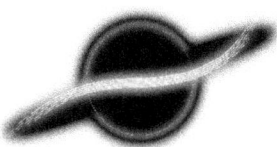

The medics had been alerted. They were working on him feverishly. Dina was off to one side, inconsolable. She covered her face and shook.

The AED was out. They shocked him.

Over and over again, they brought the paddles to his chest. But this time, there was no life. There was nothing.

Flatline.

Dina turned away and sunk into my arms as I wept. There Isaac lay, mouth agape, staring upward into the ceiling and beyond. His skin looked pallid and weak, his chest sunk. Yet, at the corners of his mouth, a faint trace of a smile teased.

Isaac, come on buddy. Don't do this to us. You were supposed to be well. I hear you, my friend. Come back. I hear you.

But Isaac heard nothing, and before we knew it, he was gone. The medics backed away and called it. Dina buried her head into my chest and sobbed, heartbroken. My own heart was ripped.

I let him go through. Me. This is my fault.

I didn't code everything properly.

And now, he was dead.

The connection was clear. Isaac was dead because of a problem with *Courier 4.0.* He had bravely volunteered to go through, and we had failed to bring back that brave soul. And now, he had suffered from a fatal heart attack on the coattails of what was to be his new identity, as the first person to travel through a teleportation system, be frozen in stasis, and emerge healthy in victory to show it could be done.

Through Dina's sobs, I distinctly heard one phrase, over and over again, and I lost it.

"He loved me, Dane. He told me... he loved me. He... told me he loved me! No! Isaac!"

I bit my lip, which was trembling, as all the air was sucked out of me. There, lying before us and turning a shade of purple, was the dead body of a brave soul who had grown even braver. He had told Dina. He told her how he felt about her.

For Dina, I was glad.

For Isaac, I was devastated. My faith had been rocked after his traumatic return. Now, I didn't even know if I had any at all. You could say my faith was annihilated, and I didn't know where to turn now. If I had any faith whatsoever, it was most definitely in a tailspin; and, potentially, in all likelihood, an unrecoverable one.

I needed to fix this damned system 'right quick,' as Donze had said, or no one would be able to tell *anyone* they loved them anymore.

Questions stacked perilously high in my brain as far as how to make this work successfully, and in time. I was not at a loss for questions.

I just had so few answers.

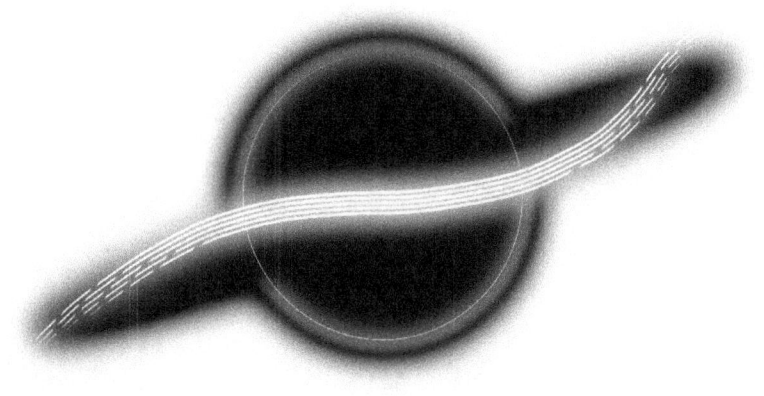

15 | Breakthrough
December 1st, 2025

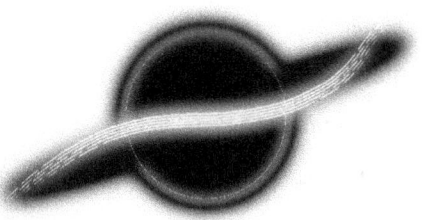

Hungry and driven, it was coming.

We all watched the feed, live, where Saturn was literally ripped apart. Its glorious rings of ice and rock disintegrated long before the planet itself did, skimming and ricocheting off Saturn's surface as they barreled across the stars into the black void that was Farragut-322. The planet went next, splintering and fracturing into large chunks, spinning and whirling crazily into the void. The molten core of the planet was exposed as portions of the crust broke off, and the temperature differential caused massive cave-ins and explosions as the quiet gas giant bellowed, gusted, and then was extinguished forever.

Our sun was also now gently being pulled toward the supermassive, helpless to resist. Its gravitational forces strove against the hungry beast drifting our way, and, at least for the present, was positioned relatively close to where it had always been. But the clock was ticking…

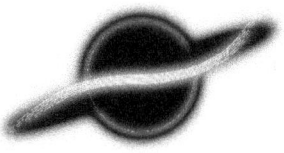

Dina was coming around again. She had to acknowledge that she loved Isaac, and it was hard for her to commit to a love she'd only just glanced off of. Her heart had been massaged by joy, only to be shattered by pain.

And as for Isaac's heart, what had caused the attack? The coroner reported that he hadn't had any congenital heart disease or defects. I sort of already figured that: in truth, going through Nova and Ava, he should have been perfected. But had the relay to Aurora degenerated something that was originally perfected in Ava? The coroner didn't think so. He had arteriosclerosis, as if he had had a high cholesterol diet or diabetes. That *had* to have happened 'coming out of the thaw,' as we called it. Something just hadn't reintegrated or settled correctly, and it was only a matter of time.

That killed me, frankly. Going through Nova had always *improved* the subject, or, at least that was initially true of Isaac when he first went through. I know it was true of Macy and me. Every time I thought about his demise I could only shake my head in frustration. What went wrong? And more importantly, *why?* I had such belief in my system, but, if pressed to be super honest, my faith in it had been perilously tested. If we were to make it, then I needed to have faith. It was that simple.

Trapper and I *did* go back and debug *CourierOS,* and we finally figured it out. It was now dubbed *Courier 5.1*, two evolutionary upgrades beyond the original success. It took us a while, but we finally discovered what caused Isaac's traumatic reintegration, and thus, would have prompted his subsequent heart attack. There were lines of subcode that could have caused my chambers – and thus, the SSD drives – to act as a cryo-freeze containment system, reducing the body's functions to the barest minimum. In all honesty, I had programmed in coding to strip the human element down to its core functions for stasis, but I had not reduced the pattern to all zeros. There were ones in there, not just zeros.

Something got lost in translation in the relay, and it took us a while to figure out where the breakdown occurred. Eventually, we determined, that in the handoff from Ava to Aurora and in the RAID array of the drives, the pattern was being split unevenly between the two drive partitions, and in the reintegration process, *Courier 4.0* had been simply trying to parse out both drives and stitch them back together. However, what it was ultimately doing was *pausing* the second partition's data and only reading the first. When the second partition was then assimilated, it overwrote the first partition, effectively resetting it to a cold state.

Thus, if we had used only single, and not *mirrored* partitions, Isaac would have emerged from Aurora as whole and alive as he had been when he was sent to Ava. I had to rethink the whole process and ensure that both partitions were read *and* assimilated simultaneously.

For now, however, neither one of us were willing to go through the teleportation relay that was Nova-Ava-Aurora. Not yet. After seeing what happened to Isaac, Dina certainly was out of the running, and we would never ask that of her. Nonetheless, a clock was ticking there as well: someone would eventually *have* to step up and volunteer, or we would never know if this whole 'cockamamie plan,' as Donze had once referred to it, would work.

In my heart, I knew who would have to volunteer. There was one person who screwed it up, and there was only one person who could redeem their mistake.

In my heart, I knew it was going to have to be me.

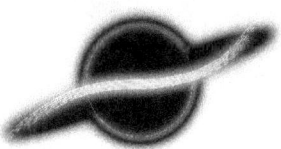

After the autopsy, we had Isaac buried outside the base on a beautiful, hot, late November day. The very phrase, 'hot, late November day' seemed so oxymoronic. And it was getting hotter, even with the sun drifting toward the black hole, because we were now *also* drifting toward it – and the sun – as well.

Farragut-322 was named as such in honor of its finder. This was something that Isaac had not wanted, and we all knew that he would be rolling over in his grave if he knew that the scientific community, and indeed the whole world, was now referring to it as such. It would have been the death of him all over again.

As for us, we resolved in our hearts never to call it that. We resolved to still call it Norma. After all, naming it after a horrible ex-wife seemed far better than naming it after a beloved colleague and friend whose research of it, and escape plan from it, had killed him.

The President held another national address, but was mumbling and incoherent. Something was happening to him – and, arbitrarily, to others around us, we had noticed – as if our very lives and consciousness were also being pulled toward Norma, in some kind of inadvertent and unwilling tug into a diminished consciousness that was not representative of their original selves.

Their mental acuity was being eroded, as if the oncoming gravity of Norma could work on the soul, and they slowly slipped into a dementia-like state. I had talked with my mom and dad at intervals, and I noticed it with them as well. A few of our techs stationed at the lab here exhibited some warning signs. It seemed to strike indiscriminately.

The medical community documented it and started referring to it, informally, as 'the slide.' Those who showed initial signs of the slide were monitored and prescribed things like Modafinil and Piracetam: nootropics and wakefulness-promoting agents, almost as if they suffered from narcolepsy.

Just as the galaxy was being affected, so were its citizens, pulled irresistibly toward a miserable end.

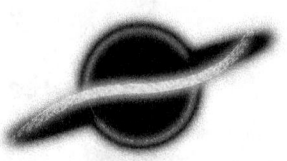

December 2nd, 2025

And now, early this morning, I sat in my Washington, DC apartment, brooding over, literally, everything.

Macy came up to me, and for some reason was extra affectionate. She would not leave my side.

"Hey, baby girl," I said to her, reaching out and enveloping her with a giant hug. She was doing fine here, which was something I feared. I'm sure she missed the familiar sights and scents of Seattle. We had been able to walk her in the narrow gaps between fierce research.

As I sat on the couch, I looked her deep in the eyes and rubbed her ears, remembering how much Isaac loved to do that. He really loved my dog, and I'm sure she missed him in some canine sentience.

I thought back to the UW lab, and all the days Dina, Isaac and I spent working together monitoring the stars and the systems out there. That dark room pinpricked with light from all of those monitors full of celestial maps and charts, wondering what we were looking at, or even looking for.

A memory of Isaac suddenly came rushing back at me from the recesses of my memory. It was from the early days of our tenure at the lab, just the two of us, talking freely.

"What do you plan to do once you graduate?"

"Me?" I asked. "I'm not sure yet. My family's down in Alameda, that's where I grew up. Just always loved the Pacific Northwest and wanted to go to the U. I think I'll try for something around here. I like it here. How about you?"

Isaac shook his head. "I don't think I'll stay. I want to get out and see the world. I'd love to chase extraterrestrial life, ya know? Ever seen *Contact* with Jodie Foster? Great movie."

"Oh yeah, that's a good one."

"Yeah," Isaac replied, "her dad said something to her at one point, like 'if we're the only ones out here, it seems like an awful waste of space.' I'd love to visit other worlds and prove or disprove their existence. Don't know until ya go, right?"

"Definitely. Don't know until ya go."

And just like that, the reverie faded, but Isaac's words remained in me, reverberating through my memory.

Don't know until ya go.

Was that why he wanted to be the first through the relay? I knew that he didn't appreciate the association with Norma, but had he also gone through because he wanted to be the first to get out of his own body and test this whole process of interplanetary space travel?

Regardless of the reason, I was moved, and once again found myself choking up. That old conversation motivated and inspired me. As before, when it was just Nova and Ava, a sudden resolve washed over me to see it through. We couldn't afford to wait, and I couldn't afford to carry the shame of what had happened to Isaac. We didn't need shame on PCb. We would need to start our new lives there whole and confident, ready to start anew.

I scratched Macy on the head and gave her some Isaac-worthy ear rubs, grabbed my things, and headed back to the lab, texting Trapper to meet me there as soon as she could.

No time like the present, right, Isaac? Norma wouldn't wait, and there was only one simple truth here:

Don't know until ya go.

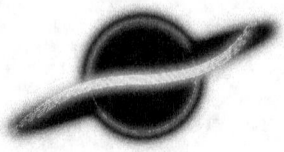

I stood before her, unashamed, and unafraid.

Correction: I was afraid. Yes. There was no denying that. What I was about to do was scary. But I was definitely unashamed. I *had* been ashamed over what had happened to Isaac, but frustrated rumination finally gave way to action and ownership. So, now I stood before Megan Trapper, with her at my laptop, ready to send me into the great unknown. Afraid, yes.

Ashamed, no.

Only she and I knew the game plan. I would be gone for a week. We needed to test this out at greater intervals. If we couldn't stand a week, then we wouldn't be able to stand a month. If not a month, then not a few years. And if not a few years, then we wouldn't be able to stand the approximately eighty-five years it would take to reach PCb.

Someone had to go, and that someone was me.

Don't know until ya go.

She didn't argue, she didn't protest, and she didn't try to talk me out of it. Megan Trapper knew what needed to be done, and she, like me, had the innate sense that I was the one who had to do it. This wasn't nobility here; it was strictly necessity due to there being no more time to be noble.

She looked me up and down, and then approached me. The countdown was running.

She had everything on, and I had nothing on. I stood before her, and she embraced me, fully, in a manner that I was unprepared for.

Megan Trapper was spunky, but there was a beauty there that I beheld perhaps for the first time. She removed her glasses and gazed deep into my eyes, staring into the well of my soul. There was no smile, no affirming words, just… understanding. And for the first time, I gazed into eyes that I had before found to be shielded; aloof. Now, this close, and this connected, I found them alluring. Tempting. Human. Gorgeous beyond words.

I smiled at her, and then took a deep breath, glancing back briefly at Nova, with its open door beckoning to me.

If I didn't come back, Trapper would have to spearhead this herself. But the reality was that she was nearly as good at coding as I was, and she knew *Courier 5.1* well enough, and the stars even better. PCb was, after all, her idea. If I didn't return, everything would be in competent hands. I had do this, and she knew it.

Trapper pulled me close, wrapping her hands around my naked back, holding me tightly. I reciprocated, wrapping my arms around her, smelling her hair, pulling her into me. It was the sweetest hug I think I had ever experienced.

"I have a note on my desktop to give to my mom and dad, should I, ya know…" I mumbled.

"Don't," she said, firmly. It was almost a plea, commanding yet breathy.

I stopped, exhaling, and finally nodding, steeling myself. "You're right. Don't think that way. I'm coming back. I know."

She crinkled her nose, and tilted her head at me. "No, you dummy. Don't *ruin the moment.*"

And then Megan Trapper reached up and pulled my face down toward her own. She kissed me deeply, and then buried her face into my chest, turning her cheek to my chest and resting softly against my own.

We both turned toward the laptop. Thirty-seven seconds. "Go," she said, pushing me away. "And come back, or I won't have anyone to call 'pudgy,' *Pudgy.*" She playfully slapped my left butt cheek.

I giggled through my nose, and then pulled away, walking briskly and resolutely toward Nova. My eyes went to Ava beside her. She was ready. Further, my eyes were drawn down the seventy-five foot line to the waiting Aurora.

Everything was set to go.

I stepped in.

The door whirred and then closed silently behind me and locked. The floor felt cold, but not frightfully so.

I remained standing, unapologetic and confident. This was it. All or nothing. Go time. All in, right here.

I closed my eyes. I didn't want to watch the countdown. I had done this before, and it would be fine, I told myself as I whispered a silent prayer to whomever might be listening. I felt Megan watching me through the glass.

My hands were at my sides. I craned my neck toward Nova's ceiling and fanned my arms out slightly, as I let the sequence break me down into a trillion particles under a complex DNA profile, reducing me to a data stream in the most peaceful moment I have ever experienced… just like Isaac had.

Images flashed through my mind. Dreams. I saw the Earth, old and new, I saw my parents, myself as a baby, our planet ripping apart in a horrendous crumpling show of force by Norma. I witnessed friends and family wishing me well and sending me off, and then they were burnt to smoldering ash in the heat of a supernova. One remained whole and well. I knew him. It was Isaac. He was in there only as a residual memory, I realized, but it felt so tangibly and hauntingly real, as if his spirit had left some imprint on the SSD's partition.

And then all was silent and still, as I was breathlessly whisked into a vortex of peace, riding me on the soft sails of ships steered by stars, gliding me through the galaxy. I heard laughter and tears, joy and pain, sobbing and cheering, all fused into a funnel of sentience, tingling my flesh and coursing through my arteries. Life and death merged into a single stream as I filled a partition on a drive…

…and slept.

Don't know until ya go.

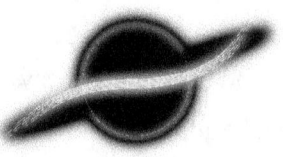

December 9th, 2025

"Well, you're still pudgy," a voice said, and then someone hugged me in unbridled laughter, bolting toward me and leaping into my arms as my eyes blearily came to, struggling in the bright light. If I didn't know any better, there were tears forming in those eyes as I strained to see them.

Megan Trapper stared longingly into my eyes and kissed me deeply. A faint whimper emitted from her as she continued to kiss me. *I could get used to this kind of wakeup call*, I thought, and realized that the thought was my own, the inherent body heat I felt inside me was mine, my consciousness remembered leaving *and* returning, and the familiar sights of the lab coalesced into clarity around me, revealing my memory to be intact.

My heartbeat was strong, and it was mine.

Trapper looked at me. I didn't know or care how much time had elapsed since I had gone; she would tell me. The look on her face revealed everything had gone just as planned, and I took her in and kissed her in return as the swirling fog enveloped us and streamed out of Aurora.

It was then that I realized that a few other techs had gathered around in the background, aware of our tests and wanting to celebrate this victory. It meant something to them as well.

"I'm suddenly acutely aware that I'm still naked," I grunted to Trapper.

She just stared at me, sighing through a smile. "Some things never change. I told you not to ruin the moment!"

She kissed me deeply, and she held me.

Hungry and weary, I had returned.

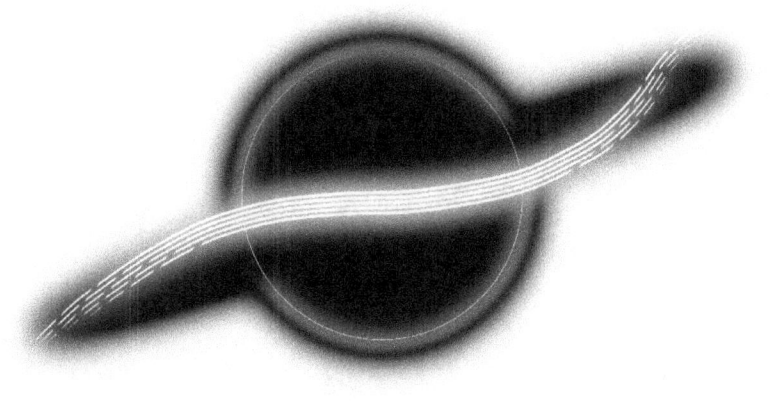

16 | Breakdown
December 12th, 2025

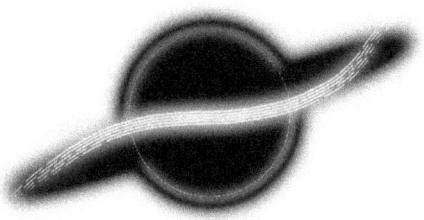

We had done it.

I had gone through, after having been in stasis for a whole week.

Dina was at first angry beyond words that she had not been allowed to be part of my teleportation, but she ultimately relented, realizing that had something gone wrong yet again, she couldn't take it. I shared with her my dream of Isaac, and she sobbed. Trapper and I embraced her and held her for what felt like a solid ten minutes as she rode that wave of longing and loss. It was precious and necessary.

I had been checked out by medical, and given the all-clear. I truly didn't feel any different. For a while I thought that Dina might be resenting my wholeness; the fact that I was relatively unaffected by the teleportation relay. After all, a whole week had gone by, and I was in stasis, and I was fine…

…and her would-be boyfriend was dead.

For the first day or so, admittedly, I felt as though I was walking on eggshells around her, hypersensitive; not sure if she was judging me, stewing in silent resentment. I thought I knew Dina better than that, and she remained her usual self, so I had to press on despite my suspicions.

A lot had happened while I was away.

The biggest news was, of course, that Trapper had also gone through a day after I had, almost as though she sought to check on me while I was in stasis. As if she even could. That news blew me away. Dina had set her up for the relay jump, and programmed her to be in a partition right next to mine. However, she only wanted to be gone for a day. That was all the risk she was willing to take at this time. Dina seconded it, and sent her through.

Trapper said that all readouts were clear and lights were green, so she felt much safer knowing that I was in there, alive and well. I felt there was something more, however, and told her as much. My *Just couldn't stand to live without me, huh?* resulted in her sporting a mocking tone and contorting her face with a *nnh, yeah, nnnh, that's it, yeah.*

I chuckled through my nervous fear *and* amazement that she had gone through before even receiving any assurance that I had successfully returned. She was brave *and* foolhardy. However, all three of us had now gone through, and all three had returned. But only Trapper and I had made the relay jump. Dina was still holding out, and we couldn't blame her.

They filled me in on the week I had missed, and nearly all of it was bleak.

Jupiter, that massive 43,440-mile radius gas giant, 11 times wider than Earth and on a far orbit close to Norma, was reluctantly answering Norma's nefarious call, sliding across the galaxy into the black void, never to return. It was not there yet, but its trajectory was being mapped, and it was on its way. Neptune was unfortunately close to Pluto on their apogee orbit, and it was now gone as well, a silent death of a planet we had never visited, and never would.

Australia had split in two. So had the Arctic and Antarctic poles. There had been seventeen deadly tsunamis in the past week alone, caused by glacier collapse. Indonesia was wiped out. Greenland was flooded. If global warming was an issue before, nothing could have prepared us for what was happening now. Norma, as it approached, was causing unpredictable gravitational disruptions. Its very presence warped gravity, causing catastrophic quakes and atmospheric collapse. The radiation levels were growing at an alarming rate, and the number of earthquakes now occurring were taking on a frightening exponential curve.

The Genesis craft was nearly ready. The nuclear propulsion component was being tested in a separate bunker deep underground at the launch site, shielded from public view and keeping us safe on the surface.

The Stock market had tanked and bottomed out, and would probably never recover, not that anyone cared. What blew me away was that Wall Street was still actually open, and there were reports of traders eagerly conducting business should Norma 'pass us by.' Ridiculous. You can't beat idealistic hubris. Humans are unquenchably hopeful.

That wasn't all of it. A collective fever was afflicting those of us who were still here on this planet, awaiting the inevitable. It was dark, and it was rampant.

President Trump had slid. 'The slide' was definitely real, and he was not immune. The slide was indiscriminate, touching everyone differently. The funny thing was, I felt fine, better than ever, in fact. As with my first teleportation using only Nova and Ava, I felt improved. Was I now immune to the slide? Time would tell.

But for the President: he had been reduced to a babbling idiot, like so many had been: a strange phenomenon seemed to just rob them of their soul, absconding with their personality, their mind, and everything that made them *them,* as they silently drifted into dementia. Exposure to Norma's event horizon – drawing nearer though still distant – was causing ego dissolution. The slide was no joke, and it grasped at us with silent invisible tentacles, gently and violently ripping our identities from us as we meandered here still.

Norma's influence had triggered a collective existential crisis. Religion was surging anew, and my mom was sharing her newfound faith with me over the phone and pelting me with faith-based messages daily. There were no messages from dad. He had killed himself while I was away. They had called my cell while I was gone, and couldn't reach me. I had told them where I was going, so they called the mainline for Chantilly and discovered that I was not here. Dad's mental acuity had been going anyway, and he jumped to the conclusion that I had died. He couldn't take it. Norma was coming *and* his son was dead? He went down to the basement where he kept his liquor and his shotgun, and that was that. I was always closer to my mom, but now I had lost him to despair, and was losing her to religion.

It was bizarre and sad, and it was all I could do to close myself off to my emotions and just *focus*.

The VP was also sliding, and thus, the Speaker of the House, Mike Johnson, was in charge of the national address. He would be on in a few moments today to announce our plans, as well as the creation of a lottery to allow those lucky six thousand souls to teleport off this rock into an uncertain future of colonizing PCb.

"Forgive me," Speaker Johnson uttered, dabbing his forehead. It was hot, but that wasn't the only thing affecting him. Johnson was also sliding.

"What I meant to say, my fellow Americans, is that we may have found a way to revive, sorry, *survive*, I mean. Through diligent work by fellow scientists, ah, excuse me, *technicians* at the University of Washington, part of the original team that had discovered the comet… I'm sorry, the *black hole*, forgive me, they have devised a method by which we may be able to leave Planet Earth and find shelter nearby. Well, not exactly nearby, but somewhere in a neighboring system. It isn't guaranteed, but it's the best chance we have to escape Farrow-," he stumbled, "Ferrisgut… I'm sorry. *Farragut*. The black hole. The one that is on its way to us here and that you've heard about."

I think we know which one you're talking about, pal, I thought judgmentally, though my heart went to him in pity, wondering if this is what my dad had gone through.

He dabbed his forehead again while we watched, cringing. This was not Mike Johnson's finest hour.

"In fairness to American citizens and to fellow world leaders, we have instituting, uh, *instituted,* rather, a lottery system. For the drawing. I mean, excuse me…," -here he shook his head quickly and then squinted to focus- "for those souls who will be chosen to board a special vehicle for passage to the system in question. You will receive an automated mailer from the Social Security Administration in the next week if you are chosen to go. If you do not receive one, I'm sorry, but we've had to accommodate a limited number of people only. Please await word and instructions, and thank you for your attention. May God bless everyone, including all of you. Ev- everyone," he said again, smiling weakly and signing off.

I turned to Dina and Trapper, eyes ringed with amazement. "Well that wasn't awkward at all. How are *you* guys feeling?"

"Fine," Dina said.

"Annoyed," Trapper said at the same time.

"Yeah, me too," I agreed. "This thing, this, *slide*, as they're calling it, I wonder if we're immune to it somehow, because we went through Nova. We've been improved, right? All of us. I had those sulfur burps. They're completely gone. Do you guys have anything that had been plaguing you that's now gone?"

Both of them thought, with their eyes roaming off into space. Eventually, Trapper spoke up.

"Oh! I had this guy who was bugging me who I actually kind of like now. He's not such a pudgy dork anymore."

"Flattering. Thanks." She nodded and gave me a thumbs up and a hearty smile. "No! I mean, I appreciate it, but I'm officially offended, just for the record. But think! Anything?" I probed.

"Well," Dina said, "I've always had some lower back pain from a lumbar injury a decade ago. Come to think of it, I don't recall... thinking of it?" She ended it with a question, verifying her own certainty.

"Yeah, well, you said my complexion was clearer the other day, Dina, remember that?" Trapper asked. "That could be something. That and the improved pudgy dork guy."

I grimaced again. "Seriously though, you know what I mean? Ever since we went through Nova, we've been 'improved' somehow. I wonder if we're immune to whatever 'the slide' is." I held out my hands, waiting for agreement.

Trapper nodded with a clenched lip, as if considering the possibilities of it. Her eyebrows flicked up. "Sure."

I turned to Dina. Her countenance had fallen, and her face wore a wry, thousand-yard stare.

"Dina?"

"We've been improved. Hmm," she finished.

She didn't need to say it. I knew then she was thinking about, and mourning, Isaac. *Ever since we went through Nova, we've been improved somehow,* I had said. Her expression resounded something else.

Except for Isaac.

I gazed at Dina with pity, and took her into my arms. Trapper rubbed her back sympathetically.

"I think with Isaac," I said to her, "there was nothing to improve. He was already perfect, Dina."

Dina sighed softly, yet heavily, into my chest. Trapper clenched her lip and studied me, approving of my sentiment. Memories of the first time Isaac went through, and his subsequent exhilaration, flowed through my mind, bringing a grin to my face. Isaac Farragut was a good man and a good friend.

"So," I said, trying to lighten the load a bit. "Lottery, huh? Sounds serious. I wonder if we'll make it."

Trapper laughed. "Relax. We're on it. Donze stacked the deck after Isaac. But I think we were already at the top of the list anyway, Dane. There was no way we were going to get left behind. Not after all we've done."

"How do you know?" I asked, a bit incredulous.

She shrugged, pulling out three government return address envelopes out of her pocket. They said, clearly, in the top left corner, *Social Security Administration*. They had our names on them.

I smiled, feeling a bit relieved, although I was never really worried that we wouldn't be chosen. The deck had been stacked indeed. I was okay with it.

PCb was calling our names, and it was only a matter of time before all three of us were reduced to data streams once more, and launched 4.24 light years into space.

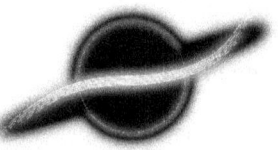

December 12th, 2025

Christmas was fast approaching, and with it, you might expect a feeling of festive Yuletide.

Not so.

Jupiter was no more, crushed to fragments.

Venus was on the same trajectory and was not expected to last the month.

Time itself seems to warp in localized pockets. Sunset was irregular, as was the occasional sunrise, changing times with increasing frequency.

New, powerful winds were rushing over our planet, and they were increasing in speed, whipping up detritus and soot in the air. Deserts were being reformed as the sand was redistributed across the globe. Most of humanity kept to themselves, locked indoors now. The three of us were no exception, but that was out of necessity while we worked feverishly. However, air travel was expected to become perilous by mid-January, and we had to get the chambers down to the launch site before then.

As governments failed and people fell prey to the slide, cults emerged right and left. Looting and violence replaced calm, stoic determination to face our demise. Those who were already reduced to a mental fraction of themselves were easy pickings for these new predators. Desperate to latch onto anything that felt more solid than their own failing hope, they were sucked right into the cultists' vortex, as we all would be into Norma soon. They preached enlightenment and peace, with a healthy sprinkling of government uprising and revolt. Many of them actually worshipped the black hole as some kind of divine entity: righteous judgment for our numerous failures as man.

Various religions amplified their messages with a fervor that they had never employed, and megaphones blared night and day from street corners proclaiming that Jesus was coming… or Brahman… or Joseph Smith… or Allah… or Taylor Swift. No one cared who was 'coming': none of the listeners regarded anyone 'coming' stronger than Norma. That was the one who was inevitably coming for them, and their fear could not be assuaged.

But even stranger – and sadder – than all of that, a new, dark phenomenon emerged. It was wholly terrifying. People who were in the throes of the slide began to report seeing alternate versions of themselves in reflective surfaces, each version representing a life they could have lived. These versions drove some to madness, others to obsession, as they lost themselves chasing these impossible realities.

Humanity was slipping into oblivion long before Norma even touched Earth's orbit.

Hysteria abounded. Mass suicides were taking hold. People were selling off possessions to people who were *actually* buying them, as if storing up goods against some kind of nuclear winter. Looting abounded. Stores and businesses closed by the hundreds each day.

Civil unrest prevailed. Violence multiplied. Discontent blanketed everyone.

Everyone, that is, except for the three of us, and others like us. If there was any hope of saving mankind, we needed to get the lottery-chosen passengers into stasis as soon as humanly possible, in order to preserve what was left of their humanity and give us a fighting chance on a new planet with people who were at least halfway sane.

Thankfully, many still remained so here, in fact. A chaplain was stationed at Chantilly with us, and, boy, was she ever busy. Her name was Rosalita… Campion, I think. Odd last name. It meant *champion*, and that seemed a bizarre name for a person of faith. She attended to all of us here with a holy determined fervor, with her diminutive stature, peeking over thick-rimmed glasses at us and speaking in a thick Mexican accent.

Trapper knew I was still bugged by Isaac and heartbroken over my failure that caused his death, so she encouraged me to go see the chaplain. And so, reluctantly, I was on my way to see her now. Why, I didn't know exactly, but I guess everyone can use a shot in the arm of faith now and then.

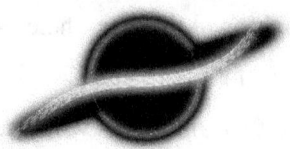

"Yes, Mr. Currier, come in! So nice to meet you," the tiny Latino woman greeted me heartily, jumping up from behind her desk and shaking my hand warmly. "If I am not mistaken, you are the head of the team that discovered the phenomenon, yes?"

"I am. I didn't discover it myself, that was my colleague Isaac Farragut, actually. Sadly, he passed away last month after testing our new system," I said, glumly.

"Yes, I had heard about Isaac. I'm so sorry, Mr. Currier. May I call you Dane?"

"Sure."

"I'm Rosie," she said, motioning me to a seat, and retreating once again behind her desk. "I think what you're doing is truly remarkable, Dane. The Lord bless you, and your team, for all you're doing and have done."

"Well, we'll see if it will be enough," I said, and I couldn't hide a slight roll of my eyes.

Rosie noticed it, sure enough. "Well, that depends on your definition of 'enough.' Is trying and doing our best 'enough?'"

I made an attempt to answer, but before I knew it, I had simply furrowed my brows and made a noisome exhale.

Rosie paused, and then snickered. "It's hard, isn't it?"

"What is hard?"

"Being forced to go see a chaplain when you're a man of science."

"I wasn't forced."

She looked at me over the rim of her glasses. "Are you sure?"

I raised my hands helplessly, but I wondered if she was somehow a fly on the wall when Trapper encouraged me to go see her. "Do you always start off your sessions by antagonizing your clients?" I asked, chuckling.

"Sometimes," she replied. "It calls them out. Brings them forth. It all depends on what you think is antagonizing."

"I guess," I responded. Pause. "Okay, ha! Fine, you got me. My girlfr-, well, my friend, Megan, she encouraged me to come see you."

"Oh? And why did your girlfriend-slash-friend do that, exactly?"

I chuckled. Rosie smiled knowingly as I did so.

"Well, because of Isaac. We've designed this really incredible thing, right? And he went through it. He *was* fine. But then, I don't know what happened, he just…"

I drifted off, staring past her and wondering what to land my eyes on.

"Passed away?" she finished for me.

I nodded, slowly. "Yep."

"And, as the person in charge, you've probably been beating yourself up because of that, most likely, yes?"

I chuckled and then shook my head. "You're good, Rosie."

She shrugged, tilting her head. "Eh. You could say I've been around the block. I've felt bad about a thing or two in my lifetime, of course. It was always making peace with it that brought me through."

My smile faded. "How do you make peace with getting someone killed?"

The chaplain just stared at me. "Is that what you think you did?"

I gritted my teeth. In all honesty, *no*, I didn't think I did that. Based on what I knew about Isaac, on his overall health, on the fact that he had already gone through the basic teleportation as I had, on the fact that we had tested it with other lifeforms, *no,* I didn't think

I had gotten him killed. Logic told me that was a lie. But my feelings said otherwise. Isaac *had* died following a teleportation that incorporated a faulty procedure I had programmed; there was no way around that. I swallowed hard and inhaled slowly.

"Honestly, Rosie, no. But he did die because of my failure to see everything clearly," I mustered.

She stared at me, piercingly, her chin resting on her fist. "When do we ever get to see everything clearly though? As a pastor, I know that the answer is 'never,' because only God can ever see everything clearly. All we can do is *try* to look with clear eyes in this murky world. It sounds to me as though you've been carrying this shame for a bit because you haven't been seeing the truth clearly enough."

"And what truth is that?"

"Well, if I told you," Rosie laughed, "I wouldn't be a very good chaplain, right? Your journey on the road to truth is your own to make." She smiled at me gently.

"The only truth I know lately, Rosie, is that our planet is on a collision course with a deadly supermassive black hole. If God can see everything clearly, I kind of wish that he would, I don't know, help us out a little more. Give us a way out. I don't know. I wish he would have saved Isaac," I finished quietly, but it felt a little like I was throwing down a challenge. "A lot of sad shit – sorry, crap – is going down, and is about to go down. You'd think he'd be interested in providing us less murky eyes in all of this. Me included."

"I understand," she said, and that was all she said. She waited and just watched me until I started to fidget. "I wonder, Dane, if all of this 'sad shit' will make sense someday in a way you didn't expect."

"I thought pastors weren't supposed to swear."

"Stay focused."

"Sorry. How will it make sense someday?"

"As a pastor, I have to believe that God is in control. That everything happens for a reason, and that everything is either God-caused, or God-allowed. That's what makes Him sovereign. Maybe one day, if He allows us to reach this Proxima Centauri b planet your team is shooting for, we'll have our answers there. Maybe we won't see clearly until we get there. With new eyes." She looked at me over the rim of her glasses and grinned.

"But why would he do that?

"Do what?"

"You know, uh, wait so long. Give us eyes to see only once we get there, instead of helping us find our way through this mess now."

"Do you not think you've found your way?"

I didn't know what to make of that question. Thankfully, she answered this one for me.

"As I just said, God is sovereign. Everything is caused or allowed by Him, remember?" she asked rather pointedly. "Do you not think that you were brought to this very moment, with that phenomenon out there barreling toward us, with eyes that see? The black hole is allowed by God, yes. But without your eyes, Dane, *every one of us* would have died here. Because of your eyes, six thousand of us might actually be saved. I have to think that because of what you've invented, God has already caused you to have eyes that see."

I didn't see that coming.

"You're talking about balance."

"Yes, I am. Cause, meet effect. Action, meet reaction. That's scientific, yes?"

I nodded. "Well, there are certainly laws that govern the natural world and bring a sense of equilibrium. Every action has an equal or an opposite reaction. Things always equalize or normalize, no matter how loud or quiet they get-"

"And where does your shame fit in that?" she asked me, interrupting.

"My shame?"

"Over Isaac."

I looked around. "I guess I'd have to say that one day it will be replaced by *no* shame."

"When you have less murky eyes to see it," Rosie said, almost before I had finished.

"So you're saying I have to accept it for it to be true."

She nodded. "Always."

"But isn't that counterintuitive to faith? Doesn't faith in something make that something more real?"

Rosie shook her head. "Nothing is more or less real just because we place faith in it. Is a chair more real because we've successfully sat on it? No. It is a chair. It's designed to hold you. You just need to *accept* that it's designed to hold you, and then you can sit on it. It's your faith that allows you to sit on it."

"So, if I understand you correctly, once I realize that everything is either caused or allowed by him, I'll have more faith?"

"Perhaps. But I think the more important thing for you right now is realizing that you *do* have the eyes. You've had them all along. So did Isaac. You both have eyes that saw our fate clearly; as such, you took what you could give to find a way through what you saw coming. You didn't have to invent or use your chambers for this purpose. Isaac didn't have to go through. But you all saw clearly, and you simply followed that vision clearly and are using them for a good purpose. There is no shame in that in God's book."

I watched her closely. I allowed the gracious words falling from her lips to fall on me and provide some much-needed warmth to the coldness of my faith, and as I did so, I could feel a weight lifted.

"Alright, Rosie. I appreciate it," I said. "I'm getting there. I appreciate it. One day I'll know it in my heart for sure, but this has… helped."

"Has it?" she asked me skeptically.

"Yes. I mean it."

"Well, you know what they say," she stood, shaking my hand and smiling endearingly at me. "You don't know until you go."

Don't know until ya go.

My jaw fell open and I squinted my eyes at her, shaking her hand. My heart warmed further at either the great, strange, mystical coincidence of her words, or the God-caused truth that reverberated all around us, and that I was only just becoming aware of.

"That's true," I said hesitatingly, studying her. "You don't. Thank you, Rosie."

"My pleasure, Dane."

It couldn't have been coincidence that she uttered Isaac's words to me just then. She had to have been given them by the God that she served.

Whatever the reason, it had worked.

That did it.

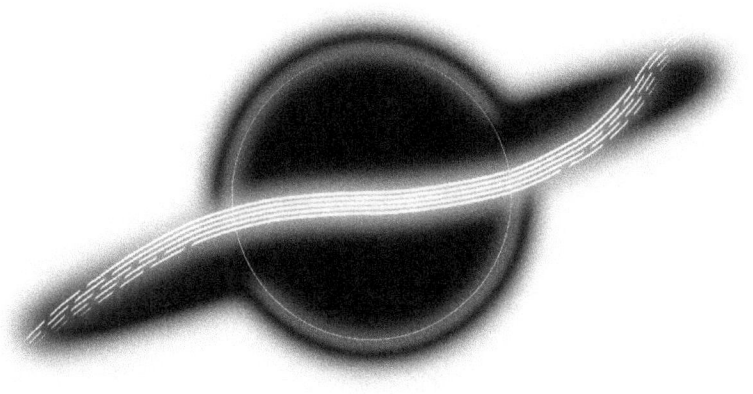

17 | Collapse
December 23rd, 2025

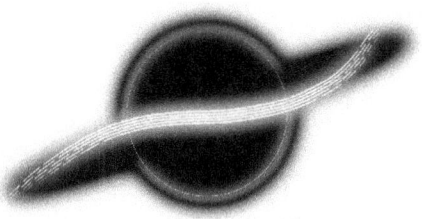

People were sliding, and we were losing them.

They were forgetting what it meant to be human. The very nuances and idiosyncrasies of what made us so special were being lost in the face of annihilation. They were losing themselves not just mentally, but physically as well. A strange 'droop' took over some individuals' visages, to the point where some simply became unrecognizable.

But recently, we all became aware of a new terror. Something horrifying had happened. Some individuals were actually *fading* as the magnetism of the supermassive irradiated them and wrestled their pigmentation away from them. Not like vitiligo; no: they were becoming transparent, and abhorrent to behold. Society labeled them *ghosts*, and they were cast out, left to die in abandon; invisible to others in more ways than one. Some of them used their invisibility to strike back, and horror stories abounded of these frightening apparitions stalking others and taking their revenge. It was utterly frightening to consider. I hoped I would never meet one.

As for those who were diminishing in their capacity, the cultists still preyed on them, feasting on their weakness, their faith, their money. It was abhorrent. Police had little power to do anything about it, much less crack down on them; they were warping just as much as those they were assigned to protect and serve.

Employees still active at DSN and other agencies discovered something unique about Norma: a tremendous amount of radiation was at its core, higher than anything previously catalogued. It was literally altering human consciousness, causing memories and identities to fragment. I know because I called my mom – she didn't even know who I was. That was a difficult call, and one that I will, sadly, never forget. I told her I loved her, and then hung up forever.

Indiscriminately, yet in large pockets of society, humanity was indeed forgetting what it means to be human. Dementia fused with Alzheimer's combined with amnesia to degenerate humans on a scale never before seen. Many were simply left to die; there was no saving them, and it was too hot outside to do so.

For the Earth was moving: slowly, as we were, mercifully, still on the far side of the sun, but surely nonetheless. We were following our star straight into Norma, powerless to do anything about it. Eventually, our small planet with its limited gravity would be pulled right into the fragmented entrails of the sun, splintering and cracking even more than it already was. The temperature outside was sweltering, heating up even more now as a result of drawing near to Sol, and our star was at risk of a supernova, that risk rising with every day Norma drew nearer. Today, in the thick of the winter season, it was a balmy 89 degrees, and even hotter down in Florida where we would launch from.

The problems the slide posed for the lottery were that some people, having already been chosen, were completely ignorant of what was happening around them, and oblivious to the need for them to escape and survive. Letters went unanswered, and lottery selections went disregarded.

That would mean only one thing: filling up the corners with those who were still sentient. Arguments and opportunistic abuse broke out; those who were not chosen insisted that they be so, *or else.* They didn't realize that it would be a difficult chore to get anyone to listen.

In the end, we knew they would simply show up, go through last after all those chosen had done so, and then they'd have to turn away the rest when our SSDs were at capacity.

Space and time became warped; stretched at times, as if the continuum was destabilized and there was no more consistent chronology.

Venus had been destroyed. In a surprise, Uranus was sucked into Norma and actually collided with the other planet on its way in. A massive burst could be seen low on the horizon late at night last night as both planets met their doom, and then were easier prey for Norma to swallow in fragments.

For the three of us, we were still okay, at least for now. But we would certainly have to remain that way. A time was drawing near where we would have to begin the cataloguing and teleportation en masse, or those poor people – and us – would never leave this planet. A long line of naked people was about to form outside our lab, and it was set for January 1ˢᵗ. In a mad hope that we would actually have a new year – let alone *any* more years – some felt the date was fitting and ideal. Those chosen by the lottery were instructed to make their way to the Washington, DC area as soon as possible, where they would be provided accommodations at one of a few local hotels that had been cleared of occupants. They were provided detailed instructions and scheduling for their teleportation.

In this Christmas season, no one even realized that it was Christmas Eve eve. We just didn't care anymore.

Five days ago, our other overgrown third chamber, Aurora, had been disassembled once more and transported to Florida at Launch Complex 39. Genesis was on its way down there as well under massive security escort, surrounded by tanks and covered by fighter patrols.

Aurora was then reassembled with care according to our detailed schematics, and finally welded to the inside of the Genesis spacecraft in prep for launch. It was online, and *Courier 5.1* was reading it in the green, five by five and ready to receive human signals.

As a last test, we sent Macy through, and they sent us a selfie with her a few minutes later. She was smiling and happy as usual. It was clear from the selfie that her tail was blurry from continuous wagging. I would see her once I got down there. Nova and Ava would also be shipped down to Florida for the crew down there to join in storage once all the passengers up here had all been teleported.

Donze was still okay as well, but he was the last survivor of the three that we had talked with. The President and Vice President were no more. Speaker Johnson was no more. The slide struck young and old, elite and common. *Many* world leaders were no more. In the scorching heat, some decided not to wait for Norma to take everything from them; it was their last act of defiance, to control their own fate and take their own lives. The President and Vice President did as many did.

The Secretary of Defense was feeling ill from overwork, but holding steady. He called me up and asked me to meet with him, and I was on my way there now.

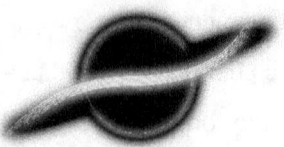

When I knocked on his door, Donze looked disheveled yet determined. His desk was littered with all kinds of file folders and paperwork, and his office reeked of BO like onions.

"Currier, come on in. Sit down, if you can find a seat anywhere." Indeed, I looked around and there were piles of files and paperwork everywhere. I glanced back at him and smiled meekly.

"I'm OK to stand, sir."

He shrugged. "Everything a go for January 1st?"

"Yessir," I replied.

"Good," he said, nodding and sliding aside a mountain of file folders. "Everyone's arriving in DC at either the Waldorf Astoria, Embassy Suites or the Hilton. They're filling up. We're gonna have to make sure everything's ready to herd them in here."

"A question about that, sir," I asked, "have they all been fully briefed as far as the process? How exactly they'll be getting to Proxima Centauri b, I mean."

He shook his head and frowned.

"The mailer should have had all that. It's the same one you got," he said. "Honestly, every time I reread that letter I'm surprised anyone took it seriously. But the hotels show they're checking in in droves, so, here we go."

Actually, I had never read my letter. Dina had read hers, and Trapper and I assumed ours said the same. "I... haven't actually read mine," I apologized. "I naturally just assumed we had been chosen, and-"

'You didn't even open it? Currier, there was specific information in there for you! Yeah, you're definitely going! This is your baby! You're the *Courier,* remember?" he sneered, playing off my name. "Of course you're going. You've got the caboose, mister. You'll be going in last and coming out first. Your other team members will go in before you at the front and the middle. But we need you to take up the rear. You and your team will populate first."

Populate wasn't exactly the right term, but whatever. My mouth fell open and I wasn't sure what to say. "Ah! OK, got it. Sorry, I should have read it. My apologies."

"Fine. Just need somebody who understands all your equipment and lingo and can spearhead the unloading of the herd. All of us naked humans on our new rock in space will need help with the initial organization."

"All of us…?"

"Well, you can bet your ass I'm not sticking around here."

"Of course not, sir," I replied, but I wondered if the deck had been stacked for Donze, or if he had stacked it himself in light of Trump, Vance, Johnson and others no longer making the journey.

"Yeah, my ex-wife is still here. So's her lawyer. They can have this rock. I'll take Proxima Centauri," he joked, lighting up a cigarette. "Sure hope we can bring these things with us," he said, shaking his head and pointing at his own smoke.

"Yessir. Well, we'll be ready."

"Good. Take this and look it over," he said, throwing me a file folder. "We'll have them coming in blocks of twenty at a time, with breaks in between to check and make sure that everyone's been demat-, disint-, broken down into data, or *whatever* it is that you wanna call it. I still think it's crazy, but what do I know? Anyway, those people will be under your care as you operate your system. It's gonna be busy, but we'll try to ferry them through as quickly as possible, Mr. *Courier*," he joked again.

"I get it, sir," I said, grinning. "Thank you. We'll be ready."

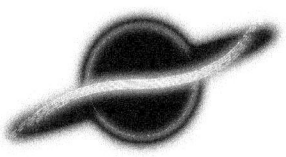

January 1st, 2026

"Hello, Chaplain Rosie," I greeted her. "Good to see you. These are my colleagues. This is Dina Jensen, part of the original team responsible for discovering Norma. That's what we're still calling the supermassive. And this is my friend and undergrad student Megan Trapper who helped me build and code the *Courier* system. Ready to go places?"

"Oh, heavens, no! I'm not leaving," Rosie said quickly. "I'm just here to encourage and bring support to any who need it. I know this will be a difficult day for some."

I tilted my head and squinted my eyes. "You're... not... leaving. May I ask why?"

"Dane, I have complete confidence I'll be taken care of, and that my God will cause or allow me to end where I should, just as He had me begin where I should," she replied. "I'll be fine."

I studied her inquisitively. She had clearly made up her mind, but I couldn't recall one person I had met who actually wanted to stay here.

"You really aren't coming," I said. I didn't intend it as a question. I couldn't believe it.

Rosie smiled and said nothing in response, just looked at me over the rim of her glasses again with that *God is in control* expression.

I took a quick look at Megan and Dina, then returned my gaze to Rosie. "Well, alright then, Rosie. Saddle up. The passengers are coming, and this could get hairy."

"Hairy is exactly what The Father is good at handling," she said.

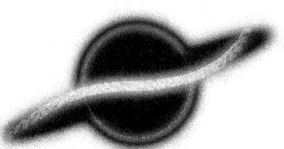

"My name is Dane Currier, and I'm the head of the *Courier* project here, in coordination with the United States government and the SSA. These are my colleagues Dina Jensen and Megan Trapper. To our right here is Pastor Rosalita-"

"Rosie," she butted in, a warm smile across her face.

"Sorry, Pastor *Rosie*, should any of you like to pray or seek counsel before going through. And to my left here is the Secretary of Defense, Mr. Erick Donze." Donze nodded to them.

They were all gathered around us. Whatever protocol SecDef Donze said he had setup regarding 'twenty at a time' was completely disregarded. There had to be at least seventy-five passengers here, all awaiting our instruction, all, presumably, nervous as hell.

Donze spoke up. "Uh, okay, has everyone read their letter thoroughly? You all understand the process of what we'll be doing?"

Various nods and *yes's*.

"Are there any questions?" he asked them.

One boy, who looked to be about six, stood in the front row, raising his hand shyly. He was missing his bottom two teeth. Donze called upon him. "What will happen when we get to Proxima Centauri b?"

"Great question! What's your name?"

"Asher."

"Great question, Asher," Donze answered. "I'm going to let Mr. Currier field questions such as those. Dane?" He turned to me.

I cleared my throat. "Thanks Asher, great question. Yes. Today, we'll be teleported into storage, and down in Florida they'll receive our signals there and get us ready for our flight. It will take about eighty-five years, plus or minus. That sounds like a long time, but when we get there, we won't be any older. We'll be exactly the same age, but in some cases, we'll be even better. If you have a hangnail, it will probably be fixed. If you have stomach problems, those should be cured. If you have back problems, you shouldn't experience those any further," I ended.

A disgruntled-looking man who looked like his father stood behind him and interjected. "Thanks, Mr. Currier. I'm Levi, Asher's daddy. We're naturally a bit confused because he and I were drawn, yet his mother and sister weren't. Do you have any explanation for that?"

Donze shifted to my left. "Uh, I'll handle that one, Dane, thank you. Levi, I understand your concern and frustration with that. This process has undoubtedly caused rifts and irritation across the world. The system had to be indiscriminate so as to not show favoritism. The lottery drew names from young and old, rich and poor, single citizens and family members, with a 2/3 ratio of males to females in order to repopulate our species on our new home world. There was no way to draw a whole family as it would undoubtedly imply favoritism and/or nepotism."

Levi cut in. "I understand that, but with the thing that's been happening to people, the slide I mean, have people dropped out or died off? What happens to their spot? Is there any room for replacements?" I didn't get a good sense of where this was going, and we watched Donze volley with him. It was an impossible question as there was no logistical or fair way to pacify all those seeking to keep their nuclear families together.

Levi burned holes through the Secretary from under his brows as he waited.

"With all due respect, Levi, that's something that we're still working on. 'The slide,' as you call it, is an unexpected phenomenon that has caused all kinds of readjustments and shifting of our plans so that-"

"So why can't you shift your plans to accommodate all members of a family?" Levi interrupted angrily, unable to suppress his frustration. He looked around briefly, as if rallying people to his cause. Those around him nodded.

The crowd began to murmur, and there was a palpable angst building. This was not something we expected or were prepared to deal with.

Various outcries erupted.

My dad wasn't chosen, but my mom was, what's up with that?

How come all the important government people were chosen? Were you chosen, Donze, huh?

Sure seems like a lot of rich people were chosen!

Donze looked around and tried desperately to keep from rolling his eyes. Rosie just stood there, her hands clasped and head bowed, presumably in prayer for peace.

Suddenly, from the rear of the lab emerged several armed guards in fatigues, brandishing M16s. They walked briskly up to encircle us in a wide arc. The crowd perceived that this was not a political forum in which to air grievances, and they began to quiet down.

Donze waited for relative silence.

"Folks, let's keep this thing focused, please," Donze said. "As I mentioned, we are working on that, and we do have some time, but I'm going to have to ask for your patience. Today is all about getting those who were initially chosen to safety. That thing out there is not slowing down," Donze said, pointing out west through the windows at the sky, "and neither should we." He turned his attention back to Levi. "I promise you that we want to do the right thing in our final hours."

Levi clenched his lips and nodded slightly, his eyes smoldering and his lip quivering. Asher was quiet as he stood with his father's hands on his shoulders.

Donze inhaled deeply and motioned back to me without looking at me.

"Yes, uh, thank you, Mr. Secretary." I felt conflicted, because I empathized with Levi and Asher. I did. But I also understood the rock-and-a-hard-place position we were all in. We couldn't save everyone. Surely, Levi understood that. "Anyone else have any questions?" I asked at last. A middle-aged woman raised her hand. "Yes, ma'am?"

"Hi, Mr. Currier. My name's Janine, and I'm curious what exactly the teleportation is like? Is there any pain?" she asked timidly. "I'm not big on pain," she giggled sheepishly. Several others giggled in response. That eased the preceding tension.

"Neither am I," laughed Dina. "I'll take this one, Dane, if that's okay." I gestured for her to take the helm. "Janine, I *totally* know what you mean. The *Courier* system is designed to teleport you quickly, painlessly, and completely, to your new location. It actually improves you somewhat, believe it or not. It's like the computer takes your DNA profile and idealizes it upon transfer. I used to have lumbar pain for years, but now that I've gone through, it's gone. Dane here used to struggle with GI issues. Those are gone," she said.

Megan shifted next to her.

"Yeah. My complexion improved, so, ya know, ready for my first date on Proxima," Megan said with a fist pump. The crowd seemed to appreciate that. I was just glad that she looked at me as she said it, thinking back to those hugs and kisses after I had gone through.

A college-age man raised his hand to my right, punctuating the laughter. "Mr. Currier and team, have you ever lost someone in teleportation?"

Oh, crap.

"Lost someone?" I asked him. Cue the knot in my stomach.

"Has anyone died from it?"

Talk about the wrong place at the wrong time. My mind raced as Isaac swarmed through it. I didn't want to lie, but I also didn't want to tell the truth. "Thank you. What's your name?" I asked him, stalling.

"Parker. Or, just 'Park.'"

That helped. "Well, Parker just Park, I appreciate you asking." I gathered air into my lungs and tried to sweep away the knot I was feeling. "I'm not going to lie. We had one accident early on, before the code was perfected. We lost our colleague, Isaac, the man who first discovered the black hole."

The crowd murmured silently. Feet shifted uneasily.

"It was…," I faltered, and my eyes fell to the floor momentarily. "It was my mistake, and I take full responsibility for it. He was my friend. I had failed to incorporate some crucial code for after he had been reintegrated. He came through, rest assured, but it was… difficult." I swallowed. I could feel Dina shifting uneasily along with the rest of them. "He had to be resuscitated, and we *did* bring him back, but then we lost him the following day. Some sort of congenital complication interfered…" -here I faltered, realizing that I was starting to actually blame Isaac's own health for his demise and how improper that was- "but the truth of the matter is that I made a mistake. I hadn't seen clearly," I said, turning to Rosie. She was watching me, and she clenched her lip in empathy. "I see clearly now. I fixed it, and we've had no issues since. You have my word. I went through after the correction, and here I stand."

"He did. I was there," Trapper instantly supported. "And I went through right after him."

Parker stared at me lengthily, studying me. I wasn't sure if my answer appeased him, but the lull in the conversation seemed to eventually satisfy the crowd. After all, it was 'take the silent plunge now of your *own* will,' or 'forever be silenced by Norma *against* your will.'

"How long will we be asleep?" an elderly voice asked next. "I'm not getting any younger," the old man jested. "Worried that I'll be meeting God before I get to the new system."

That question was twofold. I answered the first part and gave him the straightforward 'approximately eighty-five years' response. "But," I added, "your question has bearings on life and faith, and so, I think that for that, I'd like to defer to Pastor Rosie here." I turned to her.

Rosie glanced up at me, beaming. "Thank you, Dane. And thank you sir, what is your name?"

"Hudson Stigall," he answered gravelly.

"Mr. Stigall. Pleased to meet you," Rosie replied, hands clasped and addressing him directly. "As an aging person myself, I think I understand the root of your question. From what I understand of Mr. Currier's system here, you won't get any older, and you will not die, unless something goes catastrophically wrong with their system. But I have faith," she said, turning and smiling at me sidelong, "in the gift that the Father has given us in their system for such a time as this. I'd like to see another day as well. I assure you that you'll outlast the ride to the new world." Rosie winked at him, which made me smile heartily.

The old man smiled back.

I looked around, waiting for any more hands.

"Well, if there are no further questions, shall we proceed?" I asked. Various nods. "I'm sorry that we couldn't be more accommodating in terms of the teleportation, but we could not afford to mix inanimate signals with animate ones, or we'd risk fusion. Put more plainly, you'll need to all remove your clothes and go naked. We have rooms at the back where you can deposit your clothes, and you can keep your undergarments on until just before you go through, if you'd like. We'll have to leave modesty on Earth in our move to Proxima Centauri b, but I promise you I'll be among the first to welcome you to the new galactic nudist colony." I smiled, and hoped that it was disarming enough.

It worked. Big laughter, even from Levi. Asher covered his mouth in comical surprise.

Here we go.

In another thirty minutes, people were lined up, nude and semi-nude, standing in a long line scrolling toward the door, where two more sentries stood, preparing to allow in the next group when called for. A sudden chill went through me, and I sighed, realizing we might have to field these questions all over again.

Dina took the blood samples. Rosie took the prayers. Trapper took the names and checked them off a list. And then, one by one, they were sent into Nova, never to be seen on this Earth again.

Quietly, they slipped in. Some cried. Some were rooted to the ground outside Nova, desperate to will themselves to enter, reluctant to abandon everything they knew. Rosie stood beside them and prayed beside their trembling forms. A few changed their minds and ran out. There was nothing we could do to stop them, nor should we. It was their own choice to make. The hardest part was soldiers barking that they could not be readmitted.

But here, in this lab, it was finally happening, and Aurora was waiting.

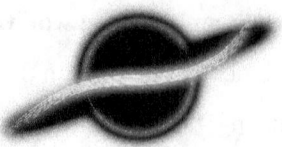

January 8th, 2026

The ghosts came last night.

Before we were really aware of what was happening, strange forms swaddled all in thick clothes, donning shades and hats, somehow overpowered the guards at the gate and forced their way onto the base. They killed the guards and stole their DBIDS cards, gaining access to the Chantilly lab. Dina was sleeping, dead tired from all the finger pricks and cataloguing all the DNA profiles of our passengers.

It was just Trapper and I in there, still transporting people and getting them catalogued as quickly as possible.

Their leader burst into the lab, brandishing the guard's M16. He trained it on me. Another few armed ghosts accompanied him, forcing the rightful lottery appointees back. Everyone screamed in revulsion.

How did we know they were ghosts? The leader removed all of his clothes, all the while yelling and insisting that he and his companions be let through. One kept his gun on Trapper while the leader marched up to her, organs and bones on full display, jostling and shifting within him as he yelled. His mournful, deathly white eyes glared at her.

If I thought he was disassembled in his ghostly form, I had never seen Megan Trapper so disassembled. She came undone, covering her eyes and shrieking. The overall cost exacted by a constant teleportation stream, long hours and exertion, fear of Norma drawing nearer, and now this, was too much for her. She screamed and dropped to the ground. The ghost grabbed her, yanking her up and forcing her to take his sample, create his DNA profile and send him through.

Someone in the crowd lunged at the leader, angered at being supplanted and echoing the urgency that we all felt. "You filthy son of a bitch beast!" he growled at him, leaping haphazardly at the leader. Another ghost whirled and gunned him down. He fell heavily and slid in his own blood.

The ghost who mowed him down turned his gun on the crowd, flanked by another who did the same. "Don't try anything! Stay the hell back! We get let through and nobody gets hurt!'

There was nothing I could do, or I would have been shot as well. I gritted my teeth and glared angrily at the translucent degenerate swaddled up in front of me, his muzzle pointed at my face.

We couldn't let them through; these apparitions would appear on PCb just as frightening as they had here, and that was no way to start a new world, with terror.

Trapper pleaded with her assailant, her hands raised in the air. "Okay, okay! Please don't shoot me!" she feebly whimpered as the pale, translucent man continued to bark orders at her. His shape shimmered as he moved, his outline flickering through decrepit patches of pigment desperate to still frame his once-human form.

Trapper pricked his unseen flesh, and then backed away, ready to initiate the teleportation relay sequence.

Alarms suddenly screeched throughout the lab, and every passenger covered their ears, many of them screaming.

The ghosts reeled, inadvertently pointing their guns at the flashing lights dotting the ceiling.

From every external door suddenly burst in squads of security personnel, brandishing their own weapons and advancing, shouting commands. A few of the ghosts whirled around, lacking the presence of mind to put their hands in the air and drop their weapons. They engaged, and were shot on sight.

Their leader, weaponless and naked, eyes bulging through translucent sinews and bone, made for his gun, but a few of the passengers, enraged at the death of their fallen compatriot, were on him before he knew what hit him.

It was all over in a matter of minutes, but we were left to pick up the pieces of man against man, grudge against trust, and abomination set fiercely against hope. This was a setback none of us needed, and it made us all the more eager to leave this place. Not only did we have to contend with Norma out there, but chilling specters here as well.

Loud curses echoed angrily throughout the lab, but eventually, order was restored. Medical personnel came in, bearing away the ghostlike figures who still breathed. As for their leader, he was choked to death by a large, lumbering man with a wrestler's build. He never stood a chance.

Megan ran into my arms, sobbing, utterly spent.

Before too long, after an extended break in which we were all reassured and provided protection, we calmly collected our breath and dutifully resumed our posts. The line of passengers resumed.

Rosie, roused from sleep, re-emerged into the lab and consoled or prayed with those traumatized by the whole ghost ordeal.

And once again, *Courier* did its job. These people were not taken captive in a place of hysteria. They were sent to a place free of madmen and death.

People were teleporting, and we were saving them.

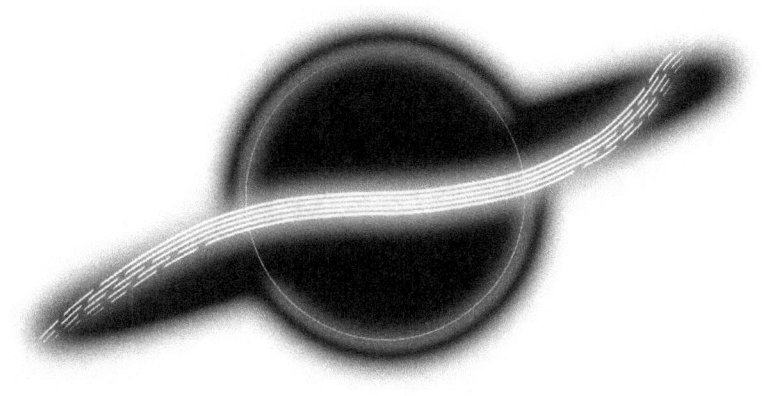

18 | Downhill
January 13th, 2026

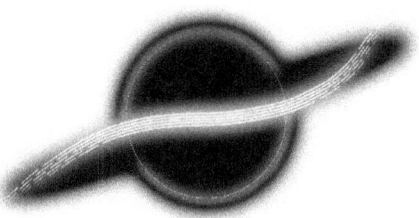

It was the most frightening thing I ever saw.

Someone came running into the lab screaming at the top of their lungs at 10:31 pm on the 10th. We didn't know what all the hubbub was about, and we were, frankly, still reeling from the ghosts of a few nights ago. Eventually, however, we determined from her frantic ramblings that something tragic was happening outside.

We raced out and looked up.

A white orb, much closer than it had ever been, now suddenly pulled away from us, and we could literally trace its movement across the sky. Norma was drawing nearer and nearer, and our moon held no strength to repel its irresistible pull. It slid over the horizon, and with it, celestial lights swirled across the dark canopy above. It wouldn't be long before the tides would respond with fury. In a singular tragedy, *one small step for man, one giant leap for mankind* became utter fiction. It eventually combusted, hurtling closer and closer to our sun like a celestial fireball, and was gone.

More people were ghosting. The radiation levels were sky-high. On this winter day in January, we were at 113 degrees. The sun was enormous in the sky, growing larger every single day. Norma was pulling in the sun, and pulling us into *it*, and pulling us toward the *sun*. Soon, all of us would be but a flicker in time; a faded memory of life and civilization.

The winds that now rushed over the earth were a combination of natural and solar winds, but they were hotter than the ambient temperature at times.

The teleportations were still going. Aside from a brief flicker of Internet outage two days ago, which saw the subjects reintegrated back in Nova where they started, everything had gone according to plan. Five thousand two hundred and twenty-nine souls were now digitized and currently resided on SSD partitions in Florida. All of the livestock had been brought in and teleported as well. It was much harder than we imagined. All of them had to be domesticated to some degree, or it wouldn't work. Thankfully, their caretakers had worked hard to ensure that they were compliant, though agitated.

Megan, Dina and I would be flying to Kennedy Space Center tomorrow, and the door would be shut for any new interested parties in Washington, DC. The last to go through would come from Florida, and then the door to Aurora would be shut forever.

If people missed their opportunities or were unable to make it to Washington, DC, there was simply nothing we could do for them or anyone else.

Except for Levi and Asher. Taking a cue from Rosie, I exercised my right to make a singular event both Dane-caused and Dane-allowed.

I had the mother and sister flown here and sent through. Maybe I was seeing clearly after all.

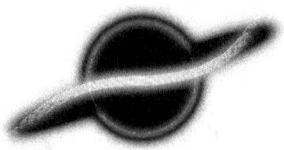

January 14th, 2026

The ground fell away below us as we soared into the clouds. All three of us were in first class. I had never in my life flown first class, so this was much appreciated. Hey, when you're working with the government, they have big pockets; first class upgrades create as little noise to them as a ceiling fan.

But speaking of wind, the flight was already choppy, and would be all the way down. The solar winds were creating havoc for pilots, and it was near time to ground all air flights before they were simply thrown out of the sky.

We were now bound for our final destination on planet Earth: Kennedy Space Center in Florida, at Launch Complex 39. That is where they would setup Nova and Ava one last time, and we would be the last ones in. I *myself* would be the very last one in.

At last count, they had five hundred seventy-nine personnel at KSC that were awaiting us and ready to go through. They were government or military, or in close cooperation with them, so they had already been briefed and their questions answered. So, we were spared that part.

Rosie remained behind. I found myself ruing that. She was a good woman, and she had imparted some invaluable wisdom to me which I would take with me to the new world. Wisdom about life, about God, about faith. Furthermore, she had helped me leave behind the shame over Isaac that had been eating me up inside. I tried to use 'Don't know until ya go' with her, but she wouldn't have it.

"My place is here," she said proudly, with a warm and contented smile. "You'll be free of this place. So will I, just in a different way."

That was the last time I saw her. But I still had the woman beside me that I was interested in, and I was really looking forward to seeing my other woman again: my Macy-girl. I smiled as I thought of the wags in arrears that she would doubtless be providing me upon my arrival. Megan held hands with me on the plane flight to Florida, but for Dina's sake, we didn't flaunt it.

The Genesis space shuttle had arrived in Florida a week ago, and she was mounted up. Aurora was securely fitted inside her. The plan was for her to close off and stop receiving signals just before launch, to protect the precious cargo of her drives, and minimize any risk of electromagnetic interference. *Burn the ships*, we said. *Don't look back.* That was the plan.

Once Genesis reached PCb, the shuttle would land, and then, Aurora would begin the reintegration process on an automated schedule. I would be first out, followed by Trapper and Dina. The rest would follow.

At this stage, we couldn't afford to wait any longer. Various safety and compliance tests were performed on the nuclear pulse propulsion. As far as everyone could tell, it was ready to go. 'As far as everyone could tell,' though, was the extent of confidence they could muster, because it had truly never been deployed commercially or privately. It would be risky. However, as we were all going to die anyway, we were all willing to engage a little risk.

Out there in the uncaring void of space, Norma was coming. Her outer reaches were now only three trillion miles from earth, and the sun was increasing in speed toward it. Norma's event horizon was approaching fast, and the tidal forces were growing in enormity, pulling and stretching our planet, tugging at its seams. Someone reported that a large land mass in central Asia had begun to fracture and bend skyward, tugging at the earth's crust and peeling it up toward Norma, pulling more and more as the earth rotated.

Soon, our planet would fracture and spaghettify, and that would be that. We were being pulled right behind the sun, increasing in speed toward it. Either we would fly right into the sun, or both the sun and the Earth would fall into a parabolic arc and fly side by side into Norma, cracking and dismembering in its flight, and then explode under strain.

More continents had split, and the new tidal patterns had inundated coastal cities, killing off poor unwitting civilians before their time. The slide took all the others.

There was no cure.

If it wasn't natural calamity, then it was the slide, and if it wasn't the slide, it was the scorching heat and the fires. And if it wasn't the scorching heat and the fires, it was the ghosts, looters and scavengers.

Earth was almost at its end, and so were its people.

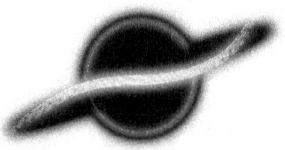

January 18ᵗʰ, 2026

Macy did not disappoint.

She leapt into my arms as I crouched there after having disembarked the plane, and in the scorching heat, she was panting frenetically, but her love was not lessened or inconvenienced in any way. I had missed her so much, and it made me so overjoyed to know that she would be coming with us. She was now digitized aboard Aurora, a belly full of treats and a tongue chock full of the scent of my face, along with many other domesticated pets.

Launch Day was tomorrow. It was upon us. Genesis had been transported to the launch pad using a crawler-transporter, and then mounted to the rocket assembly.

Before that, we would initiate the autopilot, teleport ourselves into Aurora, and prepare to leave this planet forever. Nova and Ava would be left behind. That was a melancholy realization to me, as they had served such a glorious purpose, and yet they would be destroyed within a few weeks, while we would be marooned on PCb forever, never to see them again.

But it would be harder for those left behind. Crews entrusted to our launch and automation – as well as overseeing the nuclear pulse propulsion – would remain here, nobly sacrificing themselves in the process.

Hopefully, Rosie would be side by side with them as they all hurtled toward their deaths, comforting them.

The last of the personnel from Florida had been disintegrated and loaded onto Aurora. She was holding steady, and cyclical checks confirmed drive and data integrity every ten-minutes on an uninterruptible refresh. Her solar power would see to that, as long as the sun lasted.

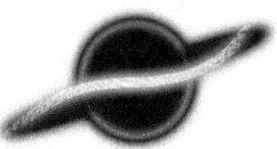

It was late. In anticipation of such a seminal event tomorrow, I couldn't sleep, and it was 11:13 pm.

You wouldn't know it, however, as it was unnaturally amber out through my curtains, as if the morning sun was already climbing up the sky. With all the space-time disruptions, it might actually *be* morning, and we wouldn't even know it.

The noise was near deafening outside my window; an unnatural byproduct of the new winds racing over our world. The A/C units were working overtime to keep us cool, but those hot winds brought with them a precarious environment which was turning our planet into an ashen wasteland.

Fires raged all across the globe now, enveloping every forest everywhere. Mount Rainier in Washington had erupted under pressure, and a quarter of the conical top blew and slid down its own crest much like Mount St. Helens in 1980 before it. The sonic boom was reportedly causing electromagnetic interference on the west coast.

Under enormous strain, other volcanoes followed suit. Hawaii had been evacuated a few weeks ago; Mauna Loa had devastated most of the islands in its blast zone, raining down hot ash that only served to accentuate the existing heat beyond human tolerance. The lava flowed nonstop, as if Earth was desperate to empty its own core. The island was buried under either burning magma or scalding hot ocean water. Drone footage revealed floating marine life dotting the waves. Dolphin, shark, whale carcasses and more littered the oceans.

My A/C was struggling to keep up in the heat, and it was muggy. It would be a long night of little sleep. I think I was *finally* starting to fitfully drift off, when there came a soft knock on my door. I turned to look toward it, and heard a quiet voice calling.

"Dane?"

Megan Trapper.

My eyes went wide with incredulity. Megan Trapper and I had already said our goodbyes earlier in the evening, and she was scheduled to go through a few hours ago. What was she still doing here?

I got up and bolted to the door. "Megan! What – how are you still here? You okay?" I looked her up and down.

"Yeah, uh-huh," she said, seemingly somewhat urgently. "Can I come in?"

"Yeah, uh, yeah, come in. It's a bit messy but, definitely, come in. Kinda lonely without Macy-girl." I plopped down on the couch facing a big plush recliner opposite it beyond a slim cherry-wood coffee table.

"I'm glad she got in there okay. You'll see her again soon, Dane. Just like Dina."

Dina had already gone through and was safely aboard Aurora as ones and zeros along with the rest of our passengers.

However, there was a strange tone in Megan's voice, and in the dim light I could see her hair was pulled back tightly into a pony tail. She glistened with sweat in the increasing heat. I looked her up and down again. "What's up? Why didn't you go through?"

She plopped down, slapping her hands on the arms of the chair in my new Florida digs. "I will. I just needed to see you one last time. Whoo! This heat, man. I know it'll be better in space. Just hope it's still better on PCb. You ready for our 25.44 trillion-mile trip?"

I chuckled. "Yeah. I have snacks. Never-ending Gobstoppers. They should last."

She gave me a confused look as if to say *you dork,* and then burst into a snide laugh. "Sure. You know, the Parker Solar Probe can go 394,736 miles per hour. That would take us 7,229 years. I'm glad this one's under a century. We won't be any older, but I have a feeling for that longer trip we *would* be. The speed of light is 11,176,920 miles per hour. Our fastest craft, before Genesis that is, can only go up to 429,988.86 miles per hour. Isn't that crazy? Yep," she nodded to herself awkwardly.

I watched her rattle off statistics. For some reason, I couldn't shake a supposition that she wasn't really here to share metrics and travel stats.

"What's up, Meg? You okay? I mean, as much as I love discussing the speed of light at close to midnight when we've got interstellar travel scheduled the next day…"

She rolled her eyes and sighed. "Fine." And before I knew it, she hopped over to the couch and sat by me, leaning against me. I could practically feel her heartbeat through her shirt. She looked up at me seductively.

"You've always been great at stating what you want," I affirmed her.

She shrugged. "Something I learned as the youngest child. Always had to fight my way through with the older brothers."

"Got it. I don't know anything about your family."

"And you don't really need to. They're all boring anyway," she said dismissively, as she stared at my lips. If she wanted to remain a closed book, she was going about it the right way.

"You really wanna do this with someone so pudgy?"

"You're not so pudgy," she said nearly instantly, and then grabbed my chin and wrenched me to herself, kissing me with wholehearted abandon.

I didn't resist. Why would I? This was our last night on Earth, as they say, and it was just the two of us.

There, in my little Florida apartment, on our last night on Earth, Megan Trapper and I made love.

Our bodies nearly combusting with heat, baking in the inescapable simmer of an ever-approaching sun, we drank deeply of life, nearly choking on the nectar as our sweat merged.

We both knew full well that the two of us, along with Dina and all those other six thousand people could die in the next eighty-five years, but we didn't care.

We just didn't care about anything else right now.

Tonight, we were alive.

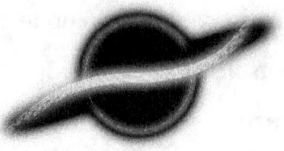

January 19th, 2026

The launch countdown had commenced! Four minutes remained from the nine-minute countdown.

Megan and I stared deeply into each other's eyes, remembering last night through our sleep deprivation. She was beautiful in ways I had never realized before, and she was mine. I thought back to our love, beaming as she stripped down, entered Nova, turned to face me, and was gone. I was the last human who would go through, assisted by the techs who remained here.

We couldn't accommodate any more, or we would risk overcrowding the drives and compromising the memory or paging file space on the drives. The remaining personnel were under strict orders to ensure the survival of the rest of our race. They seemed honorable enough to do so.

Two minutes until launch. Everything was warming up. The crews had performed meticulous inspections. The shuttle, the external tank and the solid rocket boosters all checked out. In the scorching heat, they had been further insulated to preserve their integrity.

Final assembly checks were complete. The external tank was loaded to the brim with liquid hydrogen and liquid oxygen just before the flight to minimize risk. And the risk was increasing. The crews also had to meticulously inspect and ensure the nuclear propulsion system integrity was verified.

All systems were tested including the orbiter's APUs, primary engines and all of the flight control surfaces. Pre-launch checks were done. There were no astronauts of course; it was all entirely automated: mankind's final feat of grandiosity, its final act of defiance in the face of annihilation.

The Ground Launch Sequencer was now in command, monitoring all of the flight vehicle's parameters and prepared to halt the countdown if any issues arose.

I stared out the observation window to behold Genesis as it prepared to lift off. It was treacherously difficult to try and behold it in the sweltering sun. Outside, it was blindingly bright. They say you shouldn't look straight into the sun, but looking into the sun was all we could do anymore; it dominated the horizon.

The orbiter's auxiliary power units kicked in.

I stripped down and paced slowly toward Nova. A tech acknowledged me. I myself verified *Courier 5.1* and hit *Commence Suspend,* turning to the tech and hugging him. He awkwardly leaned in and hugged the naked man who stood before him. I leaned over and kissed my laptop lovingly. And with that, I walked into Nova for the last time as Dane Currier on Earth.

10 seconds to disintegration…

The glass door closed behind me as I overheard an announcement that the GLS was handing off control to the shuttle's onboard computers and the automation kicked in.

9… 8… 7…

Nova lit up white beneath my feet. I kissed the walls and then stood still, keeping my eyes open and staring out at the brave souls who were remaining behind. I nodded to them, touched my chest over my heart, and extended it out to them. Those watching me did the same. It was so hot…

6… 5… 4…

An announcement blared that the solid rocket boosters were a go for ignition and the explosive bolts would release the boosters.

3… 2… 1…

I closed my eyes.

A flash; a blinding explosion of multicolor took me.

It was the most beautiful thing I ever saw.

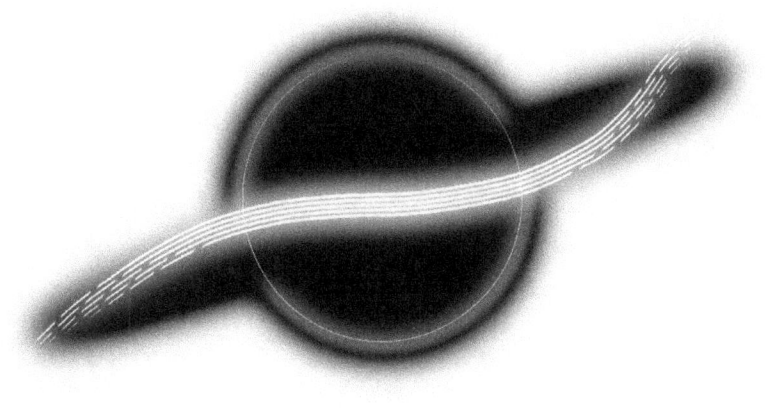

19 | Space
Date unknown

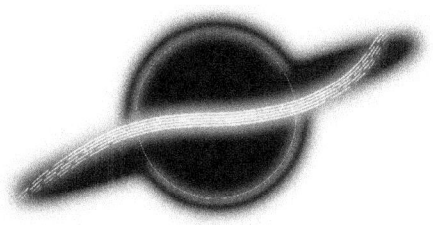

Where am I?

It was all consciousness, all awareness, all dreams, fused into one magical swirling vortex. It was enlightenment and bliss fused into a tranquil, indescribable serenity.

My body – it felt free. Floating on the wind… unrestricted… boundless. I couldn't see myself.

My mind – it saw everything. Rosie's words echoed through me as I reflected on my entire life and the whole history of all mankind. Memories I had never made echoed through me, ushered into my soul through an interconnected labyrinth of human experience.

My eyes – I think that's what they were – looked around and beheld the glory of space. Where I was, I didn't know. I panned around and could see Norma. All I could see was the supermassive, drifting there, silently. There were no planets. There was no sun.

Norma was all.

Was I still me? I felt like me, I knew me. I'm Dane Currier, I said to myself, but the sound was not there. My vocal cords seemed disembodied and intangible. Every expression was in my mind, and my mind was every expression. All around me was energy; all things were energy, and energy was all things: interconnected, tied together in harmony.

As when I stood before Nova the very first time I went through, I was aware of everything. My senses were heightened, unrestricted and free from the confines of this world, at peace with everything around me.

Suddenly, my eyes were drawn to a white speck, shooting across the stars, its stern illuminated with a deep blue-hot trail streaming behind it, heading speedily in a direction opposite from Norma.

I streamed toward it, spreading out imaginary arms in my flight. Our paths converged. It was a symmetrical shape, long and tubular, and wrapped to its frame was a familiar shape: geometric and aerodynamic.

The Genesis space craft.

Somewhere out there, in line with its current path, was a star called Proxima Centauri. And in that star's orbit was a small, habitable planet called Proxima Centauri b.

Our new home.

But where was everyone? How could I see the craft? It was almost as if I was weightless, free from the restrictions of data, free from the confines of solid state drives and all manner of physical containment, ethereal and true.

We were pinpricks of light, the craft and I, as we sped timelessly across the vastness of space. My curiosity at my own state was engulfed and absorbed by the beauty of it. Stars I saw, nebulas I beheld, gaseous clouds of luminescence I delighted in; all swirled around me in a silent reverence. Other galaxies beckoned to us as we passed, completely silent, yet their unmatched beauty was loud and breathtaking. The solar wind blew through my intangible hair.

Once more, in the midst of my spellbound state, my mind wondered back to Earth, and our recent departure. Was it recent? How far along were we on the journey from Earth? Had something gone wrong? By all rights I should be inside Genesis, fast asleep in stasis for the flight to our new star. So why was I out here, dreamlike and whole, riding the streams and wisps of outer space?

My confusion was swallowed up in delight as up ahead, suddenly, there loomed a bright red orb… a star, shining brilliantly, lit from within with an unextinguishable and indomitable fire.

Proxima Centauri. There it was.

Out here, time was a non-issue, and time was not time. The roughly eighty-five year flight was nearly complete, and our new home lay ahead of us.

We flew past it, the craft and I, almost in parallel symmetry, as we slowed in our approach. The blue light trail still emanated from the stern of the ship, aboard which slept six thousand souls in cryogenic dreamlike stasis.

I watched, hovering and floating on a multicolored gaseous stream, as the Genesis craft decelerated, its forward thrusters slowing its nuclear pulse-propelled forward momentum. Before long, it achieved a stationary orbit.

I watched as the solid nuclear pulse rocket detached and floated off silently into space. The Genesis craft slowly and silently rolled over in a calm rotation, engaging its stern thrusters as it slowly began its descent. I followed it.

It was beautiful and intrepid, placid and enthralling to watch, knowing our craft was touching down on its new soil for the very first time, and soon, all of our beloved fellow pilgrims would disembark and begin their new life.

The thick atmosphere felt stuffy... and yet not stuffy. Wisps of strata slid by me as I accompanied Genesis down to the surface. Following its programming, it gently banked, and its Harrier Jet engines rotated vertically and clicked on, firing a steady stream of thrust to slow its descent down to PCb. As silent as a drone, I followed it down in parallel, sending good thoughts its way for a successful landing.

The Genesis craft touched down. I looked around this new alien world. It was reported to be hot and cold, depending on which side of the terminator you were on. I felt neither as I slowly revolved around to take in the sights, floating in a dreamlike ether.

All was silent around me.

Eventually, a slight mechanical whining emerged from behind me, and I turned back to face the Genesis craft. Air escaped it in hissing whispers through the opening aperture at its stern. I could hear it. The cargo bay doors opened, and there, on the precipice of the ship, stood a beautiful human woman.

I knew her instantly.

Megan Trapper.

She looked around, and I hovered closer to her. I tried to give voice to her name, but it wouldn't come. I could feel it in my stream of consciousness: myself calling for her, but she couldn't hear me and didn't acknowledge my call. My ethereal brow furrowed in ethereal confusion. Why couldn't she hear me?

Megan Trapper stood there nude, whole, healthy, reintegrated, new, and breathing new air.

Beside her stood Macy, wagging and panting. Behind Macy stood Dina Jensen. They had survived. They had made it. Their hair blew lightly in the breeze in our new Garden of Eden.

But they were crying. Why were they crying?

Dina approached Megan and put her hand around her shoulder. Megan turned and embraced her as Macy scurried off to sniff out the new rock. Every step they took seemed somewhat slowed, as if gravity wasn't the same here. Far more dreamlike, it was like floating.

But, again, why were they crying?

I drew nearer to them, approaching the craft.

One by one, people reintegrated in sequence from Aurora, naked as jaybirds, some of them getting right to work on setting up equipment and handing out water. Many filed out of the Genesis craft and drunk in the sight of their brave new world and its red dwarf star. There were Levi and his son Asher. There were Levi's wife and Asher's sister. Macy ran to them and sniffed them.

But I only had eyes for Megan. She nodded to Dina, voicing something inaudible, and then heaved her chest in a belabored sigh. I watched as she turned around to the monitors. Scrolling down the screens were status reports and all kinds of data: feedback from the teleportations and the trek across the stars.

Megan appeared to fixate only on one screen. I drew near to her. She didn't acknowledge me. She couldn't hear me. Why hadn't I been reintegrated? Where was I? Who was I?

I drew close to the screen she was watching, and I read it as clearly as she did:

Currier, Dane, 28, M. Subject failed to relay. Reason: Catastrophic system failure due to ambient heat overload. Unable to return to Nova.

My intangible eyes stared with horror as the weightless truth descended me upon with all the inescapable gravity of a thousand alien worlds:

I had never made it through Nova. Or… perhaps I had made it through Nova to Ava, but the relay had failed? Clearly, one of them had overheated or exploded.

The slide had taken me: just, a different kind.

I turned to gaze upon Megan. Naked and captivating she stood there before me now, and I was unable to connect with her, or say anything to her where she'd hear me.

I scanned her beautiful form in pity and longing, and for a moment was captivated, struck by something new. Her midsection radiated a special warmth, an increased light, a luminescent presence exceeding the rest of her body heat, almost as if I was beholding two *lives.*

Two *lives.*

My formless mouth beamed, realizing the truth as my eyes and mind beheld it clearly for the first time, knowing my child was growing within her. Waterless tears filled my shapeless eyes as I silently whispered to her, "I love you," with indistinct lips that gave no voice to my thoughts.

A slight flinch. A momentary flicker of her eyes. Had she perceived my disembodied form? Had she heard me in the wells of her soul?

No.

I was a ghost on an alien world, doomed to roam forever. Megan Trapper and my child would live out their lives on this new world, without me at their side, without her 'pudgy' graduate student partner, without the love we had shared just the night before… or, more actually, a few decades ago. The only memory would be a tiny human formed from our mysterious bond of flesh and signal.

I was no longer Dane Currier. Like those poor souls back on earth deprived of their flesh, I had become a ghost. Deprived of substance, I had been reduced to a data stream, a wireless signal cursed to haunt Megan Trapper amongst the stars… for all eternity. The concrete had become abstract, and there I would remain, never more to be reintegrated. After all, Aurora had been cut off, and could no longer receive signals. Nova and Ava and everything else had been swallowed up by a supermassive black hole.

I stared once more at her abdomen, and I perceived the life growing within. Sure enough, it was there.

'That, *Rosie,' I thought to myself, 'I can see clearly.'*

I turned to watch Dina roam out and investigate the new landscape. I wondered if she silently wished to herself that Isaac was here with her in her new Garden of Eden. I wondered if her reintegrated self would yearn for him to the same degree that her previous self had. I wondered if Rosie passed in peace. I wondered if the Earth slammed into the sun, or into Norma, or neither... or both.

I wondered so many countless things as I yearned here, alone and disconnected. I was a free spirit... and yet I was a prisoner. Esoteric and ethereal oneness and bliss separated, and the intangible tear scrolled down my shapeless cheek as I drifted formless in the void.

Only one question remained, and would remain forevermore, out here among the stars on a world not my own.

Who am I?

THE END

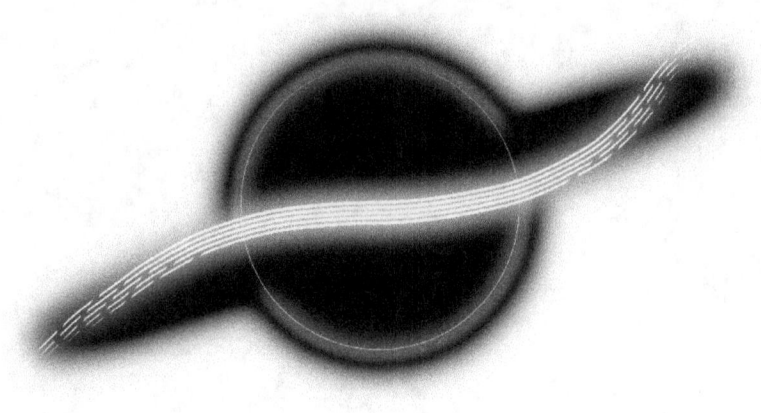

Afterword

When I wrote *Dissonance Volume IV: Relentless*, I fell in love with the hard science of it all, in the same way that I fell in love with watching *Contact* with Jodie Foster, and the scientific mumbo-jumbo that they would spit out in rat-a-tat fashion, expecting us simple mundane Cro-Magnon monosyllabic readers to arbitrarily swallow whole and pretend we knew just what the heck they were talking about. I loved the ease with which the techies spoke it, and I wanted to mirror that understanding of their own technology in the written word for that book.

When I was finished with my Christian dystopian saga *The End*, I strove to return to this novel and figure out just what so attracted me to the intrinsically complicated tech-speak which those characters wielded so fluidly. This novel is a testament to that, envisioning what it must be like to be "in the know": watching something scientifically destructive heading our way, knowing just what to call it and just how to refer to its attributes, whilst leaving the rest of us mortals floundering for a meager scrap of understanding in the process and beholding the societal collapse in the process. I love hard sci-fi grounded in reality, and *The Slide* is my tip of the hat to that.

One other element I remain fascinated with is the finality of death from the first-person narrative. If a novel is narrated first-person, and the protagonist dies, the novel is effectively over. I had already done that with *Dissonance Volume Zero: Revelation,* so, for *The Slide*, I wanted to explore an ending filled with doom and longing; unresolved and inescapable limbo filled with yearning. That fascinated me as well, and I think I've accomplished that with *The Slide.*

Some novels come easier than others, and this one proved to be an enormous challenge. In some respects, given that I knew I was writing only a singular novel, my heart wasn't in it as much as it might be for a trilogy or a saga. There were elements of it that were new to me, for example the PRE-apocalyptic nature of it. Ultimately, it turned out well, and, as with *Forecast*, it took some work, but in retrospect I'm grateful I took on the challenge, as I'm pleased with the final result. I'm not finished writing post-apocalyptic or dystopian content; nothing could be further from the truth. Those just come more naturally for me. However, I *did* want to venture into the *pre*-apocalyptic disaster realm, and see just what the emotions, the life, the environment was like before all fell apart. *The Slide* scratches that itch.

I'm excited to offer this book to you, and I hope it was just as exciting a read as perhaps *Dissonance*, *The End*, or *Forecast* were.

I want to utterly thank my ARC readers Victoria Richmond and Jeannine Dryden. Thank you for reviewing my work so ardently pre-publishing, and giving it the attention it deserves. Thank you to my beautiful wife Janine for editing so many of my works so well, so carefully, and so attentively. I hope I've done this one justice since you were busy with my other novel and other clients! ☺ Thank you to my audiobook reviewers Vance Pease, Victoria Richmond and Rhonda Davis. I so appreciate you!

And finally, as always, a HUGE *thank you* to all my readers who continue to pick up Aaron Ryan books and go "Hmm, I wonder what this one is about!" (As opposed to *Oh, no, here we go again. Honey! Ryan's put out another load of tripe, should we buy it???*) I really prefer the former over the latter.

I love creative writing. I love storytelling. I love holding it in my hands when it's done, and thanking my God in Heaven that I got the story, that I was given the premise, that I was given the characters and the narrative in order to craft something special. Thank you, dear reader, for continuing to believe in me and support me with your purchases and your reads. I can't tell you what it means to me: it's one of the most indescribable gifts I've ever received, and you all keep on giving it, allowing me to keep on receiving it.

Thank you so much for supporting *The Slide*, and I hope and pray that it blesses your library with repeat reads. May there never be a Norma, and may we as a civilization stay the course and not slide.

With love,

Aaron Ryan

FORECAST

AARON RYAN

Published in 2024, Edition 1.

Paperback ISBN # 9798990661189 · Hardcover ISBN # 9798990661172
eBook ISBN # 9798990661165

Edited by Denouement Editing. Published independently.

Cover art man by Asaf Rozanes · Cover art background by Trivuj
Rear cover art image by Gerd Altmann through Pixabay

This is a work of fiction. Any similarities to persons living or dead, or actual events is purely coincidental.

For Sweeps, Bren & AJ:
my true loves.

You are all the rain and
all the sunshine of my world.

"Consider the little mouse how sagacious an animal it is which never entrusts his life to one hole only."

- Plautus

"You must be the change you wish to see in the world."

- Mahatma Gandhi

"I am not what happened to me. I am what I choose to become."

- C.G. Jung

Part One

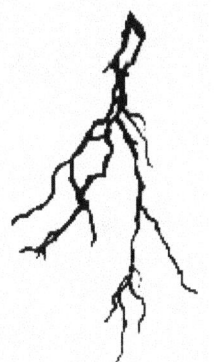

23 Days To Go

August 19th, 2001 • Manhattan, NY

It was utterly confusing, and utterly terrifying. I just stood there, wondering what all of it meant this time.

A blinding flash had lit up my mind with white once more; my body hummed and buzzed, and I couldn't move until it was all over: the same paralysis always set in and took over until the vision abated, and then I'd come to and find people awkwardly staring at me. But why was this happening?

I was still reeling, trying to catch my breath, panting hard. The sweat trickled down my temple. I clutched the pole in the subway car to steady myself, and once again everyone was staring at me awkwardly like I was a homeless drunk. Some shifted uncomfortably away from me and gawked from afar, murmuring to other passersby.

A kind, elderly woman leaned in toward me and asked "Sir? Sir, are you alright? Do you need to sit down?" She motioned to her own seat, willing to let me take it.

I shook my head. "I'm fine, thank you," I said to her, and she smiled. She reminded me of my sweet Nona, gone long before her time. If only I could have done the thing then, and staved off her death for a few more years, maybe. Who knows? It was like chaos theory or the butterfly effect, only I couldn't alter time. What the hell was happening to me?

The first one: that poor girl. I still can't shake that guilt. I could have done something. No, I *should* have done something. And the second one, at the bank: all those innocent people just…gone. I should have helped there too. I got the visions. And then when I saw the perpetrators in both situations afterward on the news, and knew that they were the same people I had seen around Jersey and New York in my mind's eye. I was racked with shame. *Racked.* That was so hard to get through.

But…this was the starkest one yet, and now I knew beyond the shadow of a doubt that this was a powerfully massive threat. How I could possibly intervene, I wasn't certain. I was just one man. I wasn't sure I could help at all, frankly, but I had to at least try.

The first two I initially chalked up to coincidences… but then each came true. I looked around. Who had triggered it this time? I didn't recognize any of the few people whose faces I dared connect with. None of them were in my vision. It had to have been someone who just got on the subway, close to me, as before. But who? People were crammed in here like sardines, and you just don't look at people.

I swallowed hard, knowing full well that I had to find a way to stop this latest one from happening. Something about planes this time. Airplanes. Large commercial airliners. A hijacking? Just snippets of images. Fights high in the sky. Dark-skinned men. A language I didn't recognize, but something from the middle East, arguably. And then…black.

The headaches were too much, the bloody noses were getting thicker, and now I was starting to pass out from exhaustion. The last time, someone stole my wallet and I wound up at the hospital, questioned by the police. I clutched the handkerchief in my pocket, readying it for the inevitable nosebleed. A woman saw me perspiring and made a face, putting some distance between us.

Everyone should technically have known who I was. I was a weatherman, for goodness' sake. I guess I looked different in real life without the green-screen weather map behind me. Now, here, they all pretended I was just some intoxicated buffoon. Maybe the sweat and the strained look made me fairly unrecognizable.

I searched around me again, anxiously, still not seeing the face that had come with that flash, doubting myself the whole time.

I'm Roland Bishop, and I know where I am, I repeated in my mind. I had to tell myself that over and over just to center myself…and to bring me back to the present.

The subway began to move once more, and I held on, headed for the PATH Station.

It had literally only been two weeks since the hospital released me. "Lightning never strikes twice," they said, but that didn't curb the tension or make things any easier. Since the strike, the air was so thick around me I could chew it, and the buzzing in my ears wouldn't dissipate or disperse.

In the New York subway system, you don't really look at people for too long. That just freaks them out and makes them tense. Penny – Dr. Penelope Eggers, that is – believed me at least, and she told me not to stare. That would just make people uneasy, and I might lose the tail. But she cautioned me to be extra careful and not go being any kind of Lone Ranger vigilante.

The roar of noise rushed over us as we made our way into downtown Manhattan. There, I knew, rising somewhere above me in vast fingers pointing triumphantly into the sky, stood the Twin Towers, the World Trade Center.

I'd never been up in them. I'd heard about the Windows on the World Restaurant and all the big businesses in there, but it was a bit imposing, and I wasn't a fan of heights, really. Down on the ground I could gaze up at them with my feet still attached here to the earth, and I was still *me* down here. I was safe.

But I'm losing me to these damned visions. I sighed. *I'm Roland Bishop, and I know where I am. I'm Roland Bishop, and I know where I am. I'm Roland Bishop, and I know where I am.*

Nope. Still confused and blurry. I probably looked like some stupefied idiotic vagrant staggering around in here, aimless and bereft of home *and* purpose. All I knew was I had to find that face before it was too late again.

More white flashes, and somewhere in the mix the hazy, barely distinguishable number *twenty-three* materialized mistily, being driven off by a wind as little bits of it splayed clumsily around. It wasn't clear what it meant.

The Kawasaki PA5 stormed over the rails, and then started to slow. People jockeyed for position to get to the doors first. I never understood why people did that. *So you're five seconds later than if you had just stayed where you were in line…big deal. Why such urgency? You don't even know what urgency is. What* I'm *doing is urgent,* I thought, disapprovingly. My head throbbed.

The doors opened. We filtered out like cattle. People jostled all around me. Someone bumped me hard and didn't even say 'excuse me.' Another person swore at the sheer idiocy of people who push and shove others out of their way. I let both go. They weren't my mark. I needed to find the face I had seen.

A good twenty or thirty of us were walking across the concrete platform to the stairs. I could feel something warm trickling out of my nose. My skin began to tingle and my head started to swim. They were close, whomever they were. Abruptly, the flashes resumed, without warning.

A plane streaking across the sky.

People screaming.

Rubble everywhere. Smoke. Dust. Ash.

A cockpit being intruded into.

That was all I needed. I was now certain that this particular vision was of a hijacking.

I looked around me. A young man met my eyes and then pulled away in revulsion at the blood I wiped from my nose onto my handkerchief. He put a few other people in between us and went on his way.

Suddenly, a face stood out to me in the crowd. A familiar face. The one I had seen in my vision.

There he is! That was him, from my vision!

I found the target shortly up ahead. He was walking with someone, briskly, and talking with them. The other man was looking back repeatedly.

My target had thick, puffy black hair, thin pursed lips, a solid clenched jawline, and beady eyes set under darkly outlined lashes. He looked around. I didn't know who the other man was. I didn't even know who my mark was. I just knew he was going to do something awful.

My head was buzzing. The mark turned to look almost right at me. Dr. Penny said not to confront people, and I wasn't going to. She cautioned me to just follow them at a distance – observe and report – but no more. I was starting to feel like that might not be enough.

Sudden white flash. And just like that, I was down.

People cleared away from me, eager to get to where they were going and not be inconvenienced. The old woman finally caught up to me and asked me again if I was alright. *God bless this saint,* I thought. The good Samaritan insisted that I should get to a doctor as I struggled to my feet and braced myself against the wall.

I shook my head and told her once more that I was fine. The buzzing lessened. He was getting away. I don't know why, but I was getting a name this time. The flashes of airplanes seared through my brain once more. I felt heat. Heat and wind.

I felt like I was going to pass out.

"Sir?" the old woman asked me again.

"M-Mohammed," I muttered. She tilted her head, confused. "Mohammed," I repeated. "Mohammed something. And…something about airplanes. I think there's going to be a hijacking."

That's all I remembered saying before I turned to look at my target again, and then the white faded to black. As my head fell to the floor and my body crumpled beneath me, I thought I caught a brief glimpse.

The man was of Egyptian descent, at the top of the stairs now, and the other man was with him. They were both staring back at me, and then rounding a corner.

The buzzing was gone. And so was my target.

And then, so was I. My Nokia 3310 fell out of my pocket and clattered to the ground, right before my head smacked into the concrete.

"Mr. Bishop?" said a voice. Smelling salts were snapped under my nose, and I awoke with a start. "Mr. Bishop, are you alright?"

My vision swam for a moment and then coalesced into clarity, gathering in focus. I looked around. *Oh great, another ambulance.* I felt *so* drained after this latest episode. That was some stark imagery.

I turned to the paramedic. "There's a man, uh, a m-man I saw down in the subway. I think he's planning a hijacking. Yes, I'm fine," I said.

I enlarged my eyes to see better around me.

The paramedic looked at me sidelong and then turned his attention to his partner. "A hijacking? What makes you say that, sir?" I'm sure he thought I was crazy. New York City paramedics must hear every story in the book thrown their way every single day. I was surprised that he didn't roll his eyes. But the night was young.

"I-I can't explain it," I said. "But I get these visions. I'm not crazy," I said, looking at both of them and putting my hands up. "Seriously. Check JCMC. They'll have a record of me being there two weeks ago. *Roland Bishop*?" I pointed at myself. "No? I was the guy struck by lightning at Millenium Park," I said sheepishly. "They said I was on the news. On my own station. News 12. I'm the weatherman there. *Keep your sunny disposition?*" I asked, desperately flaunting my tagline in the vain hopes they'd recognize it.

A look of zero recognition passed over their faces, and my paramedic looked at the other one again. Apparently, my signature forecast sign-off meant nothing to them. "You bonked your head pretty hard, Mr. Bishop. You don't remember passing out at PATH Station?"

"No, I *do* remember it. I'm not crazy. I'm just-I'm," I faltered. "I've been seeing visions since the lightning strike, and two of them have come true. I think- I'm pretty sure I just had another one. No. I mean, I *had* another one, for sure. Mohammed is his name, I think. You gotta check that name. You mean you don't recognize me?"

They chuckled. "You want us to check for a guy named Mohammed. In New York City." He turned to the other paramedic and exchanged a knowing glance of exasperation. "Take a number, pal. Anyway, we gotta take you to NYP, Mr. Bishop. That's your first stop. Your nosebleed has stopped but you gotta get that head x-ray'd. After that, you can get yourself to the police station and make any kind of report you like, but your first stop is radiology."

I started to protest, but he gently pushed me down on the stretcher. "Just lie back, sir. We're almost there."

I sighed and shook my head. I truly believed my mark was about to commit a hijacking – or *something* to do with airplanes – and yet these yahoos were insisting that it was *me* who needed the x-rays. This latest one was so real, so vivid, and this time I even had a name! Why doesn't anybody ever take prescience seriously? Why is the human race always so cavalier about what's to come?

I rode the rest of the way to New York Presbyterian in frustrated silence.

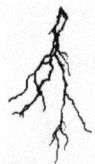

At long last, the doctor returned.

I had been in the x-ray machine for nearly an hour, and another fifteen minutes after that awaiting my doctor's return. Information is power, but I felt powerless from the moment he started speaking.

"Hello again, Mr. Bishop!" he chirped. "The good news is that I don't find anything wrong with your head. No cracks, lesions, tumors, abnormalities, or anything overly concerning. You do have a mild intracranial hematoma, but it's not cause for alarm."

"In English?" I asked, sitting up. I love it when they talk medical speak and we have no idea what they're even saying but they expect us to follow along obligatorily.

"A hematoma is usually a bit of blood pooling outside of your vessels. An injury can cause it, and I know you mentioned that you collapsed. If you hit the ground just right, you might break a blood vessel. Here, let me see," he said, coming over to me and feeling behind my head. "Right about here, is this tender?"

I winced. "Ow! Yes," I complained, irritated.

"Uh-huh. Yeah, that's this right here," he said, referring me to a darker spot on the x-ray, but fairly small still. "That must have been where your head decided to merge with the floor at PATH. You blacked out? Fell to the ground?"

"Yes," I answered, "right after I saw the man who had shown up in my vision."

The doctor tilted his head at me. "Vision? Explain."

I heaved a sigh and rolled my eyes. "That's what I was trying to do with the paramedics. They weren't listening. You wouldn't believe me or listen either if I went into it. Nobody believes me except for my psychiatrist."

He said nothing. Just looked at me and raised his eyebrows, motioning to me as if wondering why I wasn't just continuing.

I sighed again. A willing audience? Could it be? "Well," I began, "I was at JCMC two weeks ago. I'm the weatherman who got struck by lightning at Millenium Park. *Keep your sunny disposition?*" I tried again.

Still no recognition from him either. Either there are a lot more lighting-struck weathermen than I was previously aware of, or no one ever watches the weather. The novelty of my condition didn't appear to be all that exciting.

"Whatever. Since that time, I've been seeing visions. Visions of people who are about to commit some kind of crime or atrocity, and then they do, and I see them on the news. I get these…flashes… of the person's face, a kind of…montage, I guess…of what it is they're about to do, and then I get a nosebleed and pass out. Really convenient, huh? Started happening after the lightning strike. Seems like it happens when they're in close proximity."

"No kidding?" he asked, with surprisingly genuine interest. "Lightning has to exit the body. Maybe it left some residual effect in you somehow."

"Look, Doctor, uh…?"

"Walker. Dr. Walker," he replied with a smile.

"Look, Dr. Walker, I'm not kidding. It's happened three times now. Well…two times where it's come true, and I just had another episode in the subway."

"Have you talked to your psychiatrist about this latest episode?" he asked, coming over and lightly examining the back of my head again, and then peering in my ear with an otoscope while I winced.

"Yes. Dr. Penny. Well, no, actually. The others, yes. But not this latest one. Ow," I said, as he poked the inner lining of my ear.

"And what does she say?"

"Nothing. She listens. That's what I pay her to do."

"Yeah, I know how that is." He pulled away from me and crossed his arms. "You have some mild swelling in your ear canal and some general wax buildup, but nothing substantial. When do you see her again?"

"Tomorrow, actually. We keep a pretty regular schedule."

"Are you on any pharmaceuticals right now?"

"Yeah, she prescribed some benzodiazepine."

"Makes sense. There are some rare reports of benzo causing hallucinations in some recipients. I would ask-"

"You think I'm hallucinating? I'm *not* hallucinating. Not any of it. I promise."

"I believe you. I would still ask her," he said, waving me down. "I believe you that you're seeing things *and* people. I mean, you were struck by lightning. That can have some pretty dramatic after-effects. If you *are* seeing things, your mind might be making imaginary forecasts based on concrete current events or people, and it can be hard to connect the dots between the two empirically. She could feasibly help you connect those dots."

I took a deep breath. "Okay." He sounded like he was potentially a believer, but not to the extent that would have really made me feel truly heard. But it was fine; I always felt like Dr. Penny heard me, and I'd see her tomorrow anyway.

"Alright," Dr. Walker said. "You got any Ibuprofen at home?"

"I think so."

"Not much needed. It's not a big bump. Just to reduce the inflammation. Of course, an ice pack is as good as anything and then you're not messing with your blood. With those nosebleeds you said you're getting, you don't want to thin out your blood."

I nodded.

"I'll have the nurse come back in and give you your summary and then why don't you come back in a few days for a follow-up, sound good? Pretty sure I have a fairly light day on the 23rd."

"Sounds good," I said, but it didn't sound good.

What did all of this mean, and why me?

It was so confusing, and so terrifying.

22 Days To Go

August 20th, 2001 • Jersey City

I would see Dr. Penny soon.

I was home, and I had ten minutes until I had to leave for my appointment with her. She was always nice to see, but her cancellation policy sucked, and she was punctual with a capital P. But what practicing doctor wasn't these days? You did *not* want to be late for your appointment with her. Nonetheless, she was a sweet sexagenarian with a direct assessment of you. She would stare at me for the longest time over her cup of tea, burning lasers through me with those eyes of hers, until I squirmed.

Pretty sure she took great pleasure in making her clients squirm.

I made sure to feed Winston the cat with his little can of Nine Lives that Jenette usually sets on the countertop. He takes his time with it.

I took my bike and rode to 22 Woodward Street. It was only a ten minute bike ride away, and the station was picking up all medical expenses for right now. Thank God for News 12. I was actually eager to get back to my desk, and Jones would just get on my nerves anytime I tuned in and saw him. He was a decent meteorologist, sure, but he couldn't fill my shoes. I'd been with News 12 for almost two years now. I knew what I was doing, and they were eager to have me back. I was thankful for the monthlong leave they had extended for rest and recuperation. Lightning strikes aren't a tiny deal. You need time to recuperate from them.

I arrived at Dr. Penny's only slightly winded, lugging my bike up onto her porch, chaining it to the pickets, then ringing her bell. I was early. I swept my hair back and took a deep breath. Looking at my watch, it was 8:57am. I didn't like it when she waited. So, she made me wait. Because I didn't like it. Like I said, she was punctual with a capital P.

Precisely at 9am, I heard footsteps, and here came Dr. Penny down the stairs. She unlocked the door.

"Roland! Right. Good to see you. Are you ready? Come on in," she greeted cheerily, in her thick British brogue. I nodded. She had emigrated here, so she had said, in 1994, with her husband. He was a- I couldn't remember. Something about accounting, or numbers or something. Two left brains under one roof. Her thick British accent was complimented with offers of hot tea and a biscuit or two with honey each time. I appreciated it. At least that way I wasn't paying only for the counseling; I could actually get some groceries out of it too.

"Nice ride today," I said as I huffed past her into the downstairs great room, which served as her unofficial home clinic. She was licensed, and that was nice. She had it in a little gold frame up on the wall. Masters Degree, Psychology, and LMHC, Seattle Argosy Institute, 1998. Apparently, she had a practice over in the UK and had some international education credits that transferred to continuing education over here.

"Oh, good!" she bubbled. "Always nice to have good weather for a bike ride. But you know all about good weather, right?"

"I sure do," I chuckled, and just then I noticed a large red mark on her left arm that she quickly covered up, pulling her sleeve down. "Ouch, what was that, a burn? You okay, Dr. Penny?" If I didn't know any better, I'd say it resembled a big red triangle.

"Oh, yes, it's nothing. I was cooking something for dinner last night and scalded myself on the oven. Not to worry. I've got some Mineral Ice and Alocane on it. Hurt like the dickens! Don't you fret about me though, I'm fine. We're here to talk about *you*," she said, waving me away while sitting down in her chair and pulling up her mug to stare over it at me.

I stifled a chuckle, but couldn't help feeling sorry for her. That burn looked painful. "Well, alright," I said, sweeping my hair back and plopping down in a big cozy yellow Barcalounger. "I've had a few more."

"Visions. Mm-hmm."

"One was profoundly clear. Like some middle-Eastern men. Terrorists, I think. And a vision of airplanes. I couldn't shake the word *hijack* out of my head. There were two of them."

"Fascinating!" she exclaimed, tilting her head at me. Something in the way she said it made it sound like more than clinical interest. More along the lines of genuine tantalizing intrigue. "When was this one?"

"Just yesterday. On the subway in Manhattan."

"Why were you in Manhattan?"

I laughed. "Well, that's the funny thing, doc, I just can't remember anymore. I was just on the train, and then," I stammered, "it-it was only the train, and the man, and the vision."

"Nosebleed?"

"Oh yeah."

"And did you collapse again?"

"Yep."

"Hmm." She stared at me over her coffee. "And you say it basically zaps the rest of your memory, for a time at least? So you had no recollection of why you were there in Manhattan?"

"Yep."

"That is truly fascinating." She took a long time to speak again. "How intense would you say this vision was compared to the one of the girl, or the bank robbery?"

I thought to myself. "I don't know. About the same. Except," I held up a finger for her to wait, "this one felt more pronounced, and definitely longer. The visions seemed longer and more pronounced. More...clarity," I finished.

"I see. As opposed to the kidnapping victim, that was just a quick few flashes, and the bank robbery, that was a much longer series of flashes."

"Yes. Correct."

"But each time you could see them clearly, as if they were standing right before you, and their images were 'seared into your brain,' as you put it. So much so that you instantly recognized them on the news."

"Yeah, I mean, that's it. I don't know when this guy from yesterday will be on the news, or when it might happen, I have no idea. But it was just as tangible, and he was right there. And then I saw him in person at PATH. Only this time I actually got a name that I couldn't shake, Dr. Penny. An actual *name*. Mohammed."

She raised her eyebrows and lowered her mug, tilting her head at me in incredulity. "You received a *name* of the perpetrator this time?"

I nodded.

"Mohammed. Hmm. No last name?"

I shook my head. "I wish."

"How *very* interesting, Roland. This sounds like your precognition is experiencing somewhat of an evolution. If you're now able to assimilate an *identity* into your precognition, that could be very helpful for the authorities. Now, I know what you're going to-"

I rolled my eyes. "I've already tried, Doc. They just chalk me up to some weird anomaly. They didn't listen to me before; they won't again. They're just all caught up in their hegemony of incredulity and standoffishness. They won't ever open their minds to me. You know that."

"Indeed I do know that they didn't listen to you *before*, Roland," she said, waving me down. "However, someone's endorsement of you - or lack thereof - has very little to do with your trajectory. You must understand that. You are on a trajectory here that you must follow to its end, obediently."

I stared at her, grasping her words and the implications that they held for me.

"At any rate," she continued, "you went *after* those other two incidences. Goodness, Roland, if I was a beat cop or a desk jockey and had to field all those countless reports from some of the whack jobs on the streets of New York City, I would be quite skeptical as well."

"Is that the clinical term? 'Whack jobs'?"

"Stay focused."

"Sorry." I cleared my throat. "But I contacted the police, like you asked. All they did was look at me crazily, take a few notes, and stuff it into some file somewhere at the bottom of a cabinet. I'm just a 'whack job' to them. And they all know that I'm on the air and wonder why I'm resorting to parlor tricks and crystal ball crap."

"Well that's nice, I should think. At least someone recognized you, yes?"

I rolled my eyes. "Yes, I suppose that part was nice," I said, and then the tension grew palpable between us. I let out a giggle, and so did she. "Fine. Yes, that was nice. It's nice to be recognized, for crying out loud. I get struck by lightning, and no one knows I'm the guy who predicts lightning, Dr. Penny. It's ridiculous."

"Well, it is quite serious, Roland. This is not unprecedented, what you're describing. Whether it's Nostradamus with his numerous predictions, or Mark Twain predicting his own death, or Ferdinand Foch predicting World War II, all of them predicted the future with some measure of accuracy. I'm confident that in each case they were also, like you, shown visions for what would take place, and by whose hand it would take place. It's not unreasonable to assume this is the case with you."

"Yeah, but, these guys weren't struck by lightning. They just had a natural gift."

She held up a hand. "But therein lies your saving grace and spares you from being an anomaly, Roland. They were given that gift, certainly, at some point. You were also given a gift, supernaturally, vis a vis the lightning strike which you suffered."

"You think that was a *gift*?" I asked her, sneering. "Doc, I get *nosebleeds*. I pass out in strange places. I've had my wallet stolen already. Cops think I'm a nut job. People lean away from me when I start bleeding. This is *not* a gift."

Dr. Penny said nothing.

So, neither did I, just looking at her. The ticks of her grandfather clock were maddeningly loud.

Finally, she looked out the window, took her mug and put it on the table to the side of her chair. "Roland, I want to tell you something."

I said nothing.

"In life, we all have two dials. A pain dial, and a willingness dial. Most of our lives we have no control over our pain dial. It turns itself. Sometimes, it will be cranked up to ten," -here she mimed turning a dial up with her right hand," -and sometimes it will be at zero," she said, as she mimed turning the dial the other way back to zero. "What we *do* have control over is our *willingness* dial. If one were to live their entire life with their willingness dial set at level zero, they would be quite miserable. Not even fluffy newborn kittens or winning the lottery could extract a smile from them. Their willingness to deal with anything painful is nonexistent, so they've shut themselves off from the rest of life. Therefore, they resist the truth of the matter, and it's what Wesley said to Buttercup in *The Princess Bride*."

My therapist is going to counsel me with movie quotes. Awesome.

She waited for me, presumably to see if I knew the line of movie tripe she was going to feed me. I just sat there, trying to make her squirm this time.

"He said, 'life *is* pain, highness. Anyone who says differently is selling something.' When you start turning up your willingness dial, the pain becomes more bearable. The anguish of the suffering decreases as your willingness to deal with it increases. The intensity with which you resist being *willing* to deal with pain? *That* is in fact what is causing you pain. Might I suggest that you crank up your willingness dial in order to be able to deal with the suffering that is transpiring all around you? I think then you'll find that the intensity and specter of all that discomfort and pain diminishes once you see the greater good that can potentially come of this."

I was watching her intently. "And just what is the greater good? That's what I'm having trouble seeing."

"No you're not. You see it, and you know it. That's why you came to me. You wanted to help those people. You saw what happened to them before it had happened to them, and the guilt that you feel compelled you to come here and deal with it. Even now you've turned up your willingness dial to at least level two, because your newest vision compels you to act, and to intervene. For that, I commend you. But I urge you to take it higher. I think you've been chosen to help save lives, plain as a pikestaff."

"Is that a British expression?"

"Indeed," she said, retrieving her mug and drinking deeply. "I save the good ones for my most challenging clients." She smiled faintly, peering at me.

Granted, this was only my third session with her, but she was intuitive, definitely. Sometimes the light would reflect from outside, through the windows, glancing off her spectacles and dazzling me with a glint. I think she arranged all of her furniture that way, specifically to that end.

I heaved a big sigh and exhaled noisily.

"What do I do about Mohammed?"

She clenched her lip and thought for a moment. "Well, the last thing I would suggest in good conscience would be to tail *anyone* you suspect as a malefactor. You could be placing yourself in considerable danger. Let me make a call to a detective I've spoken with and see if she would be amenable to receiving your reports and treating you with a bit more respect and dignity. That might help you even crank it up to willingness level three," she said, and a faint smile spread across her lips.

"Level twenty-two would be nicer."

"Yes," she agreed. "I'll make the call and let you know. Detective Byers, Roxanne Byers. Until then, you have a few more weeks until you have to return to work, Roland. Use them to your advantage. A lightning strike is no laughing matter in any respect. Take care of your health, make sure that you're being safe, and that you're being good to yourself in all of this, yes?"

I nodded. "Is this where you tell me to lay in a hot bath and play some Kenny G?"

"I am allowed to smack my clients solidly in the head at least once per session, you know."

"Noted."

"Now, tell me about Mrs. Bishop. What's new with her?"

Big sigh. "Nothing, really. We still aren't speaking."

I thought back to my last conversation with my wife, right as she was leaving. After all, that's what had made me head to the park for some fresh air, and that's when the lightning struck, right in the middle of the day, on a relatively cloudless afternoon.

Jenette and I were having problems, for sure, but the fact that she hadn't come to the hospital to check on me, hadn't called or emailed to wish me well, and hadn't made any attempts to reconcile, was very concerning. I'm sure she wasn't watching News 12 daily to see where I was, but she had to have heard that I wasn't there, and had to have at least asked why.

Maybe not. Maybe we truly were finished.

"Well, there's certainly no harm in reaching out to her. After all, the first person to apologize…wins."

"Is that a fact?"

"Mm-hmm, yes it is. I've always maintained that humility is the doorway to harmony. It's the hardest door to go through, however; those who go there must enter on their knees. It's a painful entry to that which we desire most: the other side, where usually lie all of our hopes and dreams. If Jenette is indeed a part of that, choose humility, Roland. I'd suggest the same thing for this new gift of yours."

My eyes narrowed at her. "Meaning?"

She squinted back. "Meaning, accept this new gift. With humility. It might be just the fresh start and good reset that you need."

I squinted harder.

After all of the small talk and lesser details about my life, I had written a check to Dr. Penny, and we were once again back out on her porch. A blue sedan pulled up on the street as I was readying my bike and helmet. *Might be her next client,* I thought. *Prepare to be squinted at, buddy.*

"Do keep me posted if you have another episode, Roland," Dr. Penny said. "And do keep your cellphone handy. Those blackouts once cost you your wallet. It would be a shame if they ever cost you more. Promise me you'll take care of yourself out there."

"I promise. I will. Whoa...*ow!*" I exclaimed, as I doubled over in pain. A thick shock passed through my gut and a blinding flash seared through my head.

"What is it? Oh dear! Roland?" Dr. Penny put her hand on my shoulder.

"Here, here, let me, dear," said a voice. I looked over.

An older man in an outdated fedora and a tweed coat was huffing up the walk to the porch, wearing round spectacles. Dr. Penny backed off. "What is it? Young man, are you quite alright?"

I looked over at him. A flash jolted behind my eyes, and I recoiled and steadied myself. I could feel the hot fluid in my nose preparing its downward march as my head pounded. "Oh, man, yeah, just headrush I think," I stammered, looking at the two of them, and I started to sweat as well. My legs buckled momentarily. "I just need to sit down for a moment." I did so, and fetched my water bottle from the cylinder holder on the bike stem.

"Dear, this is my client Roland, he was just leaving," Dr. Penny said to the man. She looked to be on edge at my instability. Hell, her client was sitting here with a bloody nose and weak knees on her front porch, about to vomit, right in front of her husband. "Roland, will you be alright?"

I looked up at her strangely for a moment, and then back to the man. This was not her client, but her *husband*. I had never met him before.

"Yes, I think so, I'm sorry. I-" I started, and had to shake my head and clear my vision, reaching for my handkerchief to wipe my nose, "I- it's just-just aftershocks of the strike. I was hit by lightning a few weeks ago, Mr. Eggers. Sorry, I'll be just fine."

Without warning, another flash of white shot through my mind and clouded my vision momentarily. I looked up at Dr. Penny and then back down at her left arm. Her sleeve had ridden up when she had steadied me, and I could see the red mark again. She quickly covered it. I winced and looked back at her face incredulously, then back at Mr. Eggers. Then back at her arm. Her face. She looked at me sidelong for a moment.

I swear that I saw her eyes flash to Mr. Eggers almost imperceptibly, and then back to meet mine. There was something there. She knew that I knew, and she was terrible at hiding it.

Dr. Penny was tense, and I could see it. She was nervous, and I perceived it. She was afraid of him, and I knew it, *plain as a pikestaff*, as she put it.

"I'm-" I started, and then my eyes went wide, and I had to take a deep breath. "I'm sorry, I'll be just fine. I get them all the time. Not to worry, Mr. Eggers. I'll see myself out. Thanks."

"Well, that does sound rather nasty. If I were you, I'd head to the emergency room straightaway," Mr. Eggers insisted. "A serious predicament, to be sure. Well, come along, Penny, let's go inside. Good day to you, Roland," he said, quickly tipping his hat and heading into the house.

As he put distance between us, the buzzing in my ears decreased, and the colors around me swam less. I could see clearly again.

Emergency Room. That's practically where I had just come from. I caught my breath and waved him away. Dr. Penny watched me. I looked at her, and inhaled a deep, labored wheeze. She watched me curiously. I looked down at her arm, and then gave her a faint clenched lip smile of understanding. I wanted her to know that I sympathized. I had no idea if she knew what I was thinking.

Without a word, I hoisted my bike up in my arms and took it off her porch, staggering up the walkway to the street, setting it down and wheeling it into position. I flung my leg over to the other side and donned my helmet.

Just before I pedaled out of there, I cast one slow look back. Dr. Penny was standing on the porch, studying me, her arm covered, but she was holding it as if it was needing some fresh Alocane, or perhaps a coating of the freedom of truth.

I summoned up a weak smile of understanding her way, but it's really hard to smile at someone properly when your brow is furrowed, especially when it's furrowed because you knew how she got that mark, and you knew her husband would someday kill her, and you knew exactly how he would do it.

I shook my head at her, and all I could do was mime a willingness dial being dialed back to zero, hoping she would catch my drift.

I called her a few times from home. There was no answer. "C'mon, Doc, pick up." I was getting edgy and nervous. It didn't help that Jones was on News 12 giving the forecast for tomorrow, and he was just so damned formal and unattainable. Made me sick to watch it.

My gut had already been roiling since seeing that vision with Dr. Penny. Could I have been mistaken? Was it just a fluke, some figment of my own imagination that I was now lumping in with 'the gift?' That mark on her arm was a burn for sure. Was it an iron? I didn't know. It looked like one. But I *knew* Mr. Eggers did it. And I *knew* what he would do next.

Someone picked up. "Hello? Dr. Penny?" I asked. The line disconnected almost immediately. I did the only thing I could, and redialed. I went straight to voice mail. *That's it,* I thought, *I'm going back there.*

I tore through the house as a panic zipped through my bones. I had to get there. I wondered how long Mr. Eggers had been hurting her. I wondered how much of this she had dialed up her willingness to accommodate over the years. I just couldn't accept that someone so keen could be with someone so mean.

When did it start?

What lies or excuses had she told herself to make it okay?

What inescapable threats had she silently borne to smooth things over and sleep with the enemy?

All of these thoughts raced through my head – which still throbbed – as I got closer to their house.

I saw the lights from three blocks away. The facing houses were awash with flashes of blue and red, and the looky-loos were out in full force, scattered across the adjoining sidewalks in curiosity. There were several squad cars, and an ambulance. A fire truck was parked a little further up the street.

I had tried to call a few more times on the way, hoping I'd have enough breath between pedals, and then resigned myself to just pedal and stop trying to call. *There wouldn't be an answer anyway,* I thought. Almost lost my balance and crashed as I tried to call, swerving nearly into a garbage can on the sidewalk.

A crowd of onlookers was gathered. There was a dense throng outside her house. No one could advance beyond the police tape.

A body was being wheeled out.

I'm too late. Oh no. I'm too late!

A lump formed in my throat as I saw the white-sheet-draped silhouette on the gurney, being loaded into the medical examiner's car. I shook my head and looked down. *I'm too late. Dr. Penny had been killed! I could have prevented this one too! I failed!* That refrain bounced and thundered throughout the caverns of my shame and guilt.

And then I saw the perpetrator. Standing there, on the porch, ushered out of the house. I recognized the face. It was a face I had seen before. Police were escorting them out in handcuffs.

To my amazement and dismay, it was Dr. Penny. My head tilted in confusion. And then I realized it, as the cold truth hit me plain as a pikestaff.

She wasn't murdered. She *had* murdered.

She had turned it around and had killed Mr. Eggers.

What?? I could only hope then and there that it was self-defense. She had to know that I knew. Beyond that, this was the quickest turnaround from vision to death yet. The others had been a few days apart, each. This was only hours.

No. Dr. Penny was not dead. She had killed her own husband. She had cranked her own willingness dial back down to zero, and had refused to endure any more suffering at the hands of her now-deceased oppressor. All the very opposite of what she had just counseled me. But the very counsel she had given me would have imperiled herself, doubtless. She was no longer willing to receive his abuse. She had returned to zero and had burned the bed.

I watched her in shock. I had literally just sat across from her a few hours earlier, receiving instruction and wisdom from her. All of that instruction and wisdom had crumpled and imploded within her, and she had killed him.

She turned, as if sensing me out in the crowd. Or looking for me? Hoping that I would be there?

Our eyes met. I looked at her, and she at me. She was far away, being led into a squad car as she walked, but I swear she smiled, faintly, in understanding and full recognition of the gravity of these developments.

Deep in my heart, a dim, radiating awareness was growing that I may have actually saved her life. But had I? Maybe she was extra vigilant tonight and saw his attack coming? Maybe her counsel to me was actually meant for herself? Perhaps she was more prepared for his attack, and had her own fair dose of bleak prescience: her own 'gift' as she had called it, and had used it to save herself from her husband.

I would find out soon, I figured, because I knew what I would be doing tomorrow.

I would be seeing Dr. Penny soon.

21 Days To Go

August 21ˢᵗ, 2001 • Jersey City

There was no escaping the truth.

I was at the Jersey City Jail, and was waiting to see her. She had used her one phone call on me, and the Caller ID was not a surprise at all.

I knew instantly who it was.

That was last night, late. She must have been interrogated for hours beforehand, alone in a small room with the whole good-cop-bad-cop routine performed on her. I told her I'd be in as soon as I could the next day.

I rode there and checked in, got fingerprinted, and the Visitations Officer actually recognized me. *Finally.* Always a nice touch. Nice to be missed. *Right, Jenette?*

Now, I was just waiting to see Dr. Penny. Ridiculously long wait. It had been twenty-one minutes so far. At long last, they led her in. We were in a small bank of chairs set between dividers, and there was thick glass between each one. I grabbed the intercom phone on the wall and held it up to my ear as she approached.

Granted, I had only seen her three times in the two weeks since the lightning, but each time, she had a decorum to her; a classiness. One that could easily make you look up to her and respect her. One that made you admire her for her collective wisdom and her air of confidence.

But now, Dr. Penny was reduced to a shell of her former self. Her hair was flattened, her glasses were missing and replaced with cheap readers, she was without makeup, and her shoulders were somewhat hunched. The chirpy intellectual wisdom-giver had been replaced by an alleged killer, and her eyes were downward.

Wordlessly she approached me, and sat down. She slowly lifted the intercom to her ear. It was some time before she looked up, but I think that was more out of a realization that we were on a time limit as opposed to a desire to meet another human's eyes.

"Hi, Dr. Penny."

She looked at me, confused, and didn't reply.

"Are you okay?" I started, and tried to make light of it, looking around. "Quite a change of pace from yesterday afternoon, I bet," I fumbled. "Are they taking care of you?"

She slowly nodded.

Awkward pause. "I'm knackered," she said, quietly. "Very tired. Didn't sleep well at all, you know."

"Can I...do anything for you?" The very question seemed so antithetical to our relationship thus far. She was the one helping me, not vice versa.

She seemed too wrapped up in guilt to answer.

"Look, Dr. Penny, you called me. I want to help. And," -here I looked around the room briefly- "I saw it," I said, clenching my teeth and squinting at her.

She looked at me.

"Yeah. I saw it. *I know.* I know about your arm. I know that he was planning on denting your skull in last night with the iron. I saw the whole thing."

She flinched. "The iron?" Her head tilted.

"That's what I saw."

"The iron," she said, and this time it wasn't a question. "He-he never got that f-far," she stammered, mumbling quietly. "But the iron, oh my goodness," she finished.

"What about the iron?"

She seemed to be searching in her memory, then she did a double-take and finally sighed, looking at me. "He gave me this," she said, holding up her red-marked arm. "With the iron. He," she stammered, and managed a weak smile, "he said I never ironed his shirts well enough. So he wanted to show me how to do it properly. This is how he showed me."

She paused again, taking a deep breath.

"But apparently I still hadn't mastered it," she finished, and then clenched her lips into painful acceptance.

"So, he was going to kill you with it."

She slowly nodded again, then inhaled and exhaled a deep, labored, acquiescing sigh. "Our marriage had been crumbling for some time. He could be so cruel. He beat me fairly regularly, you know."

All of this slowly tumbled out of her as if we had done a role reversal. I now had the tea in her front room, and was squinting at her over my cup.

"He deprived me of food and beat me if I spent his money without his approval. I-I was *never* quite good enough," she faltered, and her head dropped. And just then, a solitary tear trickled out of her eye and graced her left cheek. I wanted to use some of whatever this power was that I had to be able to reach through and cleanse her face of it. She began to cry, clearly, covering her head in her hands. Her cheeks and eyes flushed red.

"You know, they teach psychiatrists everything there is to know about pulling people out, but nothing whatsoever about letting people in. I just…I just couldn't let anyone else in to the truth of how I really was inside. This… this… *masquerade*," she ended, sobbing into her hands.

I took a deep, intense breath. "Dr. Penny," I breathed slowly through the intercom, "I'm so sorry. I'm *utterly* sorry. You *are* quite good enough. You didn't deserve this. I-I've only known you a short time now, but you've helped me crank up my willingness dial. But," -here I knocked on the screen to make sure I had her attention, and she looked up at me slowly- "sounds like you had your pain dial at 10 for a long while. But, see? You had your willingness dial up there too. To my eyes it looks like you finally cranked down that willingness dial, and because of that, your pain dial is down now as well. I'd call that a fresh start."

She stopped, and looked at me, remembering. Dr. Penny smiled faintly, receiving her own wise counsel back to her as she regarded me. "And a good reset," she echoed slowly, flat and monotonous, eventually managing a feeble grin.

We looked at each other for a moment and just savored the connection of empathy.

"Thank you, Mr. Bishop," she finally breathed faintly, and then looked around sheepishly as if reluctant to say my name too loudly. Whether that was out of caution to keep me from being a witness at her trial or something else, I don't know. They already had a record of me visiting her. She had to know that. But then again, I was pretty sure she was unacquainted with the judicial system. Pretty sure this was her first incarceration for murder. "You've certainly kept 'your sunny disposition.'"

"You're welcome," I said back to her, smiling enough for the both of us. "I'm just sorry about all this. I-I wish I had seen something sooner."

"How could you have?" she defended me. "You'd never been near him before. Isn't," she stuttered, "isn't that how you get your premonitions, you have to be near the eventual offender?"

"Well, yeah, I guess you're right. Only with you, he wasn't 'eventual.' Sounds like you've been living under this cloud for a long time, Dr. Penny."

She nodded, quietly, taking a slow, deep breath.

"I just wish, I don't know, maybe we could have had more sessions, or more at different hours or something, so that I could have been around to, I don't know, *run interference* or something like that. I don't know," I ended in a whimper, running my hand through my hair with a labored groan. "And it's really, *really* odd that I only saw his offense, and not-" I stopped short and looked at her.

"Not…mine," she acknowledged. "Hmm. Yes, that is odd. Maybe his sin was greater. Or, maybe mine was just."

"Well, I'm no judge of sin or justice."

"Neither am I. But it seems you're good at detecting it." She looked at me inquisitively. "Have you had any more of them since my husband?"

I looked back up at her. "No. Not since him. But I knew. I guess I knew as soon as I saw the mark on your arm. You didn't do a very good job hiding it."

"No, I suppose I didn't."

"Do you have an attorney yet?"

She nodded briskly. "Public defender. At least for now. We have a family attorney, but I couldn't reach him last night. But yes, I have someone I was able to talk to instead. She supposes a good case can be made for battered wife syndrome. I hate that term," she muttered, shaking her head.

"Yeah, I know what you mean. I do too. But," I tried to reassure her, "if the shoe fits…right?"

She summoned up another meager smile that I could see right through. "Right." Dr. Penny tried to shield her eyes with her left hand, and I saw her burn mark with increased clarity up close this time, wincing as I saw it.

I looked at her. "How long?"

She met my eyes.

"How long has it been?"

Her left arm dropped, and she raised her eyes to the ceiling. They were glistening. Evidently the years piled up on her answer far heavier than I knew.

"Nine years," she said stoically.

My heart sank. He had been beating her for nine years. Three thousand two hundred eighty five days of living in fear, trapped in abuse. How many times had she promised herself in the dark to take action, to flee, to deliver herself from him, to call for help, only to finally react and murder him? Being a weatherman was what I did. I understood living under dark clouds all too well.

"How did you do it?" I flinched, incredulous that I asked her that; it had just slipped out.

Her quick reply surprised me. Apparently, she was ready for a confessional. "Sledgehammer," was what she said, and that was all she said. My mouth dropped. "He was sleeping. I had brought it up from the garage last night and hidden it in the bedroom."

My eyes widened, and I think she actually chuckled. It wasn't a sinister chuckle, however; instead, it was the chuckle of someone who was actually now free to laugh, liberated from the shackles of abuse. Released from the threat of constant control and violence. It surprised me.

"Wow, that'll do it. You either wake up with one helluva headache, or…" -here I paused and my eyebrows went up- "you just…don't wake up."

"Well, Mr. Eggers chose Door Number Two, I'm afraid. Door Number One would require *taking* some painkillers. Door Number Two required someone *being* a painkiller. I chose to kill my pain."

I nodded. "Thus, the good reset."

"Thus, the good reset," she said, and she smiled again, and as she did so it seemed many lines of care were smoothed from her aging face.

Dr. Penny and I bantered a bit more, and she dared to ask me questions about my own situation while marinating in the gravity of her own. I indulged her and shared about my symptoms, about Jenette, about News 12, about my last real flash prior to Mr. Eggers. About Mohammed, and the airplanes.

"Well, it looks as though I'm not going anywhere," she finished, "and I do genuinely care about your predicament and would like to know what comes of it. If it wouldn't be too much trouble, I'd love to be kept abreast of any new developments. The session are now, hmm, *free,*" she ended.

I smiled, grateful, but it was unnecessary. I shook my head. "Let's not call it free. Let's call it an I.O.U."

She nodded, understanding. "I apparently know something about owing somebody."
Her husband.

I grimaced.

"Well, with my debt," I said, "nobody gets hurt; you just get a check later. Assuming of course that you take checks written by anomalies."

"Your money is good here. And yes, well, we shall see. It might be better, Roland, for you to write your checks to my attorney. I'll provide his information later. I don't suppose I'll be going anywhere soon, so for now, our sessions will have to be conducted just like this."

"Fine by me. I'll come as often as I can. I promise."

"Thank you, Roland. You really are a kind soul. Jenette truly doesn't know what she's missing."

I grimaced again. *Jenette.* Still no call, no inquiry as to my well-being, nothing. It's practically as if she had been waiting for this escape hatch all along, and jumped through readily, never looking back.

"Thank you, Doc," I replied, shrugging. "We'll see what happens there. Time will tell. I've got a few more weeks to recover and then get back to work, and I'll try to work on that side of things in the meanwhile as well. Who knows? Maybe she'll get struck with lightning too. Heck, maybe she'll finally wake up to how immeasurably awesome I truly am."

"Immeasurably awesome *and* immeasurably humble," Dr. Penny corrected me.

"Emphasis on the latter," I said. "Anyway, I'll let you know. I promise."

"Just, if she does get struck by lightning, don't have her stand next to me please. She might know when I plan to commit my next atrocity." She giggled, but then stifled it, realizing it was in poor taste. I felt for her; she was obviously trying to make herself feel better about her predicament, and her new surroundings.

Her smile faded, and she regarded me carefully and somberly. "This is where I'll stay, isn't it? This is where Dr. Penelope Eggers goes to die. In here, or in some prison somewhere, wherever they'll deposit me." She sighed and nodded to herself. "Well. I suppose it's some consolation to know that I ended up here and not in the grave. That would have been most unjust."

I just stared at her. "Dr. Penny-" I began, but she held her hand up. Dr. Penny arched her back, looked up at the ceiling and sighed, meeting my eyes again.

"It's quite alright. I'm free from that pain. Now I must undergo another. But my willingness dial is back up to ten now. So we shall see how I fare as society's scourge. In the meantime, you should really go have that chat with Detective Roxanne. Although," -here she paused, her eyes dropping- "I'm not too sure she'll feel too fondly about me anymore, given what I've done." She shrugged.

"I want you to know something," I said to her.

She looked back up at me, curiously.

"Society's endorsement of you - or lack thereof - has very little to do with your trajectory."

Dr. Penny's face slowly awakened in recognition, and then the faintest smile emerged. "Thank you, Roland."

I nodded, and clenched my lip. I felt so bad for her, and for her plight.

We would see how she fared, indeed.

The truth was that she had killed her husband, and she would be cast as a murderer. We'd both have to see how her defense worked out. For now though, the truth, like her jail, were fortified and irrefutable.

There truly would be no escaping either.

20 Days To Go

August 22nd, 2001 • Jersey City

The rest of yesterday was pretty tame.

I came home, straightened up the house, made a few calls to friends and family, and started writing a letter to Jenette, not that I would send it. Maybe right now it was just for therapy. What did I want to say to her?

I fell asleep pondering that very question.

The next morning I awoke. I checked my phone. A missed call from Jenette! *Damn*...I had had it on vibrate. She hadn't left a message. I dialed her back immediately, waiting, silently urging her to pick up. I didn't really know what to say, and I didn't really know if she wanted to hear it. I just knew she was on my mind.

No answer. Why was I not surprised? I had been filled with hope for a moment, eagerly anticipating potentially rekindling our relationship, only to plop down on the loveseat in our living room, the unanswered call in my hands. *Loveseat*, I thought. *Ridiculous name.*

Jenette and I had met in Seattle, fallen in love and got married there in 1998. It was bliss. For a while, at least. I got a really good opportunity to come to the Big Apple for News 12, and I had to take it. I wasn't getting anywhere with KOMO-4, KING-5, or KIRO-7 in Seattle, even though I'd interned there and submitted plenty of demos. Meteorology isn't rocket science; it's just studying the signs and watching the patterns. Part of the time it's cheating and repeating. Everyone knows that. You hear what someone else is predicting, compare it to what you know of previous weather patterns, watch the winds, and you just go with it. Consensus wins. If you're wrong, you're wrong, no one really wants your head. You just call it a freak storm and try it again. But I rarely did that. I knew what I was doing, and I had developed an excellent track record.

Apparently, however, Seattle didn't seem to think I knew what I was doing. So, I widened my search and found a willing station on the other side of the country. But that of course meant one thing.

Uprooting.

Jenette wasn't super interested in moving here, but she loved me, and I loved her, and she promised to follow me. With that promise, we moved to Jersey in early 2000. With the passage of time, however, it became clear that she was unhappy, and just missed our hometown. Twenty months of unhappiness. Did I miss Seattle too? Sure. I just didn't have the same emotional pangs that she did, and never felt like returning. I kept in touch with my folks, and she with hers as well as her friends, but the long-distance friendships wore on her. On top of that, she just wasn't making the connections here that she had hoped for. I felt truly bad for her, as she always had been so great at connecting with people, but for one reason or another, now she felt trapped. Uprooted. Bored. *Alone.*

It was just a matter of time, really. In the spring of 2001, after only one year in New Jersey, our arguments really heated up, and she made it clear in no uncertain terms that she wanted to move back home. By that time, however, I'd become the face of weather for News 12. It's not like I could just quit. Sure, now I would have a video resume to show the three top stations in Seattle what I could do, but I'd be taking my chances with that. With me. With us. She just didn't understand that.

So, on the evening of Saturday, August 4th, we had our blowup fight, and she stormed out. She was going to stay with her one New York friend, Amanda, 'until I came to my senses.' *Yeah, well, good luck waiting for* that *to happen!* I yelled, and then realized painfully that I had insulted myself. She shook her head, and drove off in our car. Thankfully, I still had the bike.

I kicked a few rocks in our tiny backyard for a half hour, and then headed down to Millenium Park.

The lightning struck at 5:30pm, out of nowhere. I had literally just set foot in the park, and my left foot had only just touched the first blades of grass when that thunder hit. There was only one cloud in the sky, and it was directly overhead. The lightning came down before I could even look up. All I remember is being tense, paralyzed, and everything became white. The only way I can describe it is like a dense, molten, churning and blazing fiery core at my body's epicenter. And from there emanated this nonstop pulse of pure throbbing agony, as if I was being consumed by fire from the inside.

Then…peace.

That was a little over two weeks ago, and neither one of us had made any inroads toward repairing our relationship. I had called her number, and left her many messages, but there was no answer. I had tried her friend Amanda, but she never answered my calls. I couldn't help but feel like they were sitting there ignoring their phones.

Really hard to believe that my wife and I were at such an impasse, but *que sera sera.* I wasn't terrified that it wouldn't work out. As far as I knew, she still loved me. I knew I still loved her. I think.

That night, I finished with my letter *and* with thinking back to the incident. I wouldn't even know how to get it to her, because I didn't know where Amanda lived. I just shook my head in frustration knowing that this was going on *two weeks* now, with no semblance of restoration on the horizon.

I was just about to head out for some crisp clean nighttime air after cleaning the house, when it happened.

Flashes. Heat. Tremors that almost leveled me. The trickle came out of my nose almost instantaneously.

Then…the shouting.

The neighbors, Jake and Renita, were shouting at each other, and it happened so abruptly that it shook me out of my reveries. They had done this before, but something was heated over there tonight, and I wasn't sure what it was. I tried to listen through the stabbing fog, and my eyes rolled back in my head for a moment. Their baby was screaming. I couldn't remember how old he was…nine months? Ten?

Nosebleed. Both nostrils. Throbbing pounding in my head like a piledriver to my soul. I fell to the ground, and as I did so, I reached out my hand to try to steady myself against the wall. A current of energy shot through me, emanating from the other side of it.

Jake. I saw him. Swinging something over his head…what was it? A receipt flew through the air. For a moment it hovered there in the air, floating. I almost felt I could reach out and touch it. It had the Jersey City Home Depot name at the top. I could faintly make it out, but that was it, for sure. Something flashed in the night…a reflection of moonlight glinted off metal, and I heard a scream. The glint rose and fell, rose and fell, and guttural cries sounded out at each fall. A jet of crimson shot up toward Jake as the knife repeatedly fell. His expression was twisted into a contortion of rage and vitriol.

Jake was killing Renita and the baby.

I knew right away that what I was seeing hadn't happened yet, but I also knew right away that it would.

A door slammed as I was about to lose consciousness and collapse to the floor. My hand slipped and I dropped. Doors slamming. More yelling. Baby still crying, helplessly, in the middle of it. Something heavy falling with a thud.

Footsteps running down the walkway outside our apartments, angrily. The door opened and Renita shouted out something to him…muted…confused.

I fell elbow-first into the floor and lay there like a dead thing.

I came to forty-five minutes later, lying in a shallow puddle of my own blood and sweat. My face was tinted red, but my nose had stopped bleeding at some point. The pounding in my head remained, however.

Everything was buzzing.

I staggered up and grabbed a handkerchief, putting it to my nose. My bleeding had stopped, thankfully, but my nose was plugged with dried blood and blotted masses. I wiped them out gently, took a deep breath, put my hands to my temples, and stumbled out the front door, turning to face the neighbors' door.

I couldn't hear anything.

I gave the door a soft knock, and whispered Renita's name, saying it was her neighbor. Must have been Jake that had stormed out.

In a moment, I was right. *Renita.* She opened the door in a hurry, and her eyes were red and inflamed. She had obviously been quiet-crying into a pillow.

"Hey. Oh. What happened to your nose?" she asked, pointing.

"Huh? Oh this, n-nothing, I, uh, fell."

Her damp pillow was behind her on the couch, next to a baby boy. He was crawling toward me, about to fall off the couch. Joe-Joe was his name, I think. He was clad only in a diaper.

I had barely ever talked to them except when we'd needed butter or relish or some sundry crap like that. They had mostly kept to themselves.

I guess we had too, since we had never once had them over for dinner.

"Uh…your baby, uh…," I said, pointing and motioning behind Renita.

"Huh? Oh, crap. Joe-Joe, no!" she said, running back and fetching him to safety, putting him on the floor.

"Hey…I'm-I'm sorry, I just…," I trailed off. "Uh," -here I paused, assessing whether or not I should be intruding- "are you okay?"

"So you heard all that?" And then she laughed grimly to herself, folding her arms against her chest. "Duh. How could you not?"

"How could I not?" I said, sheepishly, with an understanding smile. "Just wanted to make sure you two were alright."

She shook her head. "I'm sure he'll be back in a minute. He was just going to the store. We're fine. If, ya know, *fine* means *my world is falling apart.* That kind of fine. Yeah."

The store. "St-store, did you say? Home Depot?"

"Yeah, why? How did you know?"

A panic tore through me. He could pull back in at any minute. "Oh my Go- okay, Renita, I know you're not gonna understand this, I don't expect you to, but I just need you to-" -here I looked wildly around, behind her into her apartment, and back into the parking lot- "I just need you to get stuff for Joe-Joe and stay with me. Please. I'll explain later. *Please?*" I was begging now.

She stared at me, her face askew with confusion, her eyebrows thrust downward. It must have been the way I said 'please,' because she eyed me curiously with her mouth agape. The words gradually slipped out of her. "Uh, sure, okay, gimme a minute," was all she whispered, retreating back into her apartment to get her things.

"Okay. Good. Okay," I said nervously, fidgeting. He could return any minute. "Please hurry."

She flashed a look back at me as she fetched a diaper bag, her keys, purse, a few toys, and finally, Joe-Joe.

In three minutes, they were in my apartment, and we closed and locked the door behind us and headed for my bedroom, toward the back.

It was quiet. Joe-Joe was playing with an old desk phone I had that wasn't on a landline. I plugged it in for him, and he was pressing the buttons with great delight, looking up and smiling at us, delighted at each button press. His binky bobbed slightly in his mouth. Winston scurried across the carpet and occasionally tried to bat at him. He laughed.

"It's up to you, Renita, I assure you. But I'm telling you the truth. Been going on for two weeks now."

She studied me. "That is weird. What a gift, huh?"

"Gift. Yeah. I don't know about that. But I see things, and they all, well, at least I think they all, uh, usually come true. And I-I saw him hurting you. He's coming back here. I don't want him to hurt you or Joe-Joe. Please stay."

She considered it briefly, and then she took such a deep breath and held it, I figured she would pop. At length, she released it in a forcible gust, and nodded slowly. She mumbled just above the threshold of silence, "For Joe-Joe."

"No," I corrected her. "For both of you."

And with that, we called the cops. They said they'd be on their way in fifteen minutes to take a statement from Renita for domestic assault, and from me as a witness.

What had I gotten myself into? I wondered.

The night was getting on.

"I don't know," I said. "She won't return my calls, and I don't know what to say. Voicemail after voicemail, man," I said, shaking my head.

"And she knows what happened to you?" Renita asked. "She knows about the lightning strike? And that was like two weeks ago!"

I nodded. I had left it on her voicemail of course.

Renita shook her head. "Wow. Lame. That's not cool. I'm sorry, Roland."

I shrugged. "We'll see what happens," I said tiredly, though I wasn't filled with optimism in the slightest.

At that moment, there came a knock at my door. It was the police! I motioned for her to stay back. I didn't want for Joe-Joe, or Renita, to be surprised.

I half-closed the door behind myself and walked up to the front door.

I unlocked it, opened it and stopped short.

Jake.

"Oh, hey J- uh, Jake, right? It's Jake?" I tried to play dumb. *Crap. Pretend like you just remembered his name!* "How are you and your wife doing?"

He was sweating, and he was angry. His muscles were tensed under a light, patterned button-up shirt and jeans, and his hair was mangy, as if he'd tried to smear his stress into it one too many times.

"Have you seen her?"

"Who?"

"*Renita!* Have you *seen* my wife Renita?" he suddenly screamed at me.

I jumped a little at his volume. A lump formed in my throat. *Joe-Joe, please don't make any noise.*

"Uh, no, I-sorry, I didn't remember her name, it's been a long time since we've seen you guys."

"Yeah. But you remembered my name's Jake. Dammit! You haven't seen her at all?"

"No, sorry, Jake. Uh, is everything okay?"

"Does it *look* like-" He stopped. So did I.

Joe-Joe. A little laugh, hardly noticeable. But parents, they say, can pick out their child's laugh or cry out of a lineup. *Dammit.*

Jake looked at me with betrayal written across his face. "Move!" he said, and he thrust me aside.

"Jake, now, wait a minute. I- oof!" I exclaimed, as he punched me in the gut. I doubled over and saw stars.

Winston's hair was up. He hissed and bolted.

Jake was fast-walking back to my bedroom. I leaned against the open door of our apartment and tried to catch my breath.

Jake threw open the door to our bedroom and went straight for Renita, grabbing her by her hair and yanking her to the floor, pulling her behind him. She screamed and tried to hang on to his hands to preserve her hair. Stray wisps of it trailed on the floor behind her as Joe-Joe watched them awkwardly with widened eyes.

"Jake, please, let her go!" I yelled, but my air failed me. My head throbbed as my rage grew.

"Shut up!" he said, and he was almost to me.

Something arose in me. A force I couldn't explain sent shivers through my veins and my sinews, electrifying me for action. I shot up, and all I could see was blue. Everything was blue, and looked as though it was sizzling.

I grabbed Jake by the arm, and he winced. Smoke rose from my hand, clutching his arm. Jake cried out in pain and tried to tear himself away. His arm erupted into blue flames. I released him as he frantically waved it about, shrieking. He extinguished his flaming arm with a thin blanket on my couch, but his arm was now blackened and burned.

A hoarse cry arose in me, welling up from the depths of my soul as it grew in intensity, rising like a fire through my lungs and blazing forth out of my vocal cords in a monstrous roar. I tilted my head back in agony as my flesh seared with intensity and the blue turned to hot white.

Lightning has to exit the body.

I remembered Dr. Walker's words back at the ER. Did lightning just exit my body? Was there still some trapped inside me? If so, how?

Something flashed in the night…a reflection of moonlight glinted off metal, and I heard a scream.

Renita broke free of him, running back to take shelter and shield little Joe-Joe. Jake's knife came out of his back pocket in his hand, and he swung toward me. I heard his yelling, but it didn't sound like him.

I held up my arms over my face in defense.

Gunshots. Three of them.

Jake stumbled backward, dazed, and just stood there, slowly looking down at his own paralyzed form. The knife dropped clumsily from his hands. Red circles appeared on his chest through his thin button-up, their diameter slowly expanding outwards.

In a moment, my assailant, Renita's husband, was down on the ground next to me.

The knife was beside him, next to a crumpled-up receipt. I already knew what it said.

The police had come.

Tomorrow would not be tame.

19 Days To Go

August 23rd, 2001 • Manhattan, NY

I had no idea what it was.

It was 9:20am, and here I was, on the PATH train back in Manhattan, on the way to see Dr. Walker for my scheduled follow-up.

I stared at my hand. Not a trace of the flame, or any injury from it, remained.

What had happened? How did I do what I did? Jake's arm was smoking when he ripped it away from me. Blue flame was pouring out of me. My hand felt hot. Had some residual electricity stayed? *Impossible,* I thought. There was simply no way. What would Dr. Walker say to that? I had to go see him again.

I thought back to when I had seen 'Mohammed' or whatever his name was, at the PATH station. Here I was in Manhattan yet again. Call me crazy, but I wanted to find him. Frankly, I wanted to see what my hand could do. Had I immobilized Jake? Electrocuted him? How the hell was that even possible?

Renita and I had given our statements to the police and they took Jake out to the emergency room on a stretcher. But he was already dead. I knew it before they pulled the sheet up over his face. That made two dead people I'd seen in two days. *Standard for most people in New York,* I wondered. I almost didn't care. Renita was safe. I had prevented her death. Jake was gone. I think I actually might have killed him before the police. I had to go see Dr. Penny, and before that, I needed to do a check-up with Dr. Walker.

But there was something else I had to do first.

I arrived at the PATH station and walked out. No idea where I should go, except up. So many people crowded out around me, and I felt that same stifling feeling when you're just surrounded by too many people and you crave a big open field.

In Manhattan, the only big open field you wade through is crowds.

So, I waded.

I just wanted to walk through and see if I could 'pick up' on anything. What could I pick up on? What signals could I possibly receive?

It started with sitting and closing my eyes. Just listening to the hum of the station and the bustling of my fellow humans around me.

I'm Roland Bishop, and I know where I am, I again repeated in my mind. *I'm Roland Bishop, and I know where I am.* Whereas before I used that to center myself and get a grip, re-emerging after an incident, now I was using it to focus and draw myself back in. *I'm Roland Bishop, and I know where I am.* I breathed and let time do the rest.

I could see before me, in my mind's eye, the souls of people moving throughout the station, oblivious to the needs of their fellow man, intent upon one thing only: their destination. They moved with purpose, intentionality, and speed. They projected their path ahead, and set their course, plotting the best routes through the traffic. And if someone's course converged with their own up ahead, no problem: they course-corrected with the best of them, deviating from their path and choosing an alternate route to take. They all had places to be and people to see.

Not I. For myself, I had to just sit here and *feel*. I could see them, but I just had to wait and see what happened after that.

I waited for a solid fifteen minutes, sitting there, almost statuesque with anticipation. Nothing. No signals, no flashes, no nosebleeds. Here I was practically wanting them now, when just a few days ago, even yesterday – they were still a major irritant.

What the heck had happened to my life in so short a time? I didn't have any explanations. I gathered myself up off the seat on which I was perched, and caught the bus up to East 75th St and New York Presbyterian to see Dr. Thinks-I'm-Crazy.

In the meantime, my stress was building. Somewhere out there was a middle-Eastern man named Mohammed that was going to commit a hijacking. I knew it.

Where he was, I did not know.

When he would do it, I did not know.

All I knew was that he *would*.

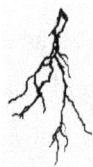

"No, no, I'm telling you my hand, like, spontaneously combusted! And then it literally burnt him - or something, doc. I'm not crazy here."

He had his hands up defensively. "I didn't say you were. The story just sounds a bit...extreme." He bit his lip as I rolled my eyes. "What does your psychiatrist say to this? You're still meeting with one, I presume?"

I wasn't about to tell him that she was now in jail. That would do nothing more than certify me as batshit crazy in his eyes. "I haven't told her yet," was all I mustered.

"Do the police know about your alleged burning incident?"

"It's not alleged!"

"Fine, Roland. Fine. Do they know about it?"

"Hell, I don't know. Everything happened so fast. They took our statements and all of that, but I didn't mention it. I suppose that the coroner will pull it up when they do a medical examination, but what does it matter? He's dead."

He nodded. "Well, let me have a look at those hands."

Dr. Walker came over and took my hands in his, turning them over and inspecting them. "I don't see anything from a cursory analysis, and there are no exit points on either of these, which is weirder, but they do feel unusually warm for being inside an air-conditioned building. Let me take your temperature for an overall baseline." He fetched his thermometer and stuck it in my mouth. As he slipped it under my tongue I briefly found myself hoping for the day when they would just have some kind of head scanners or something they could just point at you instead of putting some only-God-knows-where-this-has-been stick of glass under my tongue. He continued to study my hands, and then extracted the thermometer.

"97.6," he muttered blandly. "Nothing special or unorthodox about that. Let me have a look inside your eyes and ears for a sec, there, Mr. Roland."

"Bishop." I complied, letting him stare deep inside my soul, perhaps searching for some oddly giddy lightning ball dancing around in there just longing to escape out of its human incarceration.

Incarceration – that reminded me, I needed to go visit Dr. Penny. I glanced at my watch. 11:15am. Visiting hours start at noon today.

"Got somewhere you need to be?" he asked.

"Yes- well, no, just...curious," I stumbled, still not ready to let on that I was going to see my incarcerated counselor.

"Yes-well-no. Hmm. Seems that lightning may have affected some motor skills with regards to decision making," he joked.

I gave him the stink-eye. It didn't do anything.

Dr. Walker laughed and sloughed it off. "Relax. I'm just teasing, Roland. Your ears and your eyes look good, are you still taking your benzodiazepine?"

I nodded. "Yep."

"Okay. Might want to talk with your shrink – sorry, I owe my wife a quarter; I'm not supposed to call them that anymore – might want to talk to them about upping your dosage slightly. The only thing I think might really be working on you is some increased anxiety. This sounds like a byproduct of that, and if it's having physical manifestations as you say, a higher dosage working to calm you might counter that."

I shrugged and slightly shook my head. "Okay, fine."

He smiled. "By the way, speaking of shrink – there's 50 cents now – did you get a load of that woman who offed her husband a few nights ago in Jersey? Freakish. She was a psychiatrist, no less," he said, turning away from me and staring at his computer to tap in an update about my condition, presumably.

I swallowed hard. "Yeah, I heard about that."

"Just goes to show you that they don't know everything. *Physician, heal thyself!* Right?"

"Right," I tacitly agreed, wanting to get out of there as he had just subtly insulted one whom I now considered a friend.

"Anyway. I'll update your chart here. I think you're doing fine. My job is to make sure there are no lingering physical manifestations of that lightning strike, and to make sure you're working properly. Everything looks okay from my vantage point."

I almost gasped. *Physician, heal thyself*, I directed at him in my mind. "Nope! All good here, doc. No lingering physical manifestations except for electrocuting other humans. That sure sounds like I'm working properly, wouldn't you say?"

"Well, that aside," he uttered.

"Right," I sneered, looking away.

"Check in with Judy on your way out and she'll schedule you for your next follow-up. Next I have available is the 19th. Mmkay?"

"Alright, doc," I reluctantly agreed.

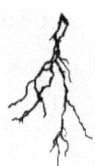

"How's the chow?" I asked her.

"Oh, certainly nothing to call home about. Has Roxanne Byers called you yet?"

"Who?"

"The *detective*, Roland. The detective I mentioned that I would call on your behalf."

"Oh!" I exclaimed, recognizing the name. "No, not yet. I'm sure she's busy. It's fine."

"Well, she will, I assure you. She was not happy with what I had done of course, but she's busy enough. And, as there was nothing to 'detect' in my case, that lightened her load. So, her schedule should allow a call sometime soon, I should think," said Dr. Penny.

I nodded, pressing the intercom phone up to my ear as I looked at her. Her mood and countenance had improved and lifted, respectively. She was adapting to her new surroundings, 'keeping her sunny disposition' as it were, and for that, I was glad. My brother was in prison back home in Seattle, and we hardly ever spoke. He was a changed man: prison had hardened him. But so had the murder he had committed. Maybe prison would harden Penny as it had Burt.

She was of course headed for prison; there's no way she'd get a light sentence and stay here in jail unless they won some kind of crazy battered-wife-syndrome act-of-passion case that had the jury falling over in the aisles. She would end up there. That would make *two* people in my life doing serious time. But for now, she looked lighter, and her shoulders weren't as hunched as last night. She was accepting the reality of her new predicament.

She smiled at me, lifting her eyebrows. "Anything new since yesterday?"

"You wouldn't even believe me if I told you."

Her head tilted. "Oh?"

I shook my head and let out a steam of air. "Let's just say I've had more than my fill of murders lately." At that, she flinched somewhat, her eyes widening, as if she was uncertain about the gravity of her own crime. "I-I don't mean that, Dr. Penny. I just-" I stammered, "I had another vision last night. While I was at home. I was going to go out and get some fresh air, and…"

"And what?" she said, eagerly. "Another vision of a tragedy?"

I nodded.

"My neighbors. A man and wife. Fighting. Oh, there was lots of noise, big commotion, yelling, doors slamming, and then he left. All the while I could *feel* them through the wall. I knew what he was going to do. I saw the visions."

"And what? What, Roland? Did you stop it?"

I looked at her. "I stopped it," I conceded.

Her face lit up. "Roland! This is *wonderful news!* What a development! Tell me more, did you go over there? What *precisely* happened in your vision?" I tried to start answering. "Did you find out that he was going to do it exactly as you foresaw?" I tried once again, my mouth clicking shut as she continued. "Did you tell her what you saw? And she believed you? Tell me!!"

I broke into wild uncontrollable laughter, and it felt good, I must say. "Which question do I answer first?" I jested.

"Now, stop that. I'm very eager to hear what transpired," she said, practically lifting off her seat and panting. "You did it, Roland!"

I calmed myself and took a deep breath. "Yeah, I did it." And then, I recounted for her the visions of the Home Depot receipt, the knife, his angry face, the stabbing, Joe-Joe, all of it. I told her what I said when I went over there, and walked her through Renita's surprise and acceptance. I shared with her what happened when Jake came over and burst into my apartment looking for them. How I grabbed his arm and it burst into flame. The roar from my soul.

"*Incredible.* Simply incredible. You are one daft individual, taking him on, do you know?"

I chuckled. "Yeah. But apparently he was just as shocked as I was – literally. I don't even know how I did it, Penny. Oh, sorry – *Doctor* Penny."

She clicked her tongue. "Tut-tut. Stop that. Penny is fine," she said, her chin resting on the fingers of her left hand.

"Very well then, Penny," I said, still laughing and sporting my best English accent.

"Now, now, *that* is *not* fine," she corrected me with a stern look.

"Sorry," I gulped, stifling a laugh. "Okay."

She regained her composure. "Oh, Roland," she said. "How extraordinary. Let me see your hand please. Hold it up to the window." I did so, and she examined it up and down. "How…extraordinary. What did it feel like?"

I didn't actually know the answer to that. Everything had happened so fast. "I don't know, Doc- uh, *Penny,* it just, all of it happened so fast. I just wanted to grab his arm to stop him, to defend myself, and then, it just shot out of me."

"Sounds like irrepressible emotions manifesting into physical symptoms. Much like *Firestarter.*"

"Firestarter?"

She gawked at me and leaned back. "Roland Bishop. Are you not a weatherman, and have you never seen the movie *Firestarter*?"

"I guess not."

"Amazing movie. Movies today are rubbish. Too much fluff. That one had a lot of heart. It was originally a book by Stephen King, you know. Remarkable bloke, and a cheeky author to boot."

"Cheeky, huh? Okay."

"Indeed. Anyway, the main protagonist is a little girl named Charlie. Last name, 'McGee' I think, if memory serves. She was endowed with special powers. I know that sounds a bit dodgy, but there was science that started it all. And Roland, do you know, whenever she would lose control emotionally, she could project fire onto whatever object of scorn she directed it at. Rage," -here she waved her arms about- "consumed her, and that little girl could suddenly make an entire building explode into flame. She could make people spontaneously combust, you know. All because of her emotions at play."

I stared hard at Penny. "Okay. Right. Sounds intriguing. Are you saying that I was overly emotional last night and that's how I fried Jake before the cops shot him?"

She clenched her lip and shrugged her shoulders. "It's certainly conceivable. How else do you explain it? I would look to Occam's Razor."

That one I knew, and I nodded. "All things considered, the simplest explanation tends to be the right one. So now I'm a superhero."

Now it was her turn for wild, raucous laughter. "Oh, codswallop, Roland. Your head needs to be tightened back on, my friend."

I let her simmer down while I watched her, laughing. It was surreal yet welcome, watching her. She was my senior by a few decades, but here she appeared as jovial as a child. This newfound freedom allowed her to jest, to relax, to let her hair down, and to fully be herself. It was truly refreshing to see, given her circumstance.

Here she was, facing even perhaps the death penalty for what she did – who knows? – and yet she laughed in the face of circumstance. My situation helped her do that. I brought her a fresh dose of lightness. Maybe I truly was a superhero after all.

If only Jenette could see that.

"Well," she said at last, "whatever it is, I think you're now far more gifted than I had at first suspected." And then she calmed, as if sensing some greater gravity descending upon us. "And now you must find a way to control it. That's where I slipped, Roland. I did not grasp my own power over Mr. Eggers. I used what power I had to destroy him. I'm certainly not saying that's what you did with your neighbor, Jake. Not in the slightest. But what you did is astonishing, Roland, and this is yet another gift you've been imparted."

She looked at me, trying to convince me, trying to play the part of the counselor from the other side of this glass, but I was stuck on something she said earlier. About her husband.

"What was his name, anyway?"

"Who?"

"Your husband."

She paused, perhaps reticent to in any way resurrect him through the invocation of his name. The color slightly drained from her face. Her brightness faded to gloom.

"Geoffrey."

I wasn't sure I wanted to ask the question, but I did it anyway. "Do you miss him at all?"

"Oh, bollocks," she blared. "Hell, no. Certainly, not. Do I miss what we *used* to have before the nine-year mark? Perhaps. You might say I miss the *old* Geoffrey. But I'm certainly not ready to ruminate on any of that yet, Roland," she said.

Dr. Penny lost her composure, and a tear trickled out of her eye, trying to make its downward slide. She briskly wiped it aside. The pain was definitely there. I thought of the best thing I could possibly say.

"I think somebody has permission to turn their willingness dial back up now."

Penny looked at me thoughtfully, and then crinkles began to appear at the corners of her eyes as her lips slowly spread into a smile. "Yes, I do believe you're right. I can receive again, can't I?"

"Of course you can, Penny. We can do it together."

My counselor sat there and just let me appreciate her as we thought about all that had transpired over the past few days. I'm sure this was a breath of fresh air for her, and a much-needed one.

"We can do it together. Thank you, Roland."

I smiled at her.

And then I felt something for Penny – something very maternal and binding. Something I had missed from my own mother, aloof and dictatorial, who had never let me be right and never let me fly. I had a troubled relationship with her, and my brother did as well, obviously: it had landed him in prison. After all, Burt had killed my mother, and he was never getting out. My dad had run off when I was three, so he wasn't even in the corner of my mind.

But sitting here, with Dr. Penny – now, just *Penny* – I felt kind of like I had not just a mother, but a *mom*. Headed to prison, for sure, but a new mom nonetheless.

I had the strangest clarity about all of it.

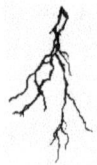

18 Days To Go

August 24th, 2001 • Jersey City, NJ

It was her.

Jenette. She was calling me back, finally.

"Hon! Good grief…where are you? How are you?" I said, snatching up my phone and speaking right away. I was lying in bed, ready to take on another day, wondering what I should do, and hoping for a call from Detective Roxanne, actually. This call, however, was so much more needed.

She stopped me. "Roland, listen, I'm sorry I haven't called. I've just needed time to think. To really think, ya know? I heard about what happened, but I only heard about it five days ago."

"The lightning strike?"

"Yeah. Amanda told me. I'm sorry. I'm glad you're okay, truthfully. She didn't want me to get all worked up, and she was just protecting me. Don't be mad at her."

"Mad? I'm- I just-," I faltered. "What? Honey, I don't care about Amanda or what she's doing or any of that. I care about *you*. Where are you, and where are *we*?"

Silence. And then a long, drawn out exhale.

"I don't know, Roland. You tell me. Where are we?"

"Jenette, you know where I am. I want you back, and I just want you to be hap-"

"No, I mean, *where are we?*"

I stopped in my tracks. "I don't understand. I thought I was answering your question." I sat up, running my hands through my messy bedhead.

"I mean, *where are we*?" She repeated. "We're still in New Jersey. I hate it here, Roland. I've told you that. I still do. I don't want to be here anymore. So, I've made a decision."

"What's your decision?" I asked in a monotone voice, growing weary with the one-sided conversation.

"I'm going back to Seattle. I- I love you, Roland. I do. But this, this upheaval, this move…I wanted it to work, okay? I did! But it hasn't. I know it's worked for you, and that's great. I'm happy for you. I am. But it hasn't for me, and I no longer want it to."

"You no longer want New Jersey to work, or you no longer want *me* to work?"

She sighed again. "You know what I mean."

"No, actually, I don't, Jenette. Why don't you tell me?" Now I was standing up, walking around in nothing but my boxers. The bright sunlight streamed through the window, and I closed the blinds as people were strolling by outside.

"I think you just said it. You called me 'Jenette.' You never call me by my name."

"What do you mean? I called you 'hon' at the beginning of the call! You haven't called me that once in our call. So, who's not wanting this relationship to work?"

"I just- ugh! This is not what I wanted for us. This is not where I wanted this conversation to go. I should just hang up. I just wanted-"

"Wanted *what?*"

Awkward pause. "I wanted to say goodbye."

And then she hung up. And, well, that was her saying goodbye. My phone-holding hand dropped to my side, and I clicked the end button.

And then I threw my little Nokia against the wall. Luckily for it, it survived. I wasn't so lucky, because I felt shattered inside, as things were shattering around me.

There was a knock at the door. Thankfully, it hadn't come while I was showering. I hated missing visitors. The doldrums of this waiting period were starting to wear upon me. I felt like I needed to get back to work, but that long, exhaustion-defeating shower felt good.

I went to the front door and opened it.

"Renita, hi!" I said, greeting her with wide eyes. "You wanna come in?"

"No, no, I can't," she said, balancing Joe-Joe on one hip. The brisk morning air filtered in behind her, and she was dressed more for fall or winter than summer. "I just wanted to pop by and ask how you were doing. I stopped by yesterday but I missed you."

"Oh, I'm fine, yeah...sorry. I went to the doctor for a follow-up for the nosebleeds and all that."

"From the lightning strike?"

"From the lightning strike." Joe-joe giggled for some reason. I looked at him and smiled.

"Well, I've got to pay a visit to the coroner today."

"Oh. Yikes," I said, grimacing. "Fun times. Do you need me to go with you?"

"No, I'm good, thanks. Just gotta do the duty and get his clothes and all that."

I nodded. Awkward.

"Anyway, doctor said you're okay? Everything okay?" she asked, biting her lip.

I gathered some air into my lungs, breathing out an uncertain *Yeah!* "Yeah, I think so. I mean, first time I've ever electrocuted somebody. I'm just glad the cops finished him off, and not me."

Insert foot in mouth, you idiot.

Her face contorted into a scrunched mess. Jake was her husband, after all.

"I-oh man- sorry, I didn't mean-"

She shook her head and closed her eyes. "No, no, it's fine. I understand," she said, tilting a shoulder as Joe-Joe tugged on some free strands of her hair under her knit hat. "Anyway, just thought I'd check in."

"No, yeah, thank you…I…appreciate it. And hey, if there's anything I can do, or if you wanna get together for some coffee or something sometime, I'm here. Here's my number." I handed her my business card with my mobile number *201-555-1818* on it.

"I'd like that," she said, and she meant it. And then she heaved a big sigh and clenched her lip. "I want to tell you thank you, Roland."

"Thank you? For what?"

"You saved my life. I believe your story. I believe what happened to you. I wanted to tell you thank you for saving Joe-Joe's and my life." She looked around awkwardly.

I just stared at her for a moment. Had I really done that? Is that what warning someone of impending doom means, that I saved their life? In this case, it most certainly did. Jake was clearly coming home to murder her.

"You're…welcome," I answered, slowly accepting the reality of it. "I just, hey, I'm happy that I could be there. Happy I was here to hear the commotion and to try to, I don't know, intervene somehow."

"Well, you did, and I'm grateful. Thank you again."

"You're welcome, Renita. You too, Joe-Joe!" Her little boy looked at me in recognition, and then smiled and turned away sheepishly, burying his face shyly against his mama's shoulder.

"Well, let me know if I can do anything for you."

"Will do. Have you heard from Jenette?"

"Uh, yeah, we, uh, spoke this morning."

"Eek. That bad, huh?"

I stopped, words failing me for a moment in the back of my throat. "Oh hell. Everything's, uh, gonna work out just fine, I think. Eventually."

Renita smiled at me.

"Well, I've gotta get going…got a full day of errands. No rest for the weary, right?" I laughed. "Be sure and keep your sunny disposition," I said, employing my tagline to try to elicit some laughter.

"Ha! Alright. Sounds good," she said, turning away with a smile. "Bye, Roland."

"Bye, Renita. Take care Joe-Joe!" Joe-Joe waved at me shyly, his head still buried in his mama's shoulder.

I closed the door behind me and sighed, leaning against it. There was a reason I was supposed to be here the day they were arguing. There was definitely a reason I needed to be here in order to avert that murder.

It was Renita.

15 Days To Go

August 27th, 2001 • Manhattan, NY

I couldn't take any more of it. I had to get out.

The weekend had passed with extreme boredom, except for cuddling with Winston here and there. I was so surprised that Jenette hadn't taken him with her; he was always more her cat. But he was a snuggle-buddy, and always nice to wake up to.

I got caught up with cleaning the apartment after Jake was killed, and I had to rearrange a few things to purge the lingering sense of tension. It was like a hovering specter in the front room: a looming presence.

I couldn't really walk around in the front room without seeing Jake's body there. It was eerie and disquieting, as if his spirit somehow lingered: a foreboding presence hovered in that room. His body was gone, but it was as if the heavy cloud of his felt rage remained.

I left Monday mid-morning at 11:15am, throwing on a light windbreaker over a T-Shirt, jeans and sneakers. I figured I could just stalk Manhattan once more on a busy weekday morning, and see what I came up with. Every superhero has an origin story, right?

So here I was, once more in the Big Apple. I didn't think I had a prayer in the world of finding that man, but I figured the PATH Station would be the best place to hang out and people-watch.

I'd done so much passage through here over the past few years; I never thought I'd be *loitering* in here one day, intentionally searching for someone, much less searching for a killer.

I knew he was a killer. Everything in me told he was going to commit a hijacking. Either he or the other man with him was. Or, maybe both of them? But I never saw the other man's face.

Jenette passed briefly through my mind, and I wondered if she was leaving today. No sense calling her. Her calling me 'Roland' and not 'hon,' us continuing to argue, her perpetual dislike for New Jersey, my throwing the phone: all of it communicated *we were through*. And the worst part of it was that I didn't feel bad about the fact that I didn't feel bad. That said much more than everything else combined.

I took the same perch that I had before, leaning against a concrete column midway through.

People ambled by, on their way to who knows where.

Young and old, business and casual, rich and poor, it didn't matter. Everyone met at PATH Station. All walks of life passed through this place, getting to where people needed to go.

Sooner or later, I would find him, I assured myself. Sooner or later I would see that familiar fa-

A shudder passed swiftly through me. A quick flinch, a brief spasm, and my head throbbed. I looked around, quickly. I had only been here for 15 minutes, but the truth slapped me coldly. *Someone else was here.*

I glanced around in all directions, frantic. I started to sniffle. The inevitable and unmistakable first sign of a nosebleed. Here it came. And then the hot flashes once more. Here they came. Suddenly I was bending over myself and clutching my stomach.

That first one felt more powerful than any other first had felt. A pang wracked my body, and this time it felt like a wave of nausea. And then I saw him.

Not the middle-Eastern man I had been looking for. No…through the halls of my mind a vision flitted of a mid-twenties man in a blue Mets baseball cap and grungy clothes. He had a grim, determined look about him.

White flashes.

Someone beating someone soundly. Pummeling them. *Flash!* Fists flying high, sailing through the air, crashing down on someone's skull, neck and back. *Flash!* A face flew out of view, too quickly for me to see who it was.

And just as quickly, the nosebleed came. Only, this time, it was thicker. I extracted my handkerchief from my pocket and held it up to my nose.

And then I saw him. There he was! Up ahead, heading up the stairs and outside. He was following someone.

My heart thudded within me. I did the only thing I could do. I followed him. I had to follow him! Despite Penny's advice to the contrary, I had to follow him. I had these abilities, and they weren't given to me for nothing.

My head swam, and I nearly collapsed, but I willed myself to stay up. To stay here.

I was at PATH Station. That's where I was. And I knew all too well who I was and what I had to do.

I'm Roland Bishop, and I know where I am, I repeated. *I'm Roland Bishop, and I know where I am.*

I followed them.

And then my phone rang suddenly. I quickly extracted it, not daring to look away and lose my target. "Hello?" I asked annoyedly. "Who is this?"

"Hi, is this Roland Bishop?" It was a woman. Whoever she was, she had a heavy giveaway Bronx accent.

"Yes it is, who is this?" I asked, panting.

"This is Detective Roxanne Byers. Your name and number were given to me by Dr. Penelope Eggers," she said, and then she paused. "Are you alright?"

"Yes, well, no, not exactly, Detective. Now's not a good time. I'm sort of in the middle of a situation."

"A situation? Are you okay?" she asked curiously.

"Did Dr. Penny tell you a bit about what I'm going through?"

"Yes, she did. A little."

"Yeah, well, it's happening again. I'm tailing somebody because I had another vision." I bumped into someone going the other way, trying desperately to keep my eyes on my target.

"Excuse me, you're *tailing* someone did you say? Are you following a perp?" she asked.

"Yes. At least I think so. I have to go now. I'll call you back in a bit, I promise."

"Wait-" she tried, and then I hung up. I couldn't be on the phone right now.

There he was, up ahead. As in my vision, there he was. Scruffy, wearing a blue baseball cap. Everyone was heading somewhere this morning: to work, to business, to see loved ones. This man was heading to a murder. But who was he pursuing? And why?

I tailed him, looking around. At one point I had to catch my breath.

We exited up the stairs and out of the building onto West Broadway heading north to Tribeca. People passed me by. I could tell they were gawking and staring. My nosebleed had stopped. The flashes, the pounding and the blood remained.

Blood. There would be blood, according to that man, I thought. And then, just as swiftly, the thought occurred to me: *not if I can help it.*

He was about thirty feet ahead of me, still heading north. The man was oblivious to me. We continued north, and I could feel the sun on my face washing over me as we passed Park Place and the Tribeca House. Where was he going? I glanced down at my watch. 11:51am. I quickly polished off a drop of nasal blood that had dripped upon it.

I looked back up. *Where did he go?* The man was gone! In the blink-and-you'll-miss-it moment I looked at my watch, I lost him. I frantically looked around through the sea of people out headed to lunch, or wherever they were going.

My phone rang again. I sneered and blew out a frustrated grunt and gust of air as I wrenched my phone from my pocket, my eyes dancing all around to find the mark. I quickly glanced down at the caller ID. Same one. Detective Byers again. I declined the call once more and looked back up, searching.

There he was! He had crossed the street over to the west side, heading toward Murray. His gaze was firmly fixed ahead of him at someone some distance ahead. I couldn't see who it was.

Suddenly, competing images flashed through me and I cried out in pain, clutching my temples. White flashes once more. Hot pulses shot through me. Other signals, mixed with indistinguishable noise and unintelligible signals swamped my vision. I shook my head to clear it out. Thankfully, they passed, but now I had a new problem.

The man had heard my cry – as had everyone else around me, some of whom drifted away from me or averted their path to avoid a homeless weirdo. I didn't look strange, I thought, other than the nosebleed. People are so superficial.

But now the man had glanced back at me and perhaps knew he himself had a tail, though he was tailing someone else. *But who!?*

He resumed his quick pace and hung a right onto Chambers Street. I followed him. By now I was sweating, trying to keep up with the feverish pace of the man. Who was he? Where was he going? Why was he pursuing whomever it was he was hellbent on destroying? Whomever he was tailing was faster than both of us.

I turned the corner onto Chambers, cautiously, and spotted him heading into The Frederick Hotel. For a moment, I thought I caught a glimpse of someone up ahead of him walking briskly inside. And then I noticed the subway stairs in the sidewalk and wondered why they both hadn't just taken that. Maybe neither one of them wanted to be in a crowd of people, or in close quarters. Either way, my target headed into the hotel, and I followed him at a distance.

My phone. One more time. Stupid phone. It was the Detective again. "Mr. Bishop, are you in danger? Please tell me where you are!" she requested calmly yet forcibly.

I grit my teeth. "The Frederick Hotel," I said, and then hit 'end' and walked in.

A voice stole my focus and attention and I jerked to my right.

"Welcome to the Frederick Hotel, can I help you?" asked a concierge at the counter as I walked in. She looked at me strangely as she took note of my handkerchief.

I waved her off with a brisk "no thank you, uh, I'm meeting someone here." She nodded and continued to stare.

I couldn't find them. *Think.* Elevators. Maybe the signals would persist and grow stronger once I got closer; after all, the man in the Mets hat had increased the distance between us. I ran to the elevators. I was going to have to take my chances. Two of them were already in operation, which gave me a 50/50 choice. Both were going up. The south elevator stopped at the third floor. I chose it and pressed the button repeatedly.

Slowly, eventually, it came back down. *Come on, come on, come on*, I thought, wringing my hands together. I glanced back at the female concierge and she quickly averted her eyes. I knew then she had been staring at me virtually the whole time.

The elevator dinged, and then opened. I practically hurled myself in there and pressed the *3* button. All at once a man appeared out of nowhere, wanting to get in. I stuck my hand out, palm outward, and they stopped short and squinted at me. I showed them my handkerchief. That did it. They backed off and put their hands up as if to say, *no blood for me, thanks*. The doors silently closed.

Third floor. I emerged quickly, and scanned up and down the hallway. I was right. Immediately, my head began to throb. I started heading west. No change in the throbbing. My heartbeat quickened, but that was it. I could feel the sweat starting to roll down my neck. I wiped the back of my head with the sleeve of my windbreaker. No flashes, no increased nosebleeds, no further change in my heart rate. I could stand properly.

I reversed direction and began to head east instead, toward the adjacent building.

I knew they were in there somewhere. Not because I started experiencing another nosebleed, or because of a quickened heartrate, or flashes.

The noises alerted me first. Strange, scuffling noises. Thumps. Thuds. Quick breaths. My eyes widened in alarm and I raced down the hall. A door was ajar! Room Number Fifteen, the last suite on the right, was slightly open. I crept in quietly. Immediately white flashes surged through my eyes in intense heat. The room lit up in scorching bluish-white ardor.

There they were! I could dimly make them both out.

The Mets man was on top of the other man, trying to choke him. His possessions were scattered across the floor: car keys, a license, some breath mints. The man's wavy black hair was in disarray as the Mets man pummeled him with one fist and had him in a chokehold with the other.

But why?!

My phone rang yet again, chiming loudly and vibrating against my keys. *Dammit, Detective Byers!*

The Mets man was suddenly aware of me, whipping around and glaring at me threateningly. His face sported a large red bruise. He looked in the very throes of breaking the other man's neck, whose face I couldn't see. It was turned toward the window.

Suddenly, the Mets man loosened his hold on the man's neck, and he fell to the floor, coughing, retching and gagging. The Mets man lunged at me, hurling us both back into the wall. My phone continued to ring. The man on the floor continued to cough.

Everything in me wanted to stop what he was doing. Why had he been pursuing the man on the floor? What the hell was going on?

My thoughts were cut short as I received a punch to the stomach, and then another. Then to the face. That sent me into a rage. Molten lava spilt through me. Suddenly, the words of the good doctor Penelope Eggers rang through my mind: *And now you must find a way to control it. That's where I slipped, Roland.*

Was I slipping? I didn't know. All I knew, lying there with the full weight and anger of the Mets man on top of me, being pummeled left and right, I was getting angrier and angrier. Visions of Penny murdering her husband flew through my mind. Visions of Jenette. Of Renita. Of airplanes being hijacked and passengers screaming. Hot flashes. Searing white behind my eyes.

My stomach tensed. My skin tingled. I erupted.

Firestarter.

And then, suddenly, before I knew what hit me, I was ablaze with fury. I craned my neck to look up at the man on top of me, and I caught and clutched his fist midair as he threw. I squeezed as hard as I could, and his fist burst into blue flame and splintered down to the elbow. With my right I reached up and grabbed his neck, as energy exploded through my limbs.

My vision skewed to blue. Everything around me was on fire in my mind. Bolts of energy coursed through my flesh and exited from my hand, straight into Mets man's neck, and he spasmed and choked with eyes wide. Wicked blue pops as if from erupting circuits sizzled through the air.

Smoke poured from his ears. His head fractured. And then flames. Flames. *Flames.* Bluish flames licked up and consumed him entirely, as he staggered backward and fell to the ground, crying out in agony, moaning, and rubbing his own body all over in a desperate and mad attempt to swat out the flames.

And then, he dropped and lay there, burning. A charred husk of a man, incinerated before my very eyes, went up in black smoke, rising toward the ceiling and choking both of us left in that hotel suite.

My phone continued to ring. I didn't pick it up, but suddenly I heard a different voice, crawling toward me, desperate to evade the blackened fumes swirling around us and enveloping us both as we lay there, panting, recovering.

The voice had an accent. "I don't know who you are, but I thank you with my life," it said. And then I looked over.

Horror coursed through me as my eyes met the eyes of the man who was being assailed. I recognized him.

His thick, wavy chestnut hair.

His pronounced middle-Eastern accent.

His Egyptian face.

His thin, pursed lips.

His solid, clenched jawline.

His beady eyes set under darkly outlined lashes.

I breathed out one word in horror.

"Mohammed," I said, and then screaming white hot flashes overtook my vision. My skin tensed, and my stomach churned. My nose freely bled yet again, streaming down my face. I staunched it with my handkerchief as I jerked away from him in revulsion.

Planes. So many airplanes. Commercial planes taking off for their destinations, and yet any one of them were going to be used in a hijacking. I just knew it. Tremors ran through me and my body quaked, this close to the source of those dangerous and terrifying visions.

And the number *fifteen*.

He looked at me in confusion. "What is wrong? I am thanking you for saving my life, sir," he sputtered amidst choking coughs. And then he reached out his hand to me.

Before I knew it, I was out of there, sprinting down the hall, ripping off my windbreaker and stuffing it into a garbage can, hurling myself violently into a stairwell. I raced out the back entrance and set off the door alarm, throwing myself down Chambers Street toward God knows where. I just had to get away.

That was the man! That was my target! What had so seized me that I had to flee?

I had just killed a man.

This man, Mohammed, was undoubtedly going to kill others. Yet I had just done what he was going to do.

Mohammed.

I screamed east, not knowing where to go. Before I knew it I was at City Hall Park, panting and hiding under the trees. My phone wouldn't stop ringing.

I couldn't stay in that hotel. I couldn't be near him. He was a terrorist. A freaking *terrorist!* And I had just saved his life! I had just enabled him to continue in his atrocity!

Penny would have a thing or two to say about this. So would the detective, and perhaps many others.

I couldn't take any more of it. I had to get out.

14 Days To Go

August 28th, 2001 • Jersey City, NJ

There had been too much in this day for me.

It was the dead of night when I returned home. I checked the clock. 12:14am.

I couldn't stay here, that much was certain. I didn't know if they had any cameras in that hotel or in the periphery, but it was a foregone conclusion that they did. Somewhere, at least. I just tried to stay in crowds and make myself less conspicuous.

Thoughts screamed through my head. One stood out from the rest.

I was now a fugitive! I had just killed a man. Out of this new uncontrollable power, this freaking 'gift,' as Penny called it!

And what was that number *fifteen* from yesterday? What was that? Now, for some strange reason, I was seeing, dimly in my mind, the number *fourteen*. Fifteen, and then fourteen? Was it some kind of code? Was it one minus the other? One plus the other? What did it all mean? I had no idea.

I was panting, and reeked of body odor. My body was tired, tired, *tired.* Sweat adhered my clothes to me, and I was chilled from the night air and hiding.

I wanted to stay away from the PATH Station, from the subways…anything. I had finally made my way back to the Holland Tunnel entrance and hitched a ride from someone who finally took me in and dropped me off close to home.

It was the weirdest feeling, walking back at night. I was caught in a tempest of desire for answers and a toxic brew of self-recrimination and scorn. *I had just killed a man!* I couldn't shake the guilt nor the memory. I didn't know who he was. But he was trying to kill Mohammed.

Maybe I should have let him. That thought passed through me like a fiery and wistful surge. He must have known about Mohammed too, right? Why else would he try to kill him? So many questions.

When I had walked to the Holland Tunnel just a few hours before, the twin towers soared into the sky overhead. I had stopped and drank in the view. They were like bastions of strength: soaring high like two twin sentinels, guarding America against the east. Briefly I remembered the 1993 parking garage bombing we'd heard about. We weren't in New

Jersey at that time. But ever since we moved to Jersey, we could look out our apartment window over the Hudson and see these towers standing there, strong, tall, defiant against that attempt, and still watching over all of us there and here. They glimmered and glistened to their very crowns, and conveyed strength to me last night as I passed under their shadows, and now once more as I stared at them across the Hudson.

Be strong, Roland. Just like them.

Now I was home. I plopped myself down on my couch to just think, and to collect myself. At any moment I expected the NJPD or NYPD to burst in with guns drawn. They'd already been here once recently for Jake.

Jake. I stared down to where he had collapsed on my floor after the police took him down.

That detective had to know. She tried to call me, I'm sure, but I turned off my phone somewhere at City Hall Park. I didn't know if Penny had given her my last name or my address, or that I worked for News 12, but she was going to find me. I couldn't stay here.

A sudden urgency took hold of me, and I turned on the midnight news to see if there were any reports. Of course there would be, but I just couldn't stay here to see them. I switched it off. I needed sleep so very badly.

Scouring the apartment, I searched for whatever I needed for a life on the run. I was essentially already a fugitive. Good thing I hadn't taken my bike into New York yesterday or I would have left it at the hotel. Just another thing to identify me by.

Even now my mind raced.

I wondered what cameras I may have appeared on, or who may have spotted me. What news reels may have shown a man in a white t-shirt and jeans fleeing the crime scene. Whether anyone found my windbreaker. I laid my head back on the couch and ran my hands through my wet, sweaty hair.

I needed a shower. I had to at least manage that.

The shower done, I was cleaned and refreshed with a second wind. I quickly dressed and grabbed my things, glancing at the clock. It was now 1:14am on Tuesday morning. I had no idea where I was going to go, but I just needed to get to a motel or something…anything to get away from here. Dare I even bring my phone? I was scared to turn it on. Couldn't they track things like that?

I reached for some quarters. I could call my voicemail from a payphone at the very least, and see what messages might have been left for me.

Stealthily, I made my way down the path with my bike. I thought, if there's anywhere I could go, perhaps I could just ride it out and wait for the morning off of Hudson River Waterfront Parkway. There were a few coffee shops there, perhaps even one of the new Starbucks, and I wasn't sure if any of them were 24/7, but I could try. Or a 7/11 or something. *Man, I need sleep,* I groaned to myself.

In ten minutes I had biked to the waterfront. It was chilly out, and passersby were sparse. I was wary: on the lookout for the cops, on the lookout for hooligans, on the lookout for anyone and everyone.

I didn't want any white flashes, any nosebleeds, any episodes….any *anything*. I hated this gift right now, because it just wasn't that: *a gift.* I reviled what it was doing to me. It was actually a curse, and now that curse had enabled me to do something horrific. I knew Mohammed's name; I had no idea the name of the man whom I had killed. He was now nameless and faceless except for his Mets cap.

I could still see Mohammed's face, lying there on the floor and crawling eerily toward me. His thick accent echoed in my mind. I could practically smell the burning flesh of the Mets man, crying out in horror as his skin went up in smoke only feet from me. I still felt the wind racing against me as I fled from The Frederick.

There was a payphone on Sussex Street right before the Paulus Hook Pier. Dismounting my bike, I chained it up to a bike hoop and figured I'd walk for a bit. The Twin Towers twinkled from across the Hudson as I looked out, and it was breezy.

I dialed my own number and entered the pin. "You have - *fourteen* - new messages," the automated greeting said. I rolled my eyes and sighed. Fourteen, in the span of a few hours.

I stopped, wide-eyed. *Fourteen.* The number fourteen. What did that mean? I had seen that in my mind's eye this morning. What did it mean? I tried to parse through it but I wasn't coming up with anything.

Back to the voicemail.

The first was from Jenette, who had called me and had forgotten to hang up. I could hear her chattering, faintly, in the background with Amanda. The next few were that pre-recorded greeting from the Jersey City Jail. Penny had tried to call me.

And then the fourth call. There she was. Detective Roxanne Byers. It was during the assault yesterday when I didn't pick up. I could hear her curse into the recording when I didn't answer. Finally, she left a full message for me at 6:02pm last night.

Mr. Bishop, this is Detective Roxanne Byers. Her voice sounded hushed. *I'm looking for you. You need to meet with me. I know about the Frederick Hotel, Roland. I know what happened to the man you were following. It is in your best interest to call me right away at this number. I don't care what time it is. You need to call me. Please. Thank you.*

The voicemail ended. No mention of "turn yourself in" or "we're coming to get you?" It didn't sound nefarious. It sounded secretive. Could she know? Would she understand somehow? I warred with myself, struggling between suspecting entrapment and two choices: avoid her entirely and throw my Nokia into the Hudson, or trust her.

Wasn't that the right thing to do? Shouldn't I turn myself in? Shouldn't I trust her? Running just made me look guilty. She knew anyway. I wasn't going to get far, and I was incredulous that I was even still free.

And then a third choice presented itself to me.

Penny. I had to go see Penny. With everything that was in me, I had to ride this out and go see Penny as soon as humanly possible, perhaps one last time.

My skin crawled, suddenly. I felt someone watching me. In a reflex, I whirled around. On the other side of the street, a short, middle-aged Latino woman was standing there, watching me. She had thin black bifocals on, and was dressed in a red knit coat and a scarf.

"Kind of late to be out and about, isn't it?" Her eyes glinted at me suspiciously, but with a kindly, knowing smile. "Or…perhaps kind of early?"

"Right," I said, dismissively, in no mood to engage anyone. I glanced around, awkwardly.

"You look like you're running on vapors."

"Is that a fact?" I grunted. "And what does 'running on vapors look like, exactly?"

She chuckled, and didn't answer me. "I'm up here with my mother for a symposium. Couldn't sleep. My mother is in medical school down in Nashville. I'm considering it as well, and we thought we'd take a trip up to Manhattan together to see The Big Apple," she said cheerily, walking toward me, slowly, her hands in her pocket.

"Oh? Sounds interesting," I said, watching her curiously. "Your mother must be starting medical school late."

"She is. I'm thirty-six, almost thirty-seven. She's sixty-one. Never too old to make a change for the future, though, right?" She had drawn near to me and now eyed me curiously on the sidewalk.

I stared at her for a moment, assessing what she might want from me. "What can I do for you, ma'am?" I asked her, tentatively.

She smiled, graciously. "Oh, nothing. Just making chit-chat. You looked lonely and disheveled. You looked like you are running from something."

"Maybe I am, and maybe I'm not."

"Maybe you *are,*" she insisted. "But wherever you're running from or to, make sure and breathe." She looked out over the Hudson. "Peaceful, isn't it?"

I looked with her. "Yes, definitely."

The middle-aged woman turned back to me.

"I'm Roland. And you are?" I asked her, curiously.

"Rosie," she greeted me with a smile. "Well, look at that. Two 'Ro's' out for an early morning stroll. Except only one of us is running from something."

"I didn't say-"

"You didn't have to, kiddo." And she eyed me curiously. "I could tell from your body language and how you reacted to listening to your own voice mails."

"You're that perceptive, are you?" I said, suspiciously.

She hmmed and hawed it away. "Maybe. That's why I'm not sure about medicine. Something greater has always called me. Something not of this world."

I raised my eyebrows. I was sure I was dealing with a whack-job now. "Oh?"

"Yep," she said, sighing. "I'm a Christian. I serve God in Heaven. I'm just not sure if I'm supposed to serve Him in medicine, or, just in being where people need me."

"And is that what you think you're doing now? Being where people need you."

She smiled at me with a knowing smile, but didn't answer right away. "Maybe," she said at last. "I don't find the people. The people just seem to find me. It's nicer that way. Less pressure." She smiled and cocked her head at me through her bifocals.

I gave her an inevitable smile. "And did I find you tonight?"

"I don't know what you found, nor why. I just try to be where people who are in need....are."

I looked her up and down. "Well," I said at last, "sounds like you've found your calling. I really have to be on my way. It was nice meeting you."

"Somewhere you need to be at 1:30 in the morning?" Her question was loaded with sarcasm.

I chuckled. "Well, not really, but-"

She was ready to interrupt me. "My advice to you, though you haven't asked – and that's fine – is to stop running. Stop hiding. One day, something even bigger than what you're currently running from will come. And how you deal with this will determine how you deal with that."

I furrowed my brows, confused at the unanticipated advice from this unexpected stranger. "You sound like my psychiatrist. You wouldn't happen to know a Dr. Penny, would you?"

She shook her head. "I know only those the Father sends my way. And for some reason, this morning, here, He sent you. And that's what I'm supposed to say to you. Stop running, Roland." Her eyes twinkled in the night.

I didn't know what to say, but I gathered air into my lungs, stared down at her, and sighed. "Okay. Sounds good." I wasn't entirely sure if I meant that to get rid of her, or if I believed it. But it seemed to be enough for her.

"Okay. I wish you luck, Roland." And with that, she turned to walk away.

"Uh, yeah…good luck, uh…"

"Rosie," she said, over her shoulder.

I walked that waterfront back and forth for a few hours, wondering what to do, and pondering Rosie's words. Such a complete stranger, but I wondered if fate truly had her in store. She seemed wise beyond her years, and maternally sweet, just like Penny.

But my legs felt thick and my indecision weighed a ton.

My life was in limbo, and all I could do was stare helplessly out over the Hudson and watch the river flow by. That's all my life was doing now: my old life flowing by on the tides of time, off to somewhere else while I was stuck here in flux. I quickly grew tired of checking my watch, and stopped altogether. That allowed me a bit of surprise joy as I finally saw the first light of the rising sun spring up over Manhattan.

I found a coffee shop that opened at 7am. Visiting hours for Penny's block started at 10am today. I biked up to Grove and 7th and parked my bike. I was taking a bit of a risk, I figured, but I had to see her. She had to know, and I needed to know what to do.

As I pulled up, I noticed the baseball diamond across the street. I had seen it before, of course, but something had changed, or, at least I had changed and was now seeing it differently. There were kids playing on it, and their laughter brought an innocence to my ears and my soul that I think I needed. Once you've killed someone, and had someone killed in front of you, life sort of…changes.

I was inordinately tired, but I gathered myself together and took a deep, cleansing sigh before walking up to visitation.

Before long, I was seated there, and here came Penny once more. She practically ran to her little booth and snatched up her intercom.

"Tell me it isn't true," she said, leaning forward close to the glass that separated us.

I didn't reply. I didn't know what to say.

"Roland!" she whispered. "Tell me. Did it happen?"

"Penny, I-," I tried to play dumb. "I don't know what you mean."

"Oh, bollocks, Roland. You know perfectly well what I mean." And then she looked around her and up at the Guard behind me. "The Frederick," she whispered, and I tensed up. "The Frederick Hotel. Detective Byers visited me and told me. Did you?"

I suddenly lost all composure and felt the wind sucked out of me. A sigh forced its way out of my lungs and I shook my head mournfully. "Penny, I- I don't know what happened. It was all a blur."

"Was it the same way that it happened with your neighbor? The blue fire? The burns?"

I nodded.

"Only this time, you-"

I clenched my lip and just stared at her. "Is there room for one more in there?"

"Nonsense, Roland. It was an accident. Mine was intentional. You know that quite well. Detective Byers is a good woman. Has she tried to contact you?"

"Yes, many times. I turned my phone off."

"Whatever for?" she asked, her eyes widening, her face pressing further toward the glass.

"I don't know, Penny! Look!" I said, growing frantic and trying to keep my voice down. "I don't know what to do! If you saw what I did, your mind would be totally blown!"

"Listen to me, Roland Bishop," she hissed through her teeth. "I want you to go down and call Detective Byers back straightaway. Straightaway! You just might regret it if you don't, and it sounds like you really need an ally right now. Running only makes you look guilty."

I blew out hard air. "Tell me about it. I told myself the same thing."

"Well then?"

"Well then what? Penny," I said, lowering my voice even further, "they'll take me into custody right away. That man was trying to kill another man, and I stopped him!"

Her nose crinkled at the bridge. "What other man?"

"The man *he* was tailing."

"Wait – slow down," she said. "The man you tailed was not the one you told me about a few days ago, the one you saw in your vision with the planes?"

"No! It was someone completely different!"

"Oh dear."

"Yeah, *oh dear* is right! This new guy – he was wearing grungy clothes and a Mets cap – he was following someone, and that *someone* turned out to be the middle Eastern man I saw in my vision. Mohammed. But before I could get to Mohammed, the Mets cap guy had him in a chokehold on the ground in a room at The Frederick, and I got in and tried to prevent it, because I saw *his* attack in a vision too!"

"This is getting *decidedly* more complicated by the moment. So if I understand you correctly, you received a new vision for a new assailant – Mr. Mets Man – and you tailed him while *he* was tailing Mohammed to The Frederick."

I nodded.

"I wonder why he was tailing Mohammed just as you were previously."

"Exactly."

She paused for a moment, thinking.

"It doesn't matter."

"Pen–"

She stopped me. "Tut-tut!" she said, putting up a finger. "It's minutiae at this point. Insignificant for the moment. For now, your only concern is to contact Detective Byers at once. Is that clear?" She looked at me scoldingly.

I shook my head, incredulous. "I guess so. I mean, it sounds like I don't have any other option."

"You don't. Unless you want to fill your days tailing people who are tailing people. Sounds like everyone is tailing everyone out there while I'm eating shit on a shingle."

I stopped a guffaw. "What is that?"

"Deplorable breakfast food. Don't ask! What I wouldn't give for a biscuit."

I smiled at her through my frustration.

"Alright, I'll call her. Do *you* need anything?"

She looked at me sternly. "I need my clients to follow my directions. I didn't pay nearly a half-hundred-thousand dollars on a degree so that I could yip useless advice at passersby, Roland. Hmmph!" She clicked her tongue and looked away in what she would call a 'snit.'

I had to let out a chortle. "You know, you really are British, aren't you?" It wasn't a question.

"Irretrievably," she said, whipping her head back to me. "Now go call her, Roland. For your own good."

"Ya know, you've gotten pretty uppity since you've been in there."

"Just wait until I'm back out. We'll see how uppity I've become."

She shook her head, but I could see a trace of a smile in there wanting to jump out at me. And then she softened.

"Just look at us," she said. "My, how the tables have turned in just seventy-two hours. It used to be just me on this side of the glass. Now it might be you as well."

Her observation elicited a thick sigh on my part, looking at her, pressing that intercom up against my ear. "Can't believe it."

"Nor can I, Roland. But what matters now is *now*. What do you do with *now?*"

It was a good question. I knew exactly what I needed to do. Or, at least I knew what I needed to do to not get *tut-tutted* again.

My phone was still around sixty percent at least, so that was something.

It was now turned back on, and my fingers hovered over the *1* button to call my voicemail. I listened to her number again and noted it down, taking a deep breath. There would be no going back once I made this call.

I dialed her number into my phone but didn't hit 'send' just yet. I stared down at my little red Nokia, knowing full well the ramifications of calling her. It stared back at me apathetically, emotionless, with zero regard to what I had been through nor what I might go through after this.

Point of no return. My legs were trembling. My arm was spasming slightly. I made sure to stand close to my bike in case I needed to race out of there.

I pressed th-

My phone rang! My arm jerked back and my body quaked in surprise. Everything in me tensed up.

Reflexively, I accidentally hit 'answer.' I cursed in frustration, the phone at my side, but then slowly brought it to my ear.

"Hello?" I greeted slowly.

"Oh, thank God. Mr. Bishop, is that you?"

"Who's calling?"

"Mr. Bishop, it's Detective Roxanne Byers again. I'd like to meet with you. I know you're scared. *Please* don't hang up. I just need to meet with you. Where are you?"

I need to meet with you. My cynicism was on full alert. Was that cop-speak for *I'd very much like to arrest you now, if it's alright with you?*

Those words felt tinged with imminent betrayal: a lure with the good-cop routine, only to spring the *Gotcha!* bad cop routine and throw a net over me once she had me in her sights.

"Okay…," I slowly breathed in response.

"Where are you?"

"Jersey City."

"That doesn't exactly give me proximity. Where about?"

I sighed. "Listen, what's this about, Detective? I don't mean to be rude, bu-"

"I think you know what it's about Roland. Cut the crap. I've been trying to reach you all night. I'm asking nicely. Please," she said. The way she said *please* somehow had the ring of truth to it. I waited.

"Roland, are you there?"

I shriveled.

"Jersey City Jail," I offered glumly. "I just visited our mutual friend."

"No problem. I'll be there in five minutes. Please wait out front."

"Will do." I hit 'end.'

Nothing in me wanted to comply, and everything in me revolted. They were going to be here in five minutes. If they were going to take me in, she had my location, so why wouldn't she just call Jersey City Jail and have someone come out behind me, walk down the steps, and arrest me? I waited. No one came. No shouts of "Freeze!"

Penny strongly advocated for me to talk to her. Would Penny set me up? I didn't think so, but I began to suspect her of concealing dark designs now as well.

After all, she had hid them from her own husband, so why not me?

My view was colored. It had been colored blue yesterday with electricity. Now it was just colored green – green with suspicion and fear.

I thought back to Rosie on the waterfront. It was time to stop running.

"Mr. Bishop?" There was that Bronx accent again.

She stepped out of the Ford Bronco, and my legs were trembling. Trembling from fear, from lack of sleep, and now, from overwhelming beauty. She was ravishingly beautiful, stopping my heart with her billowing curly hair blowing in the breeze, and that tan blazer fitting her form perfectly.

And speaking of legs, hers were long, and every bit the looker.

"Detective Byers, I presume?" I asked tentatively.

She stopped just in front of me and looked me up and down. "Have you not had much sleep?"

"How could you guess?"

"Well, I know you were on the run, and you weren't answering my calls, and this sort of thing happens when someone feels guilty for something they did."

Feels guilty? I thought. *I* am *guilty, you hot-to-trot vixen.* I was gobsmacked by her immeasurably captivating looks, her figure, her power.

I started to speak, but no words came.

"Can you come with me, please? Time is pressing."

"Wh-where are you taking me?" I asked.

"I'm not *taking* you anywhere, Roland. I'd like to go somewhere with you. Please. You must be hungry."

What the hell was going on here? I had killed somebody. She knew that. What was with the cloak-and-dagger business? *If you're going to arrest me, just arrest me and get it over with,* I thought. My knees were shaking, but I followed her.

"I am hungry. Thanks."

"Let's go." Thankfully, she was alone. That was less intimidating than it might have been had she had a partner with her. She even allowed me to sit in the front seat.

She held the door open for me, and I looked under my eyebrows at her briefly as I passed by her, smelling her intoxicating perfume…similar to stuff that Jenette wore. Vera Wang 'Princess,' I think, or something like that. My eyes locked with hers, and there was understanding there. I think she also glanced briefly at my lips.

"What about my bike?" I asked her.

She shook her head. "We'll come back for it later."

"Will I be home tonight? I need to feed my cat."

"You'll be home tonight."

Maybe Penny was right after all. If we were coming back for my bike, that meant she wasn't arresting me just yet.

Or…did she mean that she would arrest me, and she and a partner would come back for it?

Maybe Penny was wrong after all.

We had gone through a drive-through and she had bought me a few tacos and chips. I could barely even eat them, my nerves were so wracked.

"Is this the part where you say something? Or do I kick off our convo?" she asked me.

I looked over at her, sheepishly. "I don't know. You obviously know something, and this is a little too cloak-and-dagger for my taste."

She giggled maturely. "Cloak and dagger. You ever see that movie?"

"What?"

"*Cloak and Dagger.* Have you seen it? Dabney Coleman and the kid from E.T."

"N-no, I haven't," I said, furrowing my brows.

"Yeah. 'Jack Flack always escapes.' Cute movie. From 1984 I think. The kid pulled a 'crossfire gambit.' Like, a double-cross move and had the bad guys shoot at each other. They ended up killing each other off. Always loved that as a kid. Great movie. I'd love to try that someday."

"Interesting," I said nonchalantly. "Are there some bad guys we're about to talk about?"

She just looked at me without answering.

I'll take that as a yes.

"Where are we heading?" All I could tell was that we were headed back south.

"Certainly not The Frederick Hotel. But we are headed that way. We've got an office over there I'd like to take you to. Oh, by the way, here's your windbreaker. Thought you might want it back."

She reached behind the seat. I flinched. "Easy," she said. Byers fetched my windbreaker and set it in my lap. I looked down. Sure enough, there it was. Looked like it had some blackened marks on it that resembled burns. I gulped.

She reached for her car CB radio. "Byers to Armstrong, come in, over?"

"Armstrong here," came the answer over the CB.

"Subject apprehended, bringing him in, over."

"Roger that, see you soon."

"Yep." She clicked the CB radio into place once more.

"Apprehended?"

She smiled at me. "Just relax. *Keep your sunny disposition.* We just need to talk first."

A laugh inadvertently escaped my lips, and I snorted. She knew my tagline. Good detective work. "So, where's your office?"

"Manhattan."

My eyebrows flicked up. "Been there a lot lately."

"Yeah, it sounds like it."

An awkward few minutes passed as we drove through the Holland Tunnel and emerged on the other side. Once again, there were the two towers looming over us.

"Never gets old, does it? Just look at 'em."

"Yep, they're beautiful, alright," I mumbled back, tossing a glance her way, my eyes accidentally stealing to her legs. *Cool it, Roland. You're still married. Jenette might come take you back,* I thought. But an unsettling question steeped in me. *Did I really want her back? Did she really want me?*

I averted my eyes and sighed.

"Something wrong?" Byers asked me.

"Nope," I said, staring up at the towers and trying to focus on them, but instead visualizing superimposed long female legs pointing up into the sky.

"Alright, we're here," said the Detective.

I looked around and took in the view.

"Please come with me, okay?"

I didn't say anything. Exited her Bronco and shut the door behind me. We were off Lafayette Street, entering a large white building with rusty garage doors flanking across the bottom. My mouth dropped open. It was the Wanamaker Building, all that remained of a legendary Astor Place department store that few New Yorkers remember. I had been here once only, on a brief New York sightseeing tour after Jenette and I moved here. Large, elegant letters rode high above one of the doors, which we passed, entering the double doors on the right.

I followed her silently through the doors. We stood in front of an elevator, not acknowledging each other. She depressed the floor button, and stared up at the descending numbers. I glanced over at her. She didn't glance back.

The door opened and we rode up together to the sixth floor. The bell dinged, the doors opened once more, and she motioned me out. And there, waiting for both of us, were two men in suits.

"Hey, Armstrong," Byers greeted him. He nodded back and then looked at me.

"Mr. Bishop?"

"Yes?" I answered nervously.

"Could you please place your arms out wide, sir?"

I did so, and the other agent advanced toward me, feeling through my shirt. My eyebrows muddled. Was he looking for a wire or something? What the hell? He felt all over, patting me down. "Ah, watch it, buddy," I said, as his hands patted up my inner leg.

"He's clean," my frisky agent said to Armstrong with a heavy New York accent. He took my Nokia and handed it to Armstrong.

"Hey – do I get that back?" I asked Armstrong.

"Chill out, Mr. Bishop," he said, but that did little more than test my patience.

"Why do they need my ph-"

"Detective Byers," Captain Frisks-a-lot acknowledged her to my right. "Come with me please."

Armstrong disappeared down another hallway with my phone.

I cast an awkward glance over at Detective Byers. Her face was nondescript, accustomed to this procedure, and she showed no signs of alarm or surprise, which I took as some measure of comfort. Nonetheless, this thing was getting more spy-movie by the minute.

After a seemingly interminable walk to the upper quadrant of the building, we were led into a suite, past a bank of cubicles, and into a collection of offices that looked north toward Astor Place. There was a conference table in a side room. Another agent was waiting there for us.

The previous agent, Captain Frisks-a-lot, motioned for me to go in. Byers followed me, and we sat down. They closed the door behind us. The second agent was seated at the conference table with a few file folders in front of him that he must have retrieved from a file cabinet that was situated against the wall close to the window.

"Could someone please tell me what this is all about?" I asked, trying to hide my nerves.

Captain Frisks-a-lot pulled out a tape recorder and sat down next to the seated agent, hitting record as he did so. "You don't mind if we record this, do you, for the record?"

"Well, actua-"

"Great," he said, and continued to record. The other one pulled out a notepad and began jotting down some notes. Then he turned to me.

I squirmed uneasily in my seat.

"Mr. Bishop," he said, with an equally heavy New York brogue, "my name is Agent Ryan Phelps, and this is Agent Rob Fox." *That second one being aka Captain Frisks-a-lot. Got it.* "We're with the FBI."

That jarred me to attention. I flinched and eyed them in incredulity. My eyes traveled to Detective Byers nervously. "The FBI- what the hell is this?" Byers just watched me blandly. "You're with the *FBI??*"

"That's correct, Mr. Bishop. Please just listen."

"Listen, Roland," urged the Detective.

I tried to sit back and relax in my chair.

"Would you like something to drink, Roland?" asked Fox, and I didn't like the way he said my name so informally. I shook my head.

Fox looked back at Phelps, who continued.

"Mr. Bishop, Detective Byers was contacted by a Dr. Penelope Eggers who we understand is your psychiatrist, is that correct?"

I nodded.

"And that you've been seeing her following some abnormal episodes you've been having following a lightning strike that took place a few weeks ago in Millenium Park, yes?"

I nodded again.

Phelps paused. "You do speak English, yes?"

I let out a quick sigh. "Yes. I speak English, Agent Phelps. Could you please tell me-"

"Would it be safe to say that yesterday was the result of another one of these abnormal episodes?"

I didn't answer, just held still. I didn't want them to pry it out of me, but I also didn't care to feel any more like an anomaly than I already did.

"Look, I don't know wh-"

"Mr. Bishop," interrupted Fox, "you're not going to be arrested. I can imagine you're experiencing some fear and trepidation about what took place yesterday, and what the fallout will be. Let me assure you that you've been brought here because we need your help."

My head tilted seemingly of its own accord as my eyes narrowed. "Help...help with what? And where's my phone? When do I get my phone back?"

Phelps started up again. I looked over quickly at Byers who eyed me dispassionately and then returned her focus to the agents. "We understand that you've been having some visions, some *particular* visions, about a particular person, and we'd like to discuss that with you. Would that be alright?"

Mohammed. They didn't have to even say it. I knew. I gathered myself for a long breath.

"What does the FBI want with this man?" I asked.

Fox started to say something, but Phelps waved him down. "Please, Roland- Mr. Bishop, if I may. We have a lot to get through."

I shrugged my shoulders in acceptance. If they wanted to lead, they could lead.

"We believe the man you've been tailing is named Mohammed Atta." I flinched at the name. I knew it. I saw his face crawling toward me in The Frederick once more. "Born September 1st, 1968 in Egypt." Phelps opened a file folder, pulled out a dossier and placed it in front of me.

Mohammed Atta. That was him, sure enough.

"He studied architecture at Cairo University, graduated 1990, and studied at Hamburg University of Technology in Germany after that. While there he joined a mosque, and it's become apparent he is now part of a terrorist cell that had its roots there. Perhaps more than once he's been in contact with a man known as Osama bin Laden. Does that name ring a bell?"

The Al-Qaeda terrorist leader. I nodded. I had watched a documentary on him and knew that he had ties to the 1993 bombing at the World Trade Center.

"Osama bin Laden formed al-Qaeda in 1988 for the purposes of jihad. In August 1996 and again in February 1998 he declared *fatawa*, declarations of war, against America. He was indicted for the US embassy bombings on East Africa in 1998. He's regarded globally as one of the most dangerous men alive."

Fox cut in. "Yeah, FBI's got him on their Most Wanted Terrorists and Most Wanted Fugitives lists. And just two years ago the UN officially designated al-Qaeda as a terrorist organization."

"So, what does that mean for Mohammed Atta?" I asked. This time Phelps welcomed my question.

"I'm glad you asked. While in Germany, Atta formed a cell with several other men the FBI have been watching of late, and monitoring chatter." He flipped through Atta's dossier. "Marwan al-Shehhi, Ramzi bin al-Shibh, and Ziad Jarrah are some of the members of that cell whom we've been monitoring."

I heard a quick sizzle to my right and looked over. Byers had lit up a smoke. She recoiled, surprised. "You don't mind, do you?"

I shook my head. Somehow that made her even sexier.

"Atta, and members of the Hamburg cell, had been recruited by bin Laden as well as another man, Khalid Sheikh Mohammed, for an operation we believe will be here in the states, involving airplanes and possible hijack situations."

The wind was sucked out of me. I gasped. "Oh my- that's what I've been seeing. Those are the exact visions I saw."

"In these, these…abnormal episodes you've been having," said Fox.

"Sure," I said to him. I was beginning to dislike Fox. "Anyway, yeah, that's what I've been seeing ever since August 19th. I'm also now seeing *numbers,* though I don't know why. You guys think I'm crazy, don't you?"

Neither one of them nodded or shook their heads.

I'll take that as a yes as well.

Frankly, I was getting excited that some pieces were finally starting to fall into place. "Anyway, numbers. Today was fourteen. Yesterday was fifteen. I don't know."

"Fourteen. Fifteen. Could be a code of some kind. Do you have any lockers or PIN numbers that have that?" Fox asked.

"No, no, he said *fifteen-fourteen*, in that order," Phelps clarified. "That could be a mathematical equation, could be a countdown. We'll look at that in a bit. I would like to talk to you about your visions, specifically, Roland. What happened with them, and what happened *in* them?"

Byers blew out a long trail of smoke. Apparently she'd already heard this from Penny. I wondered if she even believed me.

"Well," I started, "I don't know what will trigger it except that it seems to be when I'm in close proximity with my target. Target- that's what I call them. Anyway, I starting having these…these white flashes, I get a heatwave pass through me, my head throbs, nosebleeds, passing out, the whole shebang. Before I know it, I'm on the floor.

"But," I paused, holding up a finger, "before I go down, in those shockwaves, I get all kinds of visual signals, like, I don't know, videos, of things that happened. Only none of them have happened yet. Detective Byers," I said, turning to her, "you know about the bank robbery where they killed the security guard and blew up the bank in Queens a week ago. And the twelve-year-old girl who got kidnapped out of Brooklyn and they found her body later?"

She nodded.

"I saw those too. I saw both of those incidents *before* they happened. I needed to talk to a shrink – sorry, psychiatrist," I said, remembering Dr. Walker's faux pas, "because I saw them on the news afterwards. Each time they had caught the suspect, and each time, I knew *that's* the suspect I had seen in my visions. I was near them only a day or two prior to their crime."

"So you have to be near them," said Fox, eyeing me curiously.

"Yeah. I mean, but don't mistake me, I don't know where they'll be, or when the images will strike. I've gotten all kinds of imagery lately. Just the other night I saw our neighbor killing his wife before it happened. And…" I trailed off, looking at each of them in turn.

"And what?" Phelps asked.

I glanced back at him. "I-I don't know, I was able to avert it somehow. I knew precisely how he'd do it, and who he'd do it to, so I took her in and kept her safe in my place. But eventually he found out where she was, and he barged into my apartment and tried to kill her. I," -here I took a deep breath, not knowing how much of this they'd actually swallow- "I somehow managed to disable him."

"Disable him? How?" Phelps asked again.

"I don't know exactly how. I don't know what happened to me. Like some lightning got 'stuck' in me, or something? I don't know. All I know is I grabbed his arm, and the next thing I knew his arm had burst into flame, and I was seeing white-hot blue vision and screaming with every fiber of my being and the fire of a thousand suns. It was electric. Powerfully electric."

They stared at me.

"Interesting," Phelps said, feeling the stubble of a beard on his chin.

Fox looked a bit incredulous, but was still at least listening.

"And this guy, this, Mohammed Atta," I asked them, "he was the same, a few nights ago. Only his hasn't happened yet. My neighbor Jake's happened within the span of a few hours. And the guy yesterday at the Frederick, well, his happened within an hour."

"So?" Fox asked.

"*So,*" I enunciated, "I think something in me is sensing that maybe the timeline is being sped up with some of them. I don't know. All I know with that guy is that he was trailing Mohammed Atta. I know that now because I-"

"You what?" Fox asked me quickly.

Answering his question, or completing my sentence, would potentially incriminate me. But they already knew that I had been onsite there. Byers confirmed that. She took another drag of her cigarette and blew it out heavily.

"Because he was there, Ryan," she said to Phelps. "He's the one who burnt your partner to a crisp."

I looked back at Phelps in horror. "Partner?!"

Phelps shrugged. "Not exactly. We're FBI, Mr. Bishop. He was a CIA operative working in coordination with us. You have to remember that there are some branches of us that don't exist and aren't supposed to. Agent Mulligan was tailing Atta and tracked him into his hotel. He tried to subdue Atta and take him out. That was his assignment."

"Wait, are you telling me I killed a federal agent?!" I asked in complete dismay.

They both sported blank slates. Maybe they didn't like Mulligan. Maybe he didn't technically exist and was expendable. Either way, they were expressionless. Perhaps they had just already come to grips with it and had moved on. Or maybe the FBI was just as cutthroat as I had always heard them to be: emotionless and all duty.

"Guys," I said, putting my hands up, "I had no idea. You have to believe me. I had *no* idea that's who he was. The vision didn't tell me who he was nor what he wanted. They…they don't give me any backgrounds or morality lessons on any of them. All I saw was him beating up and trying to kill someone else. I had no clue that someone else was Atta. And I had no idea that he was your partner. You gotta believe me."

They both looked at me quizzically for a moment. Fox spoke first. "We already know you were there. Nice windbreaker, by the way. Byers here tipped us off when she heard about your little, shall we say, 'gifts' from Dr. Eggers. So she told Agent Phelps here. In a very special kind of way, I might add."

"Special?"

"Fox, cut it out," said Phelps, briskly. "A little decorum, please."

I felt Byers stir along with him. "Ryan is my ex-boyfriend, Mr. Bishop. Got it?" I got it, but I wasn't happy about it. *At least it's 'ex,' I thought.* "So Penny tells me, I tell Ryan, Ryan thinks you might be valuable in finding out what our little Egyptian friend is doing, we bring you in. *Capisce?*" she said, sporting some Italian.

It made sense now.

"So you had no idea before hearing about it through Penny. Uh, Dr. Penelope Eggers," I clarified. She shook her head.

"Can we get back to the subject matter, people?" Fox asked annoyedly. "We're trying to stop Atta forward in time, not go back in time and recreate the love exchange."

Phelps rolled his eyes and pinched the bridge of his nose. "Mr. Bishop, what we're trying to tell you is that we have a potentially serious event about to go down in or around New York City at the hands of Mohammed Atta and others. We don't know what it is yet, but he and his accomplices have taken flight training here in the US. They obtained instrument ratings in May.

"We've tracked passports of other potential accomplices of Atta's who have begun their westward migration, coming into the states over the past year. People loosely affiliated with Atta but who could potentially be part of their next operation. We suspect they're going to hijack airplanes and take the hostages with them back home. Last month Atta himself flew to meet with one of the other terrorists, who we think is Ramzi bin al-Shibh. We lost Atta in Spain. Came back to the states eventually.

"And now," he continued, "over the past few months we see that he's been conducting what we assume are 'surveillance' flights, garnering information on whatever it is they're about to do."

"Wow," I breathed. "So, you think they're going to conduct a hijacking?"

"Confidence is high, yes," Phelps said.

"I'd like to come back to this numbering thing you mentioned, Roland," Fox said. "Maybe there's no rhyme or reason to it. Maybe it's not part of any kind of identifiable pattern. Might be random. But we should be looking at that too. You didn't see numbers associated with either of the previous crimes you previsualized?"

I shook my head. "No. Those were just the crimes themselves. But there have actually been *six* now, Agent Fox. The first two were the bank robbery and the girl from Brooklyn. Next came Mohammed Atta. After that it was Penny's – Dr. Penelope Egger's – husband. That turned out to be Penny herself, so my vision was incorrect... or... something. I don't know. Then my neighbor Jake, and now Agent Mulligan. None of those other ones beside Atta had any kind of numbers associated with them. The numbers thing just started yesterday. I can't really explain it yet. It's not like I saw the number six prior to my sixth vision or anything like that."

"But you think because some of them have been incorrect, or the actual tragedy differed from what you originally saw, that the numbers thing might be perhaps insignificant?" Fox kept at me.

"Not insignificant, but coincidental, certainly," I argued. "It's something that, again, I can't explain and that I, I don't know, hope gets clearer with time. In any event, they don't seem to correspond with the number of visions I've had. There's too much of a discrepancy."

"The reason I ask, Mr. Bishop," Fox said, "is because we had a bit of a surprise here ourselves that we can't explain."

"Oh?"

"Several of their guys had tickets purchased for Saturday, September 8th. Two groups of them booked together across two separate planes. Atta was with a group of two other men on one flight. An accomplice of his, Marwan al-Shehhi, was leading another group on a different flight. Then, a few days ago, on the 20th, something changed." He looked at me suspiciously.

"Something...changed?"

"Yeah. Something changed. There were no longer two groups on two different flights. There were three groups on three different flights. The two men previously listed, and then a third, led by yet another associate on a different flight. Hani Hanjour is his name. Another terrorist cell member."

I thought to myself. "Well, the night of the 19th is when I saw Mohammed Atta and the other man with him at the PATH Station. They had been on the subway with me before that. Maybe they changed their plans if they thought they were being tailed?"

"Maybe, maybe not. But then their plans changed again." I tilted my head as Fox continued. "After your little tussle with Agent Mulligan, and your subsequent encounter with Atta at The Frederick, the flights changed once more. Now there's only a single plane involved, and Atta isn't on it."

"How can that be? Did they call in and change the flight plans?"

"No. It's like they were booked that way from the very beginning. We're also tapped into bank accounts, and no further funds were exchanged, credited, or expended. That's why we've been having trouble pinpointing the exact date or manner in which they plan to conduct their hijackings."

I thought about both incidents. Both happened directly after my run-ins with Atta. And then both future plans changed. I was seeing the future! Was it possible that Atta was as well? Or was it possible that by intervening, I was altering the course of the future somehow?

No! I'm not that powerful! I thought. But that didn't explain the change of travel plans, or the fact that there was no financial or airline record of the change. That was a mystery that neither the FBI nor I could explain.

But there and then I found myself questioning *all* of the episodes I had had. Did I in some way accelerate or decelerate their transpiring? *No! It couldn't be!* There had to be an alternative explanation for it.

"I'd like to switch for a moment. Mr. Bishop, why don't you now tell us exactly what happened with Agent Mulligan at The Frederick Hotel yesterday," interrupted Phelps. "Did you meet Mohammed Atta? Are you certain that the man that Mulligan was tailing is the man pictured in the dossier before you?"

"It's him." I sighed, recollecting the haunting memory of that man crawling toward me across the floor. Of Agent Mulligan erupting into flames and burning before my very eyes. Of tearing out of there in a frenzy.

I walked them through everything I could, as best as I could recall, of how I tailed Agent Mulligan up Broadway, unaware that he himself was tailing someone else. What he was wearing. How I had the flashes and cried out in pain, and he stopped and looked back at me. Our encounter in the suite. What happened when I burnt him, and he erupted into flames just like Jake. Mohammed crawling toward me. What Mohammed had said to me. How I tore out of there.

"Got it," said Phelps. "And now, for the record, I'd like you to describe in exacting detail what you saw in your visions concerning Mohammed Atta."

I tried to think back to nine days ago on the subway, and then at the PATH Station. That sweet old lady who asked about me. The people bustling about. The sneers and disgusted look-aways because of my bloody nose. The heat. The sweat.

Mohammed.

I told them what I saw, as best as I could recall. And suddenly, as I began to prime the pump of my memory, I was seized with white flashes. As if on fast-forward, all the images came racing back, and my eyes fluttered.

Airplanes.

Large commercial airliners.

Fights high in the sky. Dark-skinned men, many of them. A middle-Eastern language.

A plane streaking across the sky.

No. *Multiple* planes.

People screaming.

Rubble everywhere. Smoke. Dust. Ash. The jet had obviously crashed into the ground, I figured. The images of the hijackers intruding into the cockpits of the planes. The visuals were jumping backward and forward with no cohesive timeline.

Screams.

Screams.

SCREAMS!

The anguished cries of thousands of people. Thousands? A massive rushing sound like concrete collapsing, pancaking one against another. Billows of smoke and dust. Yellowish ash clouds the size of buildings.

And then...blackened silence.

I was breathing hard as all of it cascaded before my eyes in a macabre montage of agony. My mouth was open, and I was sweating. I seemed to be floating in a black void.

I'm Roland Bishop, and I know where I am.

I'm Roland Bishop, and I know where I am.

I'm Roland Bishop, and I know where I am.

My heartbeat slowed. Gradually, as if through a fog, the mist cleared and I could dimly make out the shapes of Detective Roxanne Byers, Agent Ryan Phelps, and Agent Rob Fox, just staring at me.

The clock on the wall behind them read 6:17pm.

6:17pm?? How could that be? Had we been there that long?

Detective Byers had only just gotten us lunch on the way over. Had we talked that long? Or had my flood of visions taken me down some kind of wormhole?

Sweat trickled down my forehead, and I felt warmth trickling out of my nose. A cavalcade of images had just swamped me. I felt faint, still panting, looking at them incredulously.

"Th-they're going to hijack," I breathed out.

Byers reached out to steady me as I swayed.

"Hij-jack…multiple pl-planes," I said, and then I toppled over. Byers did her best to try and stop my fall, but it was too late.

I slumped over and then hit the floor hard on my already-pounding head.

As my mind faded, I reflected on the fact that I couldn't take many more hits to my cranium. Dr. Walker would have a thing or two to say.

So would Dr. Penny.

"Can I have my phone ba-" I started, but my tongue felt swollen and my lips failed me.

I dimly heard their voices calling for me. Someone slapped my face a little too hard, trying to rouse me. I bet that was Fox. All their voices seemed far away, too dim to hear through the lurid ringing in my ears.

There had been far too much in this day for me.

13 Days To Go

August 29th, 2001 • Manhattan, NY

Once more, I awoke feeling rested and calm.

Detective Byers was shaking my shoulder. "Good morning, Roland. How are you feeling?"

I felt nauseous, as well. "Not so good. What happened?"

"You blacked out."

"What time is it?"

"Almost 2am on Wednesday the 29th."

Dimly I took in my surroundings. She wasn't lying; the clock on the wall echoed the time. It was dark outside and inside. A dim corner lamp lit up another room in this cluster of offices. No sign of the agents or anyone else. There was a futon in here, and they hadn't pulled it out; I was just lying on the couch version of it, covered with a thin, knitted blanket that didn't really do much except snag your fingers. "Where is everyone else?"

"Home. Catching some shuteye. I took a nap and came back here to check on you. Armstrong is still downstairs, and other agents are on night shifts doing their own stuff, in and out."

"Does anyone else know the FBI has a field office here?" I asked her.

She shrugged. "Covert crap. Beyond my paygrade."

I groggily sat up and rubbed my eyes. "I thought you were sleeping *with* the higher paygrade though, ri-"

"I never said I was sleeping with him!" she instantly protested. "Watch it, Bishop."

I pulled my knuckles out of my reddened eyes and just stared at her. "Sorry. I didn't mean-"

"It's fine," she dismissed me. "Good Catholic girl. You assumed too much," she grunted, as she pulled out a smoke and lit it up, blowing a purplish-white plume out into the room. I waved it away from me. Never was fond of side stream smoke.

"Again, sorry," I said, and then I couldn't help it as a wild yawn escaped my lips and stretched my mouth until I thought it would rip. "Will I ever get my phone back?"

"Relax, Roland, you'll get your phone back soon," she said. *Yeah, if soon means 'sometime before Jesus returns' I thought annoyedly.* We sat there in silence, dimly illuminated by the glowing lamp.

"That was so odd. I've only ever passed out from the visions *during* the visions. Not while recollecting them. I guess plunging myself back into all of them jumpstarts the physical effects or something. So, what's next?"

"I don't know, exactly. Phelps and Fox will be back in the morning at 9am to debrief their superiors I think, and then they've got to file a report with Washington DC. Whatever directives come after that is up to DC."

"As in FBI Headquarters? Whoa," I breathed, taking it all in.

"Yep," she said in a monotone.

Another awkward silence for a while.

"Why did you say that?"

I turned back to her. "Say what?"

She pointed at me. "That thing you did, that *Roland Bishop I know where I am* thing. You said it three times. Is that something Dr. Eggers taught you?"

I nodded. "Yeah. She said it might help to 'center' me. Keep me grounded. Keep me here. Something. I don't know. I wish I could talk with her right now. This crap has grown exponentially far-reaching and crazy."

"Yeah, well, she's not going anywhere for a while. You can talk with her today. I talked with her last night after you blacked out."

"You did?"

"Yep. Told her you were safe, and that we were talking. Didn't tell her anything else. Classified, and all that." I swear she rolled her eyes at that last comment somewhat, and it made me wonder why she had dated Agent Phelps. "She sounded very relieved."

"How long have you known her?"

"Since '99. She was a good lady. Sorry. *Is* a good lady. Obviously made a very bad choice last week. But how can you blame her? She took back control of her life. They'll go easy on her. They always go easy on the battered wives." She heaved a big sigh as if she didn't approve. "I swear every time one of those comes across my desk, I already know how it's going to go down. Slap on the wrist. Not that I blame them," she said, adjusting herself in her uncomfortable side chair. "Sleeping with the enemy isn't something I envy. But neither is injustice."

"Injustice?"

"*Yeah*, injustice. You can't just kill someone because they're beating on you. There are a million and one things you can do beside that."

"Such as?"

"Gimme a break. Protective services. Witness protection. Restraining orders. Moving. Hell, using a tranquilizer gun instead of a *real* gun. But all of them seem to want to burn the beds of their oppressors. Goes against everything C.G. Jung said."

"Who's C.G....C.G....?"

She snorted, apparently offended that I didn't know. "*Jung*. Probably not your typical reading fare. He said, 'I am not what happened to me. I am what I choose to become.' I think that's pretty darn spot-on, Roland, don't you? All those people who take justice into their own hands and turn it into vengeance, well, they're becoming what happened to them instead of choosing to become something better."

"And you think that's wrong?"

"I'm a Detective, Mr. Bishop. It's my job to reveal the wrong that people do."

"Why are you opening up to me? Aren't I the perp, and you're the perp catcher?"

She raised an eyebrow at me. "Perp? Let's get something straight, Roland. You've been granted temporary immunity by the Attorney General. We'll see if it sticks. For now, they need you. We need you."

Please say 'I need you' next. The thought bounced around in my head, and then I felt guilty because I had also felt an attraction to Renita. And very little for my own wife Jenette anymore.

But she didn't say *I need you.* Instead, she looked away and blew out a plume of smoke, looking off past me with a thousand-yard stare. Until she realized that I was still watching her, however, and her eyes slowly drifted back over to me with the slightest hint of a seductive smile. That was enough to know that there were possibilities.

I giggled and looked away. That was sufficient for now. That, and wondering if something had happened to her that made her choose to become something else, like Jung had said.

"Crap – I need to get home at some point and feed Winston."

"Winston?"

"Our cat. I should have fed him last night."

"I can swing by if you give me your key."

I eyed her curiously. "Are you going to search the place?" I smirked.

"I can if you want me to."

That elicited a giggle from me. "Nah, I'm good. I wouldn't want you to find my secret stash of MMMbop cassettes and Britney Spears collectible magazines. Here you go." I handed her my keys and she was off with a wave of the hand. I thanked her, and laid back down to catch some more shuteye.

Just like clockwork, the agents arrived at 9am. Phelps and Fox strode in together, coffee in hand, wearing almost identical Savile Row suits. Both of them disappeared into another office, presumably to talk with DC, as Roxanne had figured earlier. I watched down the hall briefly to see if they would re-emerge, but they remained. There was nothing for me to do but lay back down and wait.

I awoke again at 8:37, yawned and stretched toward the sky, got up and paced around for a bit. There was a small bump on the back of my head, and it was tender to the touch. Dr. Walker would tell me that I was turning into a pickle with all of these bumps I was accumulating, and then he would owe his wife another quarter for telling me to relay that development to my shrink.

Someone had brought me coffee and placed it on the end table next to my pillow, along with a pack of Little Debbie's honey buns. I devoured them. My stomach had been rumbling from the moment I woke up.

Roxanne was nowhere to be found. I wrapped the light blanket around me and just sat there on the futon in the side room. I guessed it was her who had brought me the pastries and coffee. Staring out the window, I ruminated on how my life could have changed so much in such a short amount of time, shaking my head.

The lightning strike.

The visions.

Jenette.

Dr. Penny.

Mr. Eggers.

Renita & Joe-Joe.

Jake.

Mohammed.

Agent Mulligan.

Fleeing.

The FBI.

And then, crossing my mind briefly was the sheer audacity that I might have had something to do with Mohammed Atta changing his plans. How on earth was that even possible?

But then again, how on earth was a man receiving visions from the future after a lightning strike possible?

I shook my head to clear it off. I wished then that I had my bike and could just ride off into the wind and forget all of this. I wondered if it was still chained up outside Jersey City Jail, and whether or not someone had taken it, or whether I'd ever be coming back to it. I had no idea. I was now in the clutches of the FBI, and I had been imparted information that would not see me simply released back out into the wild to ride my bike freely once more.

Life had changed so much, and some premonition within told me it would continue changing.

My thoughts were drawn beyond myself as I furrowed my eyebrows. This was just my own life, centered around me. But what if Mohammed Atta and his terrorist cell should succeed? Who was he working with? Where was he now? Where would he go? And what about the others? Where were they? And when would they strike?

Without warning, I began to feel cold. I wrapped the blanket more tightly around myself and shut out the chill. As I did so, dimly in the halls of my mind came the number *thirteen*.

"Mister Bishop," said Agent Ryan Phelps. He held out his hand, and I shook it. His breath reeked of cheap convenience store coffee. Fox just looked at me without offering to shake my hand. "Did you get a good night's sleep? Nice to see you on your feet again," he said.

"Yeah, thanks. Nasty bump but I'll live. Do I have you to thank for that futon?"

He smiled. "Least we could do. You gave us some valuable intel last night and we're going to need more. Seems the best thing to do to get you ready would be to at least let you sleep off the initial intake."

I snickered. "Yeah, okay. Have you seen Detective Byers around here anywhere?" I asked, looking around.

Fox cocked a sly eye toward Phelps.

"No, I haven't."

"Well, is there any way someone can hook me up with a phone to call into the Jersey City Jail and talk to Dr. Eggers?"

"Sure, right this way," Phelps said. "Fox, meet you in the conference room in five." Fox nodded and was off. I fell in line behind Phelps on the way to a phone.

"Listen," he said, "don't worry about Byers and I, by the way. Fox likes to stir things up a bit. He can be kind of an ignorant meddling prick, but he's a good agent. He was friends with Mulligan, and Fox doesn't have many friends. So, he's less partial to you now than we are. Don't pay it any heed. Here we go," he said, leading me into his office. "Here's my landline. Jersey City Jail is in the book here. Just call the main line and introduce yourself as being with me and give them authorization code FFA926B. They'll put you on hold and then bring her up. It's not calling hours there yet, but this is sort of an override. Got it?"

I nodded.

"You find your way to the conference room we were in last night when you're done, yeah?"

"Okay, sounds good. Thanks."

"Oh! And here you go," he said, and then handed me a little sealed envelope. "Though you probably want to save your battery, I imagine. You can still use mine," he said, and sauntered off to the conference room.

I opened up the envelope. There was my little red Nokia, seemingly unharmed. What had they extracted from it? I wondered. But then, just as quickly, the thought came to me:

They're the FBI, idiot. Everything.

"Jersey City Jail."

Be professional. Be confident. You got this.

"Uh, hi, I'm calling with Agent Ryan Phelps for Penelope Eggers, authorization code FFA926B please."

"Say what?"

"Inmate Eggers. I'm using authorization code FFA926B." For a moment I felt like I was lowering my voice to sound more adult.

"One moment," came the curt voice.

After being on hold for a seeming eternity, there came a familiar voice on the other end. "Hello?"

"Hi! Penny, it's Roland. How are you?" I asked eagerly. "Are you doing okay?"

"I'm sorry, who is this?" She sounded muffled and withdrawn somehow.

I laughed in spite of her – and myself. "What? It's me, Roland. Are you okay? I might sound muffled because I'm on a differ-"

"I'm sorry, Roland *who*? Can I help you?"

I paused, uncertain. "*'Can you help me?'* What do you mean, 'can you help me?' Penny, it's *me*. Roland Bishop."

Pause, with nothing further from her.

"Hello?"

"I'm sorry, but you must have the wrong number. You've contacted the Jersey City Jail, and I am unfortunately an inmate here."

"Yes, I know. I-I just-" I faltered, losing patience and understanding. "Penny, what happened, are you okay? I know about Dr. Eggers."

She gasped. "What? Who told you? *Who is this and what do you want?!*"

There was an inexplicable certainty to her confusion. *She didn't know me.* And then it hit me – had her future changed as well? Something I said or did? I shook my head. It cannot be! I am *not* that powerful! "Listen to me. I am Roland Bishop, and I'm your client. What's up, Penny?"

"Please call me Penelope, sir. And what's this about 'client?' Client for what? I really should be going now."

"You're my psychiatrist and I'm your cli-"

"No. No! I don't know you, I don't know you! Never call me again, sir, please!" She hung up loudly.

I pulled Phelps' phone away from my ear slowly, staring off into the distance and wondering what had happened, searching with my eyes for answers that I would not find.

Penny didn't even know me. She had no clue who I was. My mouth dropped open and I swallowed hard with my eyes furrowed. Shock took over and I trembled, wondering what had been done – or undone – to make her completely oblivious to who I was.

I would not find an answer today.

"Welcome back. You okay?" asked Phelps.

I slowly trudged into the conference room, my mouth still cavernously agape. Bats could have flown out of there. I had no idea what had just happened. "I just, I-" I faltered. "I-I just got off the phone with Penelope Eggers in your office, Mr. Phelps," I said, turning to him. "She didn't even know who I was. She didn't even…" I trailed off.

"Who?" Phelps asked.

I looked hard at him. "Penny. Dr. Penelope Egg-"

And then it hit me. He had no idea who she was, just as she had no idea who I was. My eyes turned slowly to Fox. His face showed he also was drawing a blank.

What the hell?

"Wh-where's Detective Byers?" I asked. "I need to find her. She needs to know about this!" I looked away from them, down the hall to see if perhaps she was on her way, those big flowing brown ravishing curls waving behind her shoulders.

I almost knew what they would say before they said it. A tremor ran through me.

"Detective who? What's going on? Are you feeling alright? You look a bit peaked."

"Oh my Go-" I started. "No. *No.* What do you mean, *Detective Who*, Phelps? Your ex-girlfriend. Detective Byers from, I dunno where she works. Jersey? Manhattan? What was that that she told me? I can't remember!"

I clutched my head. A white flash tore through me.

"I think she said Manhattan. But where in Manhattan, I have no idea. You're kidding, right? You don't know who I'm talking about?!"

Now I was just shaking. This was all too much. Penny couldn't remember me, and they couldn't remember Byers.

"No, man, we don't," said Fox. Well, at least some things hadn't changed; he was still an ass. "Who is this Dr., what did you say, Dr. *Egghead?*"

"I'm married," Phelps said, turning to Fox, lifting up his hands as if to swear on his own integrity. "I don't have a girlfriend, much less an ex-girlfriend. What are you talking about?"

My knees buckled and I crumpled into the chair opposite them. Phelps stood up to try and steady me. Fox simply sat and gawked at me. "What's going on?"

I stared at them with narrowed eyes. Heat passed through me. I felt like I was starting to sweat. "Why did I just use your phone, Agent Phelps?"

He stared at me blankly for a moment. "You… said… you wanted to call your father back home and tell him you were okay. Did you get ahold of him? Was it something he said? What's going on, Ethan?"

My heart froze. *Ethan.* Ethan? What the- I leaned toward the table and propped my elbows on it, cupping my mouth in my hands. I stared wide-eyed at them. Suddenly, in an impulse, I reached into my pants pocket and pulled out my phone.

My blue phone. It said 'Motorola V60' on the front of it, and I nearly dropped it in fright, yelling and backing away. It was a flip phone, totally different than my Nokia! *Where was my little red Nokia??*

I looked slowly back up at them in dismay.

"Tell me everything about last night. Tell me *everything* I told you. Please. *Tell me everything! Tell me now, please!*" I yelled at the top of my lungs, frantic. The tears were coming. I felt like I was having a breakdown. What was going on!?

Fox put up his hands. "Whoa, whoa, settle down Mr. Stiles. We'll get this worked out."

I froze in horror again. "Mr. *Stiles??* What do you me-"

I stopped mid-sentence and stood up quickly. Fox mirrored me and reached for his gun. "Hold it!" he said, but Phelps restrained him. "Rob, wait!" he said.

I dug my wallet out of my slacks – *slacks! I was suddenly wearing slacks and not jeans, what the hell?!* – and ripped open the Velcro on it.

There, in plain sight for all of us to see, was my license, clearly displaying the name *Ethan Parker Stiles.* My DOL picture was right next to it.

But it wasn't me.

"Take a picture of me," I said.

"What?"

"Take a picture of me and let me see it!" I yelled. Fox reluctantly did so, and held his phone up to me.

That was not me in that image. I was older, with graying hair, about late fifties with a five o'clock shadow, thick eyebrows and a solid jawline. "What the hell?" I felt around my face, up and down. The man who stared back at me looked familiar somehow. I just couldn't place him.

"Mr. Stiles, what's going on?" Agent Fox asked me in a flustered tone.

"Ethan!" cried Agent Phelps.

I crumpled to the floor in a heap.

Once more, I was unconscious, in agony and fear.

3 Days To Go

September 8th, 2001 • Manhattan, NY

Something shook me to my left.

I awoke out of a mesmerized trance, standing there in Central Park.

"Hey, Roland," said Detective Byers. "You okay? You got this, or do I need to call another clairvoyant?"

I stared at her. "B-byers," I breathed in amazement. "Roxanne…you're-" I stopped, mouth agape.

"What the hell, Roland? We're gonna lose him, are you with me or what? Get in gear, knucklehead!" She pulled out her gun.

Get him? Get *who*? And how was I Roland Bishop all over again, and not Ethan Stiles? What the *hell* had happened yesterday? Was she talking about Mohammed Atta? Were we tailing him together?

"I need you to tell me when you sense him. This is where we got the APB."

It *was* Atta. I sighed, shaking off what must have been the most barbaric state of delirium I had ever encountered, and gathered my wits, snapping to attention. "I'm- yeah, ok, I'm-I'm ready. Let's do this," I said. "Do I get a gun?"

"Not a chance, man. Get up there and see what you can feel out," she said, smiling at me with an adventurous look. "Be careful, hotshot," she said seductively once more.

I cleared my vision and nodded. I pulled my eyes away from her beautiful flowing hair – it suddenly struck me how much she looked like Andie MacDowell in *Groundhog Day* – and tried to expel the heavy air that had settled into my lungs, steeling myself for action. *I am not what happened to me. I am what I choose to become.* And then I changed it. *I'm Roland Bishop, and I know who I am. I'm Roland Bishop, and I know who I am. I'm Roland Bishop, and I know who I am.* That ought to keep whomever this 'Ethan Stiles' was at bay for a while.

And with that, I was heading deep into Central Park, trying to find a terrorist. I cast a glance back to see her, and the officers with her, leave the Bethesda Fountain area heading for Wagner Cove. Suddenly my head was filled with memories of a conversation that I don't remember having. Standing there at the Fountain, their plan, she had said, was to go around north and then hem them in south. I was to proceed south toward the Naumburg Bandshell and then head west through Skater's Circle and Le Pain Quotidien, straddling the Sheep Meadow to its north as I moved toward Warner LeRoy Place. That's where someone reported a potential sighting of Mohammed Atta.

I had been to Central Park a few times with Jenette – I hoped to God that was still her name – and just remembered the trees. There were so many trees.

Suddenly, I remembered my cellphone. With widened eyes I reached down into my pants and pulled out a familiar object. My little red Nokia. I accessed the contacts and quickly found Dr. Penny. Jenette. Amanda. Thank goodness. Things were back to normal.

Concentrate, Roland, I told myself, stuffing my phone back into my pocket. I needed to relax and focus. I needed to see what I could see and feel around me, searching for signals for the terrorist that they were looking for.

I tried to calm myself.

Breathe, Roland. Breathe. You got this. He's somewhere around here. You can find him. In and out, big guy. Nice and slow.

I paced, steadily, walking westward. I tried to breathe as slowly as I could, channeling my focus and my vision into one steady stream of consciousness.

But the flashes didn't come. No flashes. No nose bleeds. No sudden pangs of anxiety. No heat waves. I was confused, and a deep-seated desire to talk to Penny was welling up inside me. *Well, the last thing I would suggest in good conscience would be to tail anyone you suspect as a malefactor. You could be placing yourself in considerable danger.* She had said that to me nineteen days ag-

Wait. *Nineteen days?* I looked again at my Nokia.

Sure enough, the date read 9.8.01 and 3:16pm on the screen. But how was that possible? Yesterday was August 29th! How was today September 8th?

I was losing my mind. I suddenly felt nauseous. I had to talk to Penny. I tried to focus, to breathe, to do whatever I could to keep my radar up and see what signals I could receive that might possibly lead to where Atta was.

And then the memories came flooding back. Memories from the past ten days – from *this* timeline, the *real* timeline – flooded back. Memories that had happened, but in my mind had not. Not as Ethan Stiles, or any other name, but as Roland Bishop, my real name.

Jenette calling me on the 3rd to tell me she had filed for separation and was now back in Seattle.

Being very near one or both of the terrorists on Labor Day, September 4th, and passing out yet again after a series of visions seeing four planes hijacked again. That number kept growing, seemingly. And bodies…bodies falling.

Roxanne getting shot on the 4th but recovering.

Phelps – seeing him gunned down on the 4th by an unknown assailant, and a car veering off, leaving me there with blood splatter on my clothes. Seeing Fox killed.

Running into Mohammed Atta again on the 5th. And then tailing Ziad Jarrah on the 7th as well, one of the other terrorists Phelps had originally mentioned.

Me on the run again on the 5th. I felt funny while I was running…my legs felt different. My chest felt different.

Awash in these 'memories,' I began to see the number three. *Three.* Why three? Walking through Central Park, trying to visually scout around for Mohammed Atta, why was I now seeing the number three?

I didn't understand. I just didn't understand any of it.

And then, suddenly, as I drew near to Tavern on the Green, I heard a ringing in my ears. My heart fluttered. My eyes blinked in a series of spasms. A cold wave passed through me, followed by heat.

And then the flashes.

They were here. Somewhere.

The nosebleed started.

My phone rang. Byers. "Bishop, what's your 20?"

"Huh?" I asked her.

"Your location! Where are you, Roland?"

"I'm getting close to the Tavern on the Green. And close to them, I think, Roxanne. Detective Byers, I mean…I think one or more of them are- *ow!*" I clutched my temple. Flashes of white. Back-to-back and searing. I could see the planes lifting off, all four of them in tandem. There were four now! They were flying and launching together, all of them eventually diverging outward toward different destinations.

Suddenly, in stark clarity, I got an image of a strange building with five sides. But it was smoking, charred, and burning in one quadrant. Something had rammed into it like a missile with a vengeance from hell. A triangular gash had been torn through it, and all of the support structures in that area had collapsed.

The Pentagon.

I could see it clearly now, as from above. But then, as my eyes were narrowing on it and the unabating white flashes took hold once more, everything was obstructed from view in a dense cloud of yellowish-white ash and dust. A billowing, blustery cloud enveloped all, shrouding the Pentagon from view.

"The Pen-Pentagon," I stuttered, stumbling. "That's one of their targets," I breathed.

"Stay there, we're coming!"

I looked around wildly to see if she was in fact coming, and if so, from where. Sweat pooled in the small of my back. The lower ends of my hair above my neck were sopped with sweat. It was only sixty degrees outside, but I began to drip. I didn't have a handkerchief, and now my nose flowed freely. I kept my phone pressed to my ear.

And then I saw him. There he was! Clear as day, Mohammed Atta was walking briskly, looking back over his shoulder toward the north. He had two other men with him. They were all neatly groomed.

"Attaaaa!!" I cried at the top of my lungs, and everyone around me must have heard it. Atta stopped and stared at me, rooted to the ground.

And the world whirred around me. I felt dizzy and spasmed. As if by some supernatural force that spun the earth like a top, my vision swam. Everything flew out of view and was replaced, dizzily, by something else. The entire scene was exchanged in a crazy patchwork. The latter took the place of the former, the new substituting the old in a dizzying trade, as a wild, howling wind rushed around me.

I toppled to the ground, my nose bleed unabating, and my head throbbing with pain. There was thunder in the wind, and there was lightning in the thunder. A rising tide of swollen undulating tone permeated everything around me. Rocks cracked around me in the vibratory pulsations.

My hand gripped my phone to the point of crushing; I couldn't bring myself to let go, and my mind would not will my hand to do it anyway.

White flashes.

Lightning strikes, all over again, zipping through my flesh, carving out domain in my blood vessels, seizing my peace and shredding it into ribbons, replacing it with agonized cries of sheer pain. I felt suspended and whisked about, nearly ready to vomit.

In ten seconds, it was all over, and I was dropped to the ground, breathing hard, covered in sweat and vomit and blood. People moved away in disgust, murmuring "did you see that guy?"

I took off my outer shirt and wiped away my sweat, my vomit, my nose, and gathered my senses. I looked up.

Atta was gone, along with his accomplices. The temperature felt more like a balmy seventy-two. Rain clouds were on the horizon.

I glanced slowly down at my hand, knowing full well what I found there would not be what I wanted or needed. In my hand I held a blue Motorola V60 flip phone.

I grimaced, burying my face in my hands, breaking down and crying right there in the park. Detective Byers was nowhere to be found in Central Park. She was nowhere to be found in my life, or anyone's life for that matter, and I was nowhere to be found in anyone else's.

I wept out of pure insanity, not knowing where I was nor who I was.

I'm Roland Bishop, and I know...

I'm Roland Bishop...

I'm...

I couldn't even complete it, and I crumpled to the ground, my body prostrate, my face in my hands.

Sadness took me, and I left.

Part Two

9 Days To Go

September 2nd, 2001 • Manhattan, NY

I didn't know what to think anymore. I was starting to lose everything that was me.

When the lightning tornado subsided, I didn't know where I was at first. The images around me blurred and colors were muted. There was a familiarity about the air and the noises, and that's all that I had just experienced: *noise*. The peace of this new environment was beyond compare, and as the images unblurred and coalesced into clarity, I realized I was sitting on the edge of my bed, back in my own apartment.

However, my disorientation still deepened.

Maybe it was all just a bad dream. One horrendously realistic and politically-charged bad dream, loaded with clandestine spy thrills and frenetic tension. I took a long breath to push out the past, and shook my head.

Just then my phone rang, and I looked down. As I did so, I glanced at the clock. 9:09am.

Jenette. I gasped. I lifted up my cellphone, and it was my little Nokia again. I shook my head and gritted my teeth, fighting between surprised joy at Jenette's call, and the unexplainable phenomenon of having memories I sadly didn't remember.

"Jenette?" I asked.

"Yeah, babe, hi…hey, Amanda was wondering if she could come over tonight for dinner so you could finally meet her. I could make her my world-famous white bean turkey chili. What do you think?"

Tears streamed from my eyes, and I didn't know why. Was it that we were still married, and apparently happily so? Or was it that I seemed to be in a moment of peace here from all the hysteria? Maybe a combination of both? I just had no clue who even knew me anymore, let alone whom I knew. Somewhere out there was a Dr. Penelope Eggers, and I needed to know if she still knew me.

"Uh, sure, hon, that sounds great," I said, muscling up a smile, and the tears continued to flow. I was so confused, and tears were the only clarity.

I wiped my eyes, and as I did so they were drawn to the counter to see if Winston had eaten his food. A can of nine lives was sitting there unopened. "Oh, come here, buddy," I said. "I forgot to feed Winston," I told Jenette.

"Aww! He'll live. He'll be fine. Okay, so, can we plan for 6? I figure we can chat for a bit after that. She just needs to be home by nine."

"Yeah, hon, that sounds just fine," I said. Something tingled my skin. I called out for Winston and clicked my tongue to summon him. A tiny gray lump burst up on the counter. He had already smelled it as I cracked open the can, and heard the *pshickt* of the can opening. "Can I pick up anything from the store for you?"

"Uh, sure, if you want, Jellybean. I think I'm out of Tropicana."

Jellybean?? My face scrunched up for a moment. She had never called me that, to my knowledge. "Huh? Since when do you call me Jellybean?" I laughed.

"What are you talking about? That's your nickname," she said cutely, and giggled. My skin tingled again for some reason. Was it cold in here? "And can you pick up some more chamomile tea please? I think I'm out."

Whatever. "Sure, hon. No problem." I was just glad to be doing normal things again with no psychiatrist, no lightning, and no FBI. "I-I love you," I stammered, and it came out weirdly.

"I love you too, Jellybean. Be home soon. Oh! Are you swinging by the library?"

Just like Jenette. My lip curled up at the end. She always remembered things right before she hung up.

"I can."

"I forgot to return the books that I got from the library for Joe-Joe, you remember him? The little boy next door?"

"Uh, *yeah*, I remember him." She had no clue, of course, about what happened a few nights ago.

"They're on my nightstand. It's the Nine Lives Series. About cats. I thought Amy could read it to Joe-Joe."

Something in me flinched, and I stopped scooping out the cat food into Winston's bowl. I looked at him, and he stared up, perplexed, licking his lips.

"Who is Amy?"

"*Amy,* silly! Amy and Terrell next door? Joe-Joe's parents! Are you okay??" she asked, confused.

I was not okay. I was not okay at all.

"Hon, are you there?" she asked.

My skin started to tingle, and I could feel my blood pressure rising. The phone fell out of my hands and clattered to the floor. Winston hissed at me and retreated under the bed in our room. I could hear him from far away growling at me as I steadied myself against the countertop.

Amy and Terrell? What the hell happened to Renita and Jake?

I heard Jenette's muffled voice coming from the floor out of the tiny earpiece on my phone. "Hon? Hon! Are you okay?"

I felt like I was going to vomit. My stomach started to churn violently. My vision swam as if I had been on a boat for hours. And then the flashes began.

A string of flashes, one after the next. And always, every single one of them, tinged with a number.

Nine.

September, the ninth month.

9:09am.

Nine Lives.

Jellybean had nine letters.

So did chamomile.

So did Tropicana.

Nine.

Someone was trying to tell me something. *Someone* out there was trying to send me a sign.

Fox's face came into my mind. As from a photographic memory, his words rang back through my mind with crystal clarity. *I'd like to come back to this numbering thing you mentioned, Roland. Maybe there's no rhyme or reason to it. Maybe it's not part of any kind of pattern. But we should be looking at that too.*

And then – just then – I started to awaken to the truth. Slowly, as a fog enveloping the land, it rolled over me, revealing truth after truth about my situation. My jaw dropped and my skin tingled, nervously. Suddenly, *I knew.*

In desperation, I snatched up my phone from the floor and hung up on my wife. "Call ya back," was all that I said. Winston hissed again.

I grabbed my coat and called the Jersey City Jail. I was rolling inside, but I tried to gain my composure and steady myself. I was getting more nauseous by the moment. Sweat dripped off me. I lost my balance as my legs buckled underneath me.

As I fell backward, my right hand shot out to grab onto something. From my palm emitted a blazing blue light, and a bolt of lightning arced from my hand to the lamp on our end table. The bulb burst and shattered, sending shards everywhere.

"Jersey City Jail," came the greeting.

Come on, you can do this. I breathed in carefully. "Hi, this is Agent Ryan Phelps. I need to speak with inmate Penelope Eggers. Authorization code FFA926B."

"One moment."

It was more than one moment. Flash after flash hit me. Wave after wave of nausea.

I couldn't hold back. Vomit spewed out of me all over the countertop, and I was about to pass out. *No....NO...* I willed myself to stay awake, and alert. I couldn't let any more time pass.

Whatever loop I was stuck in was consuming me, but I knew the truth and it couldn't stay here. *Must... stay... conscious...*

All of them. Nine.

"Hello? Sir, are you there?"

"Penny! Is this Penny?"

"Well yes, of course it is...? Is this...Roland? I thought it was Agent Phelps again."

"You remember me!"

"Well of course I remember you, you nitwit! When are you visiting me again? Have you heard from Detective Byers? I certainly hope you are keeping your sunny disposition!" She chortled.

"Oh Penny, you're too much. I'm coming to you. Stay right there."

"Yes. I'm in jail. I shall remain right here. Brilliant idea, Roland."

I rolled my eyes and tore out of there. *Hiss at me all you want, Winston. This has got to stop.*

"Oh, man, Penny. You have no idea how good it is to see you, and for you to kno-" I started to say, but she would have no idea what I was even saying. I'd have to tell her about my new bike even. I had a blue BMC before. Now, suddenly, I had a green Schwinn.

I didn't even notice it until I hopped on it. It was as if some little elves had unlocked it from in front of the jail, switched it, and brought it back here to me, transformed entirely. Now I had this one instead. Just like how my phone kept changing.

I swear I was losing my mind.

"I'm losing my mind, Penny. Seriously."

"Whatever do you mean?" She tilted her head and looked at me quizzically. Her eyes squinted. "Has something happened?"

My eyes went wide and I gasped in laughter. "Has something happened? Ha!" I couldn't repress the sick humor of it all. "*Has something happened!?* Well, yes *and* no! A lot *and* nothing, Penny! I don't even know what to think anymore! It's like nothing *and* a double serving all at once, backward and forward, side to side, and I don't even get to drive."

My laughter faded as she just watched me, unsure what to think, and waiting for the slow unraveling of my thoughts. My eyes gradually fell down to her left arm. There, as a testament to a sure past that I could at least rely on for the next five minutes, was an iron-shaped burn. I sighed and shook my head.

"You're not going to believe any of it."

"Try me," she said instantly. "There are three things in life that you should never discredit, Roland. They are one, a woman, two, the elderly, and three, the British. I'm an elderly British woman. So try me if you dare."

I took a deep breath and just watched her. Her mouth was pressed into a pulled-back smile, clenched and ready for whatever truths I was prepared to unfold upon her.

"Okay. But don't say I didn't warn you."

I don't know what that authorization code thingy did, but it granted Penny a visit far outlasting any of the other inmates in her block. It wasn't just to reach her at any time; it was to give her – and me – all the time we needed. I didn't understand the power of it, but I was thankful for it.

We spent hours talking about the most infinite details of what had happened since she and I had last seen each other on the 28th, which was five days ago, and yet it was also eleven days ago.

I began to lose count of the many *fascinating!* and *how intriguing!* and *spellbinding!* and *riveting!* and every other adverb she could conjure up as she listened, hanging on my every word, captivated and enthralled. I was positive that there was no psychology or psychiatry course that covered any of it. She was in uncharted waters just the same as me.

Her incredulity was matched only by her good humor for the sheer inanity of it all.

"Wild, huh?" I asked her.

"To put it mildly," she grunted. "But it is not outside the realm of possibility, Roland. I said before that this was a gift. I mean it! But just look at all the gifts that came with it."

"Oh, Penny, I'm still not convinced this is a gift. This has been a whirlwind of upheaval. First I'm married to Jenette, then I'm not, first I saved my neighbor, then I didn't. Do you have any idea how many different phones I've had this week alone?"

She cocked her head.

"Every time something changes, I get a new phone, or a new bike…or a new wife….or a new name! Or…it's something else! *Something* changes. I get a number that changes every single day. It's so odd. It's like every time we get closer to Mohammed Atta, something in the future – or the past – changes, and has to adapt. Whoever is running all these timelines has got to have their head spinning by now."

"Hmm," was all she could say. "That *is* fascinating, truly. You should indeed get that to the agents straightaway. If you're correct, we still have some time. But not much. The clock is ticking, Roland."

"Have you ever heard of C.G. Jung?"

She shook her head, squinting her eyes at me, her fingers to her lips.

"He said, 'I am not what happened to me. I am what I choose to become.' Detective Byers shared that with me in one of the timelines, though now I don't remember which one anymore. It could be any one of them. Or all of them. Or, tomorrow, it could be none of them. I seriously have no idea." I took a long, cleansing sigh. "I'm losing it, Penny."

I cast a quick look up at the clock. I nodded her to it. She sported a confused look and turned around to see what I was seeing.

5:27pm.

"I think you missed chow time."

She turned back around, smiling. "Roland Bishop, if you think this right here isn't food for my soul, you've another think coming. And if you think jail food is actual food, you've yet another lined up beyond that one. I think all of this is marvelous. A ripping good time hearing how you've been faring out there. Quite apart from the nosebleeds, that is."

"A *ripping* good time, did you say? Ha! That sounds appropriate. It sounds as though there's been a rip in the space time continuum or something like that."

"A very astute observation." She looked at me hard and just held my gaze for a moment. It was almost as if she was trying to hypnotize me. My mind recalled being back there in her front room while she stared at me curiously over the rim of her mug. Life was simpler then.

"Here's what I would suggest, Roland. Keep something with you at all times: something you know to be constant. Something that will never change."

I tilted my head at her.

"By all appearances, you seem to be running on parallel tracks of time all streaming into the future full steam ahead. It doesn't appear that you'll know which one you will be on at any given point in time, and your choices seem to be altering your trajectory *and* the trajectory of others. If what you currently possess is changing frequently, day by day, this might be a grounding element. It might stop the erratic jumps and keep you on a straightforward track. It also…"

She stopped, and I crinkled my brow at her. "What? Also what, Penny?" She appeared sad.

"Well, I daren't jump too far ahead or project us into any far-fetched doomsday scenarios, but, well, I'm a psychiatrist, Roland. I've seen patients enter a state of psychosis. It's not pleasant. They lose the best part of themselves in the process. I don't want anything like that to happen to you. You are my friend, Roland." She smiled at me, motherly and kind.

"You always told me to say that thing to myself. *I'm Roland Bishop, and I know where I am.* I actually twisted it the other day. I said I know *who* I am. I needed to. I wasn't sure if I was Roland Bishop or Ethan Stiles. It was eerie."

"Hmm. That may be all it takes. But I encourage you to find something tangible. Something that is uniquely and irrefutably *you*. Carry it with you at all times. It would be a disagreeable tragedy to lose you, Mr. Bishop," she said, leaning forward on her elbows and staring at me endearingly.

I smiled back.

"Is that my psychiatrist talking, or my British friend?"

Her smile grew wider.

"Well, I was an Amazonian enchantress wielding a staff of light in another life. You may address me as Lady Divinitus," she said with a giggle. "So I'm part friend, part psychiatrist, part superhero myself."

"Wow," I said, and I couldn't hold back the chuckle.

She laughed a gentle laugh and stowed her laughter. "In all sincerity, you have full right to call me 'Penny' until the end of days. Yours or mine." And then she put her hand up against the glass pane between us, fingers outstretched.

A warmth spread through my chest, radiating from her heart into mine. This was a special lady who had conquered her own pain and used it to turn the tide against the cause. I was so proud to know her.

I slowly reached out my hand to touch hers through the pane. Simple glass couldn't separate us.

She pulled her hand away and started right back in. "Now. Tell me about the numbers. How they keep changing. I'm especially interested in that. They're not going to let me talk much longer, and I'm starting to feel a bit peckish."

"Oh, Penny, it's insane. The numbers I've been seeing! Today, I got *nine*. It's September 2nd. On August 27th I got *fifteen*. When I jumped forward to September 8th, I got *three*."

She stared at me blankly.

"Penny, don't you see? It's a *countdown!* I have to get this to the Detective and the FBI guys. It's a countdown, Penny. With each new day I get a new number, and depending on which day I'm on, that tells me when the hijacking is supposed to happen. I'm almost sure of it.

"It's *September 11th*, Penny. That's when they're going to do it. It all makes sense. The more days away from September 11th I am, the higher the number. The closer I am to September 11th, the lower the number. I put it all together in my head today when the number *nine* kept appearing out of thin air during a call with Jenette."

Penny still didn't say anything. She had stopped moving. *What?* "Penny?"

And then...flashes. White hot flashes. Electricity shooting through the transparent surface, connecting us and bridging the gap with pulverizing light and energy.

I couldn't pull away.

On the other side of the glass, it seemed Penny was retreating, being slowly pulled back by a tether, dwindling into the distance, all the while frozen in time, frozen in a maternal expression of interest in my story.

A vortex opened up behind her, glistening with rotating light and color, flashes of iridescent and spatial light emanating from it, shooting out like galaxial emissaries, seeking me with some connecting message of love from her.

Yet, somehow, Penny was continuously being pulled magnetically backward, and I couldn't move toward her. I was stuck in a fixed position, immovable, paralyzed. The glass acted as an eternal barrier: translucent and impermeable.

I watched as Penny's arms stretched endlessly, stuck to the table while the rest of her withdrew into the recesses of time and space.

Keep your sunny disposition, I heard a faint voice urge me. Was that just me? Or had she whispered that to me from the other side of time?

And then she was gone. Her mind, body and spirit: gone. My counselor was taken from me.

I didn't know what to think! I had just lost Penny, and thus, a little piece of me.

1 Day To Go

September 10th, 2001 • Jersey City, NJ

I woke up today feeling frightened and tense.

Uncertain of the future, and unsure of who I really was in all of it. Would there even *be* a future?

What had I just witnessed? Penny had literally evaporated, *dissipated* into thin air right before my eyes on the other side of that glass. It was calmly brutal and brutally calm, the taking of my counselor. I had no idea what to think.

I rolled over to check my clock on the end table. My eyes felt glossed over and clouded. I blinked hard to clear out the night's gunk and the confusion, and tilted my head up at it.

September 10th, 2001. 1:01am.

That couldn't be right! No! I bolted up in a pang of fear, awash with tension. How could it be only one day to go?

Tomorrow was when the frightening and intense attacks would hap-

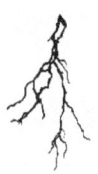

1 Day To Go

September 10th, 2001 • Jersey City, NJ

My eyes opened and I gasped in frustration.

Everything seemed to freeze for a moment. In the dim morning light streaming through the window, dust particles hung in the air, unmoving and ambivalent to my dream.

I was in a cold sweat, and my muscles were tensed as I panted heavily.

What a horrible dream! I had this knowledge in me that was more of a curse than a blessing, equipping me with neither realization nor awareness. No. Instead, it kept saddling me with caution and anxiety.

I let out my breath slowly. I still had time. It was okay; it was just a nightmare. Pain stabbed through my head fleetingly, and I closed my eyes, swallowing hard and attempting to regulate my breathing.

That's when I saw the number *one* dimly appear in my subconscious, and my eyes slowly opened once more, ringed with alarm.

I whipped over to the clock and saw the readout clearly:

September 10th, 2001. 1:01am again.

No! It wasn't a dream! Not again!

My eyes closed and I gasped, still here, trapped in this damned frustr-

8 Days To Go

September 3rd, 2001 • Jersey City, NJ

I woke up, hung my head and cried.
It was just like the old song:

The other night, dear, while I lay sleeping
I dreamed I held you in my arms
But when I woke up, I was mistaken
And I hung my head and cried...

Penny was gone. Dr. Penelope Eggers, my friend, counselor, murderess, witty sage, bastion of encouragement and direction, taken from me without warning. But what caused it? I hadn't seen any warning signs, no premonitions or visions, nothing to hint that she was departing.

Nothing.

The only constant friend I had, the only thing that seemed to remain, was Winston. He was rubbing up against my leg, and his tail was slicing the air against me, twitching. He looked up at me and meowed. I managed a meager smile, reaching down and scratching the scruff of his neck. The soft purr was audible in the deafening silence of the empty apartment.

None of it made any sense, the least of which was this. In the middle of it, the number *eight* appeared dim yet resounding in my mind. Had Penny moved to the other side? Was she now at some 'Clock of Life,' pushing on the hands with steadiness, using all her might to preserve forward momentum?

I didn't know. I just didn't know anything anymore, and here I was all over again at the starting line.

When I came to, it was 3:08pm. The very first thing I did was call Jersey City Jail and ask if they had an inmate named Penelope Eggers there.

"What was that name again?" asked the jail operator. I repeated it for her.

No such inmate here by that name.

Penny truly was gone. Either that, or she was trapped in whatever vortex everything else had been swirling around in, perhaps under some other name, and maybe her own knowledge was compromised as the others' had been. Another timeline owned her…at least for now.

A phone call for me this time. The ringtone sounded different. I looked at it. I wasn't sure I was ready for whomever it was, but as I lifted my phone to my face to see the display, it was a Motorola V60 flip phone. The same phone I suddenly had when the agents called me *Ethan Stiles*. Where was my little Nokia again?

It was an unlisted number. My mind scrambled for a moment, trying to think back to that whole *Jellybean* business yesterday with Jenette. I wondered what nonsense today would bring.

"Hello?" she asked. It was Jenette's voice.

"Yeah. Oh! Hey, hon."

"Please don't call me that."

My eyes squinted. "What?" I asked tiredly.

"I just called to let you know that I filed. The paperwork has been submitted like you requested. I tried to send you a text but it-"

"Like I requested? What paperwork?"

"Seriously? Are you drunk? Please don't make me spell it out for you."

"Hon, I don-"

"*Don't* call me that! I'm back in Seattle. Don't try to find me. I'm not coming back. I filed the paperwork. You should hear from my lawyer within the week."

"Seattle. Seattle? What?" I asked briskly, getting irritated. "What? You tell me that *I* requested that you file, you ask to have Amanda over for your white bean turkey chili, you call me *Jellybean* and ask me to get your Tropicana? What is all this? None of this makes sense!"

She paused: enough time for my blood pressure to rise dramatically. "What? What are you talking about?"

"Oh yeah. *Yeah. I'm* the insane one. Whatever happened to *Jellybean* and your friggin' *chamomile?!*" I screamed into the phone at her, turning and hurling it against the wall. It shattered into a few different pieces. Winston scampered away once more in fright, making for the bedroom.

I threw myself down onto the couch.

A soft knock at the door. I sighed, shook my head, cursed, and got up. With any luck it would be the Mormons. Good. I needed someone to beat up.

"Who is it?"

"Uh, hi, it's Renita and Jacob, your next door neighbors?"

My eyes widened, and I opened the door.

The woman standing outside was not Renita. The baby in her arms was not Joe-Joe. The man standing beside her was not Jake. My heart sank. How much longer would this go on?

"Hi, we're your neighbors. I'm Renita and this is Jake. And this little guy is Joe-Joe. Say hi, Joe-Joe," she teased, and the little baby leaned against her shyly, his pacifier bobbing in his mouth. "We were, uh, just getting ready to head out for dinner and we heard – whatever that was. Are you okay? Is everything alright?"

I gasped and snorted. I looked down at the floor for a moment. How in the hell could either one of them have known that people with their same names had been so prominent in my life only a week earlier, ending in his tragedy? They didn't look like Renita, Jake or Joe-Joe, but they had their names. I was truly going insane, I was convinced of that now.

"Um, I-I'm," I tried. "I'm fine. Really. Thanks. I just… bad conversation with the wife. *Ex*-wife, I guess."

"Oh, no, I'm so sorry." She sucked her teeth in. "If there's anything we can do to help?" she asked tentatively.

"Yeah, we're just right here," Jake said, pointing to their apartment.

Yeah, I know, man, okay? I just killed you a few nights ago, I thought.

"Yeah, I appreciate it. Okay. Thanks. Everything is fine. Just…blowing off some steam I guess."

They both looked at me as if yearning for an alternate explanation. "Okay, well, just let us know," said Jake, extending his hand toward me. "Take care, man. It's, uh, *Ethan,* right? I saw your name on the mailbox."

I had begun to extend my hand out toward him but then it jerked back seemingly of its own accord.

No wonder Jenette didn't call me Roland, I thought. *She had been married to Ethan.* No wonder her number didn't show up. Somewhere in the grand scheme of parallel timelines, someone was messing with Roland and Ethan's tracks and couldn't keep things straight. Some sadistic, celestial killjoy was tampering with my life, and it was a sick game of chaos theory or the butterfly effect. Sooner or later, I was going to wind up being either Ethan Bishop or Roland Stiles, and either would be in a straitjacket. I didn't care which anymore. I was just starting to get pissed off.

"Alright, fine. Thanks," I said, closing my door abruptly on them.

I was going to get answers. I was sick and tired of being messed with. In a fit of rage I swept the planter off of our little dining table a few paces from the front door, shattering it and spilling dirt everywhere. I cursed again, and pulled on my own hair, nearly yanking it out. I passed the kitchen and happened to look over.

There, on the ground, was my little phone, in pieces. I shook my head. Now I couldn't even call anyone. I couldn't call Jenette back, not that I would. I couldn't call Detective Byers, not that she would even believe me.

And I couldn't call Penny because she didn't exist.

My sunny disposition was becoming a rainy, contemplative thousand-yard stare, devoid of connection.

"Screw it," I said, disconnected and ambivalent.

I hung my head and sighed, and just went to sleep.

7 Days To Go

September 4th, 2001 • Jersey City, NJ

The future and the past were blending together in a seamless blur, hazy and confusing.

I awoke to a new day. The number *seven* almost jumped out at me from the walls. Spooked Winston. He fled to his usual haven of seclusion: the far recesses below our bed, closest to the corner of the room.

I shot out of bed feeling a resolve I couldn't explain, except for the fact that I was just tired of the inconsistency bullshit. I had to get back on my own track and find my way back to me. To life. To purpose.

To Detective Byers. I needed to call her.

Before I even got dressed, I went out to see if it were even possible to make a call on my pho-

There it was, sitting on the counter. *On the counter.* Last night it was in fragments on the floor. Yet there it was, my old Nokia 3310, lying there, fully intact, as if it had never once been thrown and never once been a Motorola V60. I picked it up and just stared at it, finally grunting and setting it back down. Why was I not even surprised anymore?

There were no guarantees in waking. Not anymore.

I wondered if Jenette had still filed. I wondered if Renita and Jake looked like their old selves…or if Jake looked like death embalmed. I wondered if Penny was still there.

Winston! That was the constant that I needed. That was one of the last things that Penny urged me to do before I lost her. *Carry it with you at all times.* So that's what I did. I took Winston's collar off him and looked at the ID tag that I had made so many years ago before we moved here. It read, clearly, *Roland Bishop*, and my phone number. But beyond that, there was a strange logo, an R and a B together, in a stylish fusion: something I had worked on in my spare time. That was *definitely* me. I loosened it a bit more, and then fastened it around my wrist.

God bless you, Penny. I won't lose this.

I moved with purpose and tightened that cat collar around my wrist until it hurt. It would be a sensory reminder that I could not ignore, and would be with me at all times.

I grabbed my stupid transforming cellphone.

I picked up Winston, scratching his chin and kissing him hard until he protested.

I threw on some clothes and a Yankees baseball cap, slamming the door on my way out. It was time to see Detective Roxanne Byers, if that was even her name.

Thankfully, she was in my contacts. "Detective Byers, it's Roland Bishop. Are you at your office?"

I had just gotten out of the Holland Tunnel and was riding slowly up West Street along the waterfront. It was a beautiful, sunny day, though the wind was brisk and gusty flowing down the Hudson with the water. There loomed up the two towers, gleaming proudly.

"No, I'm not, Roland. Hey, where did you go last night? You just disappeared." She sounded like she was in the middle of something urgent and was speaking quickly.

"Disappeared?"

"Yeah, *disappeared*. You were here in the office and then it was like you just got up and left. But no one had seen you exit the building."

"I wasn't at your office yesterday. I didn't see you at all, Roxanne."

Pause. "What? Is this some kind of a joke?"

"I'll explain later. Where are you?"

"Central Park. Got a tip that Atta is there. And Ryan says there are *four* planes now. There used to be just one, if you recall. Somehow their flight plans changed again."

A chill ran down my spine. Had that timeline been changed? I had seen him there on the 8th. That's when the whirlwind hit me. But that date hadn't come yet! It was still only the 4th! Whatever I was doing kept changing the timeline and the events leading up to it. But this one remained consistent. Why?

"Wait – Byers!"

"Hold *on*, Roland!" I could hear her talking to a fellow cop over her walkie-talkie in the background. She concluded with a "10-4" and then she was back on. "Gotta go, Roland. Stakeout. Talk soon."

"No wait, Byers, don't!"

Suddenly, the images of Detective Byers getting shot, of Phelps getting gunned down, of Atta and his colleagues in the park careened wildly through my mind.

The nosebleed started instantly. It was on replay this time, but it was still the same vision. I wasted no time.

I got on my BMC and increased my speed. I suddenly registered that the bike wasn't my Schwinn bike anymore. I shook my head and just dismissed it. I had to save Byers! I pedaled faster. It would take me at *least* twenty minutes to get to Central Park. I had to save her.

The wind sliced through my hair as I raced up Empire State Trail.

I broke off at West 52nd Street and careened through traffic. A car just missed me at 52nd and 11th, and smashed into another in the waiting intersection. A cop on horseback saw all of it and began to pursue. "Shit!" I exclaimed, whipping out my phone and frantically trying to steer my bike while calling Byers again. It rang and then went to voicemail. "Dammit!"

I pedaled harder. The sweat was building in my hair and on my neck. I could feel my shirt getting damp, but the wind mitigated it.

Only a few more blocks to 8th, and then I could head north again! A helicopter rushed by overhead, and I looked up. I traced its trajectory. Sure enough, it was heading for Central Park. I tried to call Byers again. Nothing.

I willed my legs to pump harder, and as I clenched the handlebars of my bike, Winston's collar dug into my wrist. That reminded me of who I was and where I was, at least. I adapted it. *I'm Roland Bishop, and I know who I am. I'm Roland Bishop, and I know where I'm going. I'm Roland Bishop, and I know what I need to do.*

Yellow cabs were everywhere, yellow blurs whizzing past me as I screamed north.

I slashed through 10th, and then again through 9th. 8th loomed up before me, and there was a large truck and construction working there. A few guys in orange jackets were milling around and the road at 8th and 52nd heading east was cordoned off with cones. I zipped through, and went right underneath a bulldozer. They screamed at me and hurled insults.

I had lost the first cop, thankfully, but there was another one on horseback, and he called after me, raising his horse to a gallop and pursuing me up 8th. I saw cop cars over on 7th, and then a blinding flash tore through me.

Man, I wish I had a motorcycle, I thought to myself. I had to get there! My hair was sopping now as I pedaled hard. Up ahead, a long line of cars was stopped at 8th and West 55th St for some reason. Honks sounded in a dissonant symphony of noise. I did the only thing I could do and screamed out into oncoming traffic, dodging cars right and left. One of them clipped my rear wheel as I weaved to the left, passing briefly under a long awning flanked by scaffolding and netting as workers improved the façade of the building at the intersection of 8th and 55th. Someone screamed at me. "Get the hell out of the road, ya moron!"

I spotted a yellow cab up ahead, heading north. Nothing but green lights. I flicked my head back. The cop on horseback was gaining on me. *Come on, legs.* I pumped them as hard as I could and caught up with the cab, grabbing onto the trunk edge where it met the window, and desperately trying to keep myself pointing straight. I kept my eyes on my front wheel.

Too low. A sidewalk vendor jutted out too far into the street and I almost lost my head against a cooker housing falafels in the making. My right leg clipped his stand, spinning his countertop somewhat. It all happened so fast.

I looked back. The cop was dwindling. Just then I heard yelling from inside the taxi. The driver was now aware of me and was railing at me with angry hand gestures. But he didn't slow down.

The taxi finally started to slow as we were almost to Columbus Circle. By then, I was starting to hear a ringing in my ears.

That's when the flashes started. I clutched my head in agony. White flashes zipped through my mind. I inadvertently let go of his cab as he banked around the circle and sped away. My bike wobbled, and I grabbed ahold of it. I felt nauseous. The trees loomed up and I lost my vision momentarily, swarmed with heat and flashes. I moaned in pain, clutching my temples once more. I lost my presence of mind and let go of the handlebars, and I went crashing into the trees in the southwest corner.

Dazed, I stumbled up. I had to get moving. It wouldn't be long before the 10-foot-cop caught up to me. Mounted police officers had a reputation for, ahem, *impatience*.

I ditched my bike and ran, careening through the trees onto West Drive, whipping out my phone. *Come on, Byers, pick up!*

More flashes. More searing pain. More nosebleed. I could hear the helicopter, and I looked up. It was north of me, maybe about a mile. That's when I saw other flying shapes. Four of them. The hijacked planes.

There were four of them again.

Without warning, the haunting visions flooded my mind. Shouting in the sky. People falling from above. Ash and smoke. Horror below as bodies pummeled the pavement. But where? Where were they falling from? From the airplanes?

I crashed through Heckscher kickball fields and bolted across the softball fields next, heading for East 65th Street. "Byers! Detective Byers!" I called, but my voice choked as a burst of flashes racked my brain. A series of them collided together, enveloping me in back-to-back stings. The aftermath was utterly throbbing. I wiped my nose as I hurled myself forward again. "Byers! Byers!" I called frantically.

I passed the Sheep Meadow right across the street. If she was anywhere on the south side of the park, she should be able to hear me from there. It was unobstructed. It was also where everything changed for me on the 8th, in what was for me only three days ago, despite the fact that it was only the 4th today.

More flashes, and more visions.

Before I knew it, I was racing up East Drive, my feet flying with the wind.

Flash.

Someone with a handgun jumping out of the trees, firing wildly into Phelps' chest.

Flash.

Fox lying nearby, his head blown apart, and a pool of blood pouring from him.

Flash.

Another assailant shooting at Byers as she returned fire. And then she was on the ground, but still moving.

The chopper was almost directly overhead, drowning out my cries of *Detective Byers! I need you!* I called with all of my might, but my voice was getting hoarse. I also knew that I would be drawing that mounted policeman to myself.

No reply. All I could do was keep running and calling for her. People veered out of my way. Pulling my phone to my ear once more, I tried calling her one last time before I sprinted full-tilt for the other end of the park. I thought I heard a noise behind me as I crossed the 79th Street Transverse cutting around Turtle Pond and making for the softball field in the great lawn.

Before I knew what happened, something struck me in the leg. I winced in pain and was down on the ground instantly, choking and breathing hard. The ringing in my ears grew louder and I started hyperventilating. I was just shy of the softball field, sprawled out across the path.

I groaned in agony and looked back, reaching down for my leg. Blood streamed from it. The mounted police officer was running up toward me, gun drawn, talking into his shoulder radio.

And just then, another noise behind me. Men, five of them, running. Off in the distance, I saw a thick head of billowing brown hair leaping over a hedge and chasing after them, other officers in tow. The woman cried out, "Freeze!"

The mounted officer called out "Freeze!"

I lost it. Byers was in danger. My visions happened; they became part of history after I saw them. I would not let her die. Or Phelps. Or Fox. I turned around and summoned up every bit of emotion as I was racked with white flashes and pain. Planes flying through the sky. Planes slamming into buildings. Buildings! One of them, very large. Another plane slamming into a green mass of Earth, carving a commercial jet-sized cavernous hole two-hundred twenty feet wide as a fireball engulfed my vision.

Blood streamed from my nose as I tried to stand.

"Get down on the ground, now!"

I'm Roland Bishop, and I know who I am. My skin tingled. My heartbeat raced. All I could see was hot blue coming from my eyes. As a note starting on the lowest end of the scale but escalating in pitch, blending with a crude harmonic, a hideous noise welled out of me and turned into an ear-piercing cacophony. I could feel my own ears bleeding.

The sun was blotted out by gathering clouds. The weather overhead changed. Briefly I caught a glimpse of the helicopter floundering, regaining its composure, and then vacating the area.

"Down on the ground or I will fire on you again!"

I looked at him, and his jaw dropped. He was covering one of his ears as he had his gun trained on me. But his gun was lowering as he gaped. I don't know what he saw, but I know what I felt.

I arched my back. I whipped my head forward as a tremendous pulse of energy snapped outward from my core, expanding in an unlimited and vicious diameter of radiating ire and heat.

The cop was suddenly blown backward and his gun went flying. He grunted, collected his wits and glared back up at me in shock and awe.

I raised my arms with my palms to the sky, and arcs of lightning burst forth from them, connecting with every bit of iron, steel, aluminum, titanium, and every other metal around me, seeking a grounding connection. My mouth expelled heat and I was engulfed in blue flame.

I'm using my gifts, Penny. This is my sunny disposition. I'm Roland Bishop, and I know who I am.

I could feel myself lift off the ground, and I turned back north, hovering up and above the trees as arcs and flashes of lightning emanated from my core and connected with random conduits for each burst. Through a blue mist I could see the Detective racing after someone. A few men fled from her presence.

And then, further up, I could see two men in suits sprinting back south to cut them off as they ran. Shots were fired. People fled in all directions. A whirlwind was around me and the vortex swirled chaotically, sending shrapnel, litter, loose branches and dust and dirt spinning off in all directions. I could feel the cop's eyes watching me along with others. Yet I only had eyes for Byers as I wafted over the trees, my arms outstretched.

There she was, her own gun drawn and pointed at an unknown assailant concealed in the trees. I descended upon him with wrath, bolts of lightning pulsing from my mouth and my eyes. The air swirled as I dropped to the ground. Byers looked over at me in horror as the wind whipped her hair up into a frenzy.

And then, the gun fired. I saw it, as if in slow motion, speeding out from under the trees and across from her toward the Alexander Hamilton Monument, slicing through the air. Without so much as a word, I grimaced, and a band of current traced from my fingertips, intersecting with the path of the bullet. Byers dove behind a tree. The bullet exploded in a micro-burst of shrapnel.

Phelps and Fox returned fire, downing one of the assailants. Another stood there and opened fire at them. Two more fled.

The two agents dashed for cover close to Byers. All three of them were pinned down.

Something Byers had said to me earlier. What was it? Through the blue haze and smoke, I remembered her words.

The kid pulled a 'crossfire gambit.' Like, a double-cross move and had the bad guys shoot at each other. They ended up killing each other off.

With every pulsing fiber of my distorted being, I flew between the gunner and the gunned, drawing his attention. It was Mohammed Atta himself. I faced him, swirling to my right as he watched me in dread. I held his gaze. He turned his gun on me. I moved between he and his fleeing assailants. They were now aware of me. Suddenly, all of their names flashed before my eyes.

Marwan al-Shehhi.

Nawaf al-Hazmi.

Khalid al-Mihdhar.

The two fleeing terrorists, al-Hazmi and al-Mihdhar, whipped their bodies around and opened fire, sending a volley of ammunition racing eastward at me, as Atta emptied his magazine of his remaining bullets westward in my direction.

I closed my eyes and breathed, lifting my head toward the sky. As a passing wind, I was gone, and so were the terrorists, killed in the crossfire gambit.

The cop dug his knee into my back and held me down. Winston's collar dug further into my skin as the dirt pressed it inward. "Stay down, d'ya hear me? Suspect down, suspect down," he spoke into his radio. "Move back, everyone, stay clear! Central, I'm at the 79th Street Transverse. Just west of East Drive before the field, over?"

"Roger, on our way," came the reply.

"Don't move, punk. Don't even breathe," he said firmly, and I could feel the cold steel of a barrel in my neck.

Footsteps running. Running. Men and women allowed to come closer. "I got him!" shouted the cop. "This who you're looking for?"

"Yeah, that's him!" yelled a man, breathing hard, and holstering his weapon. I recognized the voice. Phelps.

"Hold him down, he might spring," said Fox. Both men came over and forcibly pulled my hands behind my back, cuffing me.

"What the hell are you doing, Fox?" My voice sounded strange. Thick and weird. My mouth tasted like blood. They jerked me up and held me before them, finishing the handcuffs and hauling me eastward, presumably toward 5th Avenue and a waiting police car.

Phelps was alive. So was Fox. I looked around desperately. Where was Byers? She had to be still alive too!

There she was! She came running down from East Drive to meet the Agents as they led me to their car.

"Nice try, mister. Almost outran us. Your buddies weren't so fortunate either. Might wanna make plans without them for the rest of their lives."

"Byers, what the hell are you doing?"

"Shut it. I got him, guys," she said proudly. The mounted police officer rode off. They walked me eastward. It was the strangest sensation…I didn't know what was happening. Had I hurt someone? No, that wasn't it. Had I damaged public property? Almost certainly. That wasn't it either. And then I felt it.

My leg. It was perfectly fine. I looked down. No rip in my jeans. No bullet hole. No limping. It was gone.

Everything changed. Again.

I turned to Byers. "Detective Byers, you have to believe me. I'm not-"

"Shut it, Atta!" Phelps said. "I don't wanna hear it! Just get in the car."

We reached the car. I whipped back around to Agent Phelps. "What did you call me?" I asked, wincing from disbelief. My voice spoke with an accent that was not me.

"Get in the car, *Mohammed,*" he hissed. He searched me, extracting my phone from my pocket. I saw it. Splitting the front of the phone face in half was a large tactile flip keyboard, and a monochromatic screen. A Kyocera QCP-6035 smartphone. I had never had one of those before! I had never even bothered with a Blackberry.

My eyes froze upon him and a wave of fear passed over me. The squad car opened and I was thrust violently inside, my head hitting the opposite door handle. Blood streamed down my forehead.

Atta. He called me Mohammed Atta.

I glanced through to the front seat and noticed the cop's computer display. It read 2:42pm. How long was I electrified? How long had all of that taken?

I had no answers, and this was not the change I was looking for.

Byers, Phelps and Fox were alive, but now, I *myself* was the enemy.

The truth and the lie had blended together in a seamless blur, unnerving and terrifying.

6 Days To Go

September 5th, 2001 • Manhattan, NY

It was all starting to make sense to me now.

This whole terrorist plot was *going* to happen. It was inevitable. And I was caught up in the inevitability of it. We all were. But whatever I did seemed to have the most bearings on it. No matter how much I changed things, or interfered, the hijackings were going to happen and the terrorists would have their way.

I shook my head, thinking back to that damned hotel where Agent Mulligan had Atta in a chokehold. I should have just let him strangle him. Just let him kill him.

Shoulda coulda woulda as they say. That was now all in the past.

And now, they thought I myself was Mohammed Atta. Hell, my face felt different, my accent was different, and I had all kinds of memories that I never remembered, once more, fusing with the ones that I knew to be true. I was Roland Bishop *and* Ethan Stiles *and* Mohammed Atta all rolled into one. The one I knew the least was Ethan Stiles. At the very least, I remembered where it was that I had seen Stiles before, but that brought me no comfort.

Maybe Atta and I could sit down to a nice cup of tea someday and discuss trading lives in a nice Arabic language. I laughed grimly to myself. This whole thing was ridiculous.

And what the hell had happened to me out there? I thought the first episode was bad. This was much worse.

They had patched up my bleeding head, treated my nosebleed, and then tossed me into a small, windowless room at the FBI office after pulling into the parking garage and thrusting a bag over my head. I rolled my eyes. *I've already been here, fellas. I could tell you about the futon, the file cabinet at the end of the conference room, Phelps' office, and his authorization code. Been there, done that.*

Once inside, they pulled the bag off my head and searched me before slamming me into a dark office, tying me to a chair, shutting off the light and locking the door. That was at 6pm. Agent Phelps pulled out my cellphone, that strange Kyocera smartphone again.

Finished with that, he examined Winston's collar on my wrist and laughed scornfully at it, shaking his head. "Nice jewelry, Atta."

I grimaced at him. *It's more than that,* I thought, angrily.

Fox fiercely extracted my wallet and held it up to my face. "See this? This is what a scumbag looks like. You'll find out what we do to scumbags."

I just stared at it, firm and unwavering.

There, on the license, right before my eyes, was the name *Mohammed Atta.* My thin, pursed lips. My bushy, chestnut hair. My piercing black eyes set under thick black daunting eyebrows. My scratchy neck. My downcurved cheeks that hinted at disapproval. My slightly drooping left eyelid. My white T-Shirt and black button-up pulled high up my neckline.

It wasn't me, but it was me.

Just like that wasn't me, hovering there in Central Park, shooting lightning out of my ass at everything and everyone. But it was me.

It was, unfortunately, all me.

That was last night.

Now, I was sitting here, awake and alert, staring at the floor, wondering what to do in the early morning of September 5th, 2001. The number *six* kept appearing dimly, cascading before my eyes in the thick ink of that dark room, sometimes zooming into me and startling my vision.

Six days until the hijacking. I knew it. I just had to make *them* know it.

I didn't know what time it was, but there was no noise outside. Everyone must have left for the night except for the agents.

I sensed something.

My wrist throbbed. The cuffs were digging into my skin, and my arms were growing tired from being looped around the back of this chair.

And there, in the darkness of that room, I heard a voice calling to me dimly. It was a sweet, gentle voice that could be firm at times, coming across in tones both tender and resolute. A maternal voice, beckoning to me from the deeps of time and space. There was a yearning in that voice, of some kind of longing unfulfilled, some wrong never quite righted. I knew it well.

Penny.

Was she alive? Hope kindled in me and erupted into a fire, yearning in return for that sweet voice. Could it be that she had never existed in one timeline because of the choices that I had made, and yet now that everything had been flipped, she was alive again?

Anything was possible, I told myself. I had to see her. I strained my shoulders back to adjust my cuffs and stop them from cutting into my wrists, when I felt it.

There, in the dark, with no light, working by feel, I felt Winston's collar on my wrist.

I pressed it firmly. *I'm Roland Bishop, and I know who I am.* It was almost an incantation now, firm and secure, an anchor for my timeline. And just as swiftly the thought came to me, *What if I control my own timeline? What if I'm in charge? Instead of things happening to me and around me, what if I happened to it and I happened around it?"* I tried to wrap my brain around that.

The hijacking had to be stopped, whether Atta was a part of it any longer or not. These terrorists didn't operate alone. Perhaps I could even infiltrate their midst and gain valuable intel that would make the FBI, Byers, anyone, believe me. After all, Phelps and Fox – and maybe even Byers – owed me their lives. If I hadn't done my lightning thing at the park, they might be dead. I averted that future for them. They just didn't know it yet.

I remembered what Byers had said to me, that C.G. Jung quote. *I am not what happened to me. I am what I choose to become.*

My breathing slowed. I closed my eyes, blotting out the dark and the reality. I projected myself outside this cell.

It began quietly.

A faint rumble.

Winston's collar starting to feel so hot against my skin that I grimaced.

A ringing in my ears that grew in volume.

Slowly, the room started to glow around me in a faint hue of azure. Cerulean swirls, vaporous sapphire and eddies of cobalt fused together around me as my little prison blazed with light. As before, I felt dizzy and spasmed. My eyes were closed, but I could see it all. My breathing was measured, though I was buffeted with wind.

Once more, the world whirred around me. What I couldn't even see – the dark of this room – spun like a top around my *Mohammed Atta* shell sitting there in that cell, and the black flew out of my view. Once more, there was thunder in the wind, and there was lightning in the thunder. Once more, the latter took the place of the former, the new substituting the old in that same frenetic patchwork exchange, as the wind howled around me. Light filtered in through chinks in the dark, and the dark gave way in shifting segments that slid and moved out of the way to accommodate the new reality around me.

Blood streamed from my nose and ran down my adopted lips, and this foreign head I was now trapped in throbbed with pain. I didn't know the body, but I knew that cranial angina. *Mild intracranial hematoma*, Dr. Walker had said. *Oh, if he could see me now.*

The heat from Winston's cat collar burned through the strong metal of the cuffs and sent glowing embers flying as I wrenched my hands free. Scalding liquid metal dripped to the floor from their remnants.

I looked out of my cell, from a different building in a different town.

The small table to the right of the door had my Kyocera phone sitting there, turned off. I grabbed it and stepped out of my old cell into a new world: a different building in a different town. But where was I?

The heat hit me first. Hot scorching heat, and my clothes felt way too thick. Vegetation everywhere. There were bronzed hills and caves stretching for miles around me, dotted with evergreens, oaks, almond trees, pine and fir. Treeless steppes extended to the north. Uninhabitable deserts scrolled away to the south. To the east, montane conifer forests with shrubs, herbaceous cover and open woodland went as far as the eye could see.

All over, the image seemed glossy; softened edges around everything, somehow, out of a vignette. Hazy and murky, distinct from reality. Even my very air seemed manufactured.

But where I was, there were caves. And where I was, there was one not thirty feet from me. And where I could see, there was a six-foot-four-inch man with an olive complexion. He was dressed in a traditional Yemeni keffiyeh under a green army field jacket with no insignia. He had a gold shawl draped over himself. His foot-long beard stretched below piercing eyes and a hooked nose with high cheeks, outlined as he approached me.

He greeted me. "As-salamu alaikum," he breathed, and wrapped his arms around me. "Welcome, Mohammed," he said, and I smiled in a reflex, though I hadn't intended to.

"Nahar, Osama," I said, and the language came freely from my lips, though I'd never studied.

There, before me, stood Osama bin Mohammed bin Awad bin Laden.

Winston's collar made its presence known, hot against my wrist, but concealed under my black shirt. bin Laden did not notice, hopefully. I was sitting with him and his Taliban and al Qaeda militants in the Tora Bora caves. Stunningly, I could discern their speech. We were eating late in the day, taking in some of the cool evening air of Afghanistan.

They talked about their immense plans for 'The Great Satan,' as they called America, and as I listened to them, it all became suddenly clear to me.

In six days, jihad would reach an apex as they prayed to Allah the Omniscient for the restoration of Sharia law. They would move on Allah's behalf to strike The Great Satan at the core of its pride, in three key geographic areas.

Financially, they would attack the World Trade Center. The 1993 bombing had not done enough. The buildings must be leveled to the ground.

Militarily, they would attack the Pentagon.

Governmentally, they would attack the White House.

All three of their targets were now plain for me to hear, and their brothers in America were already moving. Pieces were already being moved into place and I, Mohammed Atta, was one of them.

They named all of the jihadist pilots who were already in America. Astonishingly, they named me, though I was sitting right there in the midst of them.

Mohammed Atta.

Marwan al-Shehhi.

Hani Hanjour.

Ziad Jarrah.

They even listed flight numbers, corroborating what the brothers in America had previously confirmed with them. Mohammed Atta was to take American Airlines Flight 11. al-Shehhi was to take United Airlines Flight 175. Hanjour was to take American Flight 77. Jarrah was to take United Airlines Flight 93.

I, Mohammed Atta, would strike the North Tower of the World Trade Center.

al-Shehhi would strike the South Tower.

Hanjour would strike the Pentagon.

Jarrah would strike the White House.

And all of this would take place on September 11th.

Allahu Akbar! they shouted into the night. *Allahu Akbar! ALLAHU AKBAR!!!*

That unending bellow, that deplorable din, that hideous battle cry permeated my soul and barraged my conscience. White flashes yet again, and pain, pain, *pain.* I could feel my eyes hot with tears and rage.

In a flash of a second, I saw buildings topple amidst wild explosions that sent New Yorkers, and the nation, and then the world, into a roiling panic. I saw them fall, two bastions of American strength, collapsing into a vicious cloud of all-consuming dust. And then I was propelled backward in time and caught glimpses of bodies… people… human beings, desperate to avoid being burned alive and taking their own final moments heroically into their own hands. I saw passengers storm up an aisleway to break cockpit doors and wrest control away from hijackers. With horrific clarity I saw all of it.

It was too much. Too barbaric. Too obscene.

I struggled with Winston's cat collar, gripping it and holding it to me, kissing it against my burning lips, and crying out. bin Laden and everyone else gawked at me in confusion.

White flashes. Heat waves. I stared at bin Laden and he stared right back, perceiving me and the threat of an infidel in his midst. I spasmed. He started to approach me, slowly and cautiously, making his steady way through his crowd of deluded disciples.

Visions of helicopters, one of them crashing. High triangular walls around a compound. Soldiers infiltrating a multi-tiered house. An explosion from the courtyard. Shots fired.

bin Laden looked at me in horror.

And then, I woke up screaming in the middle of the night in a cold sweat. My eyes were ringed with fear, and I called out for anyone who would heed my desperation.

It all made perfect, deadly sense now.

Part Three

5 Days To Go

September 6th, 2001 • Jersey City, NJ

No more dreams. No more visions. No more hope. All those people!

I just wanted quiet. I just wanted to think.

The terrifyingly vivid nightmare passed, and I was back to myself.

I don't know where I went off the rails and collided with Atta, but everything was so incredibly realistic.

I didn't know who I was anymore, whether Roland Bishop or Ethan Stiles or Mohammed Atta. I didn't want to be *any* of them anymore.

After the vision I was exhausted to my very core, like a weariness had crept into my very bones. I was sapped of any desire to do anything, and my arms hung limply at my side on the couch as I stared off into the nothingness that awaited all those poor people. I looked wearily at the clock: 5:05am. I desperately needed sleep.

I had had so many forward jumps and backward jumps and even *side* jumps…I was in a pinball maze designed by a very cruel maker. The only definite thing that I knew was the certainty of the cat collar around my wrist. But whether or not it would be there tomorrow, I had no clue.

That vision utterly racked me. Who was I, so tiny and insignificant, so powerless, so scant, so bereft of resources, name, ability and even identity, to avert the coming history? Who was I to do anything at all?

Revelations came to me of two giant, square pools, filled with the waters of sadness, though I had no idea where they were. They contained tears. Tears of all those who mourned all those who fell. The number *five* materialized as through a mist, and I took that to mean that there were only five days until this unspeakable tragedy would unfold. *Five days*. And then, I received different flashes, as I buried my face in my pillow, seeking to soak up my tears.

Two thousand nine hundred and ninety six.

I knew in an instant that that number meant the body count. I didn't have to ask or guess. I knew with absolute assurance that in five days, that would be the total. The people in those four targets had no idea what was coming.

Sixteen hundred victims from the North Tower, including all those who tried to rescue those dead or dying, and those on the ground.

One thousand from the South Tower.

One hundred twenty five at the Pentagon.

Two-hundred sixty-five passengers aboard the four planes that were used as missiles.

And six nameless faces somewhere throughout.

On top of that, faces rushed past me of all those in the future who would die from cancers, emphysema, exposure to dust and toxins, and other chronic lung conditions. The damage would be horrific.

The terrorists would not be hijacking the planes to kidnap the passengers and exact some unreasonable ransom. They would not be holding them as collateral to ensure their military and political demands were met. They would not be kidnapping them indefinitely. Nor would they be commandeering the commercial jetliners and dropping them off at some remote airport to release hostages once their horrendous wishes had been granted.

No.

They were going to use them as *missiles*, and drive them into the structures that epitomized American strength and resolve, taking innocent American lives with them. They were going to attempt to bring the United States of America to its collective knees through terror, and they had lain their plans bare before me.

The results would be catastrophic. I had to do something, I just didn't even know where to start.

Winston rubbed against my leg and purred softly, looking at me quizzically. I burst into tears at his oblivion to the carnage that was about to unfold.

And so, having no clue what to do, where to go, or who to be, I wept.

And weeping was all that I did.

All day long, I wept and wondered, wondered and wept. Wept as if it had already happened, mourning for souls whose names I would never know.

All those people! No more hope. No more visions. No more dreams.

4 Days To Go

September 7th, 2001 • Jersey City, NJ

There was no time for mourning what might not be.

Four.

I shot up in bed at 4am the moment the alarm went off. Winston had been perched on my neck. He freaked and leapt off of me, arching his back.

Four.

Haunted by the dream of Osama bin Laden and his jihadists, knowing what they were about to do in the future, I let my mind travel back to the past.

Just a few days ago I had visions of Byers being shot and wounded. Of Phelps being gunned down. Of Fox's head rendered a pulp of tissue and exposed skull and brains. Of Mr. Eggers murdering Penny. Of Jake killing Renita. Of Agent Mulligan taking out Atta.

Yet none of them came to be.

In some way, in some small part, I had managed to alter the course of the future. Through my own meager interference, the tides of time carried other sands to the shoreline instead of what was to be.

Could it be that my dream of bin Laden would be formative to what would happen in their future as well?

The number *four* kept pinging my brain. Four days to go until the attacks. My eyes were opened. I was filled once more with fierce purpose. I had to get information to Byers, as well as to Phelps and Fox.

I reached over to my wrist and felt Winston's collar digging into it. Winston himself eyed me curiously from across the room, unsure of what to think of the insane human staring down at him, wondering why he hadn't been given food.

A brief thought of Jenette passed through my mind, but I didn't sense that she was part of my purpose. I felt nothing for her. I hated that, but it was what it was. I spooned some Nine Lives into Winston's bowl and tore out of there once more, throwing on a grey Old Navy sweatshirt.

I entered Manhattan. I was on the PATH train once more, heading into upper New York. In my hand I clutched a familiar Nokia 3310 red cellphone, a priceless treasure from the continuity of days gone by. I had no idea how much longer I would have it, but I held it close and dialed Detective Byers.

She answered nearly immediately.

"Byers."

"Roxanne! It's Roland Bishop. Listen, I know what the terrorists are going to do, *and* when they're going to do it. Are you at the FBI headquarters?"

"Yes, Roland - oh man, dude, we need to lojack you. Where did you go *again*? We caught Atta!"

"What?"

"Yeah! We caught him in Central Park. Almost gunned us down. Somehow he got away. Phelps and Fox have no idea how. I'm scratching my head as well."

I had an idea how.

"Never mind that now. I'm on my way to you. I can be there in twenty minutes."

"I'll meet you there."

I had no bike, so I took the bus all the way to Lafayette and sprinted up to the Wanamaker Building. There was Roxanne's familiar Bronco parked outside.

Armstrong was outside having a smoke.

"Armstrong!" I greeted him.

"Don't ever say my name out here, you idiot."

"Nice to see you too." I waved him away and headed inside the building. He looked at me in disgust, taking a heavy drag on his smoke.

Byers was inside waiting for the elevator. "Well, hello there," she greeted me.

"Hey. Boy do I have a story to tell you guys."

She shrugged, and her billowing hair bounced in tandem. "Can't wait to hear it. I hope it explains how you keep vanishing right out from under our noses. Did you teach Atta that little trick?"

I snickered, but said nothing, looking up at the dropping elevator numbers.

"Ya know, I think we're gonna have to start all over here at some point and figure out what's really going on with you. Penny is as just as confused as I am."

I turned to her in surprise. "Penny's- she's still there?"

She smirked in amazement. "You really are a head case, aren't you?"

Warmth radiated around my heart. Penny was back. I mean, why shouldn't she be? I was starting to figure it out and get back on track with myself. I was no longer Atta, or Stiles, or anyone else, other than myself. I had kept Winston's collar solidly on me as a talisman, and it kept me here. Maybe in so doing it brought her back and kept her here too. Or maybe she had her own talisman. Either way, the notion that she had returned brought me hope.

"My ex-wife thinks so."

"Well, maybe she and I should go shopping together sometime. I could learn a thing or two."

"You wanna learn a thing or two about me, Detective Byers? I'd be happy to introduce you to the real Roland Bishop," I said, looking at her slyly. Whatever reaction I was hoping for didn't materialize on her face.

"Weirdo," she said, turning to face the elevator just as it dinged and opened, and I swear she almost winked. Her voluminous hair bobbed slightly in her frizzy pony tail.

We entered and went up.

Phelps and Fox were in their offices. Byers pointed to me as we walked through the hallway between them, and they both bid farewells to their respective calls, following us in. I took a long heave of my lungs and moved into the same conference room I had met them in on the 28th, only ten short days ago. We said nothing for a moment after they closed the door.

Phelps raised his hands in annoyance. "Well? You wanna tell us just what this is all about?"

"Yeah," Fox sounded. "And how you and your little Middle-eastern buddy managed to slip right through our fingers a few times now."

"Fox," Phelps scolded. Fox didn't apologize.

"He's not my buddy." Fox just scoffed.

I cleared my throat. "I know when and where they're going to strike," I said gravely. "I've seen it, and I need you to trust me. I *know*."

"Okay, let's have it," Phelps said. "Have a seat."

Fox pulled out his tape recorder once more, setting it on the table in front of me. This time I didn't mind. We all sat.

"You guys remember I've been receiving *numbers*, right? Strange numbers in my visions."

They nodded.

"They're a countdown. Today I got the number *four*. Yesterday it was *five*. The day before it was *six*, and so on and so forth. All the way back to when I had my first vision of Atta at the PATH Station on August 19th, when I got the number *twenty-three*. Don't you see? Twenty-three days from August 19th is September 11th. Four days from today is September 11th. Six days from two days ago is September 11th. Each day I get closer, the number drops. For me, a bit ago it was 9 days to go. Then it was 1 day to go. Then it was 1 day to go *again*. 9-1-1! Don't you see?"

"Could just be a coincidence," Phelps said.

"I had a dream."

"Well that's nice," said Fox. "So did MLK Junior."

"You're not hearing me," I protested. "I had a dream that I was with Osama bin Laden *as* Mohammed Atta. I was *with* them in Afghanistan. I was given names. Targets. *Flight numbers*. You have to believe me."

"What were the flight numbers?" Phelps asked furiously, scribbling down into his notepad and waiting for me. I sighed and recalled them from the frightening dream.

"They were speaking in Arabic. But I understood all of them."

"What, you speak Arabic now?" Fox squealed. "Your little friend Atta teach you that?" Phelps yelled at him. "What?! They're both pullin' the same stunts, Ryan, vanishing right under our noses."

"Give me the damn flights, please, Roland!" Phelps yelled, pounding his fist. "Rob, *shut it!*"

Fox sneered and turned to face out the windows.

I thought back. My head was pounding at the memory, and my wrist flinched, cut by Winston's collar.

"United Airlines 175. American Airlines 11. American Airlines 77. United Airlines 93. All leaving on September 11th from various airports up and down the Eastern seaboard," I told them, pounding my fist on the table. "I checked them all! United 175 departs from Boston this Tuesday. American 11 departs from Logan. United Airlines Flight 93 departs from Newark. American Flight 77 departs from Dulles. They're doing this so as to not arouse suspicion. You guys have to believe me. Every single one of these jets is going to be aiming for targets."

Both of them stopped, staring at me intently. Byers started to say something and then stopped mid-sentence. Blood trickled from my nose. "What is it, Byers?" I asked her. She didn't say anything; just stared at me. "Byers?"

I looked back at the agents. They hadn't moved a muscle. Frozen, as if catatonic, both of them. I grunted in confusion, looking them both over, back and forth. Fox had his pencil in his mouth. "Agent Phelps?" Nothing. "Fox?" I asked. Again, nothing.

Comprehension seized me.

"Oh, shit," I said with a gasp. "Now they know. I get it. Of *course* everything changes once they know everything." I stared at them, frozen there in suspended animation. It was like the Windows Blue Screen of death, and nothing could restart it except for a reboot. A system had crashed somewhere.

I reached over and pressed Byers' shoulder. It was hard as a rock and icy to the touch. Indeed, my own breath in that room seemed to be visible before me. A chill swept through. A brief thought passed of punching Fox in the jaw. He would never know it was me.

Think, Roland. Now you're going to have to explain this to them all over again. They won't remember any of this. I tried to think of where the reboots had been. They weren't exactly uniform; they had taken place in multiple locations and at diverse, inconsistent times.

But the *major* reboots – those had happened at Central Park. Going home wouldn't reset anything until seemingly the next day.

And in any event, having to tell them the same revelatory information every single day wouldn't serve any purpose in us locating the terrorists where they were *now*, nor would it give us enough time to avert their dastardly plans for the morning of the 11th. They might already be at the airport ready to launch.

I was stuck in a loop. The Inevitability Loop.

But how could I get out of it? How could I jump ship and get out of this loop, making sure to stay 'me' in the process, lest I too was swallowed up and frozen by the same space-time continuum reboot loop?

Think. Who else had been there, returned in an altered form, and yet re-emerged as themselves?

Her name jumped out at me. *Penny.*

Everything had frozen without the escape hatch of sleep, and it was a long ride back to Jersey City Jail. People were standing in the middle of the street. New York was a noiseless metropolis of a bustling standstill. A ringing was in the air, like a pent-up compression engine under strain, and it was slowly rising.

But the New Yorkers heard it not. Cars were everywhere in mid-stream, the blur of their activity trailing behind them. I stole some poor guy's bike right out from underneath him, and that was a surreal task. He stayed there, levitating, without the slightest trace of annoyance, and was in for a rude awakening once the timer ran out.

Once again I was screaming through the streets of New York City, but this time heading south. I swear I passed the 10-foot-cop that had shot me, now riding around the waterfront, his horse frozen in mid-gallop. I passed quickly through the Holland Tunnel and emerged on the other side, heading up to the Jersey City Jail.

Everyone, everywhere were stopped in their tracks. Motorcyclists in the streets leaned dangerously to pass around other cars buzzing down Hudson River Greenway, stopped entirely in a pocket of gravity. I glanced up. A commercial jetliner was up there, flying who knows where. Suspended between earth and sky, lifeless, and yet full of lives. My heart was heavy at that sight. But…I needed to press on.

I made it to Jersey City.

No one greeted me at the reception counter of the jail. I broke the glass on the attendant's security window and depressed what I thought would be the release button to allow me back into the cells where I might find Penny. By that time I was drenched with sweat and completely out of breath. But the Winston collar held fast.

I rounded a corner and traced down a bank of cells. The last one on the right had a little light streaming out of it. The heaves of my breath sounded loud and clear against the walls of those cells. Inmates in varying stages of undress were in their cells, lying about, reading, writing, or on the toilet. Two female inmates were showering together, and the rivulets of water ricocheting off their naked bodies held fast in the air, suspended in time and space as they stood completely still under the warm, frozen downpour.

And there she was. She was reading, a book in her hands, her thin readers adorning her face, with a steaming Styrofoam cup in her hands as she read. She eyed me playfully over the top of it.

"Whatever took you so long?"

"Welcome back, Lady Divinitus."

"I see you found what makes you…*you,*" she said, pointing to Winston's cat collar attached firmly around my wrist. I just stared at her. I knew her, and she knew me.

And then, there I was again, lying on her bunk, just like old times. There was a female inmate on the bunk above us, frozen in time, completely unaware of the sheer joy we were both experiencing at being reunited.

Penny sat opposite me on the cold aluminum shitter, drinking her tea and asking me questions. I answered all of them, much to her heart's content, while she listened intently and took mental notes. Pencils were not allowed in here; they all too easily made cunning shanks.

She would answer no questions about herself until she was thoroughly satisfied with my accounts of everything that had transpired since the last time we had seen each other on September 2nd.

It was so good to see her again. I had to be careful, however. I didn't want to risk sending her back through some ill-timed release of information that would necessitate a reboot. Or…was she immune to it? I wanted to prove my theory, but if I mentioned the date, or the specifics of the flights, or both, it might jumpstart that loop again.

"Penny, do you remember leaving? When you drifted away? What happened?"

She quietly sipped her tea and then pensively stared at the floor. "I don't know, Roland. I truly don't. It was the most bizarre thing I had ever experienced. You were talking, and then you just…froze."

"*I* froze? I thought *you* did!"

"Strange. I could see you, but I could not speak to you. Or, rather, you could not hear me. And then, things got very dim and, sort of, stretched away from me. Elastic and ungraspable."

I nodded, remembering.

"I waited for a while, and then pounded on the glass to catch the attention of the guard so that they could help you. But I grew frantic, I must confess. A bit gutted. The whole thing was dodgy. I was growing quite inconsolable, and a guard behind me came and had to physically remove me. I was hysterical, Roland, if you should like to know the truth. Hysterical."

Now it was my turn to *hmmm*. "And what happened after that?"

"Well, nothing, really, except I settled down in my cell and they told me that they removed you and took you away to the hospital. That was the last I heard of any of it."

"Utterly bizarre. On my end, *I* was still here and *you* were gone. I felt devastated. Exhausted. Drawn. I went home and just cried."

"Oh! You poor thing. It appears that we are both in need of counseling."

"Indeed," I said, mimicking her. She caught my impression and smiled endearingly. I wished that I could tell her the details, just to get it out of me.

"There's more to be said, isn't there," she asked, reading my inner thoughts. "You have something you wish to tell me."

I nodded. "I do. But I'm worried what might happen if I do."

"Well, out with it then. Surely, it could not be much worse than the last time you froze us and you thought I no longer existed. Or are we just making chinwag here?"

"What's a chinwag?"

"Stay on topic, Roland!"

I sighed, and sat up quickly. "I'm worried," I said, "about losing you again. I mean, all these people aren't going to stay motionless forever. Something's eventually gotta give, and the clock will have to reset, and things will be in motion once more. I'm just counting my lucky stars that you're back and that we could talk."

"Bollocks. If you think I went to the great beyond and came back all knackered and bereft of wisdom, you're certifiably mad. Besides, you've dropped enough bread crumbs now for me to decode the rest on my own, Roland."

"I have?"

"Yes! Of course you have. Have you even taken a look at my book?"

My eyes narrowed. *Her book?* She extended it to me. It was a black book with gold letters. I read the title.

The Only Plane In The Sky. An Oral History of 9/11.

I looked up at her and gasped.

"Take a look at the back cover, Roland."

I turned it over. There, plainly for me to see, was proof that she knew.

Avid Reader Press / Simon & Schuster (September 8, 2020).

I gasped again and stood up, staring hard. "No *way*...where did you... how did you... where did you get this, Penny?"

I stared at her in amazement. She giggled.

"Lady Divinitus has her ways. If you want to know the truth of the matter, I don't know. I wandered aimlessly for a while in dark hallways. Only slowly did I become aware that I was meandering through what must be the galaxy's greatest library. Full of treasure troves of books upon books to the power of books. Fiction, nonfiction, biographical, memoirs, autobiographies, reference books, romance, western, science fiction, fantasy, history, all of it. I cannot tell you where it was, nor where I was. All I knew was that I was somewhere...*else.*

"And that's when it hit me, Roland, and I became quite chuffed, really," she said, smiling. "I was *ecstatic!* I realized that I, too, had been given a gift. For whatever reason, I was transported here for answers. Not just for me, but for you. I, in my Jersey City Jail jumpsuit, roamed that hall for what seemed like years. There were dim lights and tables to read at. There were rolling ladders to access the upper shelves. Strangely, there was no one else present. I had an unencumbered visit, shall we say?

"At any rate, I proceeded to the history section to see if you were correct. I never doubted you for a second, but I wanted to make sure for myself and to know precisely what happened. I found this book, Roland. Published in the year 2020. And so, as when I counseled you that you should take something with you that is uniquely you, I made the book uniquely me. I tore out this page." She showed me the inner flaps of the book. Just as she said, page 83 was missing. "Just a random page, no less, but I did something to ensure the story's passage with me. *I ate it.* Yes! I balled it up and ate the dratted thing. It tasted of knowledge, Roland, don't you know?" She was talking faster now, excited and mesmerized by her own experience.

"Anyway, it's still in here, somewhere," -here she rubbed her hand across her belly- "and so I have it with me. I began to feel something *sliding*. Not the floor, or the ladder, not the weather…but…*time*. Time itself. A strange wind began to course through that library. It buffeted me and pushed me backwards. Colors swirled around me. Blues, mostly. There was a tremendous rushing wind that carried me out of there. I tell you here and now that I clutched that book to my chest like there was no tomorrow. *Because there might not be*, I thought! And then, before I knew it, I was back here. Right back here. Clutching this book to my chest. The guards almost confiscated it as contraband, for goodness' sa-"

A thrill ran through me. "What day was that? The date!"

She searched her memory. "What? When they tried to confisca-"

"No, no, Penny, the date you came back!"

"Ah. Let's see, it was three days ago. September 4th, Roland. Right around 2:30pm in the afternoon."

My legs quaked, and I fell onto the bunk. The inmate above us jostled lifelessly. "What is it? Whatever is the matter?" asked Penny.

"Of course. That's when I was in the park and I became Atta. Things changed. Everything changed right there. I saw the same wind."

"You became Mohammed Atta!" she shrieked.

"Long story. I can't explain it. I'm not even sure I would want to try. It was the most bizarre thing. But that's when I felt that wind – and the colors – and it plunged me into change. For the second time, I should add. And then, I was in Afghanistan, with Osama bin Laden and his jihadists. I thought it was a dream, but I can't explain the transition, nor where it happened. And then the next time I tried to explain all that to Byers and the FBI, they froze too."

"Yes but don't you see?" she asked me. "There's no risk of that with me, now, Roland. I found it out on my own. I read here that it will happen on September 11th, four days from now." My eyes widened. I reached for Winston's cat collar. "Relax, I'm not going anywhere, Roland. I know all about the history of it. The names you've shared with me, those are all in here. The history is not set yet, because not all the pieces have fallen into place, and you keep changing things. And I'm sensing that there is still more to do. You have a part to play in all of this yet."

She stiffened, and stuck out her chin. "I'm going to give you reverse counsel now. Something I cautioned you against before. Your power is evident. That much is clear. Your ability to recreate history is also growing. So I suggest you engage it. Nurture it. Go out there and see what you can find. There's still time to change the past, Roland."

"You mean the future."

"I mean both. The future *contains* the past. The present is what you have to work with to influence both. You're outside of both. So, be the change! You have your feet in both worlds, apparently. I counsel you to straddle them carefully, and to go see what you can do. Just hold onto that cat collar." She looked at it. "What is your cat's name?"

"Winston."

"Ha! A most British name. Jolly good. That really is a very great comfort to my mind."

I breathed a sigh of relief to have her back, and to expel the pent-up incredulity that continued to settle upon me. This was all far too incredible. Penny must have sensed what I was thinking. She took a sip of her tea and leaned toward me.

"Roland," she whispered. "Go be the change."

It was 4:13pm, looking up at the clock as I walked out of Jersey City Jail.

For whatever reason, I felt compelled to avoid Atta. I couldn't be sure where *any* of them were, but I didn't want to go whisking off to Afghanistan again, and he was the FBI's primary target: I might get shot. Who else should I pursue? New York City was such a huge metropolis. Where would I even find any of them?

More hot flashes. And this time, they were *welcome*. I spasmed, standing outside the Jersey City Jail, thinking and waiting. White. Blinding flashes of light that traveled from the back to the front of my brain with scalding heat. My pores opened up to expel the perspiration within. And then, suddenly, I was whispered a name.

Ziad Jarrah. He was one of the lead hijackers that Phelps had mentioned and whom Osama bin Laden had confirmed. And then I saw him! There were three other men with him, and they were all disembarking a plane, walking up the passenger boarding bridge. But when? And where? The number *four* appeared in my mind's eye again. I clenched my jaw and gritted my teeth. *Four still means today*, I thought. Was I supposed to tail them now? That didn't answer the question of *where?*

More flashes. A cockpit being burst into with a beverage cart and fire extinguishers. A plane flying out of control. Green grass looming up. The number *ninety-three*.

I opened my eyes. That was it. That had to be it. Jarrah was the lead hijacker for United 93. The four men were getting off a plane at an airport, preparing for their hijacking. But where? I clutched at my cat collar and tried to breathe.

My knees buckled from a revelation so powerful it racked my spine. I nearly collapsed to the ground. Out of a plane window, through the eyes of an unidentified soul, I could see the World Trade Center in the distance. There it was. Both towers as solid steel fingers pointing up into the sky in defiance of what was to come.

They were arriving at an airport. But what airport was within sight range of The World Trade Center?

My eyes opened wide. I grabbed my stolen bike and raced off. Newark International Airport was forty-six minutes away. I had to get there.

The sun was setting when I finally rolled up to Newark International Airport.

I was panting and sweating. The wind had served to mitigate some of that sweat, but now, slowed to a halt, my body was heating back up, and my damp clothes were paying for it.

I looked back. Far away now, I could see the World Trade Center like toothpicks, brightly illuminated and reflecting the distant setting sun.

I had no idea where to go. I had no idea what to do. People were everywhere, still frozen and statuesque as though someone had hit a celestial 'pause' button. Birds were suspended in the sky in flocks. The crests of water usually rippling along the Hudson formed tiny stabbing peaks, deadly to dive into.

Deadly – that was the word to describe the people I was seeking. They were here…somewhere. I had no idea where to look.

It had to be after 5pm now. I glanced at my watch. It was no longer there. *My watch was no longer there!* Winston's collar was still there, but memories brewed in me of never having worn a watch. *Impossible.* I knew the face of it, knew its hands, but it had disappeared entirely. Had I lost it? Or had it been stripped away in one of these mysterious interludes between the certain and the strange? Or had I just forgotten to slip it on that morning?

It was a good bet it was the former, not the latter.

Dread seized me, wondering if this was the beginning of a change I could not resist or rebel against. Change that might steal Penny from me. Or Byers. Or justice. I cast my bike aside and ran inside the airport.

I didn't have much time. I had no idea where to look, or if they were even still here. I just knew I had to find them.

I wondered if any of the people around me could still see. If they were able to perceive the one human in motion sprinting everywhere throughout the airport. I raced with all of my heart, fueled by adrenaline and raw fear. I examined every single terminal, checked out every single face, every single gate, every single baggage claim, restrooms, airport lounge and security screening area that I could.

The worst part about all of it were the flashes, and the nausea. And the nosebleeds. All throughout the airport, I became repeatedly stricken. Searching for the faces of these terrorists, I drew near to countless souls whose future held horrors. They were beyond count. Either my intuition and power were growing stronger, or the concentration was greater. In either case, the depravity of future man was on full display here. I was repulsed and disgusted. There were far too many to alert to the authorities.

Sadly, I had to face the moral quandary of whether or not to take any action. Could people survive rape? Yes. Could they survive being robbed or kidnapped, or sexual assault? Yes. But could they survive murder? No. I had to leave these people behind, and it was the hardest thing I had ever done. One particular face, as I drew near, disgusted me so much I wanted to gut him. The visions I saw that that man would commit…were unthinkable. I would have to return to him afterwards.

It's not your mission to save everyone, Roland. Just 2996 of them.

Finally, I gave up hope and stopped in the middle of the Alaska gates, my hands on my knees, my form doubled over. I was crying from the horror of all that I had seen, out of breath and spent from the miles that I had run. Exhausted and drained, I was a dog-tired and ragged wreck. I couldn't remember when I last ate, and now I was paying for it with all my calories expended and my heart broken.

I couldn't find them. They simply weren't here. Perhaps they had already left the airport and were on their way to their final destination, preparing to hide out until the morning of the 11th. Perhaps it was already far too late.

I needed food desperately: something. Anything. In a dazed stupor I found the nearest restaurant and stole myself some already cooked Argentinian Choripan and a bottled water. I held it up and said 'cheers' as I walked out, and dried my sopped hair on some poor sap's sweater, making sure he didn't topple over as I did so.

I sat and ate. It must have been a good half-hour. The black of night draped over the airport outside. I decided to go back for more as long as this time suspension worked to my advantage. But on my trip for seconds, I stopped. Halfway back to the restaurant, an idea gripped me, and I paused. I abandoned my pursuit of food, and raced back up to the main ticketing counter at the front of the security checkpoint. Newark had never looked busier with all of these people in here packed together and motionless.

I shoved a ticketing agent aside and fiddled my way into the computer system, trying to find where to go. It was easy enough. I touched the mouse and recoiled from a spark, which surprised me. Tentatively I returned to it, and I heard whirring and clicking as the computer returned to life from its dormant state. I clicked 'Search' and my fingers tapped the rest.

Jarrah, Ziad.

Within an instant, the computer had found what I was looking for. I was amazed that it, too, was frozen, but maybe it reacted to my touch. Perhaps the electricity still living in me had jumpstarted it. Whatever happened was irrelevant. What I saw on the screen, however, was.

Jarrah, Ziad S, M. FC, Spirit FLL > EWR, Arrival 1933pm, B-2.

Easy enough to decode. Ziad S. Jarrah, male, First Class, Spirit Air, Fort Lauderdale to Newark, arriving at 7:33pm at Terminal B, Gate 2.

I quickly scanned the rest of the names.

Saeed al Ghambi.

Ahmed Ibrahim al Haznawi.

Ahmed al Nami.

Ziad's fellow jihadists. His musclemen.

They were all almost here.

My eyes were drawn to the clock at the bottom right of the Windows 2000 interface.

6:48pm. I had forty-five minutes until Jarrah would arrive. I had to trigger the reactivation. I had to get things moving again. That plane had to land. Jarrah had to exit and come out so I could report him to the authorities. But how? *Think.*

What was keeping me centered and keeping everything else at bay? What had triggered the pause the first time around? I remember being back at the FBI office with Phelps, Fox and Byers. I was telling them the flight numbers and the date.

Then, everything froze.

Be the change.

I heard Penny's voice crystal clear in my mind… urging me… guiding me. Almost as if she was standing right beside me. How could I be the change?

Suddenly, my cat collar began to glow again. It pulsed and itched, heating up my wrist, hot to the touch. I wrestled with it and unclasped it, feeling the burn as I did so.

I wrenched it off of me and stared at it, breathing hard. My wrist sported a slightly reddened line spanning it. Suspending it there in front of me, I saw my logo. *RB*. There it was. *Something uniquely me.* And I was supposed to go be the change. That's what Penny had said to me.

Not even really knowing what I was doing, or if it would work, much less if it would do irreversible damage, I stared at Winston's collar. I'm sure he was somewhere at home, watching out the window, tummy rumbling and wondering if he would ever be fed again.

But here, miles away at Newark airport, I had to de-center. I had to become part of the running timeline again. I had to step back into the loop. That meant releasing that which grounded me to where and who I was.

I had to get away from everyone so no one would see it. I had to make sure that I was cleared of security and in the gate waiting area, or I would be prevented from entering and possibly accosted. I ran to the men's room and jumped into an unoccupied stall.

I sighed, and tried to summon whatever it was that I needed to do. I thought of Penny. Jenette. Byers. Atta. bin Laden. Winston. Jarrah. Phelps. Fox. The cop. Dr. Walker. The sweet elderly lady on the subway. Renita. Joe-Joe. Jake. The taxi driver. The frenzy of all of it; the whirlwind of these past few days. A tremor ran through me as I tensed my muscles and flexed my core, trying to feel every bit of emotion at what had taken over my life.

It was working.

Suddenly, I breathed out in a reflex, and hot vapor distended the air around me. Waves of heat scorched my vicinity. Winston's collar began to sizzle. I grabbed it hard and stared at it as everything phased to blue. Energy took me. I took it back. With my left hand I held his collar, as I extended my right up toward it.

A single arc of blue light shot out from my index finger and transformed poor Winston's collar into burning metal. The energy bolt vaporized it, and it melted in an instant to the floor at my feet.

As I did so, everything and everyone suddenly screeched back to life, as if a record had skipped and then realigned. The end of *Where The Party At* by Jagged Edge and Nelly was playing inside the terminal. It faded out and then *Hanging by a Moment* by Lifehouse started blaring through the speakers. *How appropriate,* I thought. *Tragedy was truly hanging by a moment here.*

"What the hell?" the man in the stall next to me shouted. I looked down and saw trousers around ankles.

"Sorry," I feebly said, exiting the stall. A group of men were all looking toward my stall in amazement.

"Do *not* eat the Choripan!" I warned them, pointing to my stomach, and walking briskly out of there. I think my profuse sweating was the clincher for them.

Be the change.

I had done it. That plane would land. Jarrah and his men would be here. Now, it was just a waiting game. I glanced at the clock again.

Only thirty-five more minutes until Jarrah's plane arrived.

The taxiing lights eventually pulled around the corner, and a yellow commercial jetliner's nose emerged from out of the black mist outside, pulling up to the passenger boarding bridge.

Soon, they were all exiting out of the gate. The terrorists were in First Class, but for some reason they didn't exit. They were in first class! They should have exited by now. Maybe they were hanging back to see if anyone was accosted, or if federal agents were coming for them, and if so, this way they could remain on the plane, commandeer it, and take off for an alternate destination.

Oh no, I thought. *I changed something again! Where are they?!*

Just when all hope seemed lost, the familiar white flashes seized me once more. *There he was.*

Ziad Jarrah. And a white flash of heat.

He was followed by his henchmen. Those who, presumably, would fight off any opposition while he assumed control of the aircraft and began their deadly flight. I tried to think back to where he was supposed to strike. The White House? Yet I didn't see the White House in ruins. Only the Pentagon and the two towers of the World Trade Center.

Then I remembered the hole in the ground. A commercial jet-sized cavernous hole two-hundred twenty feet wide, and the ensuing fireball.

Was their mission thwarted? I *had* seen passengers ramming the cockpit of United 93. Was that mission thwarted? Were Jarrah and his men rendered a failure?

There was no way to be sure. And even more frightening, there was no way to be sure if my presence here would alter that. Still, I had to try.

They exited the passenger boarding bridge with all the nonchalant confidence that the jihadist life could afford them for their suicide mission. They hardly looked around, putting distance between each other as if to make it appear that they were cellular and disconnected one from another.

How You Remind Me by Nickelback was playing as I began my pursuit of them. I tried to ignore being seen. Thankfully, my bloody nose had abated for now, and I took up my pursuit behind them with my sweatshirt hood pulled up over my head.

The flashes continued, and my wrist spasmed. I looked down, missing Winston's collar. As Nickelback's song continued, I was myself reminded of my poor cat back home, and I wished I could be there to feed him.

They continued on at a decent clip. For a moment I wondered if they would be heading to baggage claim, but then the cold truth slapped me in the face: they weren't staying long. What baggage? This was a one-way trip for all four of them.

At one point, one of them suddenly looked back and noticed me. It was the shortest of them. A flash tore through me, and the name *Ahmed al-Nami* flew through my vision. That was al-Nami! They were all following in lockstep with Jarrah further ahead.

I tried to avert his gaze and attempted to hide myself behind a large man walking in front of me, but I made the mistake of peeking out behind him so that I wouldn't lose any of my targets.

al-Nami was still watching me. He did a quick double-take, and then moved up closer to his partners. I could see him leaning into them, muttering something in Arabic.

All four of them began to move at a quickened pace, each in turn looking back in my direction.

Suddenly, they broke into a run.

White flashes! My head lit up like the sun. Visions of The White House exploding in flame and ruin. A tailfin sticking out of it, and a shower of rubble flying in all directions. Blackened smoke miles high into the air, carried away by the breeze.

Shit! I messed it up!

I started running after them.

More flashes. People fleeing and screaming. Someone trapped under concrete, pleading for their lives. And everywhere, people burning. A blackened American flag lying on the ground in tatters.

People, aware of the commotion, started to look around wildly in fright. Five men rushed past them for an unknown reason, one in pursuit of the other four, and the last one appearing disheveled and bloody.

They raced down the concourse.

I did the only thing I could. "Help! Security! Terrorists!" I yelled at the top of my lungs, screaming into the air as we all hurled our way up to the top of Terminal B where it split toward Baggage Claim and Rental Cars.

They kept running. People screamed.

The terrorists were putting distance between them and myself now.

I could see one of them up ahead lift a phone to his ear. Jarrah was calling in for evacuation: someone on the receiving end of that call was their driver who would usher them to safety. I continued to yell in hot pursuit.

A security guard leapt out of nowhere and brandished a weapon. "Thank God – security, those men are terrorists!"

"Get down!" he screamed, and he trained his gun on me. "Hands behind your head! Get down on the ground *now!*" he hollered.

"What? No!" I said, hitting the deck. "Those guys ahead, they, they're getting away!" He flicked his head back in Jarrah's direction, and then spoke into his shoulder radio. "Dispatch, possible terrorist activity, Terminal B, merging with the concourse." He turned back toward me again.

"You stay right there!" he barked at me, and I nodded compliantly. He raced off after Jarrah and the others, informing one of his colleagues where I was.

But I wasn't going to stay there.

Don't you know I'm part of the Inevitability Loop, buddy? I got up as soon as he was out of view, cautiously trailing both him and them.

I could see all of them up ahead. The guard was calling after them and telling them to freeze. People were scattering and running for cover. He ordered them to halt and pointed his weapon. Jarrah and his men moved behind columns and through passengers as if they had done it a thousand times before.

All of them were moving toward Level 3 and the loading/unloading zone. If they got into their transport vehicle it could be all over for all of us, and they would get away. I was starting to lose control. Getting hot, getting tired, still hungry, and desperately thirsty.

The anger began to course through me as I wanted to be closer to them, to tackle one of them, to do *something*.

I'm trying to be the change, Penny, I said in my head. *I'm Roland Bishop, and I know who I'm supposed to be,* I encouraged myself.

My feet started to slow as my energy ebbed. I couldn't keep it up. I had no way to get them, and no way to catch up, and no way to even try.

Jarrah and his men raced out of there, and the cop slowly fell behind. I couldn't see them. They were getting away.

My head flashed painfully and I clutched my temples.

My mind was going. Blackness was taking over the white flashes, and I grew dizzy from exhaustion and mental strain. Gradually, as if the foreground blurred and fluidly retreated, gelling into the background behind it, the rear image replaced the former in a murky swap. Hazily, I could see The White House, completely intact, remaining solidly present as Jarrah and his men escaped in their getaway car.

I looked around in a daze, exhausted. The sweat pooled in my back, and my hair was drenched. My knees buckled and I fell to the floor. I heard the security guard, huffing heavily, making his way back to me, his weapon drawn once more.

Jarrah and his goons were nowhere to be found. It was late, and darkness was descending upon New York with only three days to go until unspeakable tragedy.

My mind was fading, and wicked bolts of discomfort were shooting through my brain! My vision clouded over, and I didn't even have my Winston collar to center myself.

I was out of time, mourning what still would be.

1 Day To Go

September 10th, 2001 • Newark, NJ

The darkness was receding, and light was coming in.

I had been unconscious for a few days, in a mild coma, the voice said, and it had a familiar ring to it, though I couldn't place it. It echoed through the caverns of my muddied and contorted mind as I strove to listen clearly.

"You had quite the nasty fall at the airport. Doctor says you have a hematoma, and you had already had one that this was building upon. Lots of swelling going on in that cranium of yours. Sounds like you were causing a bit of a stir at the airport, too, yeah?"

I knew that voice.

I groggily opened my eyes and looked at her – there were her thick, voluminous brown curls, cascading down her shoulders in unrestricted, wild locks desperate to make a statement.

"Good to see you."

She stifled a surprised giggle, and looked down at me, her eyebrows furrowing. "Uh, good to see you too."

Oh, I see. Trying to play hard to get.

The TV was playing softly, suspended in the far corner of the hospital room on Channel 1. It was playing a preview of the upcoming *The Lord of the Rings: The Fellowship of the Ring* movie, coming to theaters this December. I wondered who would be around to see it, and if there would be any interest following the deadly tragedy that was almost upon us in two days' time.

Byers spoke again. "Do you remember anything that happened at the airport?"

I reached up to scratch my head and look around. My mouth felt parched and sticky. "Is there any way I can get some water?"

"No, there is no way. Do you remember the *airport*?" she reiterated with some edge this time. I returned my eyes to her and showed my surprise at her tone.

"Uh, no, well, yeah," I said. "Kinda. I was tailing Mohammed Atta. Wait – no, sorry. This time it was Ziad Jarrah. And his goons. The guys from United 93."

"What are you talking about?" she whined. "Who?"

I was in the middle of stretching my mouth when I stopped and looked over at her in disbelief. I brought my wrist up to my face and glanced at the hospital ID tag.

Stiles, Ethan P. M / 53 / Cauc.

I threw my hand back down on the bed with some force, cursing. My arm skimmed the roll-up food cart parked next to me on the other side, bouncing the ginger ale dangerously about.

"Whoa! Easy there, Mr. Stiles. You're going to make *one* helluva mess there."

"Shhhhhit! *Whatever.* It doesn't even matter anymore," I mumbled. "I failed."

"What doesn't matter? And…failed at what?" she asked me, frustrated.

I clicked my teeth and rolled my eyes, wondering if Penny was still who she was. I wished briefly that I had swallowed my own book and kept it with me. *The Book of Penny.* That way I would always have her with me. Never before had I felt so ungrounded and uncentered.

"You wouldn't believe me if I told you."

"Try me."

"No." I shook my head. "Not even *I* believe myself anymore."

"Well, the passengers at the airport sure believed you, running around and screaming about terrorists, chasing phantom bad guys. You caused quite the stir. I'm afraid that's what the cuffs are for."

I hadn't even noticed them. I guess I thought that I had some phantom sensation of Winston's cat collar and assumed it was that. But no: glancing down, I saw the cuffs and lightly tugged against them, rattling the bed rail.

The nurse came in and checked my vitals. I asked her for some water. "*Oooone* minute, Mr. Stiles," she said dismissively, heading back out, her loafers swishing on the floor. My mouth felt thick and pasty.

I grunted in disapproval and turned back toward Byers. "So, what now? Arrest? Public disturbance? What?" I said in a blasé tone.

"One thing at a time," she said, holding her hand up. "You mentioned you were tailing somebody. Who was that?"

"Ziad…Jarrah. Terrorist."

She stared at me blankly. "Is that one name? One terrorist? More than one?"

"There were four."

"The…guard that apprehended you said you were running by yourself. That you were alone."

"I was alone. No one was with me. I rode all the way to Newark from Jersey City Jail."

"That's where you're at now. University Hospital in Newark. That was the one closest place to take you," she clarified. "But the guard said that you were one. There were no 'four people' you were chasing. Just one. You."

Why the hell do I keep hearing the number one, I thought. "Wai-wai-wait a minute," I said, waving her down. "He said those guys weren't even there?"

She nodded.

"No. That can't be. Check the manifests. It was a flight from Fort Lauderdale to Newark. I'm not crazy here. It was one plane" -here I noticed the number one again...*what the hell?-* "with four of the 9/11 terrorists on it."

"9/11?"

"Sorry," I grunted, exasperated. "No one calls it that yet, I guess. September 11th. It's one of the terrorists that Phelps and Fox talked about. The attacks happen then."

"September 11th, you mean *tomorrow? What* attacks?! And how do you know Phelps and Fox?" she asked, approaching a frantic tone. "Talk to me!"

"No-no-no...today is Sunday the 9th. The attacks happen on Tuesday."

"No, today is *Monday* the *10th*. September 11th is *tomorrow*."

I stared at her blankly. "It can't be." My jaw dropped. In a reflex I grabbed the remote and flicked the channel until I saw News 12 pop up. In a ticker on the bottom, there it was. Monday, September 10th. My eyes went wide. In a moment of seizure, all was made plain, and the number *one* appeared through bursts of blinding radiance in my mind, drifting past me.

We had one day left, and less than that! The attacks were going to happen tomorrow morning! I was out of time.

"Byers. Byers!" I nearly shouted. My blood-pressure monitor started to beep a warning. "You gotta get me outta here. My name is Roland Bishop. Not Ethan Stiles. *Roland Bishop!* You gotta tell Phelps and Fox that I know when they're going to strike. When *and* where! I know all of it now!" I shook my handcuff against the bed vigorously, and she stood up and backed away. "You gotta get me out of here. *Please,*" I begged.

"No way! Stiles, Bishop, or whatever you think your name is. You're not getting out of here. I'm supposed to hold you until the FBI arrives."

I grunted and laid back in my bed. Penny's words came back to me then and there, as if from a shadow of my past, dim yet rising in clarity as they progressed.

The present is what you have to work with to influence both. You're outside of both. So, be the change! You have your feet in both worlds, apparently. I counsel you to straddle them carefully, and to go see what you can do.

I needed to straddle them carefully, indeed. If I was Ethan Stiles, I was in an alternate timeline and in an alternate identity. I had to get back. But if I told her the truth about all the names, and the flight numbers and all that, that would cause another system crash, and this freaking Inevitability Loop would suck me – or her – right out of the present. If I stayed right where I was and slept, I might never ever wake up as Roland Bishop again. And if I did either, would I lose Penny and Roxanne in the process?

I needed to straddle carefully. *Think, Roland. Think. There might be one way.*

And just then, the number *one* flashed through my mind. All these one's. I should have been paying attention. *One* meant, as all the other numbers had before it, the number of days left. Only one day left. There might be a way.

"Byers," I asked her. "Okay. Okay. Fine. What time is it?" I gritted my teeth in hope.

She looked at her watch. "2:28pm. Why?"

"I need to make a call to my neighbor at least. Her name is Renita. Or Amy. Can't remember."

"You don't even know your neighbor's name?"

"Byers! This is serious! Anyway, she said she would feed my cat. At least let me make sure that Winston is taken care of. *Please.*"

Byers stared at me with a silly sneer. "Winston?" she asked skeptically.

"Yes! I know it's a silly name. But it's a silly cat from a silly ex-wife. I do love him though. If they're gonna come haul me away, please at least let me call her and make sure she gets in."

She shook her head, still in disbelief. "Fine, Ethan. Take care of your silly cat. They confiscated your phone, though, so how are you going to do that?"

I sighed. "I can use the room phone here." I pointed to it sitting over on an end table by the wall. Byers raised an eyebrow at me and walked over toward it. She bent over, and picked up the phone.

I began my deep breathing.

She studied it for a moment, looked at me, and then started walking it over to me.

I dredged up every angry memory I had.

She handed me the phone. "Make it qui-"

I grabbed her with my free arm and pulled her on top of me, hugging her close as my body began to tense and pulsate. She elbowed me in the ribs, which only made me angrier. The handcuff on my right arm sizzled and smoked, burning me as arcs of lightning began to flash out of me. Byers screamed.

"Help! Someone, help me!"

"I'm sorry, Roxanne, I'm sorry!" I called out in wrath, my whole body buzzing with frenetic energy. "I'm sorry!"

In an instant, everything melted into a cobalt-indigo shade. All waved and flickered in the heat, and the walls around us shifted. Right on time. Byers continued to scream for help, elbowing and kicking backward into me. I took every blow. "Let go of me!" she yelled, and then screamed again as she witnessed what I was witnessing. She turned her head to look at me and screamed once more – I couldn't tell you how horrifying I must have looked because I've never looked in a mirror while it was happening.

The cuffs melted and I was free. I wrapped my other arm around her in a bear hug and I could hear her wheeze. I was not letting go. This was my new centering and my new grounding, and she was going to straddle history and future with me. At the same time I gripped my hospital ID tag hard to make sure I had a hold on it. I wasn't letting go of that either.

The vortex claimed both of us, sucking us in as Ethan Stiles kidnapped the Detective and emerged on the other side as Roland Bishop.

The light then receded, and darkness took us.

4 Days To Go

September 7ᵗʰ, 2001 • Jersey City, NJ

There we were, together, just the two of us.

Byers was on top of me on my bed, frozen in shock, having watched her entire present vanish in a lightning haze and tumultuous whirlwind. My only regret was that we were both clothed…but that could wait.

Words failed her, and she could only form grunts. In a flurry of movement, though, she was off me, jumping out and down the hall into the kitchen, staring back at me in alarm.

"What the *hell* was that?!" she screamed.

I would answer her in a moment. I reached to turn my nightstand clock toward me. To my everlasting joy and relief, there was Winston's cat collar firmly digging into my wrist. I took it and kissed it. Next, I checked the alarm clock. There, plainly displayed for my joyful eyes, it read:

Friday 9.7.01.

It was the 7ᵗʰ all over again. Hopefully, I wouldn't have to relive all of that chase. But, taking heart, I accepted the fact that I bought us some time. I had straddled the line of the present to influence both the past and the future. I had carried her with me into a *new* present, and now she would believe what I told her, because her eyes were now opened. The running date was now a variable for her as well.

Byers would know with certainty that we had skipped through it, diving in and out of the never-ending flow of Time.

Roxanne stood there now, perplexed, panting hard, hands outstretched at her side. She gawked at me out of the corner of her eyes, her face contorted in freakish misery.

"Seriously! What the hell was that?"

"What…when…who…where…all of it is pretty irrelevant, Roxanne," I said. "But I can prove it to you-"

"Yes! Please! Prove it to me *right now,* Ethan!"

"Well, first, my name is not Ethan Stiles. It's Roland Bishop. And I *was* chasing Ziad Jarrah and the other jihadists last night at Newark. They were there."

She said nothing.

"They confiscated my phone, right? Do you remember the color?"

She nodded. "Blue?" she asked, nervously.

"Tell me what that is right there," I said, pointing behind her. She turned and looked. On the counter behind her was my phone, once again a little red Nokia 3310. She turned back to me. Winston skittered across her path, and she jumped in fright. "That's my cat. Winston. Whose name you like so much."

Her eyes followed him, and then she looked around in fear. "We're in my apartment in Jersey City. Where I end up after every single one of these episodes. At least, except for one." I saved the detail about Mohammed Atta and Afghanistan for later. Not too much all at once.

"Look at your own watch," I urged her. "Go ahead, look."

She pensively brought her wrist up and her eyes finally left me and moved to it. She gasped. Apparently her phone read the same time and date as mine.

6:13pm · September 7th, 2001.

"B-but," she started. "It was 2:28 on the 10th…"

"I don't know how it happens, Roxanne. I don't know *why* it happens. But I've been jumping in and out of this time loop for weeks now, straddling multiple running storylines, always ending at the inevitable attack on the World Trade Center this Tuesday. Tomorrow you'll be in Central Park. You were there already in a previous timeline, chasing Mohammed Atta. Do you remember that at all?"

She shook her head. "No, yesterday I just happened to be at Newark following up on a lead when I got the call about you."

"Nope. Think, Roxanne. That wasn't yesterday, that was three days from now on the 10th. Yesterday, for you, was the *8th*, and you were in Central Park with your officers tailing Mohammed Atta. It hasn't happened yet, of course. We went backward in time."

"You mean you kidnapped me and *took* me backward in time!" she yelled at me.

"I had to, Roxanne. You have to believe me. Look at your watch. Look at your phone. Look at my hospital tag!" I held it up for her. "See? Read it."

She leaned in close and peered at it. "You gotta be shittin' me," she said. "Bishop, Roland J. Male, 28, Caucasian. *No…way,*" she breathed in utter disbelief. "I put that tag on you! I gave them your name from your wallet!"

I pulled my wallet off of the counter behind her by my phone, and flipped it open. She read my driver's license and closed her eyes. *Bishop, Roland J.*

"Tell me I'm not going crazy," she said, her eyes pleading with me. "Tell me that this isn't a dream."

"It's not a dream. If anything, it's a terrible nightmare – or will be in a few days. For whatever reason, I was struck by lightning and given what Penny insists is a gift – a *few* gifts - and now I'm just trying to use them as best as I can. I used it yesterday, summoning up all my emotion and opening up that wormhole, taking you with me. I don't know how. I just have to get really hot and bothered, and, I just, I don't know," I ended lamely. "It just happens."

We looked at each other in silence for a moment.

I put my wallet back on the counter.

She breathed lengthily and dropped her head. "Ya know," she said, "I wouldn't have believed you at all except that you looked so damned familiar, lying there in the hospital bed. I was fighting with myself the whole time, knowing I knew you from somewhere. I left that hospital bed so many times and walked out," -here she started pacing- "then walked back right in to lean over your bed rail and see who the hell you were! I've known you before now. I've known you as Roland. I just didn't know that I knew you."

I smiled at her, seeing her take it all in.

"In any of those times, did you happen to lean over and kiss me?"

"You wish," she said, pacing again and putting her hair up into a pony tail. "I was looking at your face and realizing maybe God had a sense of humor after all."

"Oh, thank you."

"It's the Catholic in me." She huffed, putting her hands on her hips and turning around to gawk at me.

"Dr. Penny chose wisely," I said.

"Did she?"

"She did indeed. Come here." She didn't resist me. Roxanne Byers slowly paced over to me, stopping a few inches short. I could still feel the heat from Winston's collar, but I was now feeling a different type of heat altogether.

So was she, because our stopping and staring turned into something different altogether. I leaned in, slowly, and my lips met hers. She had on cherry Chapstick, and I could taste it, as I thrust my lips deep against hers.

It was the most wonderful taste I'd had in a long time, especially after so little food yesterday. That night, we ate food together, this good Catholic girl and I. It was the food of love that we ate, while we drank deep the nectar of life.

There we stayed, together, just the two of us.

1 Day To Go

September 10th, 2001 • Jersey City, NJ

The number *one* flashed before my eyes again.

We had one day left to avert tragedy. Three days ago, we thought we had all the time in the world.

It was 5:37am. Roxanne lay still, quiet, beside me, her mind dead to the world. Yet mine was teeming with energy, full of information streaming through me: facts and data that I had never read yet somehow knew to be true.

This Inevitability Loop was carrying me through a portal of history, as if I had read the very book that Penny had swallowed.

History now played out before me in my mind, as if *all* of it had already happened:

August 6th, Atta and an associate rented a white, four-door 1995 Ford Escort from Warrick's Rent-A-Car, which they returned on August 13th. Atta booked a flight on Spirit Airlines, also from Fort Lauderdale to Newark as Jarrah had done. He left on August 7th and returned on August 9th. He went to Central Office & Travel located in Pompano Beach to purchase one ticket for a flight to Newark. He was scheduled to leave on August 7th in the evening, and scheduled to return in the evening of August 9th. But he did not take the return flight.

On August 7th, Atta checked into the Wayne Inn in Wayne, New Jersey. He checked out August 9th. On that very same day he booked a one-way first-class ticket on America West. It was Flight 244 from Ronald Reagan National Airport heading to Las Vegas.

It was clear now that Atta traveled twice to Las Vegas. These flights were known as 'surveillance flights.' They were for he and the other jihadist cells in America to plan and rehearse how to carry out their attacks that were going to happen tomorrow. It was also now clear that the other hijackers also traveled to Las Vegas at various times over the summer of this year.

Throughout this past summer, Mohammed Atta met with Nawaf al-Hazmi to bring him up to speed on the status of their upcoming attacks. They met monthly for updates.

On August 23rd, Atta's driver license got revoked. It was revoked *in absentia* after Atta failed to show up to traffic court for an earlier citation he had received for driving without a license.

The same day, the Mossad, which was the Institute for Intelligence and Special Operations in Israel, provided his name to the FBI. They said that Atta was one of nineteen US residents that they suspected were preparing to plan an imminent attack against the United States. The only four publicly-known names they provided were Atta's and fellow accomplices Marwan al-Shehhi, Nawaf al-Hazmi, and Khalid al-Mihdhar. No one knew if every one of those nineteen names were all initially going to be part of those who would carry out the attacks tomorrow.

More flashes burst through my mind. I was receiving information on the future again! As I was receiving, I felt the slow trickle coming out of my nose, and I got up to stumble to the bathroom for some Kleenex.

On September 10th – *today* – Atta would be picking up al-Omari from the Milner Hotel in Boston. I could see their car: it was a Nissan Altima. They were talking. I heard them! They were heading to a Comfort Inn in South Portland, Maine. They were far away. Cameras would pick them up pumping gas at an Exxon station in Portland later this afternoon.

I saw a number on a hotel room door. *Room 233.* I saw a bank ATM. They were making withdrawals. The logo for Wal-Mart flew through my vision. They were picking up supplies there. I saw box-cutters. The logo for Pizza Hut flashed into my vision. Atta was eating there.

And then, suddenly, it was tomorrow: September 11th. I could see Atta and al-Omari, together, driving. I watched them arrive in the early morning hours to Portland International Jetport. They abandoned their Altima in the parking lot. They boarded Colgan Air at 6am, heading to Logan International Airport in Boston.

The connection between the two flights at Logan was within Terminal B, but the two gates were not connected within security. There were two separate concourses in Terminal B. The south one was used mostly by US Airways; the north was used mostly by American Airlines. I could see Atta becoming belligerent with a ticket staffer once he was told about additional screening requirements in Boston.

6:45am flashed into my mind. 6:45am at the airport in Boston. Atta lifted a phone to his ears. It was his fellow jihadist, hijacker Marwan al-Shehhi from United 175, confirming readiness to begin.

I could then see Atta checking in for American Airlines Flight 11 just as I had experienced in my previous visions. He once again passed through security, and he boarded his flight. He was sitting in business class. I saw another number. His seat number. 8D.

The plane lifted off at 7:59am from Boston to LAX.

It had eighty-one passengers aboard.

All of them were going to die.

We had less than one day to go. I sat on the toilet clad only in my boxers, steeped in thought, my head in my hands and Kleenex stuffed up my left nostril to staunch the bleeding. How were we ever going to stop four groups of terrorists in four different planes from four different locations? I couldn't even relay all these details to anyone who could do a damned thing about it without freezing time all over again.

It was now 6:28am. Roxanne stirred in my bedroom. I heard her let out a soft moan in her sleep. She muttered something incoherent about time travel.

Winston jumped up on the bathroom countertop and meowed demandingly. "Come here," I said to him, scooping him up. Poor thing hadn't been fed properly in I don't know how many days. "When were you fed last, Winny, huh? The year 1792? I know. Daddy's all over the map," I said, setting him down and cracking open a can of Nine Lives for him once more.

And then it hit me. I stared at that can for what seemed like time immemorial as visions flashed into my brain of possible outcomes.

Over the span of the past few weeks I had lived three different lives. I was Roland Bishop *and* I was Ethan Stiles *and* I was Mohammed Atta. The lightning lived on for each of them, and they were all connected.

But what if they could be *dis*-connected? What if I could be in three places all at once?

But that would take care of only *three* of the groups.

Roxanne made four.

Roxanne also knew. She made four! She could now head one of the groups off at the pass as well. The four of us could work in tandem.

We had to get Phelps and Fox and the others to know, or we'd never make it. We had to find a way to get all of these four lives in different locations at the right times.

But I had only just received information about Atta. I didn't know where or when the others would arrive. I just knew the flight numbers.

The flight numbers! Of course. How simple! Those that would tell me and everyone else where they would each be. That is, unless by trying to intervene the flight numbers had changed, and the hijackers would now be on a different flight. But then, wouldn't Penny's book have changed? Wouldn't I be receiving visions of *different* flight numbers for tomorrow?

In my mind's eye and in my memory, the flight numbers had not changed. Maybe they were fixed, and all of us were variables around them? Were they, being inevitable, the only fixed, grounded and centered points other than Winston's cat collar and Penny's book?

We had to intervene, Roxanne and I. Even if we were the only two who knew, we had to do something and try to stop them. And we had one day left to do it.

But we wouldn't be the only two. There would be *four* of us, and I knew who they were.

American 11 would depart from Logan at 7:59am. It would crash into the North Tower of the World Trade Center at 8:46am.

United 175 would depart from Boston at 8:15am, slicing diagonally into the corner of the South Tower in a grisly inferno seen by the entire world at 9:03am.

American 77 would depart from Dulles at 8:20am, drilling into the Pentagon like a missile at 9:37am.

United 93 would depart from Newark at 8:42am, though they were supposed to leave earlier but were delayed on the tarmac. I could not see its end result.

Four locations. *Four* of us.

I raced into the bedroom. "Roxanne, come on, get up." She moaned again and flipped over angrily on her side. It gave me a chuckle. *Not a morning person. Noted.* "Roxanne, come on, you gotta get up. I have an idea. I need your help."

"Whaaa-?" she asked, sitting up and throwing a mess of her own hair out of her face. "What are you talking about? What time is it?"

"Almost seven. I need you to come with me. Now."

She didn't stop grumbling, but she did come with me. To our amazement, heading outside, there was her Bronco with us. I was thinking we would have to take the bus, but this was an added bonus. Maybe the stars were aligning. Maybe we would have a chance.

I was talking quickly as she drove. "Straight to the FBI office. We need to tell them in person because we need to take them with us."

"Take them with us? You mean like-"

"Exactly. You hold onto one, and I'll hold onto the other. You can take Phelps if you'd like since you guys used to be an item. I'll take Fox. I have a mind to squeeze the life out of him anyway. Maybe I'll grab him and cut off his circulation as a little payback. Should cut off the blood to his brain. He doesn't use it much anyway."

"Roland, don't."

I rolled my eyes. "I'm kidding! I wouldn't. We need him. We need *both* of them."

We were racing through Jersey City heading for the Holland Tunnel. It was now 7:15am. I reached into my pocket and pulled out my Nokia. I smiled. "Hey! Would you look at that? I'm still me." I showed it to her, and she looked at me and smiled crazily.

"I don't know how you're still sane, dude."

"Me neither. Let's hope we both stay that way." I looked down at my phone and called information for the numbers to the two airlines. "Man, I wish someday we had internet on our phones so we could just verify this kind of information in a browser."

Roxanne scoffed. "Ha! The internet in your hands in a phone? Yeah, like that'll ever happen." She returned her eyes to the road and sped toward the Big Apple.

We reached the FBI Office. Once more, the agent stood out front. Only this time he looked different.

"What's up, Ostrom?" Roxanne asked him as we scurried inside.

"Who the heck is Ostrom?" I asked, hurrying in behind her.

"Don't ask. I remember Armstrong too. But now I have this memory of Ostrom that I didn't ask for. So just… don't ask."

I shook my head and exhaled, following her into the elevator and up to the office where Phelps and Fox were waiting.

"Phelps! Fox!" she cried. They each emerged from their offices, coming down the hall toward us.

"Where the hell have you been, Byers?" Fox asked angrily. "I thought you were on the job at Newark four nights ago and then you vanish without a trace and don't return our calls?"

"Can it, Fox! Both of you, get in here!"

She motioned angrily for them to follow her into the conference room. Like obedient children or dogs with their tails between their legs, they followed her in.

"This is serious," she began. I was going to lead the way, but she was more fiery, and they felt it. "Bishop here has news, he has *proof* of when Atta and his goons are gonna pull everything off. We know the date, we know the times, we know the flight numbers."

Phelps' jaw dropped. "How? How did you get all that?"

"Never mind that right now. I just need both of you to stand right here."

"What?"

"Just do it, Fox!" she yelled. "There's no time! Both of you, please, come over here. This is not something we can just explain to you – it's something you have to experience." I watched her as she shepherded them further into the room on the other side of the conference table."

"Roxanne, I really don't see-"

"Shut it, Ryan! You have to trust me on this."

My cat collar began to get hot. Of course it did: we were changing the future and the past all at once, with less than one day to go. I glanced up at the clock. It was now 9:36am. We couldn't delay.

"Okay. Just stand right there." Phelps and Fox were side by side, casting awkward glances at each other. "Roland, come here." I obliged. "Stand in front of Ryan." I did so, not sure where she was going with this.

I was eye to eye with him, and we both turned to look at Roxanne.

"Okay, Ryan. Now hit him."

"What?" Phelps asked, flabbergasted.

"What?" I asked at the same time.

"Go on, hit him!" she insisted. *Oh, now I get it,* I thought, as I started to return my gaze to Phelps. *She wants me to get angr-*

Oooof! Phelps smashed his fist into my gut and I doubled over.

Oh boy, did that piss me off. I couldn't breathe for a moment, and my body was tingling with anger. I furrowed my brow and sought for air. "Don't do that again," I choked, staring angrily at Phelps. "Roxanne! Stop. It doesn't work that way."

"But you said-"

"I know what I said! That's not what I meant though. *I* have to start it off."

"Oh. Sorry."

"If you need me to do it instead, let me know," Fox offered. I shrugged him off and walked away.

Straddle the line, I told myself quietly, reaching over and grabbing my cat collar. I faced away from them, and started to breathe hard. My stomach still roiled, and I wanted to turn and punch Fox. Good. I was getting angrier. Winston's collar started to burn.

"What's going-" Phelps started.

"Shh! Just wait," Roxanne urged him.

Flickers of blue at the corners of my vision. *Straddle the line*, I said again softly to myself. I brought up every emotional thought I'd ever experienced. Every grudge, grievance, frustration, bitterness. I dredged it all up. I went all the way back to being a child under my mom's strict control. My brother Burt. The frustration of being dictated to and never heard. My dad's absence. Things I had never even told Penny. Everything from the past few weeks and the stress of it all: I summoned it to the surface.

"*Byers?*" Phelps asked nervously.

My skin began to get hot. I was churning inside. I clutched Winston's collar and dug it further into my skin, pressing the heat into my epidermis.

"Wait for it…" Byers whispered.

The wind began to blow. Both of the agents' ties fluttered, and they looked down in amazement. The clouds outside faded to a burnt auburn, underlit and eerie. Traffic seemed to slow to a grinding halt.

But for me, all I saw was glowing blue. Flickers of angry blue flame erupted out of my head, and the agents recoiled. I clutched my temples, trying to stay grounded. *Straddle the line! Straddle the line!* I heard myself yelling.

"No, Fox, don't!" Roxanne yelled. "Stow your weapon! He's not going to hurt you!"

In a reflex, my head was thrown back and I couldn't contain the buildup anymore. Blue flame burst forth out of my mouth with every word as I screamed:

I'm Roland Bishop, and I know who I am!

I'm Ethan Stiles, and I know who I am!

I'm Mohammed Atta, and I know who I am!

Straddle the line! Straddle the line!

A vortex erupted around us. The agents howled in dismay, and Roxanne screamed. Loose papers flew around the room. Before I knew what was happening, a dissonant shriek shot from my soul and split the room's air asunder. My hands went out wide and arcs of lightning connected with every piece of metal. The gun in Fox's hand was seized by an arc, and then it flashed and burst in his hands. His right hand had been completely blown apart. His chest was splattered with his own blood.

Fox screamed in agony and I could hear Roxanne trying to help him.

One by one, the glass windows blew out around us as I continued to shout.

I'm Roland Bishop, and I know who I am!

I'm Ethan Stiles, and I know who I am!

I'm Mohammed Atta, and I know who I am!

Straddle the line! Straddle the line!

Tracers of white hot light burst from me and incinerated points of the walls around us. The conference table caught fire. They were all powerless in the midst of it.

But not me. I was full of power. I channeled all of my emotion and all of my strategy into a triumvirate of focused concentration and will. It demanded everything from me. At just the right moment, I let go of Winston's cat collar as a blinding light took all of us.

For a moment, all was silent.

Briefly, everything around us was stilled. I dropped to the ground, heaving in the inky blackness. I turned and looked around me as stray remnants of the vortex danced on the periphery, fading away, rescinding into nothingness. Light filtered back in, and I saw them standing there, panting, looking all around in dismay and awe.

We were all in my living room, back in Jersey City.

The number zero flashed before my eyes as they noticed me on the ground.

All three of me.

Phelps drew his gun, recognizing one of me.

Roxanne stopped him. "Ryan, *no!* That's not him! That's *not* him! Wait and see!"

Fox was examining his right hand, oblivious for a moment to Phelps and Roxanne approaching me in curiosity. Agent Ryan Phelps had never seen anything like this. "Where are-?" he started to ask.

"Shh," Roxanne said again. "It's okay. We're at Roland's place in Jersey City."

I stood up. Every one of me stood up.

Roxanne came over and looked at me. In unison, all of me looked over at her and smiled, grateful for her help.

She heaved a massive sigh of relief. "You did it, Roland," she whispered, eyeing all of us, and then she turned to the agents.

"Guys, I'd like to introduce Roland Bishop, Ethan Stiles, and Mohammed Atta. But... they're really all Roland Bishop."

We glanced at the clock on the wall. It was 4:03am on September 11th, the day of the attacks.

The number *zero* flashed before my eyes.

0 Days To Go

September 11ᵗʰ, 2001 • Manhattan NY

They all eyed me curiously as I stood there. It was a good start.

I couldn't believe it actually worked. Oh boy, did I have a story to tell Penny.

"When you're finished gawking, we have to move out," Atta said, and their heads flipped over to me.

"Lord Almighty," Phelps breathed out, drawing closer to Atta. "You look just like him. Can you…do you…can you feel his memories, know his thoughts?"

"It doesn't quite work like that," Atta said. "I can speak Arabic, I have all of these memories from different timelines and different places. Like, I can see you, Roland, from inside The Frederick, as I crawled toward you."

"Weird," Roland replied. "That must be surreal."

"Wait-wait-wait," said Fox, still feeling his resurrected hand, "so all three of you are…*you?* How in the holy hell does that even make sense?"

"Nothing makes sense after you get struck by lightning," all three of me said in unison. Fox started in fright, backing away slightly. Phelps continued to eye Atta curiously. "Which one of you is in control?" he asked Atta.

"I am," said Roland. "I promise."

Phelps looked over at Roland, and a trace of a smile grew on his lips. "Boy, you guys weren't kidding when you said that this was something we'd have to *experience*. Why couldn't you just tell us back at the office?"

"You wouldn't have believed him," Roxanne said. "And you guys would have been frozen."

"Frozen?" asked Fox, squinting his eyes. She nodded. "What, like a meat locker?"

"You're a meathead, you know that?" she asked him. "No! Frozen in time. Stuck. In some kind of informed paralysis time loop thing. Roland, you say it."

Roland stifled back a laugh. "It's something I can't explain, guys. Once the knowledge of the exact date and time sets in, that's the truth. And when the truth hits you, it demands something of you. So you have to act on it. But the universe must not have been ready to let you act on it yet, so that's why you – and everyone else – gets stuck in time. Like a system crash. At least I think that's it."

"Incredible," breathed Phelps.

"So all of this went down after you got hit by lightning?" Fox asked.

Ethan nodded. "Ever since then I've received visions, and I've learned how to harness it and use it. I've been pinballing back and forth between dates, shuffling through this Inevitability Loop and trying my best to figure out what to do next. And where to be. Now I know where that is."

Phelps' eyebrows went up. "And where is that?"

"In four different places," said Roland. "We're going to stop some terrorists. And we don't have a lot of time, so let's get moving. I know precisely what to do."

Roland explained everything he had seen, everywhere he had been, all that he had witnessed, and all that he knew to be coming from the future, as the six of us sat down. The agents could not keep their eyes off Atta. Or Stiles. Or Roland. Any of us. They eyed us curiously, never sure who was about to speak or who was the figurehead. Ethan and Atta nodded along to everything Roland said.

By now we all knew what all the terrorists looked like, and we knew what flight they would be leaving on as well as the time. It would simply be a matter of being in the right place at the right time.

American Airlines 11 would depart from Boston's Logan Airport at 7:59am. Mohammed Atta would go there with Roxanne. Phelps was about to protest, but Roland explained that Atta would do the most damage to Atta *as Atta*.

United Airlines Flight 175 would depart Logan at 8:15am. Roxanne would handle Marwan al-Shehhi there.

American Airlines Flight 77 would depart Dulles at 8:20am. Roland looked over and nodded to Ethan. He would go there and confront Hani Hanjour with Fox.

And finally, United Airlines Flight 93 would depart from Newark at 8:42am. Roland would go there with Phelps, and they would confront Ziad Jarrah.

By the time Roland was finished, it was 6:22am.

They shook their heads wildly and sighed, widening their eyes to take it all in. It was, admittedly, a mind-job.

"So weird, Roland. How will you know which one of you is…you?" asked Roxanne.

"I'll know. And I can untether whenever I need to. I know it sounds weird, but I can feel myself in all of you," Roland said to the other two. They nodded right back.

"I can definitely. It's three streams of consciousness," Atta said. The agents muttered and swore.

"Man, you even have the accent down," Fox said.

"I don't 'have it down,' I *have* the accent," Atta clarified. "I *am* Atta…but it's just from a different timeline, and with Roland's consciousness at the helm." They shook their heads in incredulity.

Atta turned to Roxanne. "*Now* can I have a gun?"

She smiled. "Let's go. We're already late for Logan Airport, and that's two planes. We won't make it time."

"Yes we will. Trust me." Atta's eyes lit up blue.

Everyone had exchanged phone numbers. Roxanne and Atta were outside in her Bronco, once more parked at the curb. They had a date with Logan Airport. All three of me had grabbed jackets from the coat closet.

"Get there," Roxanne said. "Good luck, boys."

"See you on the other side," Atta said to them in his thick Egyptian accent. "You certainly are a handsome man, Roland," he added. Roxanne placed her hand in Atta's. They all shook their heads as a flash consumed Roxanne's Bronco and they disappeared from sight.

"Well, that's one for the books," Roland said. "Let's get a move on, Phelps. I say we try to catch these guys before they even get to their gate."

Phelps nodded and donned a fedora. "Here. You're gonna need this." He handed Roland a gun and a badge. "That was Agent Mulligan's. Use it and honor him."

Roland held it lovingly. "I will. I promise." Roland took Phelps' hand. Blue light consumed the two of them, and they vanished, somewhere along the Inevitability Loop toward Newark.

"Well, I guess it's you and me now," Ethan said to Fox. "Ready to do this?"

"*Ready?* No. Determined even though the three of you are absolute freakin' lightning-struck whackjobs? *Yes,*" Fox emphasized.

"I'll take that as a compliment," Ethan said, grinning. "There's only one thing left to do."

"Yeah? And what would that be?"

"We have to hold hands," Ethan said, grinning.

Fox grunted in disapproval and rolled his eyes, slapping his palm in Ethan's and squirming at the touch.

In three seconds, they disappeared as well.

Winston watched all of it curiously from the window.

It was a beautiful early-fall day that September 11th as I moved in three different directions, fanning out to my appointed destinations. The weather was gorgeous everywhere you looked, with not a trace of clouds.

A strong cold front had crossed the New York City metro area last night, apparently. Hurricane Erin was growing and massing out on the Atlantic Ocean last night. But the cold front had kept Erin out over the ocean, leaving the northeast in peace. It was crisp and clear and high pressure moved in, with winds up to twenty-five miles per hour. A perfect day for flying. *Or dying.*

We were all in uncharted waters and undiscovered country. We were rewriting history as we inched closer to our respective destinations, glancing off what was written, and writing our own pages as we went. Somewhere, Penny might be reading a book from 2020, watching the ink rearrange itself into different sentences.

It was election day in New York City. Voters were going to the polls for the mayoral primary, comptroller, public advocate, and more. That was the short-term, and the only thing people truly saw. No one had any idea about the long-term, and the sheer terror that was about to descend upon them if any of the three teams failed.

Simultaneously, all three of our teams emerged out of the fog together, stepped out of a churning spinning vortex that was growing in intensity.

Roxanne was behind Atta as they looked up at the Logan sign. Atta would be going for Gate B-32 to intercept the real Mohammed Atta. Roxanne would intercept al-Shehhi at Gate C-19.

My sight was taken to Ethan and Fox outside Dulles. They were heading for Gate D-26 and Hanjour.

Roland and Phelps appeared in my mind's eye arriving at Newark, heading for Gate 17 and Jarrah.

My mind swam as all three images flooded together, jockeying for attention. They overlapped, intersected, and played off one another.

One thing was certain: we couldn't call airport security or we would inform people of the plot and risk a time freeze once more. We couldn't involve anyone else, or we'd have to suck them all back through the vortex, and I just couldn't fit that many people in my little apartment. Winston would never approve of it.

The clock was ticking. As we drew near to each of our respective destinations, the flashes came. Stronger than they ever had before. I was bleeding in tandem out of all three of my right nostrils. Atta's left leg cramped up as he ran in the cold morning, and all three of us felt it.

"You okay?" Roxanne asked Atta.

"Fine," Atta said obstinately, though he needed to work out the charley horse in his calf. His nerves were on fire, and he hadn't had much water. "I can go on."

Roxanne and Atta made their way into the airport and prepared to split up.

"Your leg alright?" asked Phelps.

"Yeah, just needs massaging," said Roland. "It'll be fine. We're here. Flash your badge and let's get on our way to Gate 17." He wiped the blood from his nose.

The sun was rising in the east, and the crowds were growing, moving to their respective destinations.

"Dude, what's the problem? We don't have time to waste with a bum leg," complained Fox.

Ethan bent over and massaged the cramp out of his left leg as they slowed. Blood dripped from his nose onto the carpeted walkway. Fox was nervously looking around and scanning the boards for the respective flights and gates.

"I'm good," said Ethan. "I can go on now. Just a cramp." He sniffed and wiped at his nose.

"Fine. Let's move," Fox ordered.

Phelps went first through security, flashing his badge and whispering something to the security officer at the checkpoint.

Briefly Roland had a flash and a vision, and his head swam, stopping to grip the scanning counter. "Whoa," he said, dizzy, waiting. Finally he breathed again. "It's nothing. It's passed." But he couldn't shake the sensation of being instructed to remove his shoes as he went through security. He passed a hand over his eyes and dismissed it as perhaps an insignificant future vision.

Atta stopped in the middle of a run through the concourse, and Roxanne asked, "What is it?" He paused as if listening, and clutched his head briefly. "It has passed. It is nothing. Let us go," and he was off with the Detective once again. She flashed a badge at a security officer and was let through with Atta in tow.

At Dulles, Ethan stumbled and fell.

Fox was unsympathetic. "Man, I always get second string," he said. "Get up, dude, we gotta move. What's wrong *now*?"

"I don't know," said Ethan. "I just received a strange vision about…removing shoes? Blinded me for a moment. Something from the future, though I'm not sure where or when."

The Dulles airport was playing *Thank You* by Dido, and the music descended down from overhead speakers, filling all of our ears. I heard it in stereo: there and here.

Where my conscience was floating out there in the ether, I didn't know. The three of us were linked up somehow, and I could sense and feel everything that they could, as they could with each other.

"Can we go now?" Fox asked, annoyed.

"Yes, it's fine. We can go," Ethan replied.

Atta and Roxanne split up. "You got your phone, right?" Roxanne said.

Atta held up his little Kyocera smartphone. "You did not see, but I checked with Roland and Ethan before we left. Roland has the Nokia, Ethan has the Motorola V60. I have this." Atta smiled a thin-lipped smile at her, one eyelid slightly sagging.

"K, that's…that's great," she said a bit distrustfully. "Use it, Atta. I mean, Roland. Whoever. And be careful!"

"I will. You too," Atta said, and he felt his wrist, ensuring that his Winston collar was on snug.

Roxanne headed for Gate C-19 and al-Shehhi.

Atta raced on toward Gate B-32 and Atta.

"Here comes the gate," said Roland. "Right down concourse A." He began to feel nervous in the pit of his stomach. The gun bounced lightly inside his jacket, and he wasn't sure when, or *if*, he would have to use it. "Right down here, Phelps."

Phelps was to his right as Gate 17 loomed up.

Suddenly, Roland gasped and moved back, seeking to shelter from view. "What? What?" demanded Phelps.

"Possible sighting of Jarrah. Coming out of the restroom to your right."

Phelps retreated and held back. "Additional sightings. Roland, get over here!" They backed into the entrance of a gift shop while passengers ambled by. Phelps brought the rim of his hat downward.

An overhead announcement said something about a gate change. "Look. That's al-Nami, the little guy. You said you spotted him chasing Jarrah, right? That him?"

Roland peeked out beyond the entrance. Sure enough, there was al-Nami, sitting down talking to someone on a cellphone. They had to wait. If he was in any way communicating with the other terrorists, he could alert them to their position, and their cover could be blown.

They had to wait.

Atta continued down the concourse. Up ahead, he saw a man with a similar build, stocky shoulders and puffy, wiry black hair enter the men's room. Atta pulled his jacket up around himself and kept his eyes down.

The terrorist entered the men's room, and Atta pursued, though the white flashes persisted, and his nose began to bleed once more.

Images of people running. Of a gaping, burning hole in the side of one of the towers. Of people falling.

"For goodness' sake, Roland, wipe your nose, you're gonna attract attention," said Phelps. He handed him a handkerchief.

Roland took it from his hand and dabbed at his nose, wiping the blood trail that obeyed gravity and moved toward the floor. He looked around awkwardly as he, too, was beset by flashes of uncomfortable, blazing light stabbing through his brain. Images of a struggle in the sky. Of people screaming and a jetliner lurching violently midair. Of green grass below.

Byers had reached Gate D-26. al-Shehhi was not in sight, nor were any of his accomplices. She wondered. Had something changed, and they weren't here? It was already 7:15am. They would be boarding in a half-hour. Indeed, she thought, Atta's flight would be boarding in ten minutes.

In another area of the airport, Atta's mind continued to flash as he entered the restroom, wiping his nose.

Fox picked up his phone to dial Phelps. "Phelps, what's your 20? How's it going over there? Stiles here has a bit of a nosebleed and is going through those flashes, but nothing much yet. We think we might have seen one of the guys near the gate here at Dulles. Not sure."

"Standby. Positive ID on two of the targets at the gate. Do not engage any of them until you've ID'd all of them and none of them are on their phones!"

"Copy that," he said, and switched off. "Just wait here, Stiles. Yellow light."

But Stiles was not seeing yellow; he was stricken with white. Images of the Pentagon in flames. Of an entire section collapsed in an angular heap. Of bodies out on the grass. And everywhere you looked, smoke.

Phelps continued to watch and look inconspicuous. Someone bumped him on their way out of the gift shop.

Oh, excuse me," said the voice. Phelps turned, and it was a sweet elderly woman with a younger lady in tow, holding a bag of purchased snacks, presumably for the flight. Phelps tipped his hat at her.

The agent took a quick breath to cleanse his stress palette, and moved his vision back over to the gate.

A Middle-Eastern man was right in front of him. Phelps jumped and recoiled. "Gah! Hi. Can I help you?"

It was Ziad Jarrah.

"Why are you watching us?" Jarrah said. Roland slid out of view. If this was the same Jarrah he had pursued a few nights earlier, he might recognize him, and the jig would be up.

At the same time, Roland's mind was awash with exchanging images. A ball of fire. A clear day. Rubble. A building standing tall. They flickered together, back and forth, like a Cable TV channel with interlacing frames, uncertain which to broadcast.

Phelps played dumb. "Watching you? I dunno what you mean."

Jarrah just stared at him, and then looked around for any signs of any accomplice. Jarrah had appeared seemingly out of nowhere, and must have caught both of them watching al-Nami.

"Sir, I'm looking for my wife," Phelps invented, trying to throw Jarrah a bone. "I thought she was sitting here but I can't seem to find her."

Jarrah continued to study him with deadened eyes. "I wish you luck in your search," he offered in a detached monotone.

"Thank you, much obliged," said Phelps.

Jarrah walked away from the two of them. At that moment, al-Nami emerged from the men's room in the distance with two other men. They all sat together. Phelps pulled his phone to his ear and pretended to be talking to his wife, waving his hands around as if he was frustrated with her.

Jarrah eyed him for a moment, then spoke quietly to his fellow jihadists. They glanced up at the departures board and the time. It was now 7:20, and they would be boarding in twenty minutes.

Roland's flashes returned to normal, and a smoking jetliner-shaped crater burst with a fireball from the ground.

At Logan, Atta entered the men's room, his head down. Two men were at the urinal. One finished up and started washing his hands. Feet hung down from the furthest stall. Atta waited until the terrorist was alone, hiding around the corner from the end of the stalls.

A young man came in and noticed Atta facing him. He turned uncomfortably, aiming his body away from Atta to shield his privates. Atta turned as well, pretended to pee into a urinal but quaking with hot flashes and trembling from visions.

Movement from the furthest urinal.

The young man continued to urinate. He needed to leave! Atta quieted his breathing and listened. More movement and toilet paper being dispensed.

Finally, the young man jiggled and zipped up his fly, turning away from the urinal with one final awkward glance at Atta. He did not stop to wash his hands.

Atta breathed out slowly. Flashes consumed him, and he was sweating profusely, but he held steady and willed himself not to collapse.

The stall door opened. Footsteps. The white flashes increased in heat and intensity.

Suddenly, Atta whirled around and faced his doppelganger. The terrorist's jaw dropped in utter surprise as he tried to shove Atta out of the way and burst out of the bathroom. But Atta had the strength of three men and lightning coursing through him. His eyes lit up blue. His hands began to smoke. The cat collar around his wrist burned with a righteous light.

In the unoccupied bathroom, Atta threw the terrorist into the stall wall, and the tile cracked. Atta cried out in pain as Atta went for him again, burying his hands into Atta's neck, choking him.

The terrorist flailed about in misery, attempting to punch and strike Atta, but Atta overpowered Atta. In a moment, the terrorist's neck was broken with a sickening crack. He slumped down to the ground, pulverized with a lightning grip that fried his nerves and severed his spinal column.

Atta dragged him back into the stall, locked it from the inside, took his shoulder bag, slid back out underneath, and left the men's room just as another male patron was entering. He slid the shoulder bag over himself.

Atta then returned to Gate B-32 as if nothing had happened. His associates were waiting for him.

Roxanne looked around cautiously. She was at D-26, but there were still no signs of al-Shehhi or the other men. She took a seat at the window, waiting and wondering if they had messed everything up.

In an instinct, she pulled out her phone and dialed Phelps.

Roland was recovering from the visions, but was still trembling. Phelps was keeping up the charade of the missing wife, holding his phone to his ear.

Roland could see the four United 93 terrorists sitting together, studying Phelps. One of them reached for his phone.

Suddenly, Phelps' own phone rang. He stopped his charade, frozen in horror. How could he be on his phone with his wife if his phone rang audibly? There was no way.

The jig was up.

All four terrorists started to move away, advancing down the hallway to beat a hasty retreat. As they passed Roland, his head exploded with vision after vision, interlaced and jockeying for power, each seeking to subdue the other and uncertain which would gain the upper hand. Screaming through all of them were blinding bursts and streaks of pallid white.

Phelps dropped his phone and whipped out his gun. "Freeze!" he cried, and the four of them broke into a run. He gave chase. Roland somehow struggled to his feet and sprinted after them. As he did so, his senses were renewed as the perpetrators drew further away. His vision became clearer. His focus was sharpened. He could see them up ahead. He did the only thing he could.

Phelps fell behind him as Roland became a freight train with momentum no one could impede. He cried out for Jarrah, and this time he had him in his sights with no escape. Roland careened into the air wildly and screamed a high-pitch wail that rent the very air. Everyone within hearing dropped to the ground and clutched their ears. The terrorists, on whom he focused his belch of cataclysmic sound, dropped solidly to the ground.

And that's the last time they saw the light of day.

An airplane flying out of the ground, uncrumpling. A horrifying ball of fire receding back into the earth, utterly extinguishing.

Roland stretched out his arms as bolts of sheer power jetted from his fingers.

A 747 pointed toward the ground yet flying backward into the air, leveling off.

Lightning was released from his digits as powerful and as hot as the sun. It connected with each of the jihadists and they flailed in agony. Other passengers fled wailing and screaming. Smoke rose from the bodies as they became charred and blackened with three hundred million volts of energy coursing through them.

A commercial jetliner full of living souls, flying backward but slowing, slowing, gradually coming to a stop as wispy strata settled upon it and it froze in midair, as if a videotape reel had been spun to a grinding halt.

Phelps cried out to Roland as continued arcs flew from his body and light streamed from his eyes. The random zips of energy connected with anything metal all around them, and innocent passersby were at risk of harm.

Slowly spinning forward again, a jetliner, holding its course and staying aloft, continued to fly toward San Franciso unimpeded, unmolested, and undestroyed.

The light faded. Roland panted through it, his hair streaming with sweat, and the visions faded. The flashes dulled and dissolved to peace.

Phelps put his hand out toward Roland's shoulder and cautiously touched him. "Hey. Hey, Roland. You okay?"

And then Roland grabbed Winston's collar and the vortex opened up behind them.

Fox repeatedly called Phelps with no response. "Dammit!" he hissed through his teeth. "I can see all of them! What do you-" he stopped. "Ethan? Stiles, where are you?"

Ethan Stiles was no longer with him. Fox looked about wildly. He was walking up to Gate D-26, trembling and tremoring with all sorts of hallucinations and real images, unsure how to discern the truth from the lie. And then a sudden peace took him, though racked with visions. He approached Hani Hanjour, who had another associate sitting next to him. He motioned back to Fox. "Hey, they're right here, come here," yelled Stiles joyfully.

Fox's eyes went wide. *What was the fool doing??* He hid all traces of his gun in his pocket and played it cool. "Hey, man, what's up?" he asked Stiles.

"Yeah, these are the guys I told you about!" Stiles replied. "This is Dave, and Jack. Hey, where are Mike and Will anyway?" he asked, looking around wildly.

"Sir, you are mistaken," said Hanjour, looking around nervously. "You have us confused with someone else. And are you alright? You appear to be ill."

Indeed, Stiles's legs buckled briefly and he composed himself and stood back up to full height. "No, I'm fine, thanks. You guys were the guys we hung out with that night at the tavern, right?"

"Sir. Please," insisted Hanjour, recoiling into himself and covering his face with his hands. "You do not know what you are talking about." His accomplice did the same. "Please go away." Other passengers around us began to move away, not wanting to be part of a scene.

"Oh, no problem, no problem," Stiles said, and he was trembling. Here were two of them, together. Here was their chance to draw out the other two. An overhead speaker announced Flight American 77 would now begin boarding first class and premium class passengers. *Perfect timing,* Stiles thought. *That oughtta bring them outta the woodwork.*

Stiles' legs buckled again, unsure what to think. Competing visions flashed into his mind of the Pentagon on fire, and then completely intact. Back and forth, as he swayed.

He decided to lay it out bare. "Listen, fellas," said Stiles. "I got this problem, see? There's this building in Virginia shaped like a star. You guys know which one I mean? It's really cool. We wanna go see it but we don't know how to get there, and we musta thrown back one too many, ya know what I mean?"

Fox was now following him. He started to laugh and play along. "Ha! Yeah, I know what you mean, buddy. You talkin' about the Pentagon?"

Hanjour seemed to flinch. "Sir, I really don't know what you are talking about. If you will excuse us, we must board now."

At that moment, the other two showed up, ready to board. "Is there a problem?" they asked Hanjour. He didn't respond to them; he flashed his eyes to Stiles and Fox. They looked over at them. "Do you have a problem, gentlemen?"

Stiles winced from a flash. "No, but you do," he said, nearly falling over. At that moment, Fox drew his weapon and trained it on Hanjour. The others backed away and started to flee.

Stiles exploded. The wobbly legs turned into stoic columns of strength as he grabbed one of the men and threw him into Hanjour. Hanjour fell under the weight of the first man, and the other two fled.

"Not so fast!" cried Fox, holding them at bay with his weapon. They froze.

"Hold it!" cried Stiles. "Don't move. Don't even think about it," he warned them, leaning forward and hissing a dangerous sound as bluish light burst forth from his mouth and eyes. Passengers got up and fled from the gate. The gate agent called security.

But Stiles wasn't done. Neither were the visions. The Pentagon couldn't decide whether or not it wanted to remain intact. It was still burning. There was only one thing left to do. He grabbed his cat collar and clutched it.

Straddle the line, Stiles mumbled. "Grab each other's hands. Do it, now!" he yelled to them.

Fires slowly dying.

Hanjour looked at him quizzically. They all did.

"Now! Fox, bring the other two over here. Hurry!" Fox escorted them over at gunpoint and made them hold the hand of their fellow jihadist.

A building being raised. A star being reformed intact.

Rapid footsteps could be heard running down the concourse. Airport security. They would fire upon Stiles without the slightest provocation once identified.

The terrorists were holding hands. Stiles moved closer to them. He grabbed the hand of the nearest one. "Immortality's over, fellas. No absolution and no large-breasted women in the afterlife for you," he hissed.

A jetliner-shaped missile stopped short of its target and pulled forcibly back up into the sky.

Fox recoiled as Stiles summoned a vortex of blinding color and fury, opening up behind all of them and taking all five of them into it. Roland untethered his consciousness from Stiles. Stiles' lifeless body fell in alongside theirs, suddenly bereft of a soul, and there was screaming in the wind.

The Pentagon, symbol of America's might, unharmed, as a passenger plane continued on through the sky toward LAX.

Detective Byers was waiting patiently. She hadn't heard from the other members of her team, and it was now 7:45am. Boarding would begin for Flight 175 any minute!

As if at the end of hope, there they were. All four of them, led by Marwan al-Shehhi himself. Her heartbeat quickened. She lifted her phone and prepared to call Phelps just as the overhead announcement signaled boarding would begin shortly. She stood, carefully eyeing them but being cautious not to draw attention to herself. She was, after all, a detective. The detective knew stealth.

Passengers began to line up for boarding. The gate opened leading out to the passenger boarding bridge. Roxanne dialed Phelps and lifted her phone to her ear. All she got was static. She dialed again. Static.

Roxanne tried Roland. Same thing. In desperation, she tried Mohammed. Static.

She sighed. She would have to take them by herself. There was no way she could let them get on that plane. No way. She held up her badge and trained her gun on al-Shehhi. Fellow travelers squealed and moved away. "Detective, NYPD, freeze!" she said.

Al-Shehhi turned and sneered. "NYPD? You're in Boston, miss!" he scoffed. The other terrorists stepped away from their leader, preparing for a quick getaway.

"I said *freeze*," she shouted at them, moving in closer. They complied. "Hands up!" she said.

The vortex opened up behind her quicker than she could breathe. Roland and Phelps were thrust out of it right behind her, knocking her off her balance. Lightnings arced all around them.

Shots were fired, though she didn't know from where. An undercover cop? A security guard? A sky marshal? Everyone scrambled for cover. Two terrorists made a run at her and she squeezed off a few rounds. They were down. The third held still with his hands upraised. "Shots fired, shots fired!" she screamed.

al-Shehhi ran for the ticket agent, and grabbed her from behind, choking her. Out of his pocket he pulled a box cutter: a simple and unsuspicious purchase from the local gift shop. He held it to her neck.

Roland and Agent Phelps stumbled up, weary. Roland was beset by tremendous pressure: the multiple hematomas were acting up as visions surged through him and assaulted his mind. Dimly through the fog he could see al-Shehhi holding the ticket agent hostage.

Roland cried out in pain as images of the South Tower alternated between intact or smoking; crackling with flame, or calm and noiseless.

"al-Shehhi, drop the knife!" the Detective yelled. As she did so, distracted and focused entirely on him, the other remaining terrorist lunged at her, ripping the gun from her hand. He threw a punch at her, but she was too fast. Her billowing hair twirled angrily in her wake as she whipped around, grabbed his punching arm and bent it backward at the elbow. She brought up her right knee and knocked the wind out of the jihadist, then clobbered him with a fist to the throat. He fell over, clutching himself and retching. Phelps ran to subdue him and hold him down. Other passengers assisted him who hadn't yet fled for cover.

al-Shehhi disappeared down the passenger boarding bridge with his hostage, into the bowels of the United Airlines plane itself. It was United Flight 175.

The Detective pursued them angrily, her gun drawn.

It was Atta now on the plane in first class. He was aboard American Airlines Flight 11 with his associates, speaking no word, and staring straight ahead, keeping up the ruse.

It was 7:50am.

They would depart in nine minutes.

al-Shehhi had locked himself in the cockpit of United Airlines Flight 175.

By that time, Newark Airport was on lockdown. I knew that Jarrah and his men were dead. I knew that Hani Hanjour was trapped in a phantom zone somewhere with his associates, thrown in by Ethan Stiles. I knew that Atta the terrorist was dead.

I knew that the *other* Atta – *me* – remained alive as did his fellow jihadists, but to what end, and for how long, I didn't know the answer. Nor did I know if they would somehow break free and resume their plans with at least these two planes. Time would tell. History was already being rewritten, but the clock was still ticking, and I still had visions of at least one tower collapsing.

Roland stumbled along into the passenger boarding bridge after Byers. He could hear violent collisions up ahead: she was trying to break in to the cockpit. The ticket agent lay dead at the plane's aperture. Her throat had been slit. Roland looked away in disgust.

The airplane's engines were warming up. Instrument panels were switched on and the plane itself was starting to back away from the terminal.

Oh no. al-Shehhi was going to complete his mission!

Roxanne must have surmised what was happening, because she came bursting back forth onto the passenger boarding bridge, and a sizeable gap was now opening between it and United 175. The plane was pulling away!

Roland stumbled forward and embraced Roxanne. "You okay?" he asked, panting.

"Yeah!" she yelled over the noise of the engines and the wind. "Did Phelps get the others?"

Roland nodded. Both of them looked out toward the plane, retreating into the distance and moving out of sight past the bridge. The nose cone disappeared.

"I've gotta go after that plane, Roxanne. I'm already weakened from splitting all of me, but I've gotta do something."

She looked at Roland stoically. "I'm going with you!"

They both looked down. It was going to be a jump, with a painful landing. They were at least fifteen feet up. Neither of them would be able to pursue after a fall like that.

"Pssst!" Roland looked over. "This way, dummy. We don't have to jump." She directed Roland to the exit door of the boarding bridge, and there was a nice stairwell waiting for them leading to the ground below. The two of them scurried down. Roland just caught sight of a United Airlines tailfin disappearing around the corner of the boarding bridge once more.

They ran. Roland was exhausted already from the confrontation with Jarrah, but somehow he found the strength to press on.

United 175 was retreating from them, hanging a right up ahead and taxiing for takeoff wherever it could do so. By now the tower must have demanded that they turn back, and they would have warned other planes to keep their distance.

Painful flashes tore through Roland. The South Tower was up. Then it was down. Then it was up. Bodies were falling from it and then rising back up into it like some freakish teeter-totter.

They continued to run toward 175. It looked like it was turning right again! That meant that they could cut it off at the pass. Roland was still exhausted, but they were almost there.

They crossed onto the tarmac directly in front of it. The engines were whining and increasing in pitch. Roland looked over at Roxanne. She backed away from him, breathing two words.

"Do it."

Roland looked away from her and let emotion swallow him whole. He was so spent; tired of this whole damned thing and all these terrorists. Roland stared down that plane as the engines started to roar to life. It sped wildly toward him.

Blue-light. Emanating everywhere.

Towers falling.

The plane roared at Roland. He felt hot. His feet lifted off the tarmac as the wind took him. His hands raised palms up. Energy swelled through him and lightning struck the ground all around him. He could almost see al-Shehhi's face contorted in amazement and dismay as this tiny human lifted up and threw himself against the nosecone, climbing up toward the window.

Massive ash clouds folding back, retreating as if into a vacuum. A building erecting itself. Tiny dots – humans – soaring back up from lifelessness on the pavement back into the sky, merging with reconstructed floors above.

Flashes of heat and thunder.

al-Shehhi backed away from Roland, reclining in his seat, his eyes wide with fear.

Roland lifted his hands and pointed his palms toward the terrorist, balancing on the nose cone.

A massive jolt of energy coursed through Roland! It enveloped the entire cockpit with blazing light. The aircraft's instrumentation malfunctioned as he heard a horrible cry from within. The plane had partially lifted off the ground but then came crashing back down to earth. Yet he held there, suspended on the nose cone.

The plane screeched and slid to a halt, dark black smoke billowing from the cockpit and sparks everywhere.

Through the smoke, Roxanne saw a tiny figure shoot across the tarmac toward Gate B-32.

Despite the mayhem, American Airlines Flight 11 had been cleared for takeoff. Atta was sitting in first class next to one of his associates, in seats 2A and 2B.

But I was losing him.

For whatever reason, the connection wasn't holding, and the timelines were getting distorted and out of sync. The connection flickered under the strain, and Atta's eyelids fluttered and spasmed as multiples timelines merged together and sought for mastery.

I was losing him. The connection would not hold for much longer, and if that happened, Atta was free to do whatever he wished, to whomever he wished. American 11 would continue on toward its final jihadist target.

I had to stop him.

Roxanne and Roland sprinted for a security desk. The detective flashed her badge. "I'm Detective Byers, NYPD, working in tandem with the FBI. You got terrorist operatives aboard American Airlines Flight 11 heading for LAX from Gate B-32. Five of them. They're readying for takeoff!"

The agent turned to her radio and began communicating with airport security central.

Roland clutched his head and moaned. He was still panting and could barely stand. "I'm losing him, Roxanne, I'm losing him." Roxanne whirled her head over to Roland in fright. "And I'm losing *me* in the process. I'm already weakened from losing Stiles and from that confrontation with ah-Shehhi. I can't hold on to him!"

She turned back to the security agent. The agent nodded. "We're on it. Okay, everyone stand back and wait here, we have a major security situation here. I'm going to have to ask all of you to step back and remove yourselves from the security line and wait. Foster…Harkins…with me!" She pointed at two other agents and rallied them to her. "Alright, let's go," she said.

"Come on," said Roxanne. "I'll help you. You're the only one who can truly stop him, Roland," she said, taking his face in her hands and staring into the well of his soul.

Roland breathed deeply, and his eyes fluttered.

Atta breathed deeply, and his eyes fluttered. Something was wrong with the connection, and he was losing himself. He turned to look back at his associates. There they all were.

Abdulaziz al-Omari.

Satam al-Suqami.

Waleed al-Shehri.

Wail al-Shehri.

The four other jihadists returned the gaze without a smile, nodding subtly to him. Atta turned back and stared straight ahead. His brain was suddenly pounding.

He looked down at the strange cat collar around his wrist, wondering how it had gotten there, and what it was for.

The plane began to move. It was 7:56am.

It was 7:56am. Roland, helped by Roxanne, made their way to B-32. They were close. Other security had already been dispatched out to the runway. Security vehicles raced out toward it.

They could see it, far away, moving slowly up the runway and in line for takeoff.

"We've gotta get out there," breathed Roxanne. "But how? We'll never make it in time."

Roland's head stopped thumping for a moment as remarkable clarity gripped him. He looked up with widened eyes at Roxanne. "I know what I have to do. I have to reset everything. I can do this."

He smiled at her, as a blue light emerged through his eyes in the most tranquil and peace-filled aura she had ever experienced.

With a ferocity that surprised her and made her recoil, he reached over and ripped off Winston's cat collar and flung it from him. Spasms took him, and arcs of energy blazed forth all around the two of them together.

And then, he was gone. Roland's lifeless body fell to the floor there by the gate window. Roxanne cried out and tried to steady him. He lay there crumpled at her feet, gone.

"No. No!" cried Roxanne, and she cradled his head in her hands, his nose streaming with blood. "Somebody get me a rag, a towel, anything!"

Atta's head stopped thumping.

The lead hijacker of American 11 shook his head and massaged his temples, looking around confusedly, gathering his bearings.

Suddenly, the plane slowed, and then came to a full stop. The Captain came over the speaker. "Uh, folks, we've got a security situation at the airport. I'm going to have to ask you to remain seated and patient for a moment. We should be back underway shortly."

Atta leaned forward and gasped, wholly seized by a primal force that inhabited him from head to toe.

I looked down. The cat collar was intact around my wrist. I could see, plainly, the 'RB' logo on it.

I'm Roland Bishop inside Mohammed Atta, and I know who I am.

White blazes barraged my innards and racked my body with an epileptic reverberation. The jihadists noticed it. They jumped up in dismay. One of them started advancing toward me.

"Sir, please, I'm going to have to ask you to get back in your seat," said a flight attendant with the name badge *Betty Ong.*

"I don't know, I don't know," cried Roxanne. She was on the phone with Phelps. "It's like he just died. *Can I please get a paramedic here?!*" she shouted.

"Just hold on, Byers. Hold on. They're coming," said Phelps through the phone.

"Hold on, Roland. Hold on. They're coming," she whispered to his expressionless face.

But the blood still streamed from his nose.

"Sorry again for the delay, folks. We've been asked to disembark the plane. I'm going to have to ask every one of you to be patient, follow the instructions of airport security and do as you're told. I realize this is a hiccup in your travel plans but hopefully we'll be back underway shortly." The captain switched off.

Nearly every passenger either groaned or cursed. But not the four jihadists. I could tell that they were silently stewing, knowing that this unanticipated delay would cost them dearly and perhaps even sabotage their plans. Their brothers were underway, or were going to be. With each passing moment their risk of discovery grew.

My body, Mohammed Atta's body, was not itself. Inside this Egyptian body, there was an Italian-Portuguese American burgeoning within, controlling all his limbs and all his thoughts. I stood, and filtered up and out of the plane like the rest of them, pointed at by men with guns. My Egyptian nose was bleeding heavily. I removed my black button-up shirt to staunch the bleeding, holding it to my nose.

A small security force was gathered outside, brandishing weapons. I slowly looked back at my fellow jihadists, tilting my eyebrows up and directing them to remain calm. My head swam, awash with competing visions. The North Tower crumbled, and then it stood.

Its antenna mast descended dangerously toward the earth, and then rose back up. Over and over again, like a childish game of give and take.

I read the jihadists' thoughts. In their minds, they would have to flee. Their intuition told them that they had been discovered, and all was lost. They would never now make it to the World Trade Center.

We all filtered down the aircraft boarding stairs onto the tarmac below. A lineup of planes formed behind us. More security personnel were pulling up with men and women brandishing weapons.

Two of the jihadists were talking quietly to each other.

"Hands on your heads please!" cried the security force. "Single file!"

Suddenly, one of the jihadists, passing by a security officer, thrust his body into her and knocked her to her feet. He seized her automatic rifle. The other jihadist took a woman hostage and held a box cutter to her throat, blocking his compatriot behind him so that neither would be shot.

"Let us go, we demand it! Or you will have the blood of this woman on your hands! I swear it!" he shouted.

The security personnel fanned out and pointed their rifles at them, screaming for them to put down the gun and the knife. The female hostage started to cry and plead with her hostage-taker, begging for her life.

In a flurry, the remaining two jihadists repeated the actions of the first two, each seizing a passenger and holding a box cutter to their throat. They backed away and stood close to their jihadist counterparts.

I watched them. And then, I calmly started to walk over to them, and our eyes met. "Brothers," I said, holding my hands up. "Please. This is not the way. Listen to me."

"Sir, hold it!" cried a security officer, training his weapon on me. I was free of the others and an easy shot. My nose had ceased bleeding.

"Brothers, please," I pled. "*Allahu Akbar,*" I said calmly, continuing to stride toward them as time seemed to slow. I smiled gently. "God is great."

And then I did it. It let it all unfold, churning up every primal force within me, every urge, every complaint and lust, every fierceness and ferocity, every sadness and regret.

My eyes began to blow with a bluish frenzy, steam pouring out of them. I opened my mouth to reveal white-hot bluish light blazing forth. The jihadists froze in horror. "Allahu Akbar!" I cried once more, but the voice was different, laden with multiple dissonant clashes of notes together into an alien cry.

The four terrorist compatriots clustered together as I approached, banding together out of fear at this seeming betrayal from Allah.

"Sir, I will fire on you if you do not freeze!" yelled a voice. And without another word, in a single, blinding moment, the security officer shot at me.

The bullets did not connect.

I disintegrated before their very eyes in a dazzling explosion, and the bullets went wide. Mercifully, they did not connect with anyone else. And somewhere, a body in a bathroom stall began to glow.

All three of me were now released into the ether, becoming formless and, thus, unconstrained. Limitless. The circuit was now complete. Mohammed Atta's dead body appeared from the restroom and then dropped to the ground, pulverized by bullets. The glow faded.

I had transformed into lightning itself. I veered and swooped through multiple dimensions, returning to the tarmac at Logan Airport, the four focuses of my wrath before me, and three hundred million volts at my disposal.

A deafening roar engulfed the entire passenger crowd, swarming their eyes and making them cover their ears. The hostages were freed and bolted. The howling wind swirled amongst them, contracting, diminishing in size as it formed a diameter around the four jihadists. One shot wildly into the air, but the hurricane force winds jerked his rifle into spastic directions and he lost control.

Bodily they were lifted together and thrown about like spineless rag dolls, smashed together. The compressing lightning storm sent shockwaves and three hundred million volts of energy into each of them. Flesh seared and melted in the heat. Unearthly cries of agony – the sounds of two-thousand nine-hundred and ninety-six reclaimed victims' protests – screamed through them.

Their bodies were pulverized. Ghastly skeletons dripping with entrails burned entirely in the flashes, disintegrating and sprinkling to the ground as the storm subsided.

The wind abated, and the passengers, terrified and fearing the end of the world, were lying prostrate on the ground, covering their heads.

The security guards had been blown backward, their weapons dislodged from their hands.

The pilots stared down from their cockpit window, horrified and entranced.

The calm returned, and the sun still shined.

The five terrorists were nowhere to be found.

And neither was I. I had straddled the line to the end.

"Please, somebody, please," Roxanne cried into the air. "Isn't there a medic in this whole damned airport?" She slammed her fist into the ground, looking endearingly down upon me.

My eyes fluttered open. My lungs began to expand. I felt a sizzling pop jump through my hand into Roxanne's, and she recoiled. Electrical current coursed from me through her, as I reinhabited this human shell. But my eyes felt distant. My pupils dilated briefly into tiny dots. I could feel it. I could feel *everything*.

Roxanne slapped my cheek lightly.

"Roland! Roland? Are you okay? Talk to me!"

"Ow," I mumbled, my pupils expanding once more.

"You did it, Roland, you really did it!"

"Did I do it?" I mumbled. "Well, you said 'do it,' so I did it."

She laughed nervously in relief. "Do you always do what you're told?"

I smiled at her, taking in her beauty, hovering above me. "No. Only when ordered by hot detectives."

And suddenly, peace engulfed both of us, and we were stricken with a lungs-expanding moment. Visions were given to both of us as having borne witness to the other side of time, out there in the vortex.

Planes flew unimpeded through the sky. Bodies never fell.

Flames never licked the sides of buildings. Cancers never inflicted rescue workers.

Firefighters, policemen, and port authority workers lived on.

A grassy field in Shanksville, Pennsylvania remained completely intact.

Buildings never toppled. Ash clouds never engulfed Manhattan.

The world never wailed and mourned. Passengers never lost their lives.

Planes were never used as missiles. Terrorism had failed terribly.

Flags fluttered in the breeze, but not filled with any more patriotism than they had been before: in continued vigilance…not in unified mourning.

As in separate gifts of vision, we were taken into the air and saw beautiful vignettes of American 11. United 175. American 77. United 93.

All were coming in for a landing.

It was the purest and most beautiful thing I ever saw.

Next to Roxanne, that is.

She smiled at me, lovingly, and then bent down and kissed me, as I ran my hands through her hair.

"You did it, Roland. You exceeded my expectations and have kept your sunny disposition," she said to me.

"I sure did, Penny. But I have you to thank for keeping me on the straight and narrow along the way. Oh! And this," I said, holding up my wrist so she could see Winston's collar.

"Well, you were daft enough to keep it on *and* to take it off. Not many could manage that properly," she said, sipping her steaming tea. There was that look again, eyeing me over the rim of her drink. "It would appear that the lightning never left your body."

I shook my head. "No, apparently it didn't. Not until the very end."

"And Winston's cat collar kept you grounded through it all." Penny just stared at me, deep in thought. "What will you do now?" she finally asked me.

I thought for a moment. "Well, Jenette is already gone. Renita has someone new, and prospects with Roxanne are looking pretty sunny." I offered a sly smile.

"I daresay you've earned that. You deserve someone nice, Roland. You truly do."

I nodded in thanks. "So do you."

"Indeed I do! Honey, would you come in here please?" There were noises behind her. "Honey, this is my client, Roland Bishop. A very fine chap, though American through and through."

I laughed and stood. Mr. Eggers didn't have a trace of violence in his body, and the smooth and cheery crinkles around his eyes spelled a story of warmth and pure love for his wife.

"So nice to meet you, Mr. Bishop," he said, shaking my hand. "Penny tells me a lot about you," he said.

I narrowed my eyes. "She does?"

"No. Just pulling your leg, my boy. Patient-client privilege and all that." He winked at me.

Penny looked at him endearingly, and grabbed his hand. Her blouse shimmered at the connection, and there was not a trace of a burn to be found on her arm.

"Well, I'm off. Got to trim the lawn with the scissors and put out the garbage, you know."

"Uh, they have mowers for that," I offered.

He just winked again and waved me off, bobbing out of the front room, through the front door and down the steps to his yardwork.

She shook her head playfully and sighed. "I do deserve someone nice, don't I?" she said, and she beamed. "I really do."

"Yes, you sure do," -here I paused and looked at her under my eyebrows, holding up my bottled water in cheers- "*Lady Divinitus*. I'm glad for you. I'm glad for all of us."

She held up her tea and returned the cheers. "Here's to cranking up the willingness dial."

"To cranking up the willingness dial," I agreed.

Penny paused, eyeing me curiously. "I have only one question for you, Roland," she said, leaning toward me. "Just who was this Ethan Stiles person?"

I smiled at her. "I don't know *exactly* who he was. But he was in the park with me that day when I got struck. He must have gotten struck as well. I remember seeing him sitting on a bench as I walked toward the grass. He's been in a missing persons bulletin since then; I saw it with my own eyes. I don't know who he was other than someone who also had a part to play in all of this."

"Hmm. Well, God rest his soul. It sounded like he played his part," she concluded.

I nodded. "We all did," I said, agreeing. "All of us. We helped prevent 9/11. We all helped reset everything."

Penny and I eyed each other warmly as we sat there. It was a good reset, indeed.

THE END

Afterword

The "Dissonance" sci-fi series was *so* hard to break away from. For a whole year of my life, it was where I lived, and I didn't want to live anywhere else. With every fiber of my being and the fire of a thousand suns, I love that story, I love the characters, I love the settings, and I'm inordinately proud of how much work I put into it, fleshing out those stories in so short a time, being caught up in a whirlwind of creation from 2023 to 2024. I miss it.

But this book was something that kept calling me, and I was remiss to continue putting it off. I hated belaboring it and drawing it out, putting it back up on the shelf like a castaway in favor of returning to *Dissonance*. It simply couldn't compete. But, all things considered, I knew where I was supposed to be the moment I completed the alien invasion hexalogy.

Right back here, with Roland Bishop. I mean Ethan Stiles.

This is a story that has haunted me, and one that I really needed to tell. 9/11 looms like a specter over the lives of so many, and it still holds sway today. The phantoms of the past don't really give us breathing room, and I wanted to revisit it in a revisionist sort of way, writing historical fiction, which is a genre that I hadn't really dabbled in much before. All I knew was that somehow, in some way, I wanted to write the wrongs done to so many, and to give a reprieve. I wanted to wrest control out of the hands of the hijackers and keep those beautiful buildings towering high into the sky. I wanted people looking out their windows; not jumping from them. I wanted them to remain; not crash into the dust. I wanted the 343 firefighters and all the other heroes to live on.

When 9/11 happened, I was undergoing some personal trials that required some heavy introspection. I wasn't myself. I needed to really strip all else away and focus on who I was, and what I needed to be healthy. As such, I unfortunately missed the power and potency of the human spirit defying all odds to survive. I missed the heroism of the firefighters, the port authority workers, the NYPD, the priests and volunteers, the rescuers, the unidentified heroes, the valiant United 93 passengers and crew, the rescue dogs, the food and beverage servers, the caretakers and babysitters, the parents, the children… every single person who was involved in consoling and being consoled, rescuing and being rescued: all of them were part of the human spirit that I missed on 9/11 since I was so self-absorbed. The full gravity of what happened that day didn't hit me until 2005, at which point I wrote some poetry and music that reflected on the weight of the day, and how America was forever changed. I desperately wished to have been there, to have played a part in saving lives, to have done *something*. All of us wish we could have done *something*. Hettie Jones said of that day, "We are breathing the dead, taking them into our lungs as living we had taken them into our arms." I wished I had been there to take them into my arms and take them into my lungs. To be with them and to have shown them that they were loved before they were lost.

That's what historical fiction is: rewriting the past. Oh, if we could only do it in reality, and undo the damage and trauma caused by that single day. For now, I'm content to have offered a bit of escapism from the harsh realities of the present and the past by diving headlong into a version of history that didn't contain such an atrocity.

Ethan Stiles, er, Roland Bishop allowed me to do that.

I thank you, my dear reader and friend, for partaking of this story with me, of living it out and being willing to explore the dangerous and sacred ground of September 2001 with me, humbly, together. It's an odyssey that I hope will impact many in a healthier way than the real-life event did.

And to all the Roland Bishops and Ethan Stileses out there who desperately tried to undo it before me on the actual day-of, I salute you and honor you. I will always remember, and never forget that all gave some, and some gave all.

With love,

Aaron Ryan

About The Author

Award-winning and bestselling author, speaker, panelist, workshop presenter and voice actor Aaron Ryan lives in Washington with his wife and two sons, along with Macy the dog, Winston the cat, and the finches Inky, Pinky, Blinky & Clyde.

He is the prolific author of the bestselling *Dissonance* alien invasion hexalogy, the Christian dystopian fiction trilogy *The End,* the *Talisman* trilogy, the sci-fi thrillers *Forecast, The Slide,* and *The Phoenix Experiment*, the nonfiction books *God Is Not Santa* and *You're Going Straight To Helen (In A Handbasket)*, the children's picture books *The Ring of Truth, The Sword of Joy* and *The Book of Power,* the business reference books *How to Successfully Self-Publish & Promote Your Self-Published Book* and *The Superhero Anomaly*, six business books on voiceovers penned under his former stage name (Joshua Alexander), as well as a previous 1990's discontinued work, *The Omega Room*.

When he was in second grade, he was tasked with writing a creative assignment: a fictional book. And thus, *The Electric Boy* was born: a simple novella full of intrigue, fantasy, and 7-year-old wits that electrified Aaron's desire to write. From that point forward, Aaron evolved into a creative soul that desired to create.

He enjoys the arts, media, music, performing, poetry, and being a daddy. In his lifetime he has been an author, voiceover artist, wedding videographer, stage performer, musician, producer, rock/pop artist, executive assistant, service manager, paperboy, CSR, poet, tech support, worship leader, and more. The diversity of his life experiences gives him a unique approach to business, life, ministry, faith, and entertainment.

Aaron's favorite author by far is J.R.R. Tolkien, but he also enjoys Suzanne Collins, James S.A. Corey, Michael Crichton, Marie Lu, Madeleine L'Engle, John Grisham, Tom Clancy, Tim Lebbon, Christopher Golden, C.S. Lewis, Stephen King and Dave Barry.

Aaron has always had a passion for storytelling.

Visit his website at authoraaronryan.com, join his exclusive and private Facebook group at authoraaronryangroup.com, or check out his store at authoraaronryanstore.com. Follow Aaron on IMDb at imdb.me/authoraaronryan.

Also, if you have a podcast and would like to interview Aaron, he is regularly interviewed and shows up well on camera. He is a bestselling and award-winning author as well as a longtime speaker and panelist who would be delighted to appear on more podcasts. Three of his books have been adapted for the screen. One is currently being pitched to major streaming networks. Another has won entrance into major film festivals and even won awards for best screenplay.

He is also a voiceover artist and narrates his own audiobooks, but AI (and other factors) is eroding the voiceover industry, so he adapted and overcame adversity by returning to authoring. All his life he has been a storyteller, and he loves to tell stories! Both of his careers fit him like a glove, and he enjoys discussing both careers, but in particular, authoring, including self-publishing, creative ways to market, the threats of AI to creatives, and more.

Feel free to check out his previous appearances at

https://www.youtube.com/playlist?list=PLMnbc3h716bs6u4j5B4B31DIsoBLkktwM

.

Thank you for considering and following Aaron Ryan!

If you liked Aaron's books, please visit the Amazon and Goodreads pages for this book and leave a positive review. Once it shows up, please email the screenshot of it to me@authoraaronryan.com for a discount on your next book purchase from him! Thank you so much. Reviews really do help a ton!

Visit Aaron's website and sign up at the Blog:

Subscribe to Author Aaron Ryan

Follow Aaron and connect on Social Media:

Connect with Aaron

Feel free to check out the following links for further information on Aaron:

Subscribe to Aaron's blog for free giveaways, news and new releases at
authoraaronryan.com/blog

Join the Author Aaron Ryan Facebook community at
facebook.com/groups/authoraaronryan

Subscribe to Aaron's YouTube channel at youtube.com/@authoraaronryan

Visit Aaron's social media links to connect with him at dot.cards/authoraaronryan

Visit Aaron's website at authoraaronryan.com

Follow Aaron on IMDb at imdb.me/authoraaronryan.

Also by the Author

As Aaron Ryan:

1. *Dissonance Volume I: Reality*
2. *Dissonance Volume II: Reckoning*
3. *Dissonance Volume III: Renegade*
4. *Dissonance Volume IV: Relentless*

5. *Dissonance Volume Zero: Revelation*
6. *Dissonance Volume Up: Rising*
7. *The Complete Dissonance Alien Invasion Saga*
8. *The End: Alpha*
9. *The End: Omicron*
10. *The End: Omega*
11. *The Complete "The End" Christian Dystopian Saga*
12. *Forecast*
13. *The Slide*
14. *The Phoenix Experiment*
15. *Talisman: Subterfuge*
16. *Talisman: Nexus*
17. *Talisman: Halcyon*
18. *The Complete Talisman Series*
19. *The Ring of Truth*
20. *The Sword of Joy*
21. *The Book of Power*
22. *The Christian Kids Values, Identity & Affirmation Series*
23. *God Is Not Santa*
24. *You're Going Straight To Helen (In A Handbasket)*
25. *A Lyrical Empirical Satirical Miracle*
26. *Examining The Lord of the Rings: An independent critique by Aaron Ryan*
27. *The Superhero Anomaly*
28. *How to Successfully Self-Publish & Promote Your Independent Book: A Self-Publishing & Business Marketing Guide For The Independent Author*
29. *Reflections: A Compilation of Journals and Poetry*

30. The Omega Room (abandoned in the early 90's)

31. Autobiography (no longer available)

32. Glimmerings – works of poetry

As his former stage name, Josh Alexander:

33. Voiceovers: A Super Business, A Super Life

34. Voiceovers: A Super Fun Pursuit

35. Voiceovers: A Super Responsibility

36. Running a Successful Voiceover Business

37. How do I get started in Voiceovers?

38. Five T's to Triumph: The Secrets to Getting Cast in Voiceovers

www.ingramcontent.com/pod-product-compliance
Lightning Source LLC
Chambersburg PA
CBHW081137020726
47504CB00009B/1903